ALSO FROM JOE BOOKS

Disney Frozen Cinestory Comic

Disney Cinderella Cinestory Comic

Disney 101 Dalmatians Cinestory Comic

Disney·Pixar Inside Out Cinestory Comic

Disney Princess Comics Treasury

Disney·Pixar Comics Treasury

Disney Darkwing Duck:
The Definitively Dangerous Edition

Disney Phineas and Ferb
Colossal Comics Collection

Disney Frozen: The Story of the Movie in Comics

Disney·Pixar Inside Out:
The Story of the Movie in Comics

Disney

BIG HERO 6

CINESTORY COMIC

JOE BOOKS INC

Published in the United States by Joe Books
Publisher: Adam Fortier
President: Steve Osgoode
COO: Jody Colero
CEO: Jay Firestone
567 Queen St W, Toronto, ON M5V 2B6
www.joebooks.com

Library and Archives Canada Cataloguing in Publication
information is available upon request.

ISBN 978-1-926516-96-7
First Joe Books Edition: July 2015

3 5 7 9 10 8 6 4 2 1

Published in the United States by Joe Books, Inc.

Printed in USA through Avenue4 Communications at Cenveo/Richmond, Virginia

For information regarding the CPSIA on this printed material, call:
(203) 595-3636 and provide reference # RICH - 613704

CINESTORY COMIC

ADAPTED BY
Jeremy Barlow

LETTERING AND LAYOUT
Salvador Navarro, Ester Salguero, Eduardo Alpuente,
Puste, Alberto Garrido, and Ernesto Lovera

DESIGNER
Heidi Roux

SENIOR EDITOR
Carolynn Prior

SENIOR EDITOR
Robert Simpson

EXECUTIVE EDITOR
Amy Weingartner

PRODUCTION COORDINATOR
Stephanie Alouche

Walt Disney
ANIMATION STUDIOS

BIG HERO 6

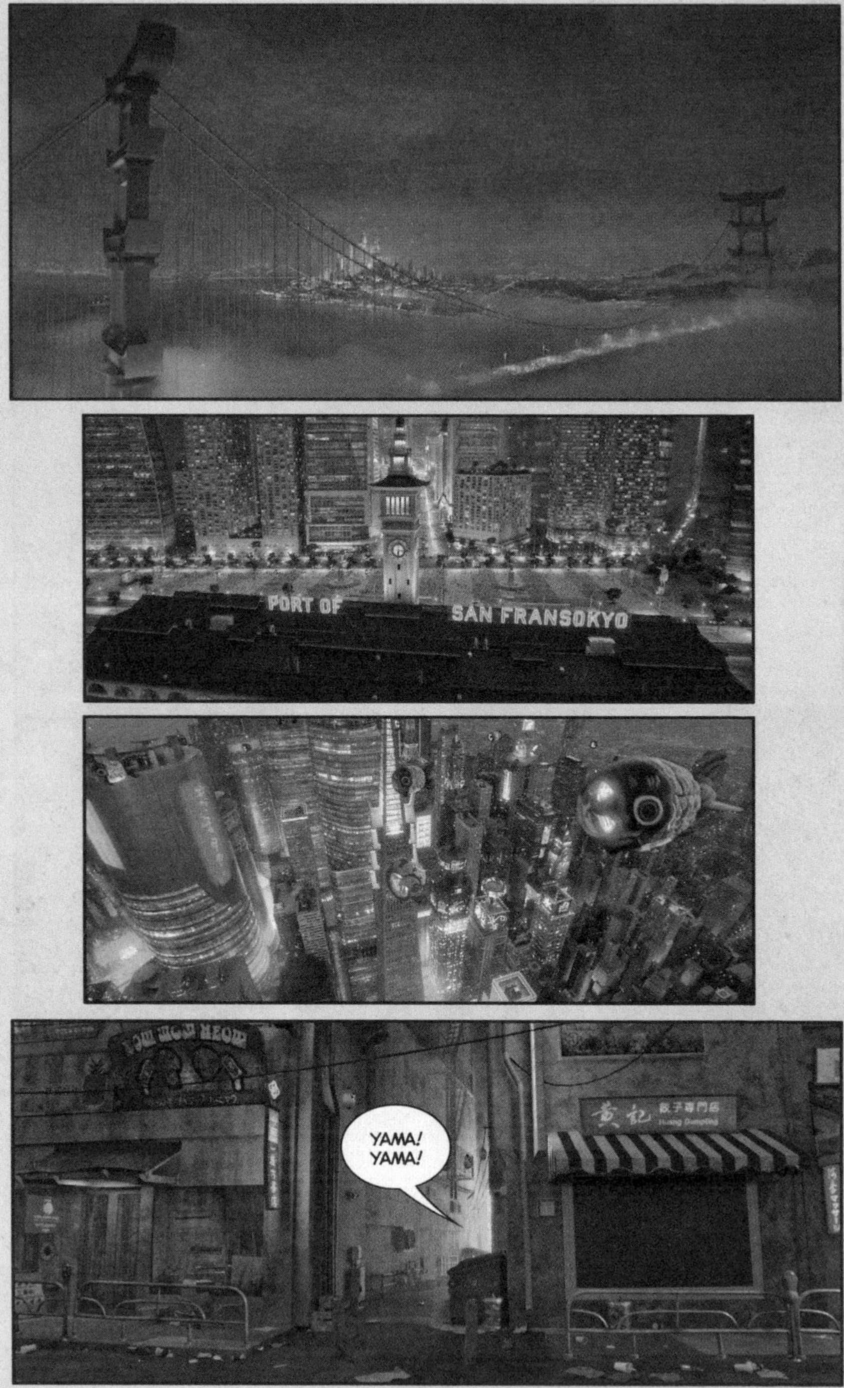
PORT OF
SAN FRANSOKYO
YAMA! YAMA!

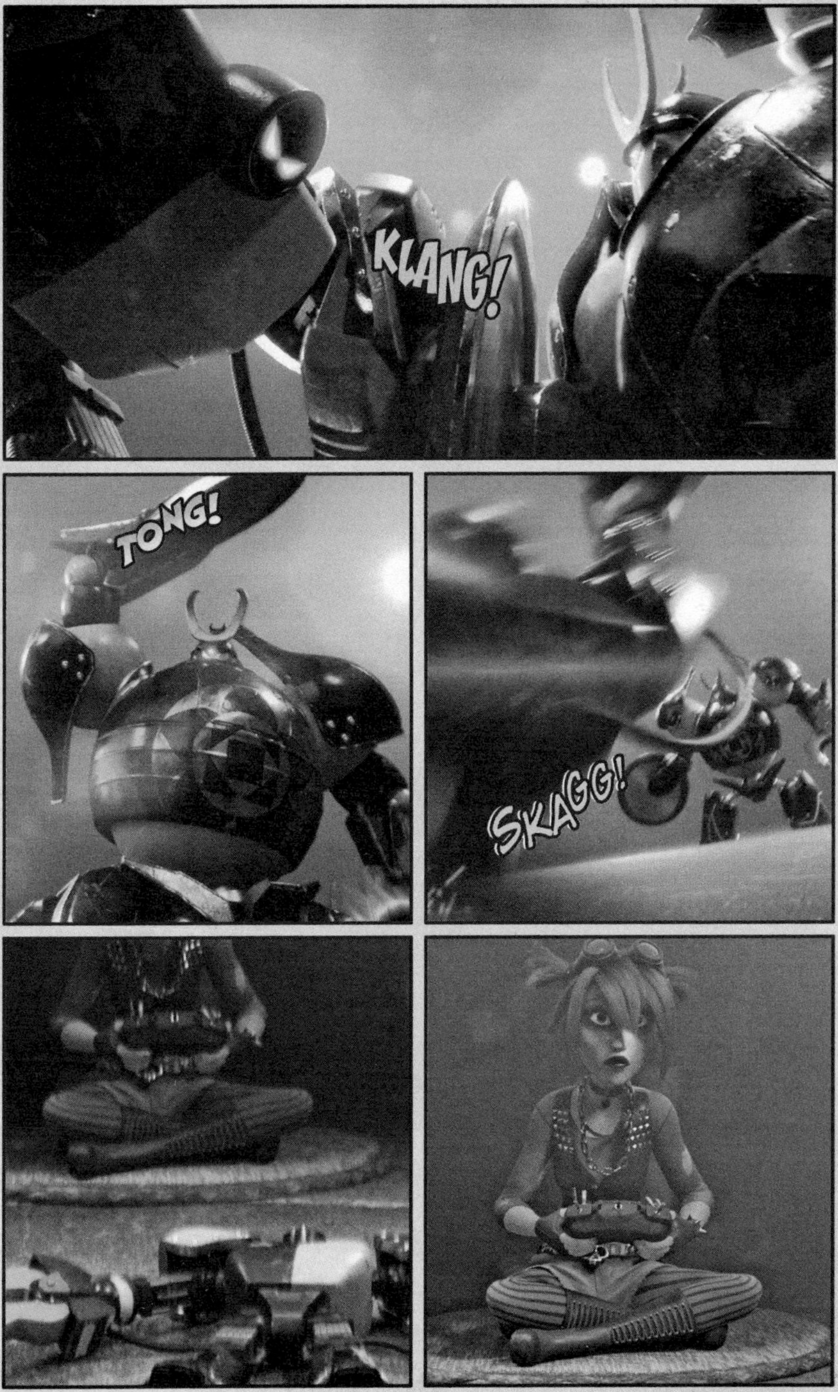
KLANG!
TONG!
SKAGG!

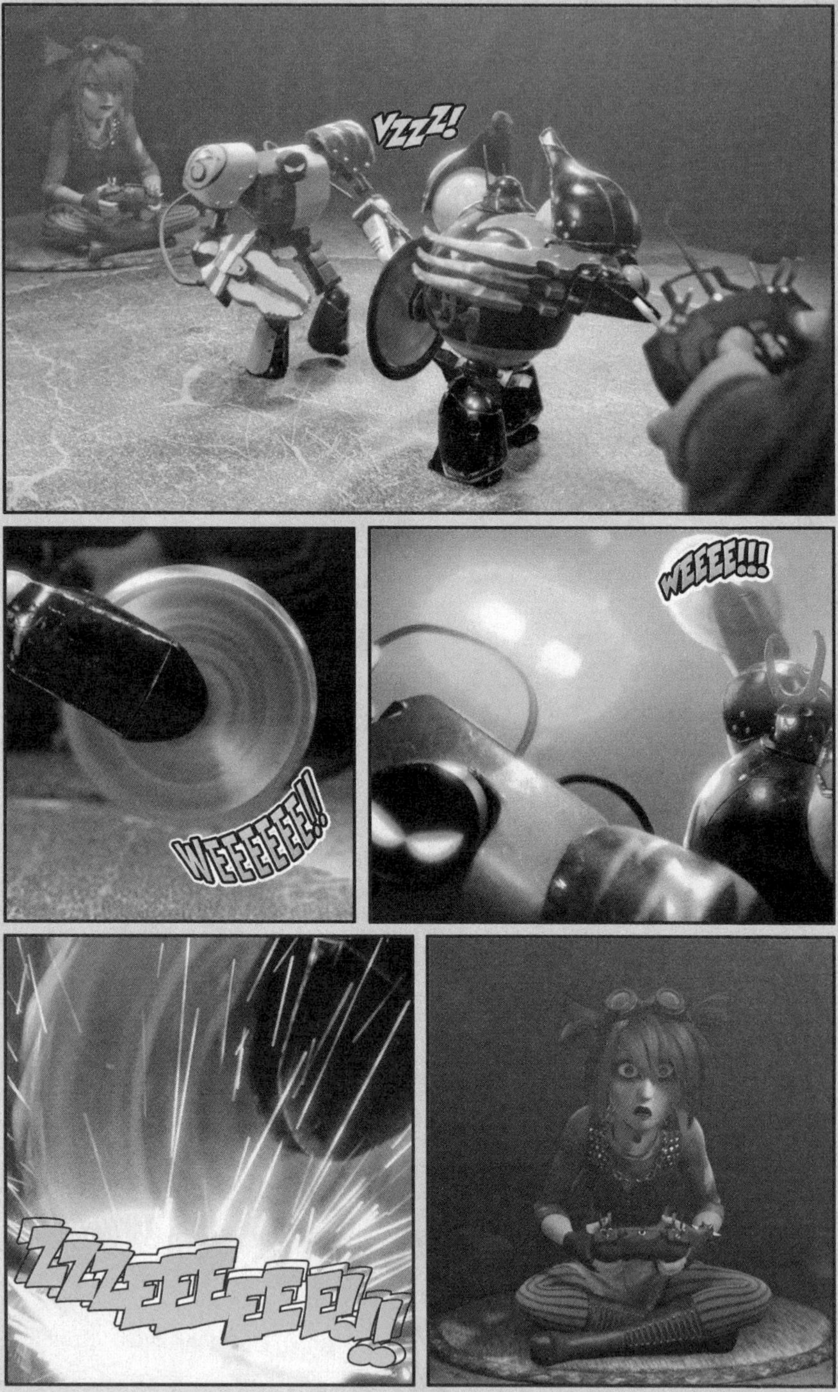
VZZZ!
WEEEEEE!!
WEEEE!!!
ZZZEEEEEEE!!

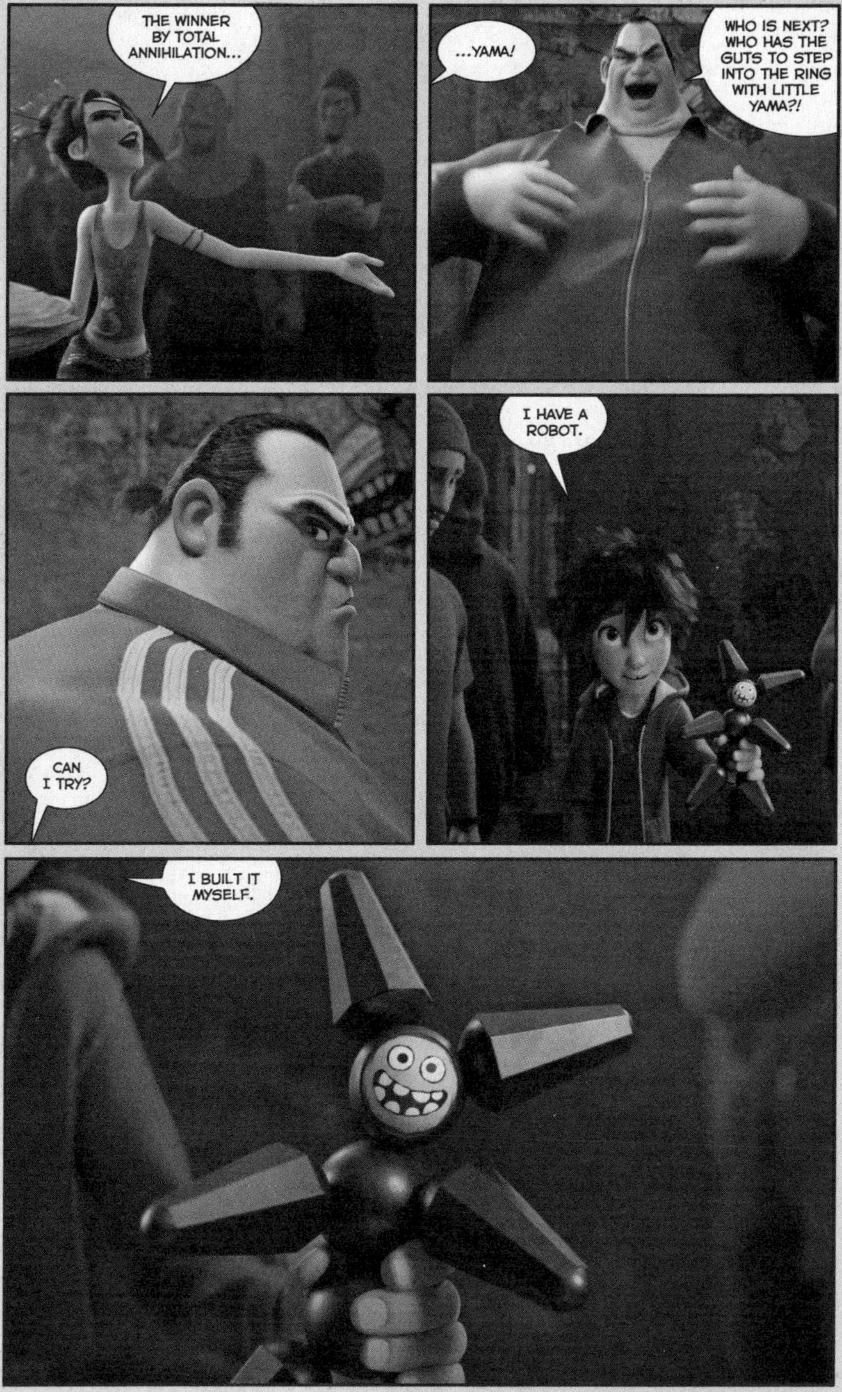
THE WINNER BY TOTAL ANNIHILATION...
...YAMA!
WHO IS NEXT? WHO HAS THE GUTS TO STEP INTO THE RING WITH LITTLE YAMA?!
CAN I TRY?
I HAVE A ROBOT.
I BUILT IT MYSELF.

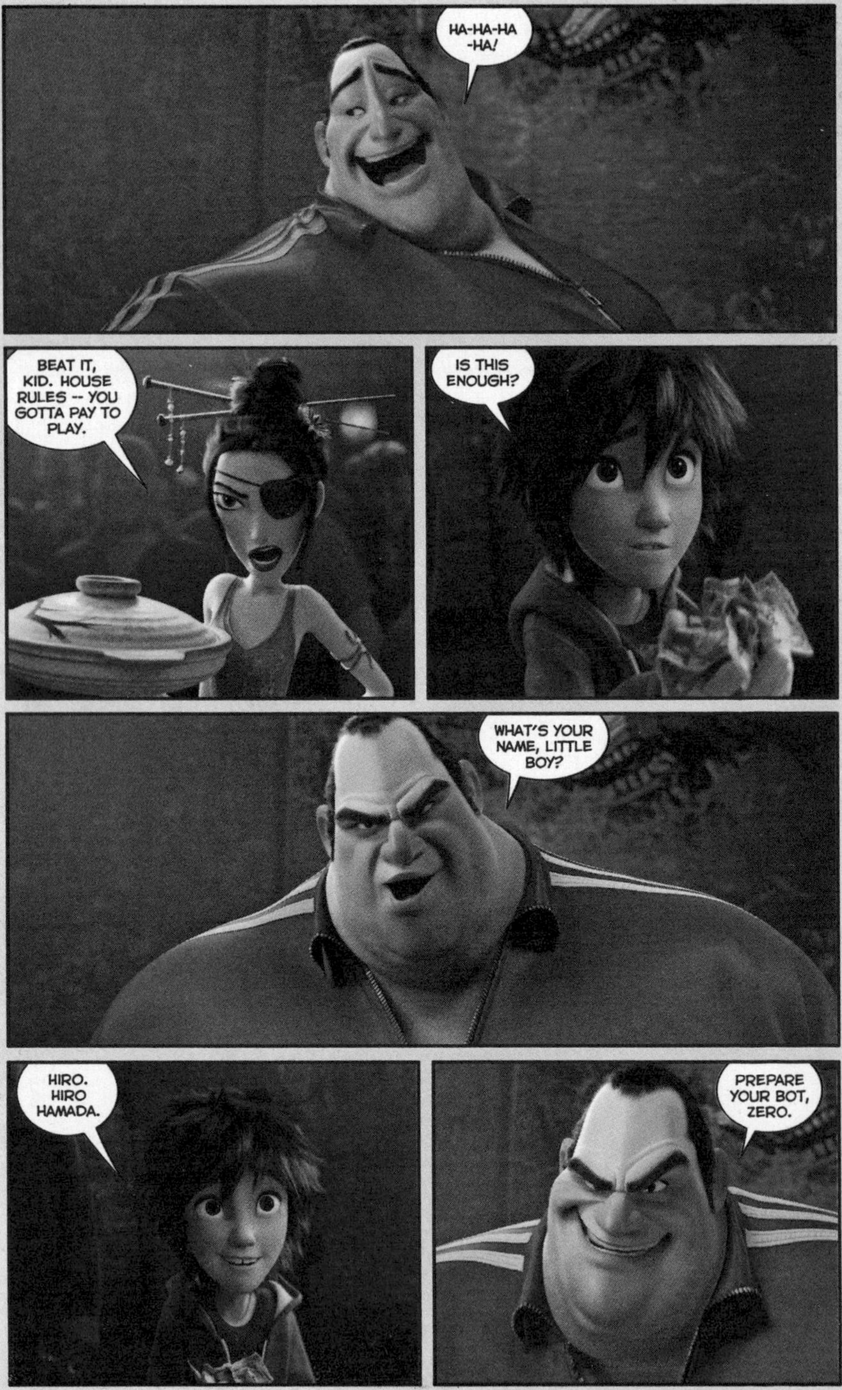
HA-HA-HA -HA!
BEAT IT, KID. HOUSE RULES -- YOU GOTTA PAY TO PLAY.
IS THIS ENOUGH?
WHAT'S YOUR NAME, LITTLE BOY?
HIRO. HIRO HAMADA.
PREPARE YOUR BOT, ZERO.

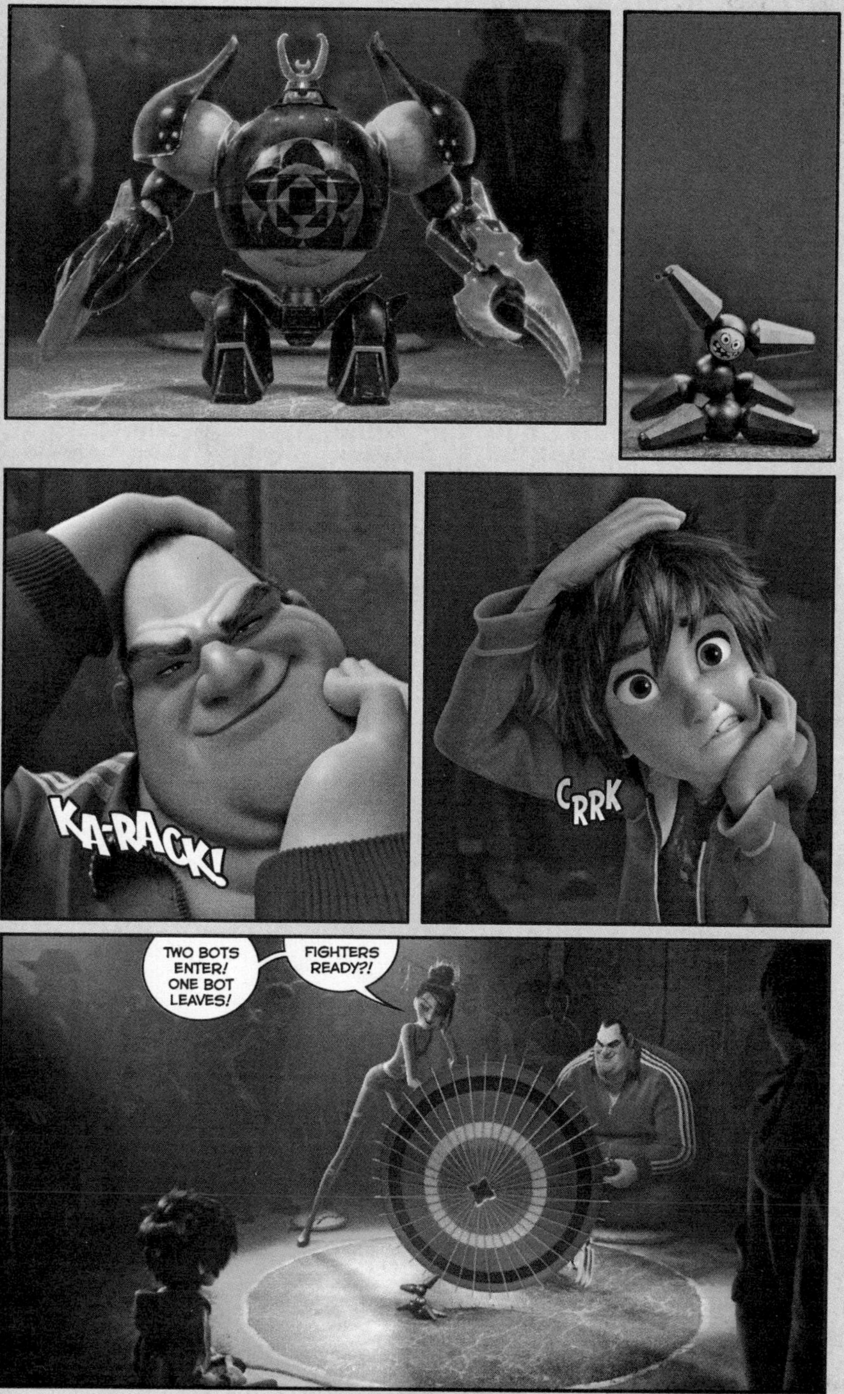
KA-RACK!
CRRK
TWO BOTS ENTER! ONE BOT LEAVES!
FIGHTERS READY?!

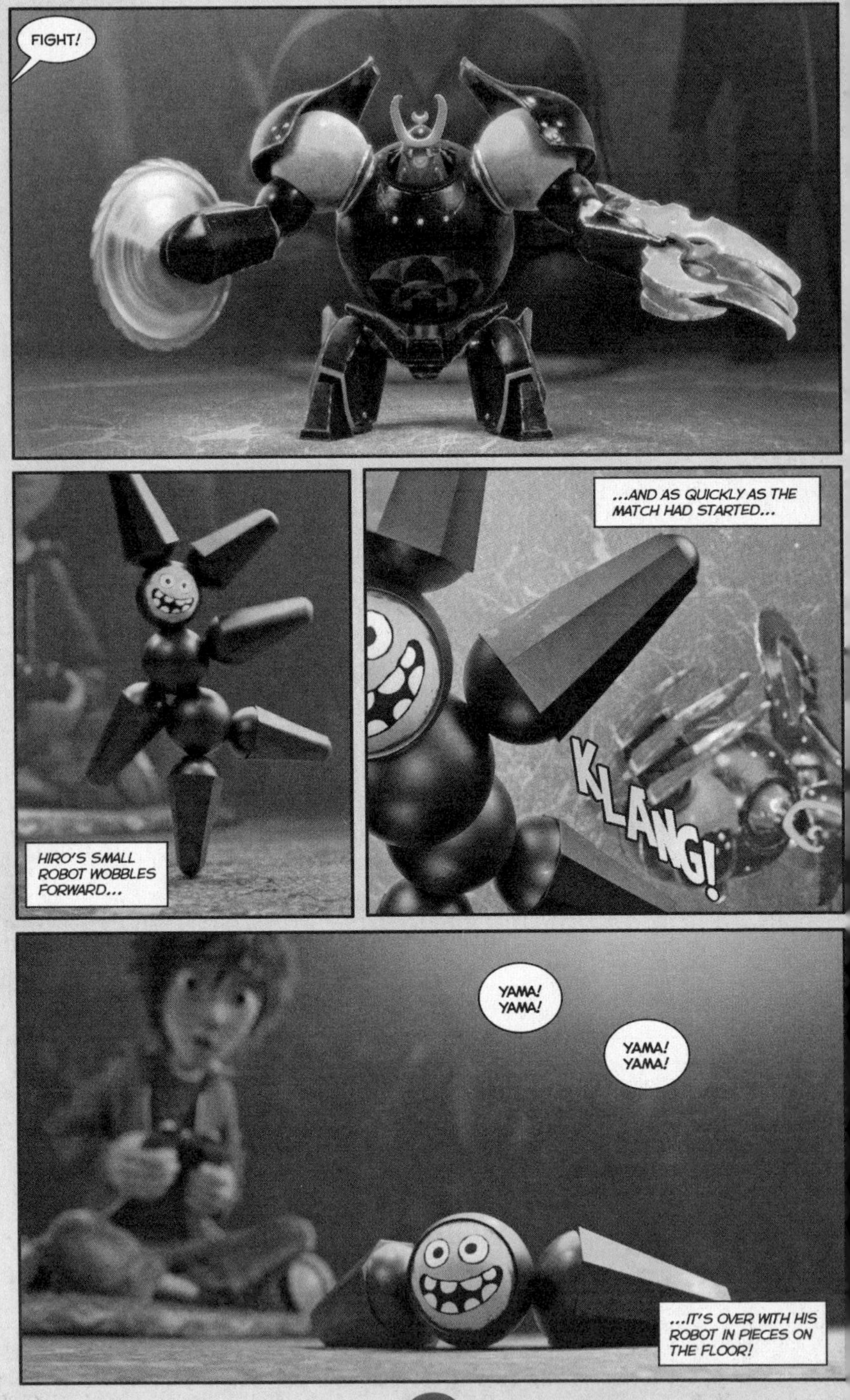
FIGHT!
HIRO'S SMALL ROBOT WOBBLES FORWARD...
...AND AS QUICKLY AS THE MATCH HAD STARTED...
KLANG!
YAMA! YAMA!
YAMA! YAMA!
...IT'S OVER WITH HIS ROBOT IN PIECES ON THE FLOOR!

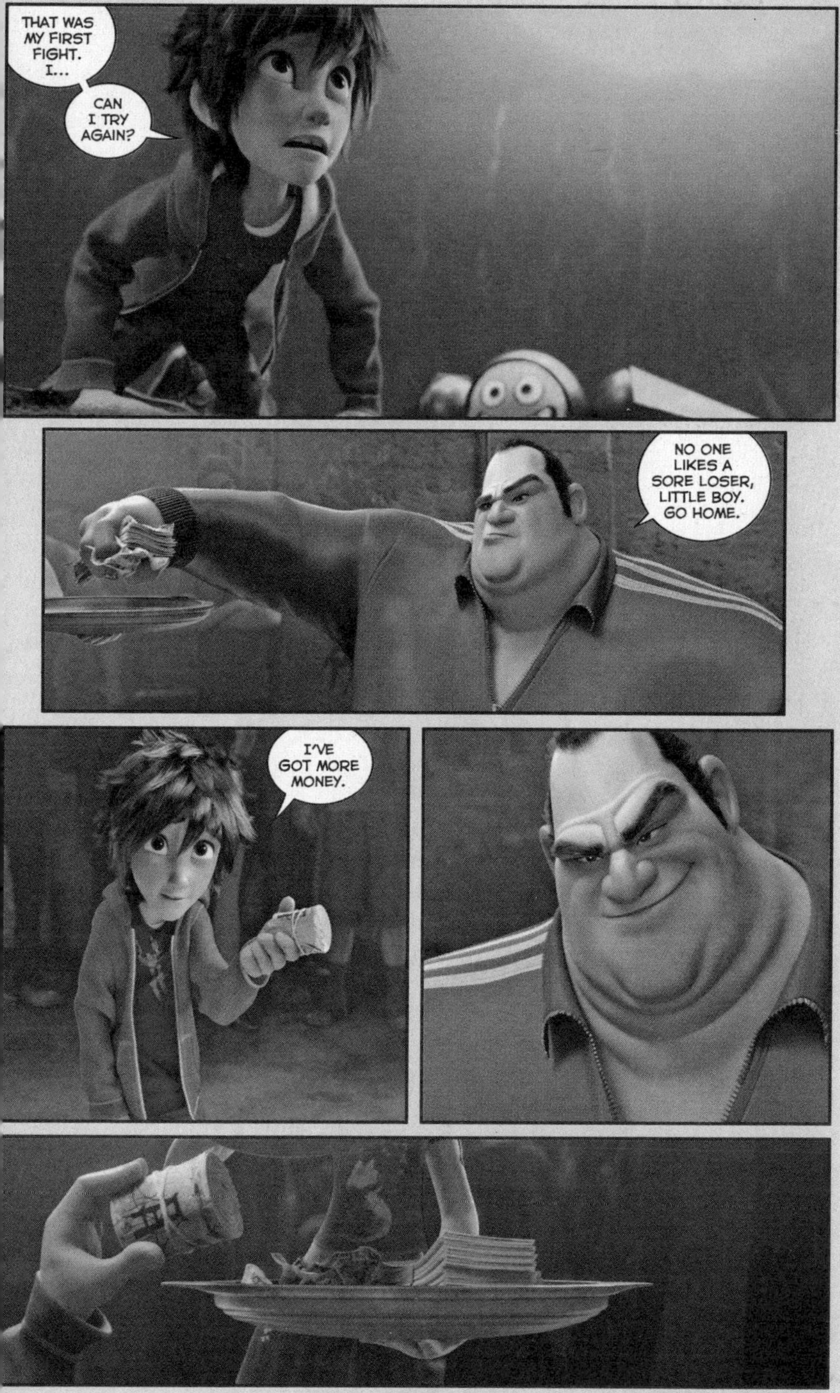
THAT WAS MY FIRST FIGHT. I...
CAN I TRY AGAIN?
NO ONE LIKES A SORE LOSER, LITTLE BOY. GO HOME.
I'VE GOT MORE MONEY.

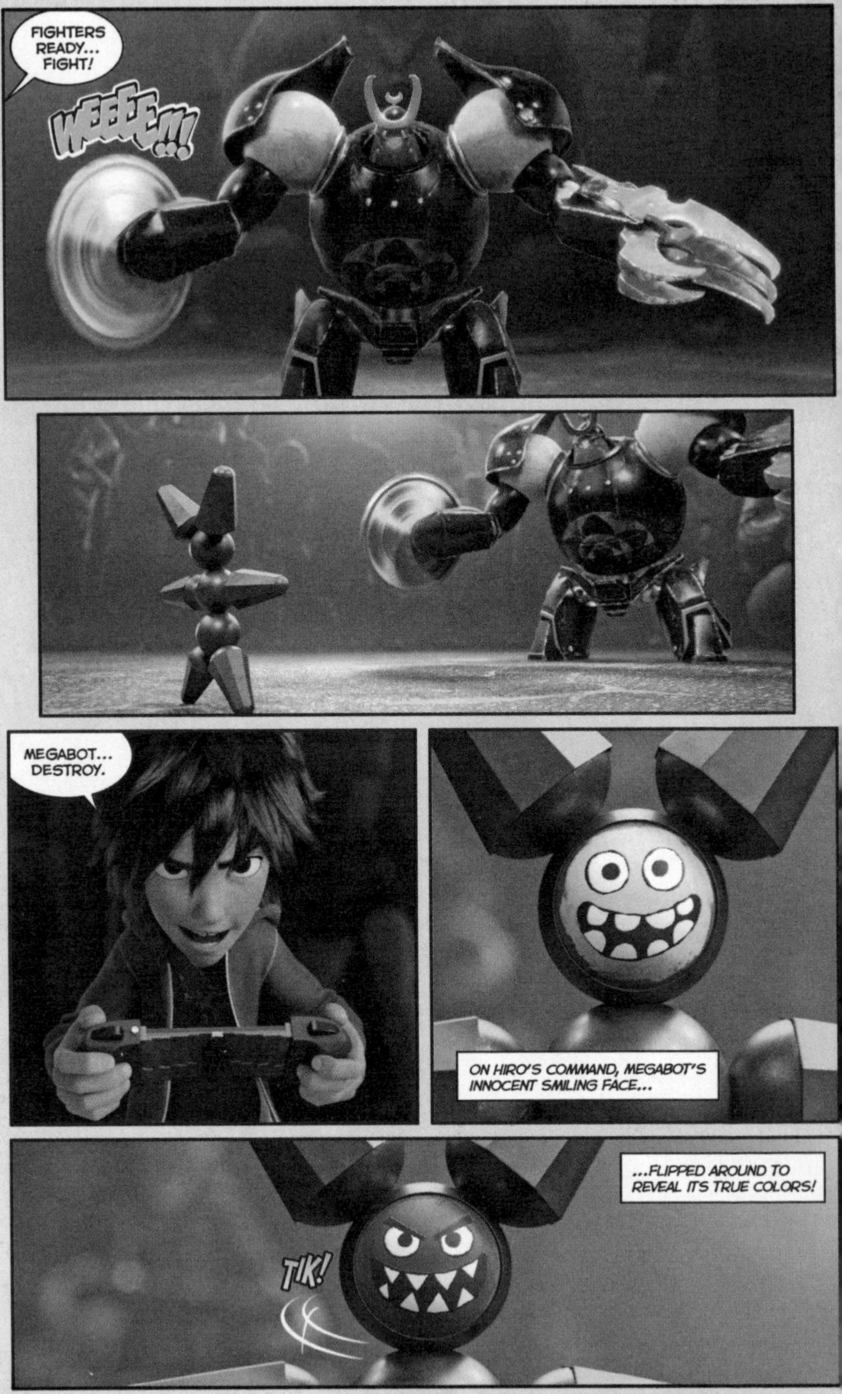
FIGHTERS READY... FIGHT!
WEEEE!!!
MEGABOT... DESTROY.
ON HIRO'S COMMAND, MEGABOT'S INNOCENT SMILING FACE...
...FLIPPED AROUND TO REVEAL ITS TRUE COLORS!
TIK!

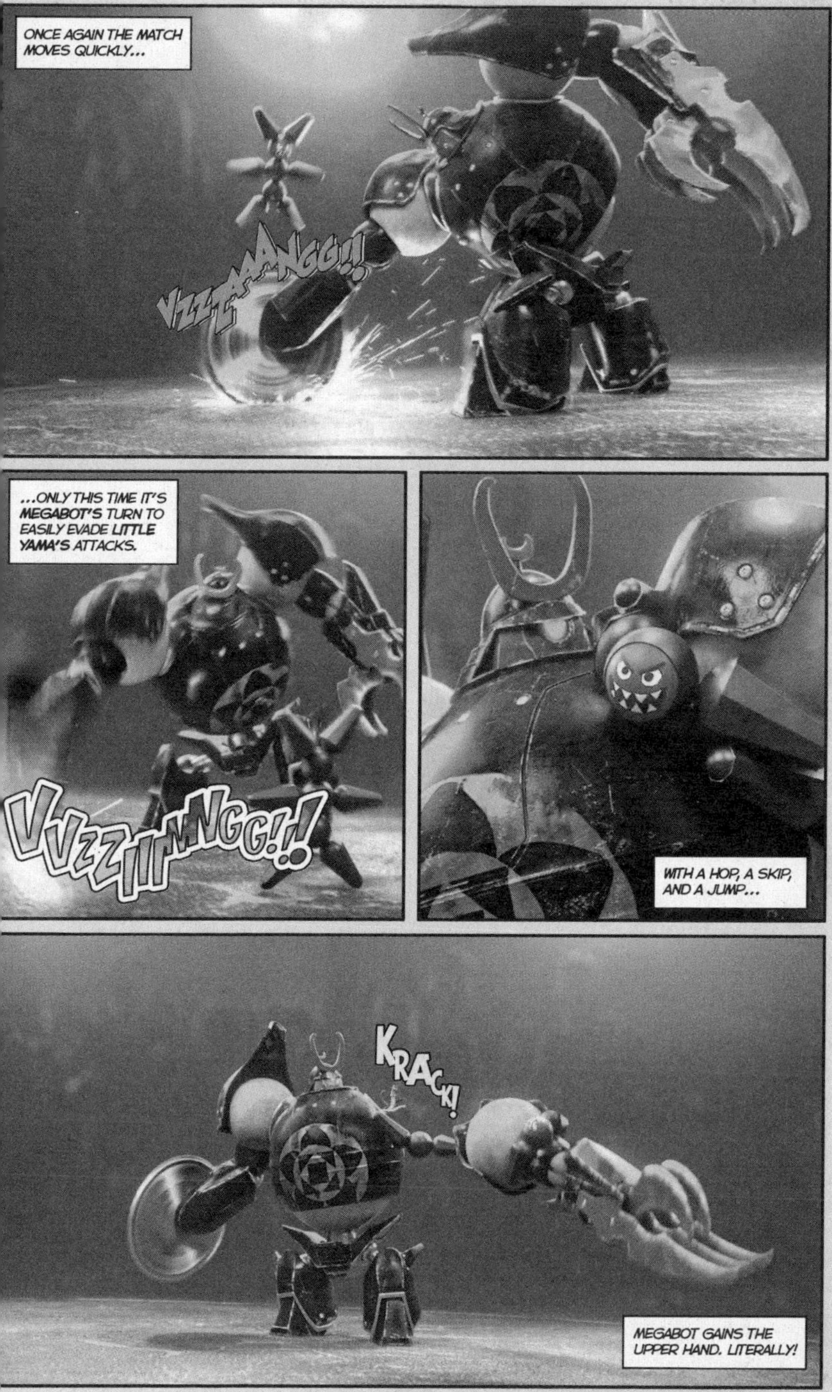
ONCE AGAIN THE MATCH MOVES QUICKLY...
VZZZAAANGG!!
...ONLY THIS TIME IT'S **MEGABOT'S** TURN TO EASILY EVADE **LITTLE YAMA'S** ATTACKS.
VVZZIIINNGG!!
WITH A HOP, A SKIP, AND A JUMP...
KRACK!
MEGABOT GAINS THE UPPER HAND. LITERALLY!

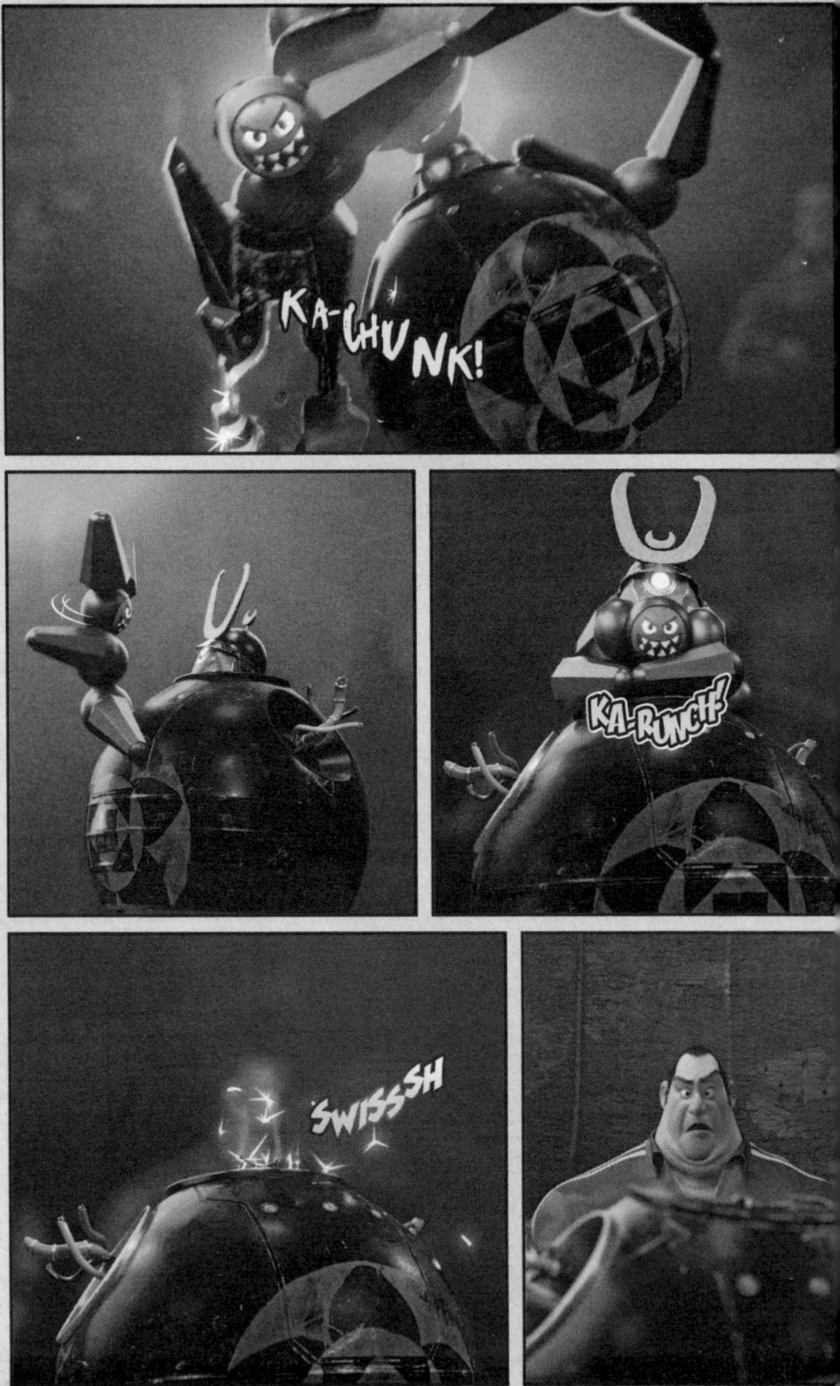
KA-CHUNK!
KA-RUNCH!
SWISSSH

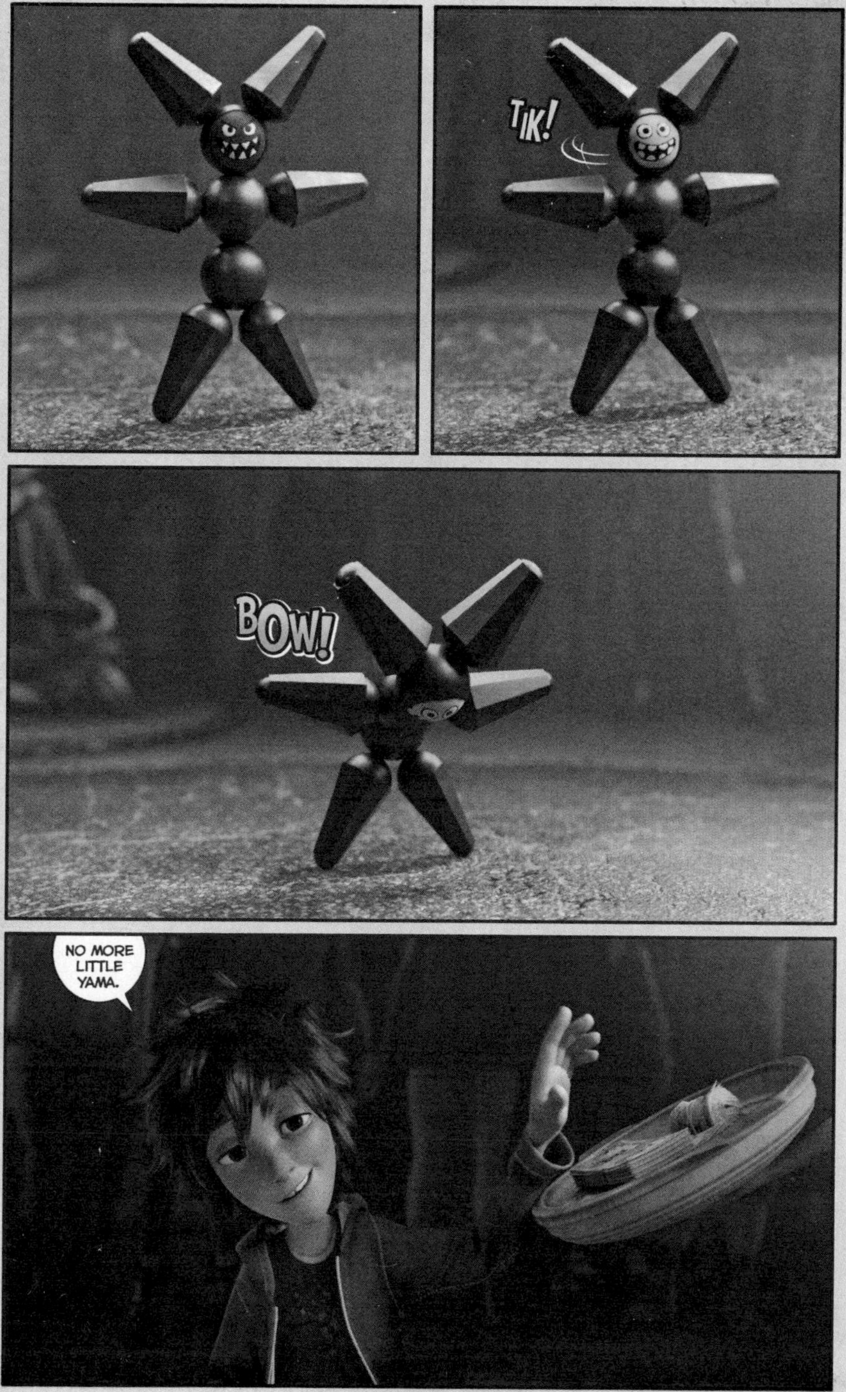
TIK!
BOW!
NO MORE LITTLE YAMA.

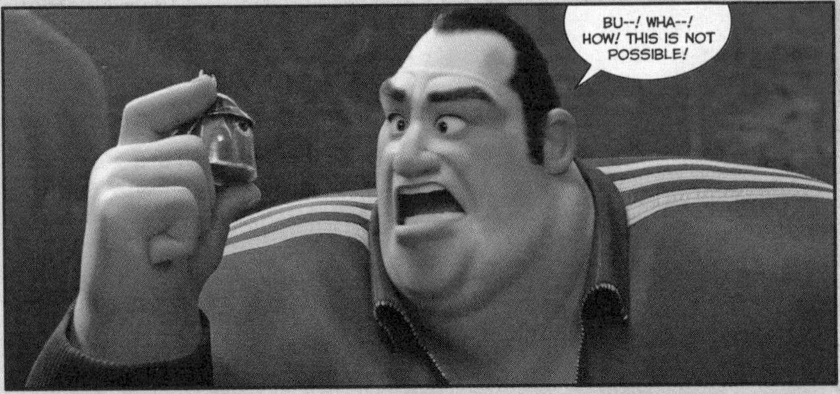
BU--! WHA--! HOW! THIS IS NOT POSSIBLE!

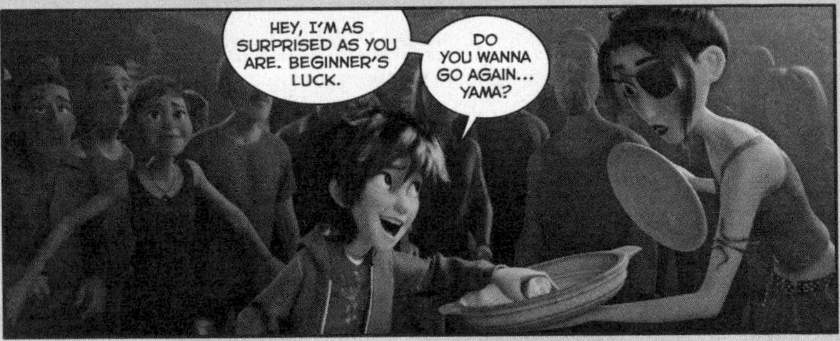
HEY, I'M AS SURPRISED AS YOU ARE. BEGINNER'S LUCK.
DO YOU WANNA GO AGAIN... YAMA?

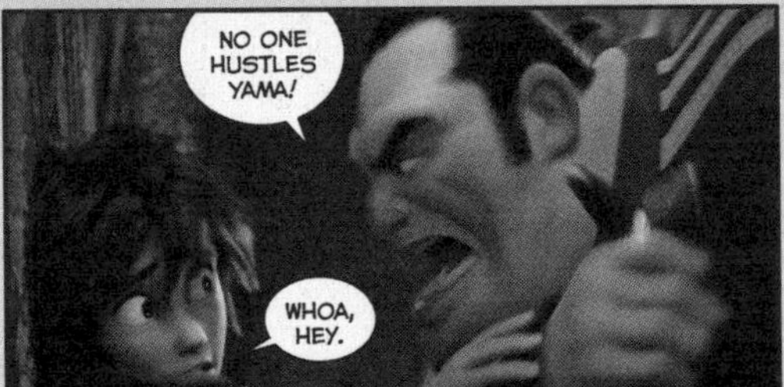
NO ONE HUSTLES YAMA!
WHOA, HEY.

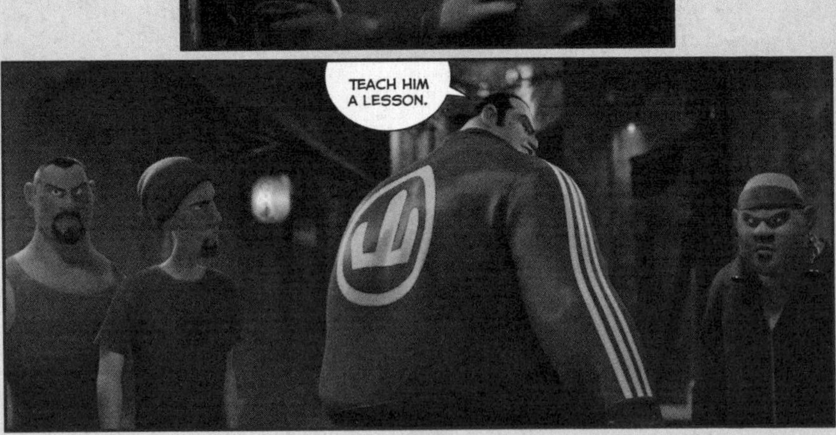
TEACH HIM A LESSON.

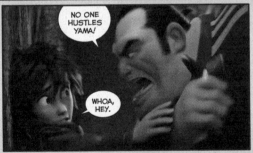

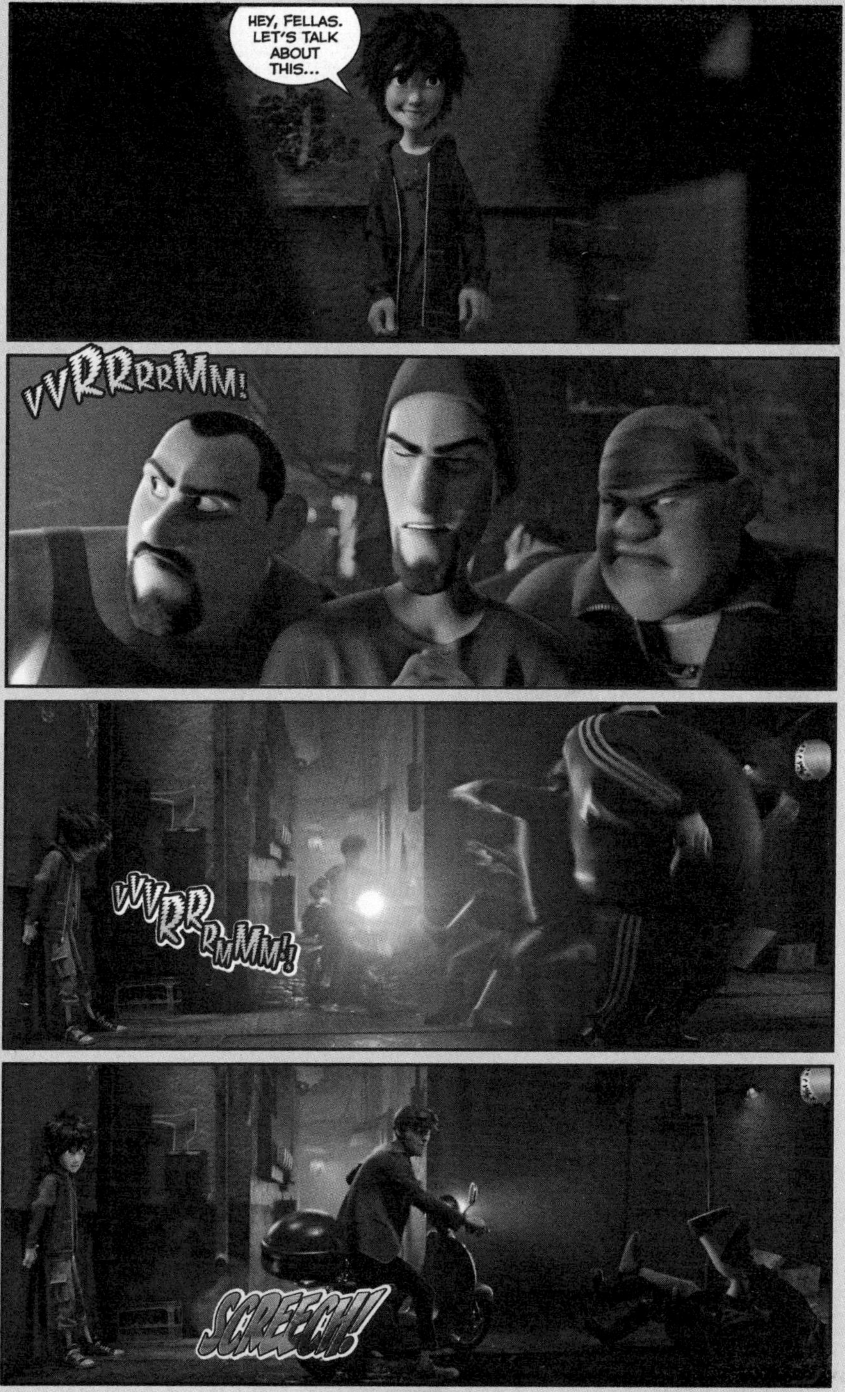
HEY, FELLAS. LET'S TALK ABOUT THIS...
VVRRRRMM!
VVVRRRMMM!
SCREECH!

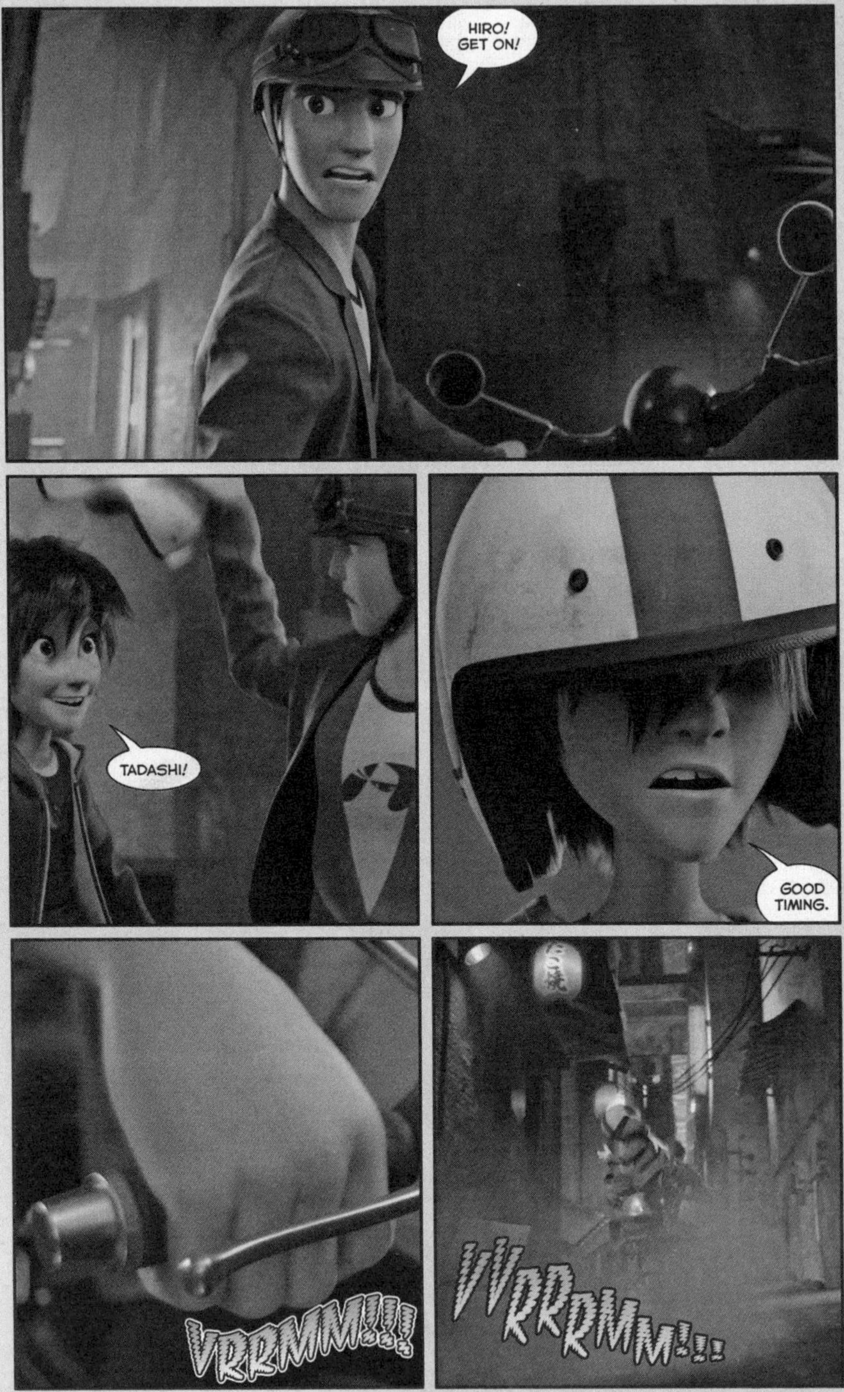
HIRO!
GET ON!
TADASHI!
GOOD
TIMING.
VRRMM!!!
VVRRRMM!!!

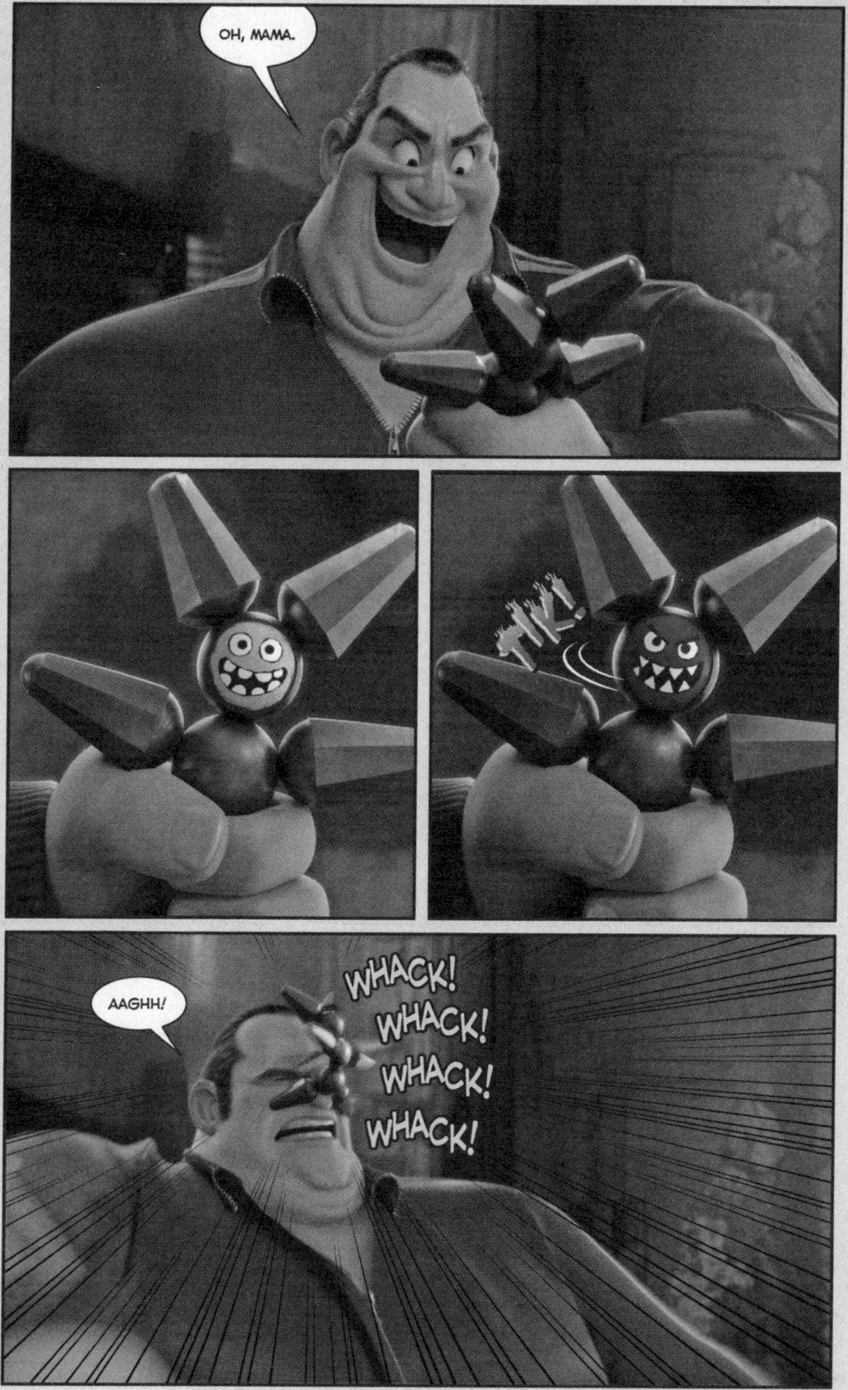
OH, MAMA.
TIK!
AAGHH!
WHACK!
WHACK!
WHACK!
WHACK!

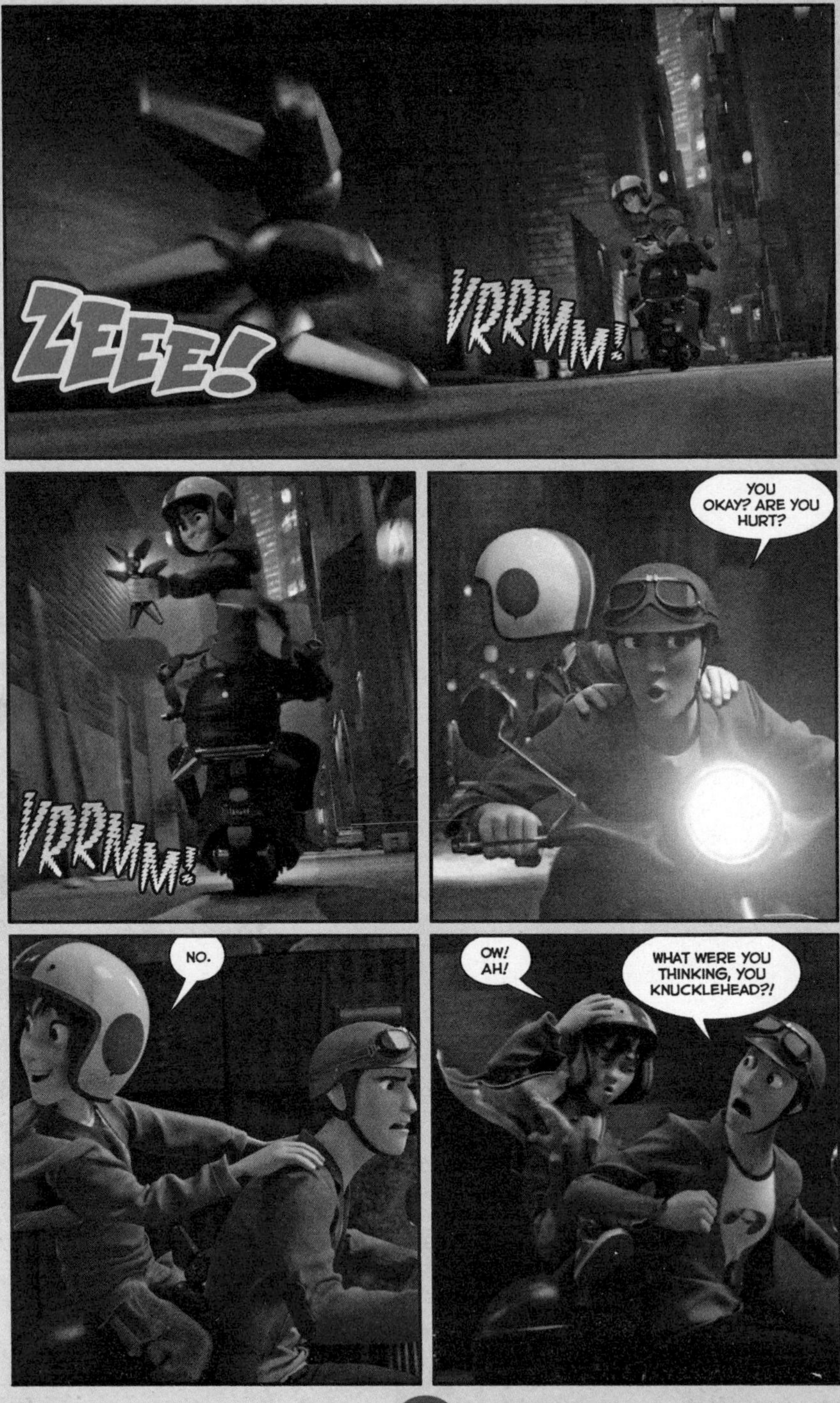
ZEEE!
VRRMM!
VRRMM!
YOU OKAY? ARE YOU HURT?
NO.
OW! AH!
WHAT WERE YOU THINKING, YOU KNUCKLEHEAD?!

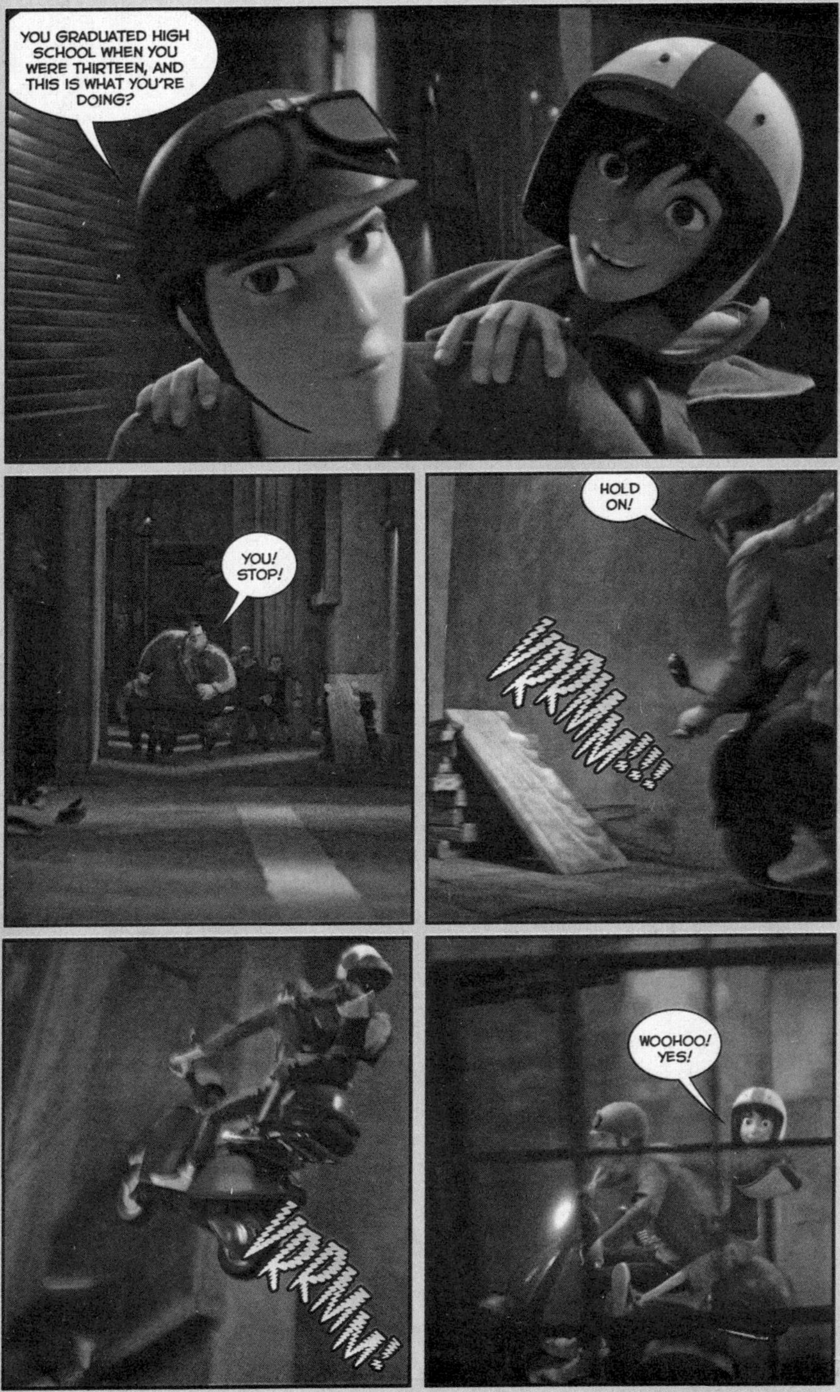
YOU GRADUATED HIGH SCHOOL WHEN YOU WERE THIRTEEN, AND THIS IS WHAT YOU'RE DOING?
YOU! STOP!
HOLD ON!
VRRMM!!!
VRRMM!
WOOHOO! YES!

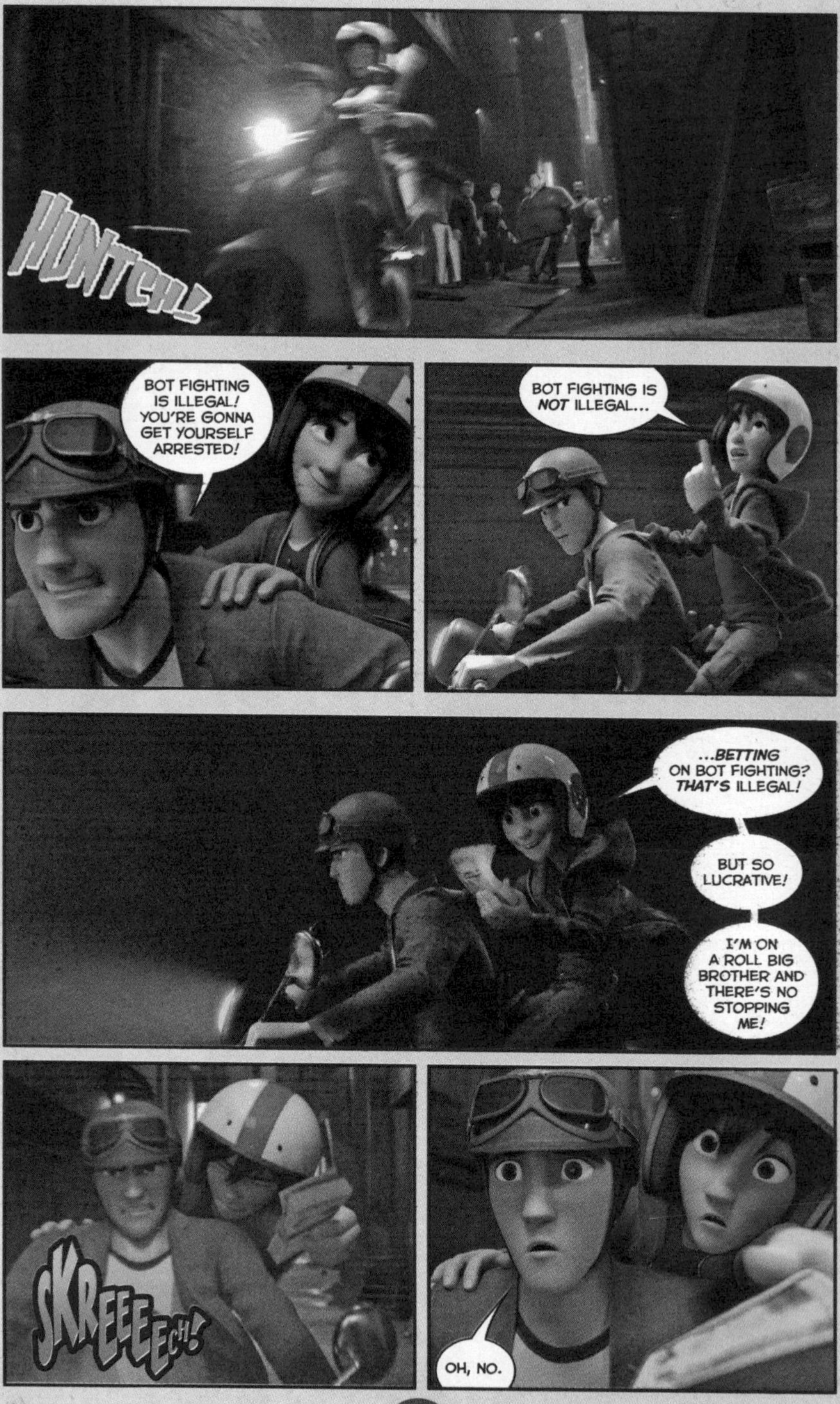
HUNTCH!
BOT FIGHTING IS ILLEGAL! YOU'RE GONNA GET YOURSELF ARRESTED!
BOT FIGHTING IS *NOT* ILLEGAL...
...*BETTING* ON BOT FIGHTING? *THAT'S* ILLEGAL!
BUT SO LUCRATIVE!
I'M ON A ROLL BIG BROTHER AND THERE'S NO STOPPING ME!
SKREEEECH!
OH, NO.

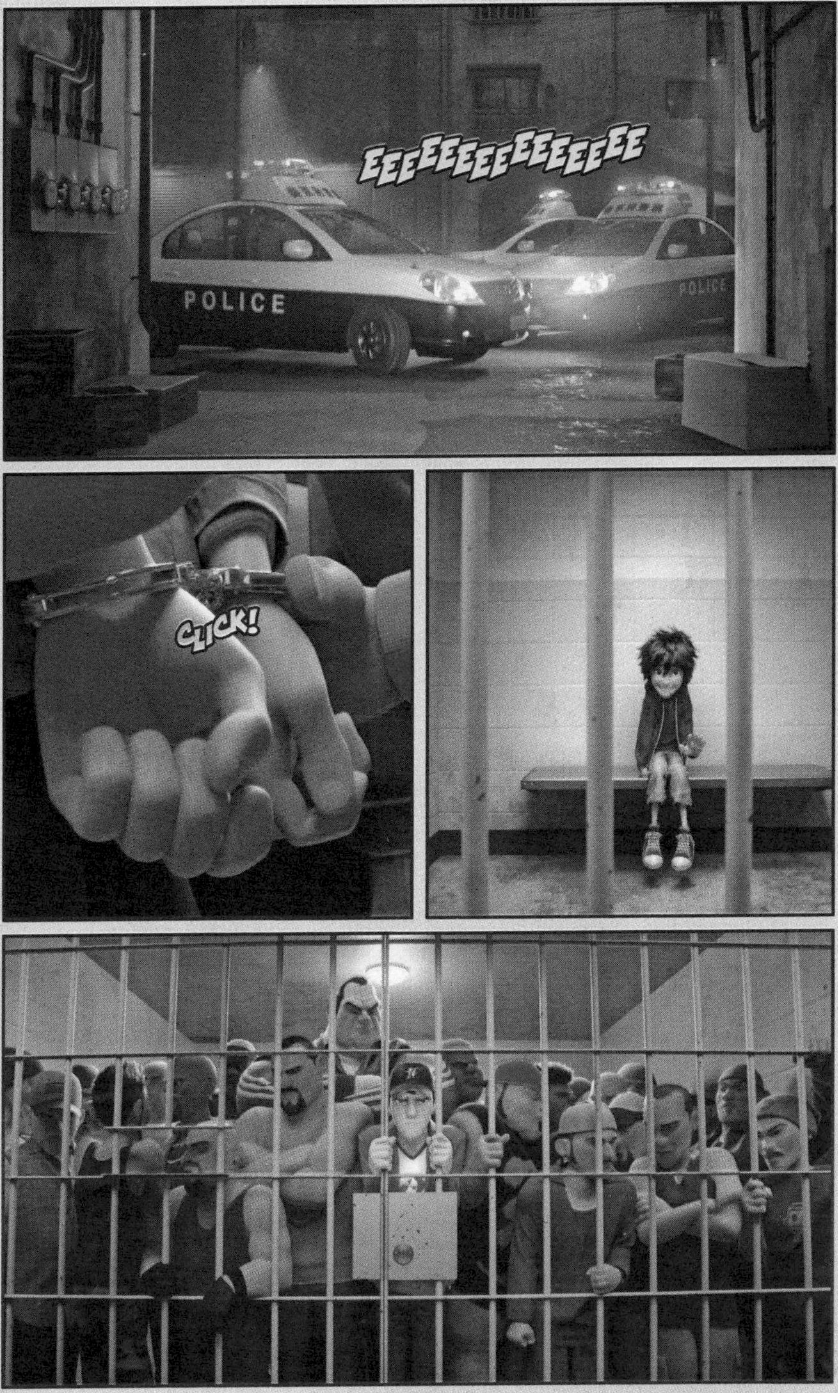
EEEEEEEEEEEEEEE
POLICE
POLICE
CLICK!

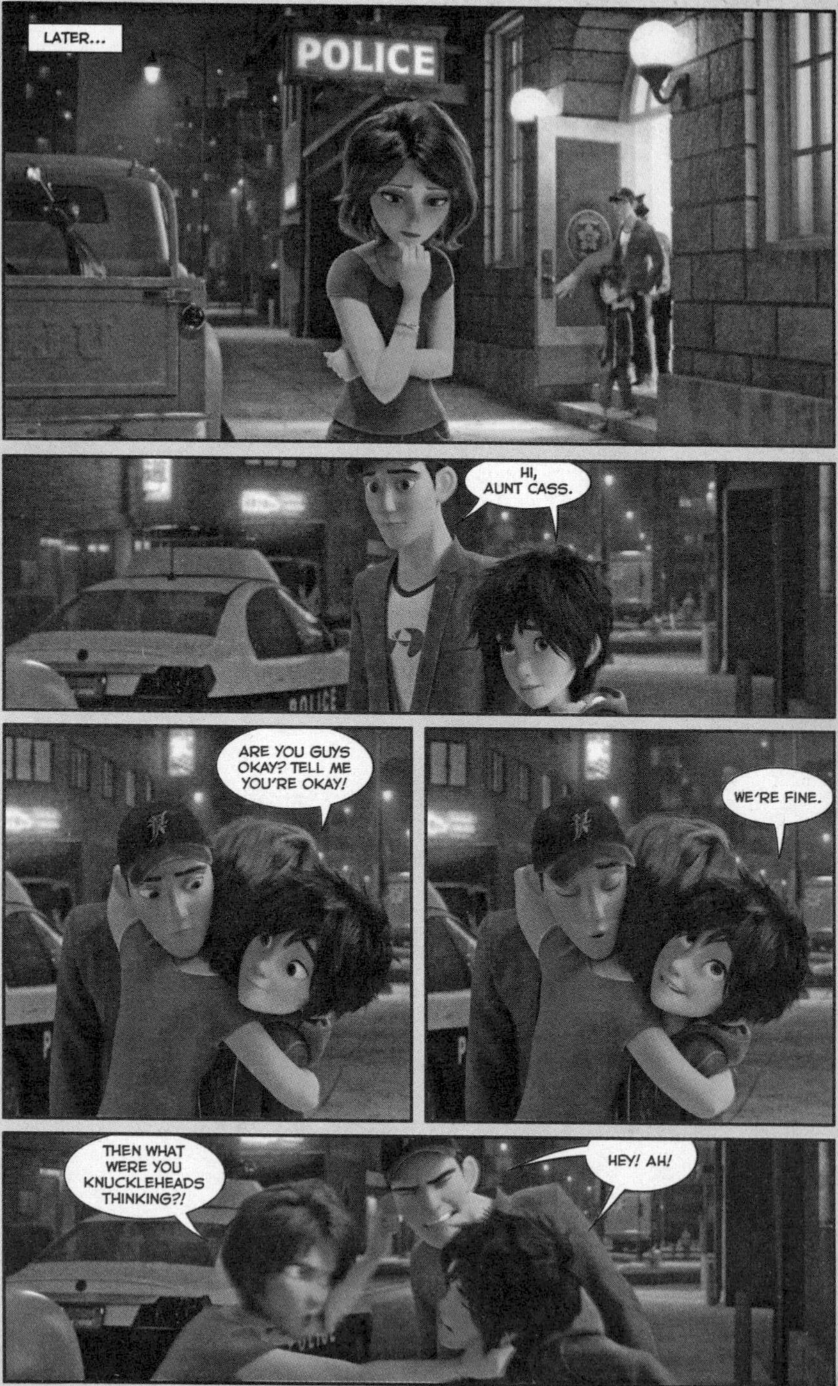
LATER...
POLICE
HI, AUNT CASS.
ARE YOU GUYS OKAY? TELL ME YOU'RE OKAY!
WE'RE FINE.
THEN WHAT WERE YOU KNUCKLEHEADS THINKING?!
HEY! AH!

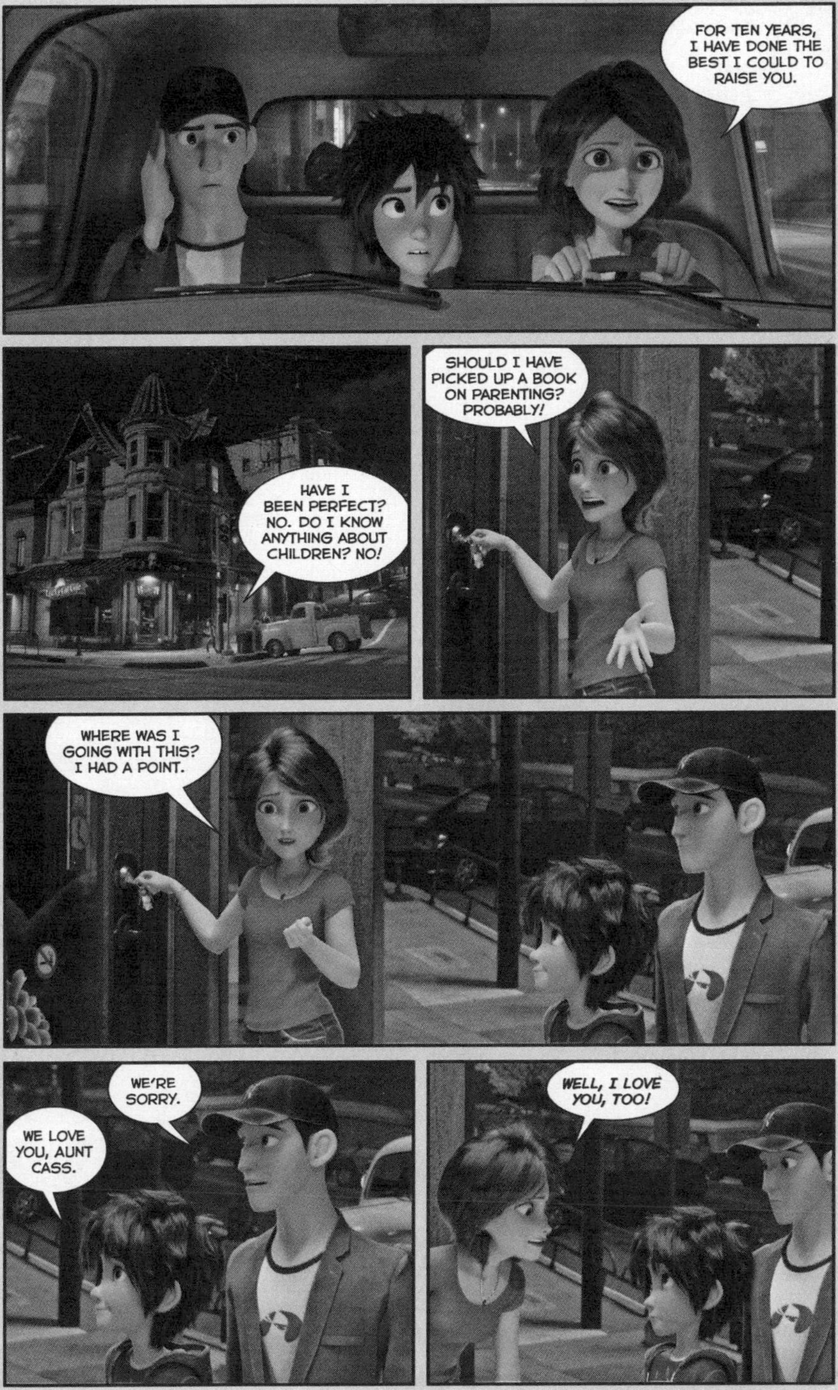
FOR TEN YEARS, I HAVE DONE THE BEST I COULD TO RAISE YOU.
HAVE I BEEN PERFECT? NO. DO I KNOW ANYTHING ABOUT CHILDREN? NO!
SHOULD I HAVE PICKED UP A BOOK ON PARENTING? PROBABLY!
WHERE WAS I GOING WITH THIS? I HAD A POINT.
WE'RE SORRY.
WE LOVE YOU, AUNT CASS.
WELL, I LOVE YOU, TOO!

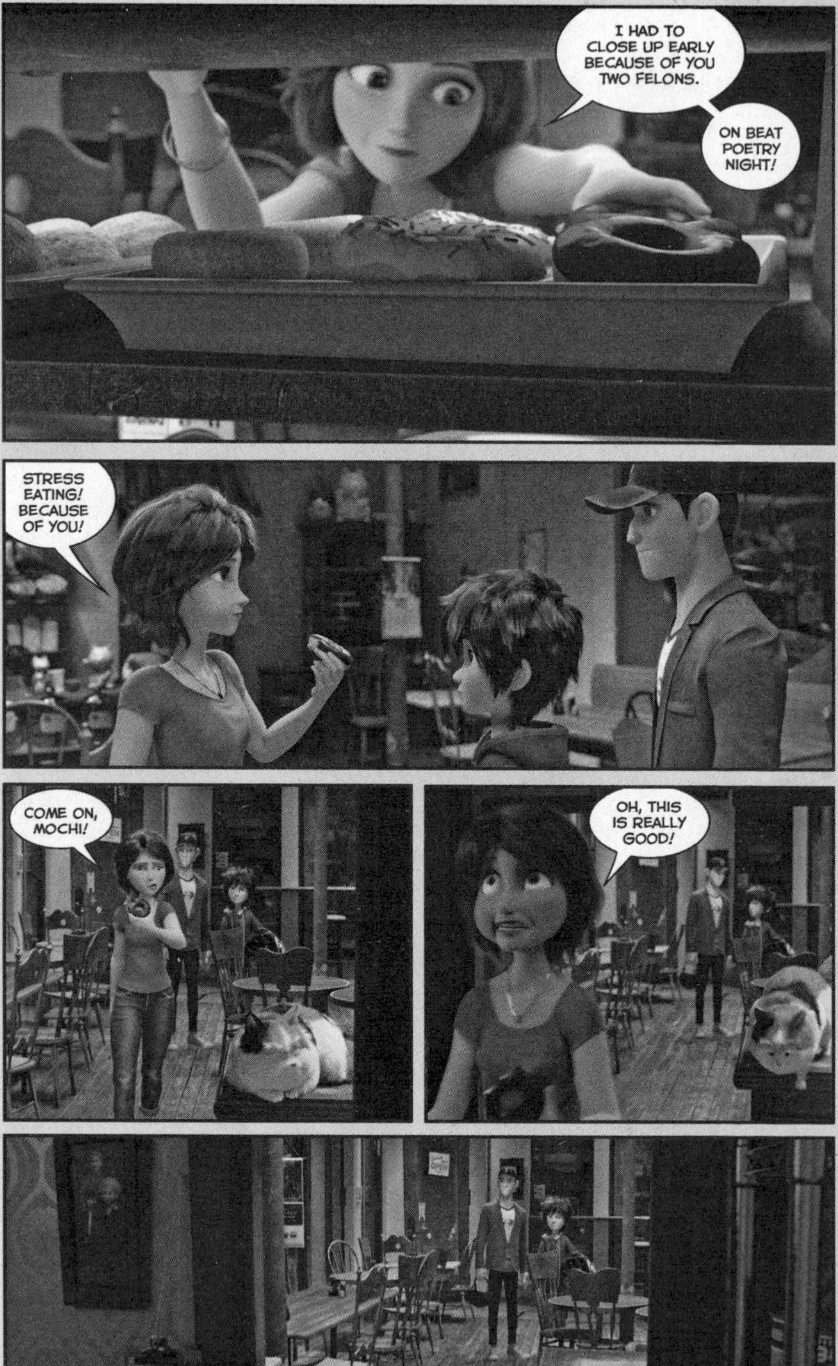
I HAD TO CLOSE UP EARLY BECAUSE OF YOU TWO FELONS.
ON BEAT POETRY NIGHT!
STRESS EATING! BECAUSE OF YOU!
COME ON, MOCHI!
OH, THIS IS REALLY GOOD!

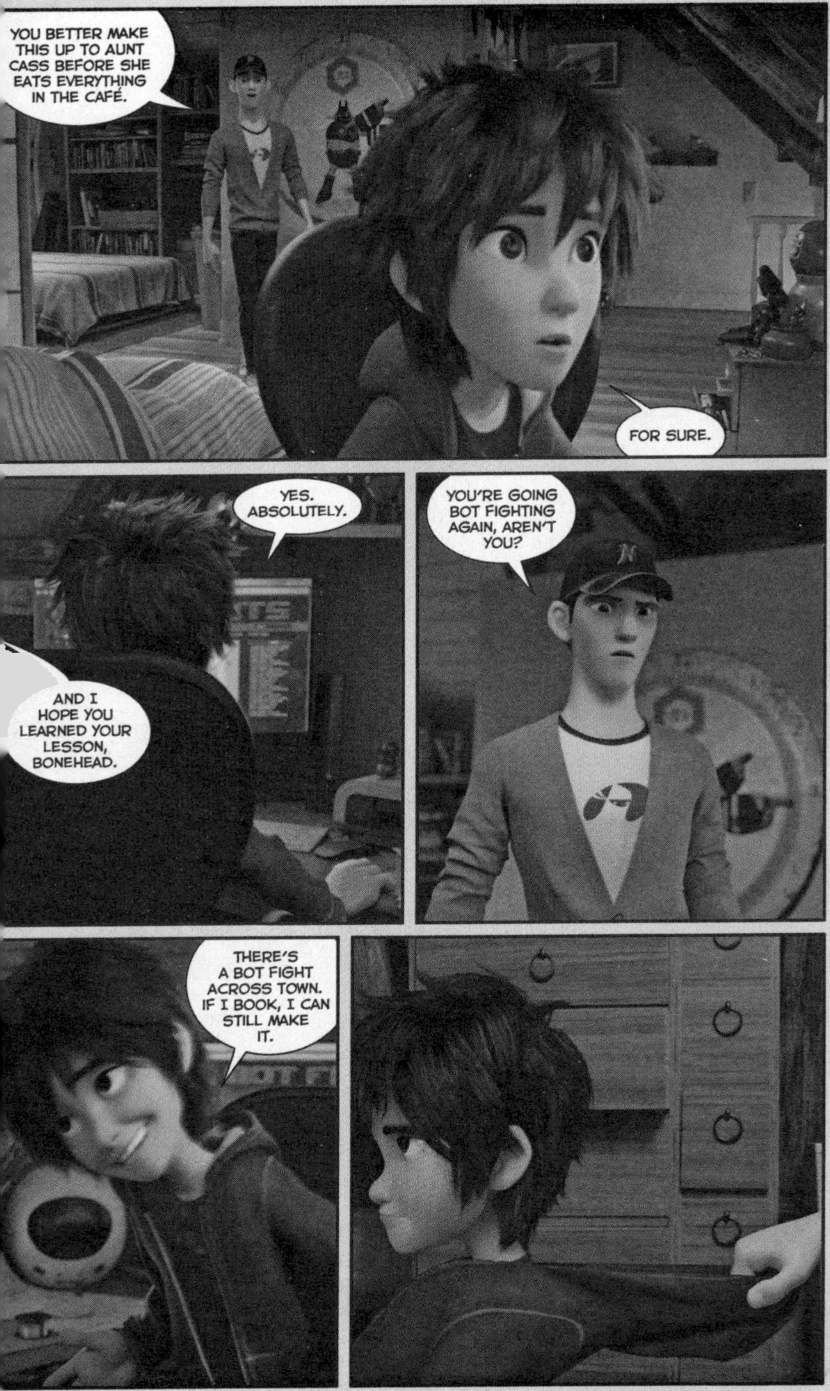
YOU BETTER MAKE THIS UP TO AUNT CASS BEFORE SHE EATS EVERYTHING IN THE CAFÉ.
FOR SURE.
YES. ABSOLUTELY.
AND I HOPE YOU LEARNED YOUR LESSON, BONEHEAD.
YOU'RE GOING BOT FIGHTING AGAIN, AREN'T YOU?
THERE'S A BOT FIGHT ACROSS TOWN. IF I BOOK, I CAN STILL MAKE IT.

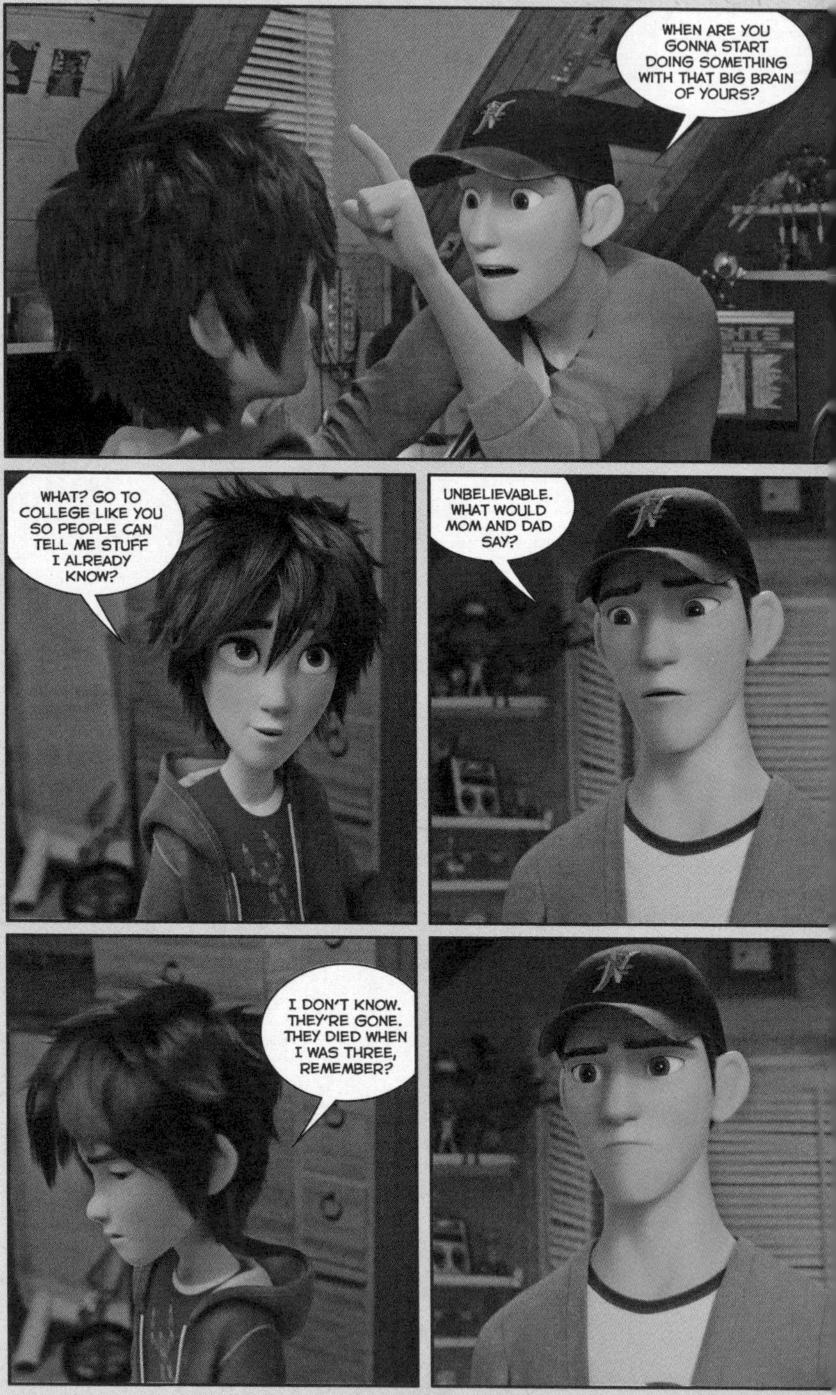
WHEN ARE YOU GONNA START DOING SOMETHING WITH THAT BIG BRAIN OF YOURS?
WHAT? GO TO COLLEGE LIKE YOU SO PEOPLE CAN TELL ME STUFF I ALREADY KNOW?
UNBELIEVABLE. WHAT WOULD MOM AND DAD SAY?
I DON'T KNOW. THEY'RE GONE. THEY DIED WHEN I WAS THREE, REMEMBER?

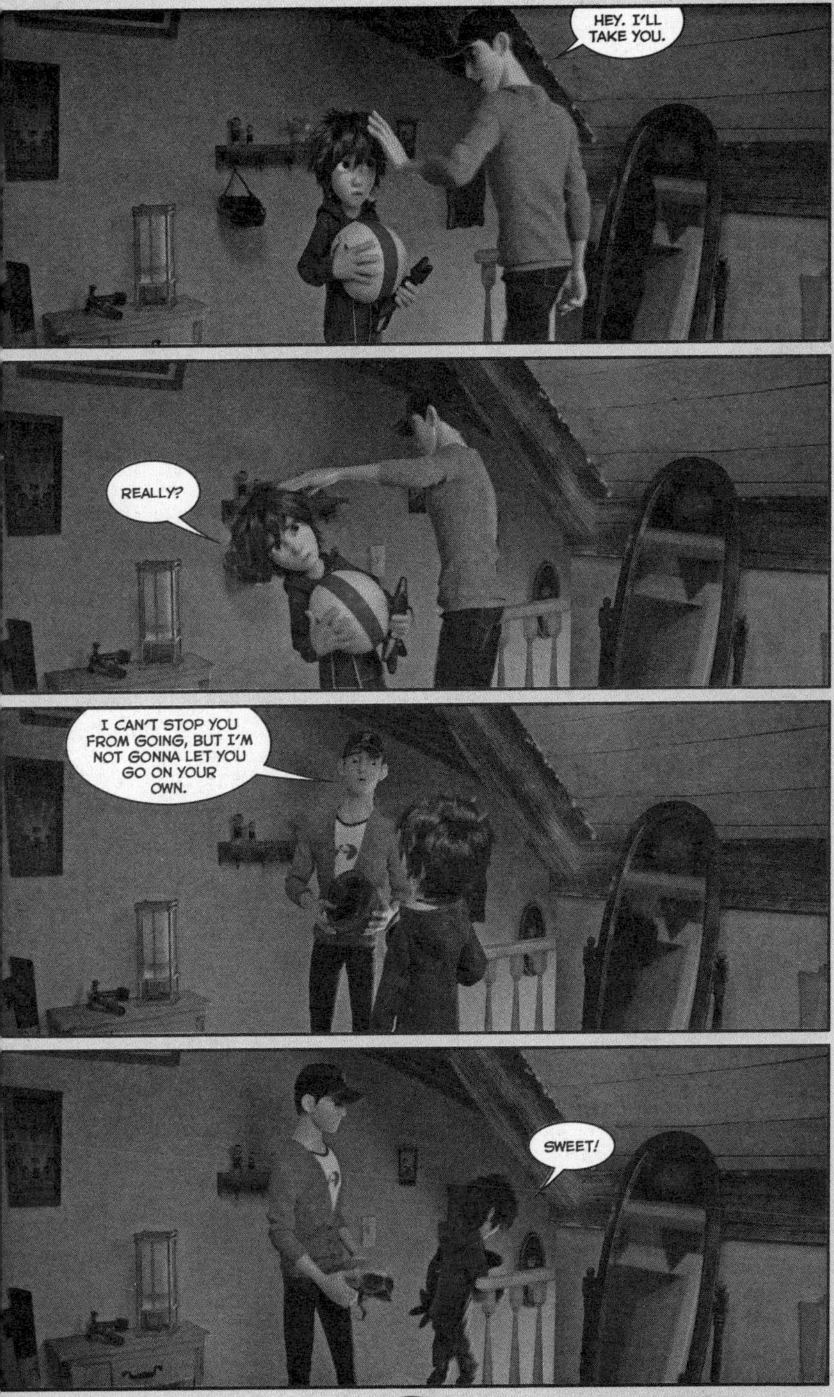
HEY. I'LL TAKE YOU.
REALLY?
I CAN'T STOP YOU FROM GOING, BUT I'M NOT GONNA LET YOU GO ON YOUR OWN.
SWEET!

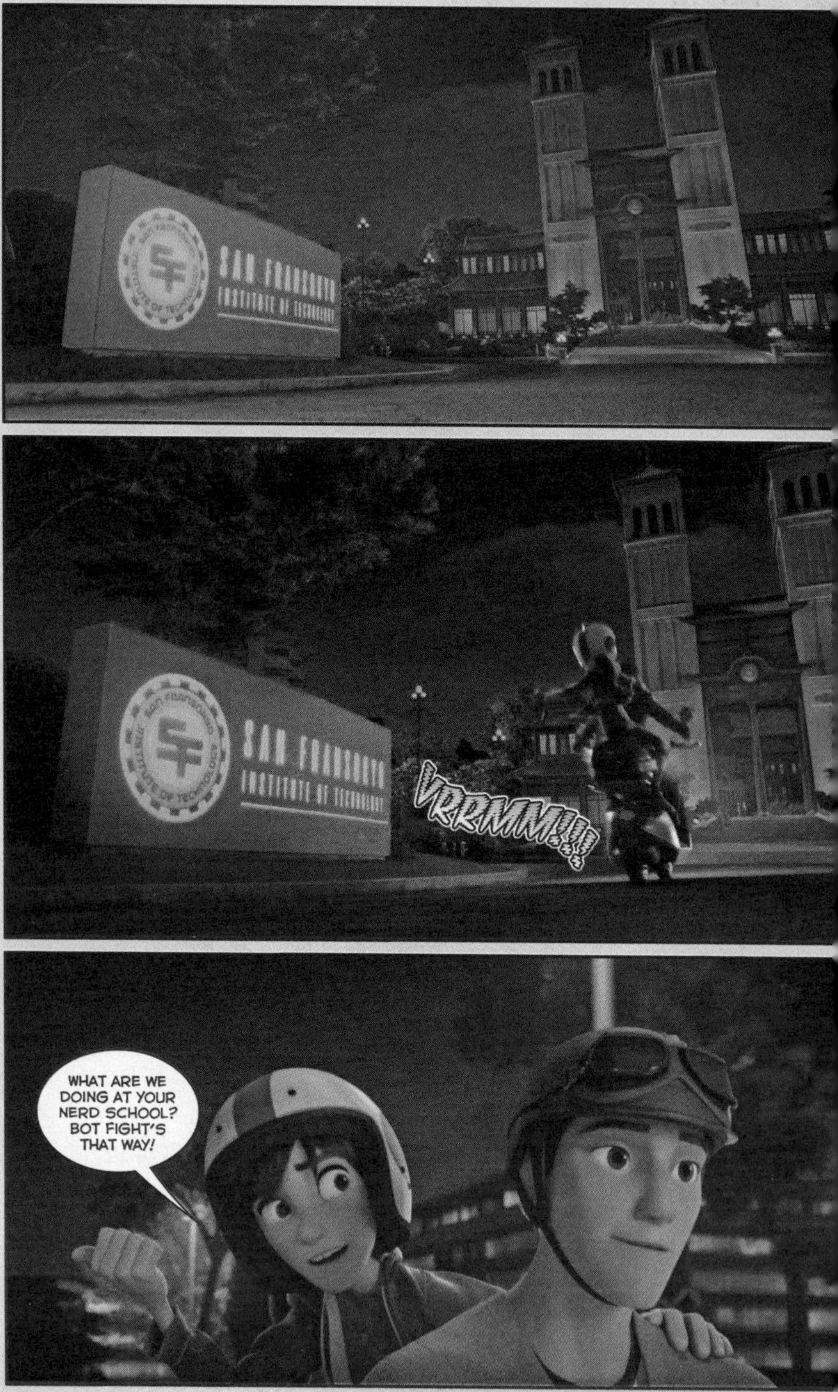
SAN FRANSOKYO INSTITUTE OF TECHNOLOGY
SAN FRANSOKYO INSTITUTE OF TECHNOLOGY
VRRRMM!!!
WHAT ARE WE DOING AT YOUR NERD SCHOOL? BOT FIGHT'S THAT WAY!

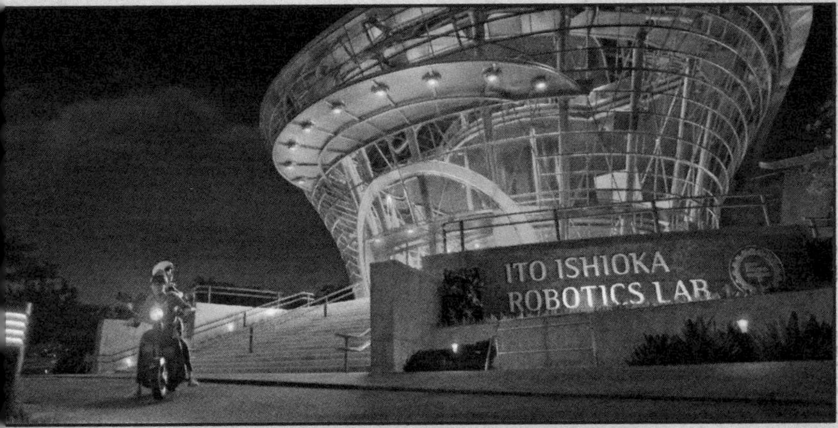
ITO ISHIOKA
ROBOTICS LAB

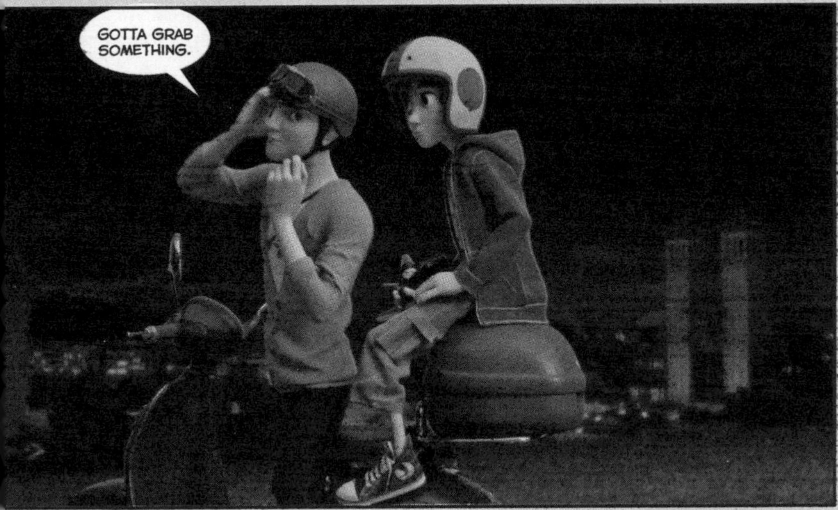
GOTTA GRAB SOMETHING.

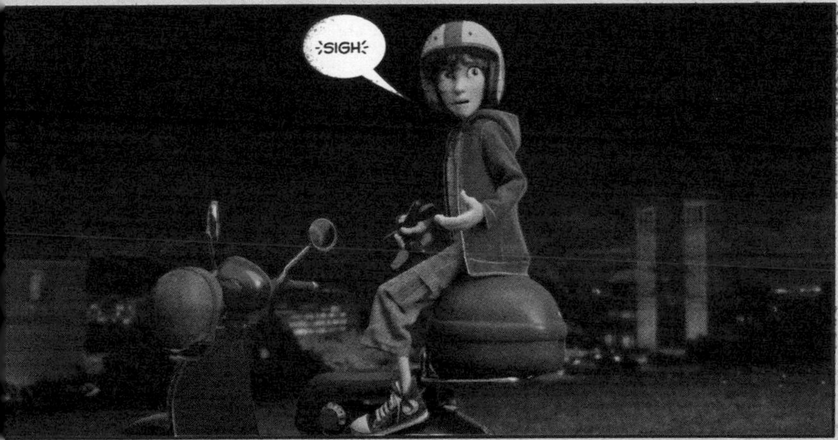
SIGH

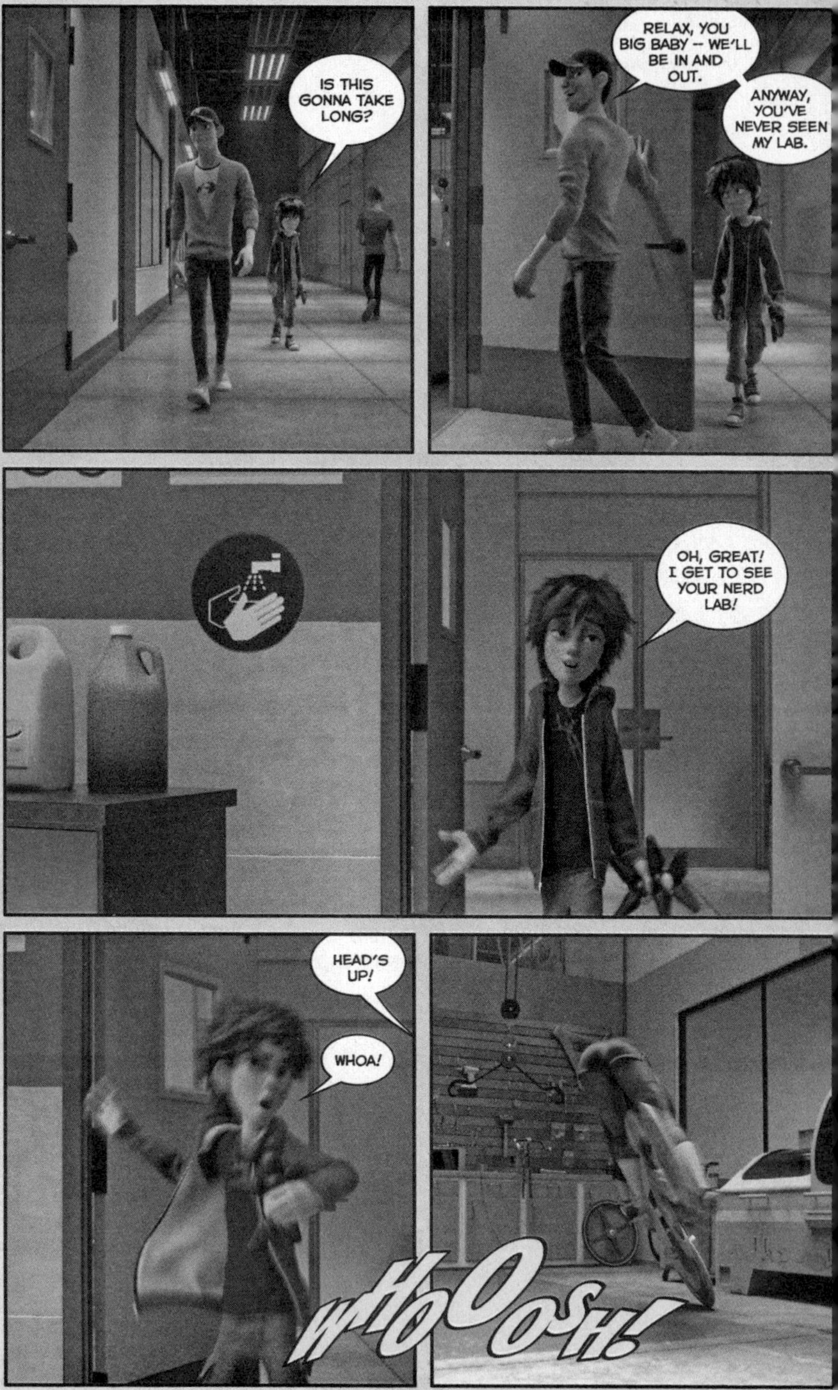
IS THIS GONNA TAKE LONG?
RELAX, YOU BIG BABY -- WE'LL BE IN AND OUT.
ANYWAY, YOU'VE NEVER SEEN MY LAB.
OH, GREAT! I GET TO SEE YOUR NERD LAB!
HEAD'S UP!
WHOA!
WHOOOSH!

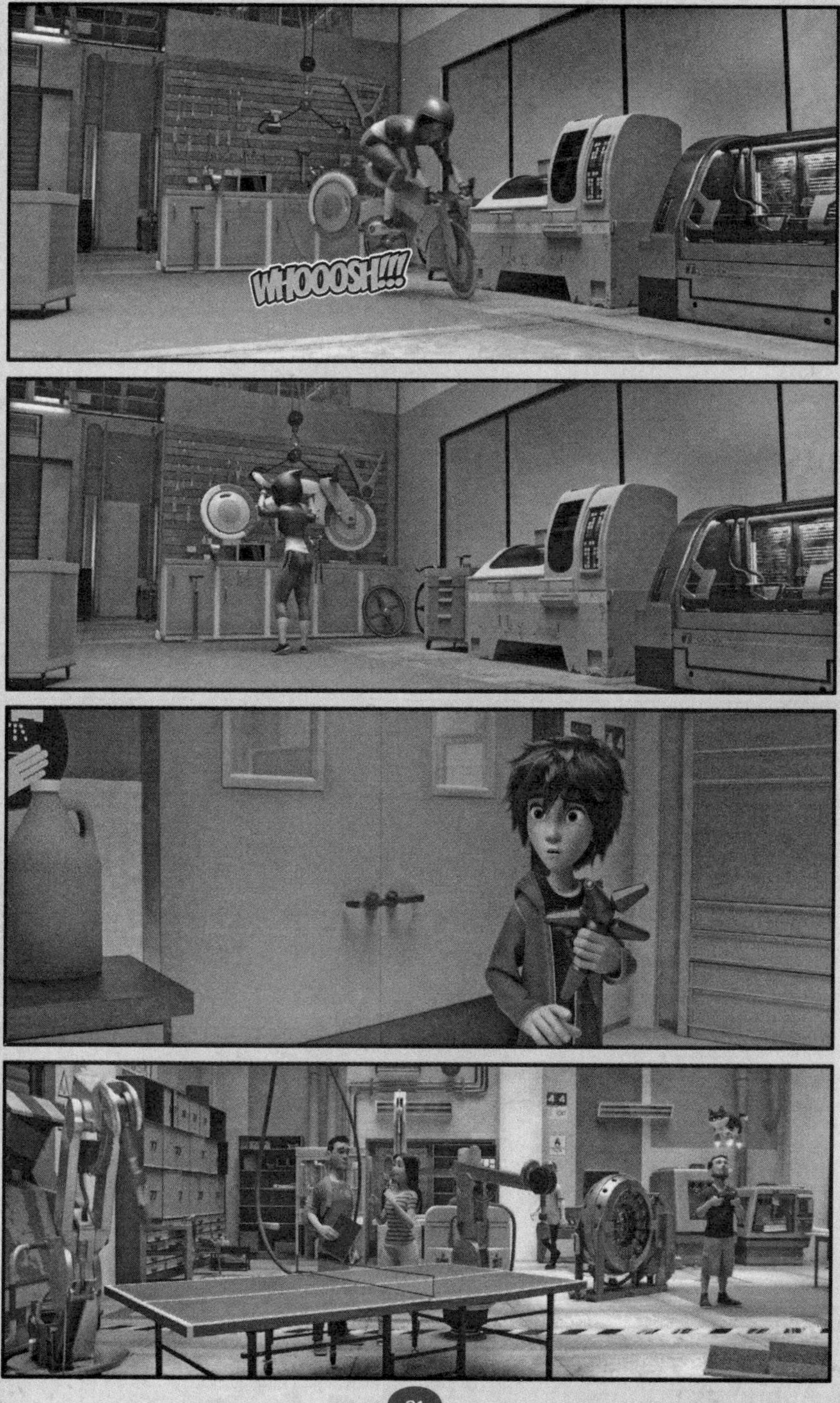
WHOOOSH!!!

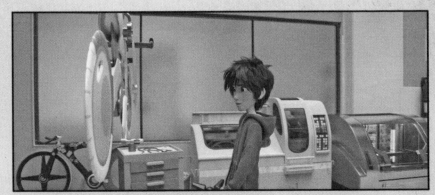

HEY!

WHOA. ELECTRO-MAG SUSPENSION...

WHO'RE YOU?

GO GO, THIS IS MY BROTHER, HIRO.

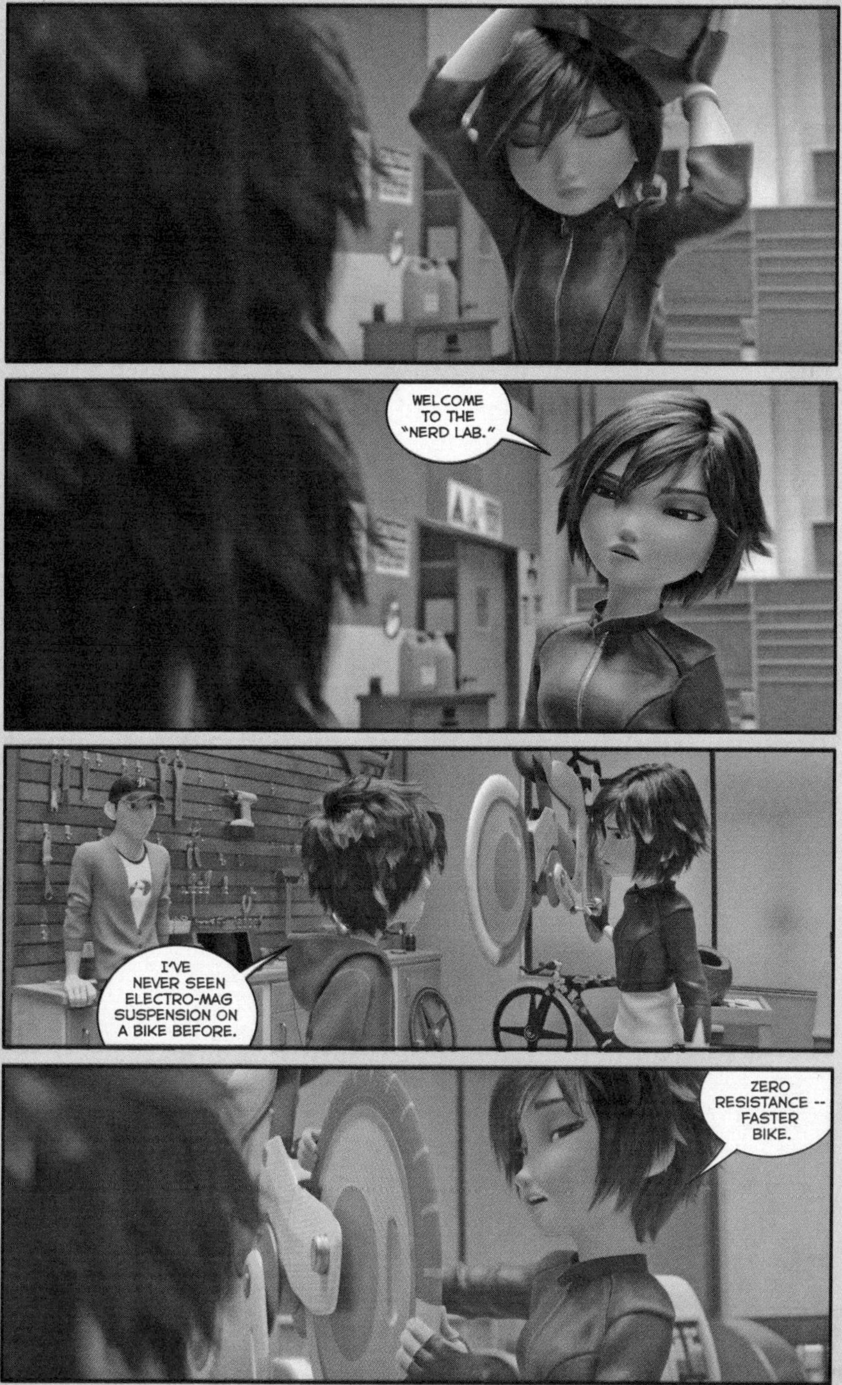
WELCOME TO THE "NERD LAB."
I'VE NEVER SEEN ELECTRO-MAG SUSPENSION ON A BIKE BEFORE.
ZERO RESISTANCE -- FASTER BIKE.

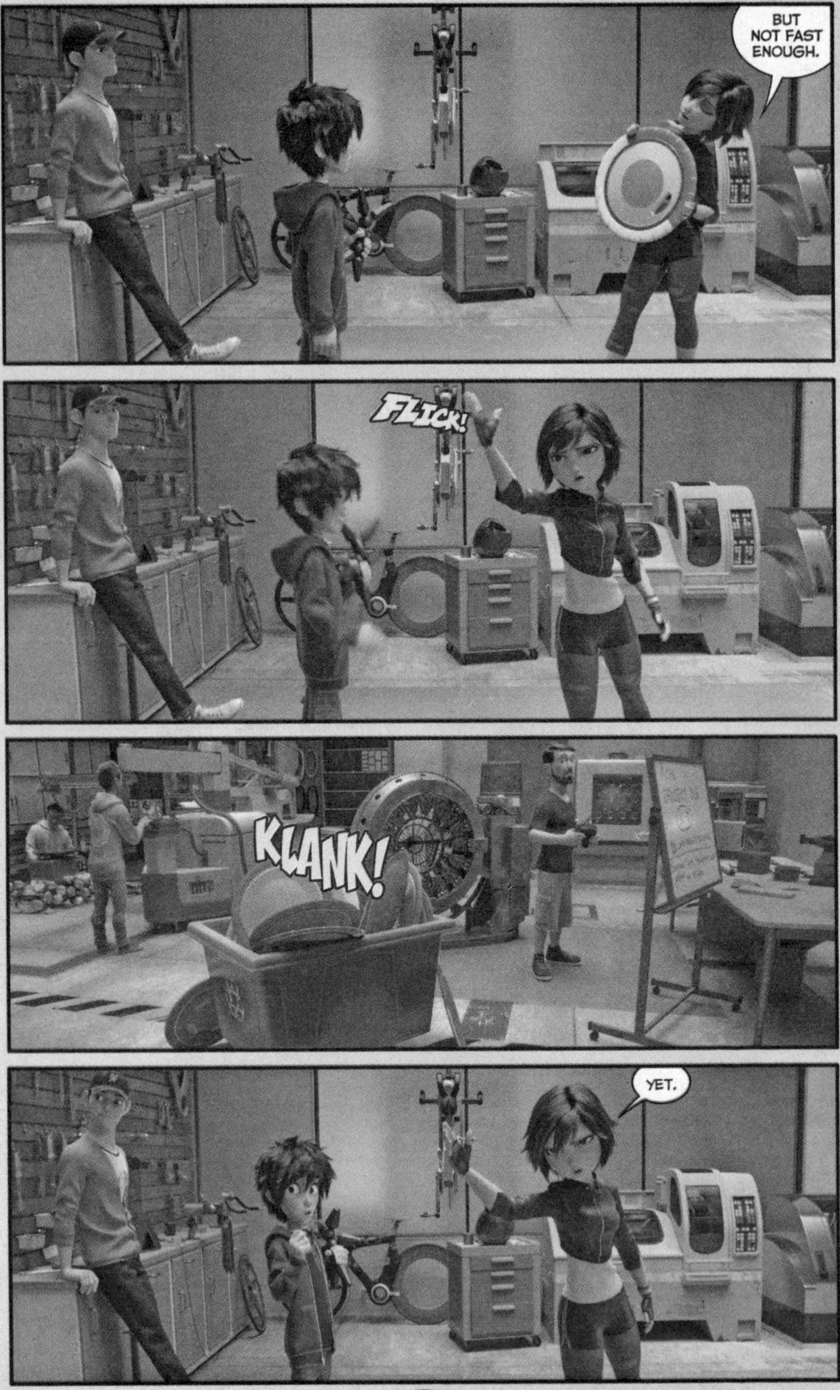
BUT NOT FAST ENOUGH.
FLICK!
KLANK!
YET.

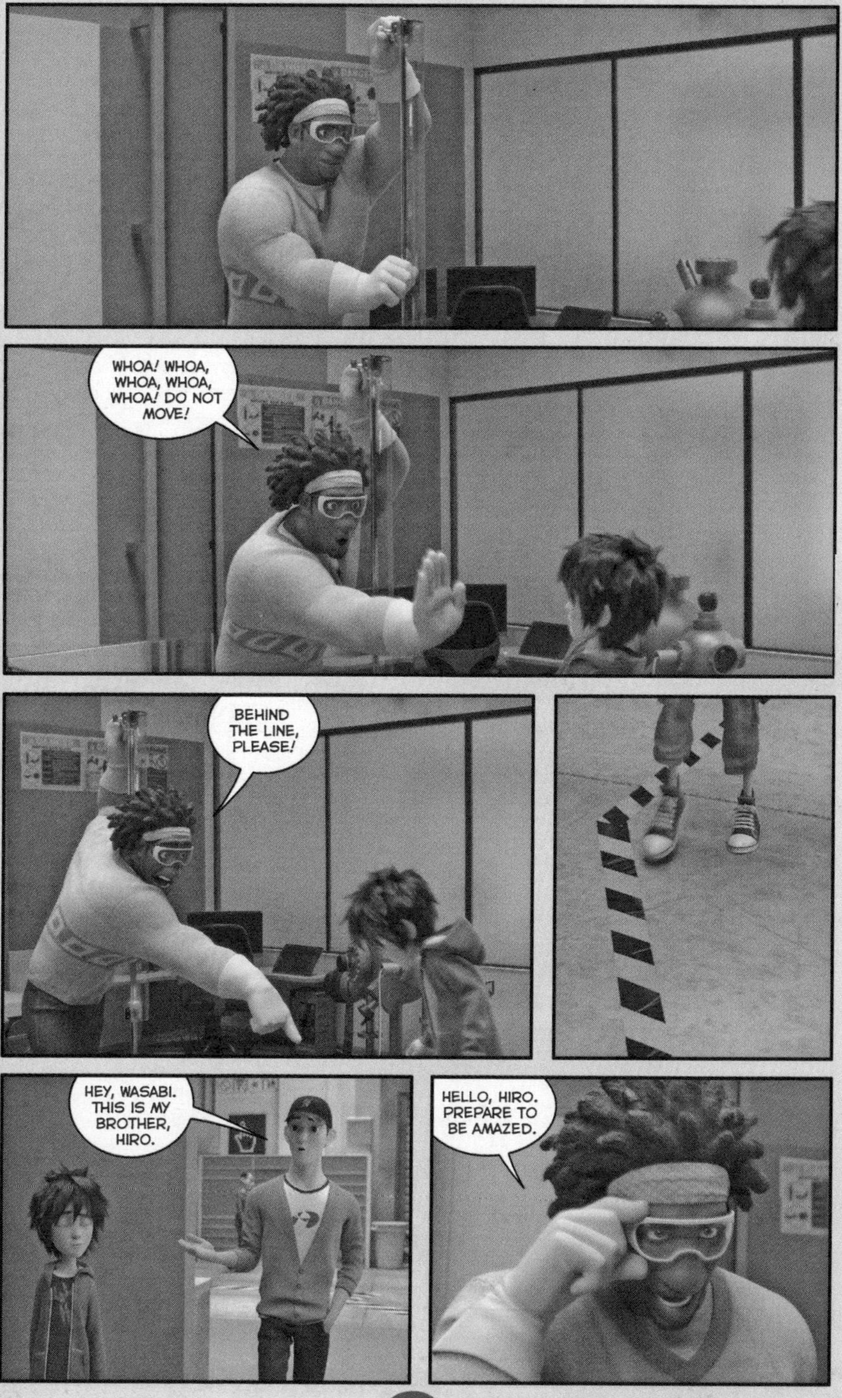
WHOA! WHOA, WHOA, WHOA, WHOA! DO NOT MOVE!
BEHIND THE LINE, PLEASE!
HEY, WASABI. THIS IS MY BROTHER, HIRO.
HELLO, HIRO. PREPARE TO BE AMAZED.

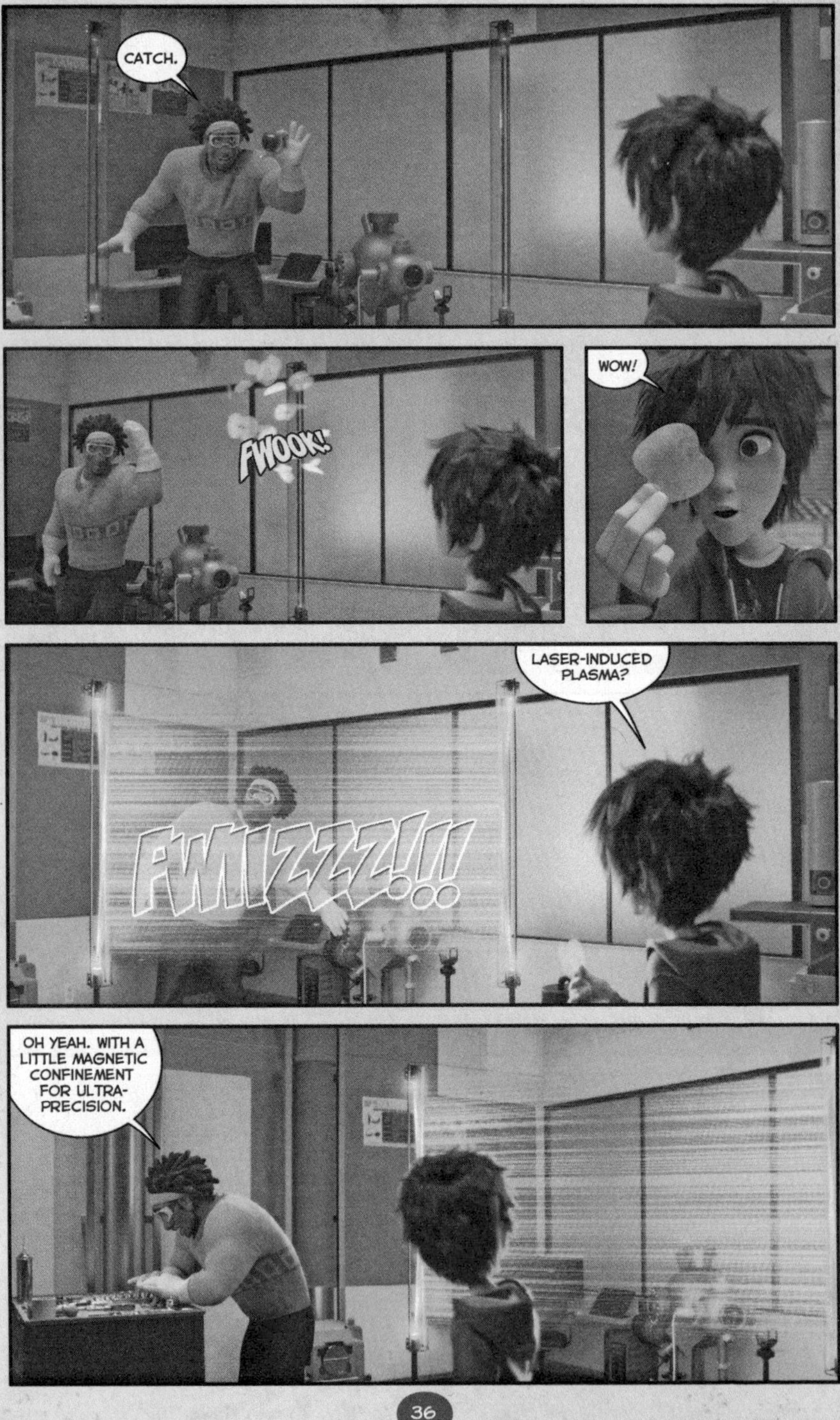
CATCH.
FWOOK!
WOW!
LASER-INDUCED PLASMA?
FWIZZZ!!!
OH YEAH. WITH A LITTLE MAGNETIC CONFINEMENT FOR ULTRA-PRECISION.

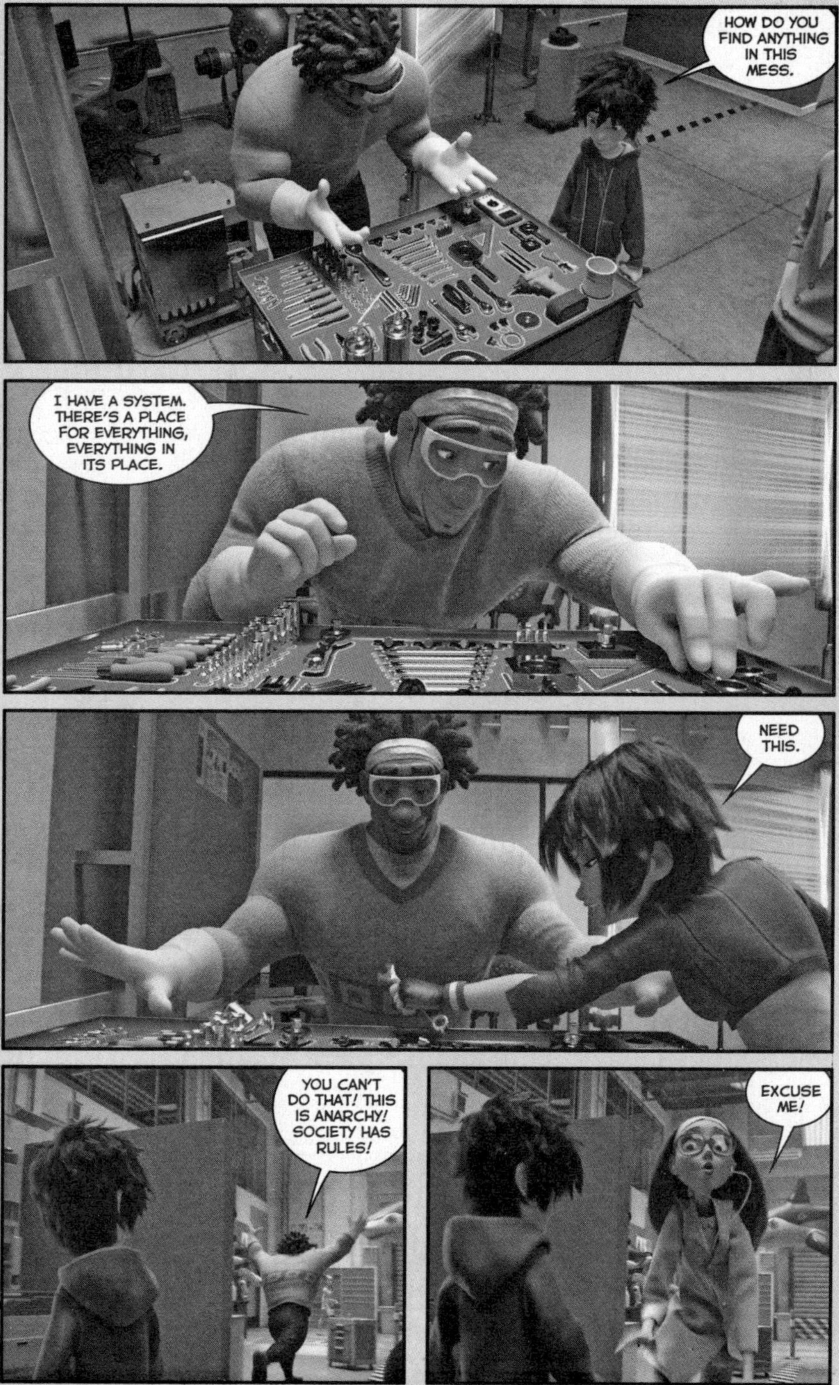
HOW DO YOU FIND ANYTHING IN THIS MESS.
I HAVE A SYSTEM. THERE'S A PLACE FOR EVERYTHING, EVERYTHING IN ITS PLACE.
NEED THIS.
YOU CAN'T DO THAT! THIS IS ANARCHY! SOCIETY HAS RULES!
EXCUSE ME!

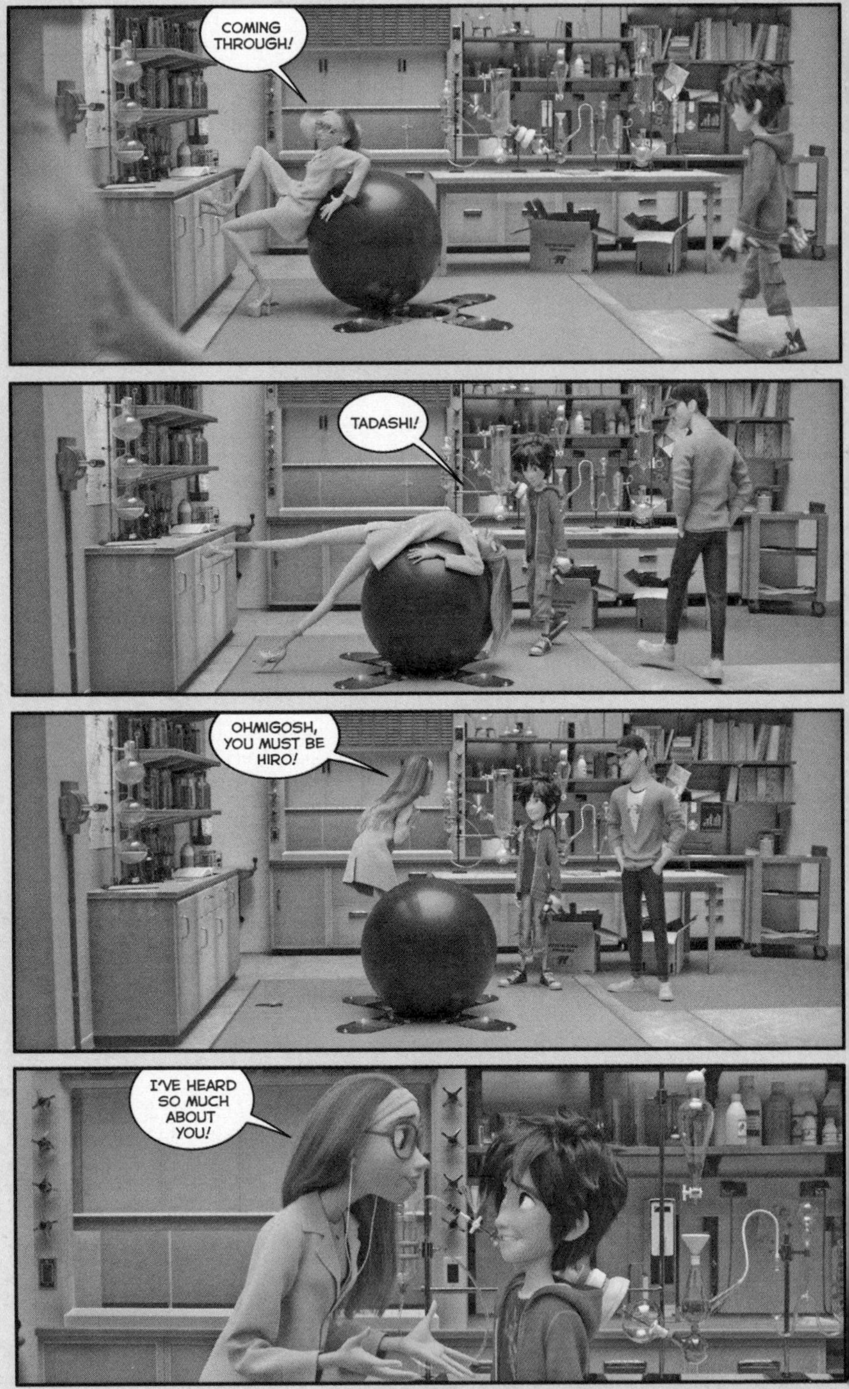
COMING THROUGH!
TADASHI!
OHMIGOSH, YOU MUST BE HIRO!
I'VE HEARD SO MUCH ABOUT YOU!

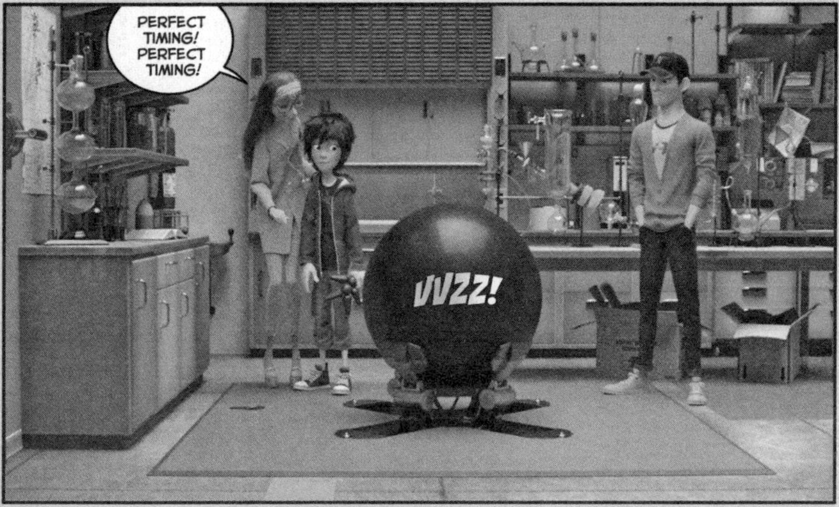
PERFECT TIMING! PERFECT TIMING!
VVZZ!

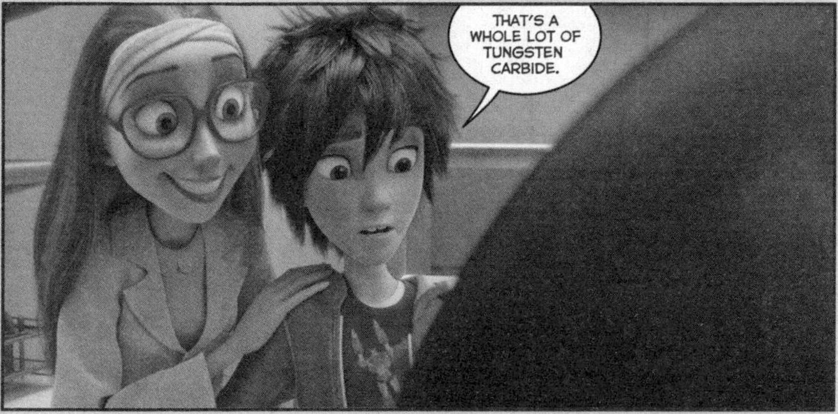
THAT'S A WHOLE LOT OF TUNGSTEN CARBIDE.

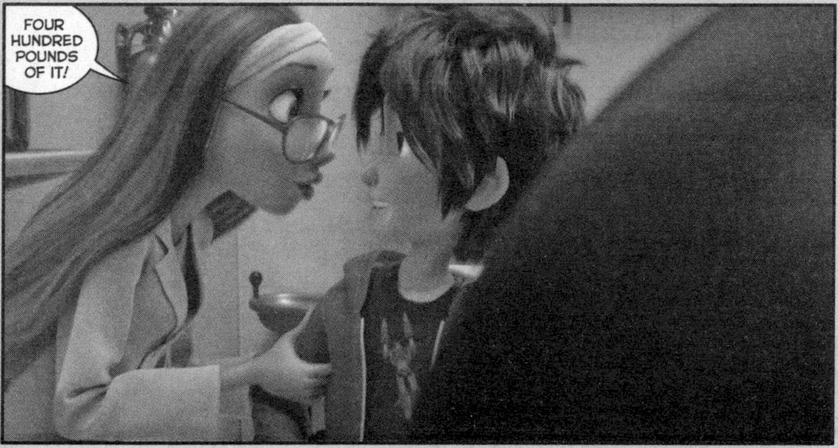
FOUR HUNDRED POUNDS OF IT!

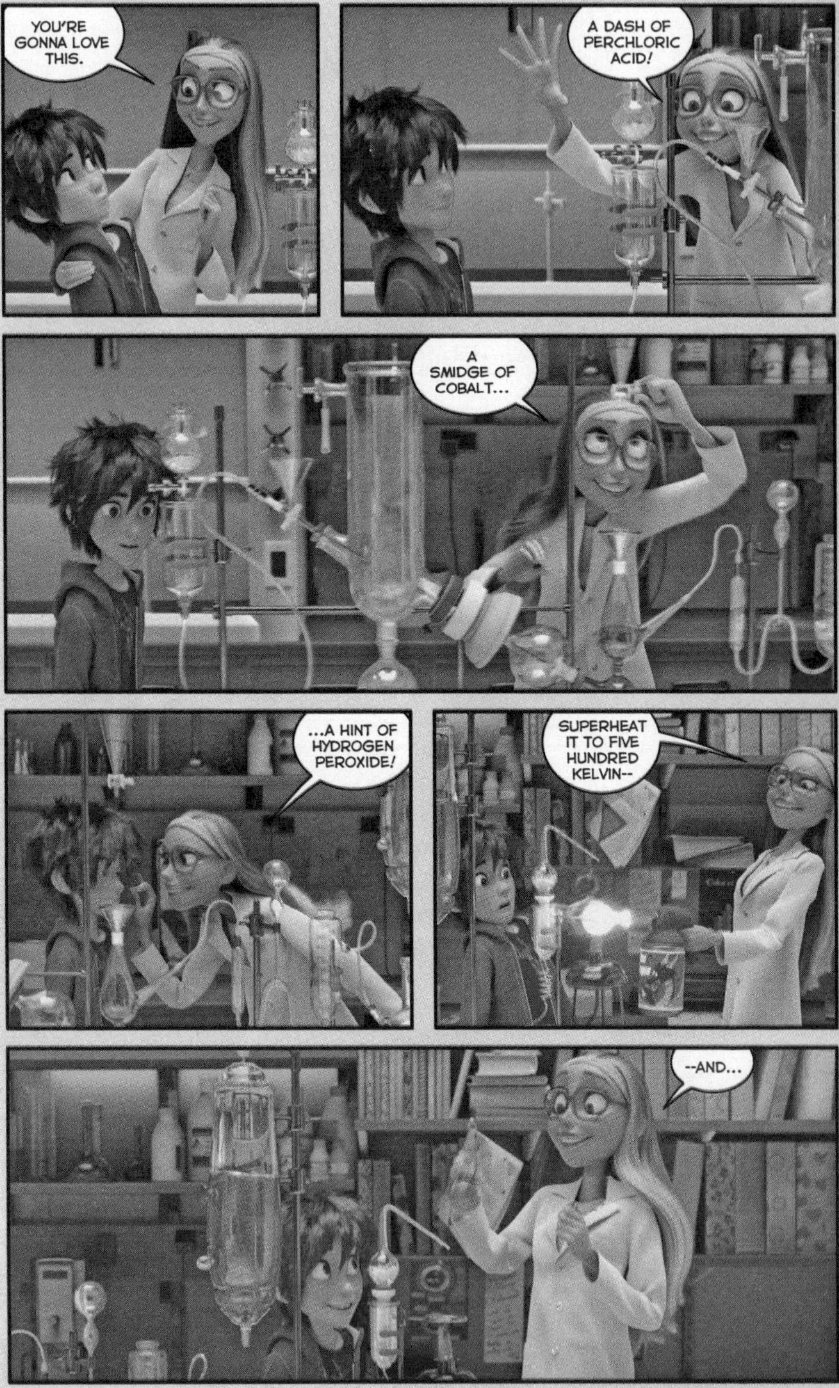
YOU'RE GONNA LOVE THIS.
A DASH OF PERCHLORIC ACID!
A SMIDGE OF COBALT...
...A HINT OF HYDROGEN PEROXIDE!
SUPERHEAT IT TO FIVE HUNDRED KELVIN--
--AND...

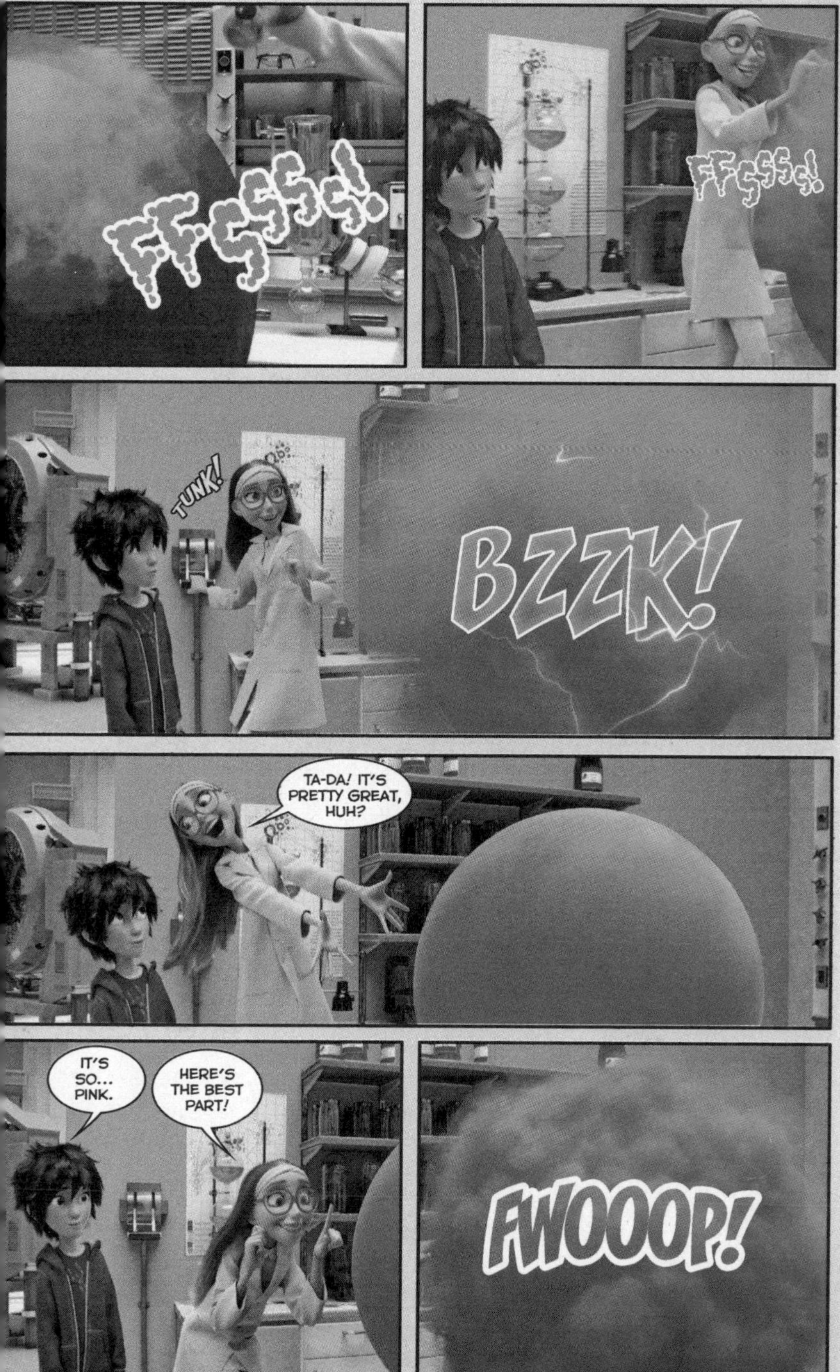
FFSSSS!
FFSSSS!
TUNK!
BZZK!
TA-DA! IT'S PRETTY GREAT, HUH?
IT'S SO... PINK.
HERE'S THE BEST PART!
FWOOOP!

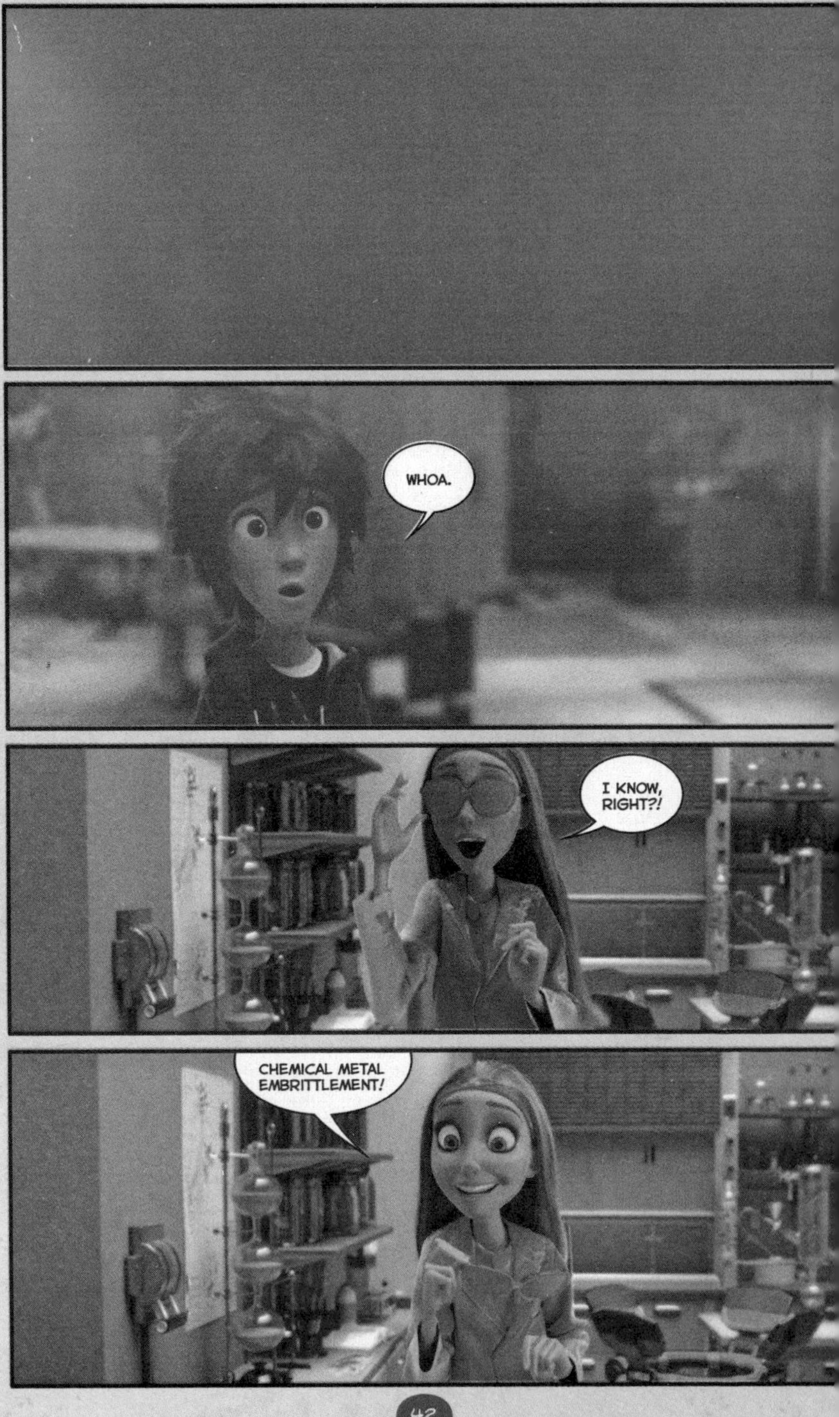
WHOA.
I KNOW, RIGHT?!
CHEMICAL METAL EMBRITTLEMENT!

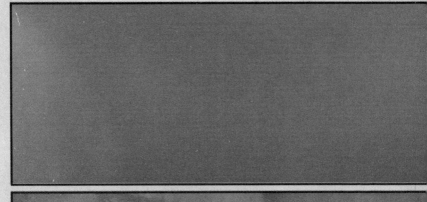

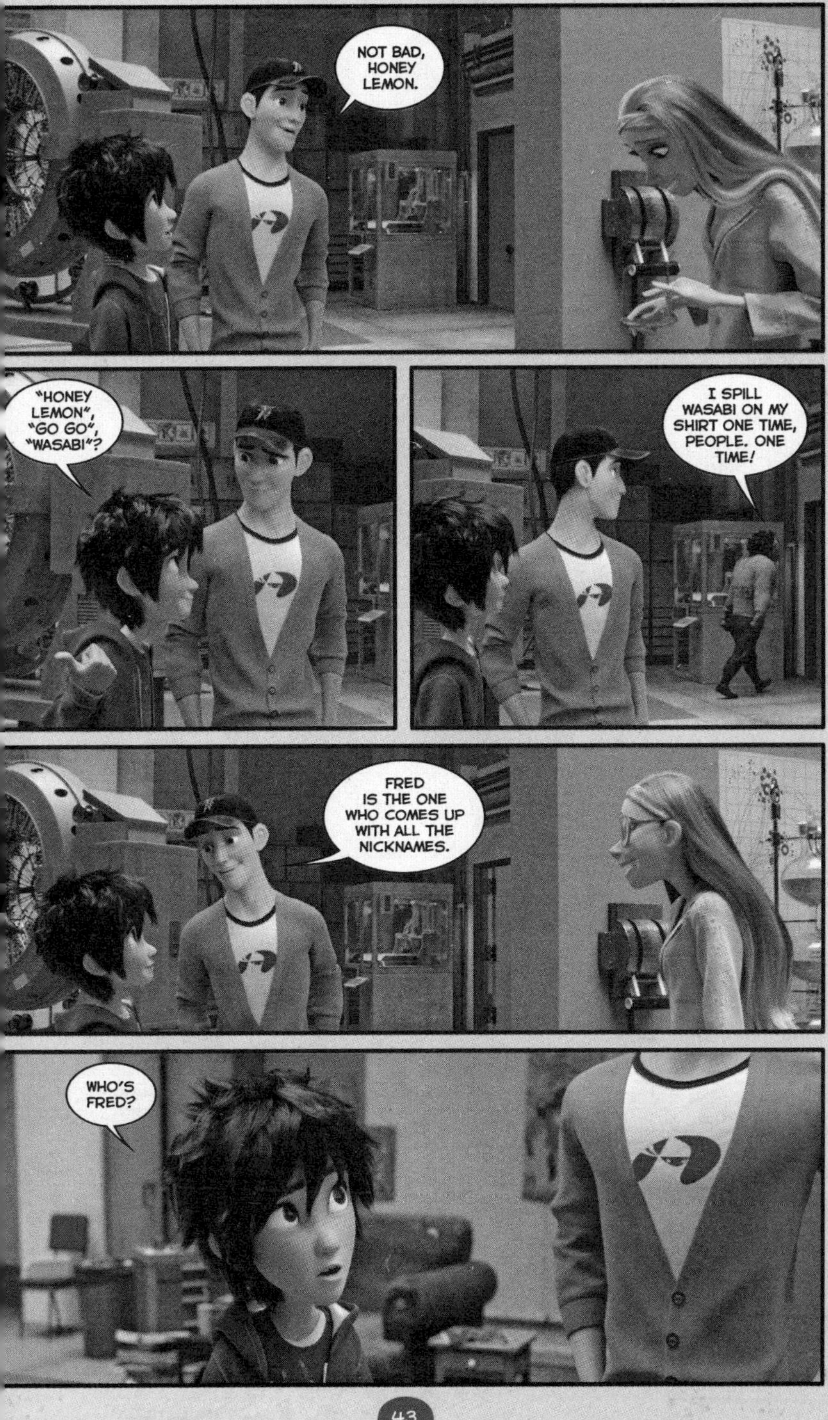
NOT BAD, HONEY LEMON.
"HONEY LEMON", "GO GO", "WASABI"?
I SPILL WASABI ON MY SHIRT ONE TIME, PEOPLE. ONE TIME!
FRED IS THE ONE WHO COMES UP WITH ALL THE NICKNAMES.
WHO'S FRED?

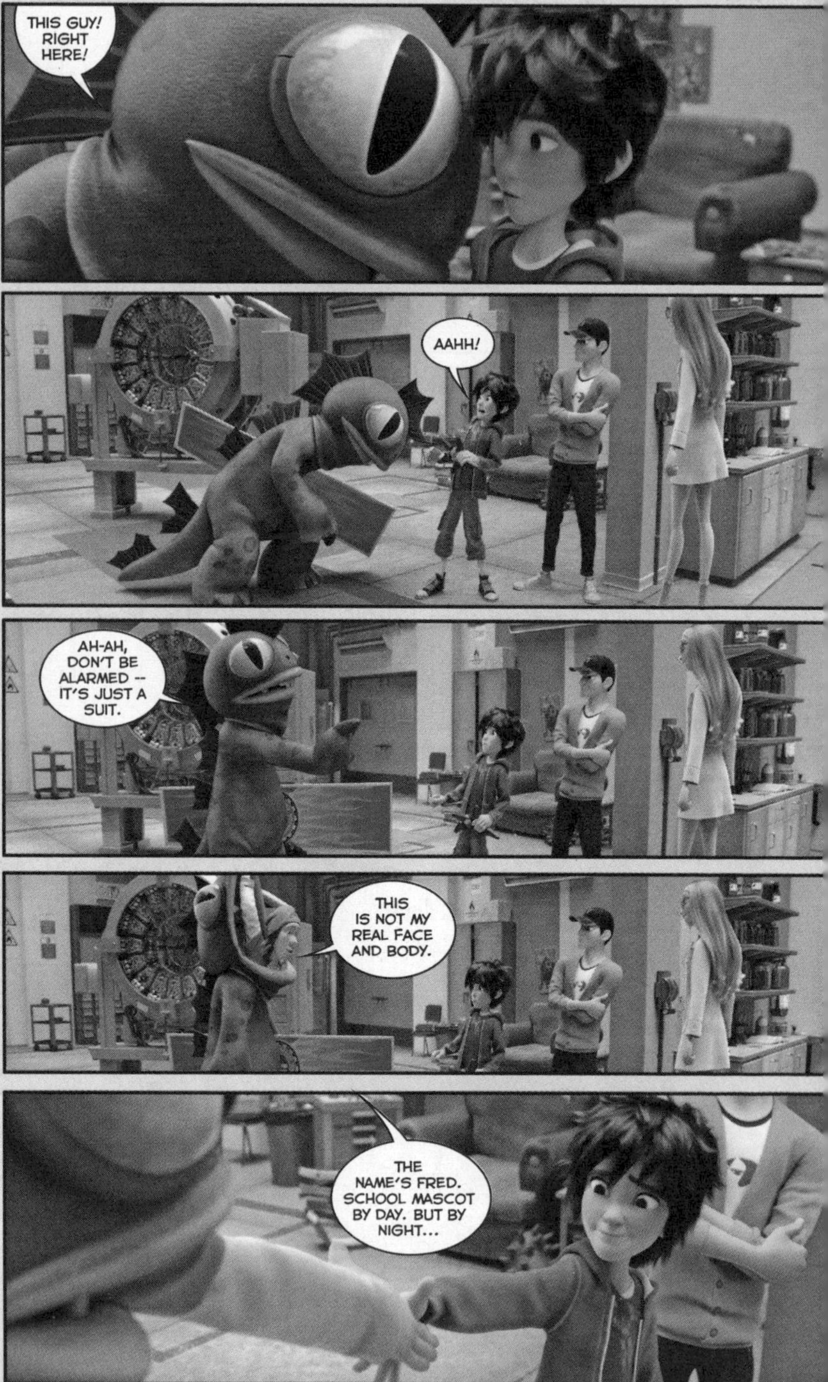
THIS GUY! RIGHT HERE!
AAHH!
AH-AH, DON'T BE ALARMED -- IT'S JUST A SUIT.
THIS IS NOT MY REAL FACE AND BODY.
THE NAME'S FRED. SCHOOL MASCOT BY DAY. BUT BY NIGHT...

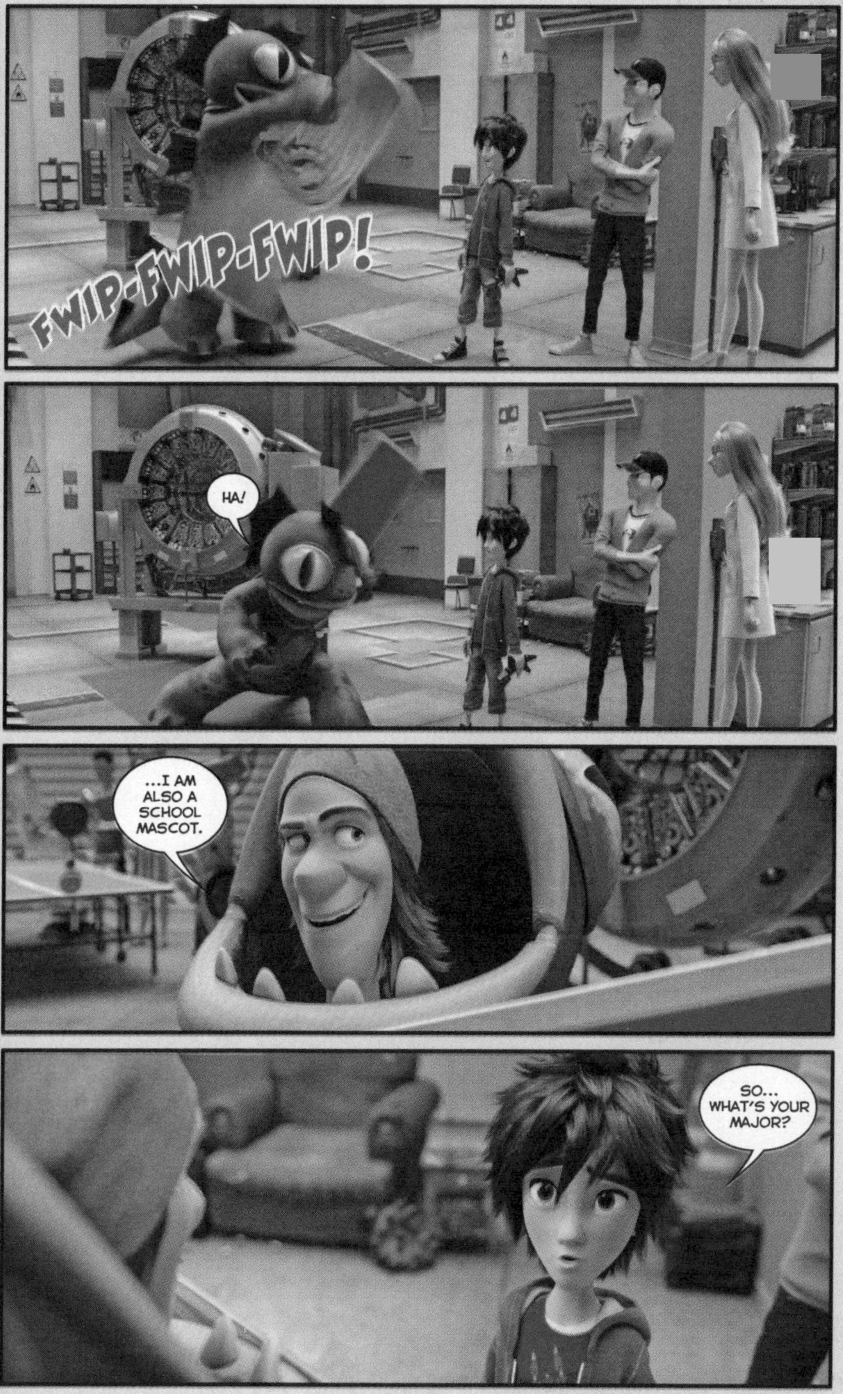
FWIP-FWIP-FWIP!
HA!
...I AM ALSO A SCHOOL MASCOT.
SO... WHAT'S YOUR MAJOR?

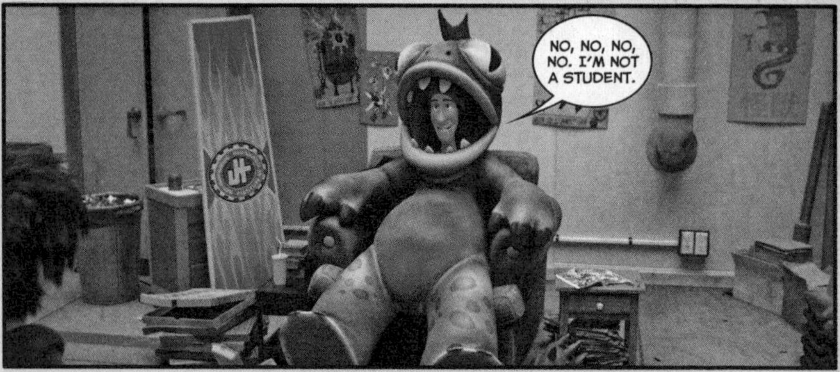
NO, NO, NO, NO. I'M NOT A STUDENT.

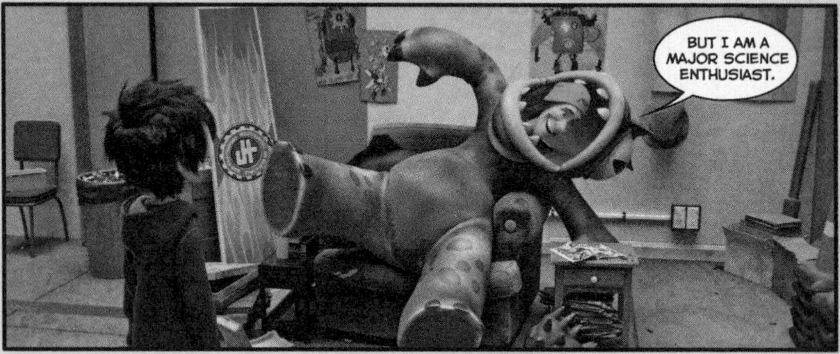
BUT I AM A MAJOR SCIENCE ENTHUSIAST.

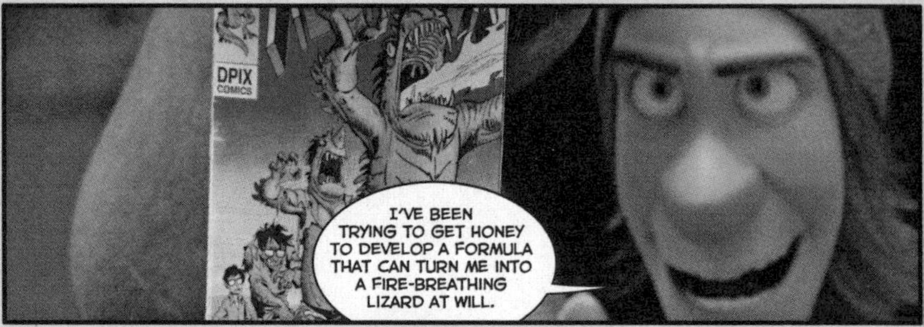
DPIX COMICS
I'VE BEEN TRYING TO GET HONEY TO DEVELOP A FORMULA THAT CAN TURN ME INTO A FIRE-BREATHING LIZARD AT WILL.

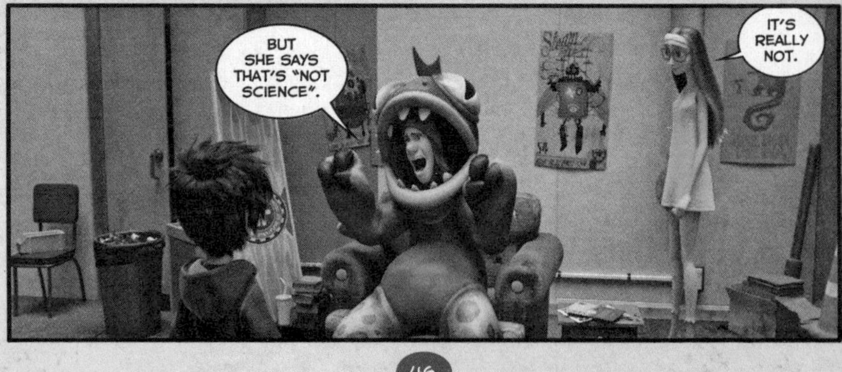
BUT SHE SAYS THAT'S "NOT SCIENCE".
IT'S REALLY NOT.

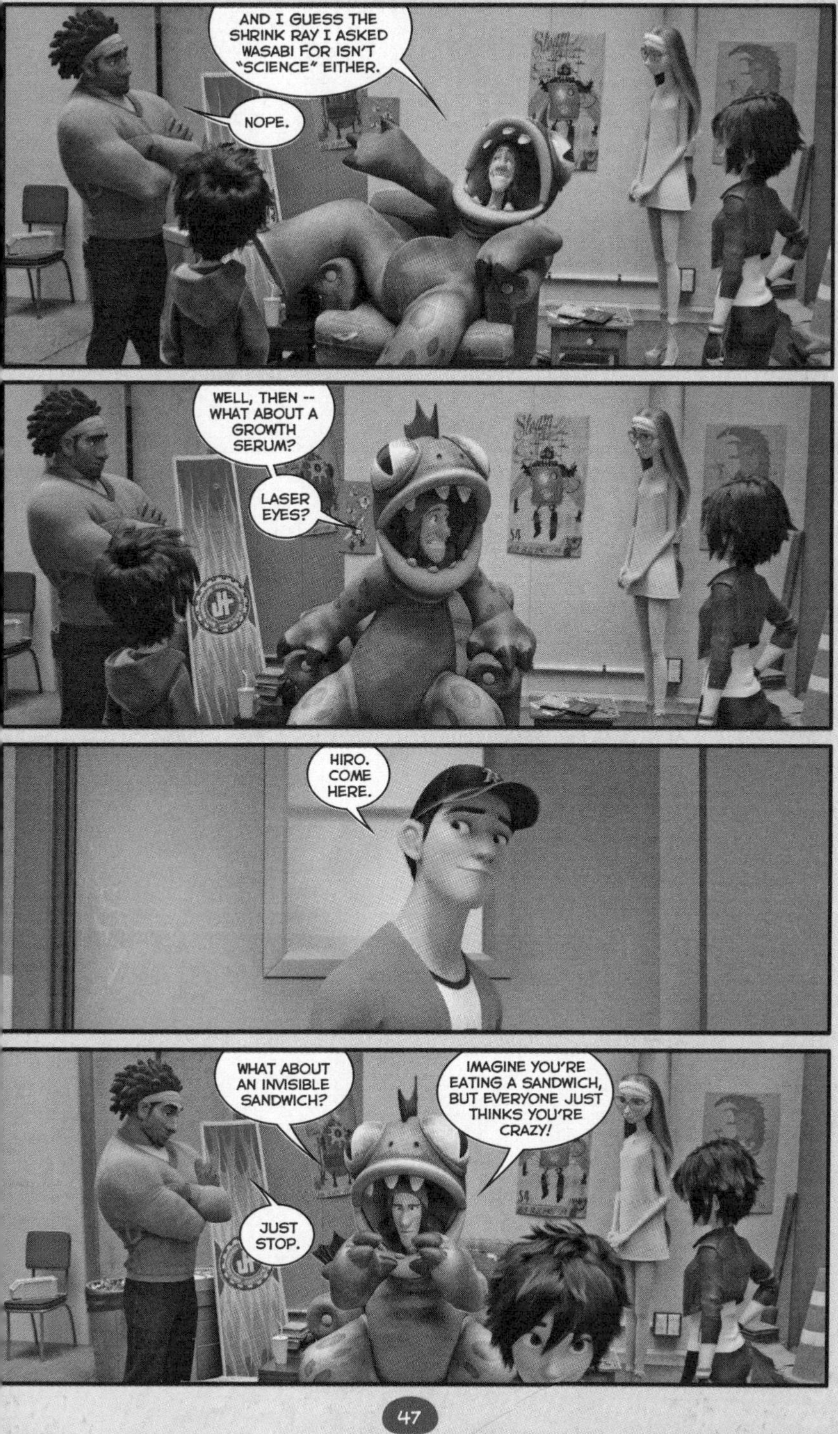
AND I GUESS THE SHRINK RAY I ASKED WASABI FOR ISN'T "SCIENCE" EITHER.
NOPE.
WELL, THEN -- WHAT ABOUT A GROWTH SERUM?
LASER EYES?
HIRO. COME HERE.
WHAT ABOUT AN INVISIBLE SANDWICH?
IMAGINE YOU'RE EATING A SANDWICH, BUT EVERYONE JUST THINKS YOU'RE CRAZY!
JUST STOP.

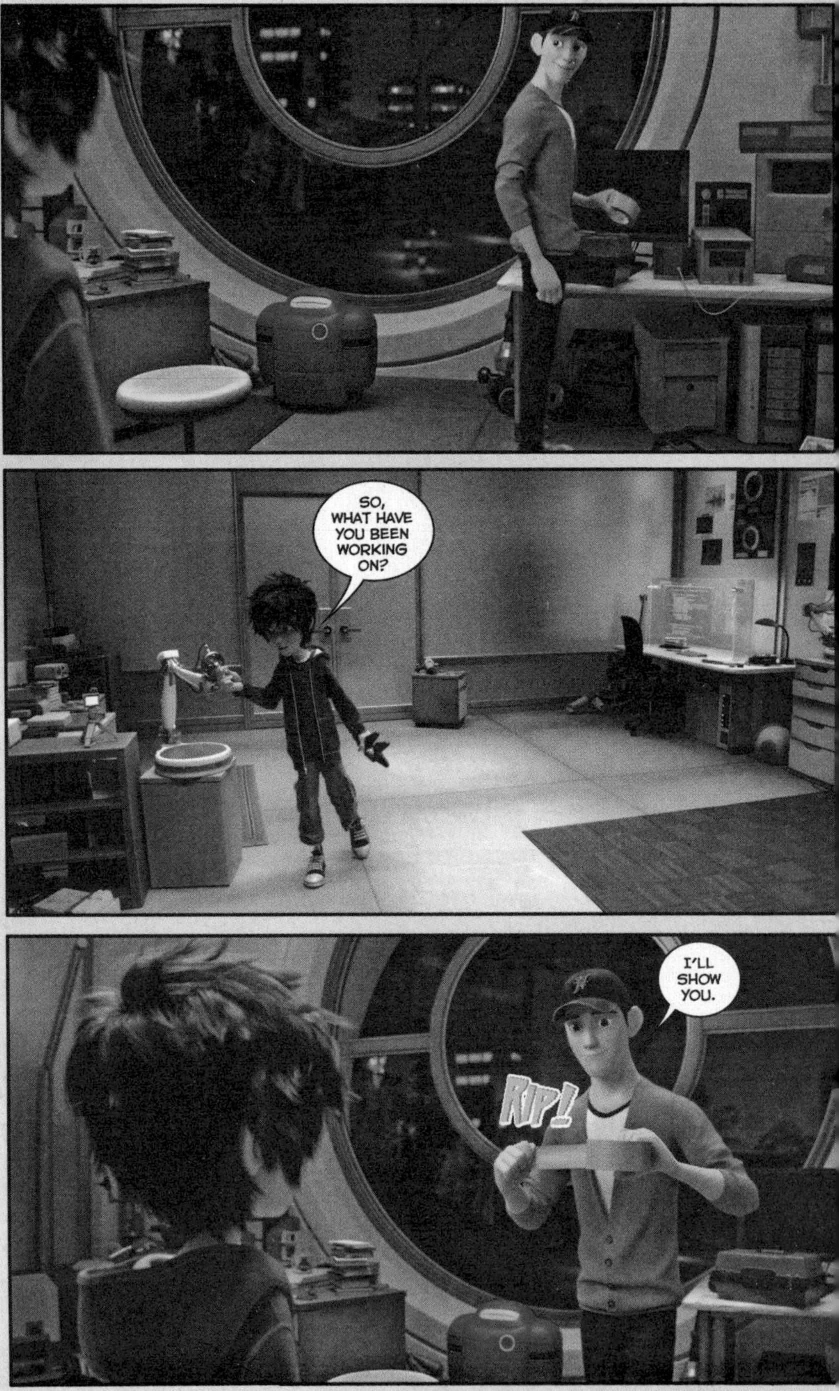
SO, WHAT HAVE YOU BEEN WORKING ON?
I'LL SHOW YOU.
RIP!

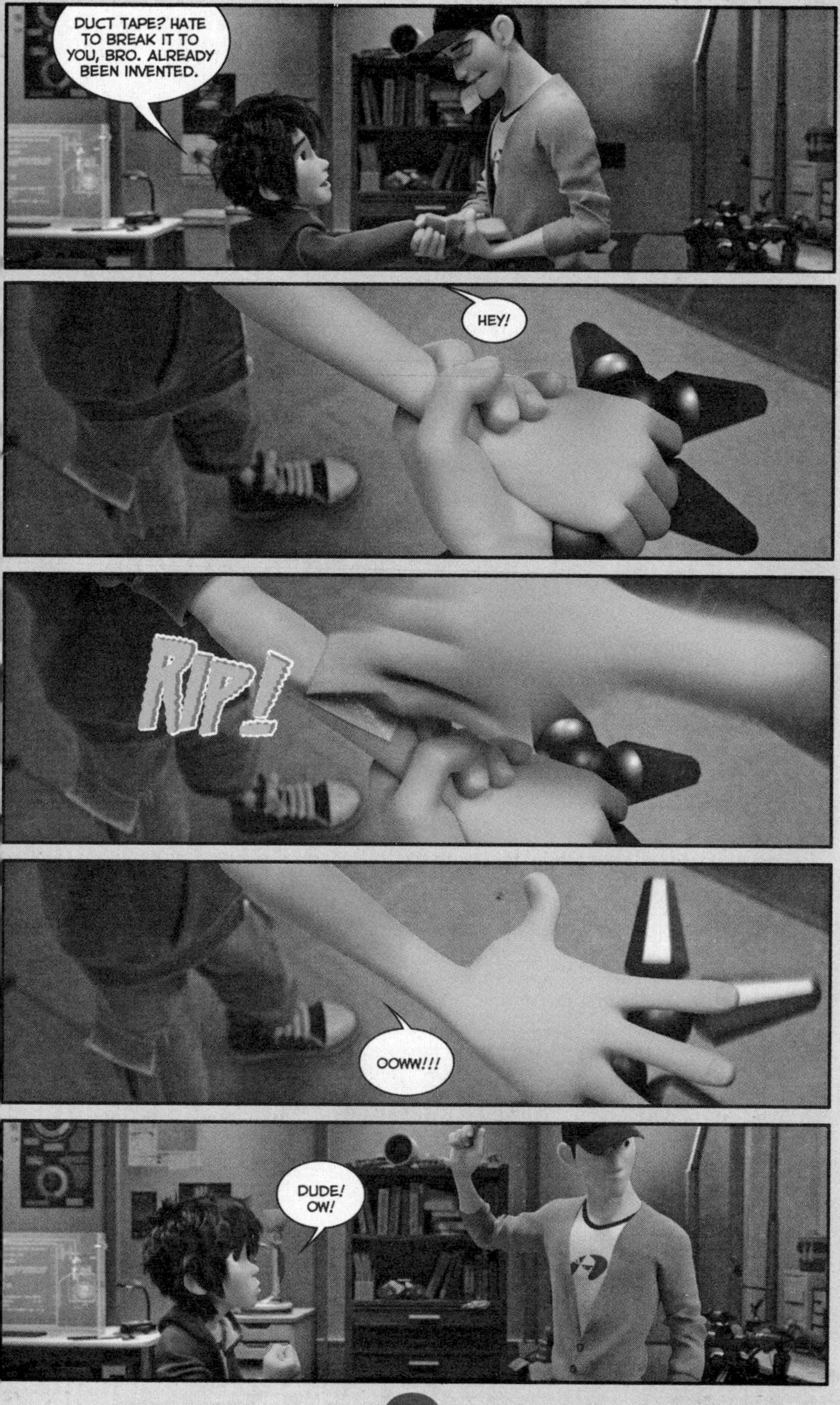
DUCT TAPE? HATE TO BREAK IT TO YOU, BRO. ALREADY BEEN INVENTED.
HEY!
RIP!
OOWW!!!
DUDE! OW!

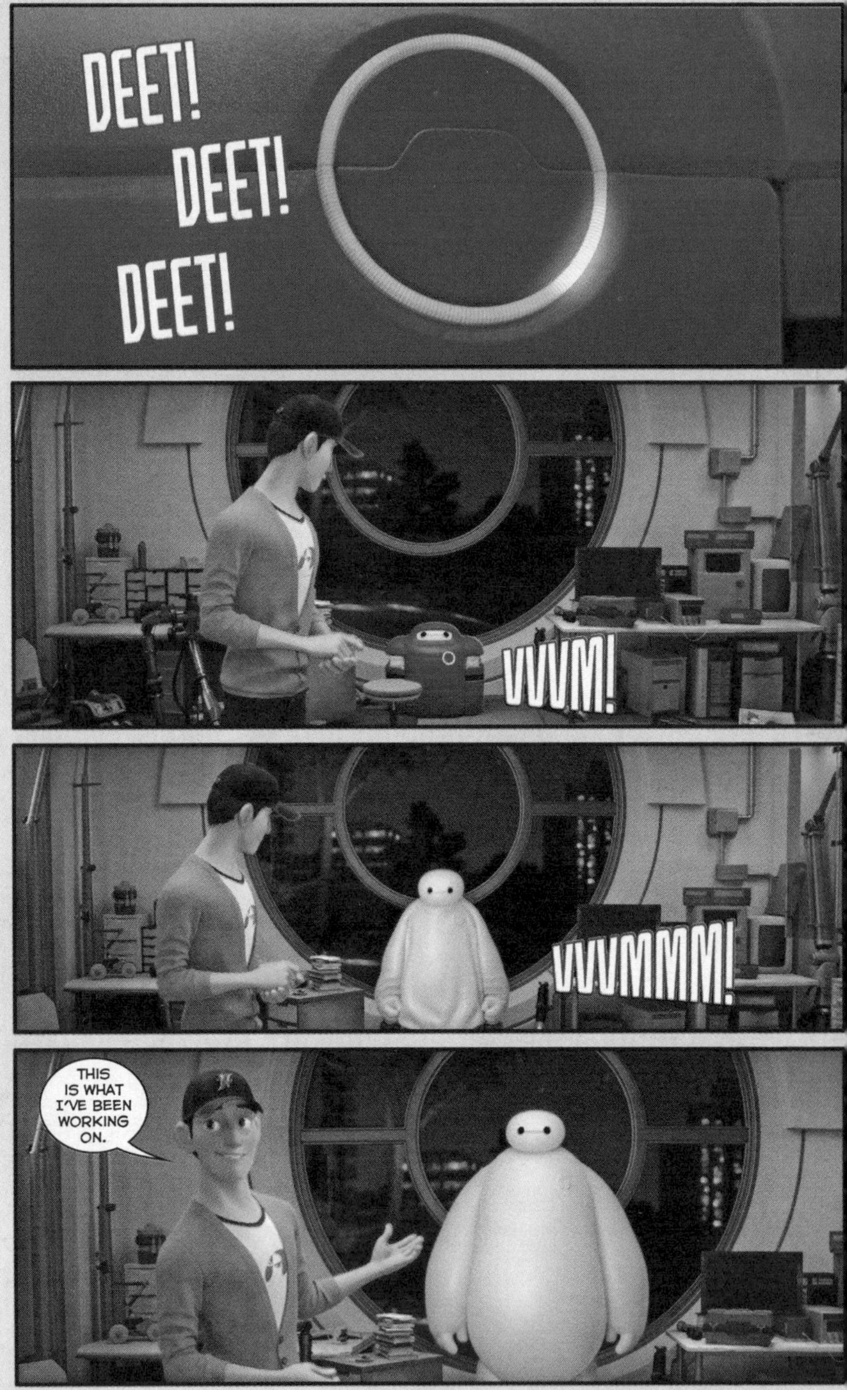
DEET!
DEET!
DEET!
VVVM!
VVVMMM!
THIS IS WHAT I'VE BEEN WORKING ON.

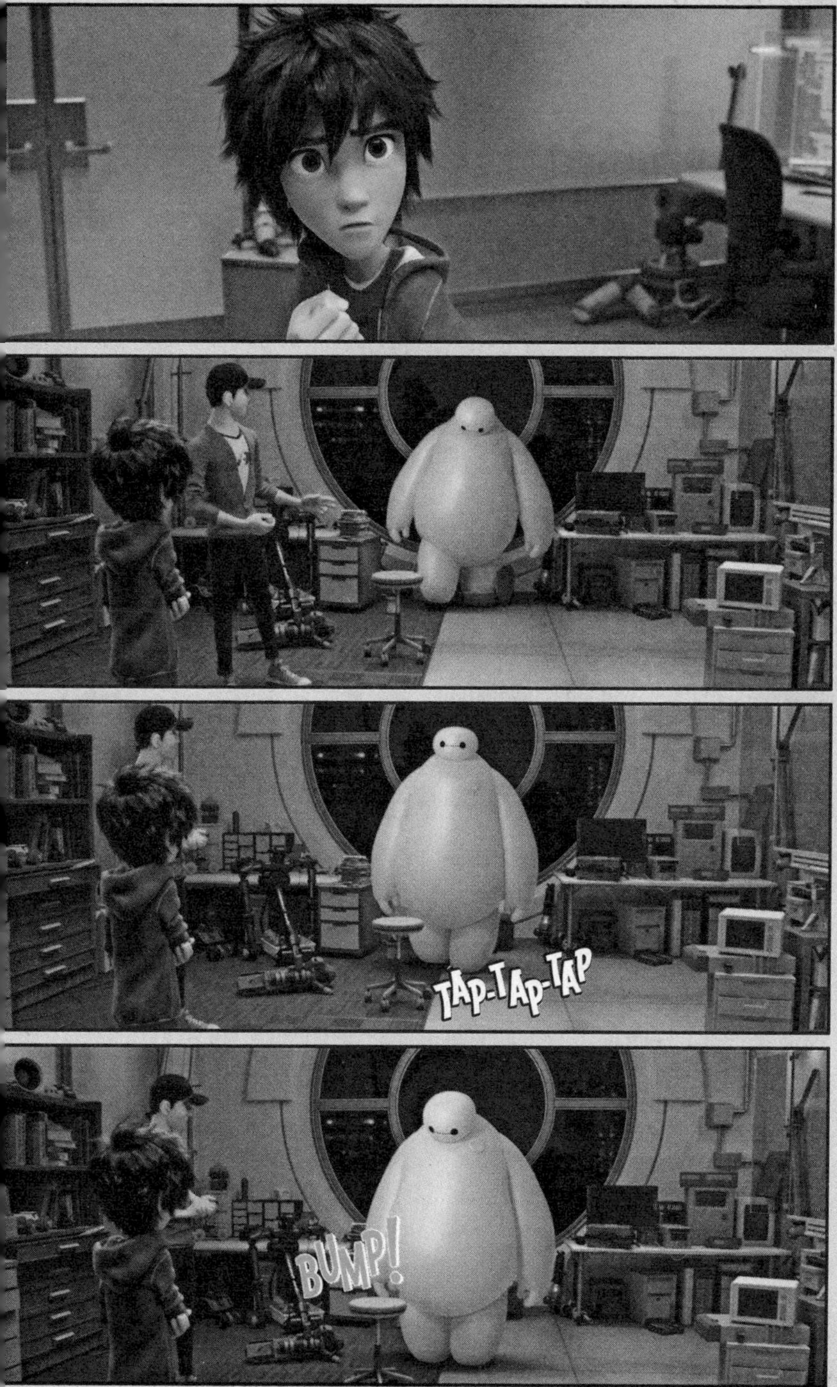
TAP-TAP-TAP
BUMP!

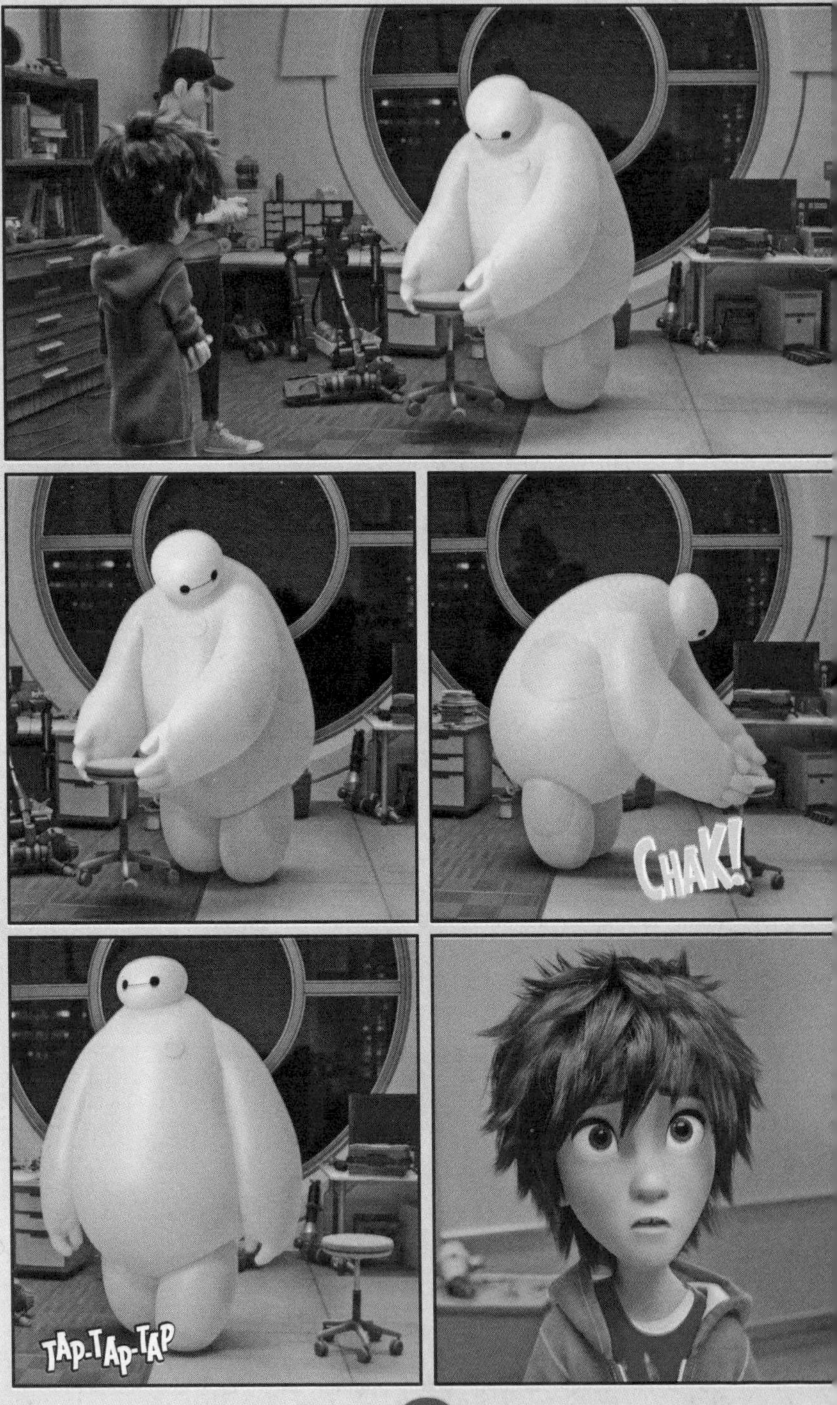
CHAK!
TAP-TAP-TAP

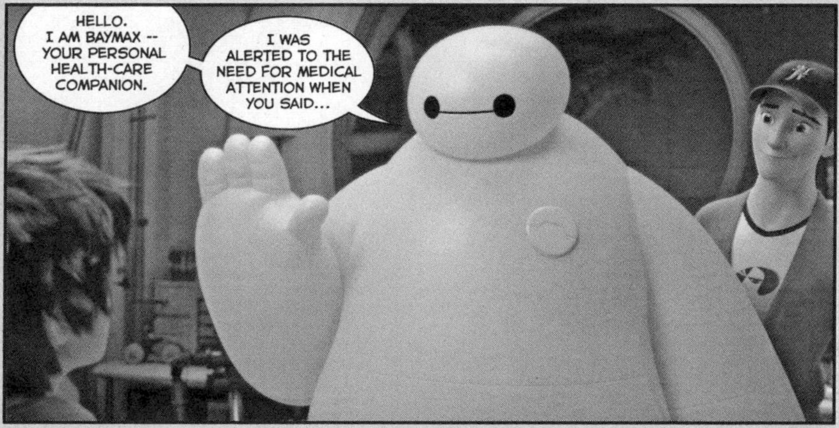
HELLO. I AM BAYMAX -- YOUR PERSONAL HEALTH-CARE COMPANION.
I WAS ALERTED TO THE NEED FOR MEDICAL ATTENTION WHEN YOU SAID...

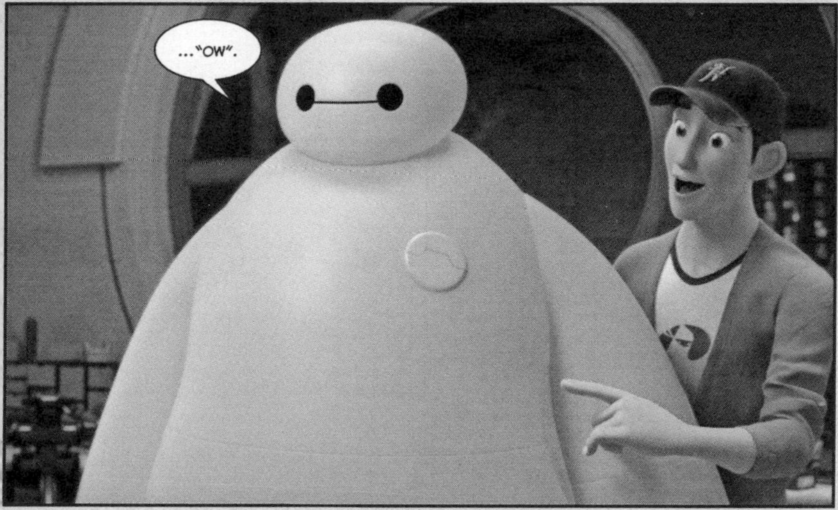
..."OW".

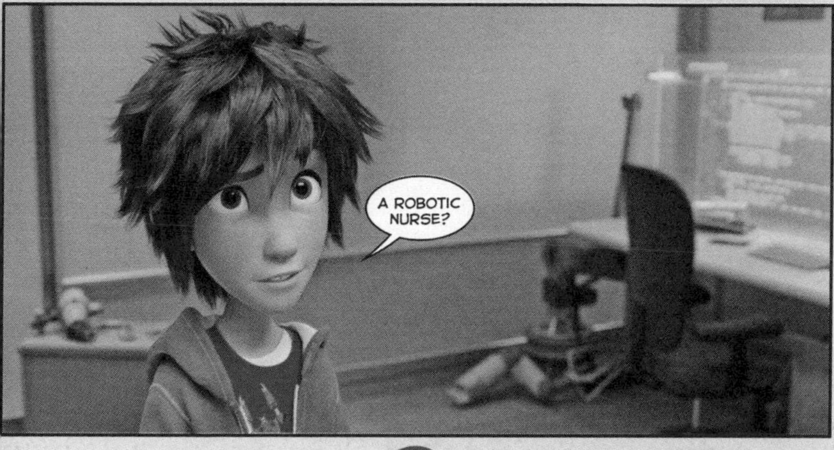
A ROBOTIC NURSE?

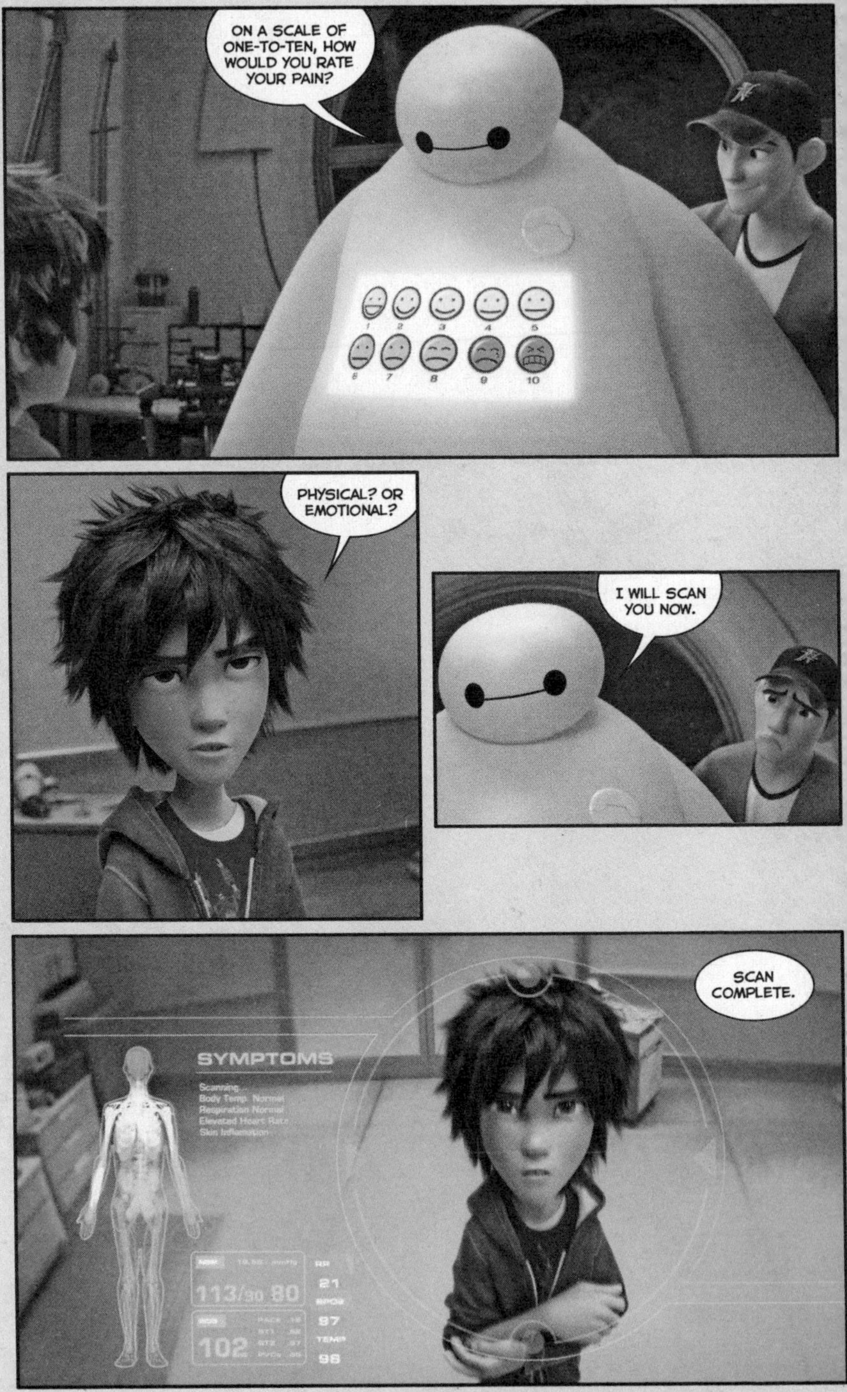
ON A SCALE OF ONE-TO-TEN, HOW WOULD YOU RATE YOUR PAIN?
PHYSICAL? OR EMOTIONAL?
I WILL SCAN YOU NOW.
SCAN COMPLETE.
SYMPTOMS
Scanning...
Body Temp: Normal
Respiration Normal
Elevated Heart Rate
Skin Inflammation
113/90 80
21
97
TEMP
98
102

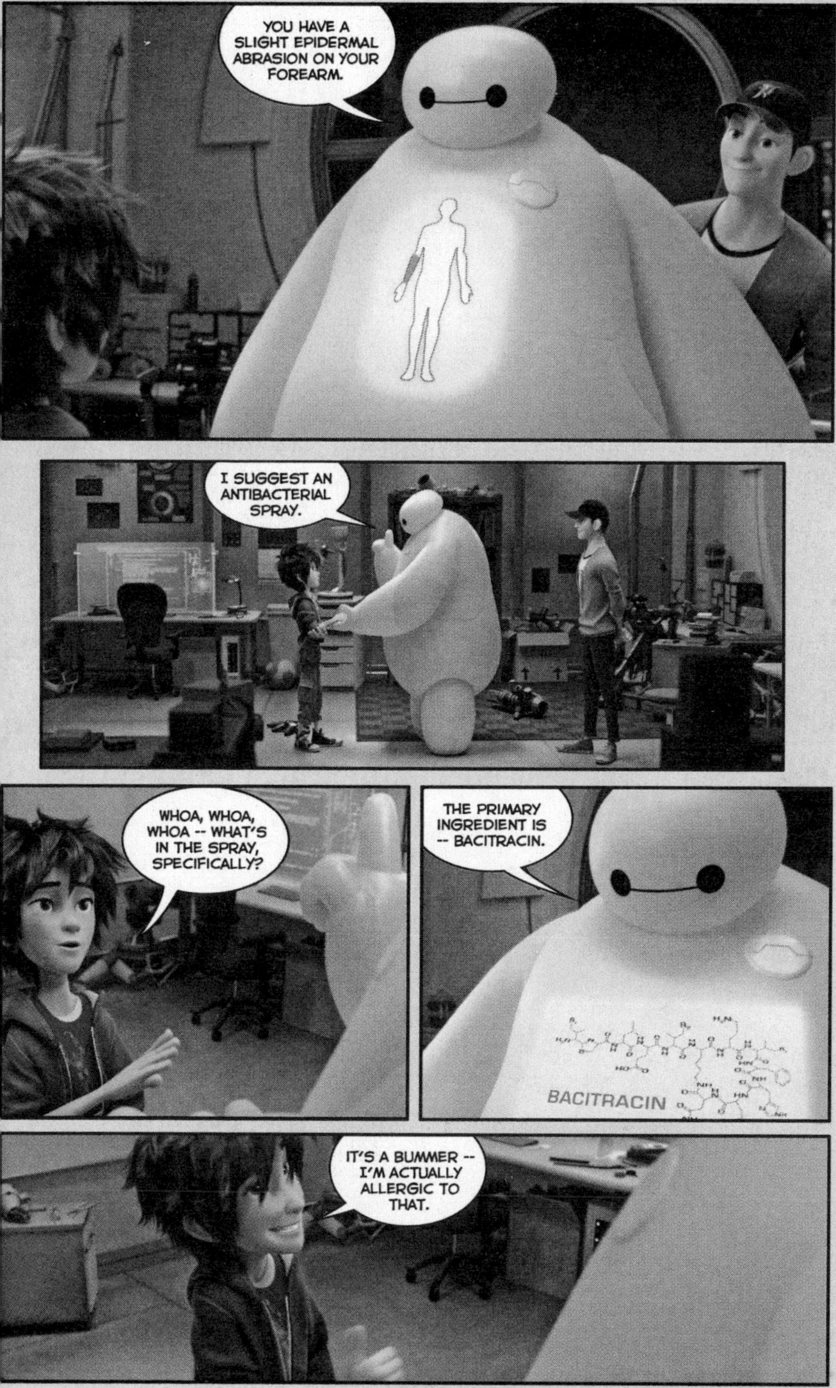
YOU HAVE A SLIGHT EPIDERMAL ABRASION ON YOUR FOREARM.
I SUGGEST AN ANTIBACTERIAL SPRAY.
WHOA, WHOA, WHOA -- WHAT'S IN THE SPRAY, SPECIFICALLY?
THE PRIMARY INGREDIENT IS -- BACITRACIN.
BACITRACIN
IT'S A BUMMER -- I'M ACTUALLY ALLERGIC TO THAT.

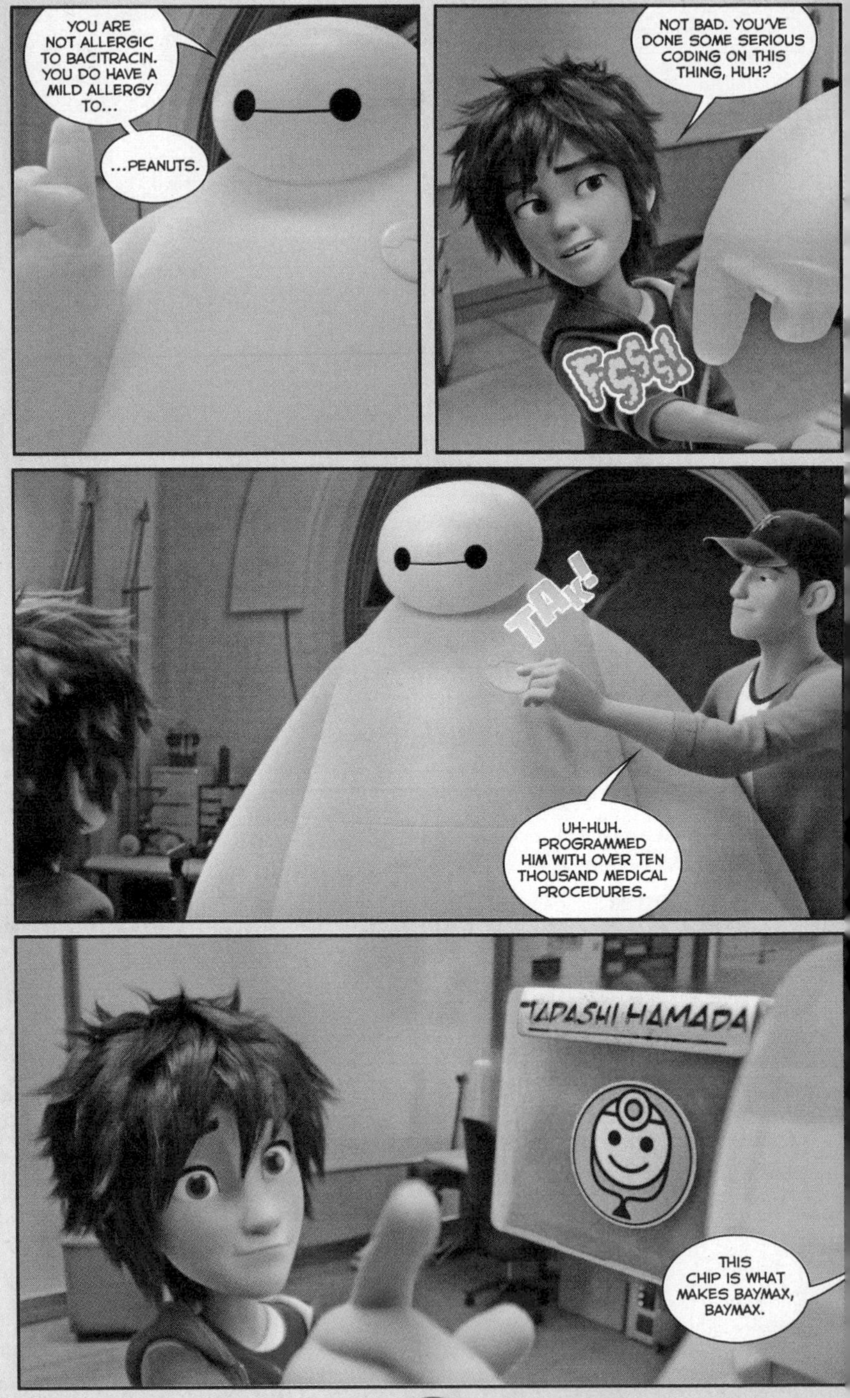
YOU ARE NOT ALLERGIC TO BACITRACIN. YOU DO HAVE A MILD ALLERGY TO...
...PEANUTS.
NOT BAD. YOU'VE DONE SOME SERIOUS CODING ON THIS THING, HUH?
FSSS!
TAK!
UH-HUH. PROGRAMMED HIM WITH OVER TEN THOUSAND MEDICAL PROCEDURES.
TADASHI HAMADA
THIS CHIP IS WHAT MAKES BAYMAX, BAYMAX.

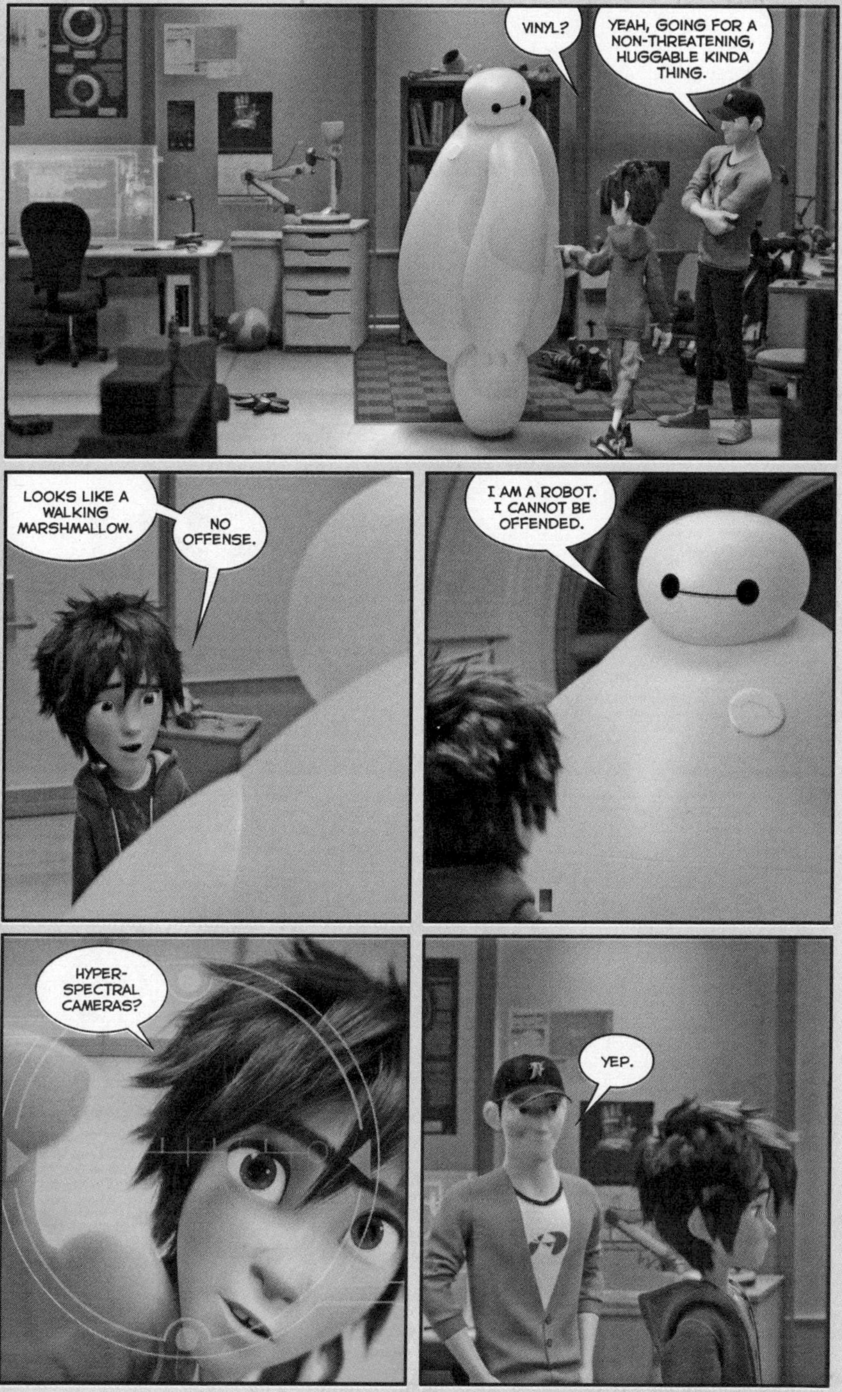
VINYL?
YEAH, GOING FOR A NON-THREATENING, HUGGABLE KINDA THING.
LOOKS LIKE A WALKING MARSHMALLOW.
NO OFFENSE.
I AM A ROBOT. I CANNOT BE OFFENDED.
HYPER-SPECTRAL CAMERAS?
YEP.

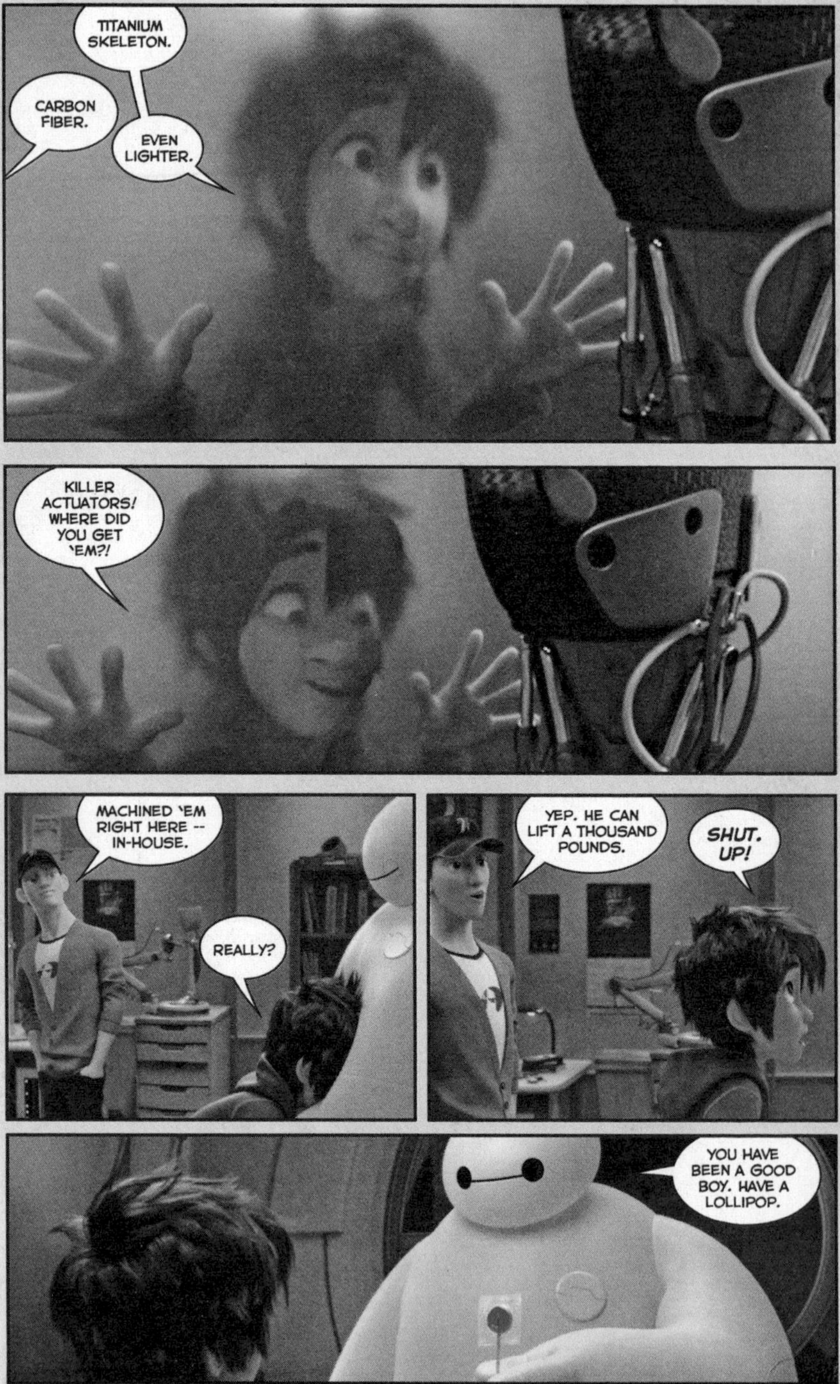

CARBON FIBER.
TITANIUM SKELETON.
EVEN LIGHTER.
KILLER ACTUATORS! WHERE DID YOU GET 'EM?!
MACHINED 'EM RIGHT HERE -- IN-HOUSE.
REALLY?
YEP. HE CAN LIFT A THOUSAND POUNDS.
SHUT. UP!
YOU HAVE BEEN A GOOD BOY. HAVE A LOLLIPOP.

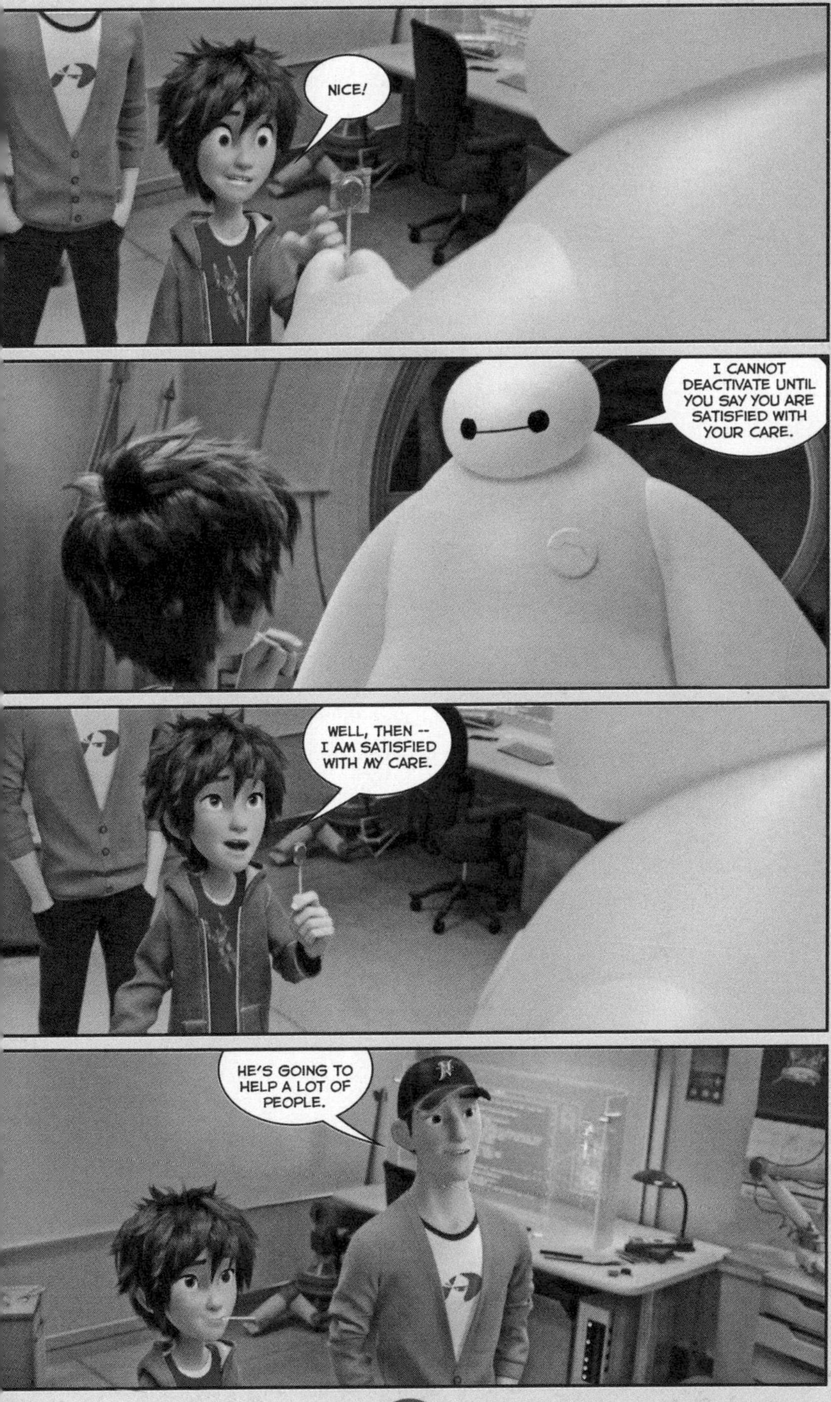
NICE!
I CANNOT DEACTIVATE UNTIL YOU SAY YOU ARE SATISFIED WITH YOUR CARE.
WELL, THEN -- I AM SATISFIED WITH MY CARE.
HE'S GOING TO HELP A LOT OF PEOPLE.

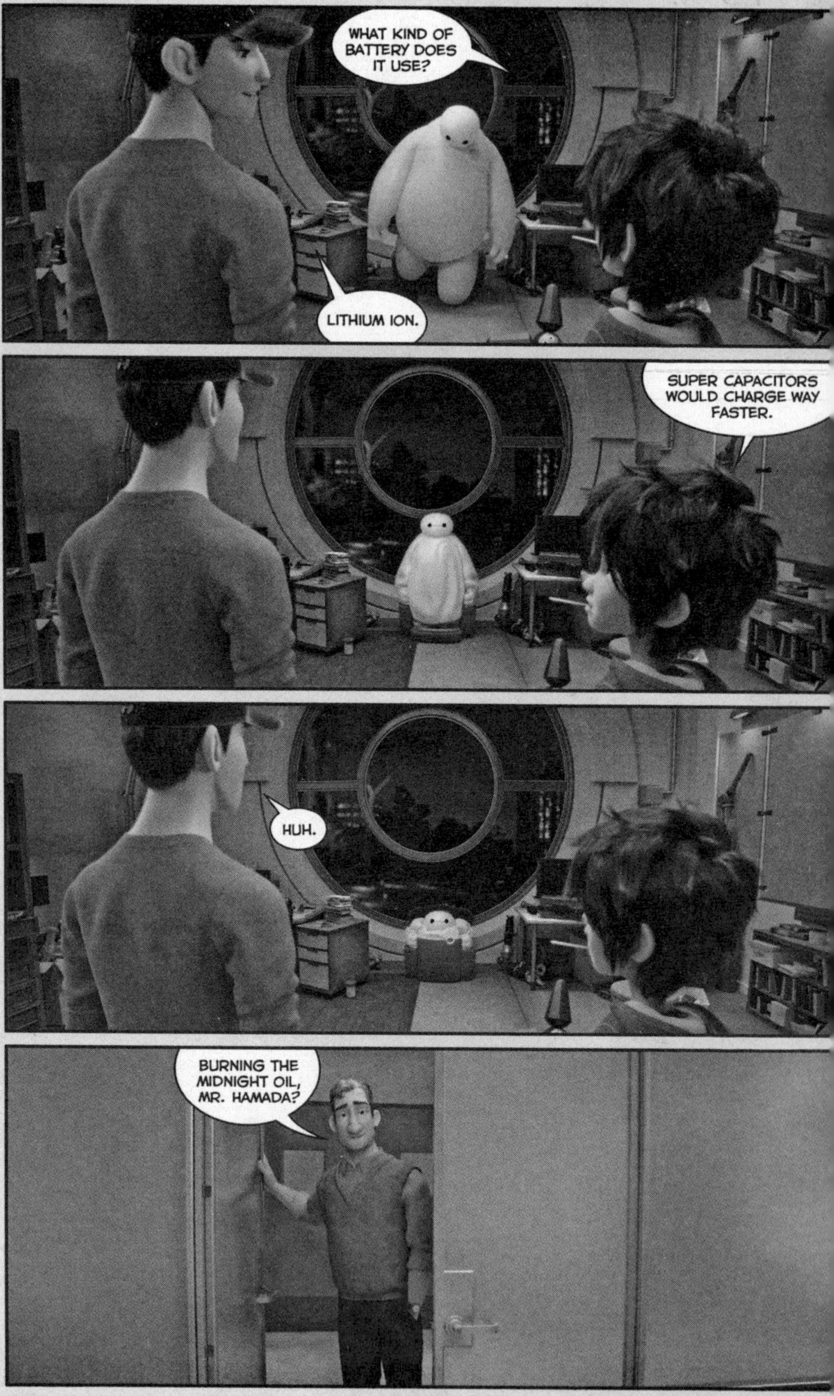
WHAT KIND OF BATTERY DOES IT USE?
LITHIUM ION.
SUPER CAPACITORS WOULD CHARGE WAY FASTER.
HUH.
BURNING THE MIDNIGHT OIL, MR. HAMADA?

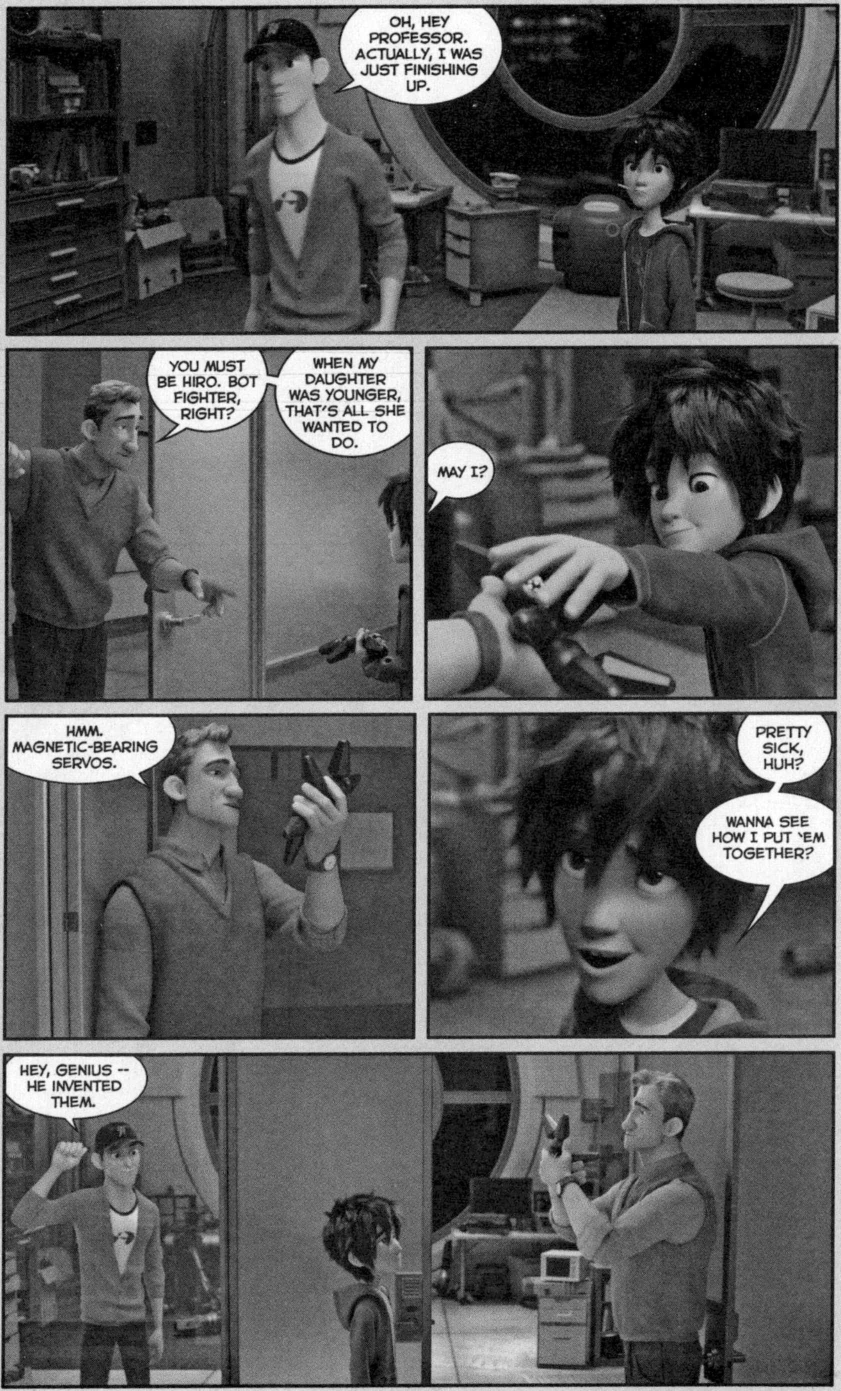
OH, HEY PROFESSOR. ACTUALLY, I WAS JUST FINISHING UP.
YOU MUST BE HIRO. BOT FIGHTER, RIGHT?
WHEN MY DAUGHTER WAS YOUNGER, THAT'S ALL SHE WANTED TO DO.
MAY I?
HMM. MAGNETIC-BEARING SERVOS.
PRETTY SICK, HUH?
WANNA SEE HOW I PUT 'EM TOGETHER?
HEY, GENIUS -- HE INVENTED THEM.

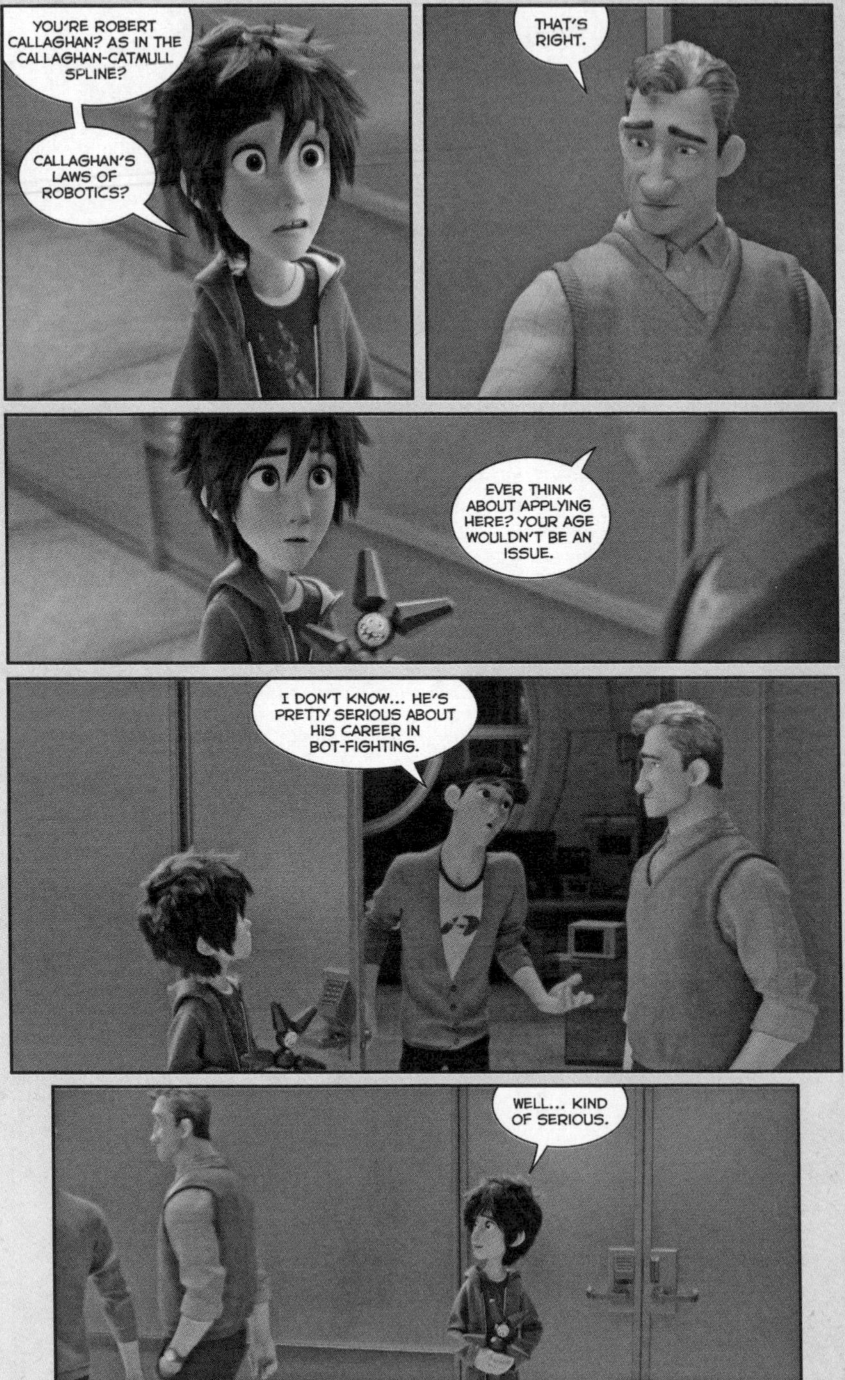
YOU'RE ROBERT CALLAGHAN? AS IN THE CALLAGHAN-CATMULL SPLINE?
CALLAGHAN'S LAWS OF ROBOTICS?
THAT'S RIGHT.
EVER THINK ABOUT APPLYING HERE? YOUR AGE WOULDN'T BE AN ISSUE.
I DON'T KNOW... HE'S PRETTY SERIOUS ABOUT HIS CAREER IN BOT-FIGHTING.
WELL... KIND OF SERIOUS.

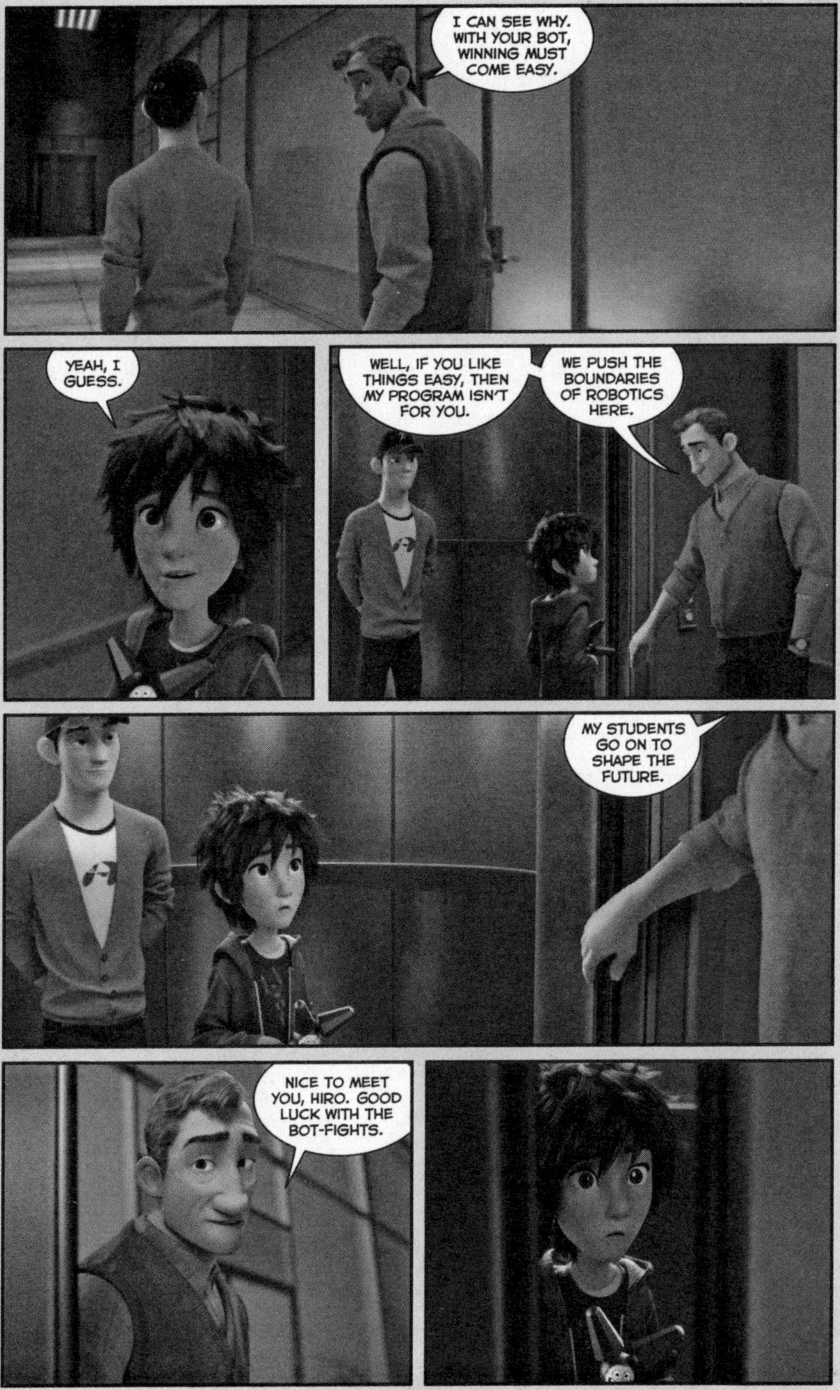
I CAN SEE WHY. WITH YOUR BOT, WINNING MUST COME EASY.
YEAH, I GUESS.
WELL, IF YOU LIKE THINGS EASY, THEN MY PROGRAM ISN'T FOR YOU.
WE PUSH THE BOUNDARIES OF ROBOTICS HERE.
MY STUDENTS GO ON TO SHAPE THE FUTURE.
NICE TO MEET YOU, HIRO. GOOD LUCK WITH THE BOT-FIGHTS.

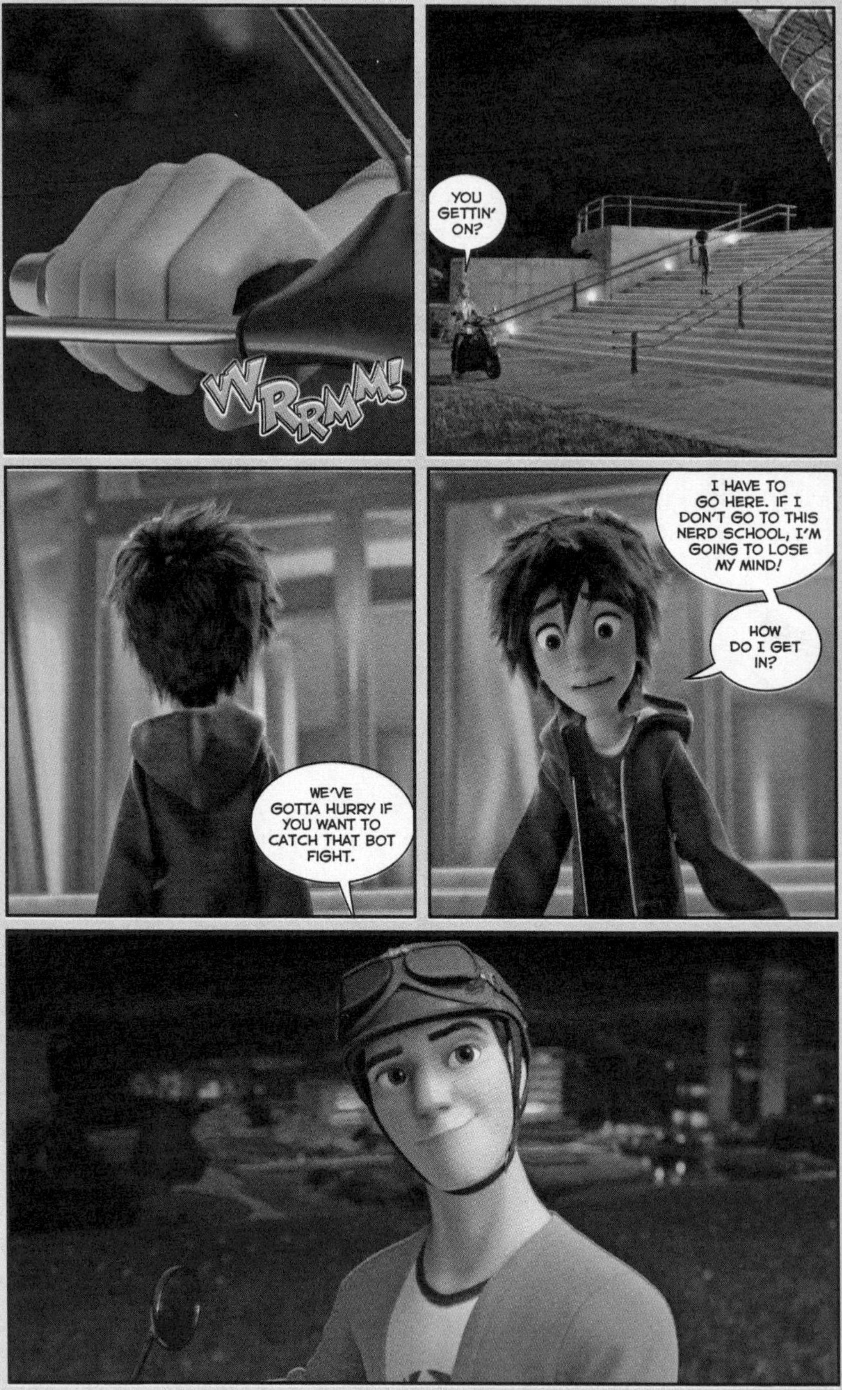
WRRMM!
YOU GETTIN' ON?
WE'VE GOTTA HURRY IF YOU WANT TO CATCH THAT BOT FIGHT.
I HAVE TO GO HERE. IF I DON'T GO TO THIS NERD SCHOOL, I'M GOING TO LOSE MY MIND!
HOW DO I GET IN?

EVERY YEAR THE SCHOOL HAS A STUDENT SHOWCASE. YOU COME UP WITH SOMETHING THAT BLOWS CALLAGHAN AWAY, YOU'RE IN.

TAK!

SAN FRANSOKYO INSTITUTE OF TECHNOLOGY

SFIT SHOWCASE

CALL FOR ENTRIES
For more information please visit www.sfit.edu

SAN FRANSOKYO INSTITUTE OF TECHNOLOGY

SFIT SHOWCASE

CALL FOR ENTRIES
For more information please visit www.sfit.edu

BUT IT'S GOTTA BE GREAT.

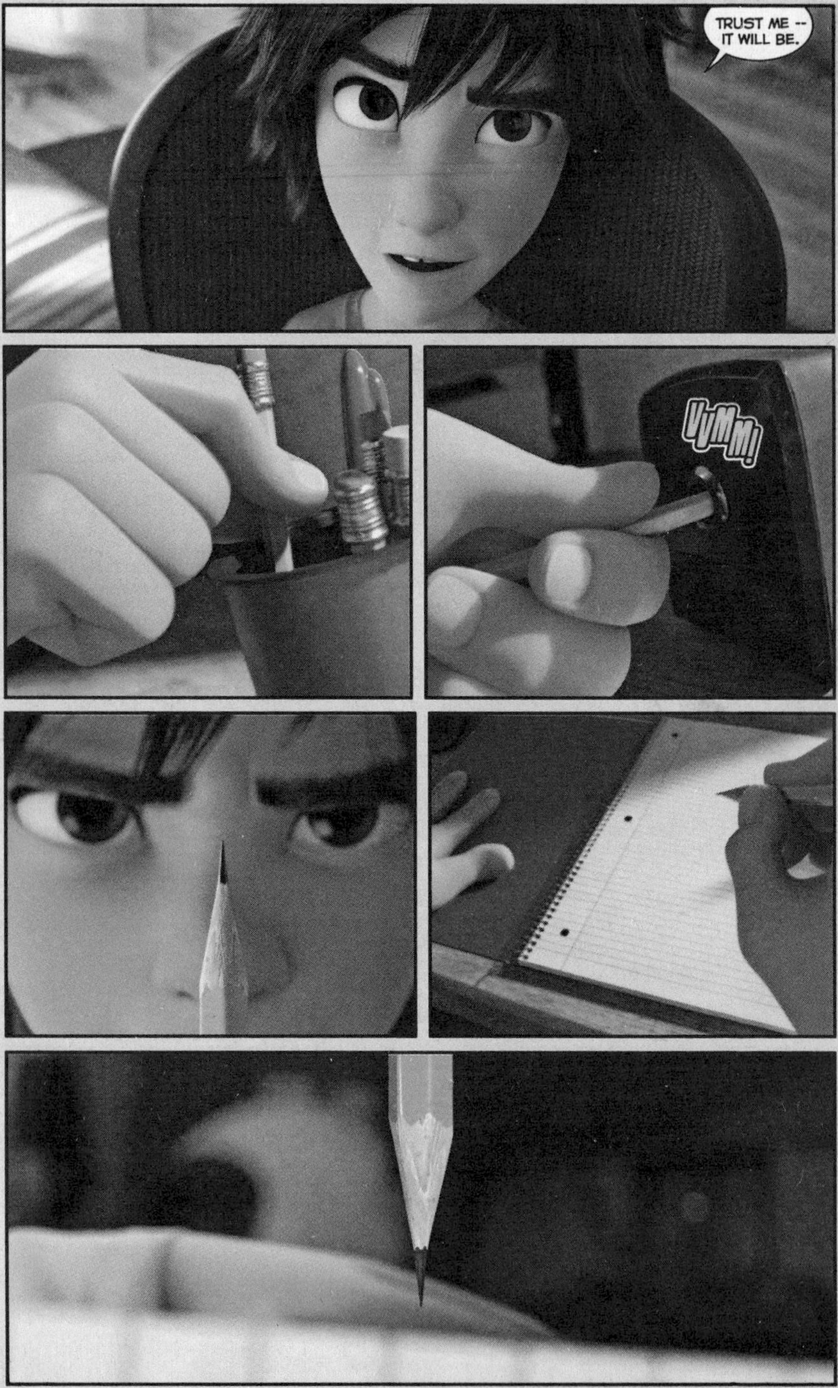
TRUST ME -- IT WILL BE.
VVMM!

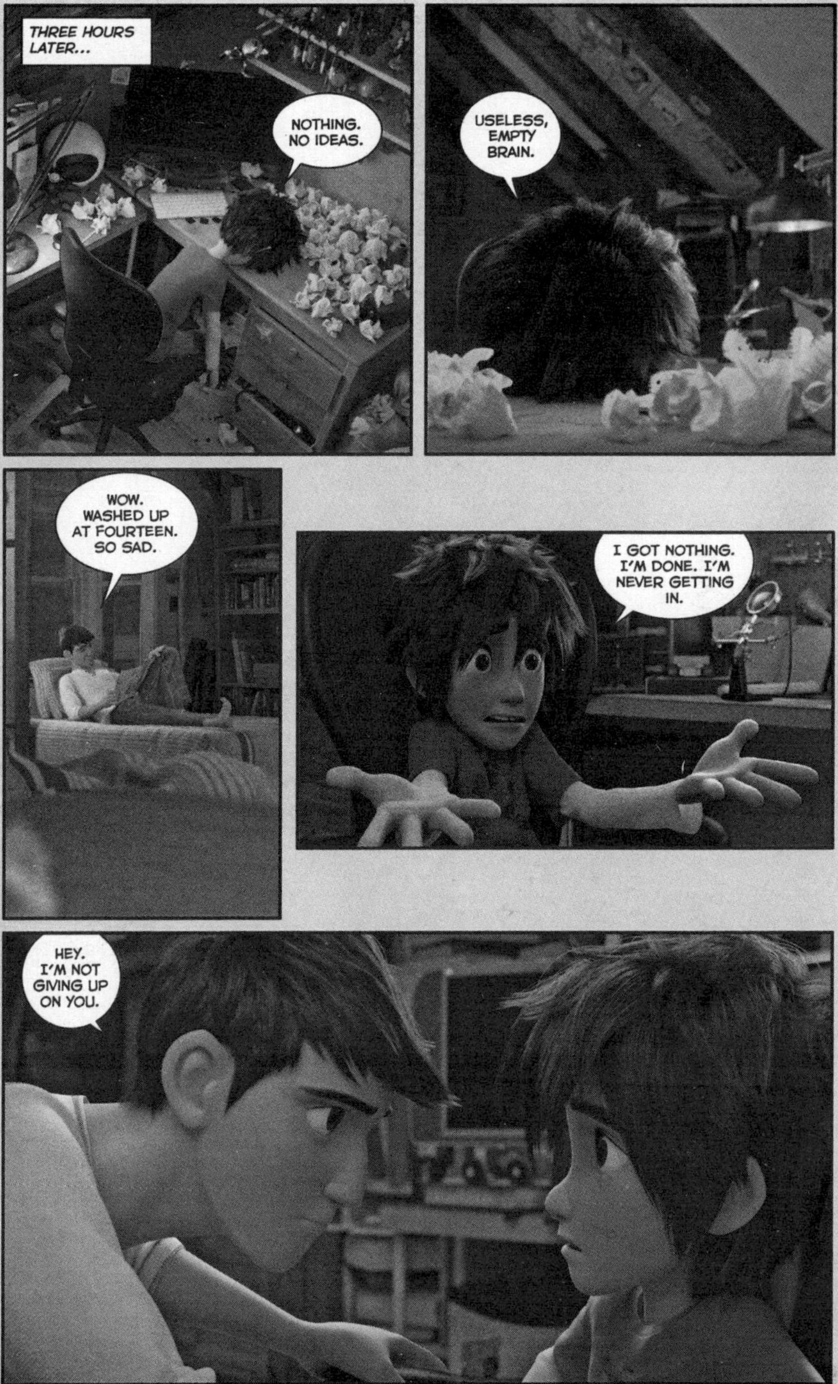
THREE HOURS LATER...
NOTHING. NO IDEAS.
USELESS, EMPTY BRAIN.
WOW. WASHED UP AT FOURTEEN. SO SAD.
I GOT NOTHING. I'M DONE. I'M NEVER GETTING IN.
HEY. I'M NOT GIVING UP ON YOU.

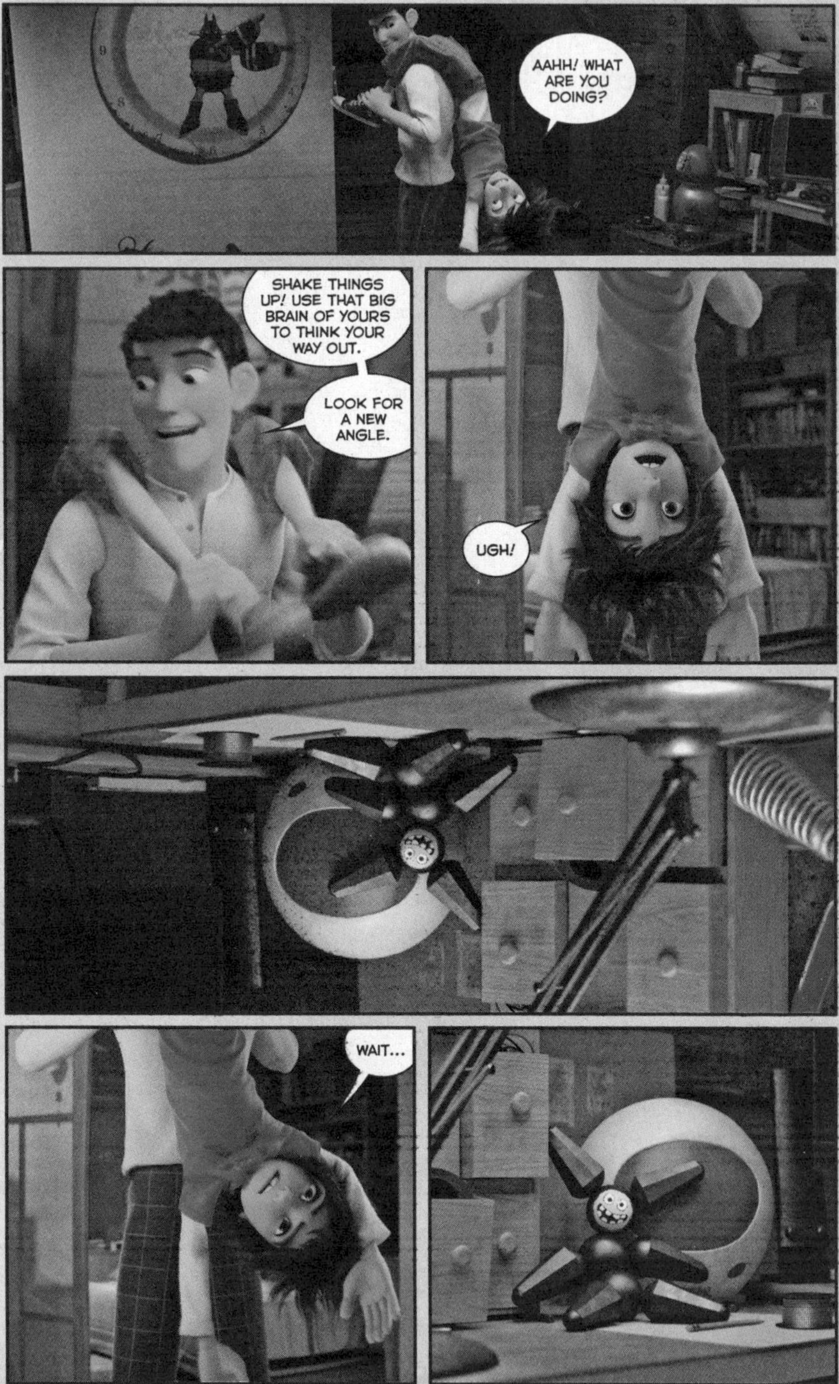
AAHH! WHAT ARE YOU DOING?
SHAKE THINGS UP! USE THAT BIG BRAIN OF YOURS TO THINK YOUR WAY OUT.
LOOK FOR A NEW ANGLE.
UGH!
WAIT...

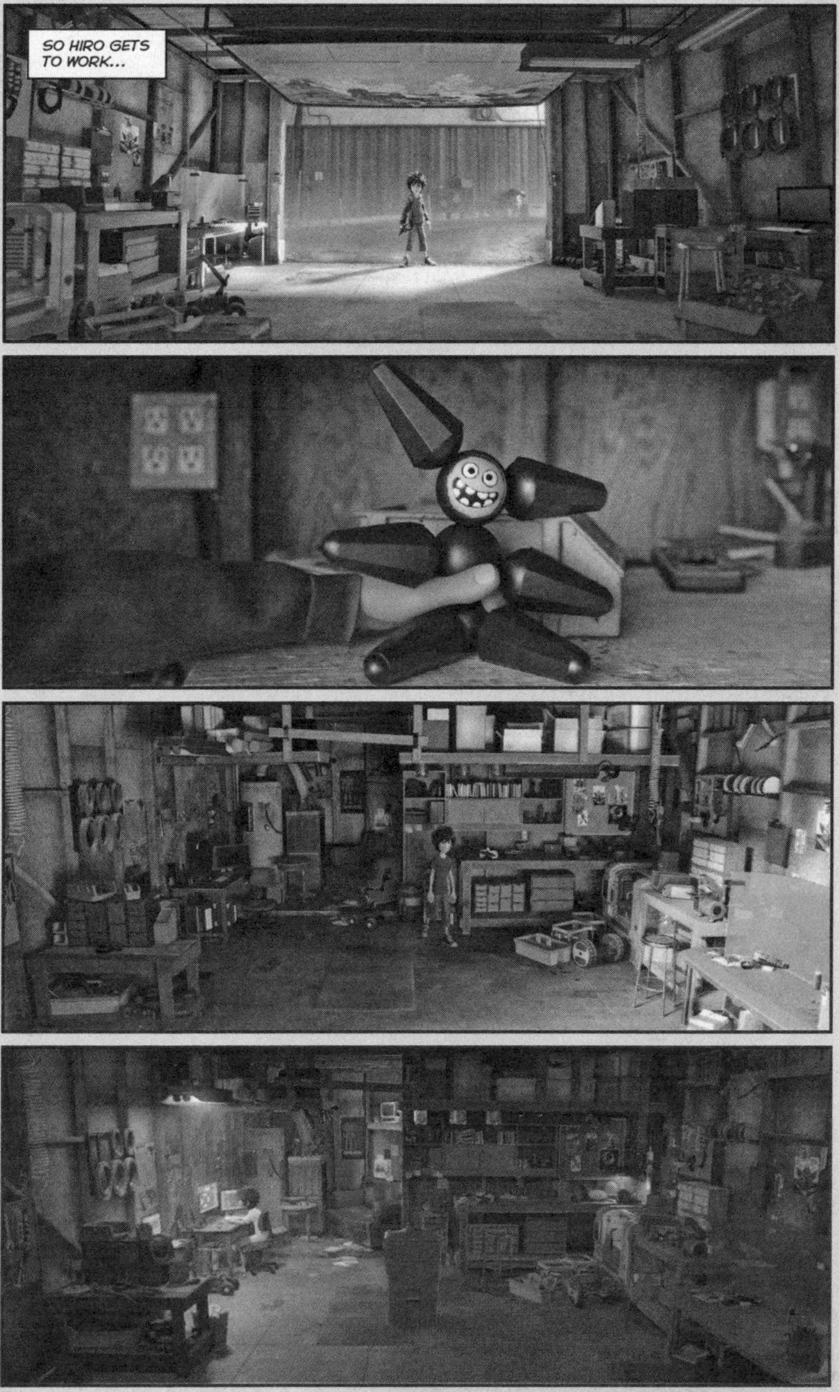
SO HIRO GETS
TO WORK...

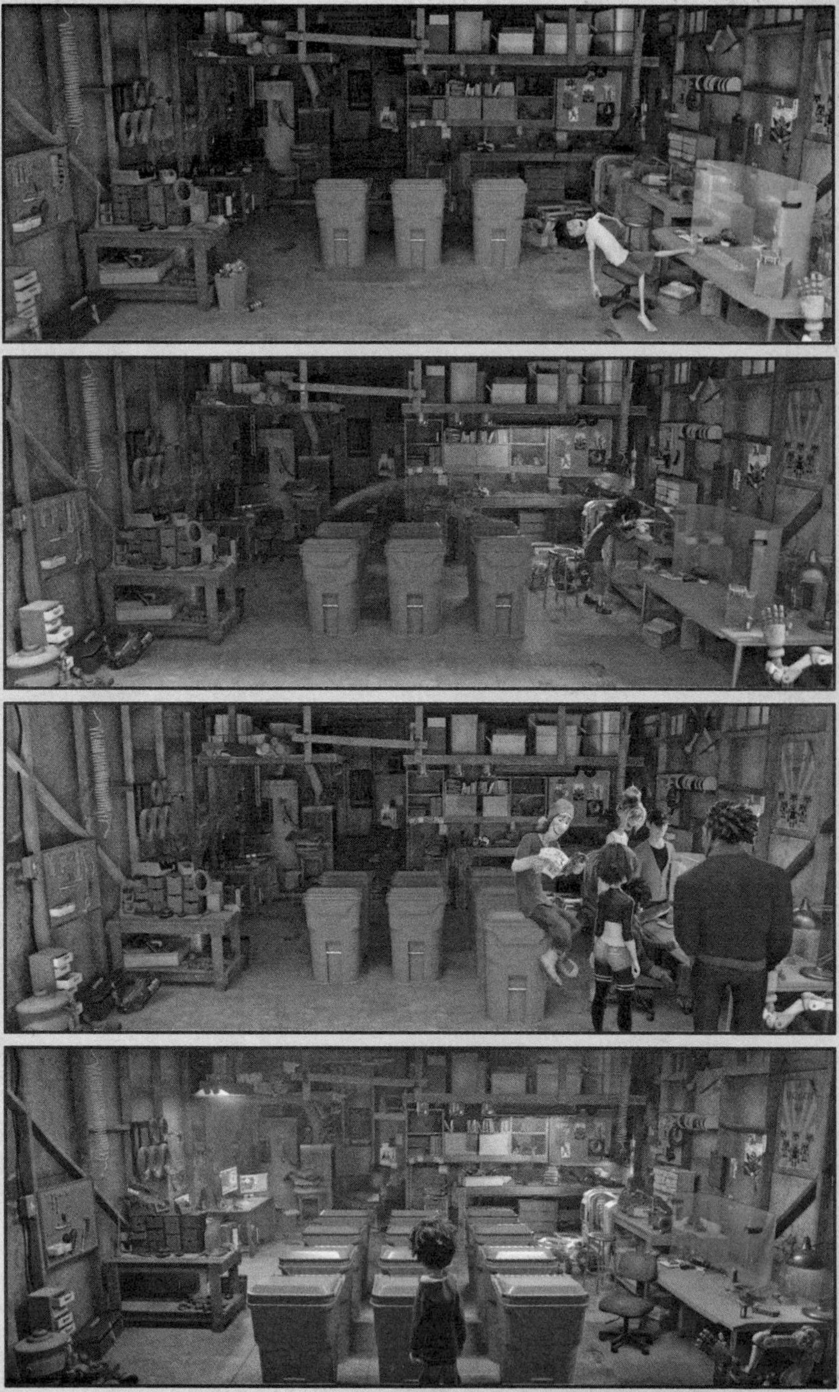

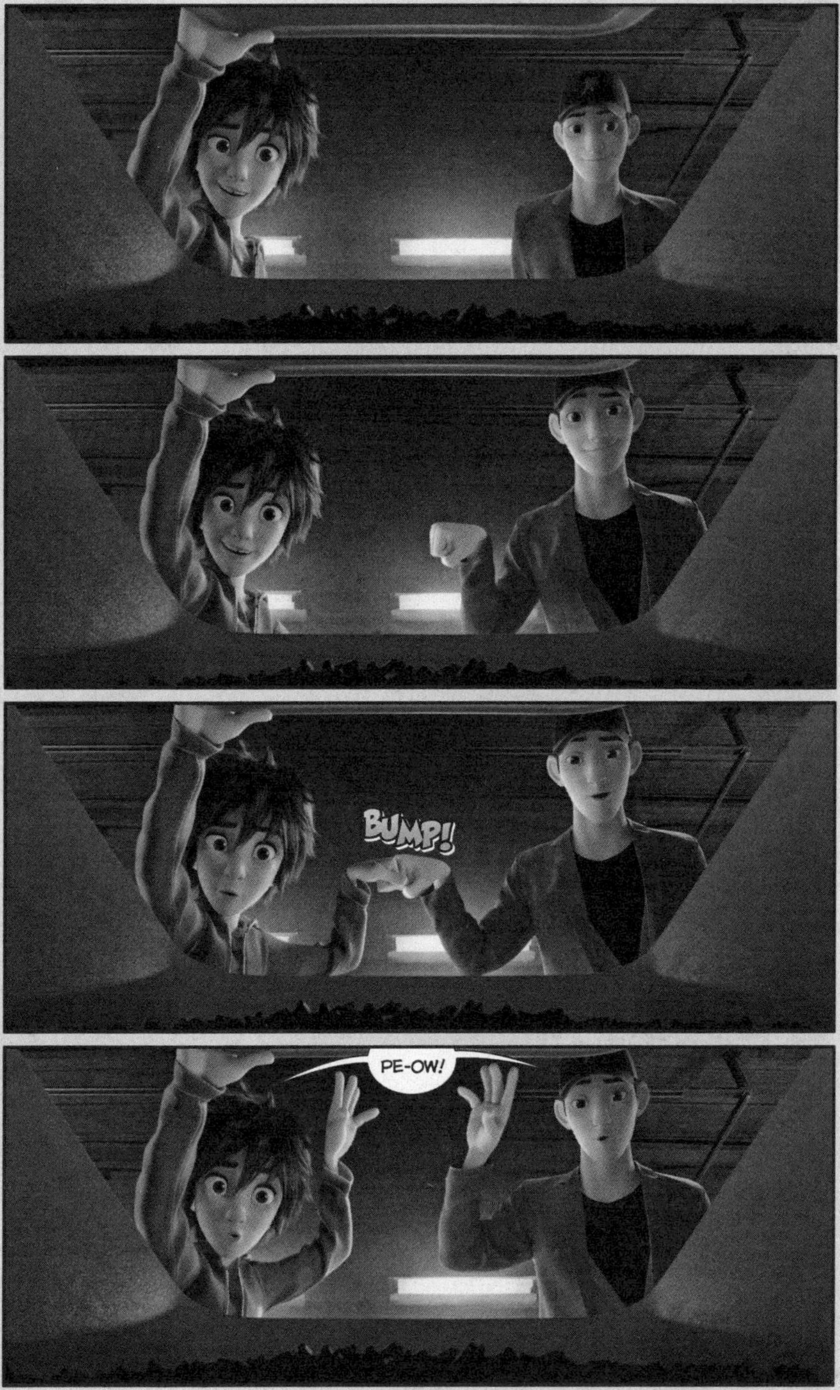
BUMP!
PE-OW!

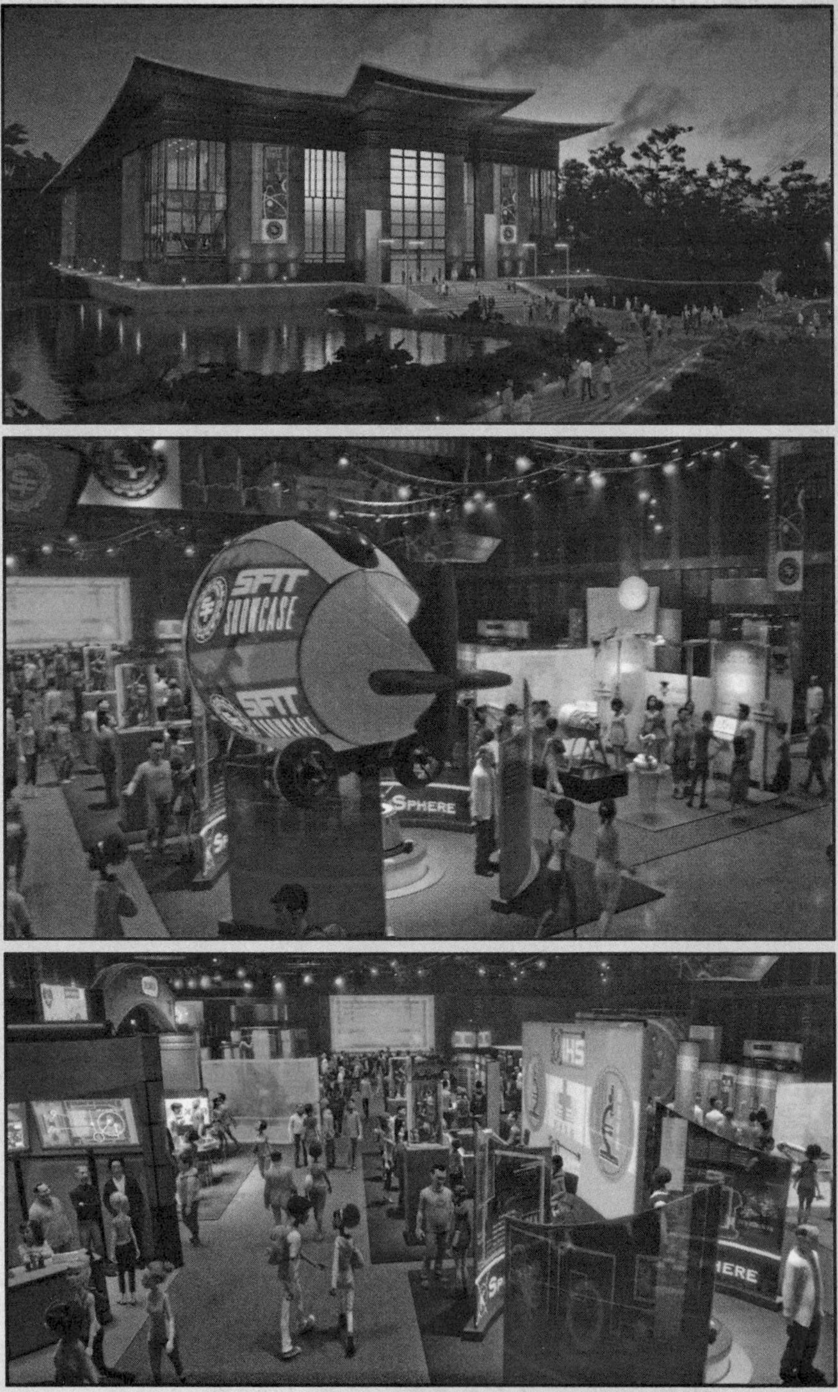
SFIT
SHOWCASE
SPHERE
IHS

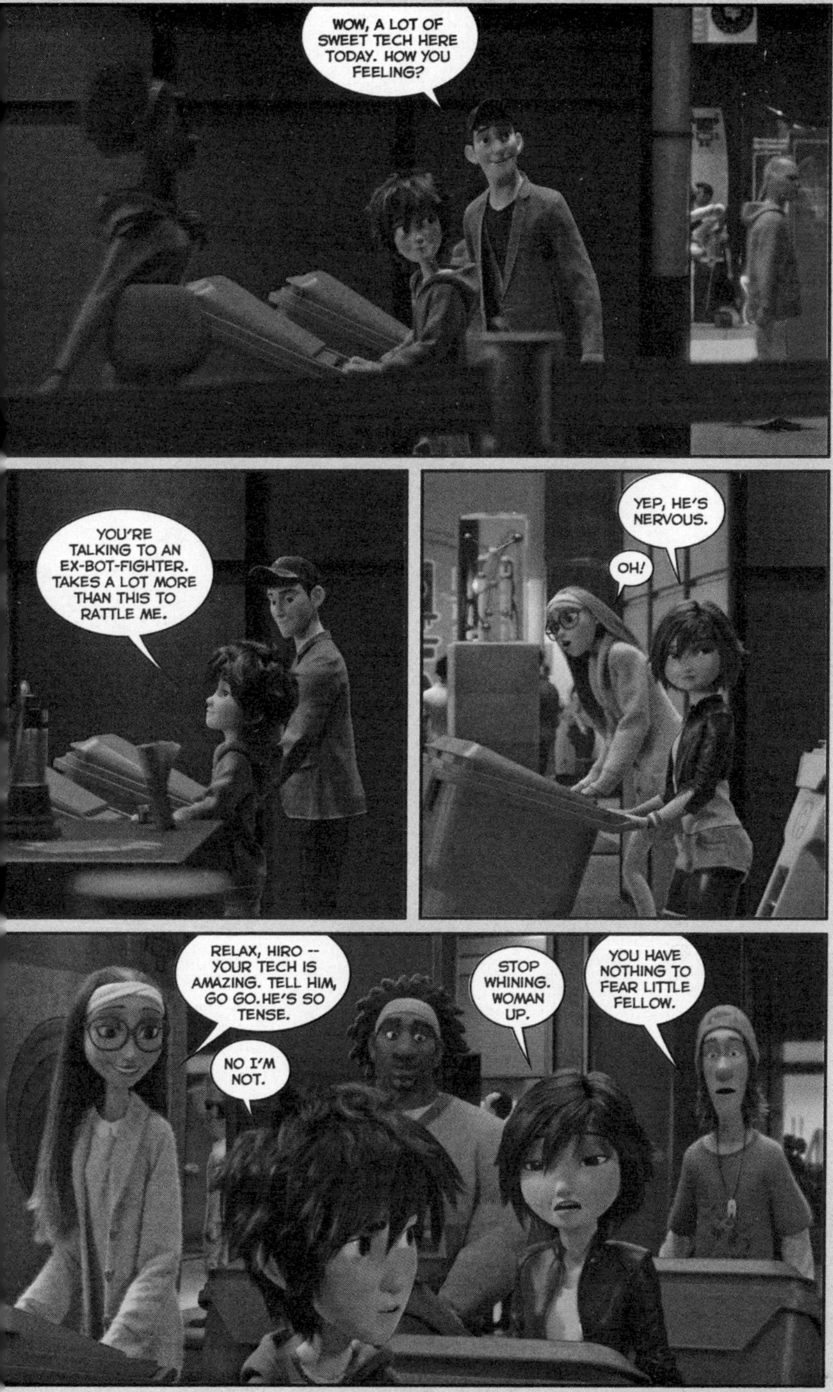
WOW, A LOT OF SWEET TECH HERE TODAY. HOW YOU FEELING?
YOU'RE TALKING TO AN EX-BOT-FIGHTER. TAKES A LOT MORE THAN THIS TO RATTLE ME.
OH!
YEP, HE'S NERVOUS.
RELAX, HIRO -- YOUR TECH IS AMAZING. TELL HIM, GO GO.HE'S SO TENSE.
NO I'M NOT.
STOP WHINING. WOMAN UP.
YOU HAVE NOTHING TO FEAR LITTLE FELLOW.

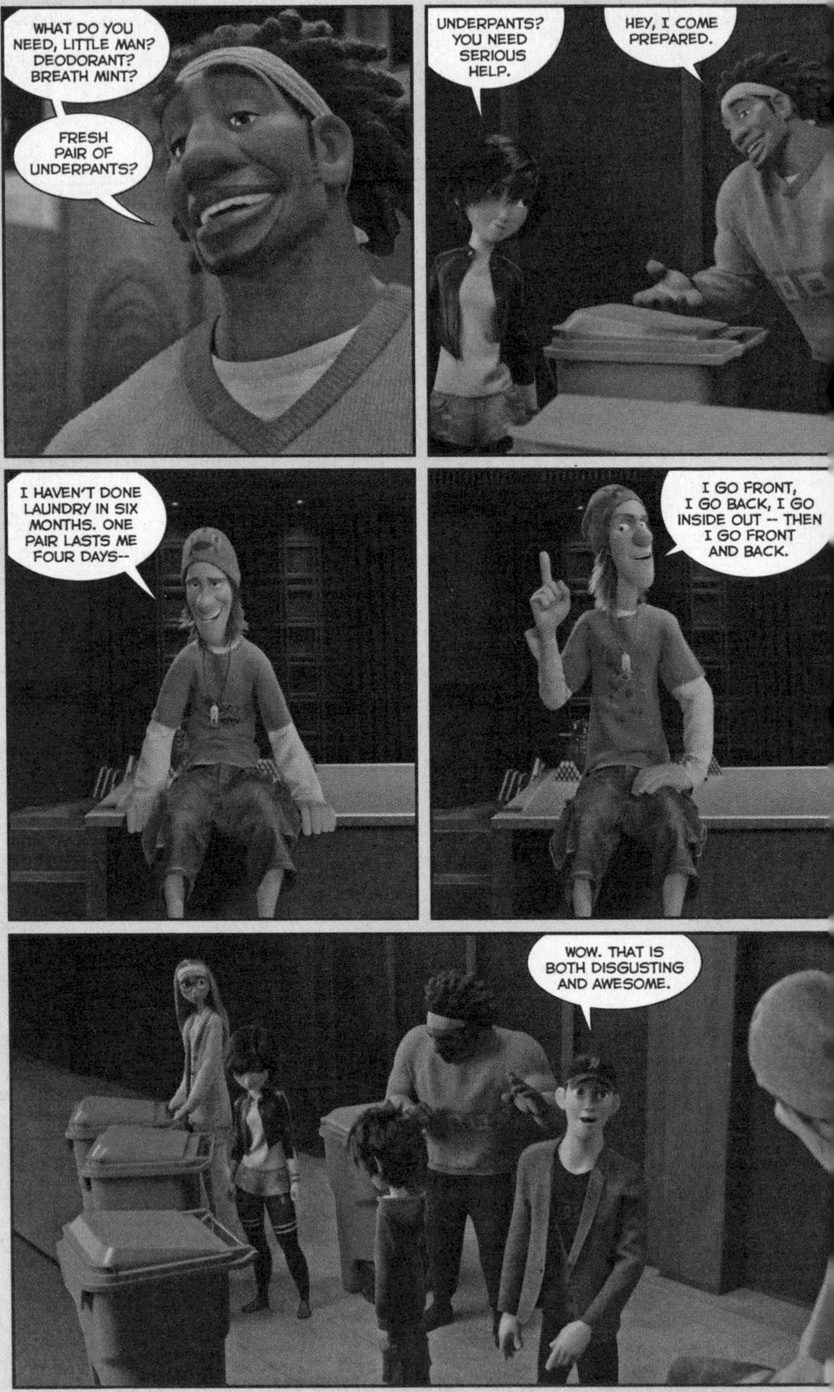
WHAT DO YOU NEED, LITTLE MAN? DEODORANT? BREATH MINT?
FRESH PAIR OF UNDERPANTS?
UNDERPANTS? YOU NEED SERIOUS HELP.
HEY, I COME PREPARED.
I HAVEN'T DONE LAUNDRY IN SIX MONTHS. ONE PAIR LASTS ME FOUR DAYS--
I GO FRONT, I GO BACK, I GO INSIDE OUT -- THEN I GO FRONT AND BACK.
WOW. THAT IS BOTH DISGUSTING AND AWESOME.

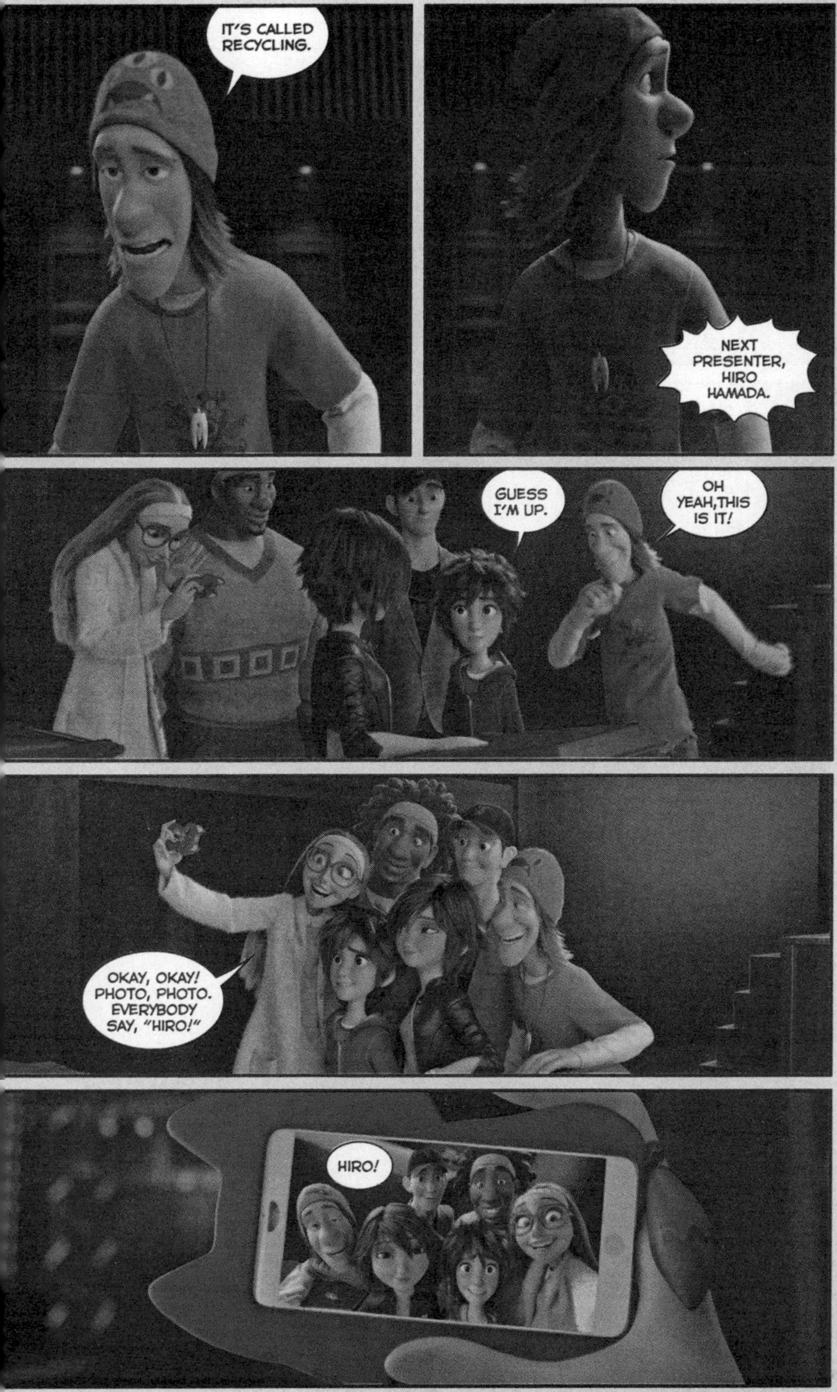
IT'S CALLED RECYCLING.
NEXT PRESENTER, HIRO HAMADA.
GUESS I'M UP.
OH YEAH, THIS IS IT!
OKAY, OKAY! PHOTO, PHOTO. EVERYBODY SAY, "HIRO!"
HIRO!

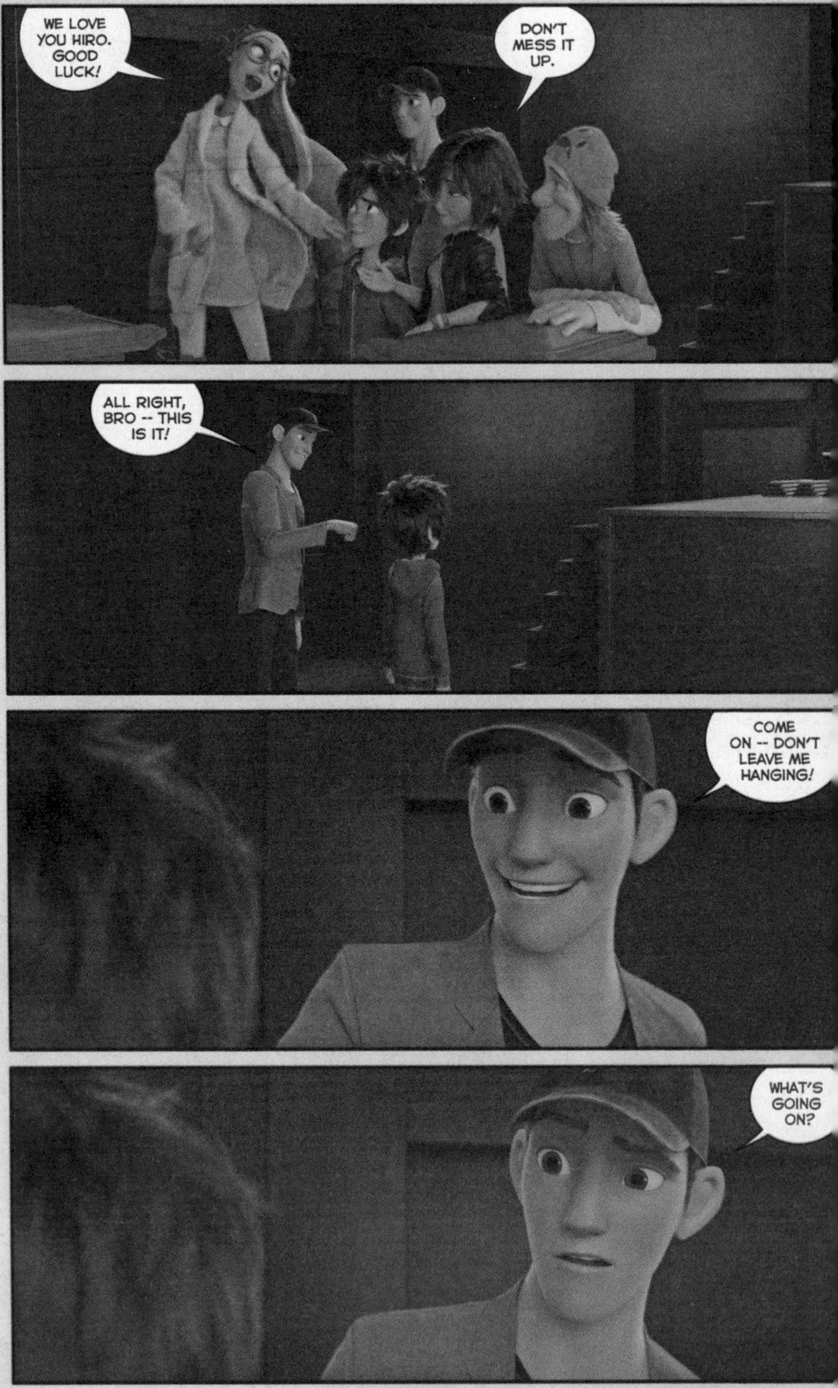
WE LOVE YOU HIRO. GOOD LUCK!
DON'T MESS IT UP.
ALL RIGHT, BRO -- THIS IS IT!
COME ON -- DON'T LEAVE ME HANGING!
WHAT'S GOING ON?

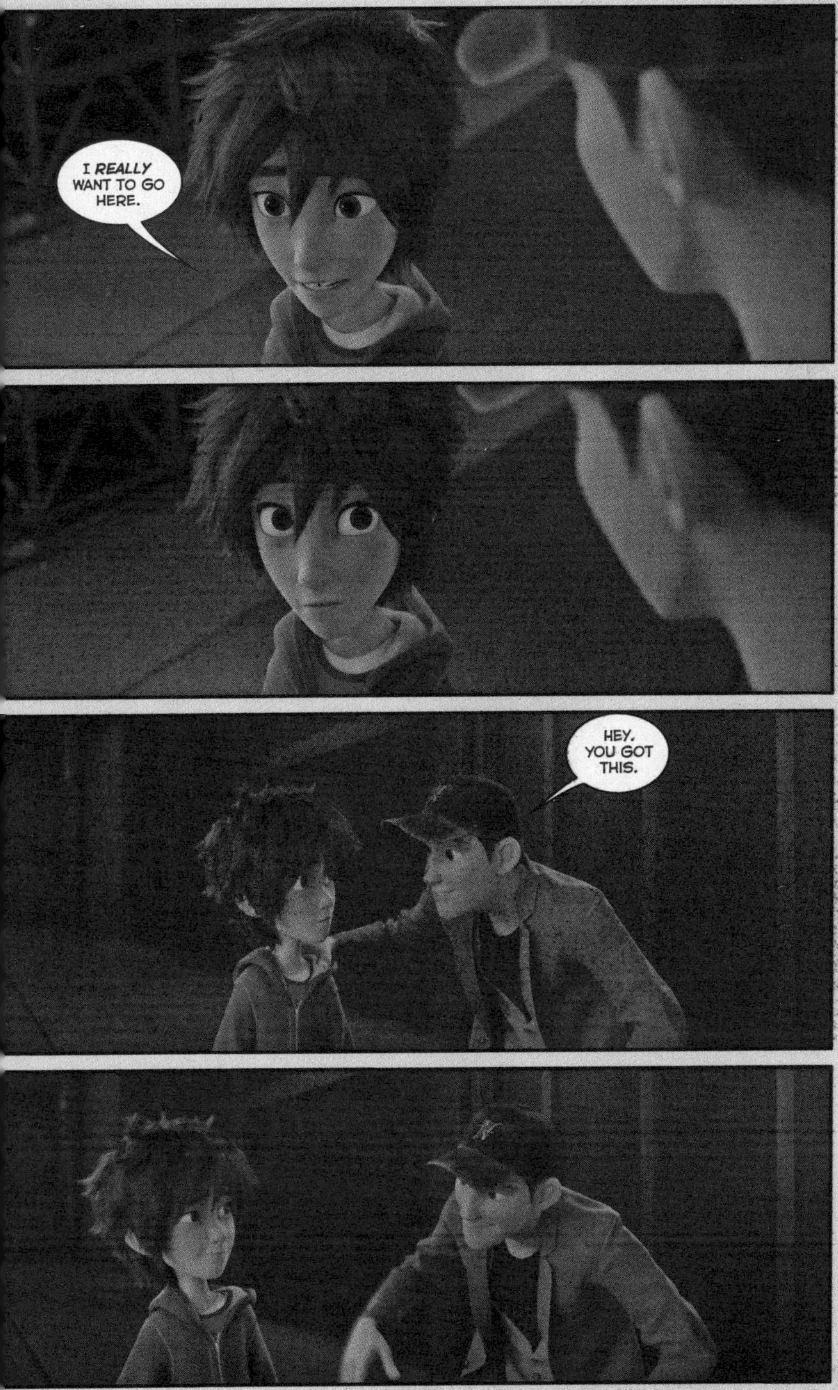
I *REALLY* WANT TO GO HERE.
HEY. YOU GOT THIS.

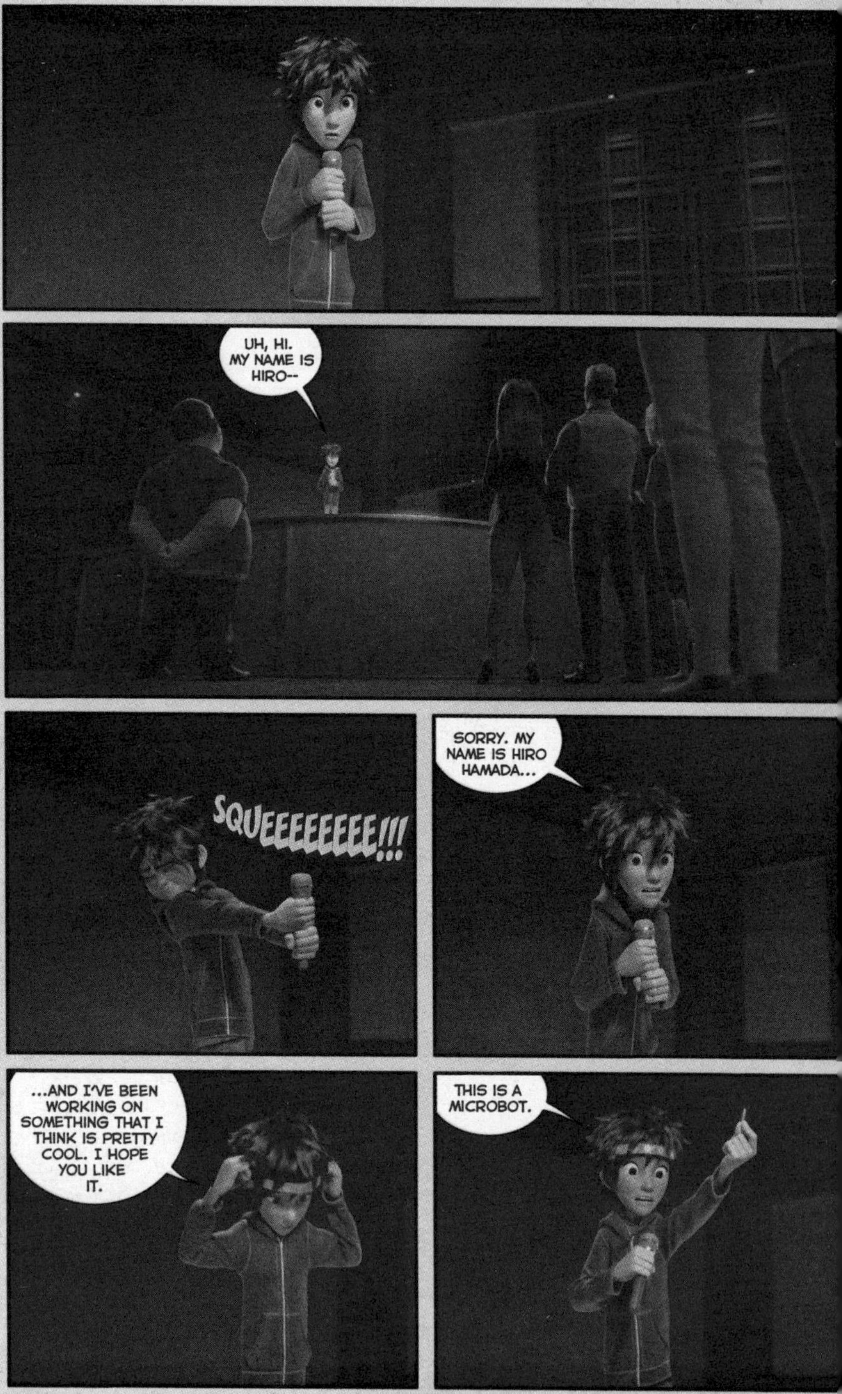
UH, HI. MY NAME IS HIRO--
SQUEEEEEEEE!!!
SORRY. MY NAME IS HIRO HAMADA...
...AND I'VE BEEN WORKING ON SOMETHING THAT I THINK IS PRETTY COOL. I HOPE YOU LIKE IT.
THIS IS A MICROBOT.

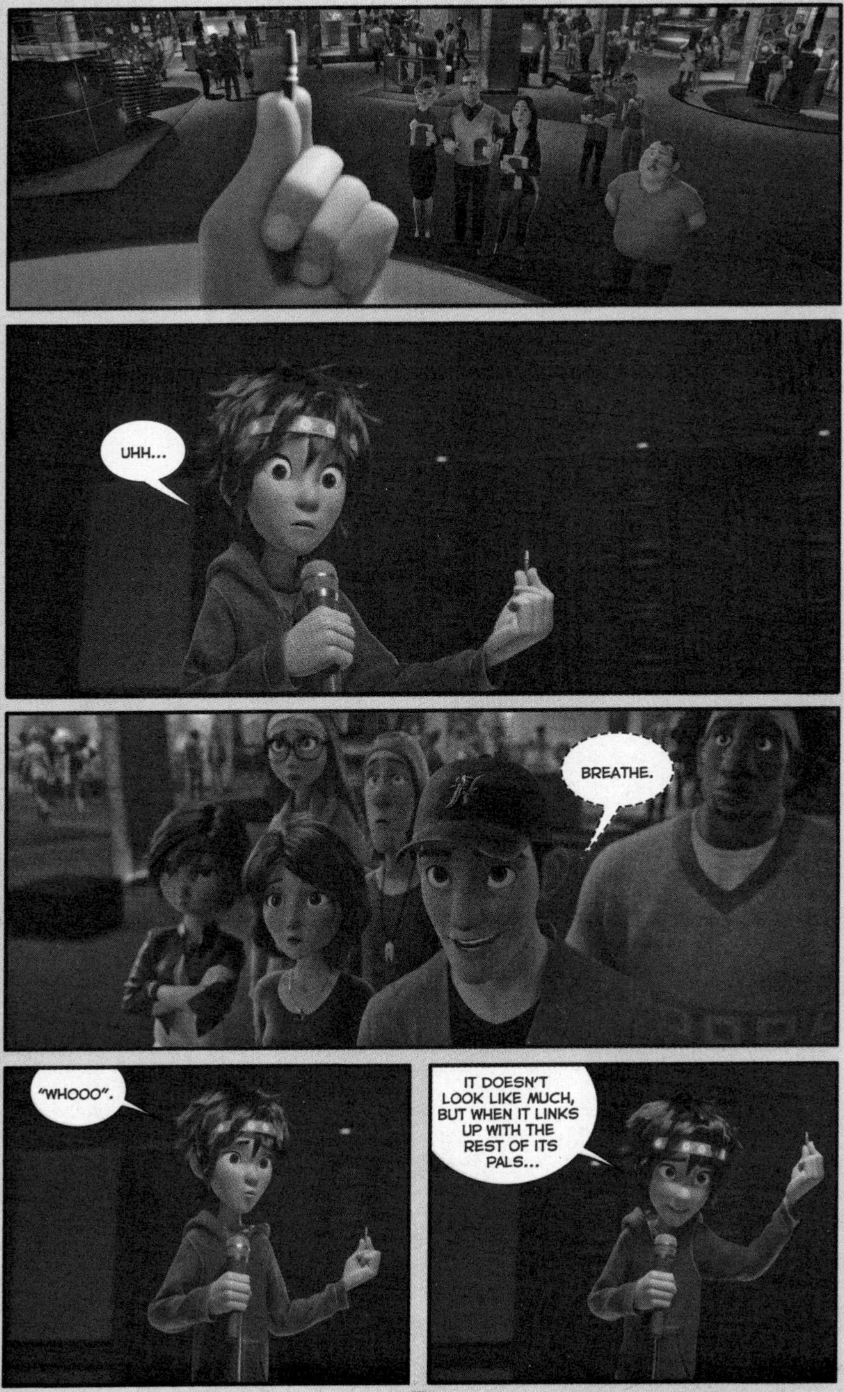
UHH...
BREATHE.
"WHOOO".
IT DOESN'T LOOK LIKE MUCH, BUT WHEN IT LINKS UP WITH THE REST OF ITS PALS...

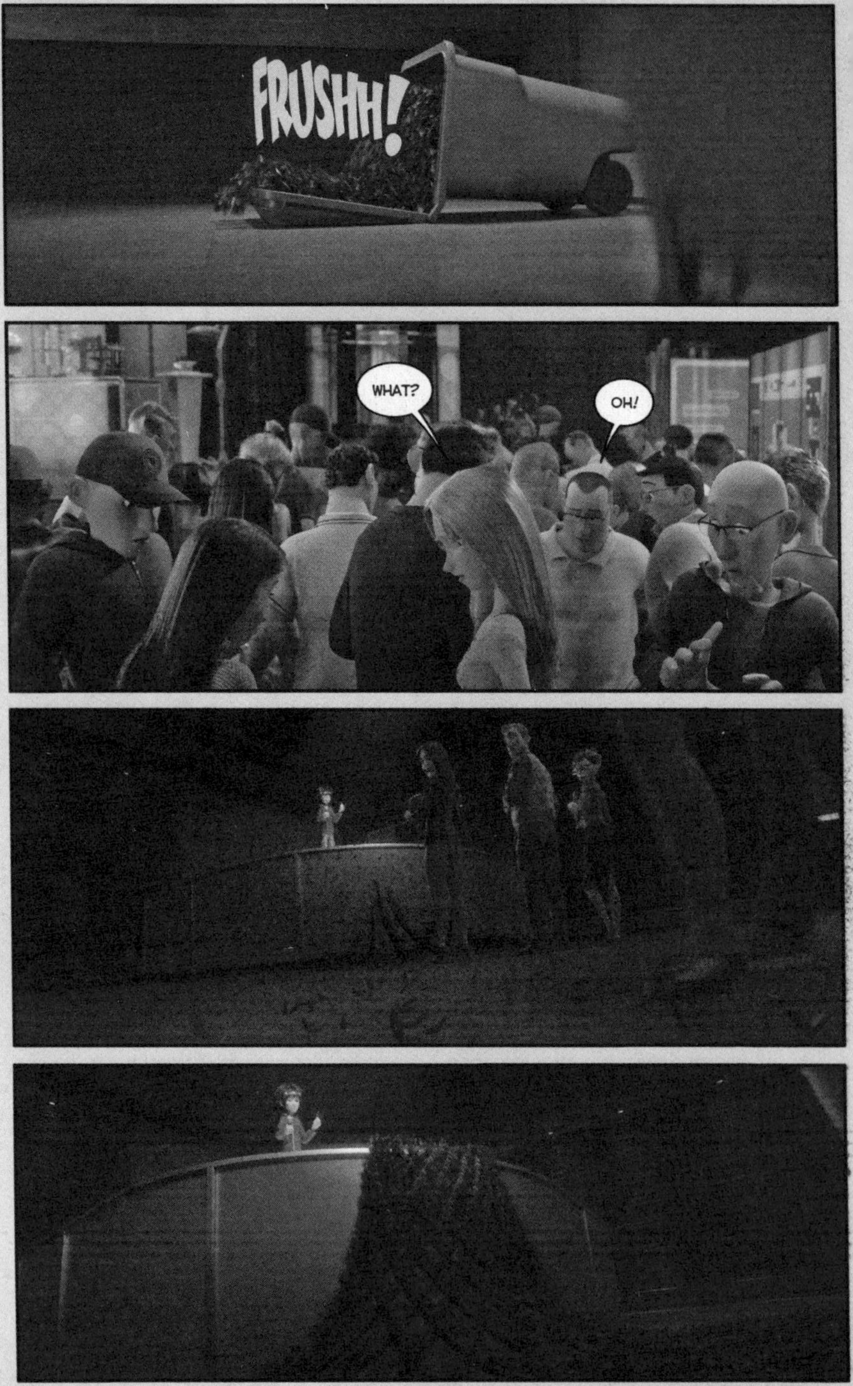
FRUSHH!
WHAT?
OH!

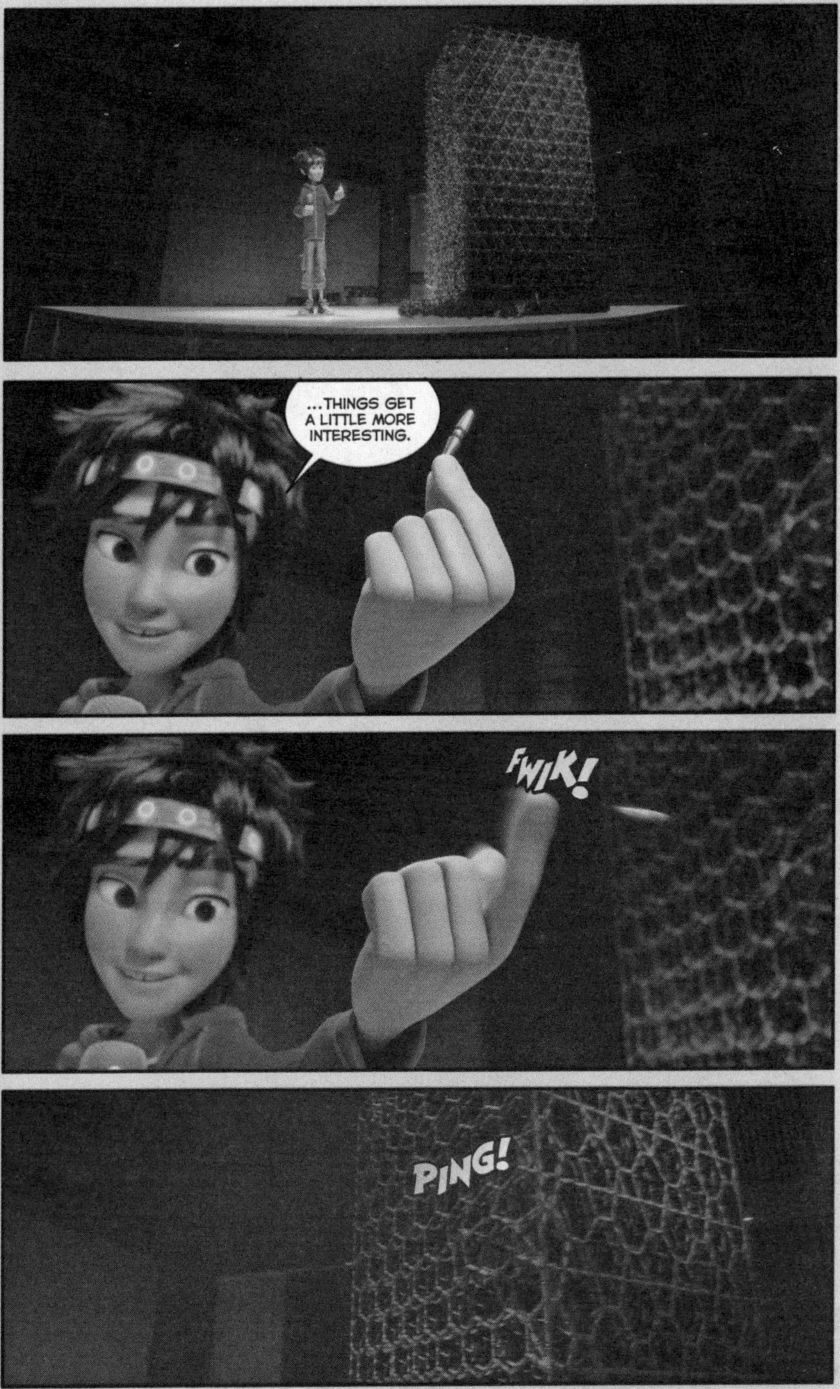
...THINGS GET A LITTLE MORE INTERESTING.
FWIK!
PING!

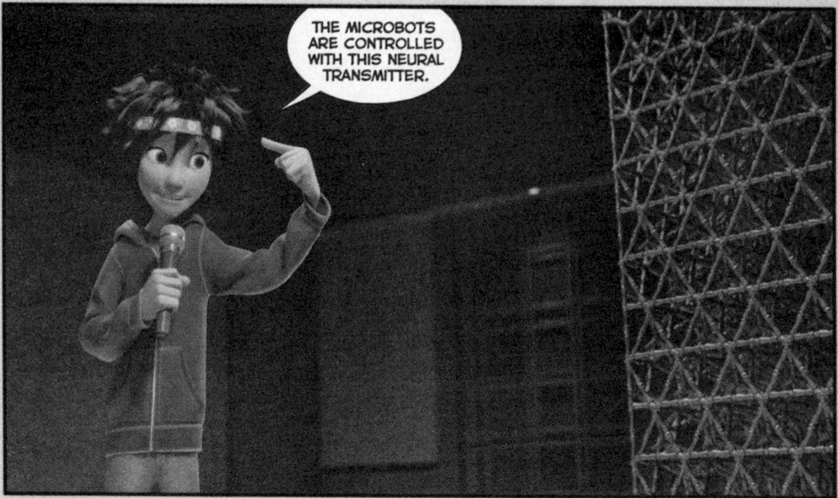
THE MICROBOTS ARE CONTROLLED WITH THIS NEURAL TRANSMITTER.

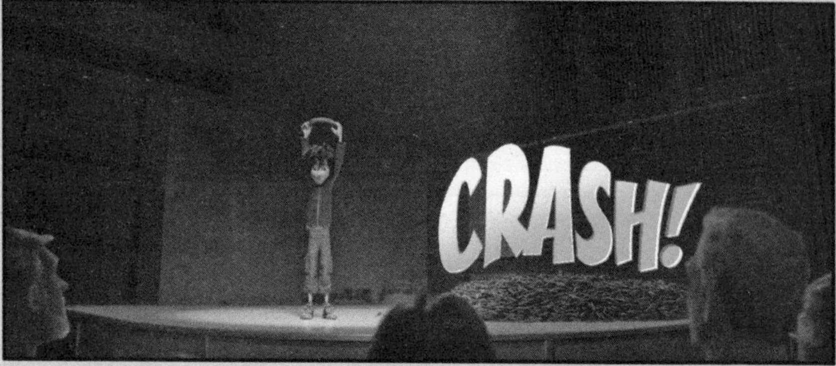
CRASH!

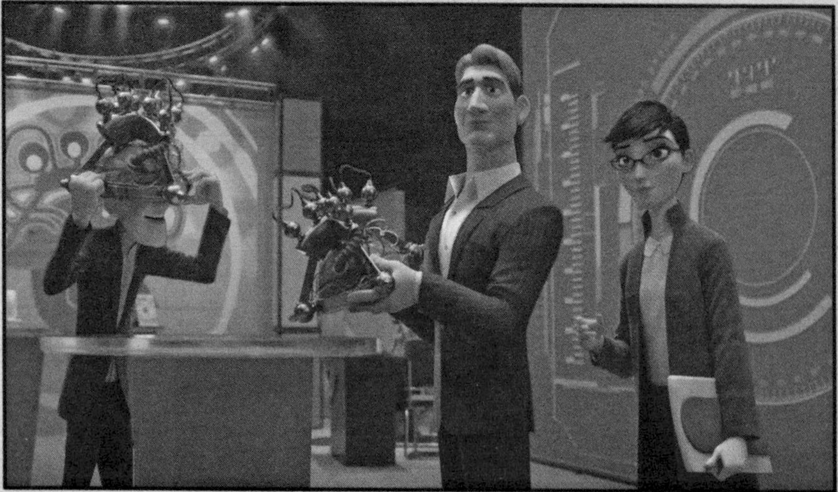

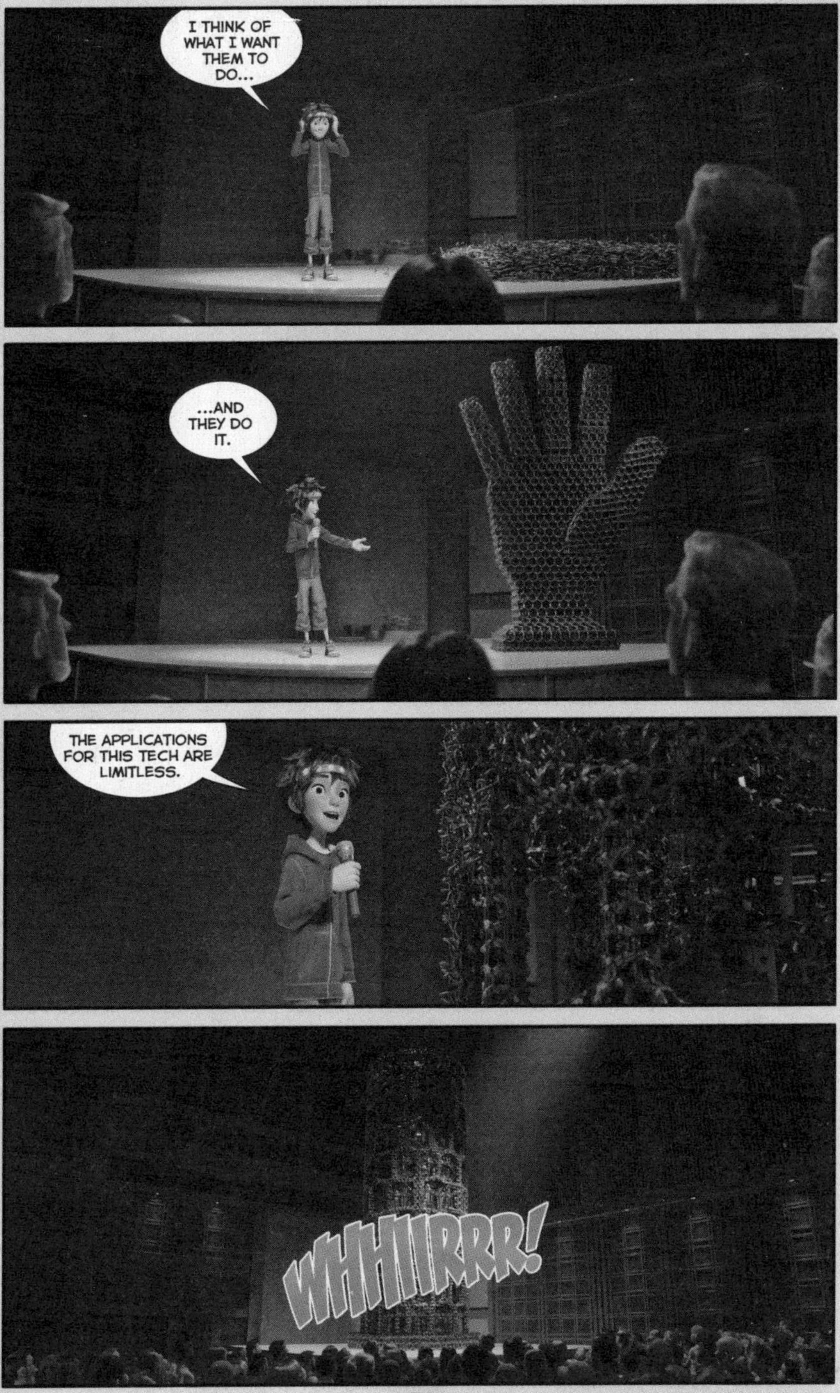
I THINK OF WHAT I WANT THEM TO DO...
...AND THEY DO IT.
THE APPLICATIONS FOR THIS TECH ARE LIMITLESS.
WHHIIRRR!

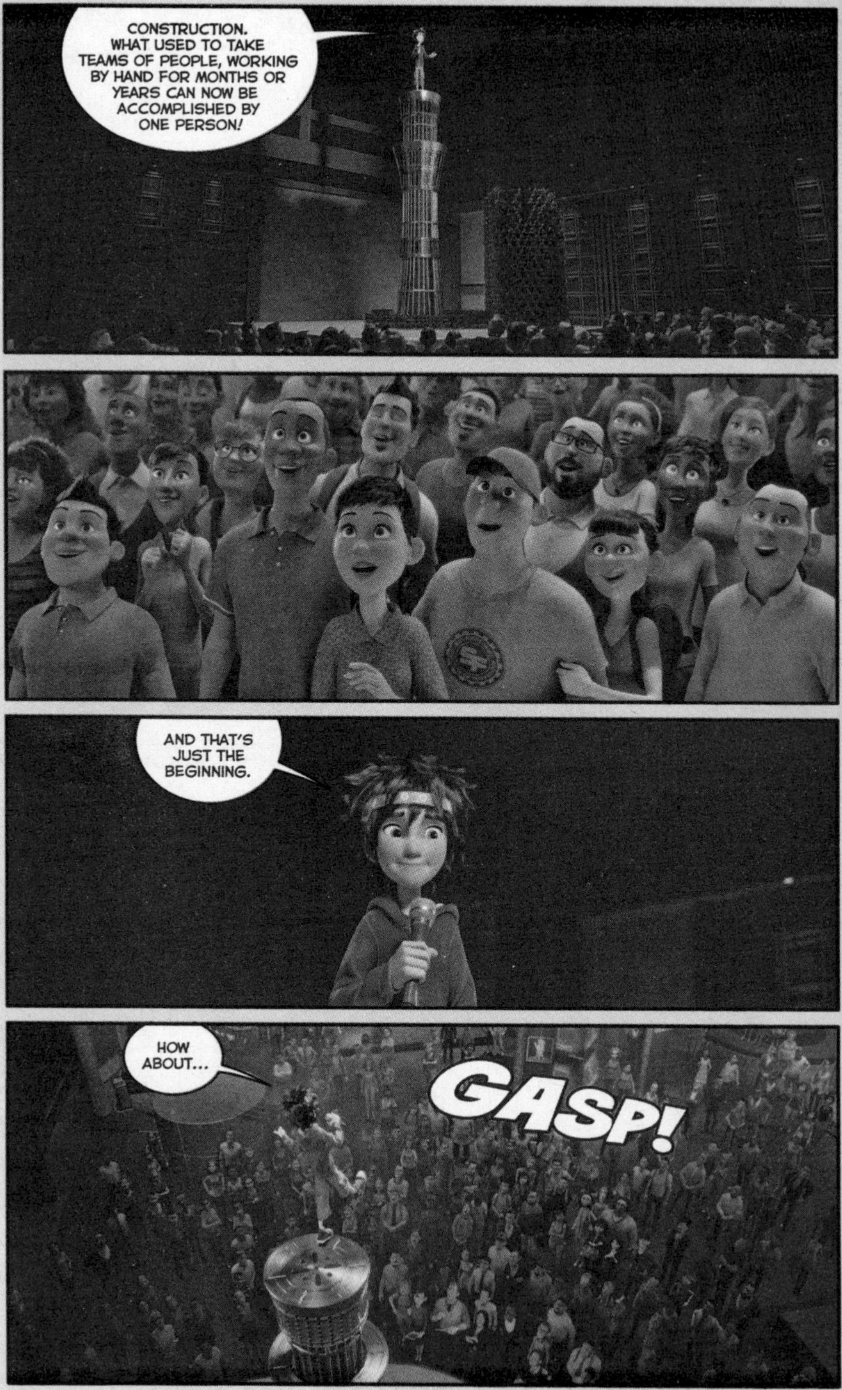

CONSTRUCTION. WHAT USED TO TAKE TEAMS OF PEOPLE, WORKING BY HAND FOR MONTHS OR YEARS CAN NOW BE ACCOMPLISHED BY ONE PERSON!
AND THAT'S JUST THE BEGINNING.
HOW ABOUT...
GASP!

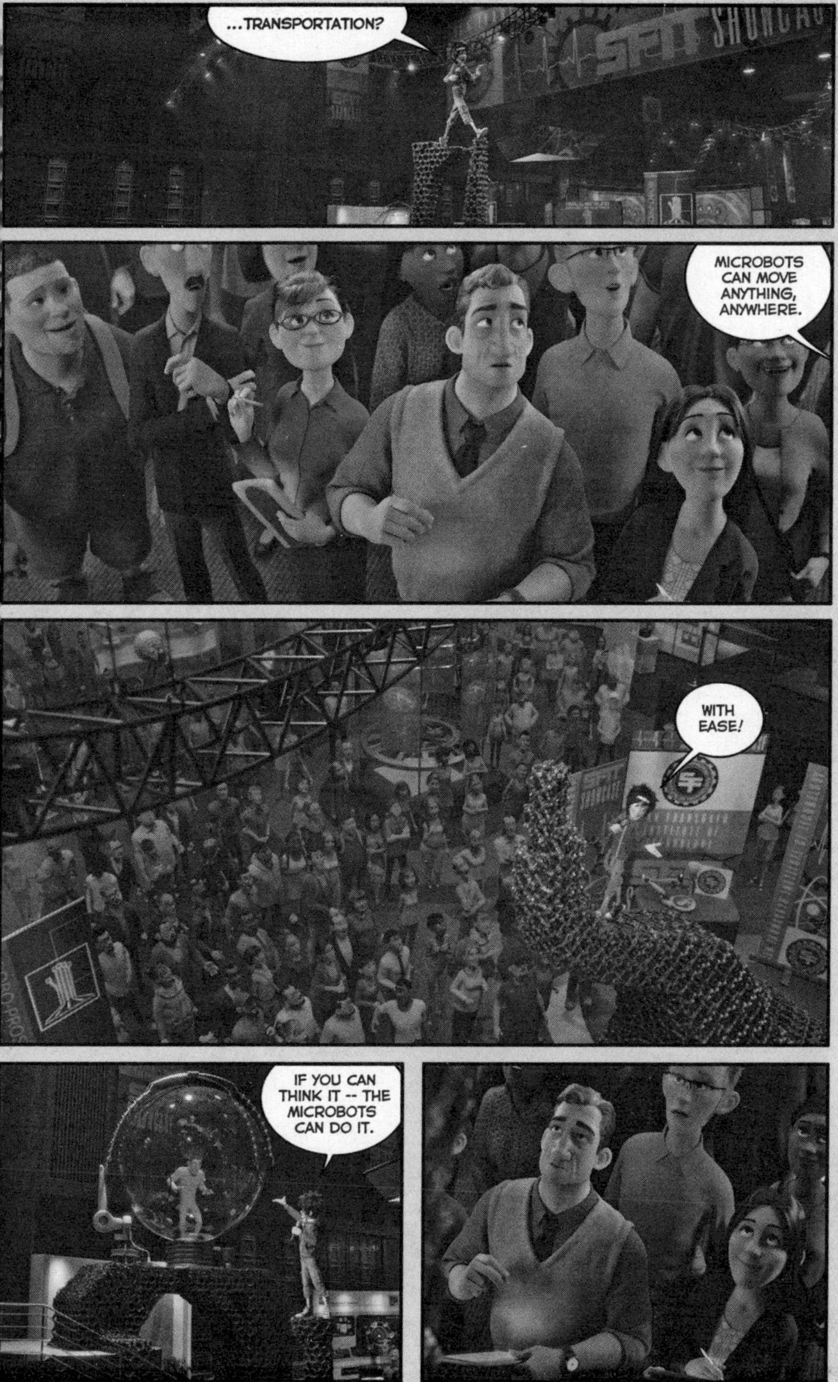
...TRANSPORTATION?
MICROBOTS CAN MOVE ANYTHING, ANYWHERE.
WITH EASE!
IF YOU CAN THINK IT -- THE MICROBOTS CAN DO IT.

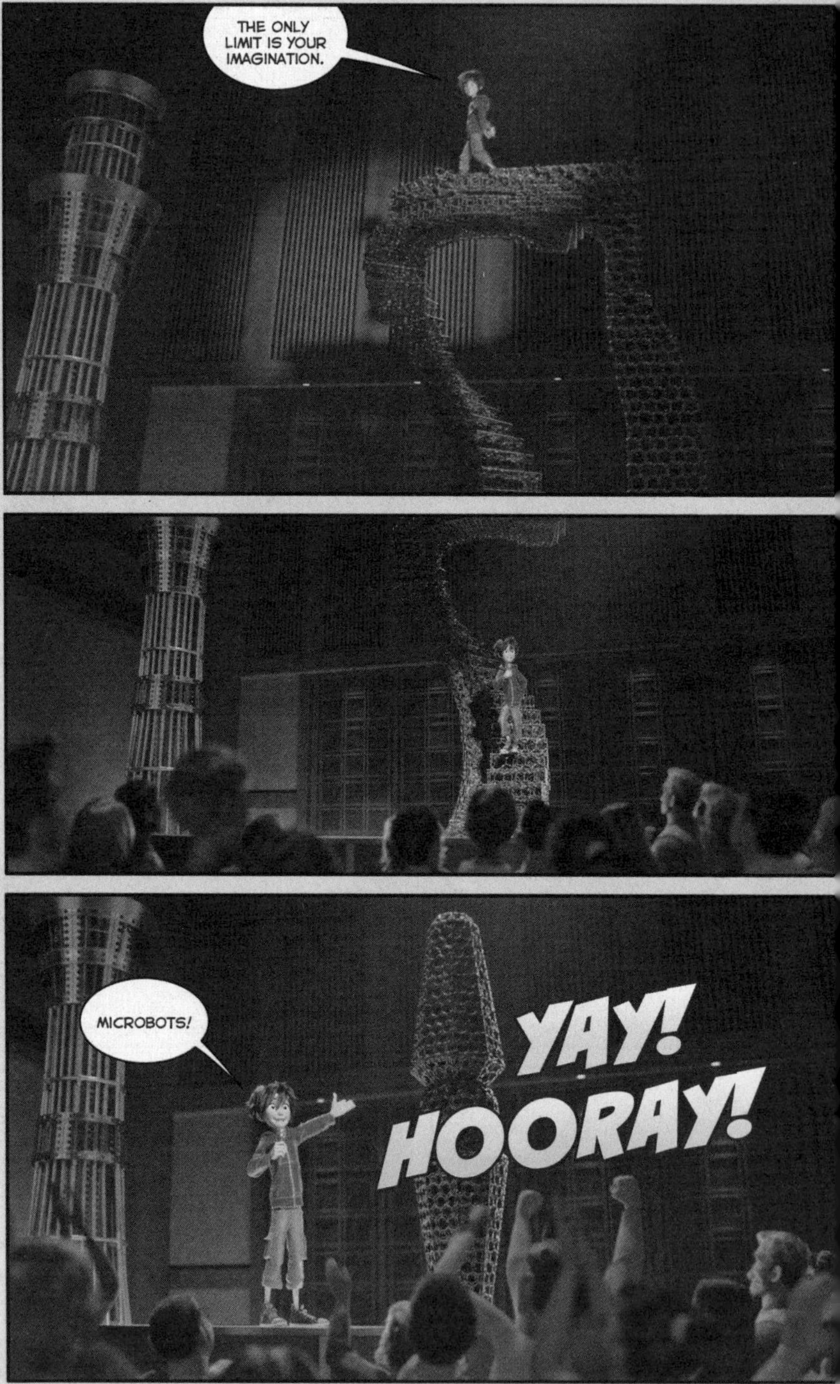
THE ONLY LIMIT IS YOUR IMAGINATION.
MICROBOTS!
YAY!
HOORAY!

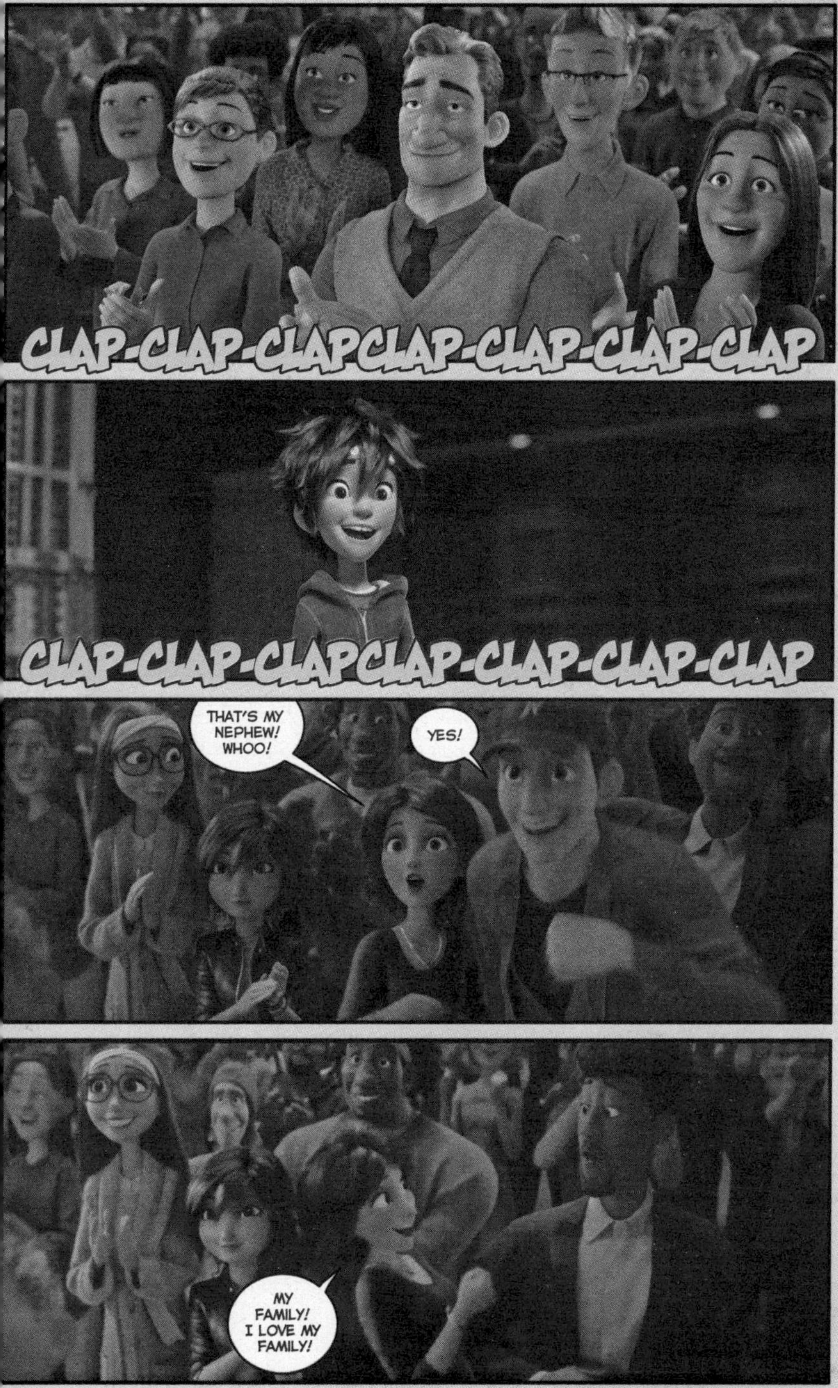
CLAP-CLAP-CLAPCLAP-CLAP-CLAP-CLAP
CLAP-CLAP-CLAPCLAP-CLAP-CLAP-CLAP
THAT'S MY NEPHEW! WHOO!
YES!
MY FAMILY! I LOVE MY FAMILY!

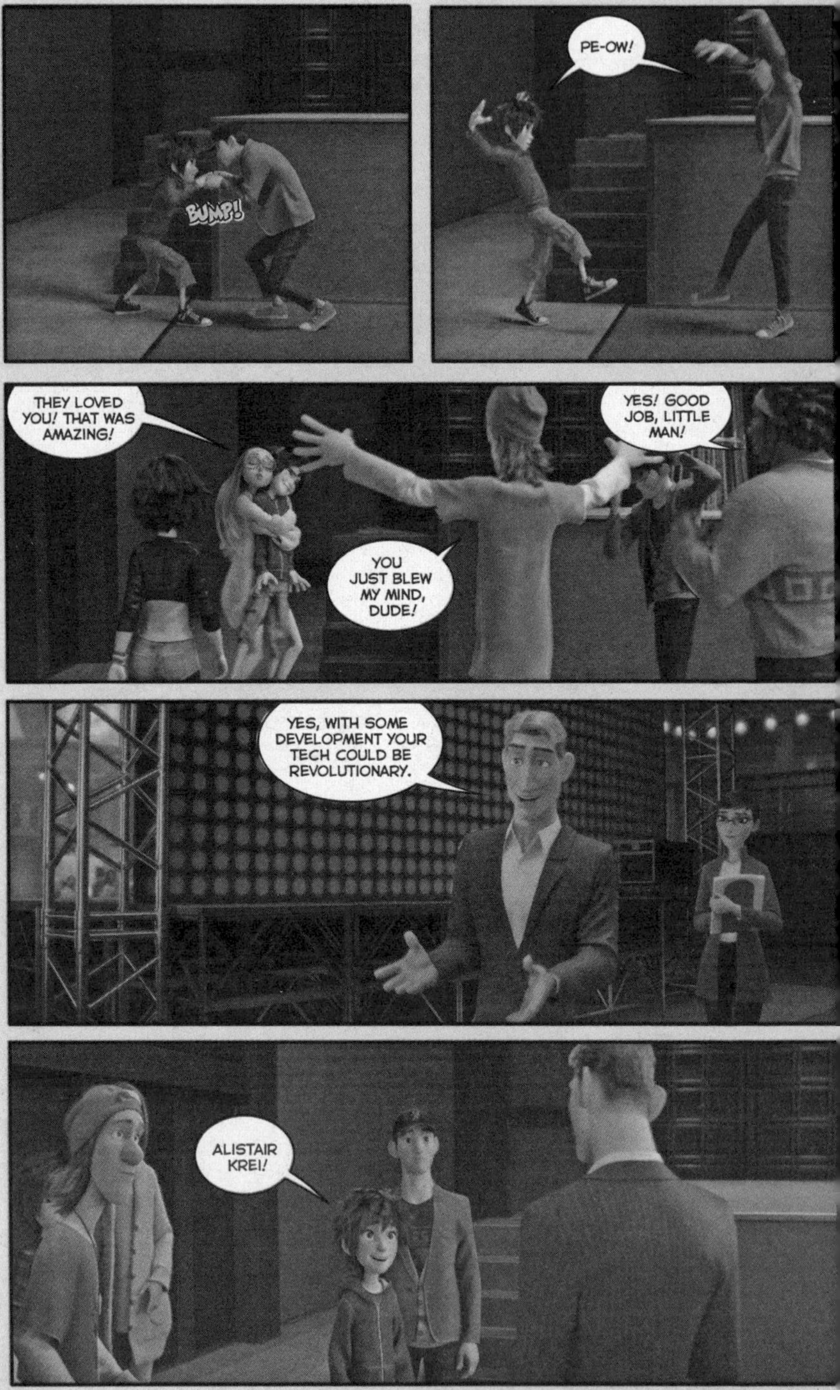
BUMP!
PE-OW!
THEY LOVED YOU! THAT WAS AMAZING!
YES! GOOD JOB, LITTLE MAN!
YOU JUST BLEW MY MIND, DUDE!
YES, WITH SOME DEVELOPMENT YOUR TECH COULD BE REVOLUTIONARY.
ALISTAIR KREI!

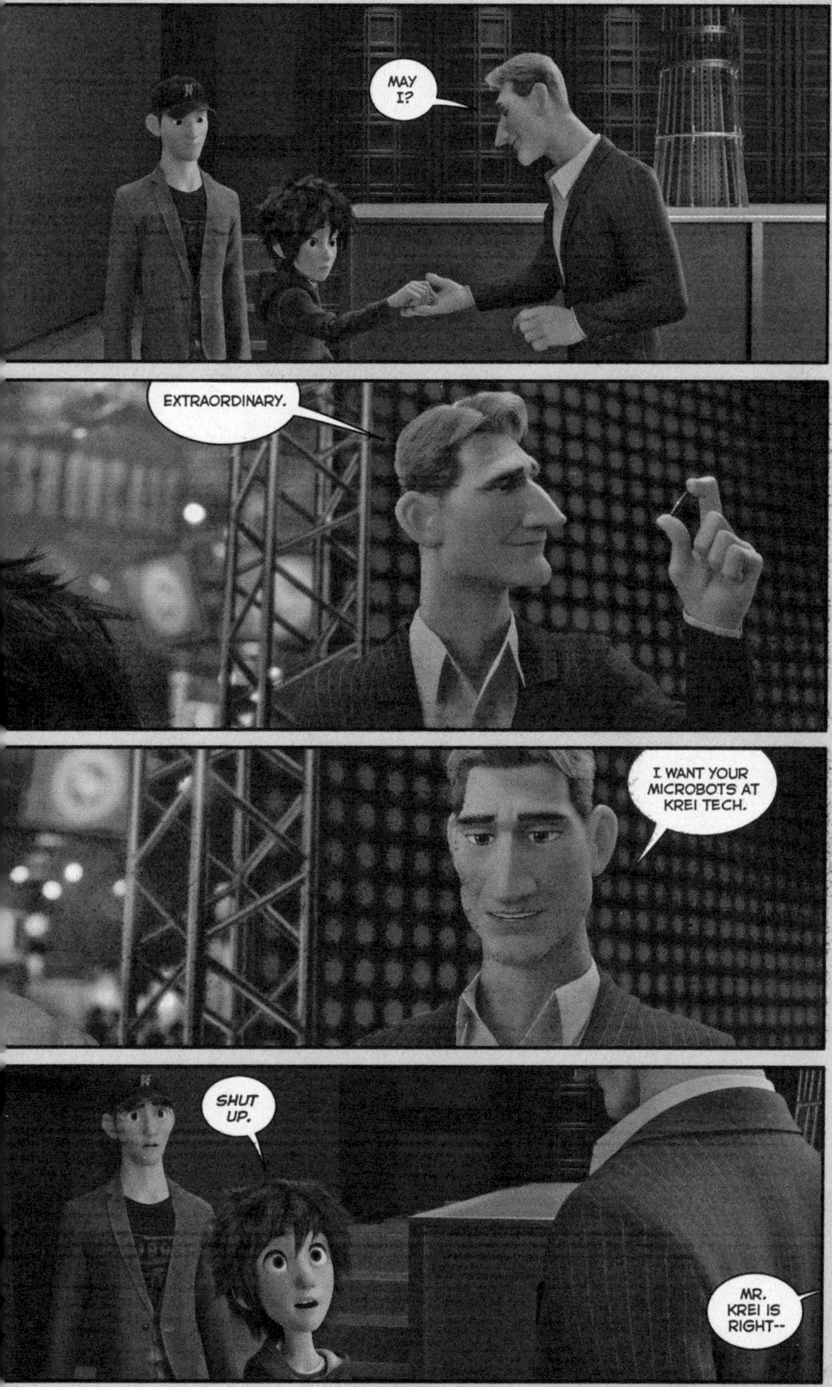
MAY I?
EXTRAORDINARY.
I WANT YOUR MICROBOTS AT KREI TECH.
SHUT UP.
MR. KREI IS RIGHT--

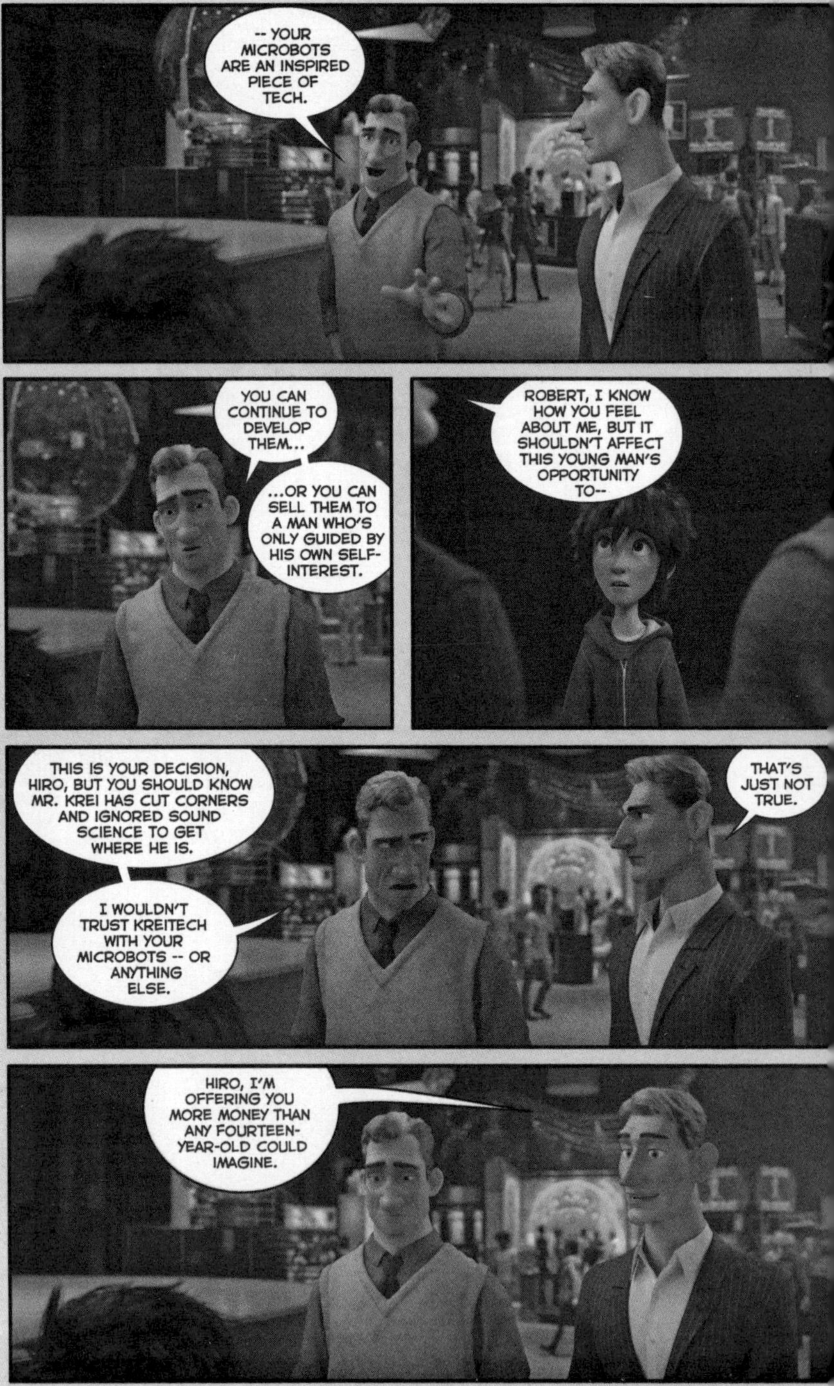
-- YOUR MICROBOTS ARE AN INSPIRED PIECE OF TECH.
YOU CAN CONTINUE TO DEVELOP THEM...
...OR YOU CAN SELL THEM TO A MAN WHO'S ONLY GUIDED BY HIS OWN SELF-INTEREST.
ROBERT, I KNOW HOW YOU FEEL ABOUT ME, BUT IT SHOULDN'T AFFECT THIS YOUNG MAN'S OPPORTUNITY TO--
THIS IS YOUR DECISION, HIRO, BUT YOU SHOULD KNOW MR. KREI HAS CUT CORNERS AND IGNORED SOUND SCIENCE TO GET WHERE HE IS.
I WOULDN'T TRUST KREITECH WITH YOUR MICROBOTS -- OR ANYTHING ELSE.
THAT'S JUST NOT TRUE.
HIRO, I'M OFFERING YOU MORE MONEY THAN ANY FOURTEEN-YEAR-OLD COULD IMAGINE.

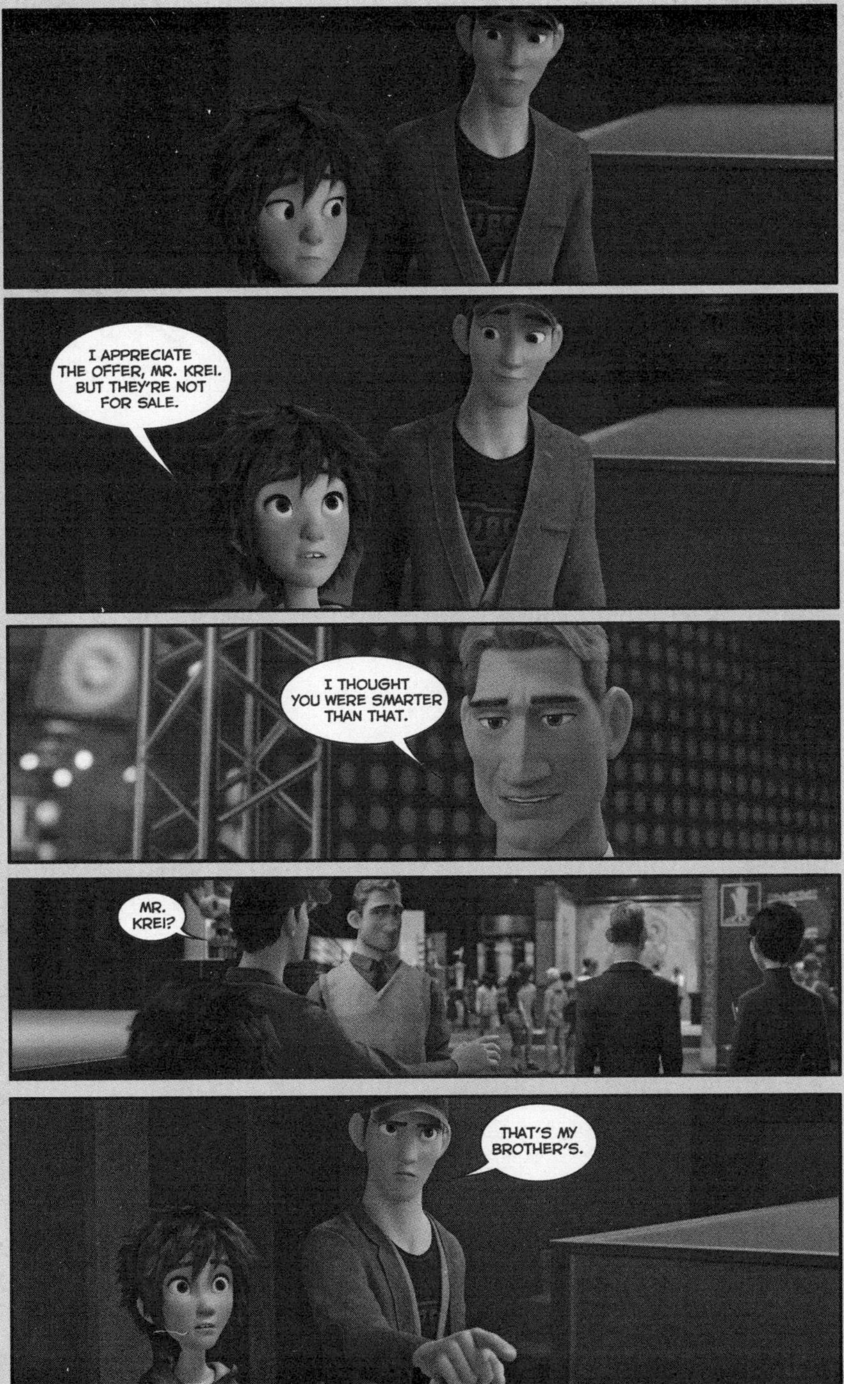
I APPRECIATE THE OFFER, MR. KREI. BUT THEY'RE NOT FOR SALE.
I THOUGHT YOU WERE SMARTER THAN THAT.
MR. KREI?
THAT'S MY BROTHER'S.

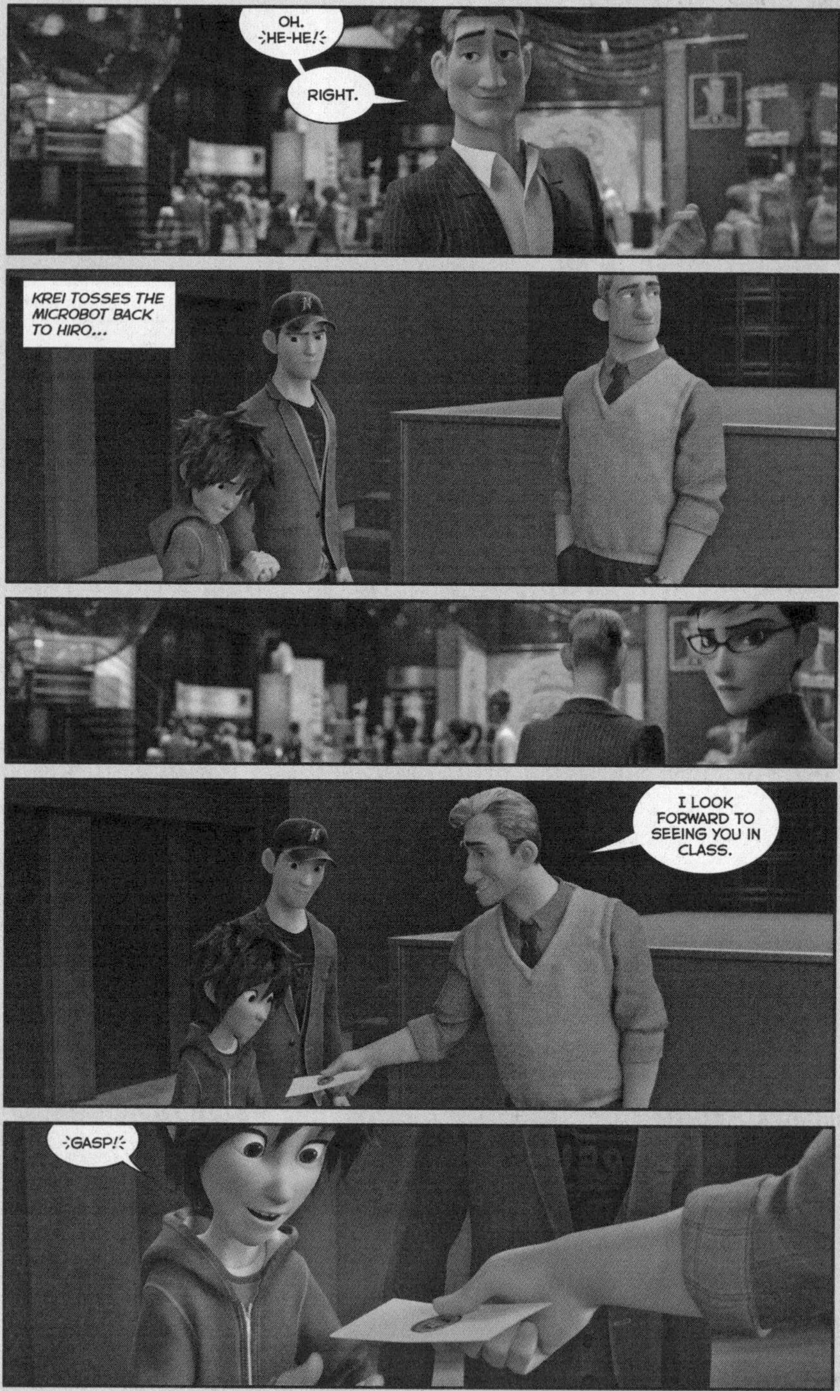
OH. HE-HE!
RIGHT.
KREI TOSSES THE MICROBOT BACK TO HIRO...
I LOOK FORWARD TO SEEING YOU IN CLASS.
GASP!

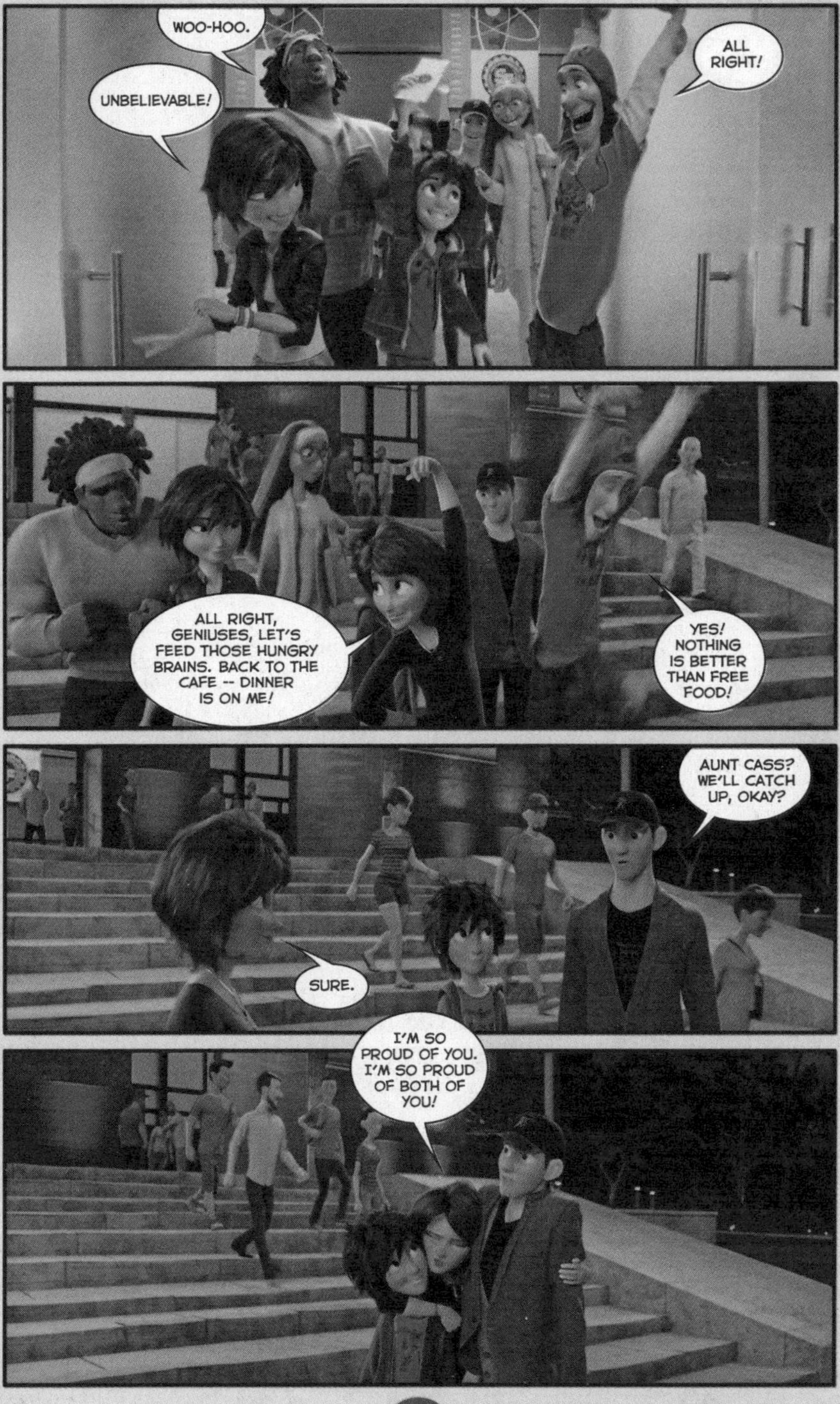
WOO-HOO.
UNBELIEVABLE!
ALL RIGHT!
ALL RIGHT, GENIUSES, LET'S FEED THOSE HUNGRY BRAINS. BACK TO THE CAFE -- DINNER IS ON ME!
YES! NOTHING IS BETTER THAN FREE FOOD!
AUNT CASS? WE'LL CATCH UP, OKAY?
SURE.
I'M SO PROUD OF YOU. I'M SO PROUD OF BOTH OF YOU!

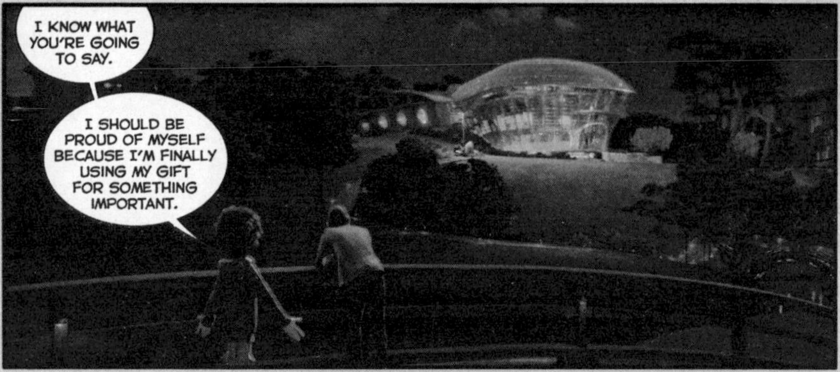
I KNOW WHAT YOU'RE GOING TO SAY.
I SHOULD BE PROUD OF MYSELF BECAUSE I'M FINALLY USING MY GIFT FOR SOMETHING IMPORTANT.

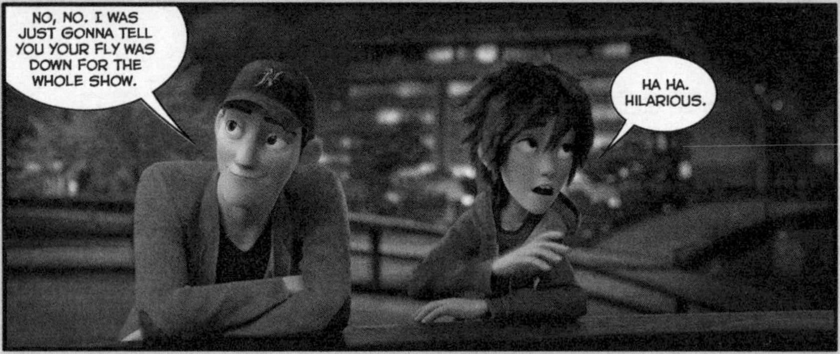
NO, NO. I WAS JUST GONNA TELL YOU YOUR FLY WAS DOWN FOR THE WHOLE SHOW.
HA HA. HILARIOUS.

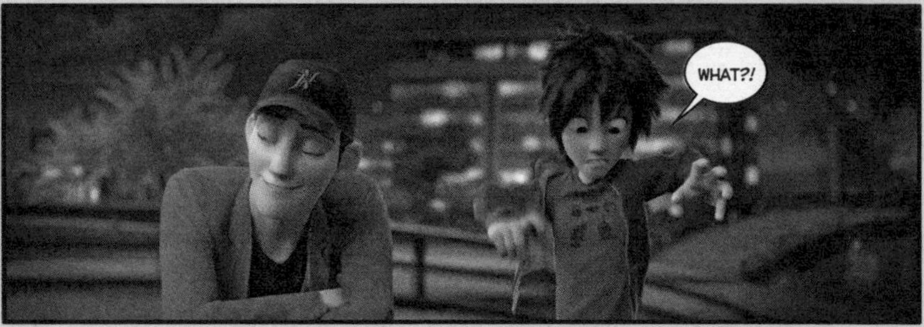
WHAT?!

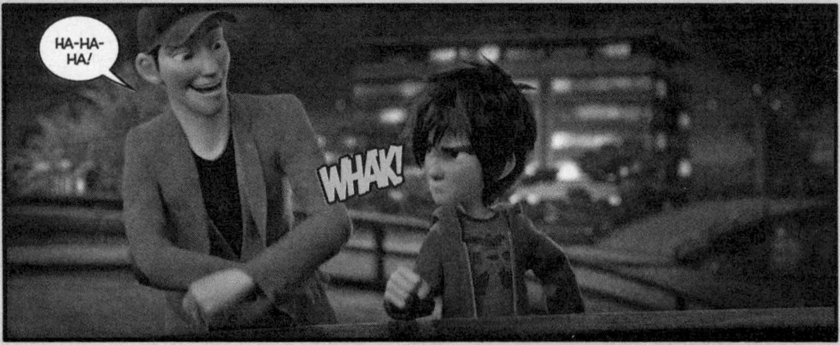
HA-HA-HA!
WHAK!

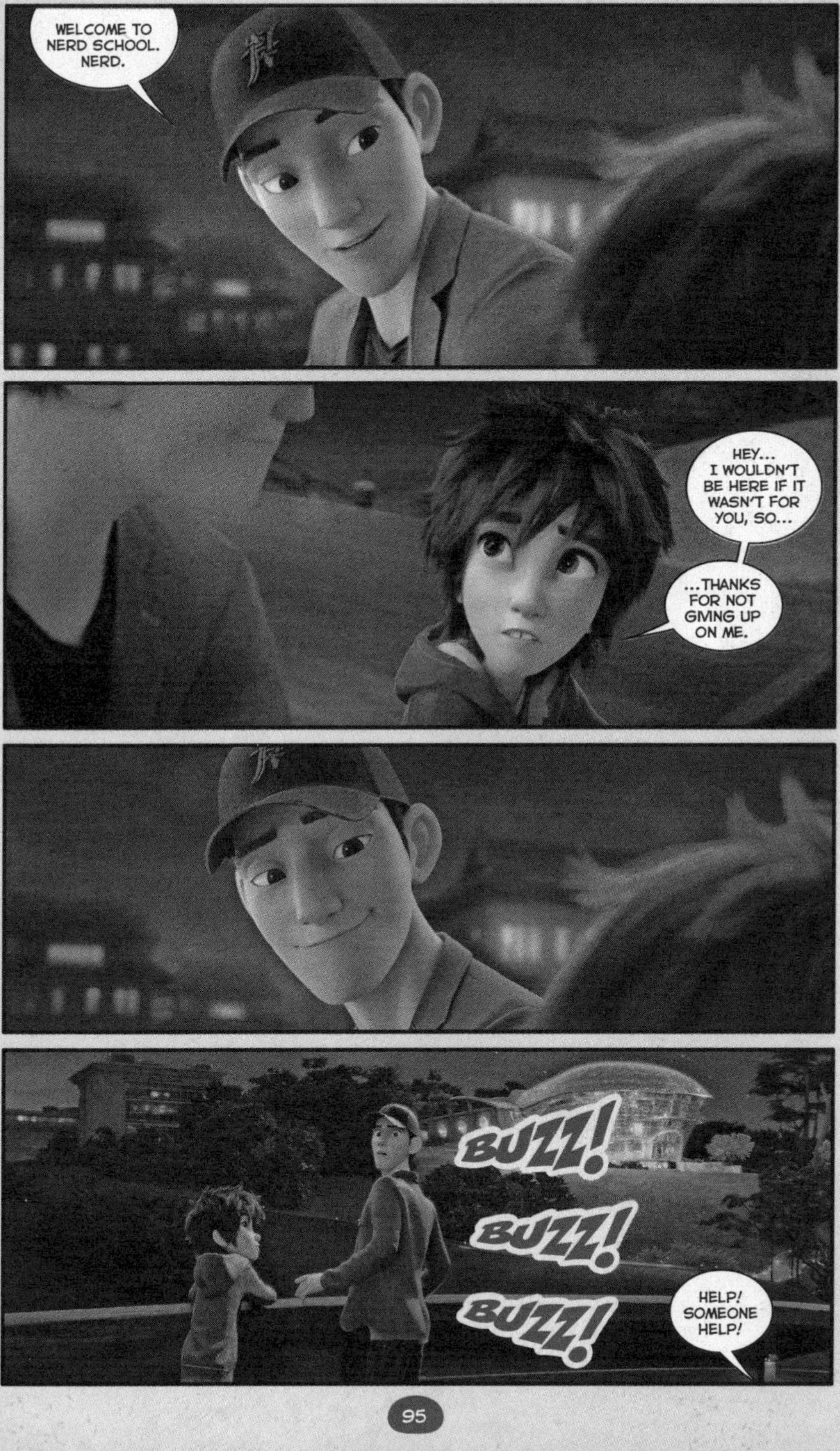
WELCOME TO NERD SCHOOL. NERD.
HEY... I WOULDN'T BE HERE IF IT WASN'T FOR YOU, SO...
...THANKS FOR NOT GIVING UP ON ME.
BUZZ!
BUZZ!
BUZZ!
HELP! SOMEONE HELP!

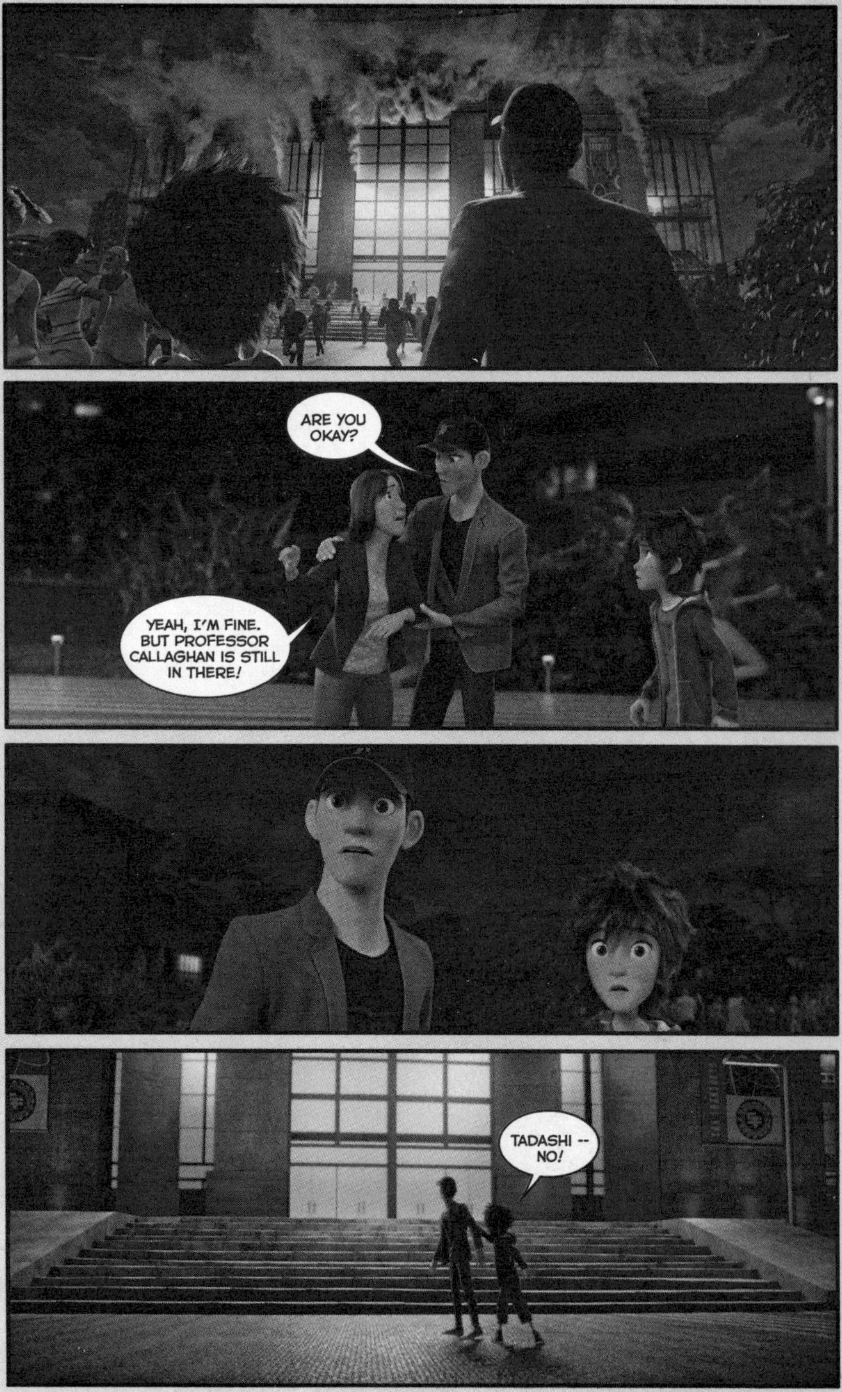
ARE YOU OKAY?
YEAH, I'M FINE. BUT PROFESSOR CALLAGHAN IS STILL IN THERE!
TADASHI -- NO!

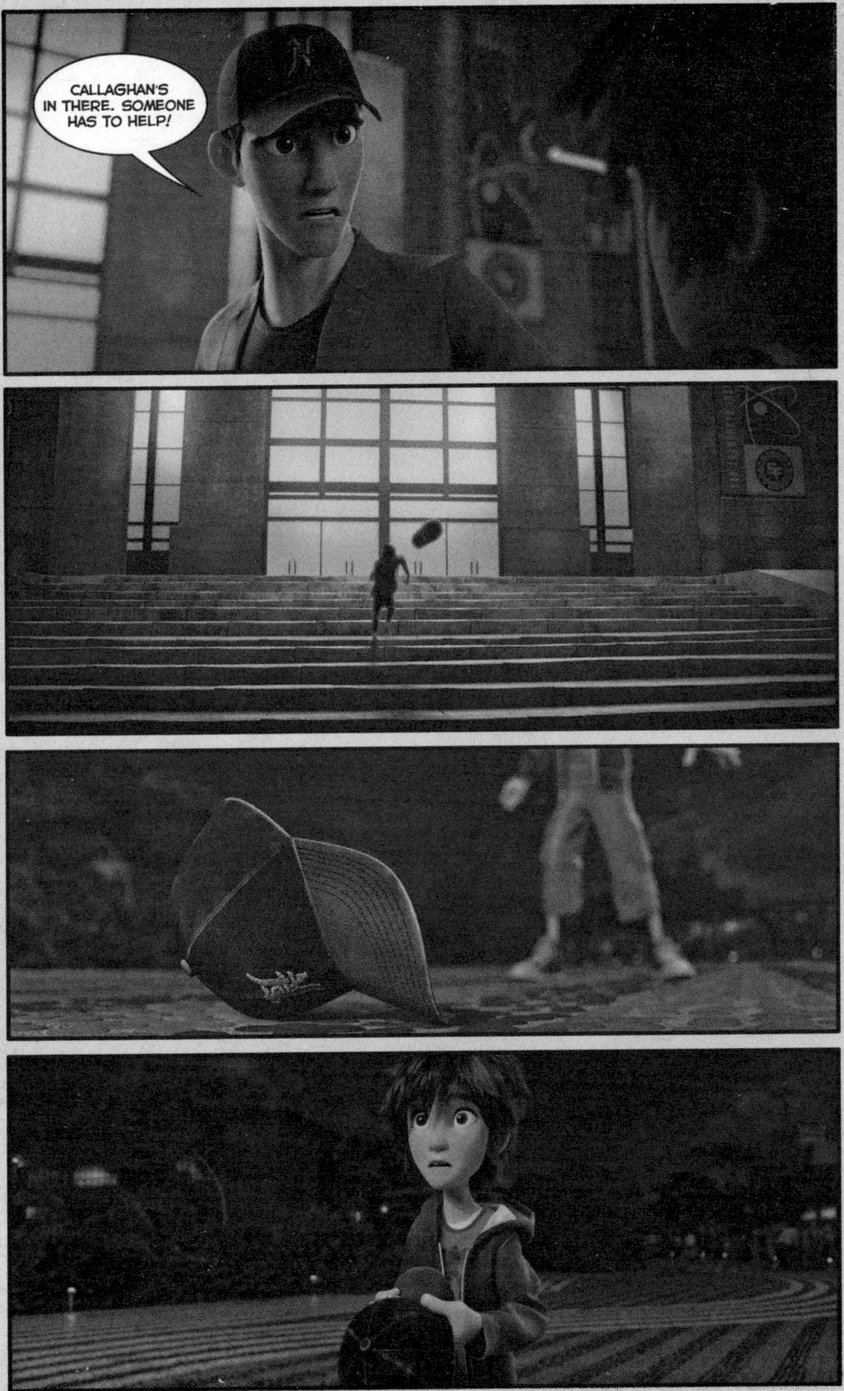
CALLAGHAN'S IN THERE. SOMEONE HAS TO HELP!

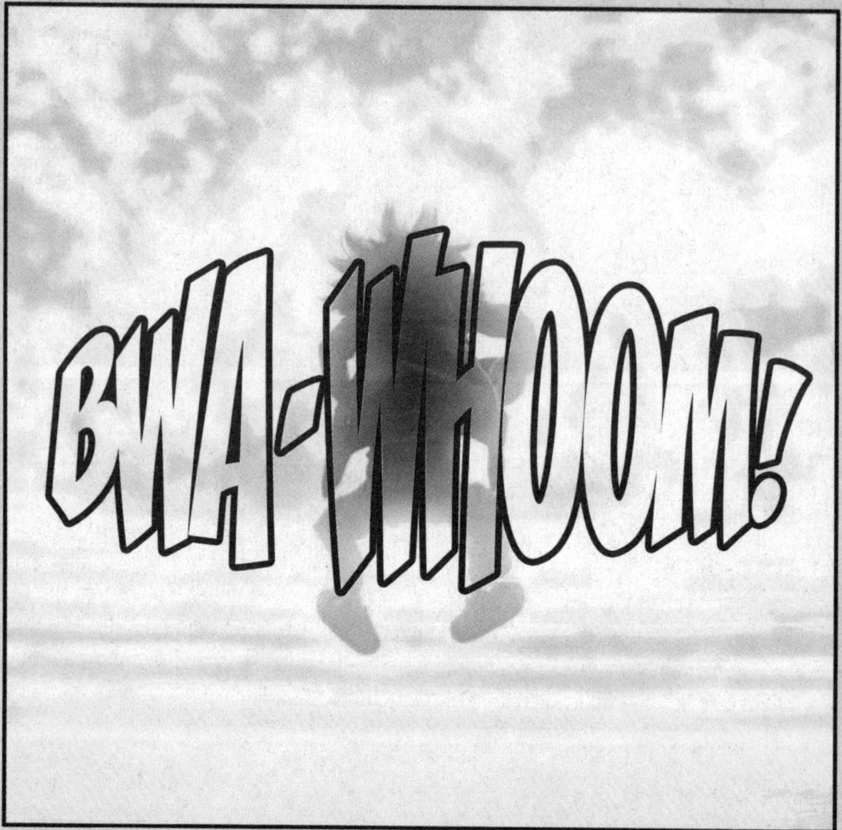
BWA-WHOOM!

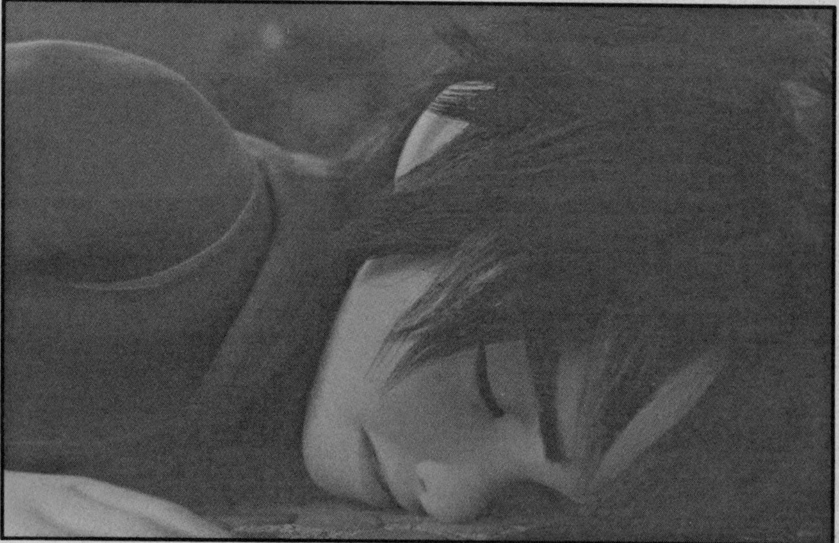

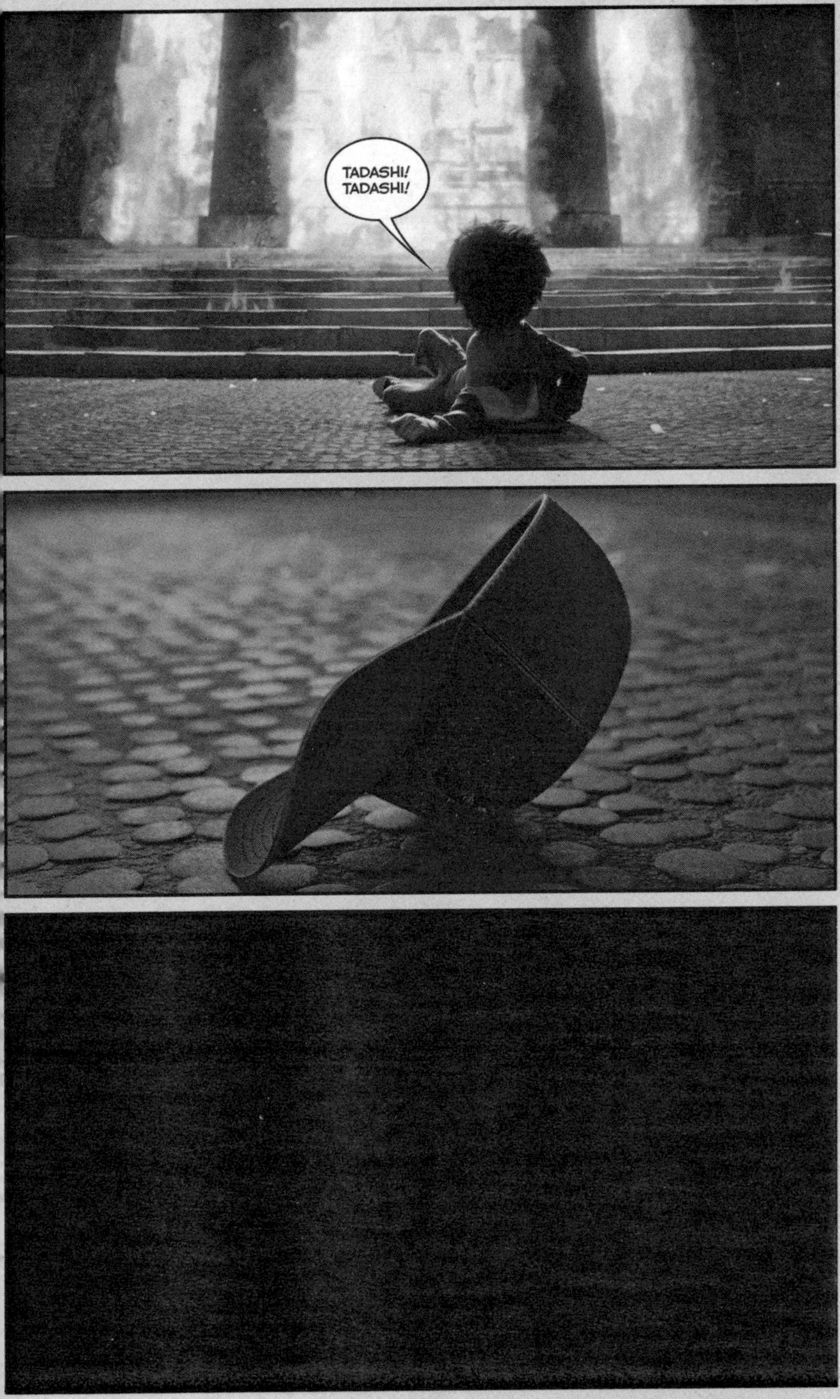
TADASHI!
TADASHI!

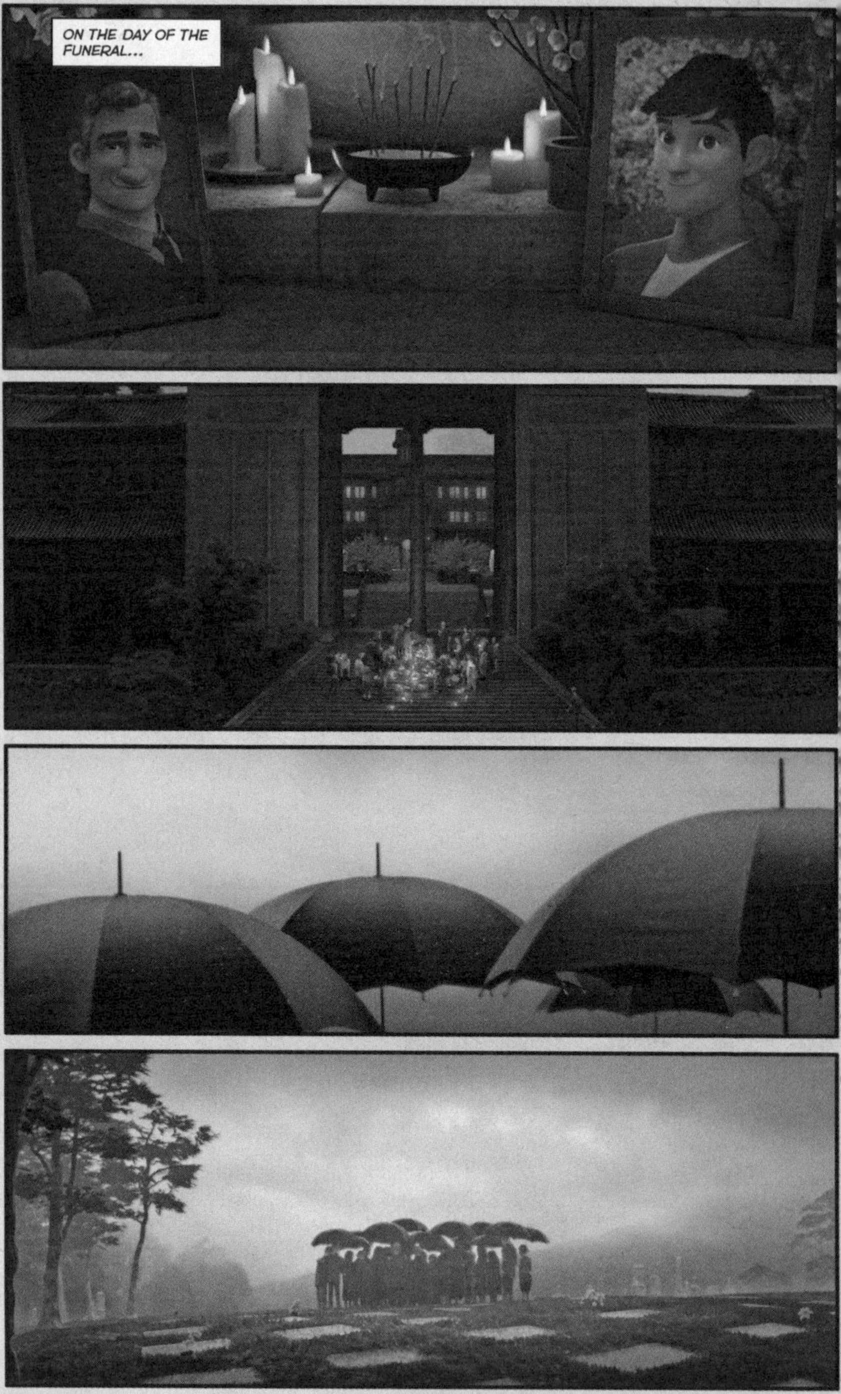
ON THE DAY OF THE FUNERAL...

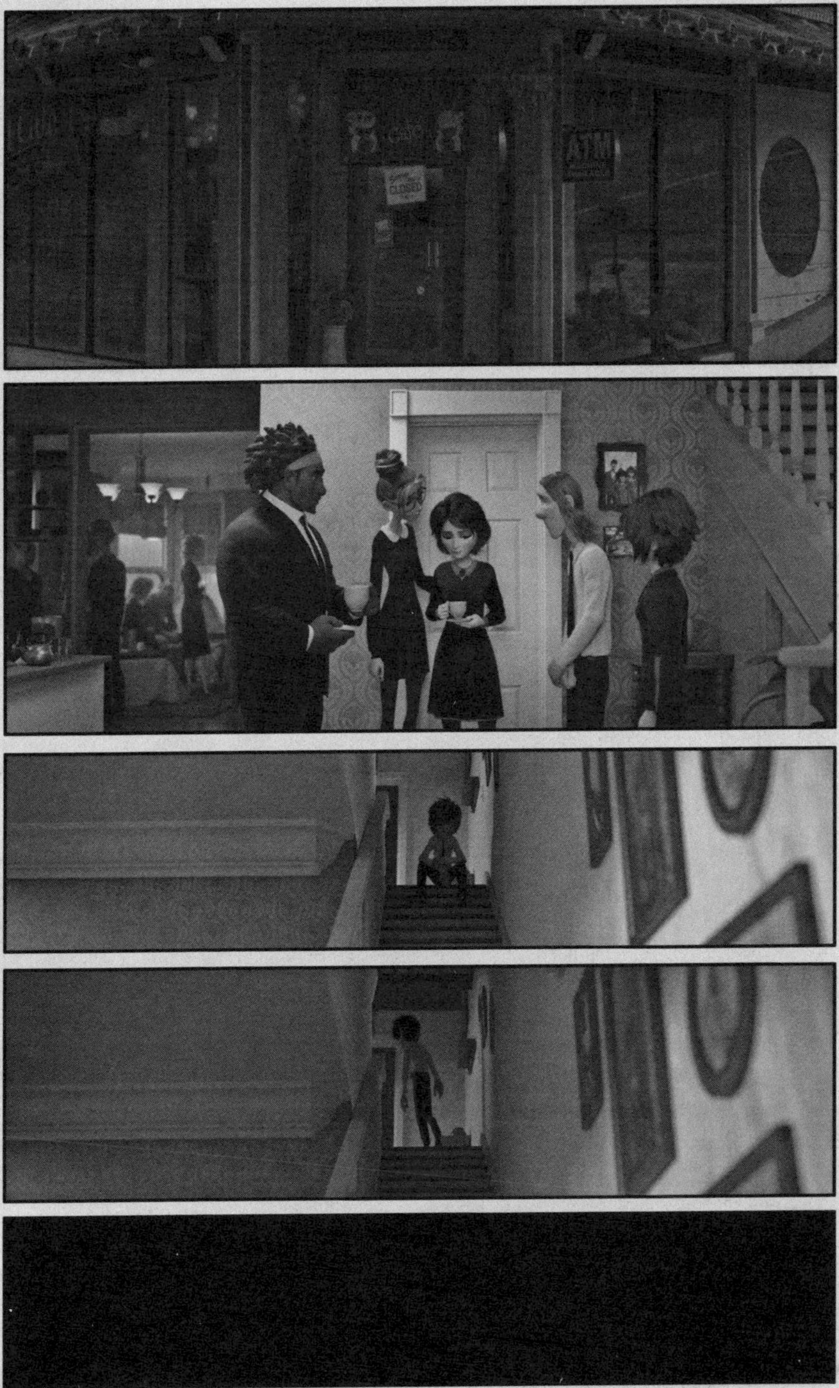
CLOSED

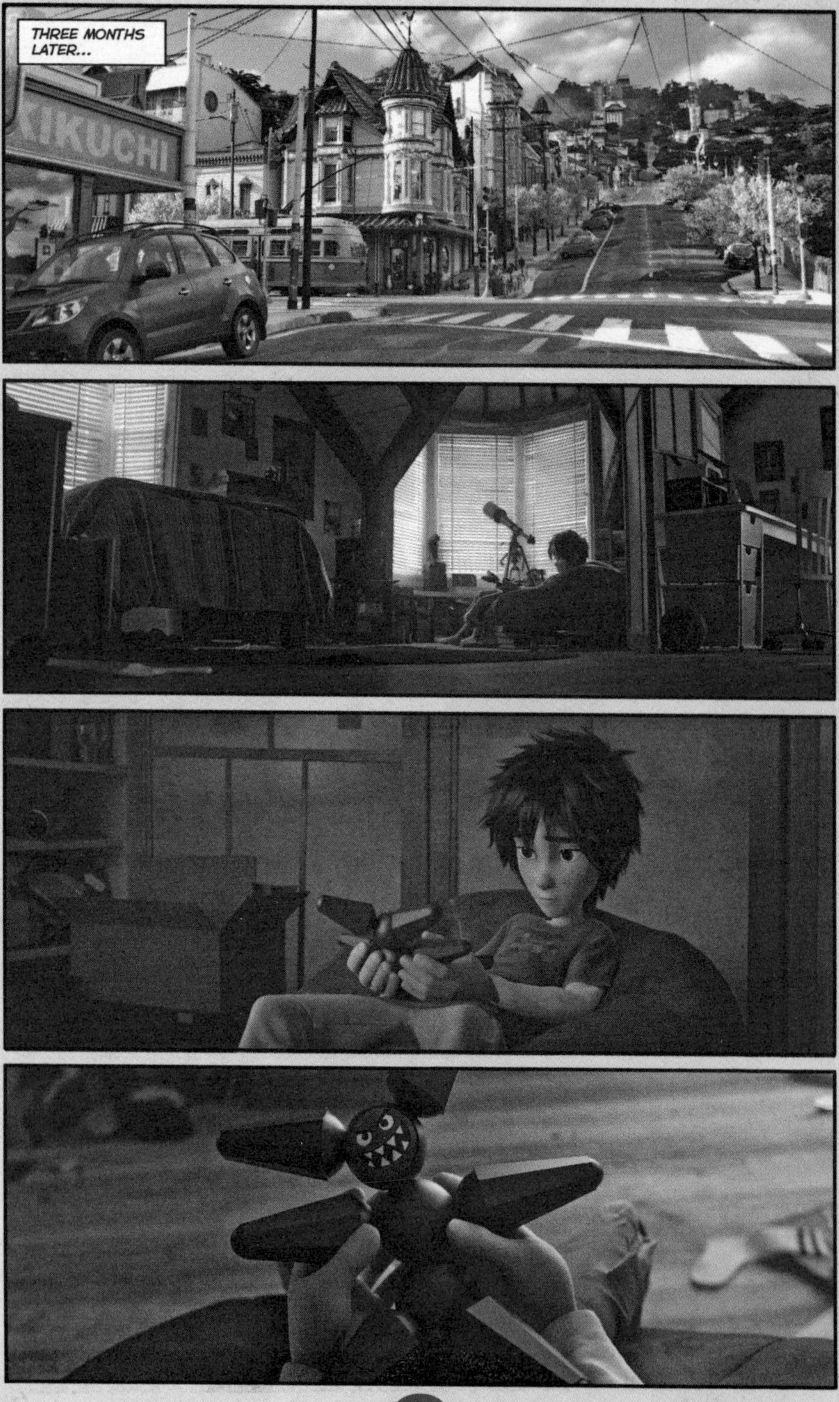
THREE MONTHS LATER...
KIKUCHI

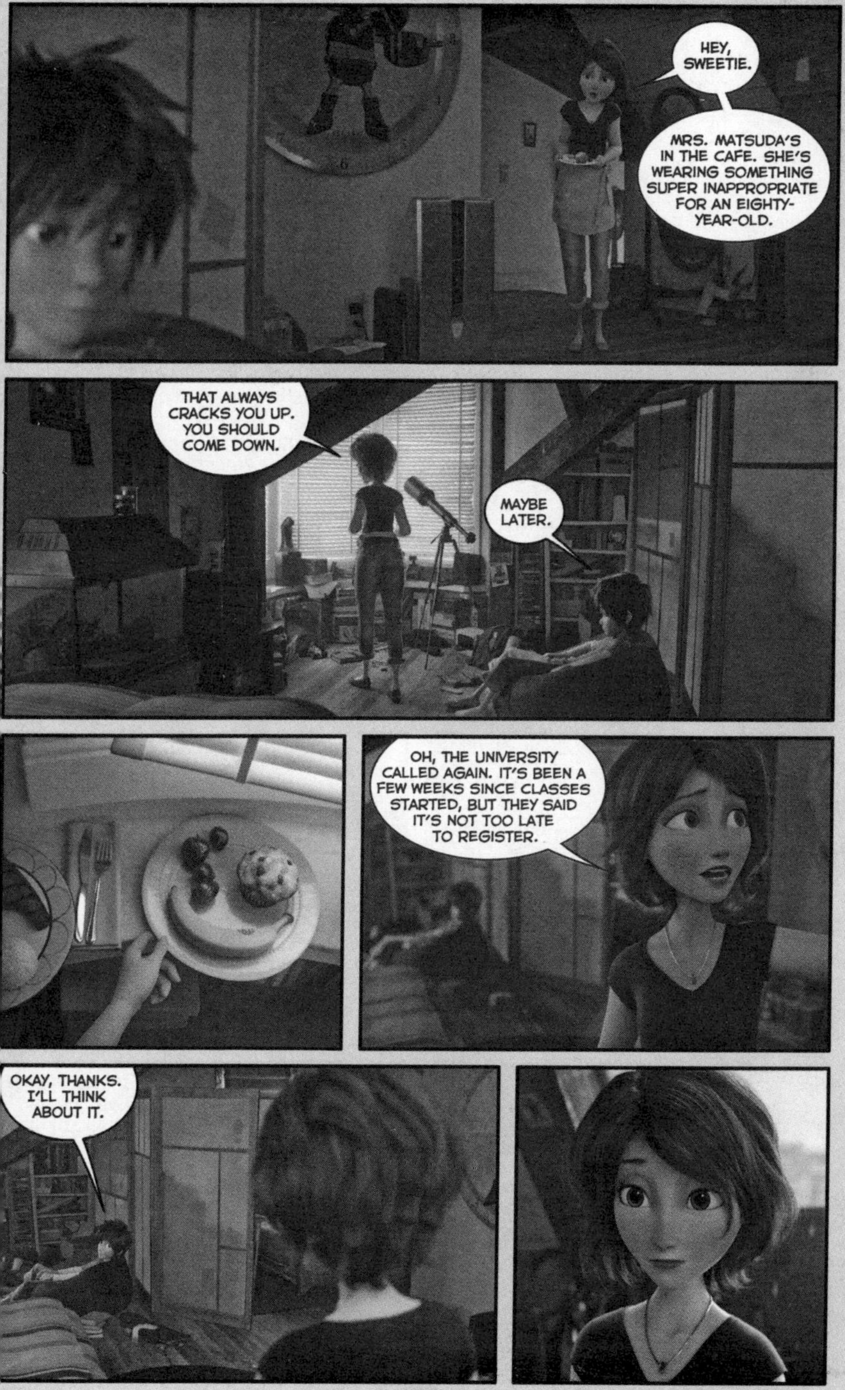
HEY, SWEETIE.
MRS. MATSUDA'S IN THE CAFE. SHE'S WEARING SOMETHING SUPER INAPPROPRIATE FOR AN EIGHTY-YEAR-OLD.
THAT ALWAYS CRACKS YOU UP. YOU SHOULD COME DOWN.
MAYBE LATER.
OH, THE UNIVERSITY CALLED AGAIN. IT'S BEEN A FEW WEEKS SINCE CLASSES STARTED, BUT THEY SAID IT'S NOT TOO LATE TO REGISTER.
OKAY, THANKS. I'LL THINK ABOUT IT.

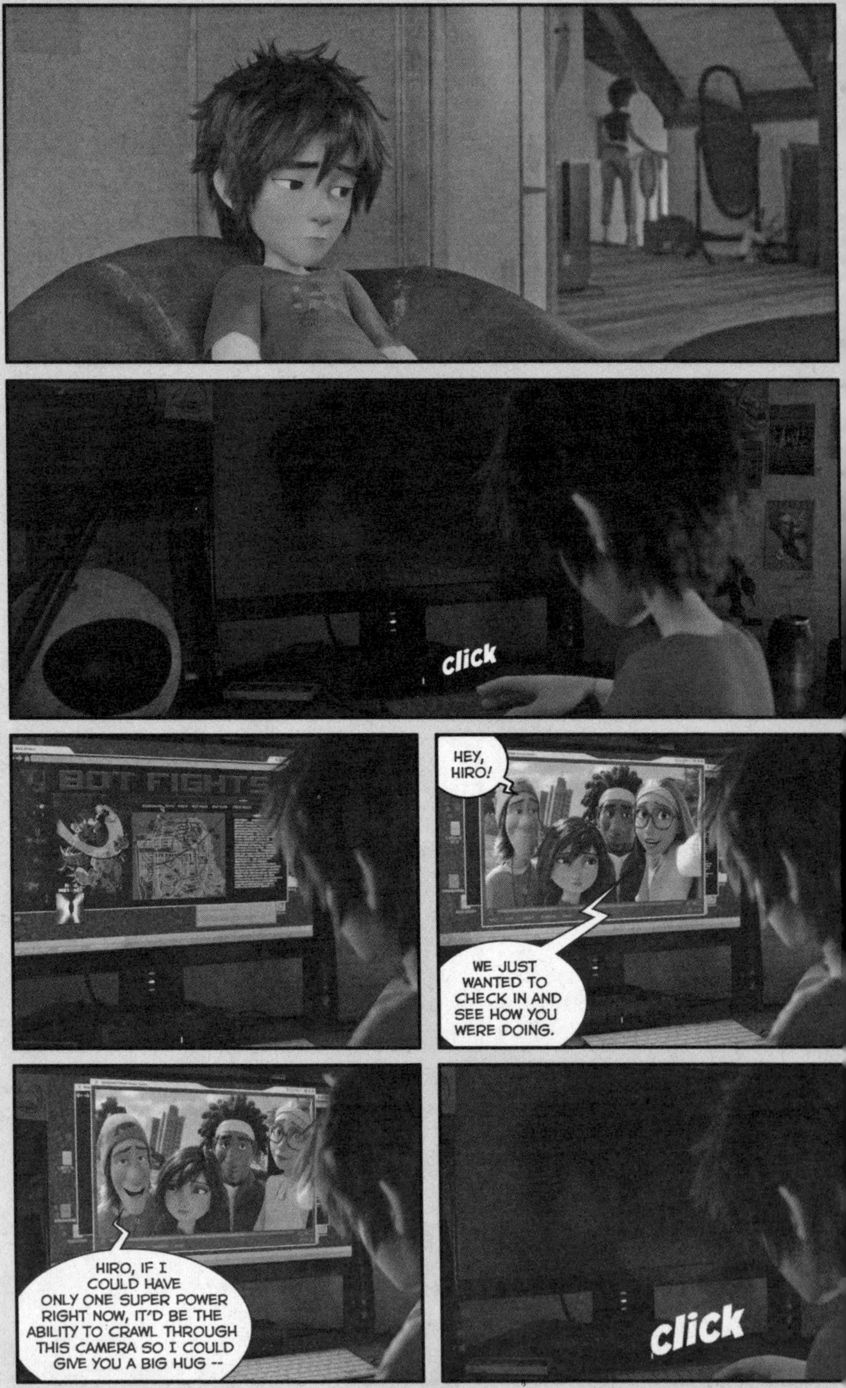
click
BOT FIGHTS
HEY, HIRO!
WE JUST WANTED TO CHECK IN AND SEE HOW YOU WERE DOING.
HIRO, IF I COULD HAVE ONLY ONE SUPER POWER RIGHT NOW, IT'D BE THE ABILITY TO CRAWL THROUGH THIS CAMERA SO I COULD GIVE YOU A BIG HUG --
click

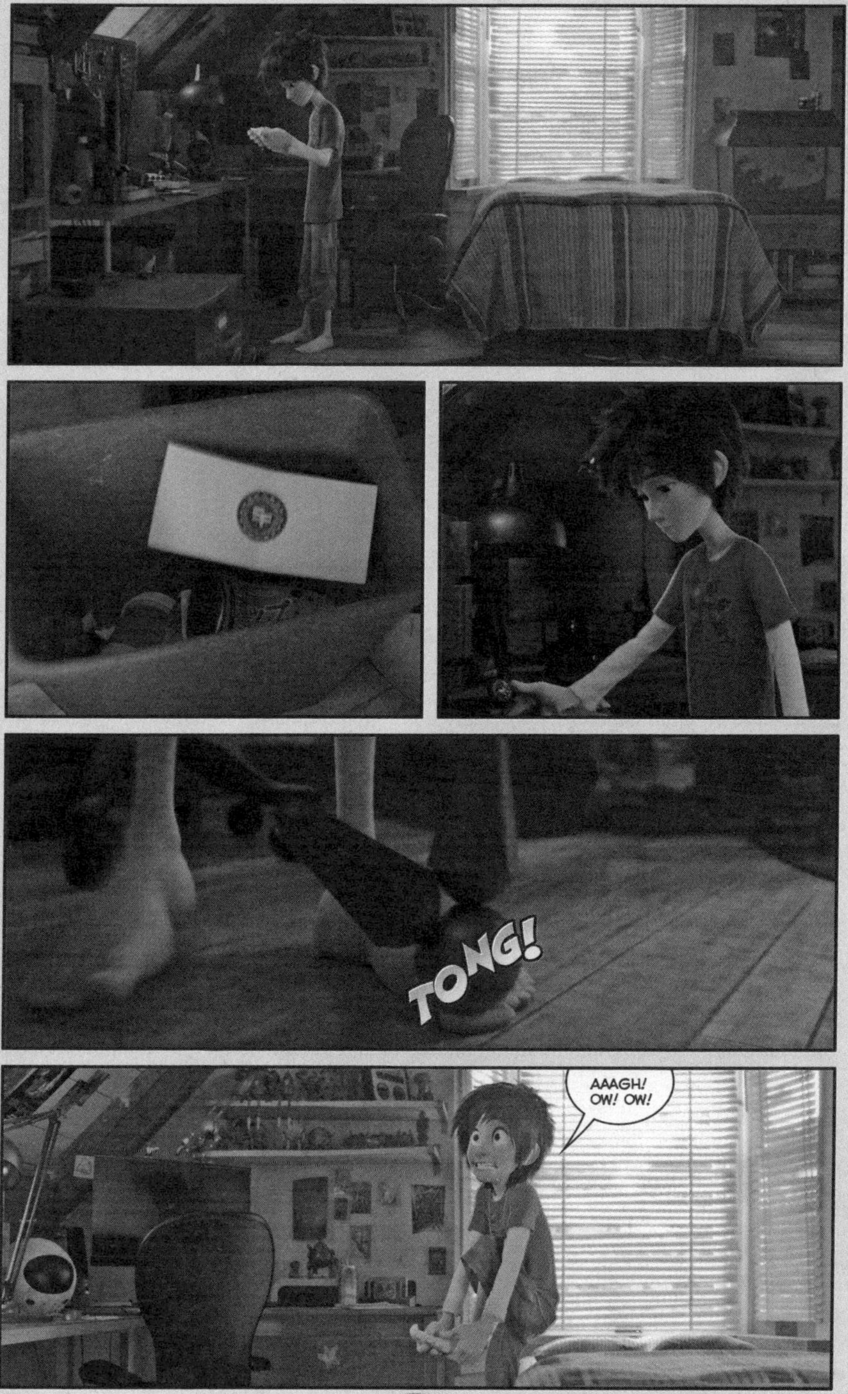
TONG!
AAAGH! OW! OW!

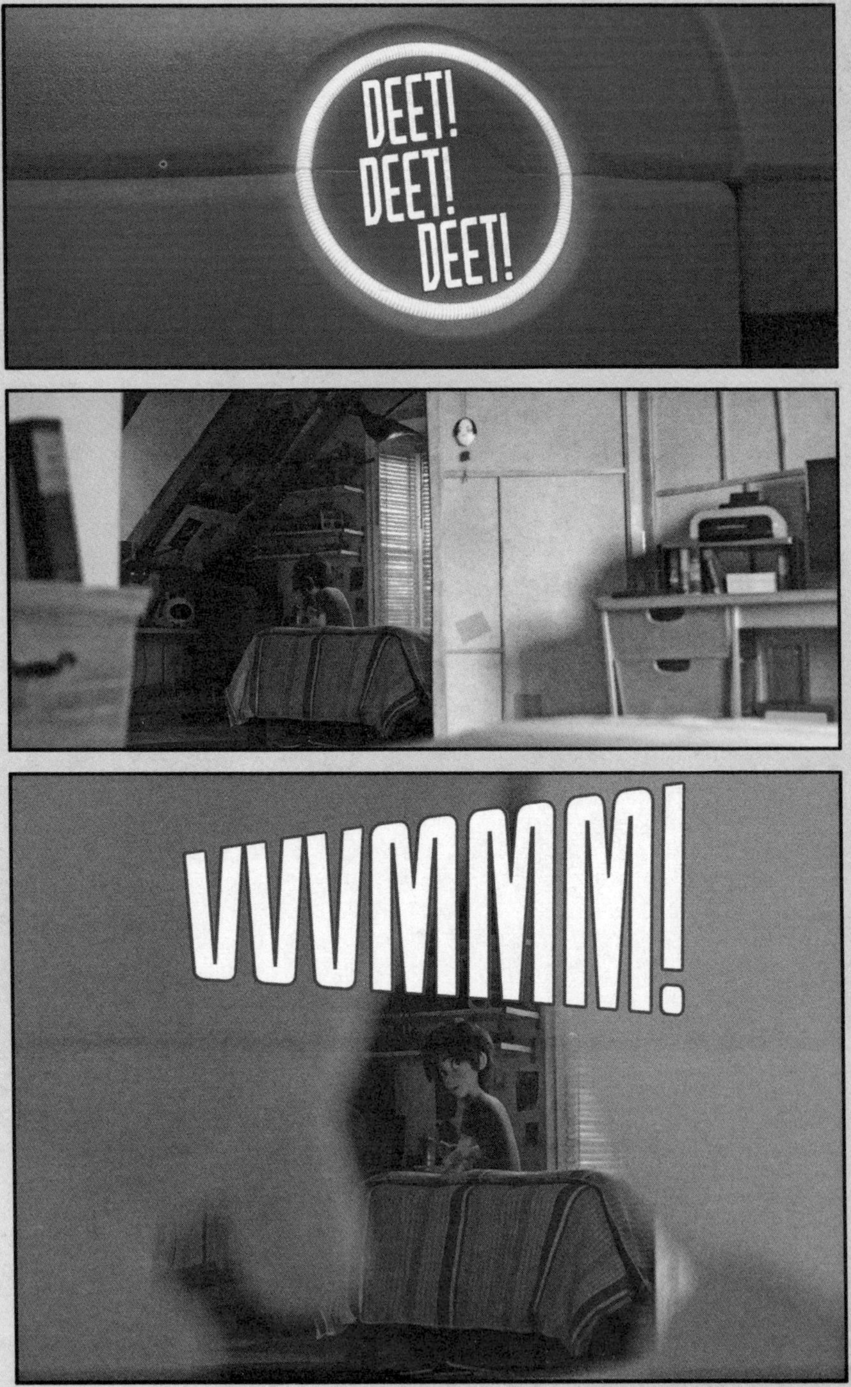
DEET!
DEET!
DEET!
VVVMMM!

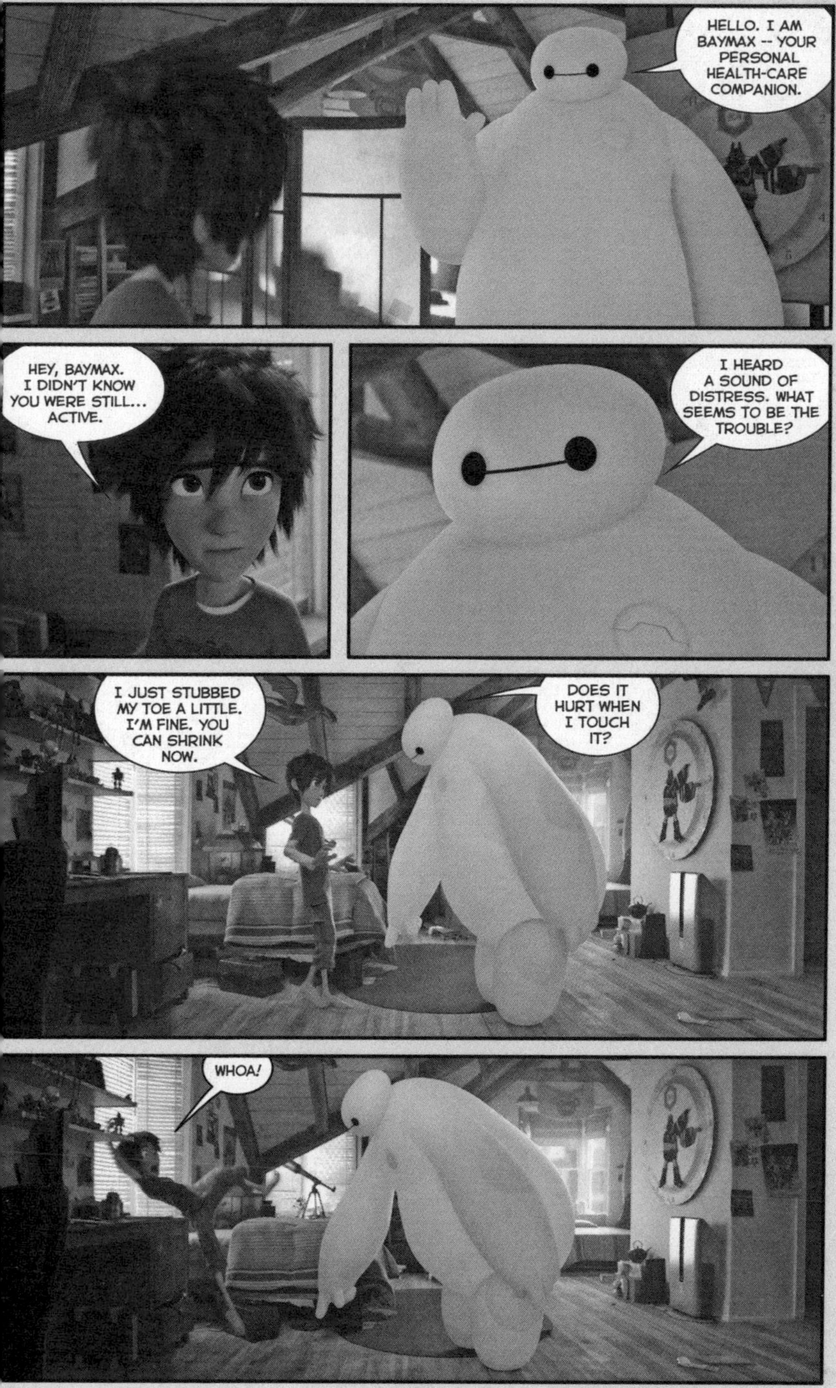
HELLO. I AM BAYMAX -- YOUR PERSONAL HEALTH-CARE COMPANION.
HEY, BAYMAX. I DIDN'T KNOW YOU WERE STILL... ACTIVE.
I HEARD A SOUND OF DISTRESS. WHAT SEEMS TO BE THE TROUBLE?
I JUST STUBBED MY TOE A LITTLE. I'M FINE. YOU CAN SHRINK NOW.
DOES IT HURT WHEN I TOUCH IT?
WHOA!

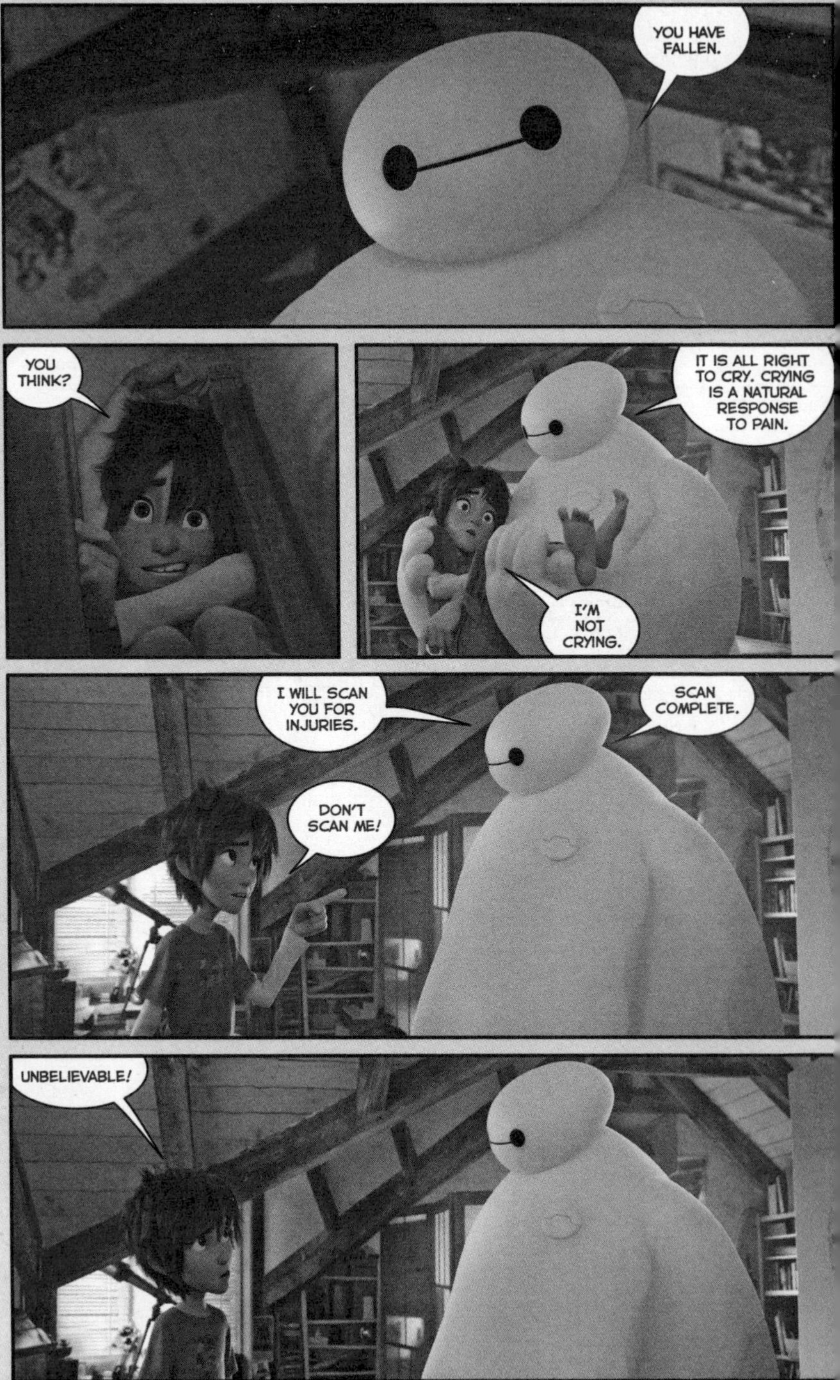
YOU HAVE FALLEN.
YOU THINK?
IT IS ALL RIGHT TO CRY. CRYING IS A NATURAL RESPONSE TO PAIN.
I'M NOT CRYING.
I WILL SCAN YOU FOR INJURIES.
DON'T SCAN ME!
SCAN COMPLETE.
UNBELIEVABLE!

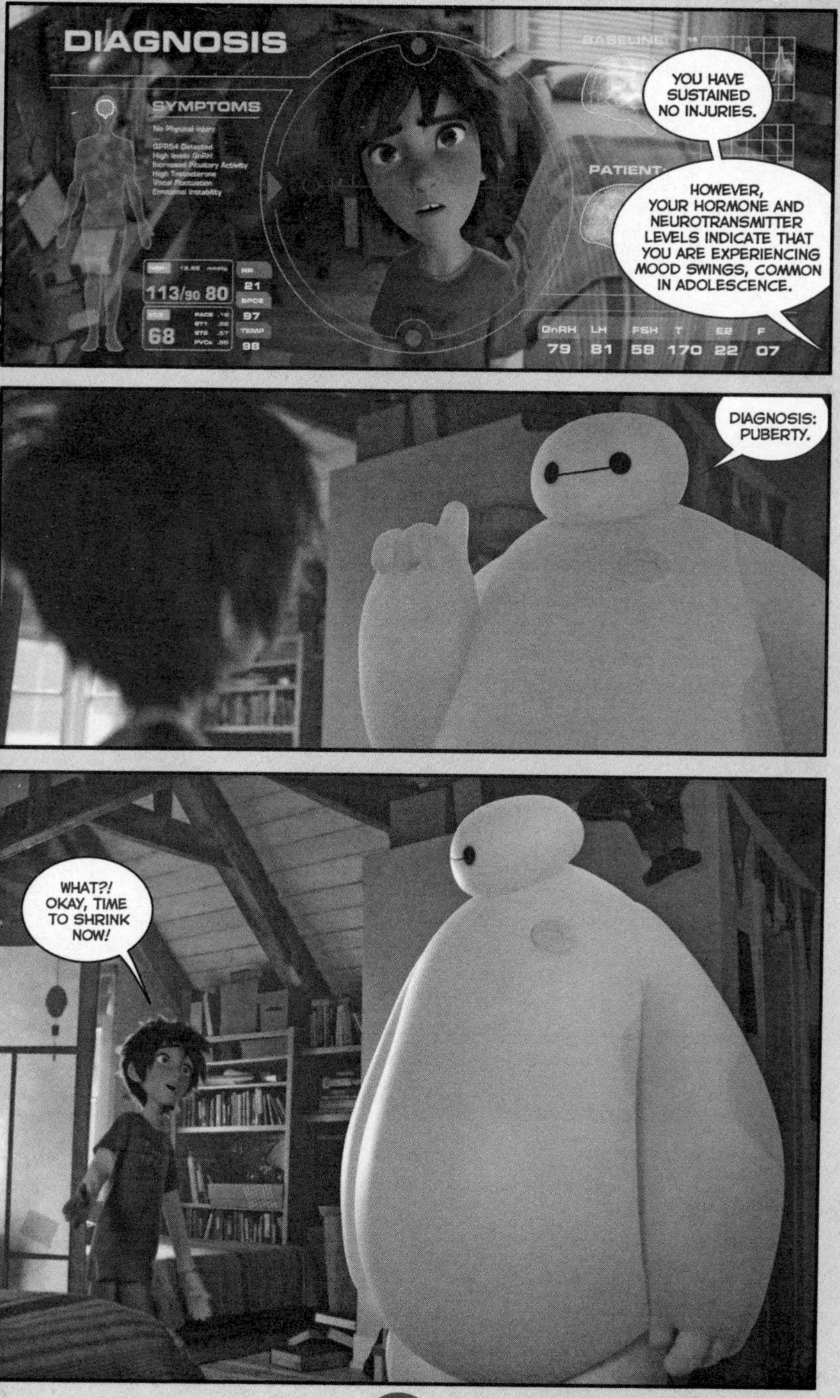
DIAGNOSIS
SYMPTOMS
PATIENT:
YOU HAVE SUSTAINED NO INJURIES.
HOWEVER, YOUR HORMONE AND NEUROTRANSMITTER LEVELS INDICATE THAT YOU ARE EXPERIENCING MOOD SWINGS, COMMON IN ADOLESCENCE.
GnRH LH FSH T E2 F
79 81 58 170 22 07
DIAGNOSIS: PUBERTY.
WHAT?! OKAY, TIME TO SHRINK NOW!

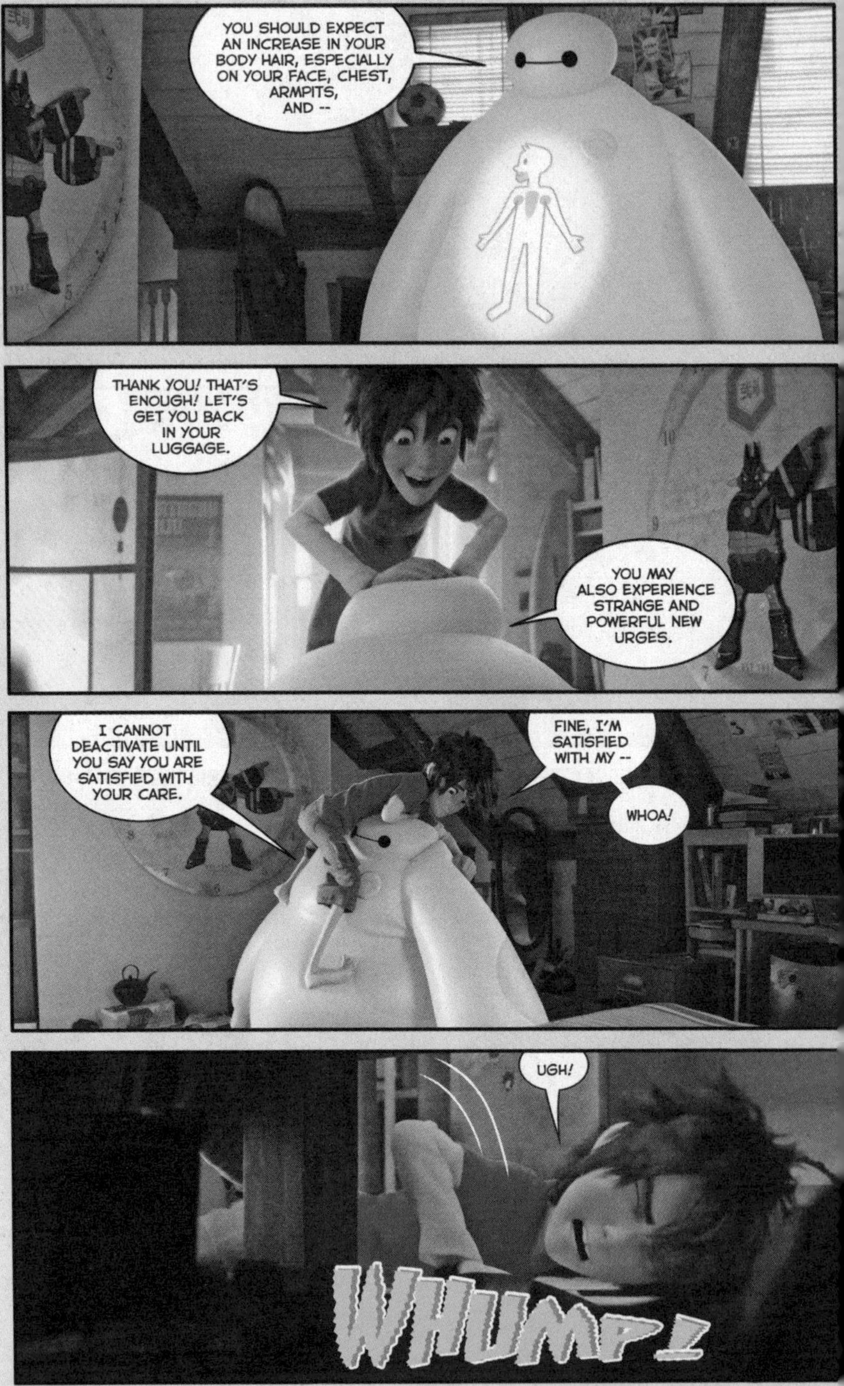
YOU SHOULD EXPECT AN INCREASE IN YOUR BODY HAIR, ESPECIALLY ON YOUR FACE, CHEST, ARMPITS, AND --
THANK YOU! THAT'S ENOUGH! LET'S GET YOU BACK IN YOUR LUGGAGE.
YOU MAY ALSO EXPERIENCE STRANGE AND POWERFUL NEW URGES.
I CANNOT DEACTIVATE UNTIL YOU SAY YOU ARE SATISFIED WITH YOUR CARE.
FINE, I'M SATISFIED WITH MY --
WHOA!
UGH!
WHUMP!

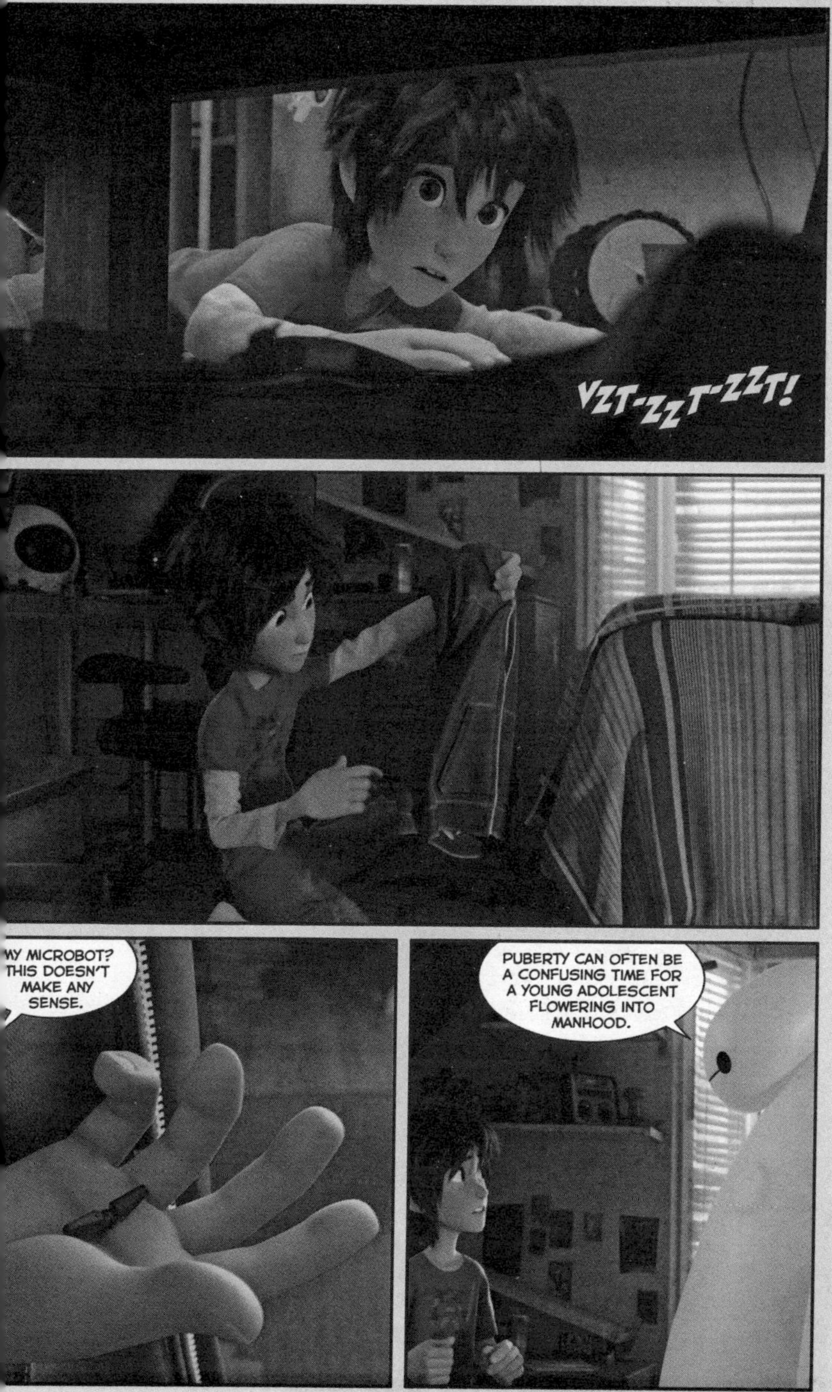
VZT-ZZT-ZZT!
MY MICROBOT? THIS DOESN'T MAKE ANY SENSE.
PUBERTY CAN OFTEN BE A CONFUSING TIME FOR A YOUNG ADOLESCENT FLOWERING INTO MANHOOD.

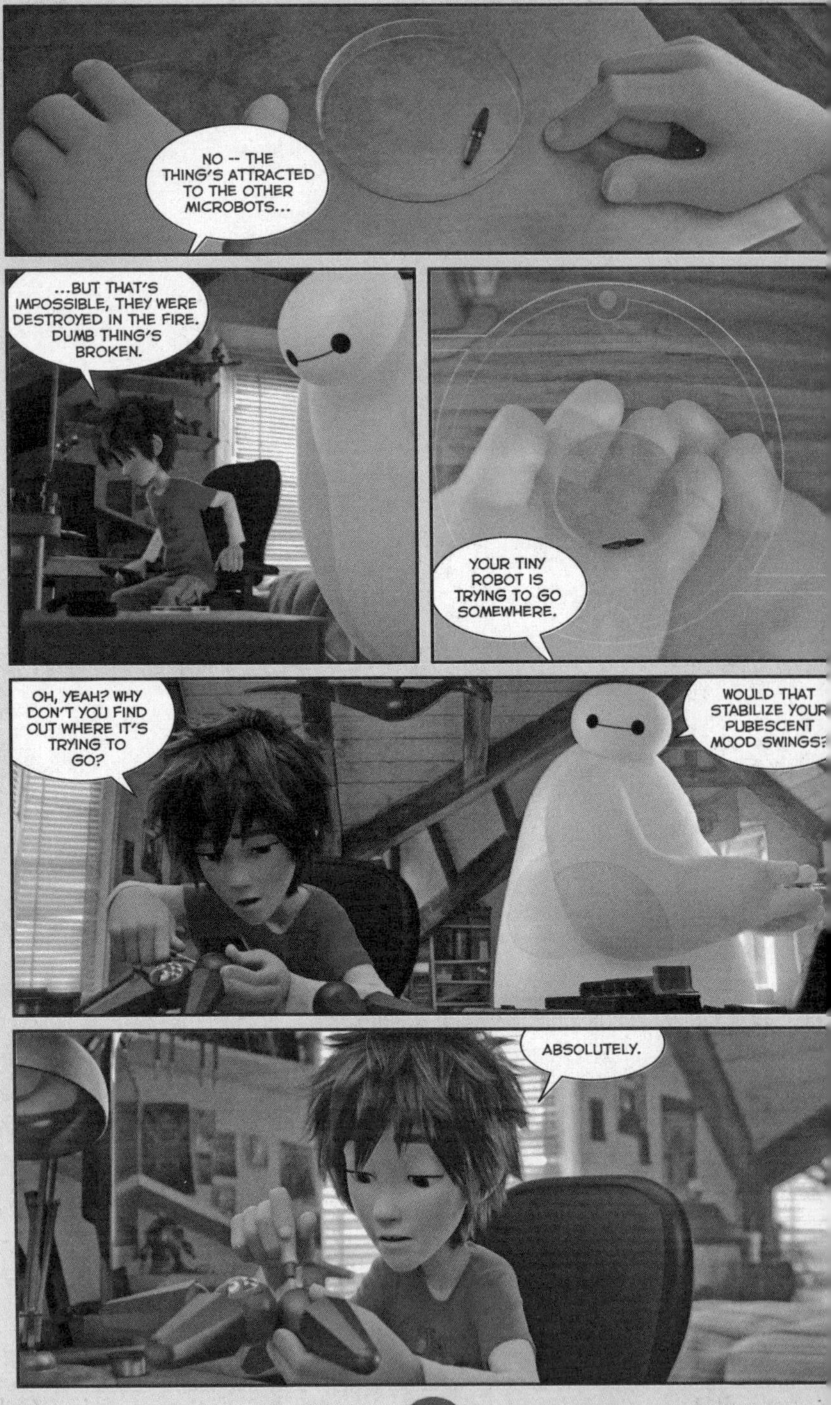
NO -- THE THING'S ATTRACTED TO THE OTHER MICROBOTS...
...BUT THAT'S IMPOSSIBLE, THEY WERE DESTROYED IN THE FIRE. DUMB THING'S BROKEN.
YOUR TINY ROBOT IS TRYING TO GO SOMEWHERE.
OH, YEAH? WHY DON'T YOU FIND OUT WHERE IT'S TRYING TO GO?
WOULD THAT STABILIZE YOUR PUBESCENT MOOD SWINGS?
ABSOLUTELY.

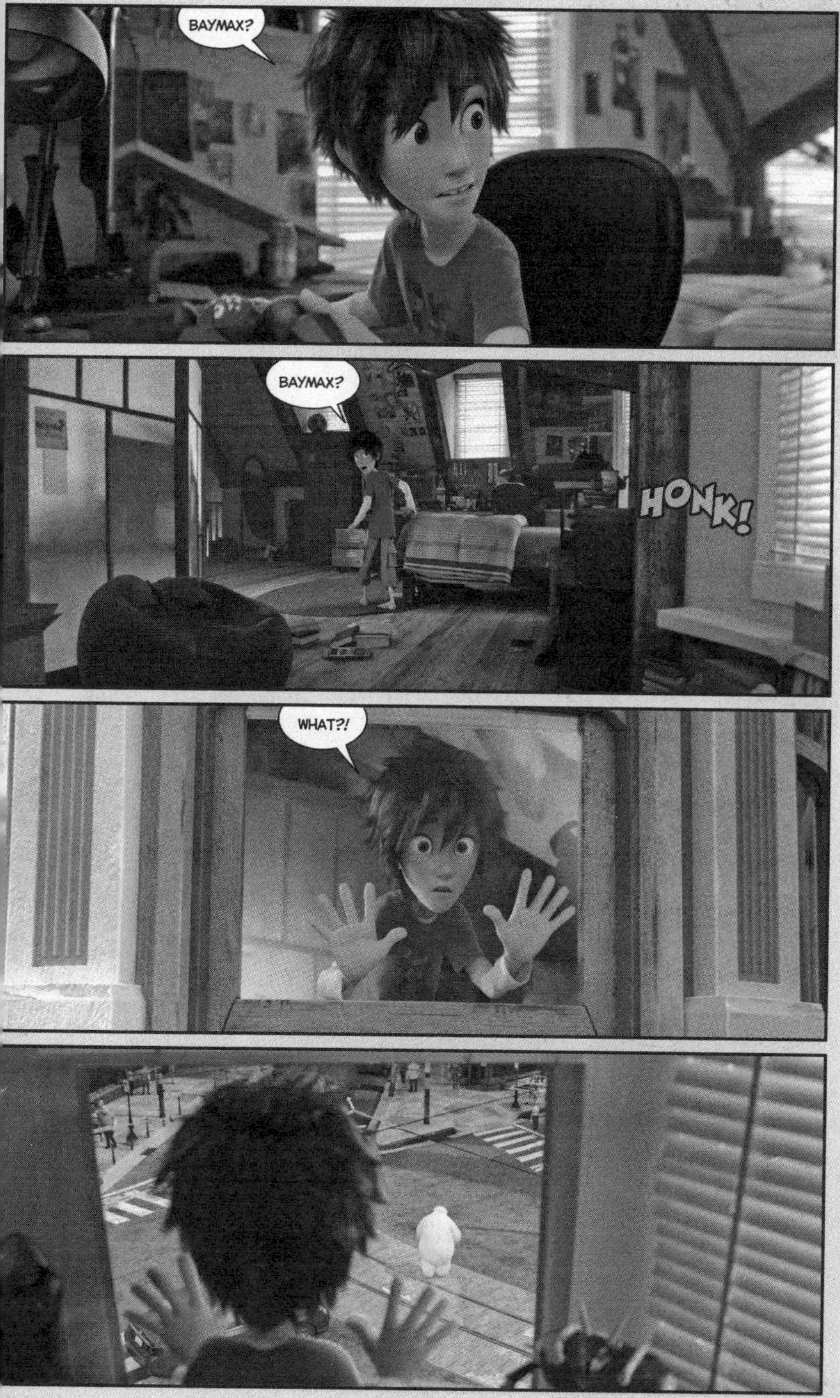
BAYMAX?
BAYMAX?
HONK!
WHAT?!

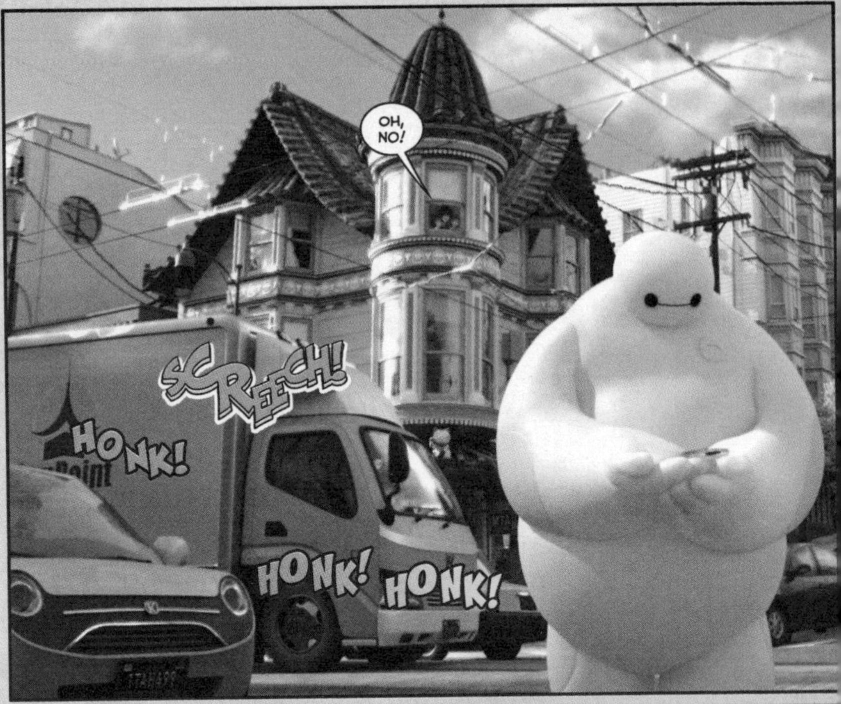
OH, NO!
SCREECH!
HONK!
HONK!
HONK!

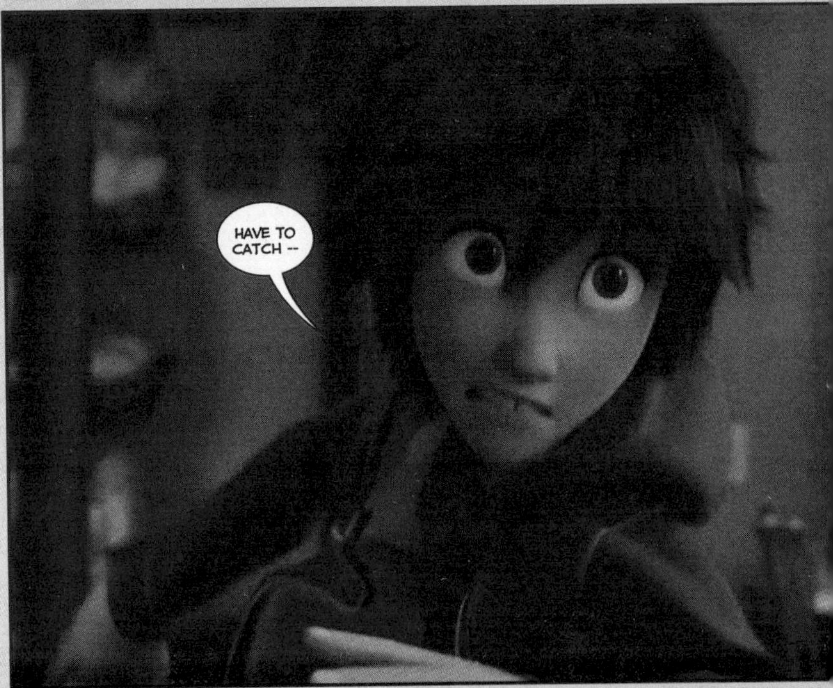
HAVE TO CATCH --

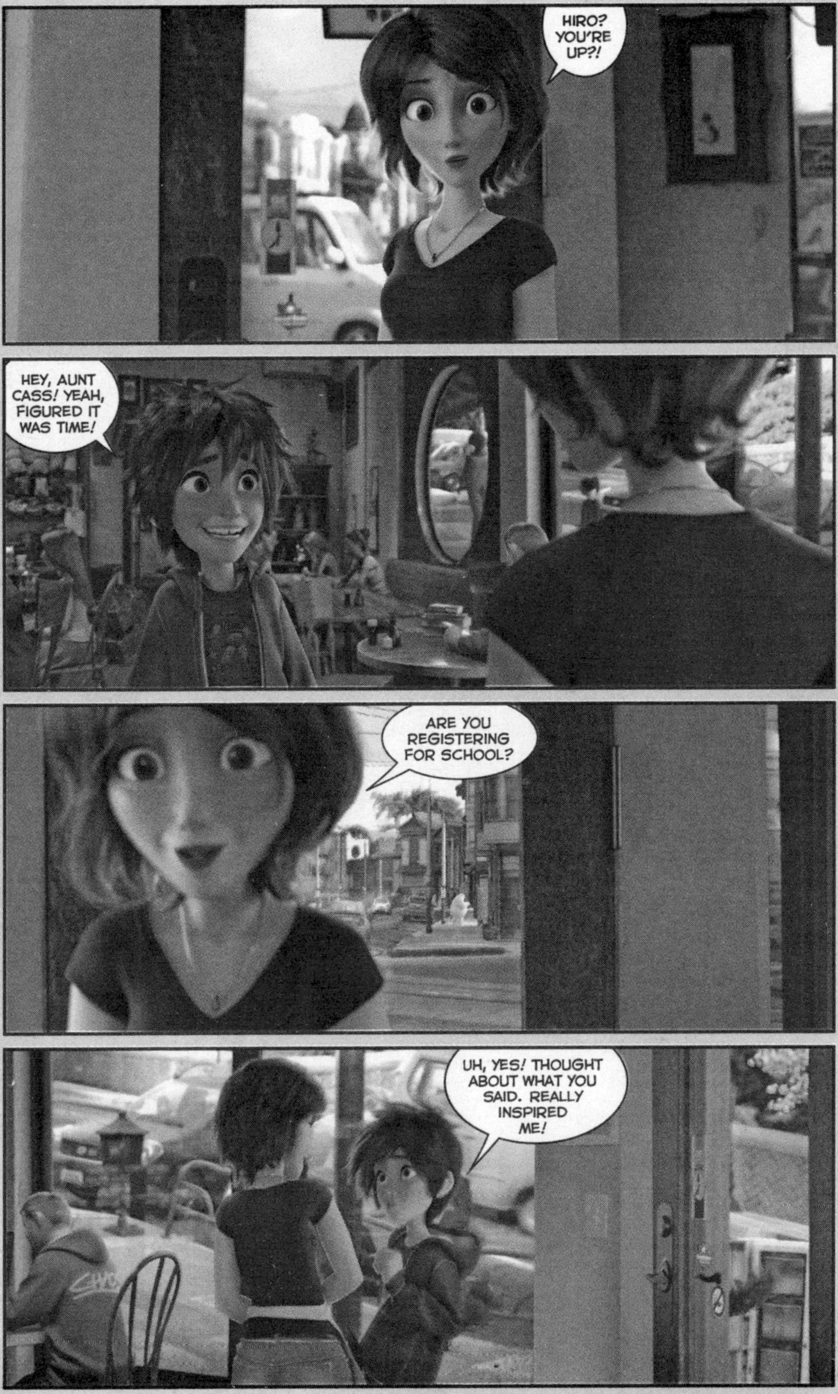
HIRO? YOU'RE UP?!
HEY, AUNT CASS! YEAH, FIGURED IT WAS TIME!
ARE YOU REGISTERING FOR SCHOOL?
UH, YES! THOUGHT ABOUT WHAT YOU SAID. REALLY INSPIRED ME!

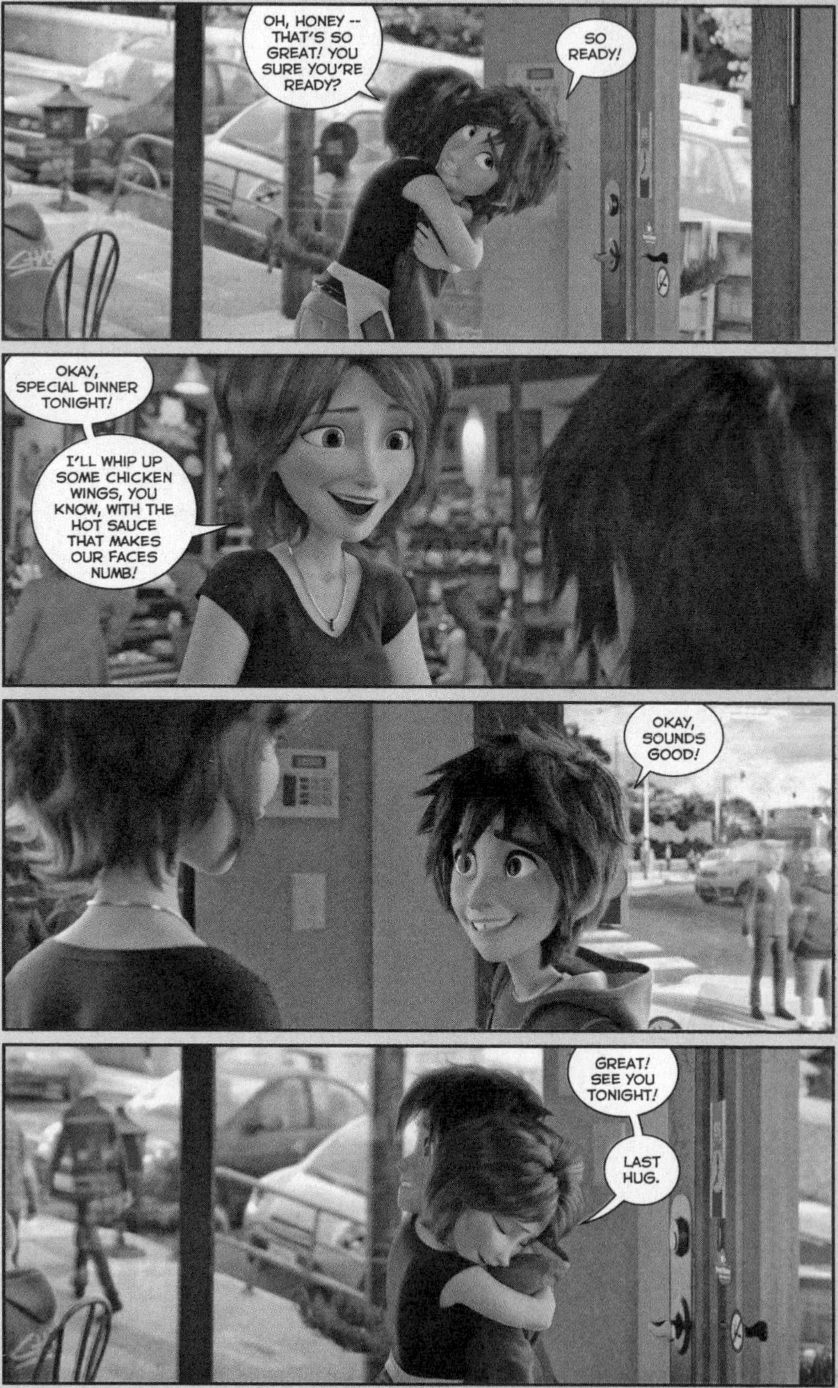
OH, HONEY -- THAT'S SO GREAT! YOU SURE YOU'RE READY?
SO READY!
OKAY, SPECIAL DINNER TONIGHT!
I'LL WHIP UP SOME CHICKEN WINGS, YOU KNOW, WITH THE HOT SAUCE THAT MAKES OUR FACES NUMB!
OKAY, SOUNDS GOOD!
GREAT! SEE YOU TONIGHT!
LAST HUG.

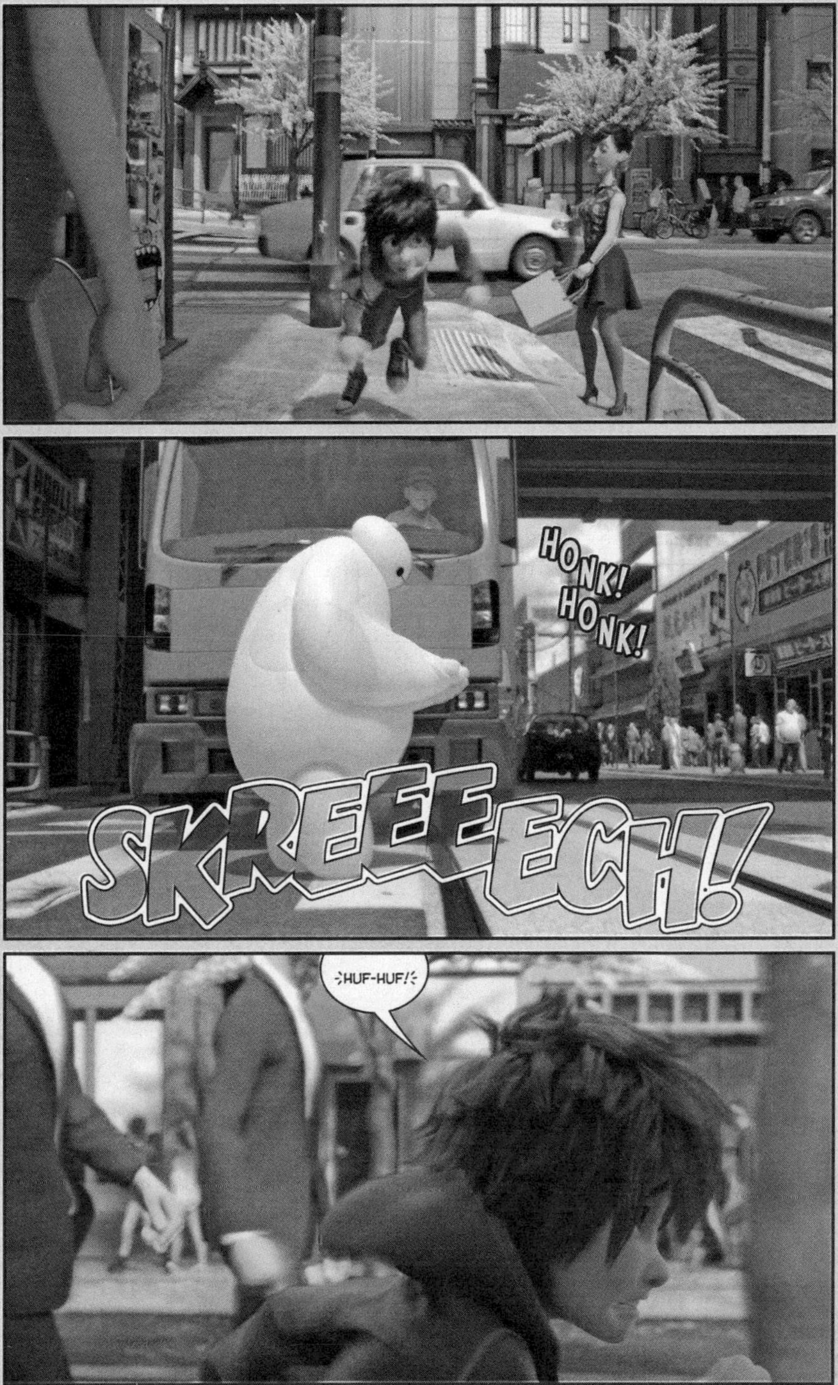
HONK! HONK!
SKREEEECH!
HUF-HUF!

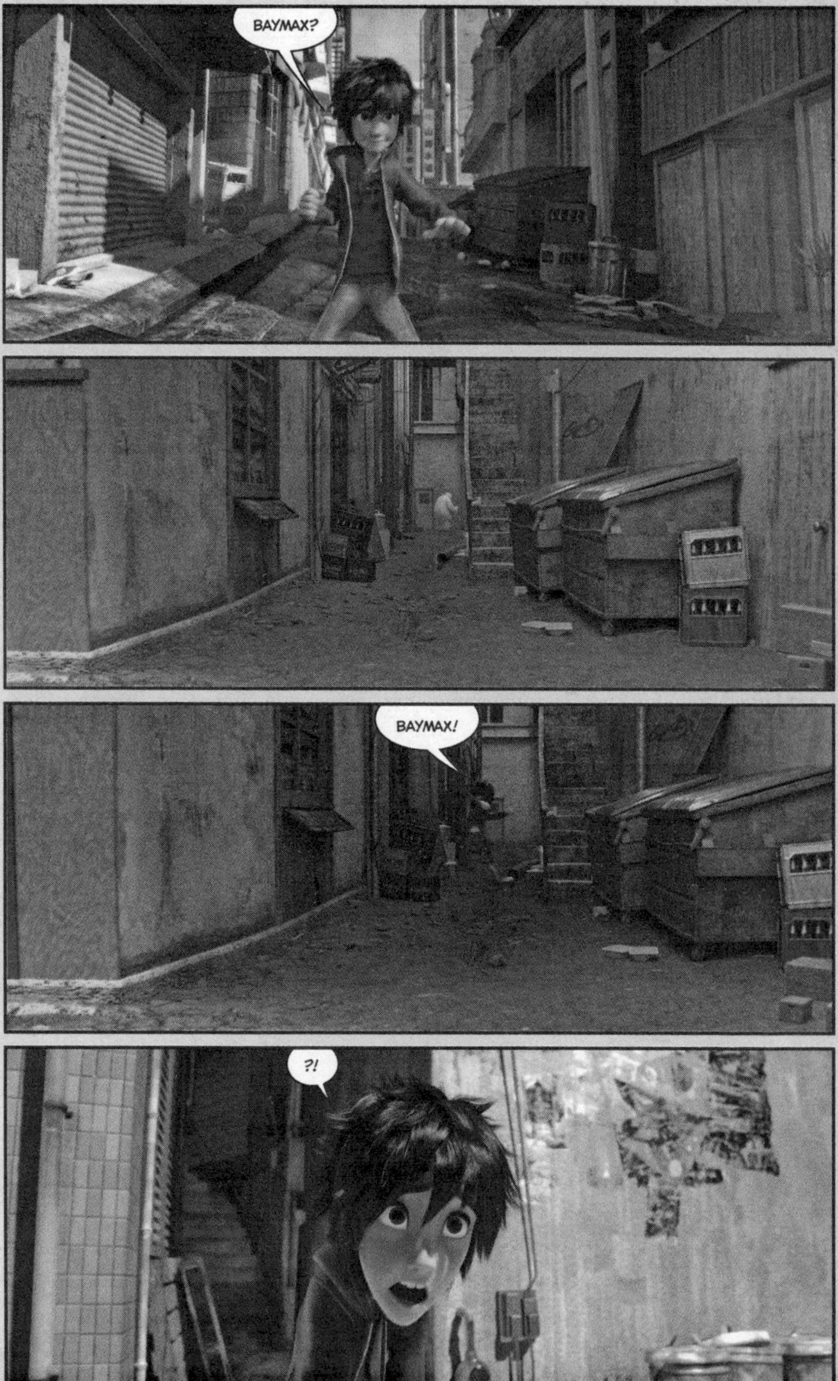
BAYMAX?
BAYMAX!
?!

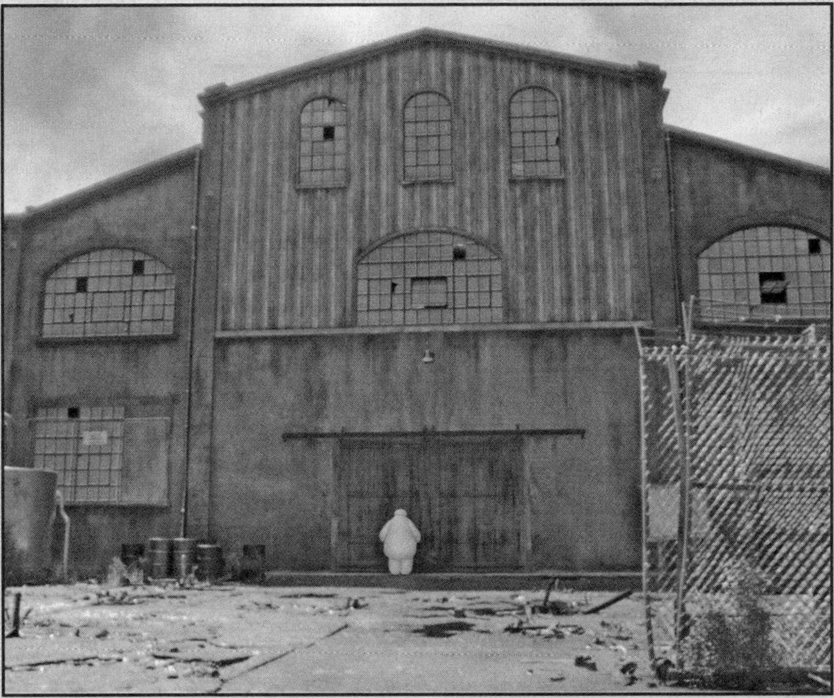

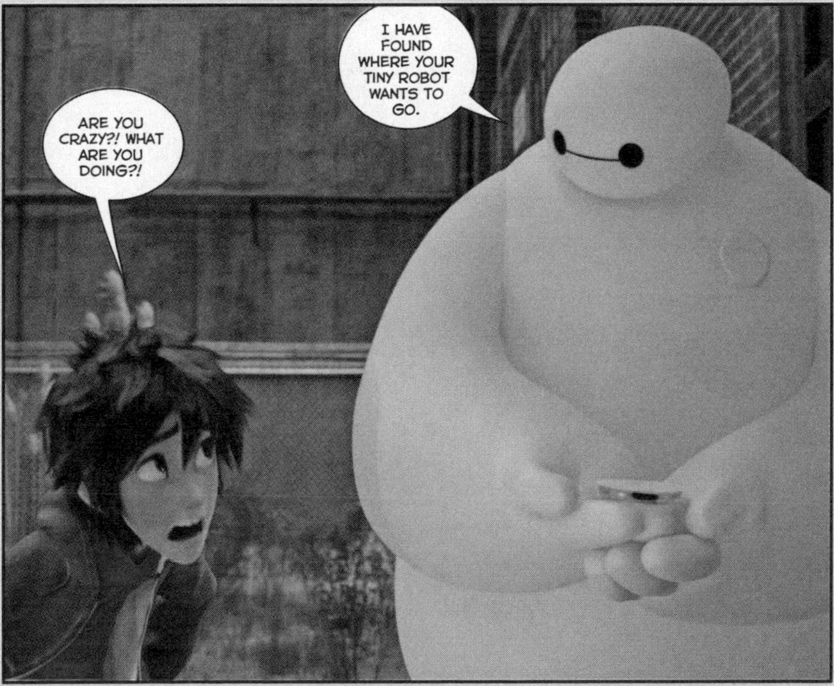
ARE YOU CRAZY?! WHAT ARE YOU DOING?!
I HAVE FOUND WHERE YOUR TINY ROBOT WANTS TO GO.

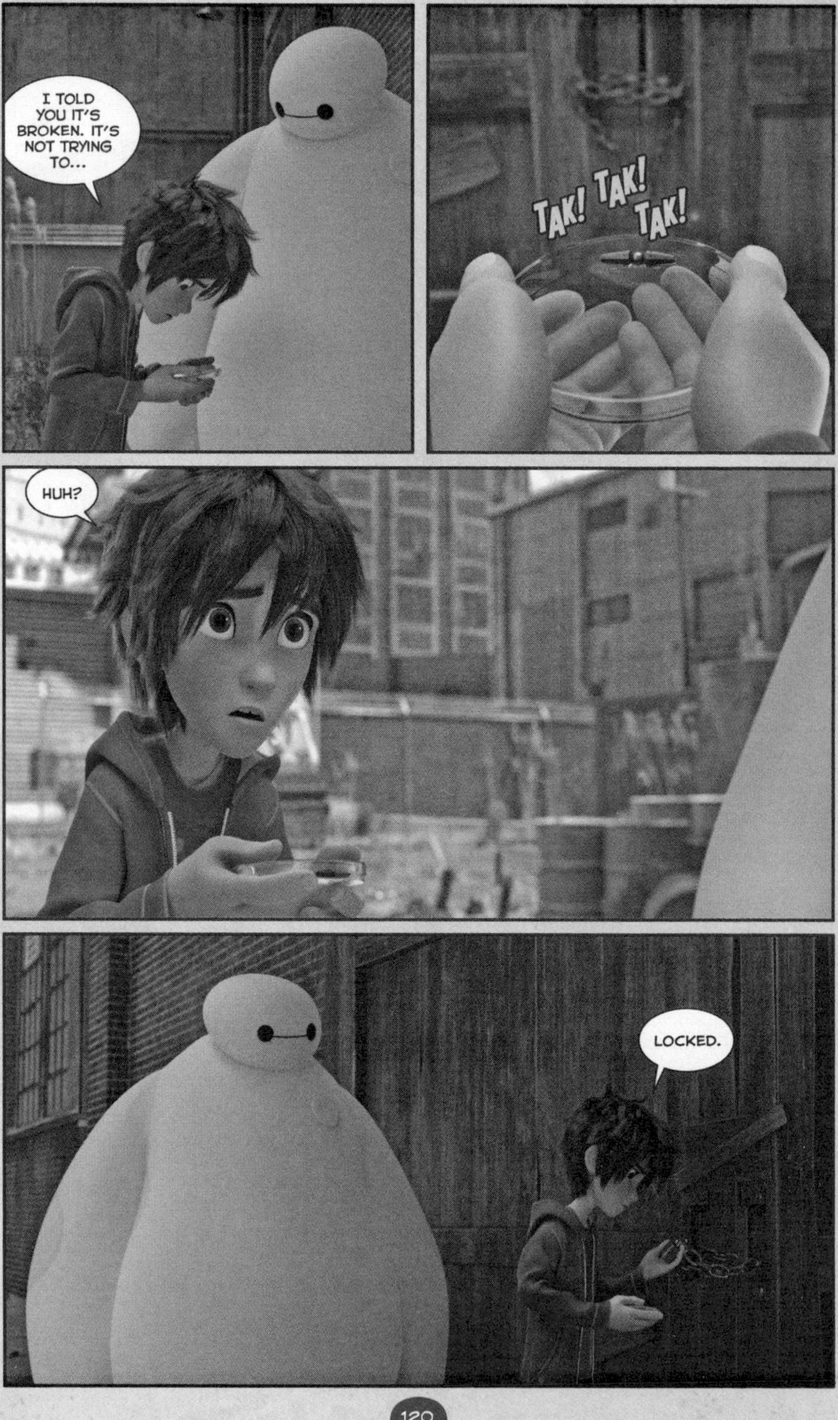
I TOLD YOU IT'S BROKEN. IT'S NOT TRYING TO...
TAK! TAK! TAK!
HUH?
LOCKED.

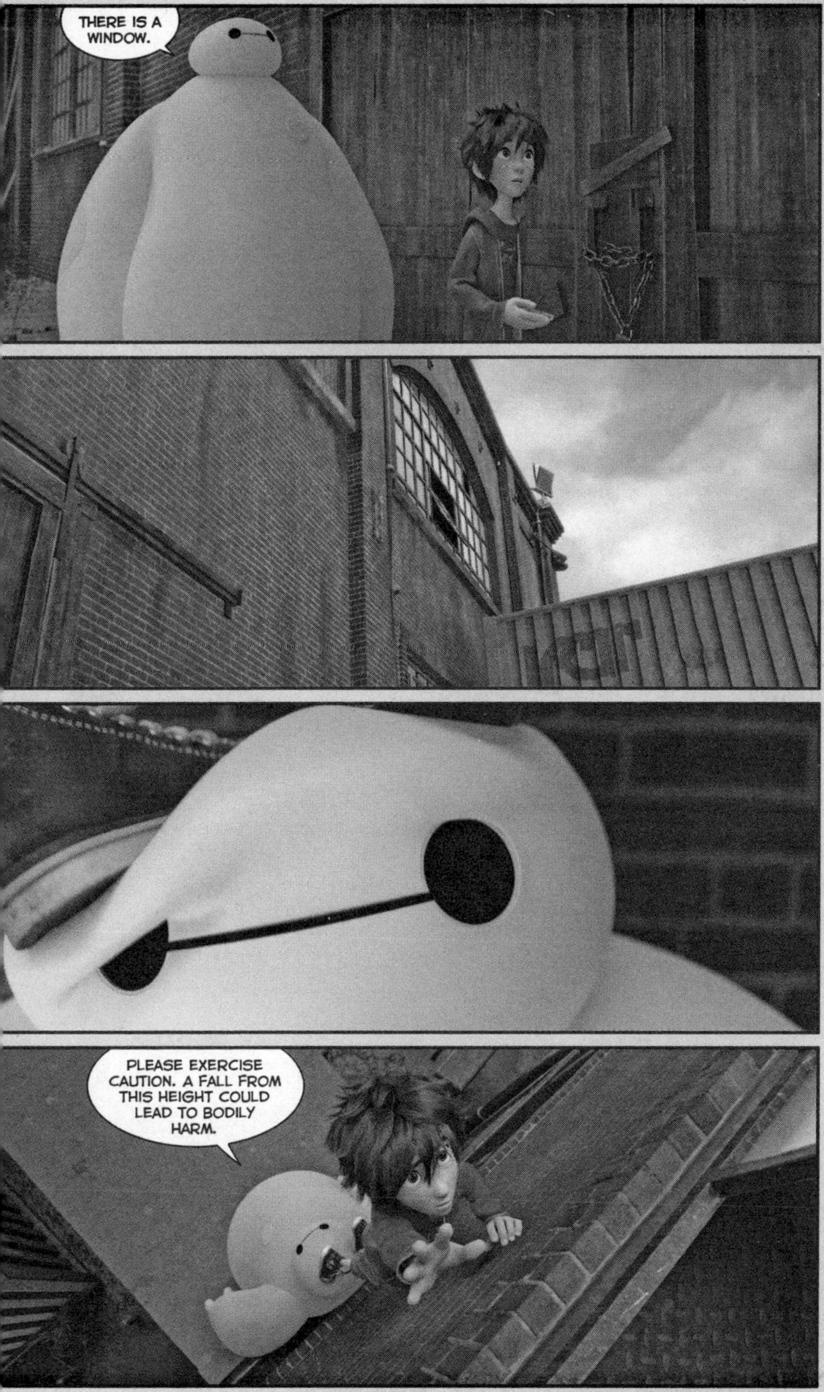
THERE IS A WINDOW.
PLEASE EXERCISE CAUTION. A FALL FROM THIS HEIGHT COULD LEAD TO BODILY HARM.

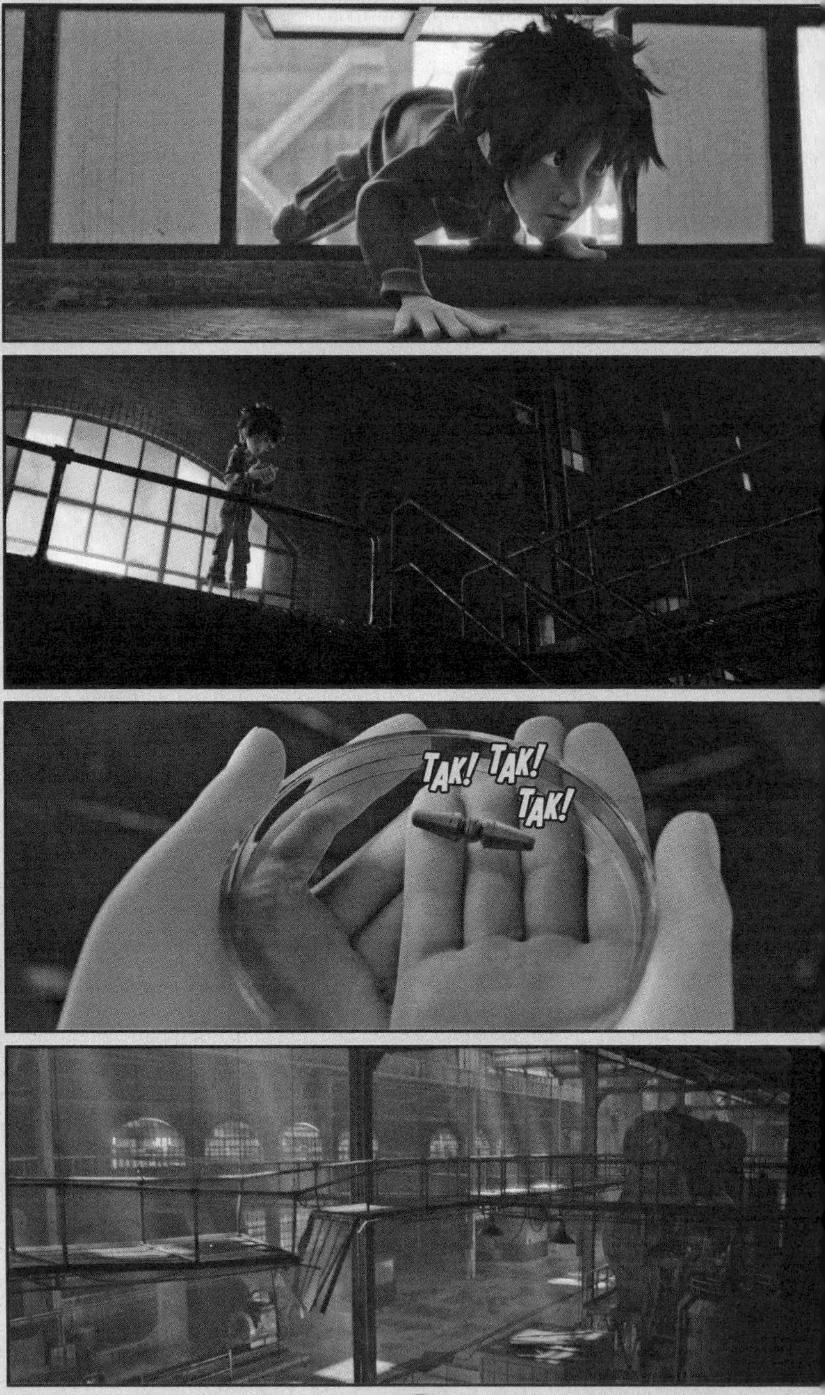
TAK! TAK!
TAK!

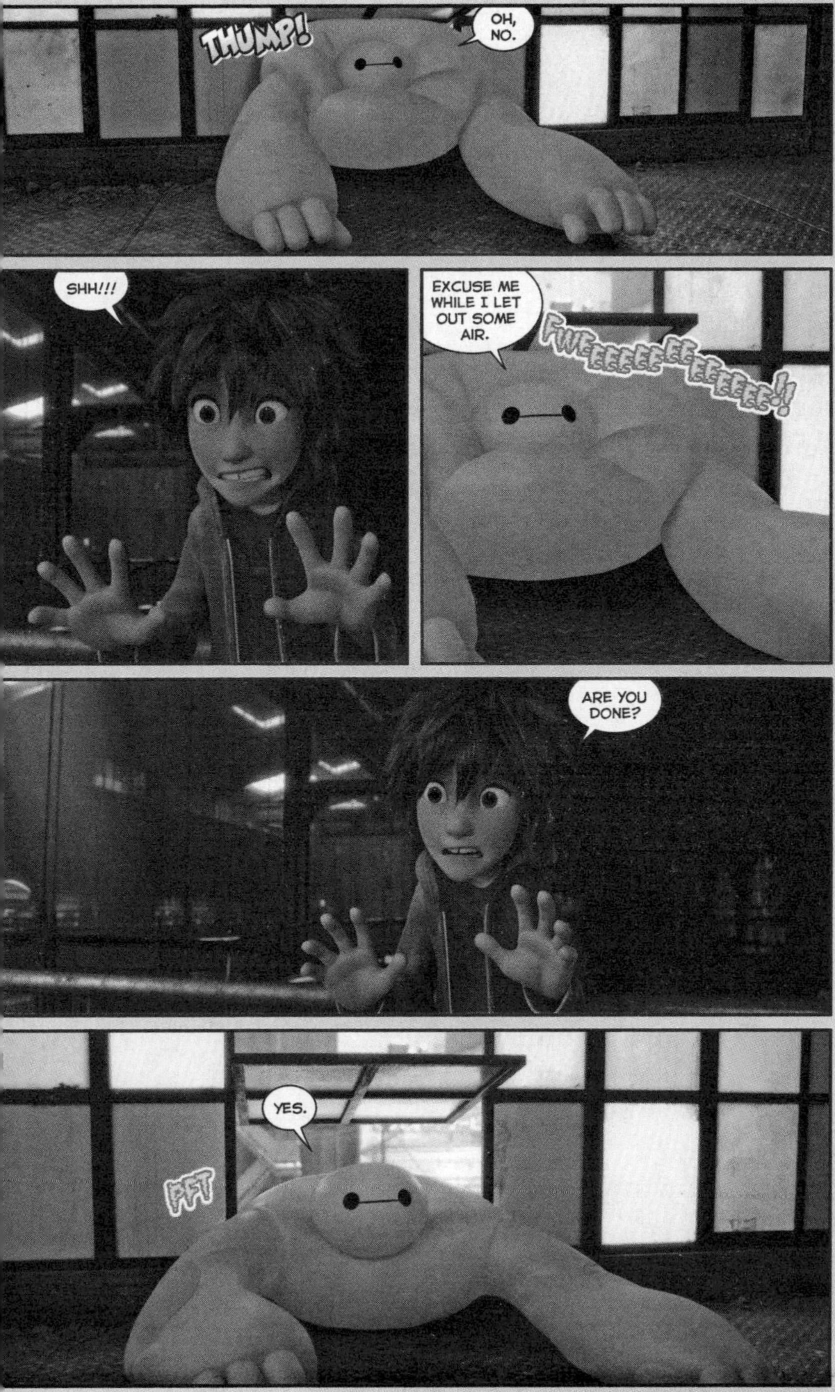
THUMP!
OH, NO.
SHH!!!
EXCUSE ME WHILE I LET OUT SOME AIR.
FWEEEEEEEEEEEEEEEE!!
ARE YOU DONE?
YES.
PFT

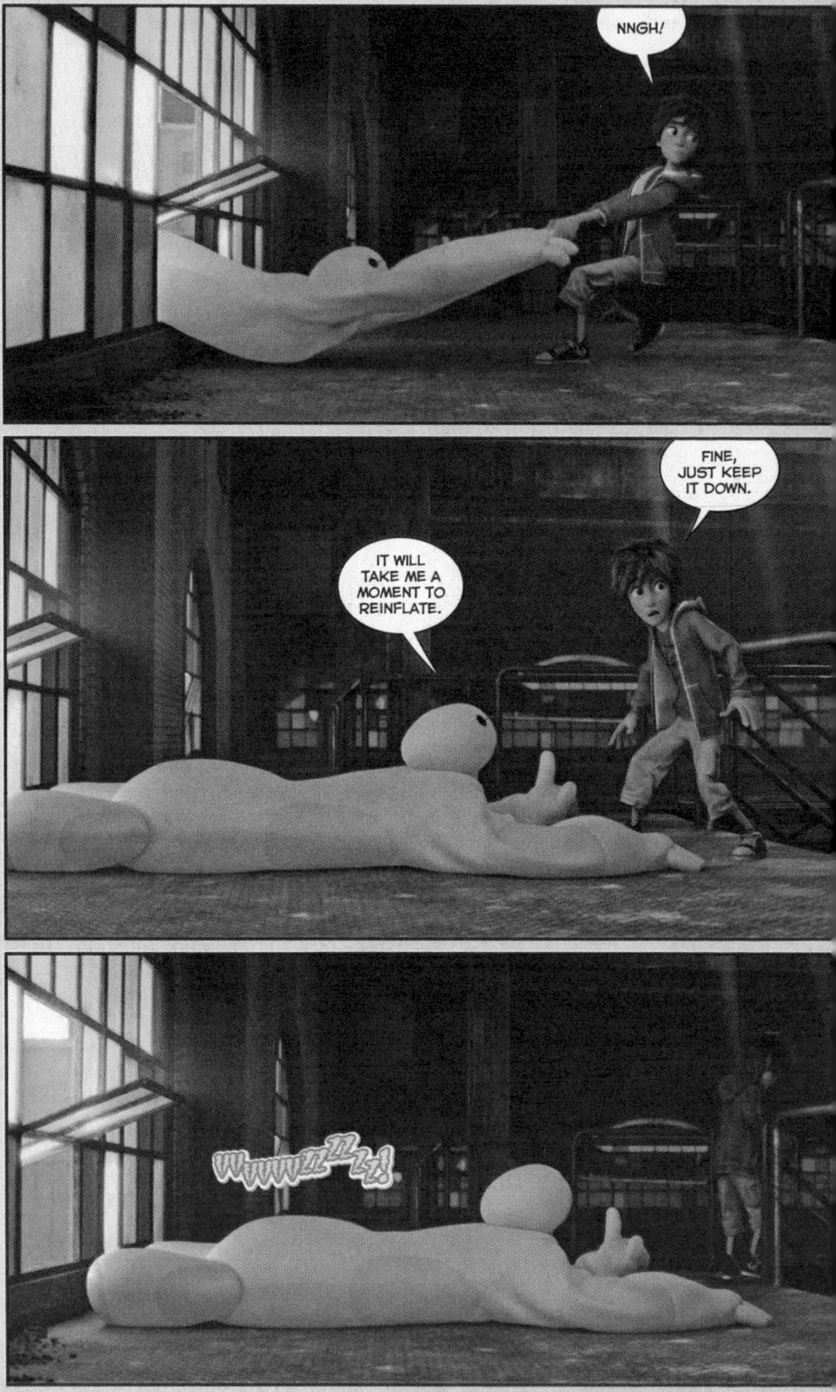
NNGH!
IT WILL TAKE ME A MOMENT TO REINFLATE.
FINE, JUST KEEP IT DOWN.
VVVVVVZZZZZZ!

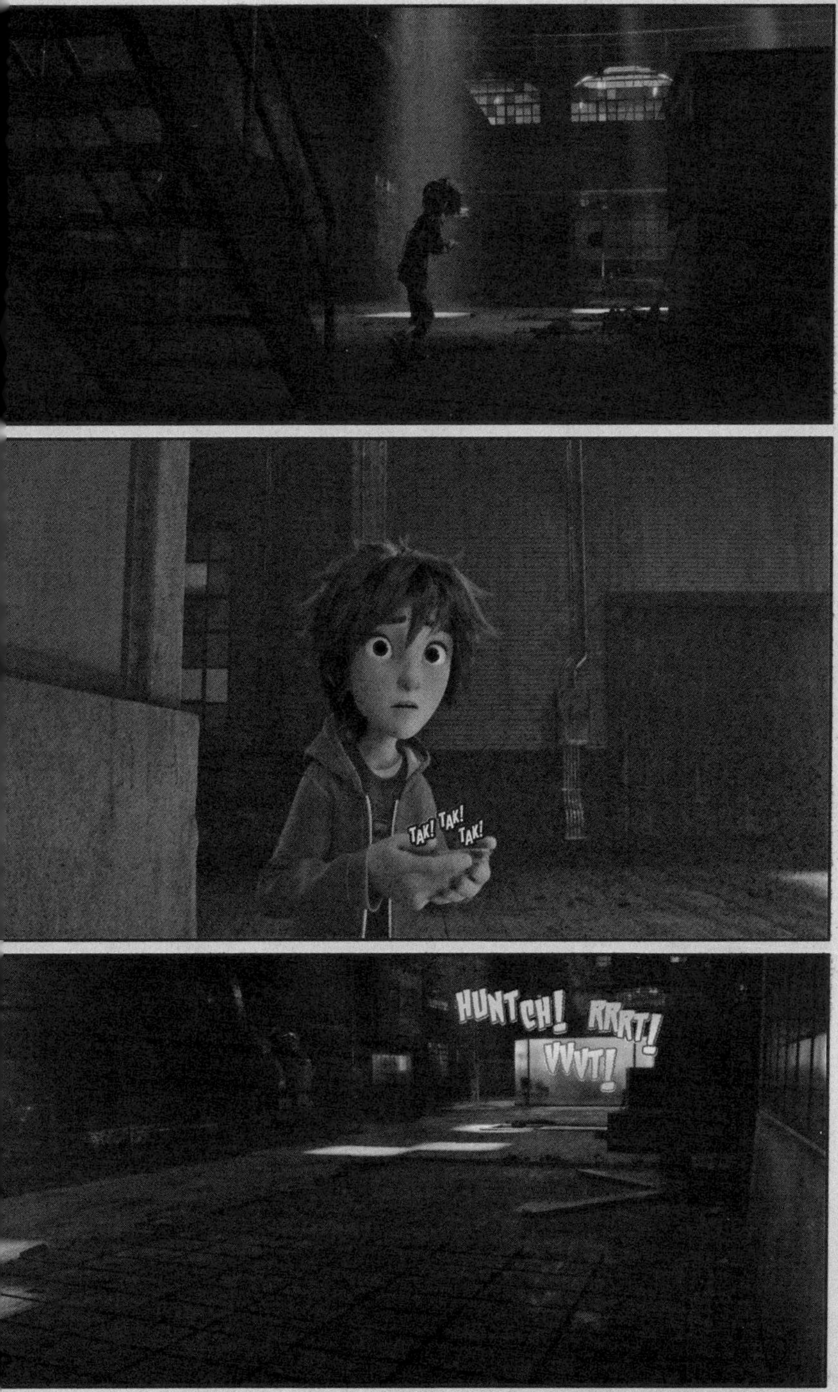
TAK! TAK! TAK!
HUNTCH!
RRRT!
VVVT!

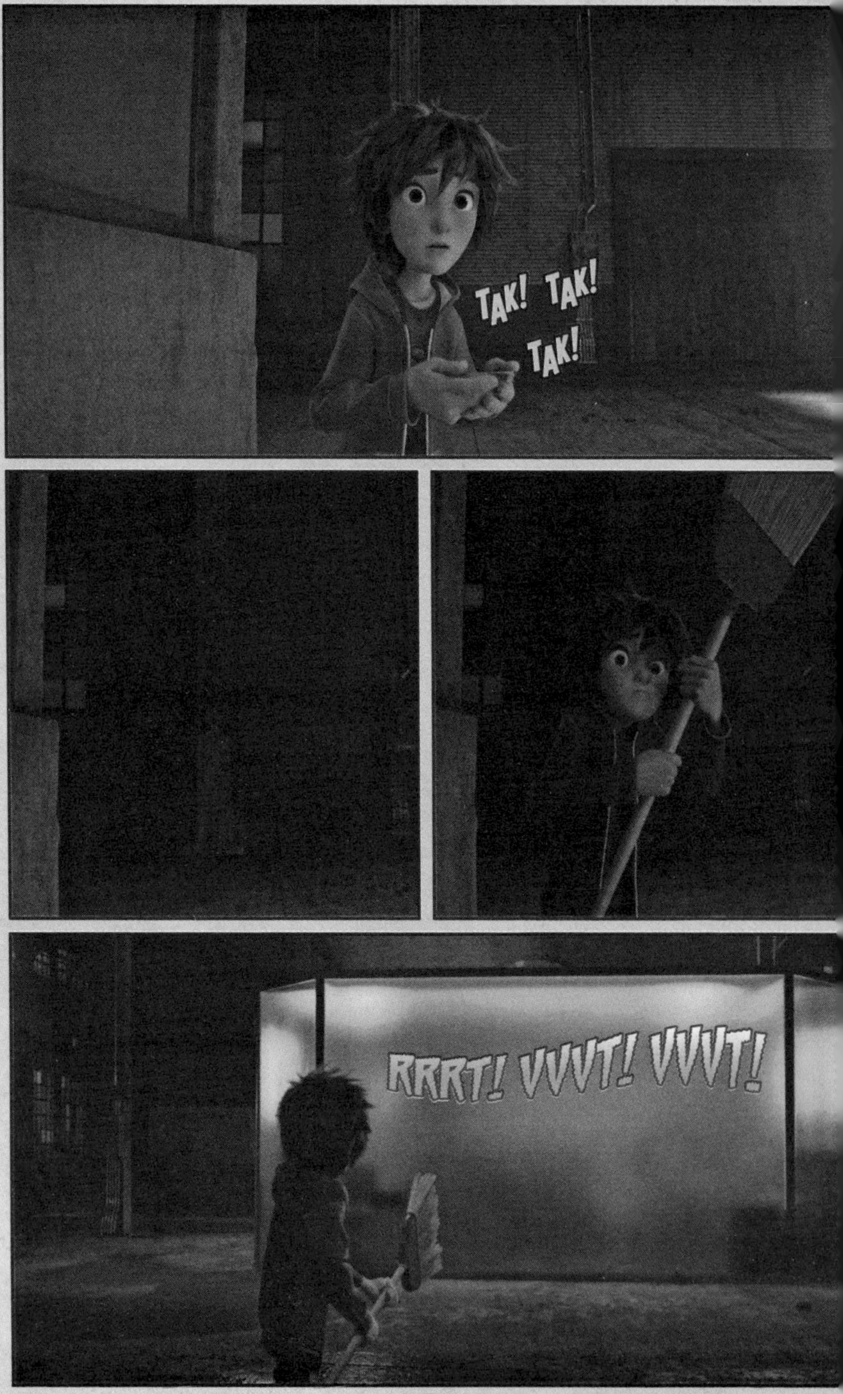
TAK! TAK!
TAK!
RRRT! VVVT! VVVT!

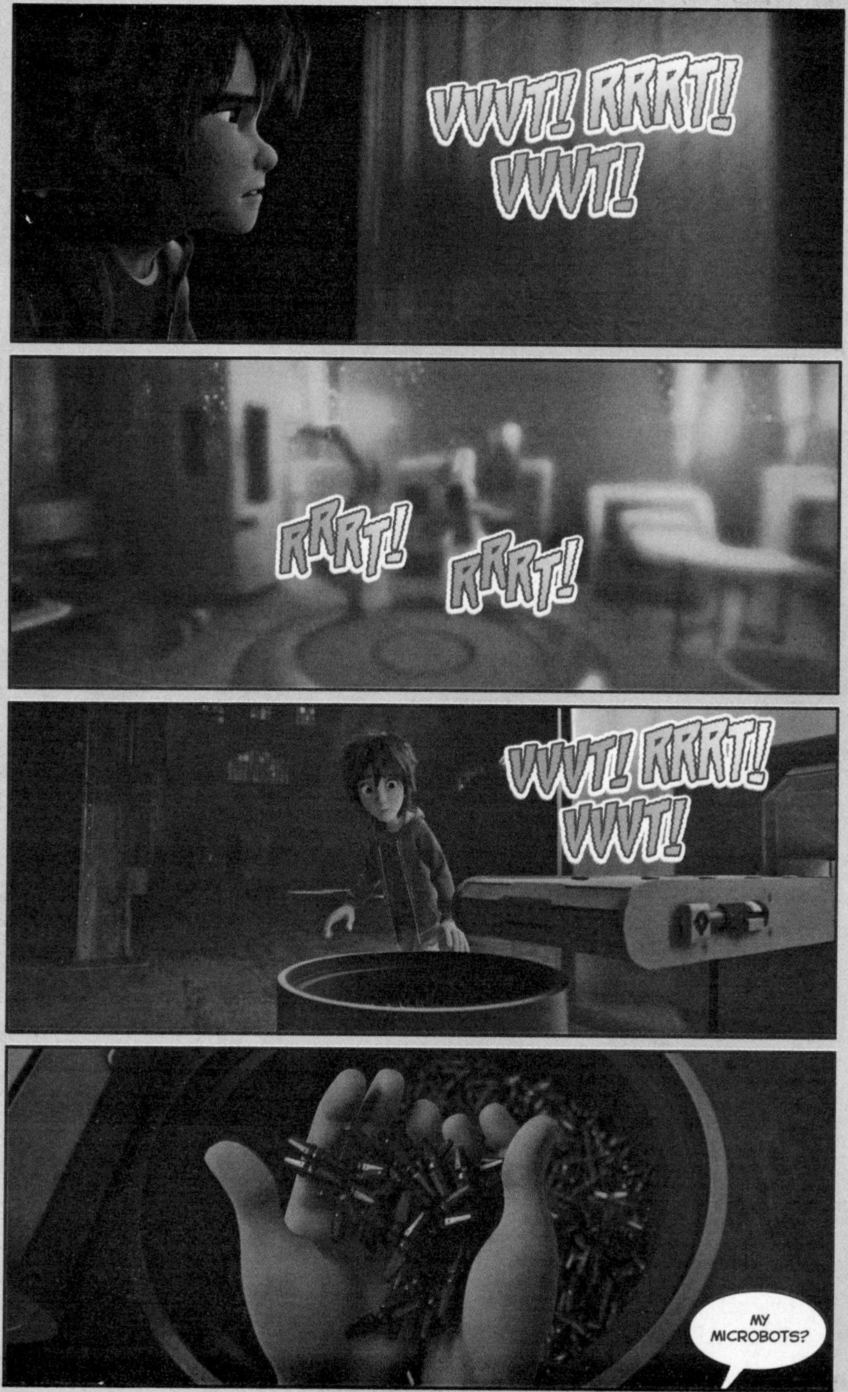
VVVT! RRRT! VVVT!
RRRT!
RRRT!
VVVT! RRRT! VVVT!
MY MICROBOTS?

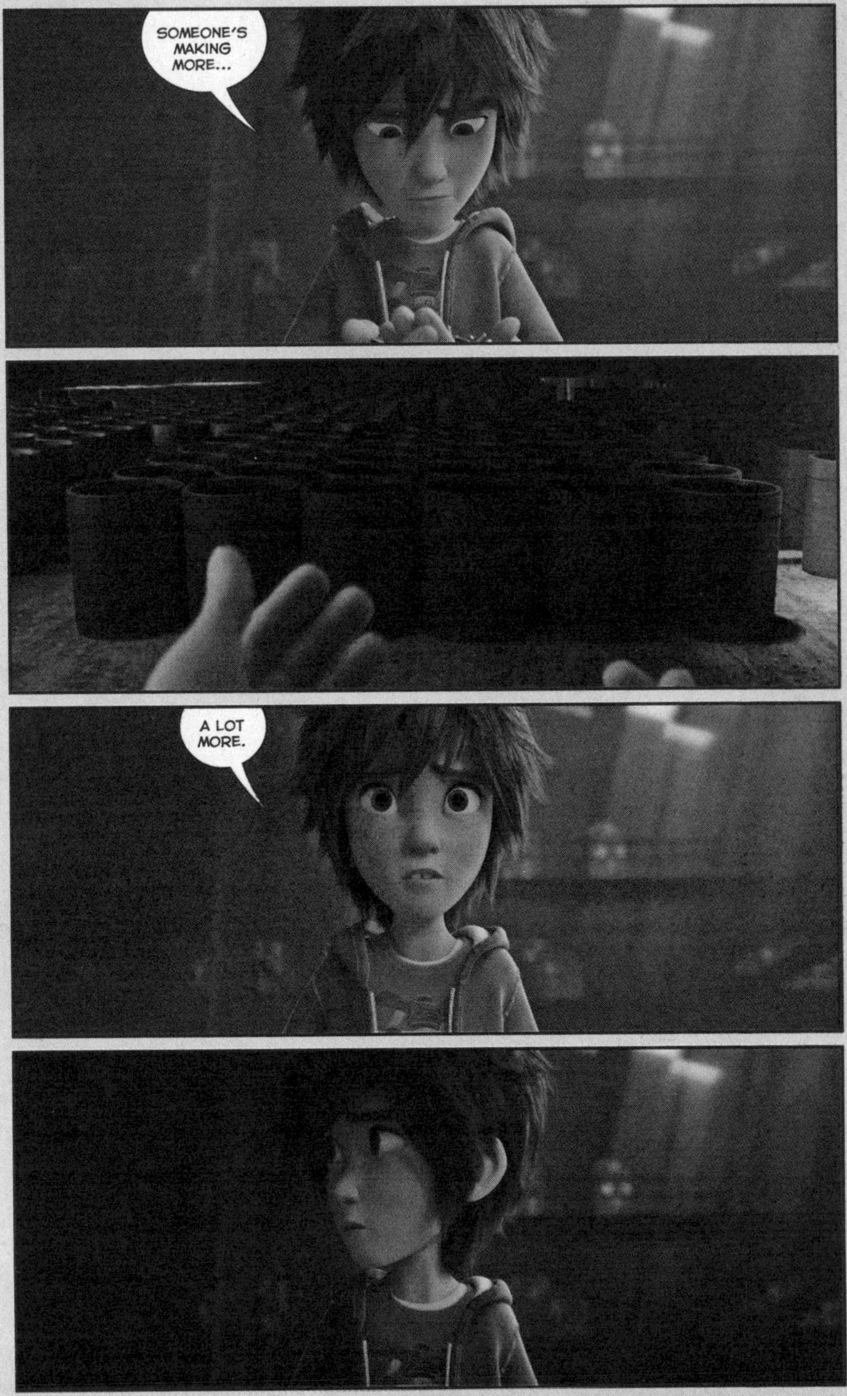
SOMEONE'S MAKING MORE...
A LOT MORE.

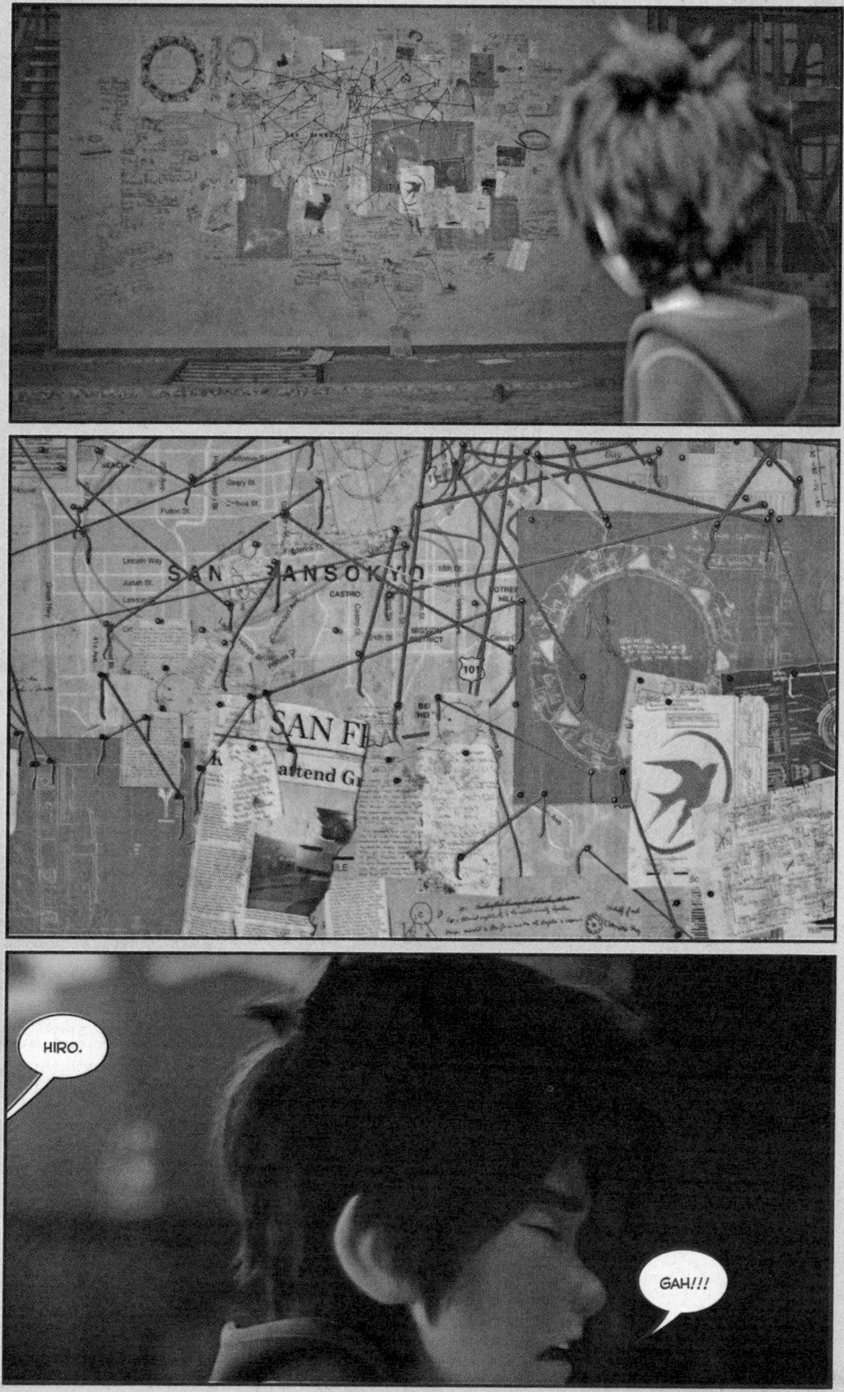
SAN
ANSOKYO
CASTRO
SAN F
attend G
HIRO.
GAH!!!

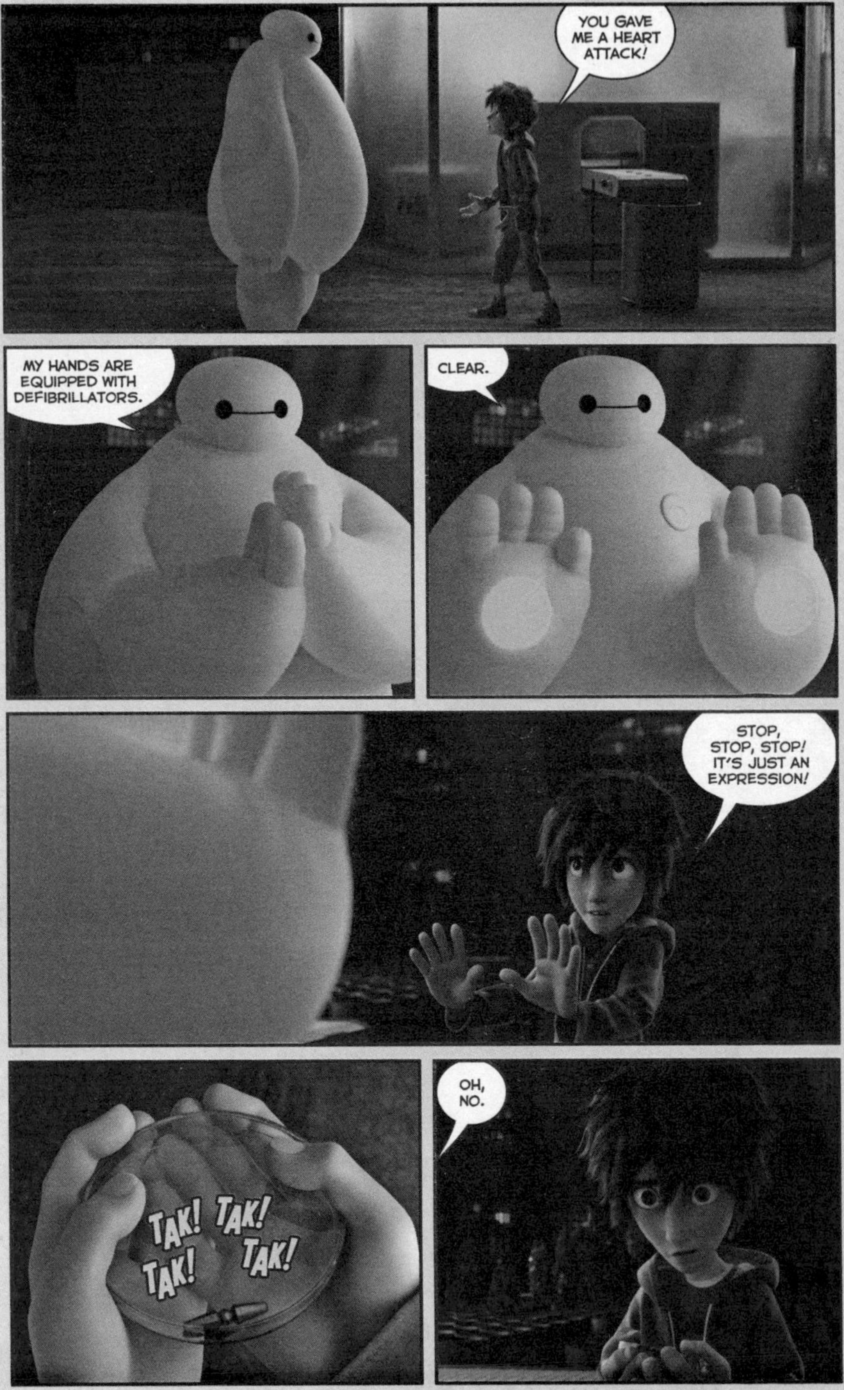
YOU GAVE ME A HEART ATTACK!
MY HANDS ARE EQUIPPED WITH DEFIBRILLATORS.
CLEAR.
STOP, STOP, STOP! IT'S JUST AN EXPRESSION!
TAK! TAK! TAK! TAK!
OH, NO.

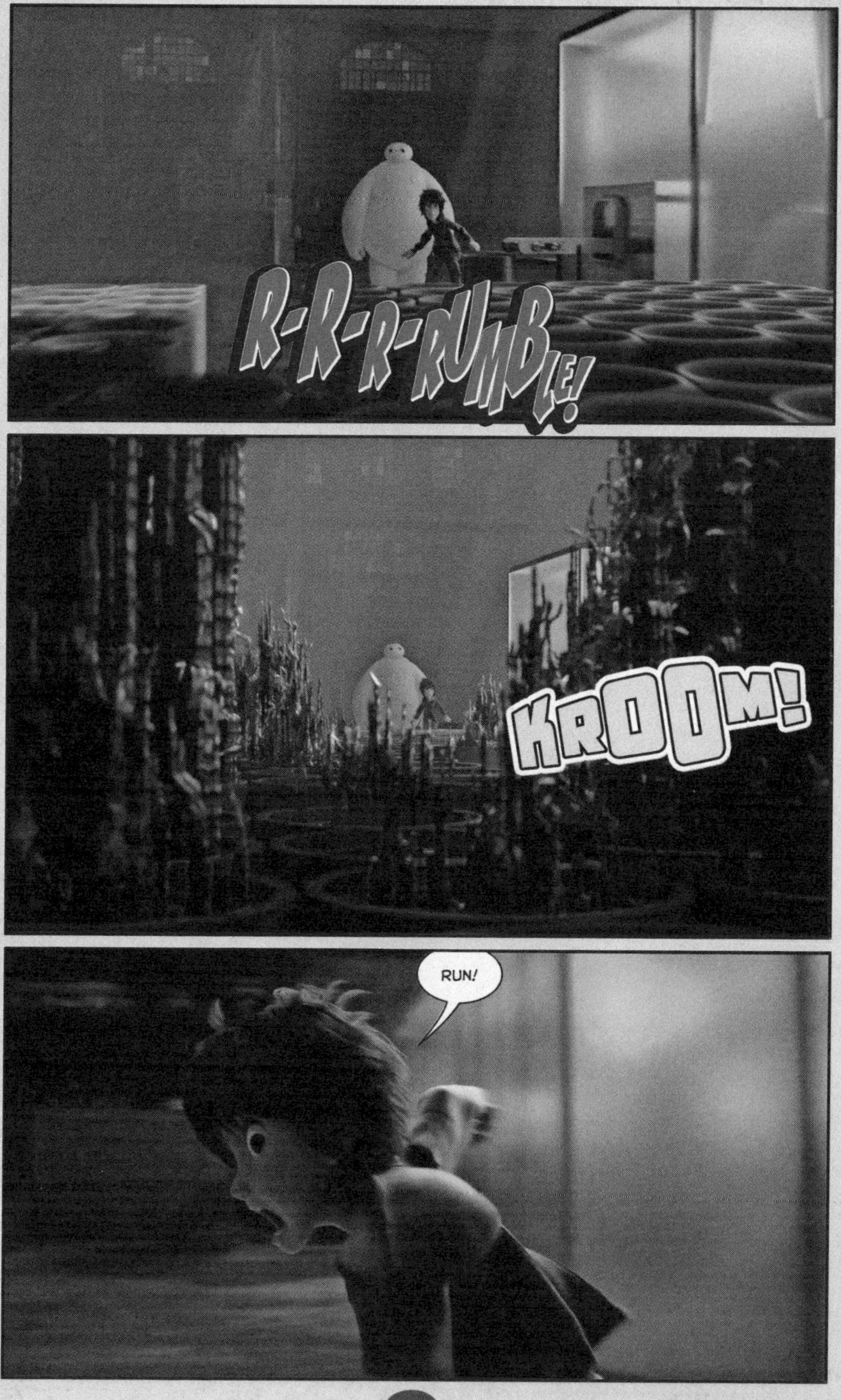
R-R-R-RUMBLE!
KROOM!
RUN!

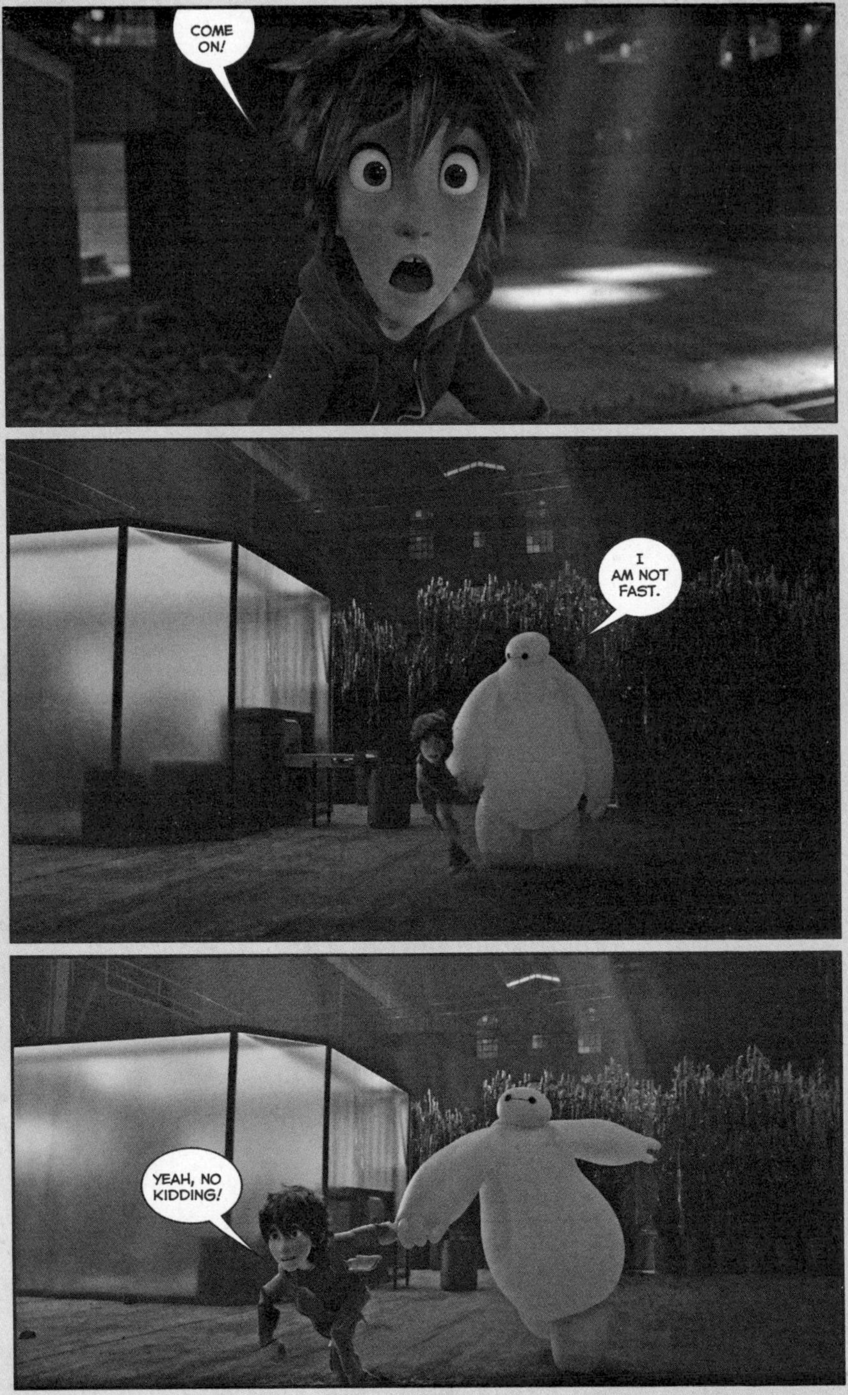
COME ON!
I AM NOT FAST.
YEAH, NO KIDDING!

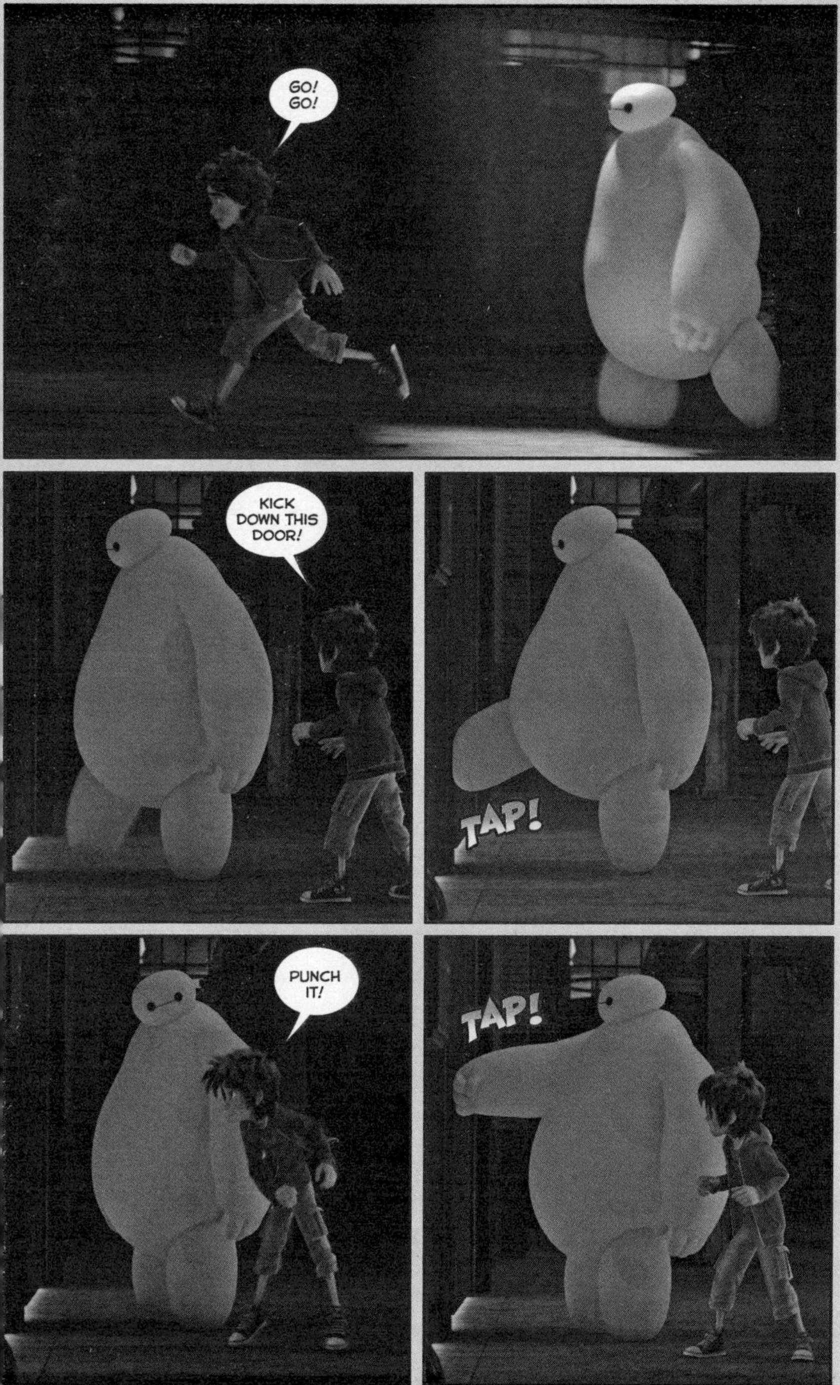
GO! GO!
KICK DOWN THIS DOOR!
TAP!
PUNCH IT!
TAP!

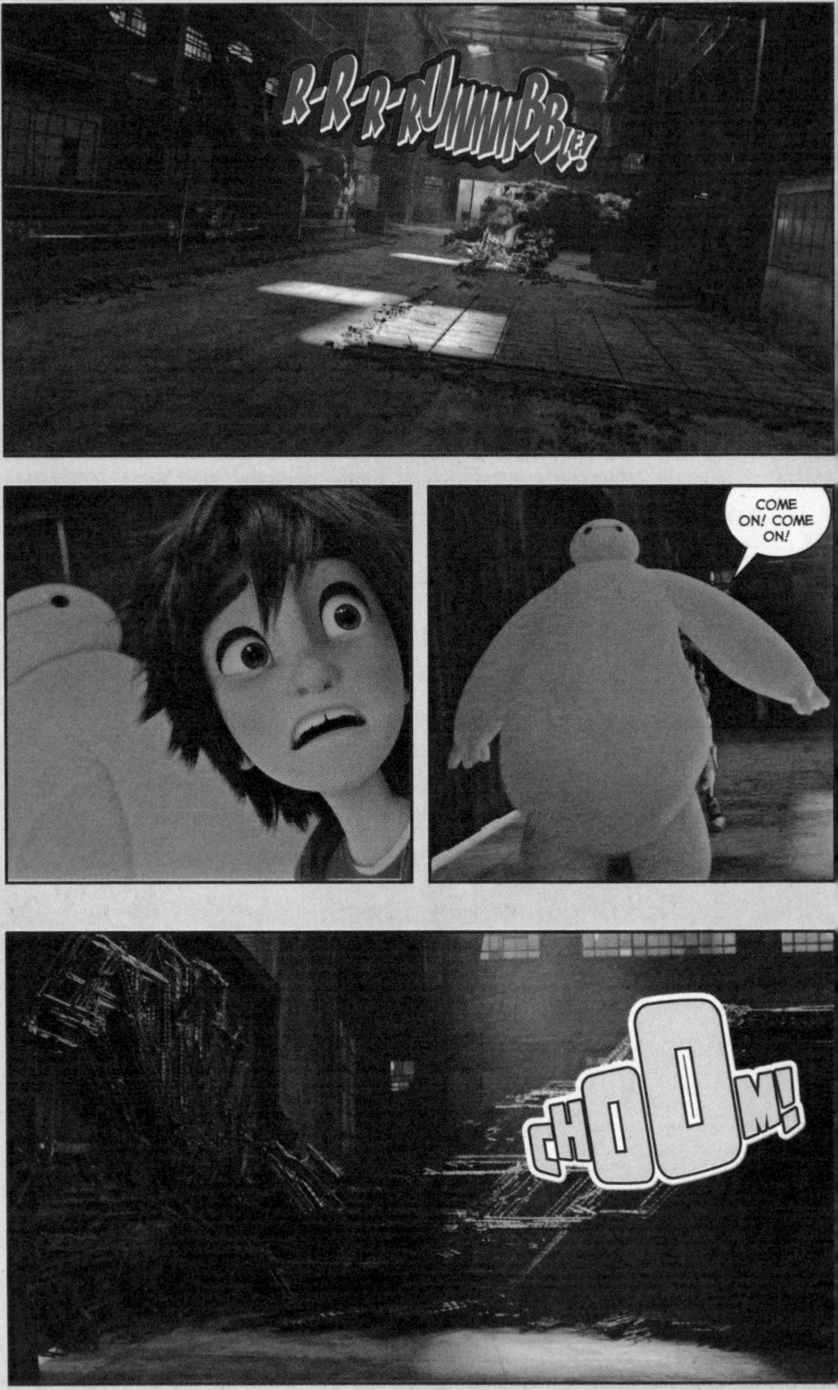
R-R-R-RUMMMMBBLE!
COME ON! COME ON!
CHOOM!

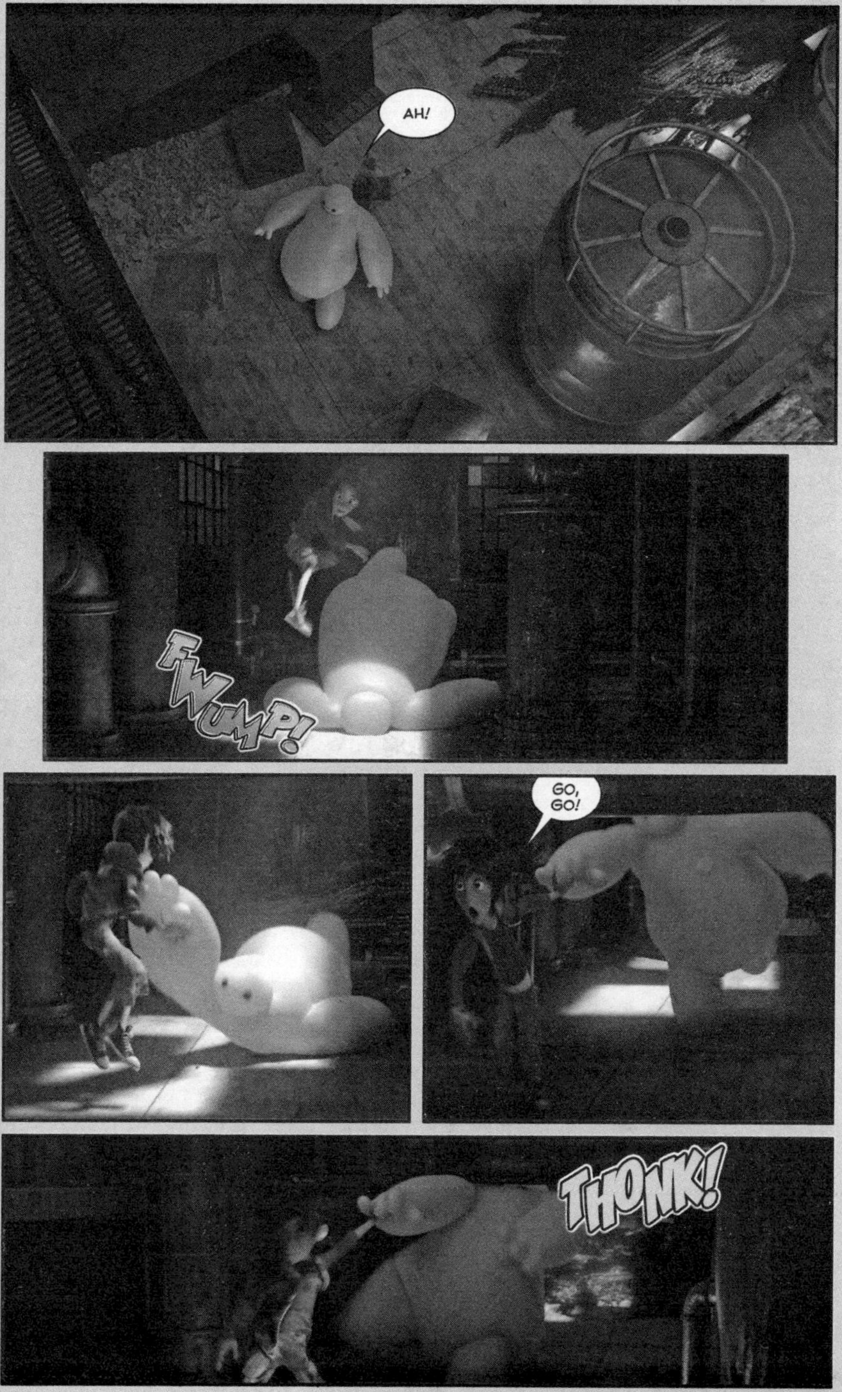
AH!
FWUMP!
GO, GO!
THONK!

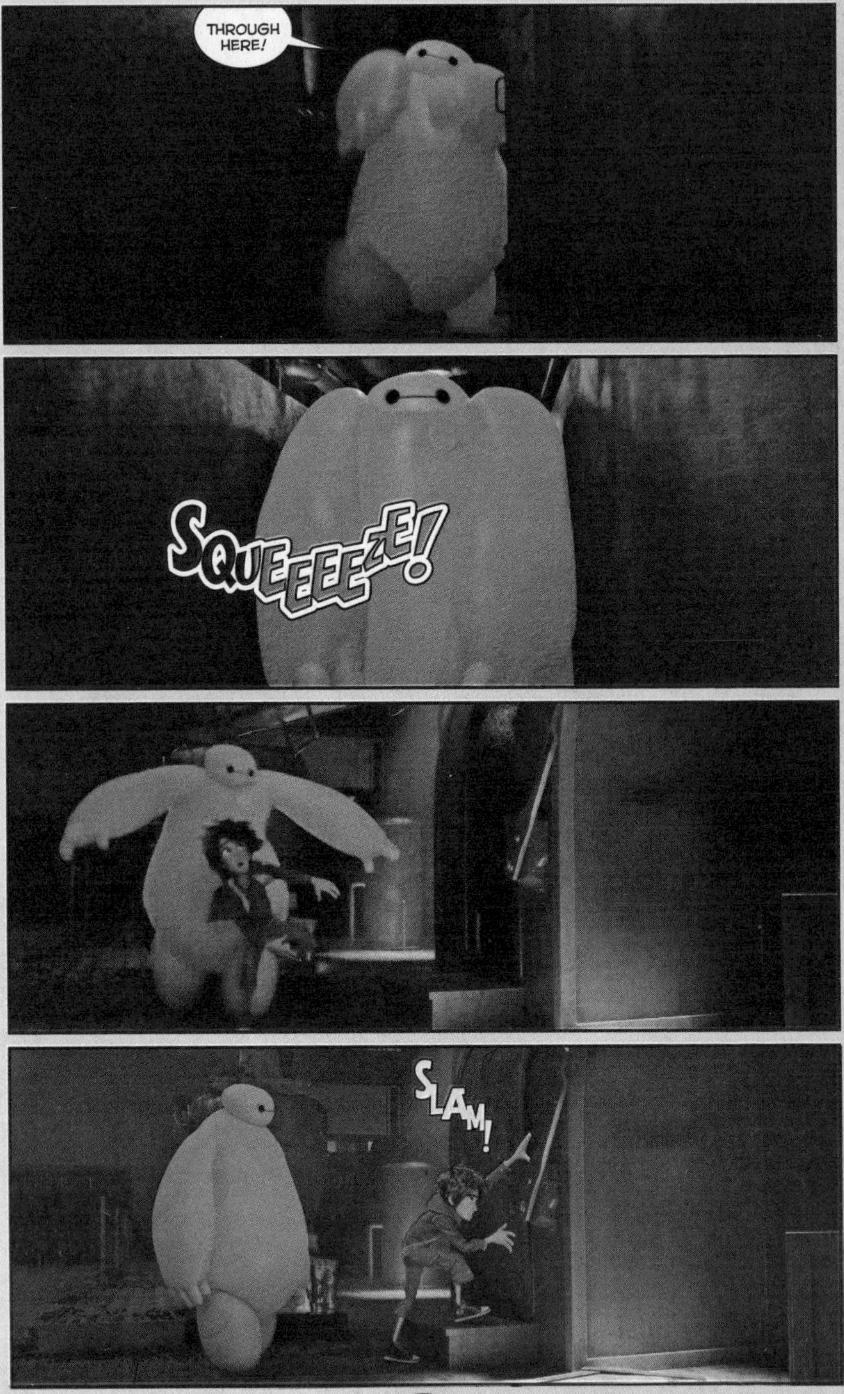
THROUGH HERE!
SQUEEEEEZE!
SLAM!

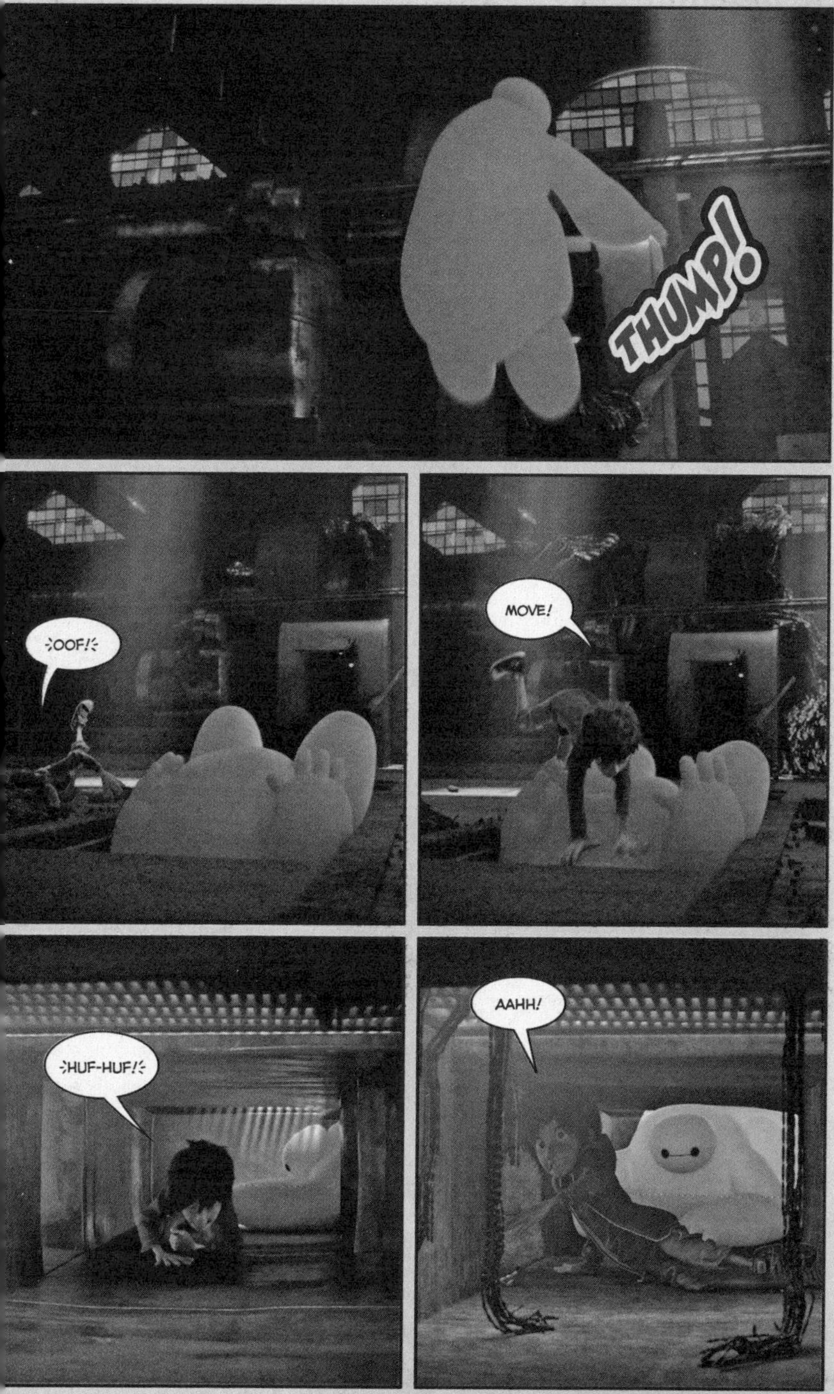
THUMP!
OOF!
MOVE!
HUF-HUF!
AAHH!

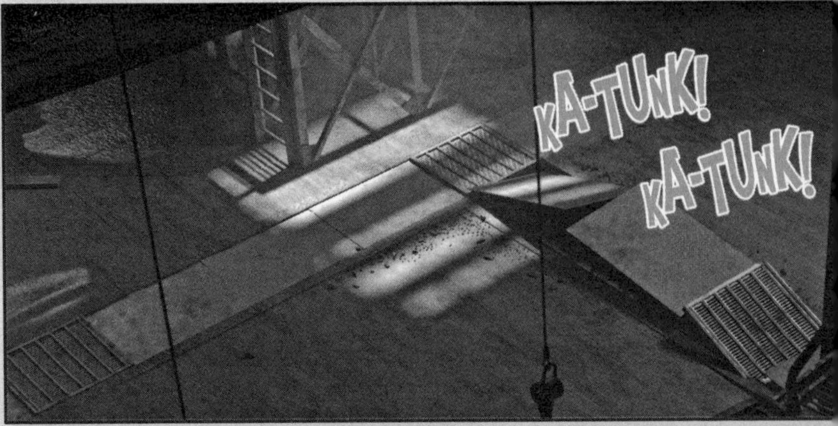
KA-TUNK!
KA-TUNK!

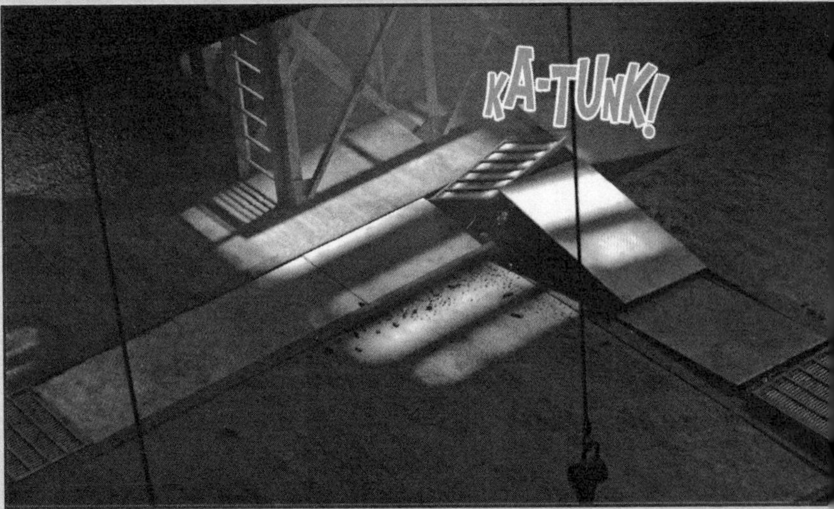
KA-TUNK!

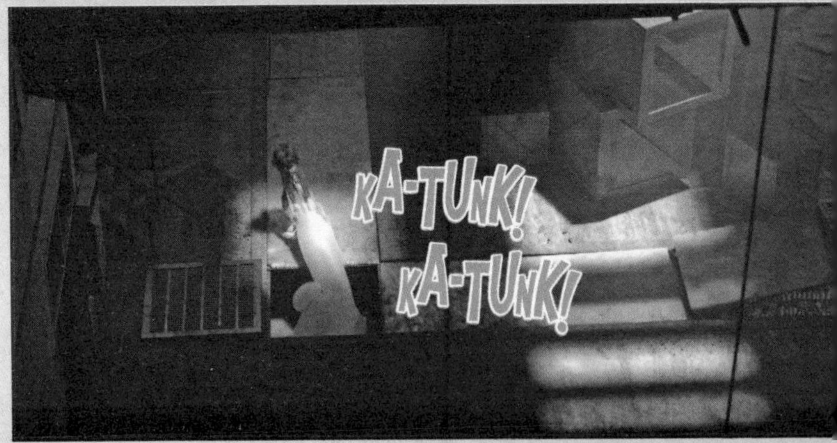
KA-TUNK!
KA-TUNK!

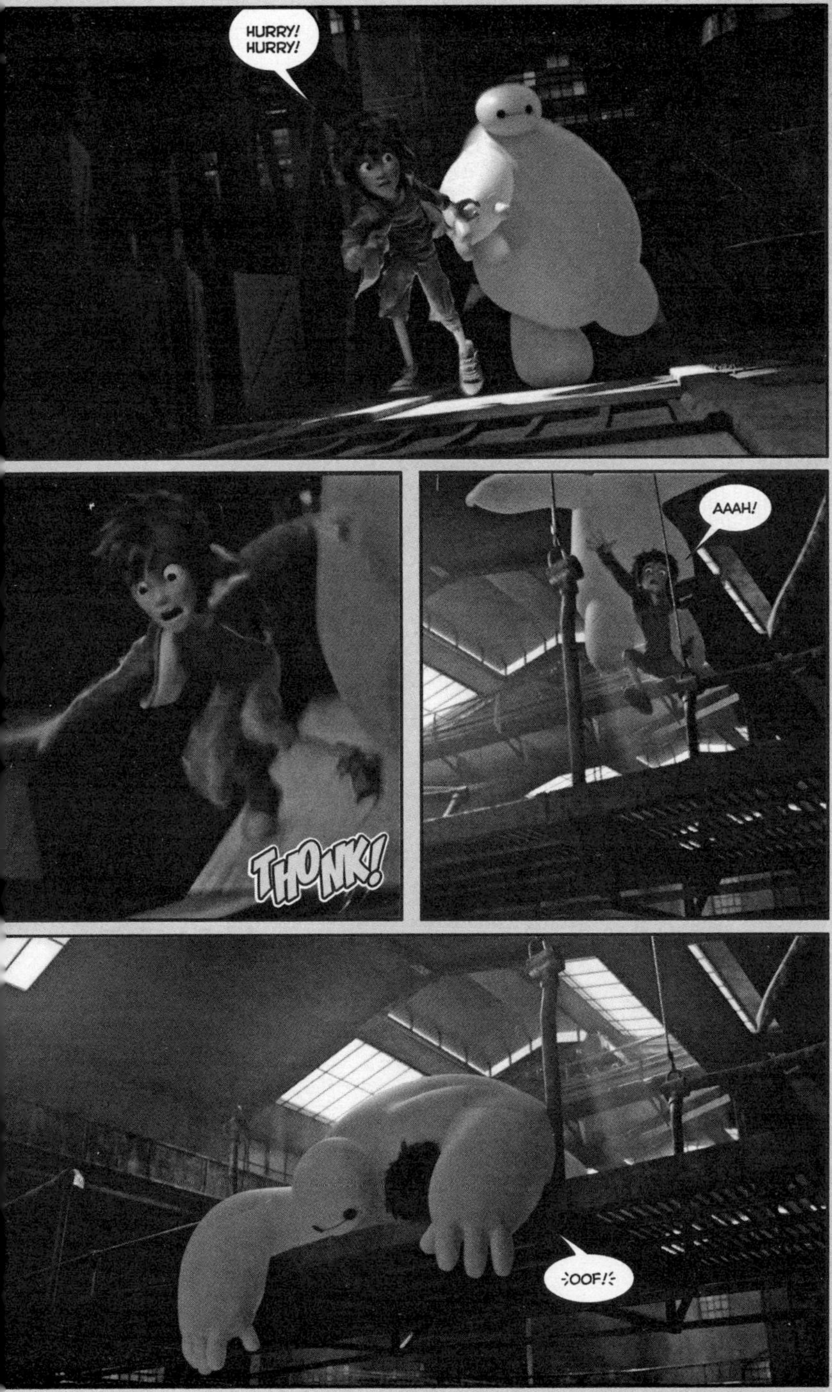
HURRY!
HURRY!
THONK!
AAAH!
OOF!

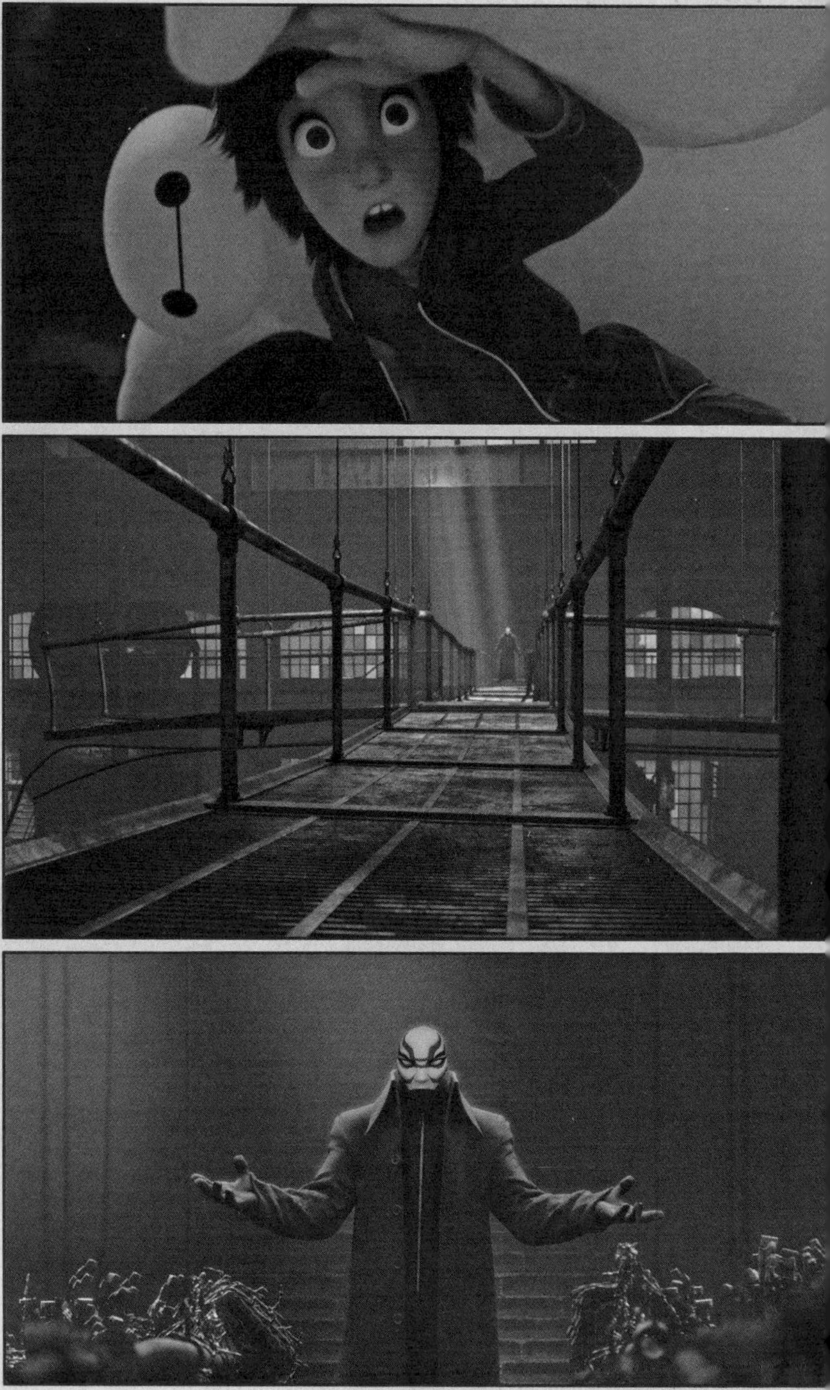

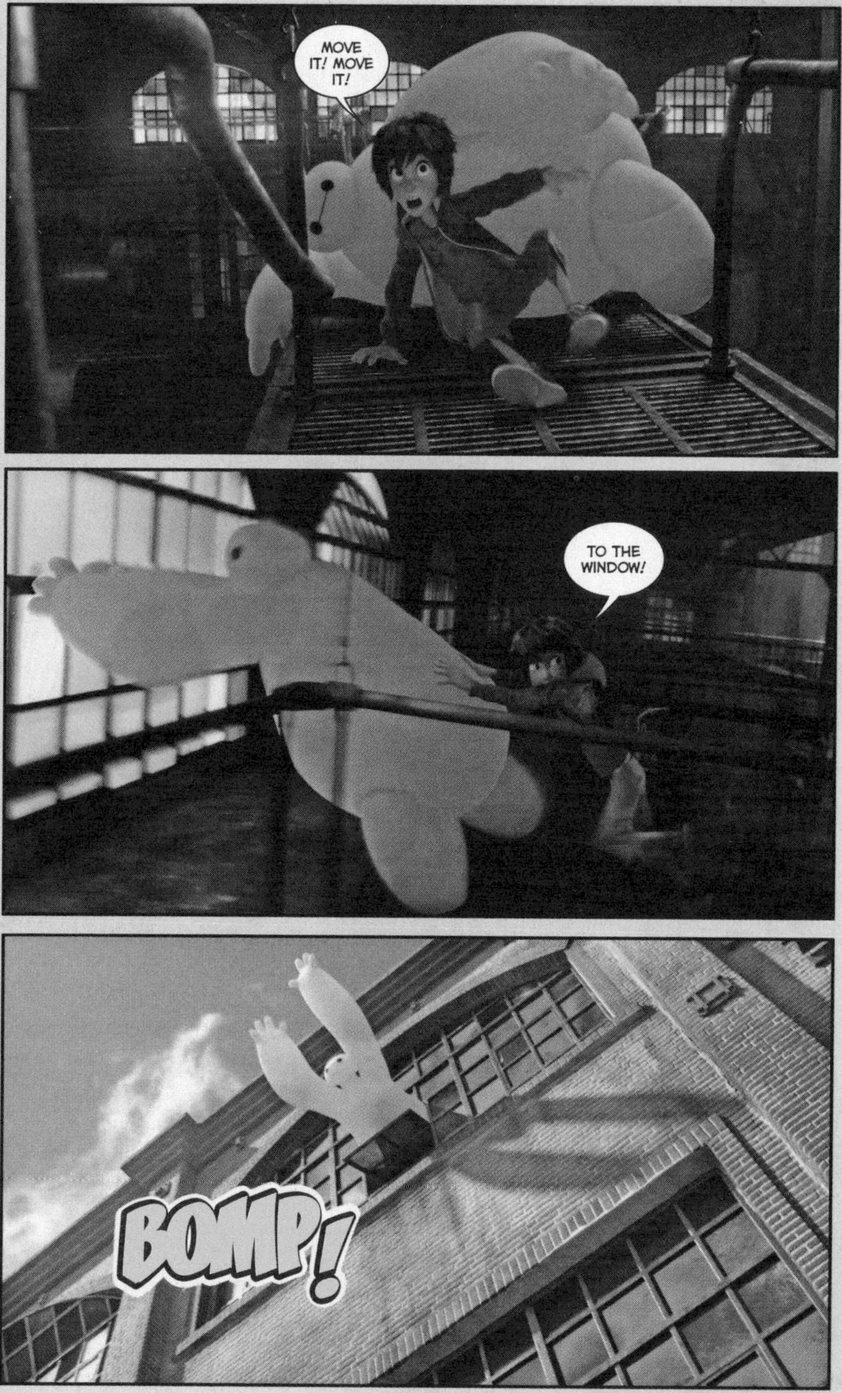
MOVE IT! MOVE IT!
TO THE WINDOW!
BOMP!

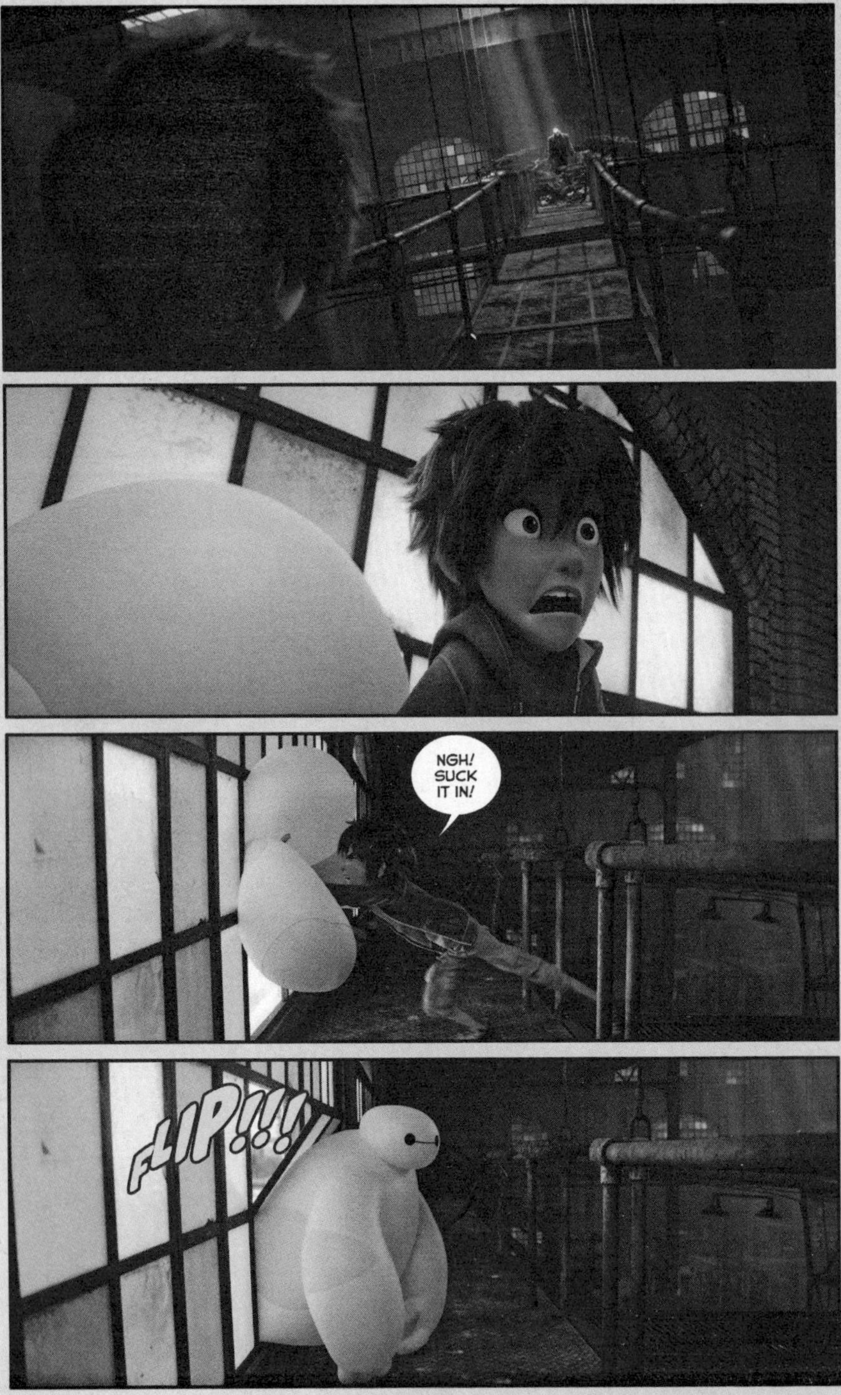
NGH! SUCK IT IN!
FLIP!!!

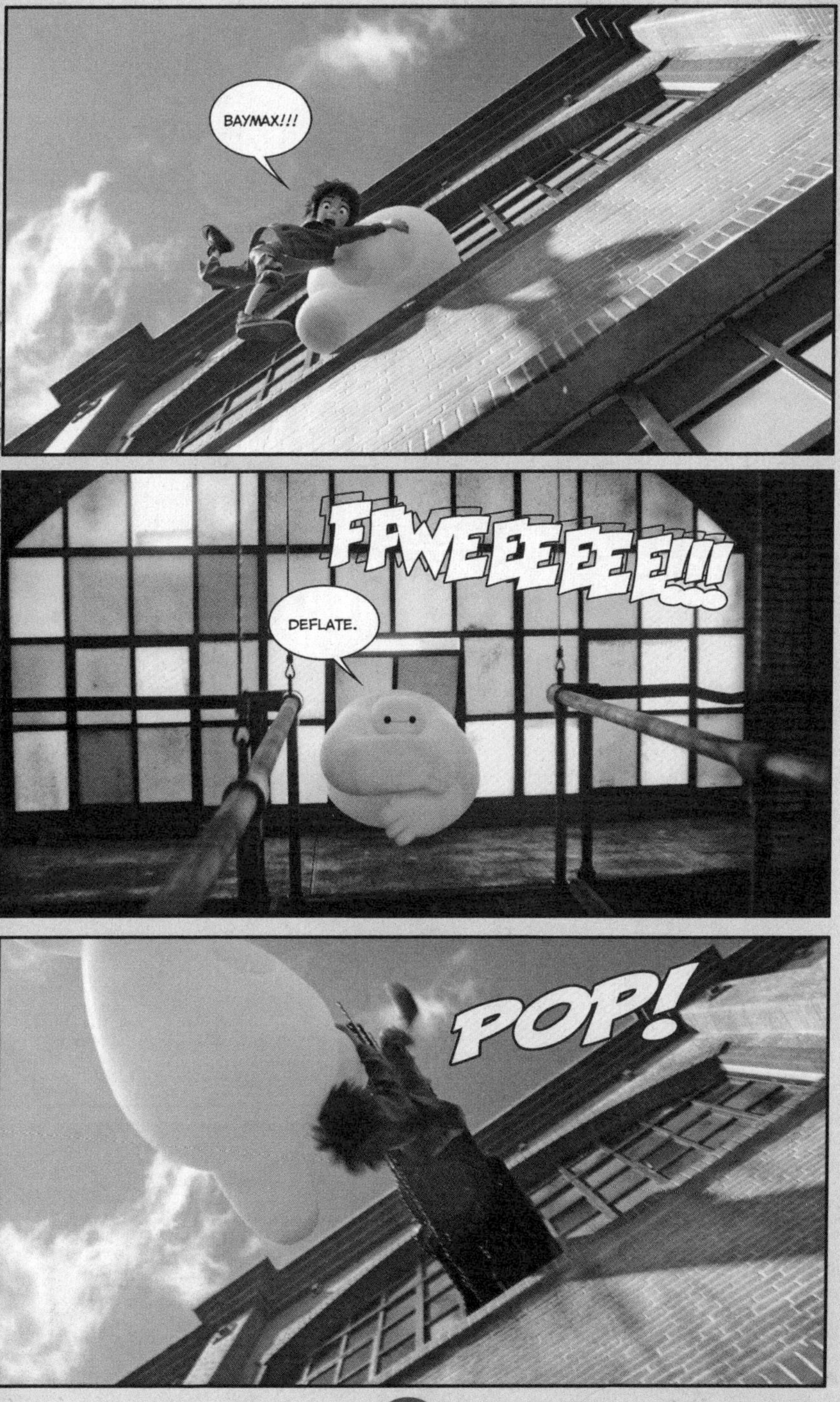
BAYMAX!!!
FFWEEEEEE!!!
DEFLATE.
POP!

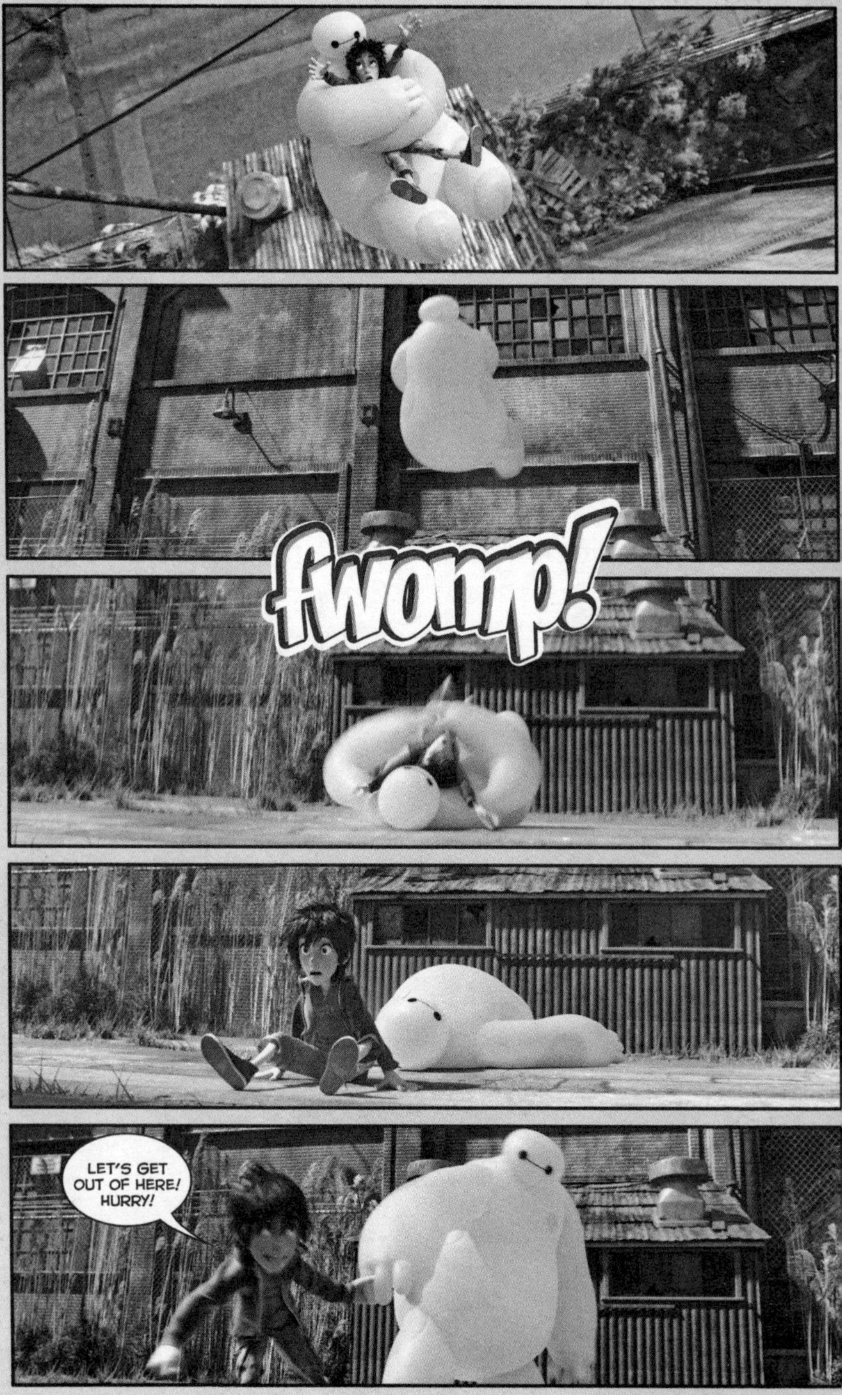
fwomp!
LET'S GET OUT OF HERE! HURRY!

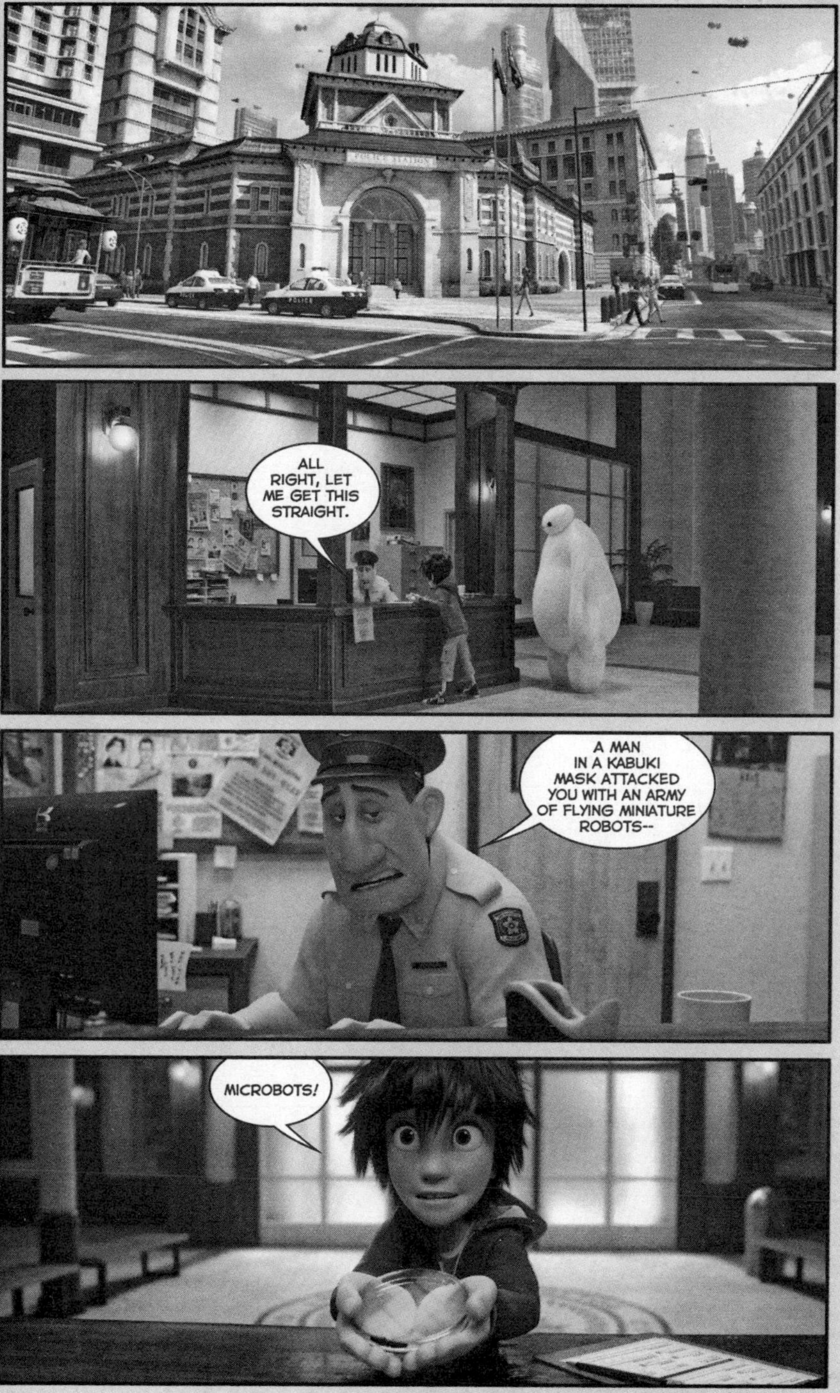
POLICE STATION
ALL RIGHT, LET ME GET THIS STRAIGHT.
A MAN IN A KABUKI MASK ATTACKED YOU WITH AN ARMY OF FLYING MINIATURE ROBOTS--
MICROBOTS!

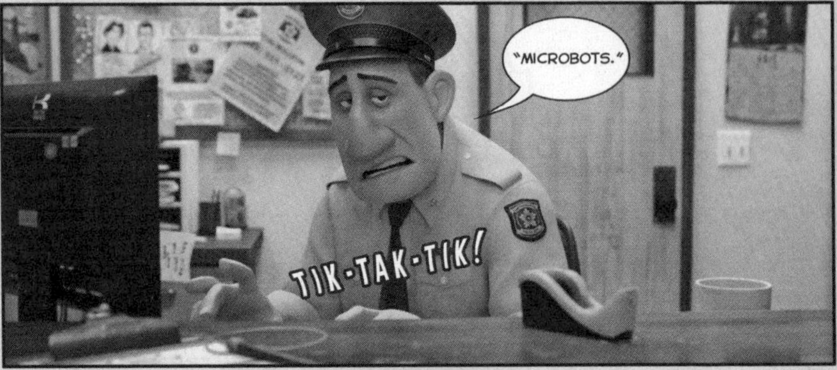
"MICROBOTS."
TIK-TAK-TIK!

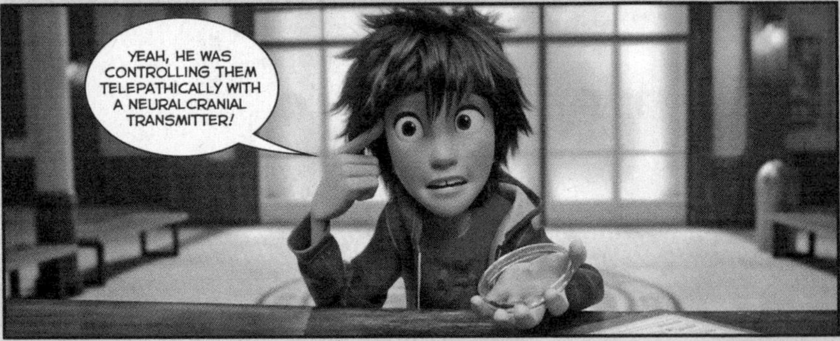
YEAH, HE WAS CONTROLLING THEM TELEPATHICALLY WITH A NEURALCRANIAL TRANSMITTER!

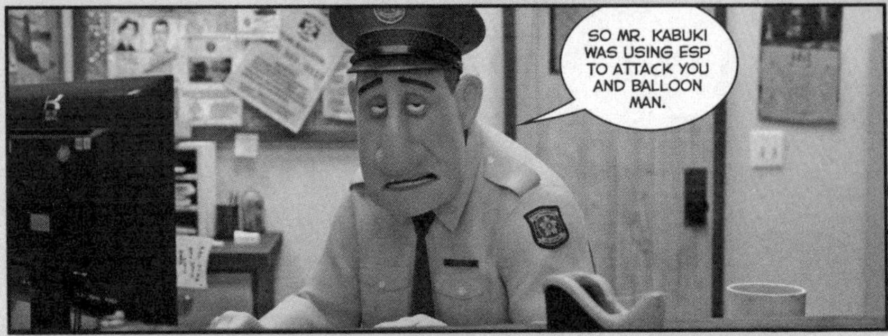
SO MR. KABUKI WAS USING ESP TO ATTACK YOU AND BALLOON MAN.

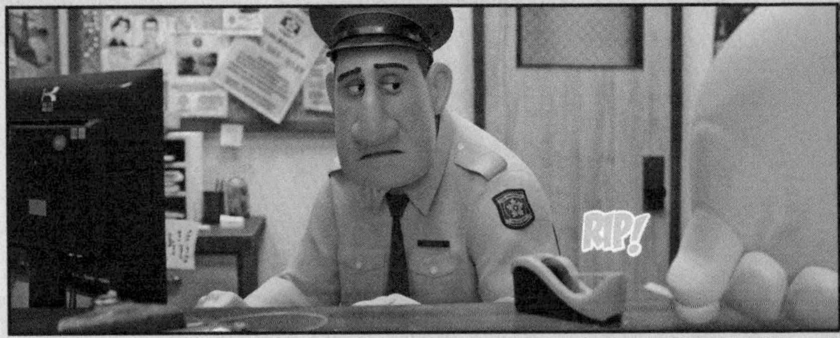
RIP!

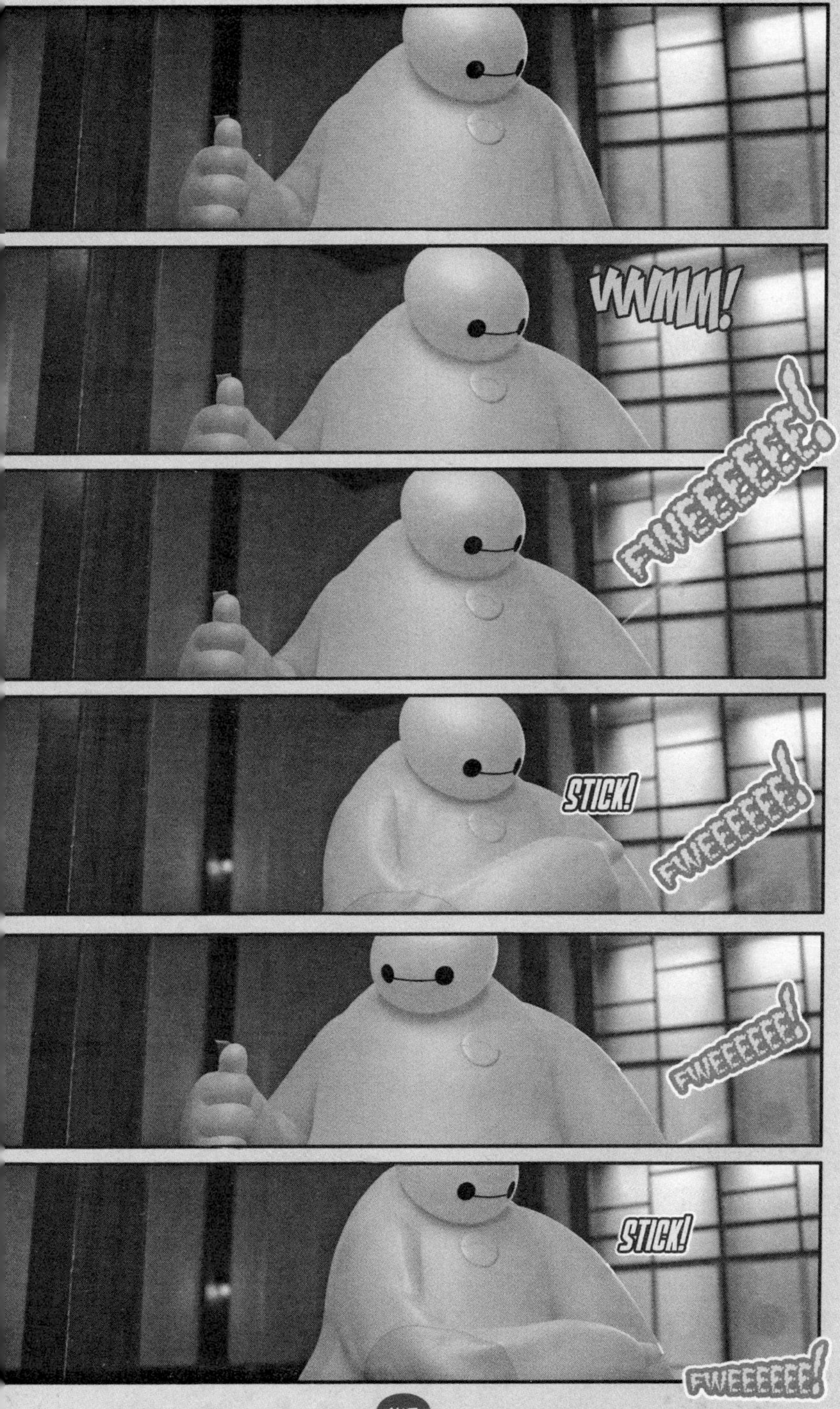
VWMM!
FWEEEEEE!
STICK!
FWEEEEEE!
FWEEEEEE!
STICK!
FWEEEEEE!

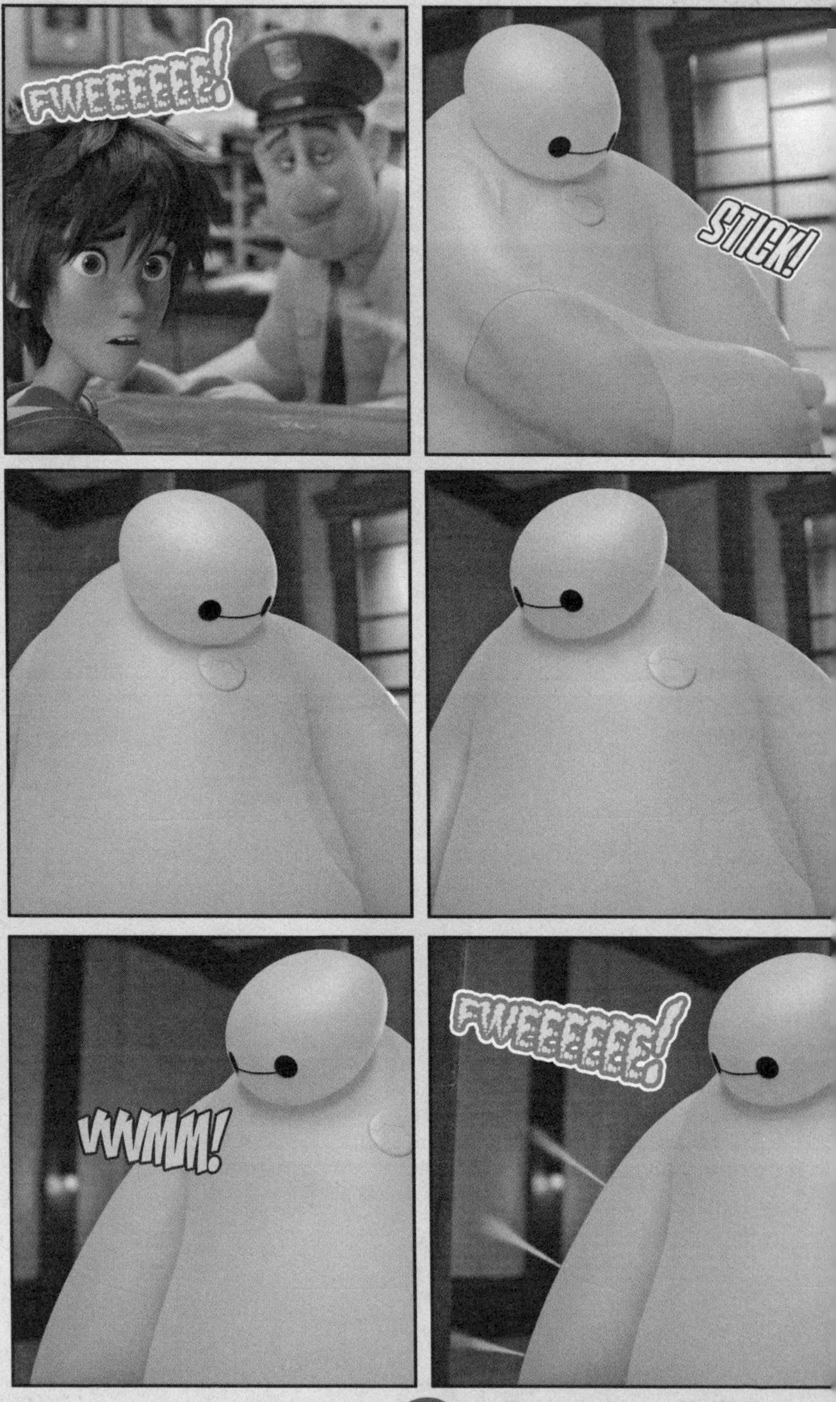
FWEEEEEE!
STICK!
VVVMM!
FWEEEEEE!

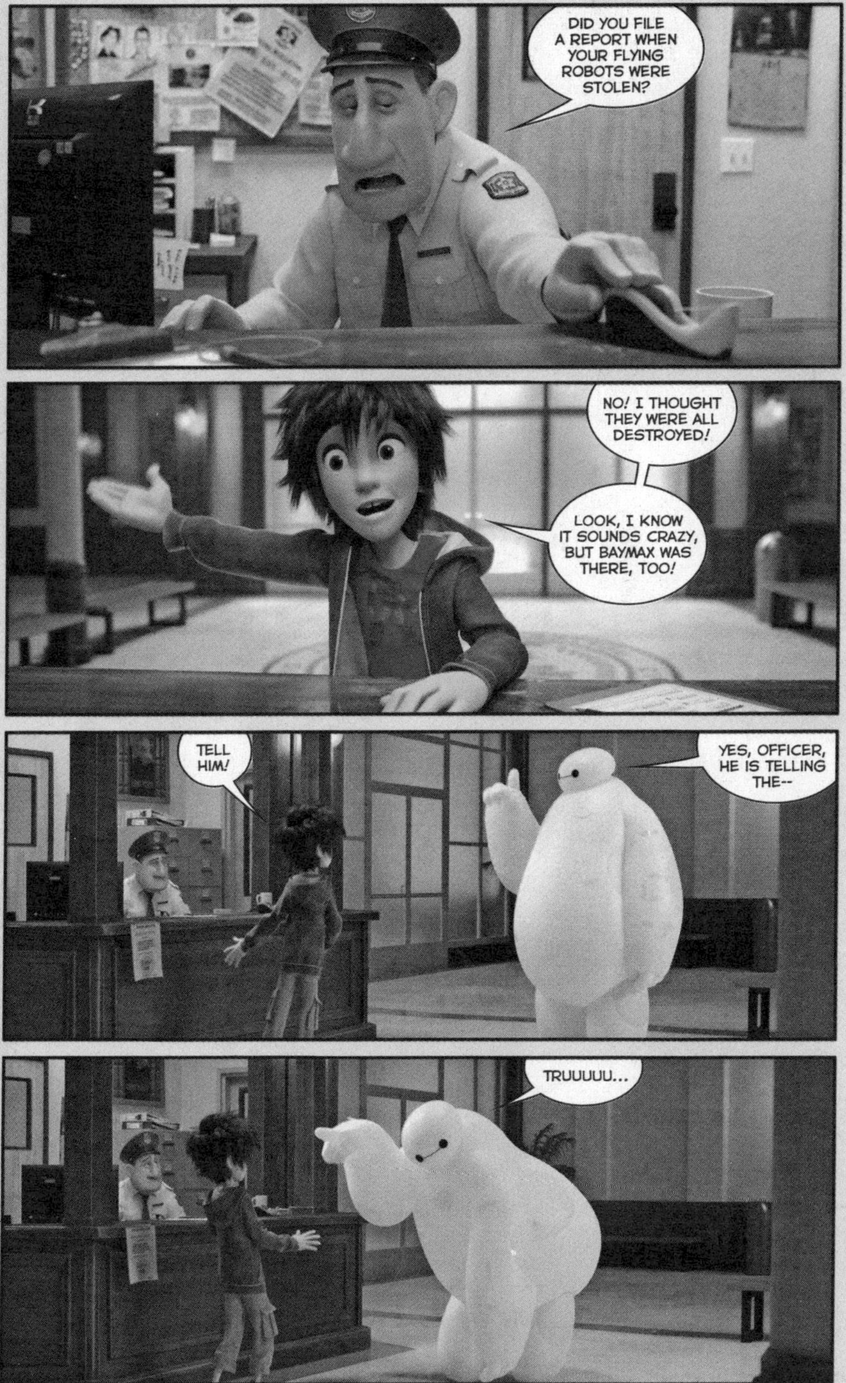
DID YOU FILE A REPORT WHEN YOUR FLYING ROBOTS WERE STOLEN?
NO! I THOUGHT THEY WERE ALL DESTROYED!
LOOK, I KNOW IT SOUNDS CRAZY, BUT BAYMAX WAS THERE, TOO!
TELL HIM!
YES, OFFICER, HE IS TELLING THE--
TRUUUUU...

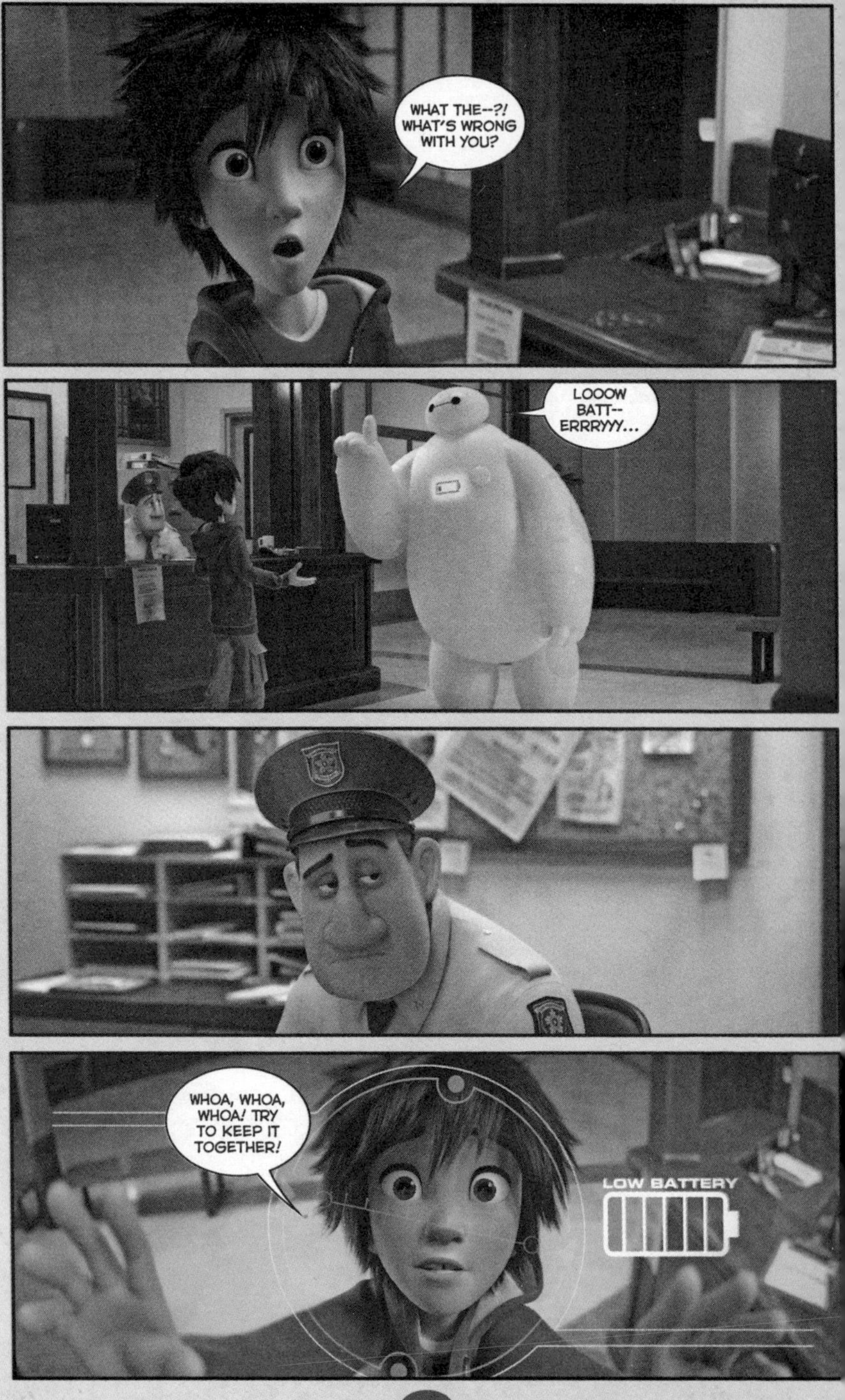
WHAT THE--?! WHAT'S WRONG WITH YOU?
LOOOW BATT-- ERRRYYY...
WHOA, WHOA, WHOA! TRY TO KEEP IT TOGETHER!
LOW BATTERY

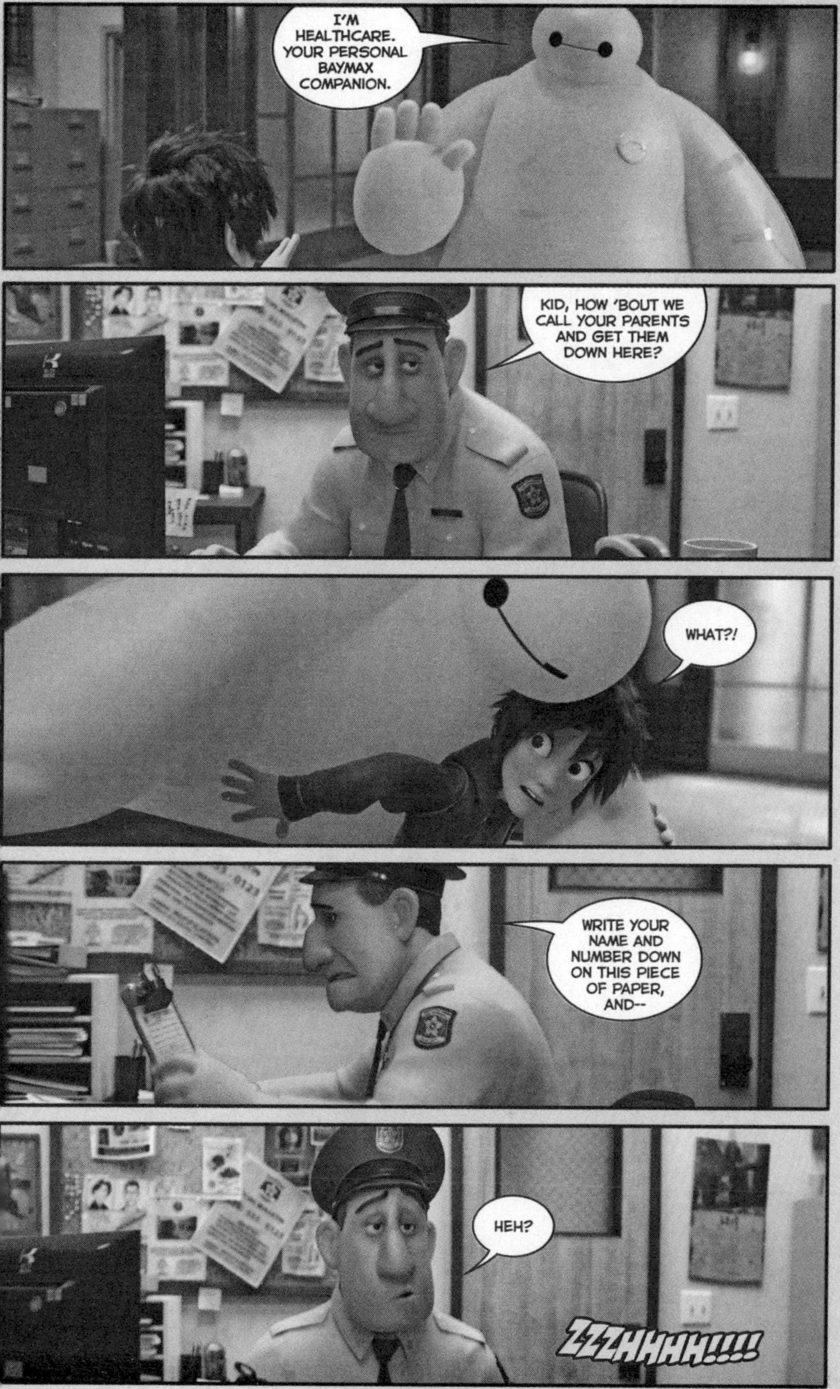
I'M HEALTHCARE. YOUR PERSONAL BAYMAX COMPANION.
KID, HOW 'BOUT WE CALL YOUR PARENTS AND GET THEM DOWN HERE?
WHAT?!
WRITE YOUR NAME AND NUMBER DOWN ON THIS PIECE OF PAPER, AND--
HEH?
ZZZHHHH!!!!

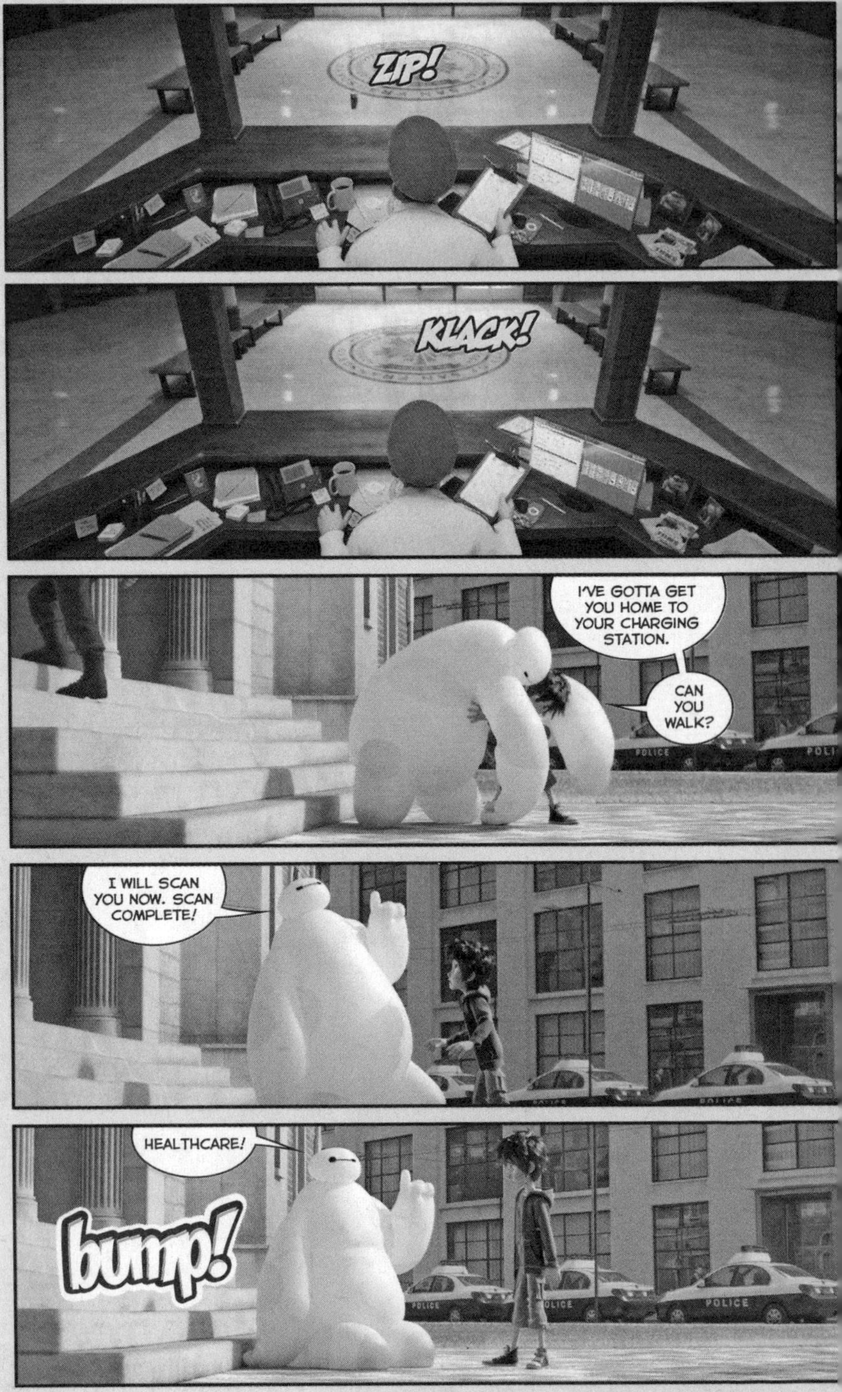
ZIP!
KLACK!
I'VE GOTTA GET YOU HOME TO YOUR CHARGING STATION.
CAN YOU WALK?
POLICE
I WILL SCAN YOU NOW. SCAN COMPLETE!
HEALTHCARE!
bump!
POLICE

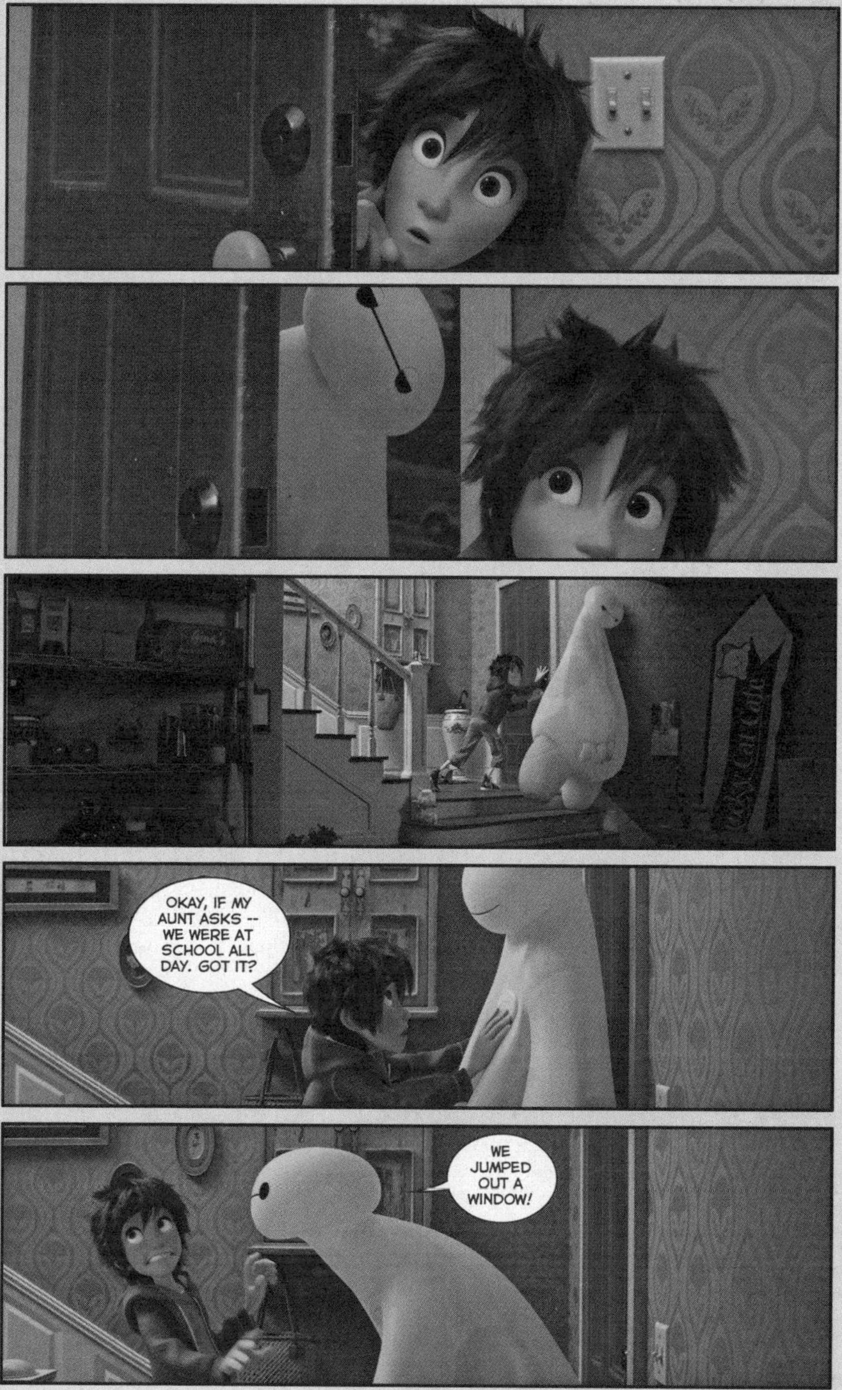
OKAY, IF MY AUNT ASKS -- WE WERE AT SCHOOL ALL DAY. GOT IT?
WE JUMPED OUT A WINDOW!

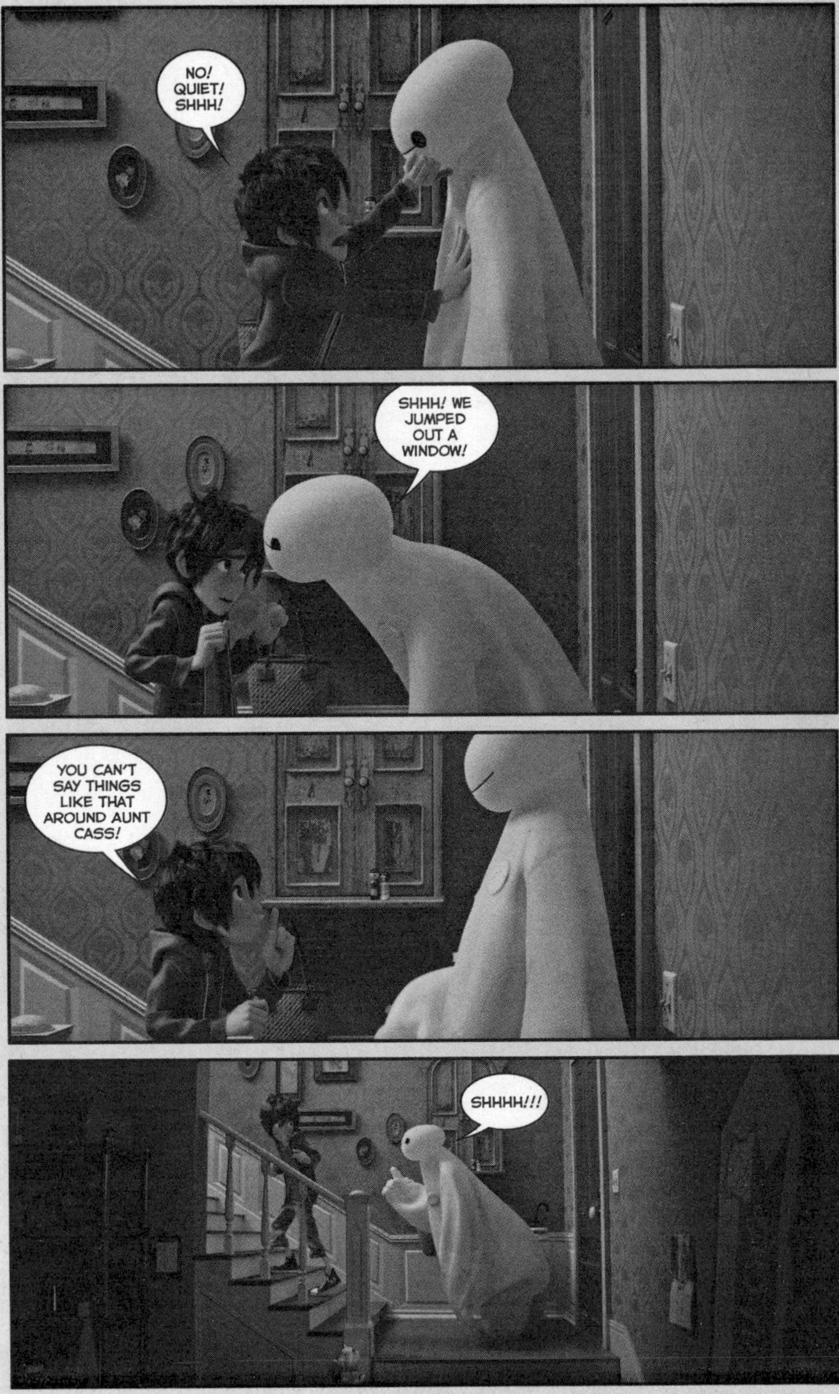
NO! QUIET! SHHH!
SHHH! WE JUMPED OUT A WINDOW!
YOU CAN'T SAY THINGS LIKE THAT AROUND AUNT CASS!
SHHHH!!!

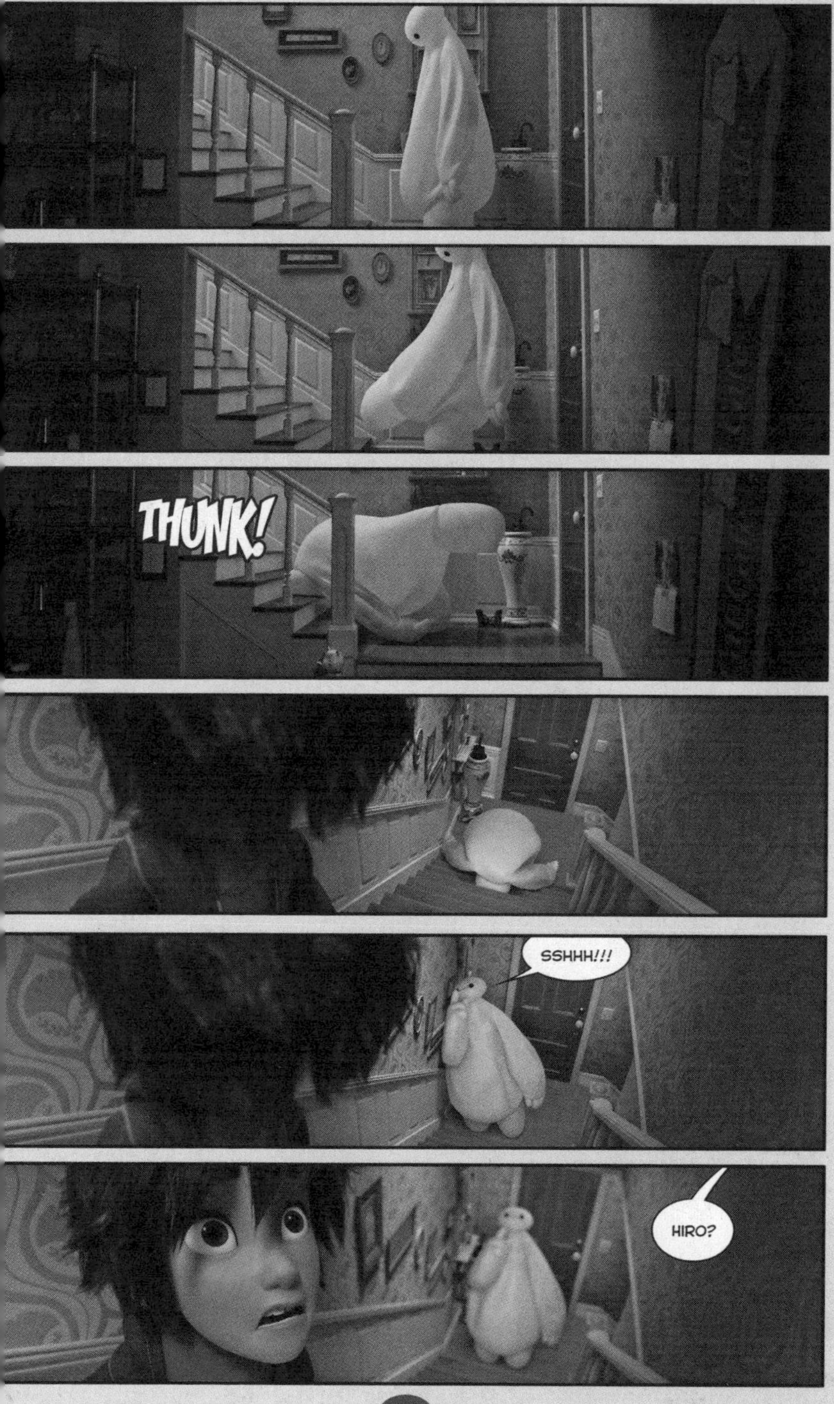
THUNK!
SSHHH!!!
HIRO?

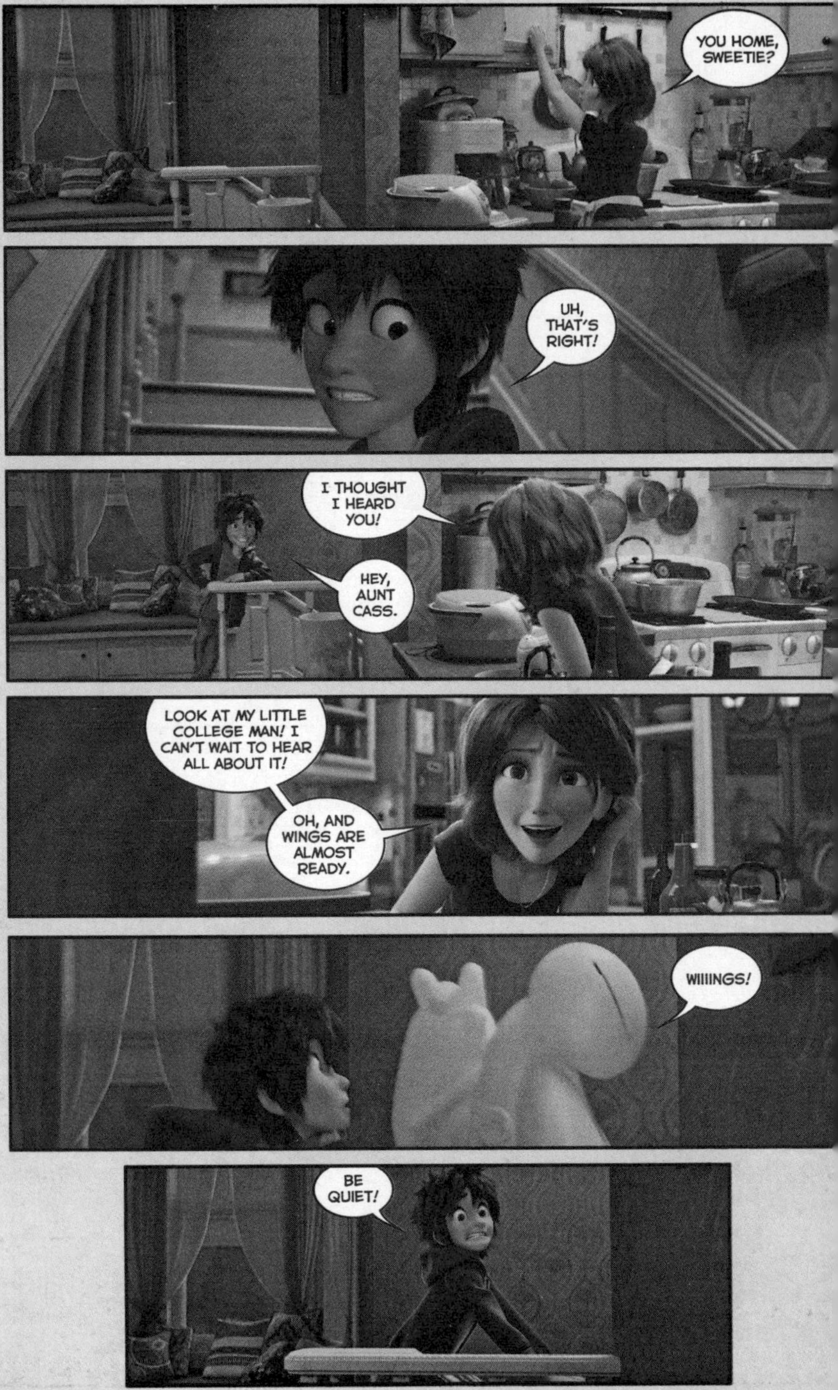
YOU HOME, SWEETIE?
UH, THAT'S RIGHT!
I THOUGHT I HEARD YOU!
HEY, AUNT CASS.
LOOK AT MY LITTLE COLLEGE MAN! I CAN'T WAIT TO HEAR ALL ABOUT IT!
OH, AND WINGS ARE ALMOST READY.
WIIIINGS!
BE QUIET!

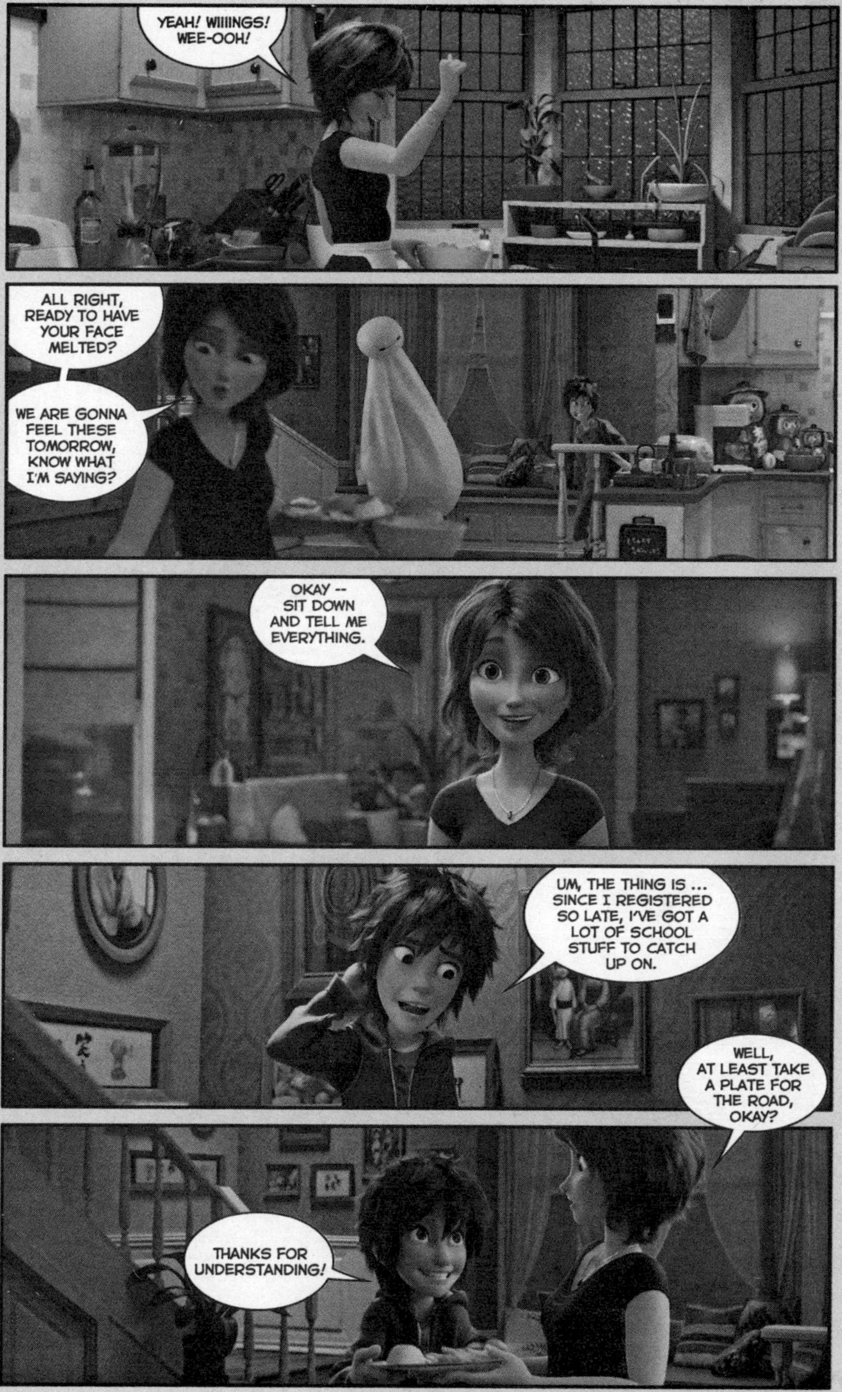
YEAH! WIIIINGS! WEE-OOH!
ALL RIGHT, READY TO HAVE YOUR FACE MELTED?
WE ARE GONNA FEEL THESE TOMORROW, KNOW WHAT I'M SAYING?
OKAY -- SIT DOWN AND TELL ME EVERYTHING.
UM, THE THING IS ... SINCE I REGISTERED SO LATE, I'VE GOT A LOT OF SCHOOL STUFF TO CATCH UP ON.
WELL, AT LEAST TAKE A PLATE FOR THE ROAD, OKAY?
THANKS FOR UNDERSTANDING!

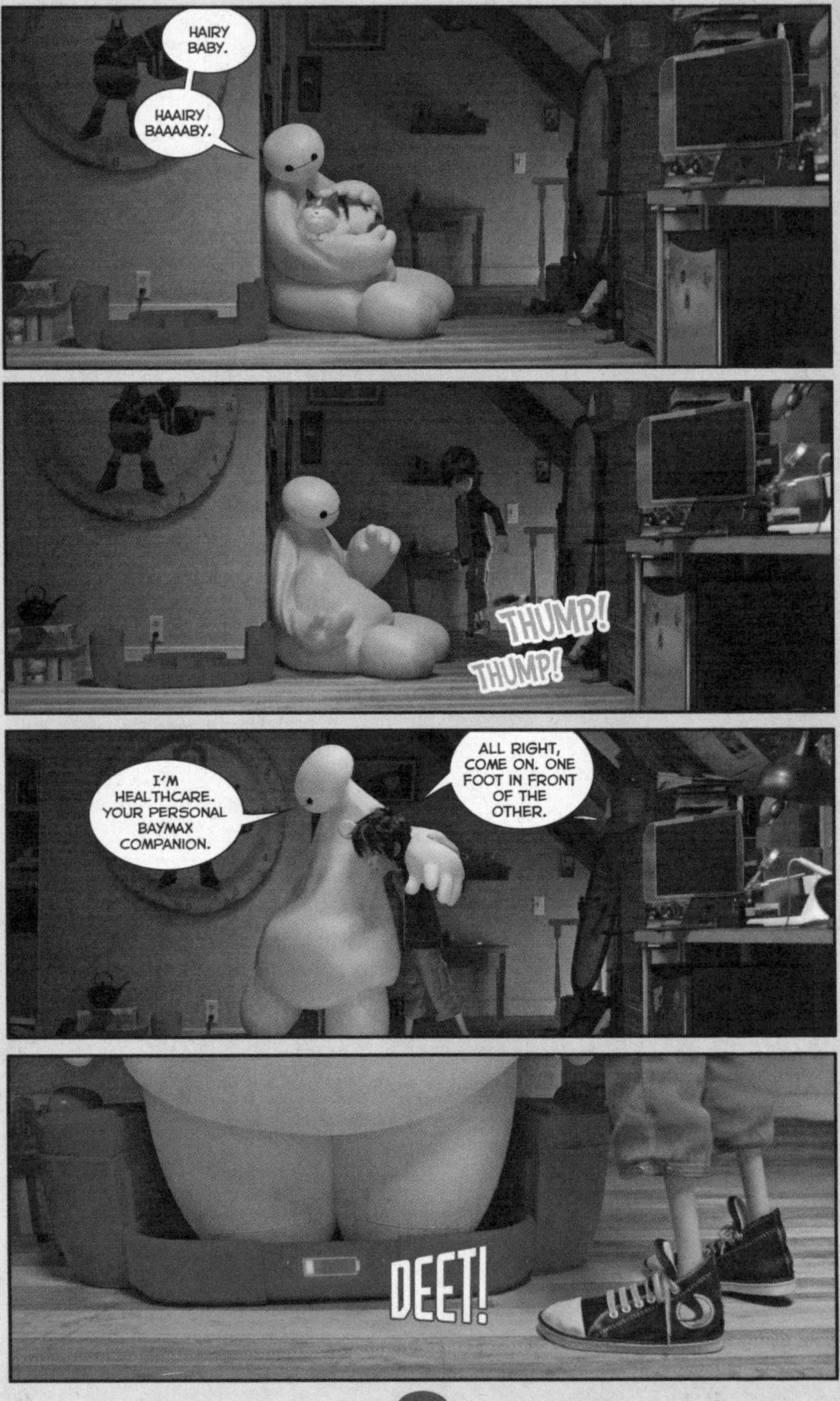
HAIRY BABY.
HAAIRY BAAAABY.
THUMP! THUMP!
I'M HEALTHCARE. YOUR PERSONAL BAYMAX COMPANION.
ALL RIGHT, COME ON. ONE FOOT IN FRONT OF THE OTHER.
DEET!

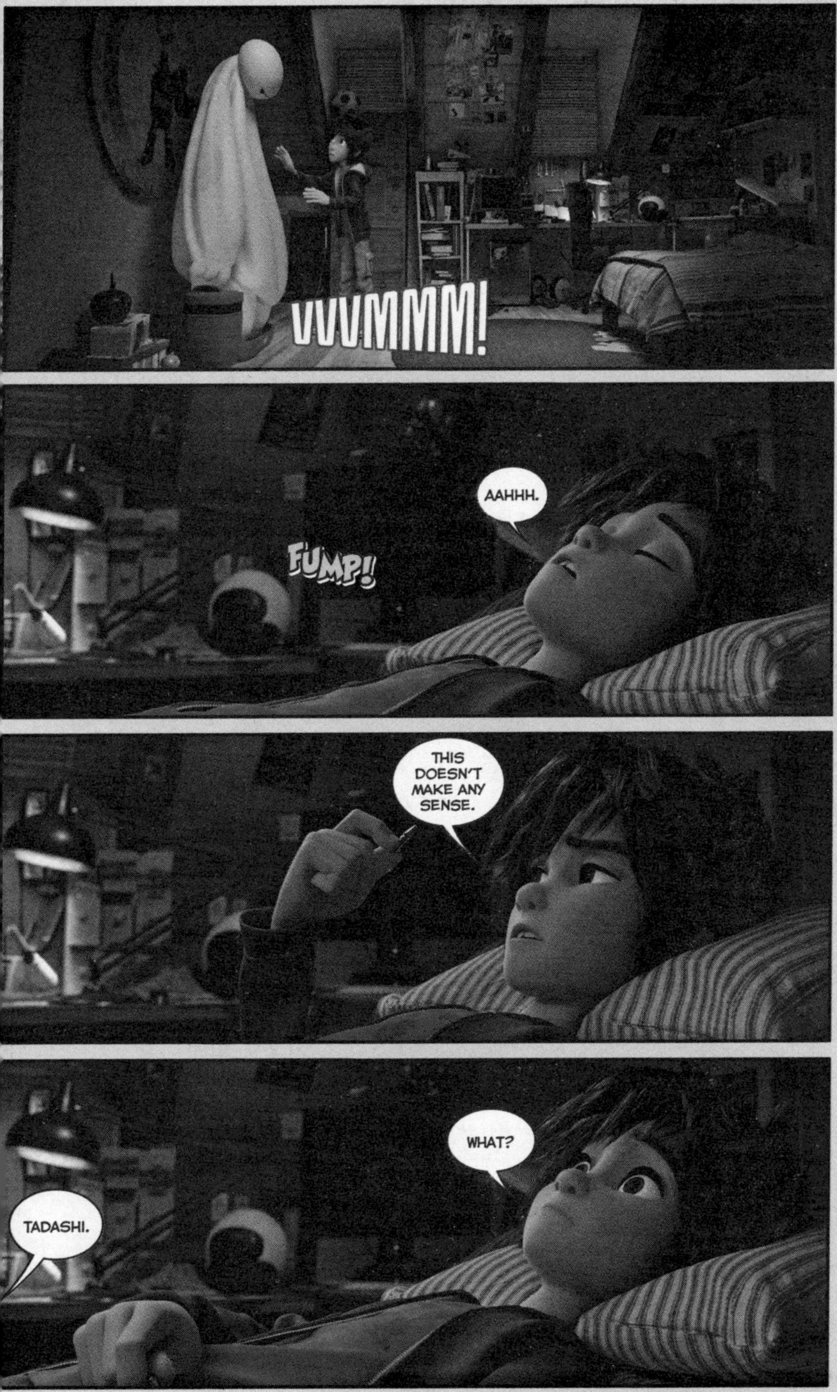
VVVMMM!
AAHHH.
FUMP!
THIS DOESN'T MAKE ANY SENSE.
TADASHI.
WHAT?

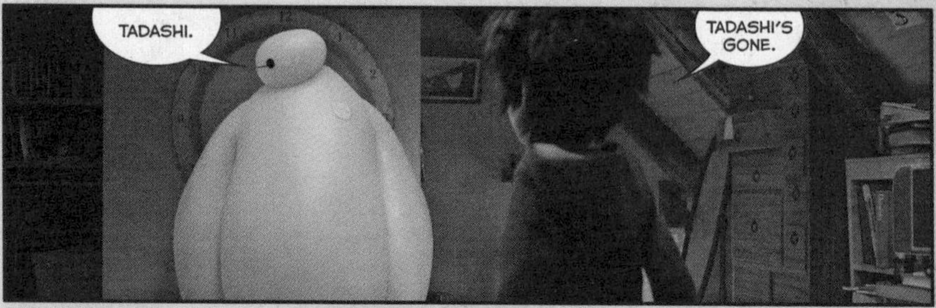
TADASHI.
TADASHI'S GONE.

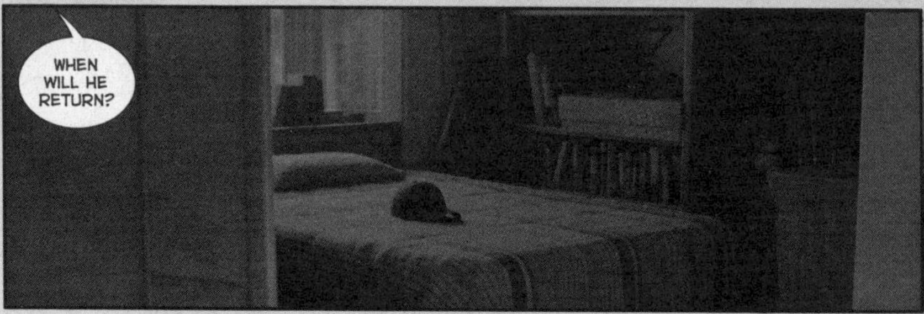
WHEN WILL HE RETURN?

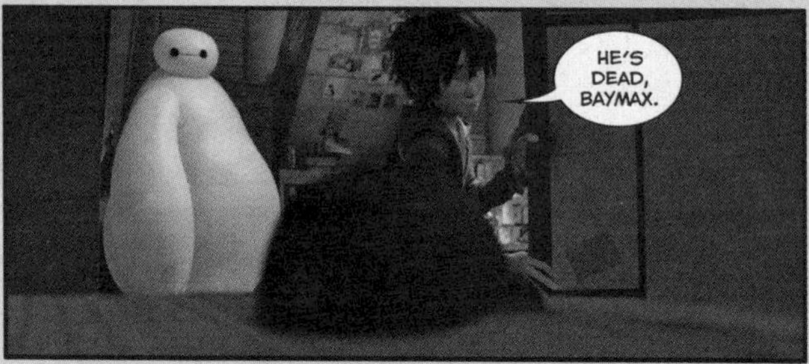
HE'S DEAD, BAYMAX.

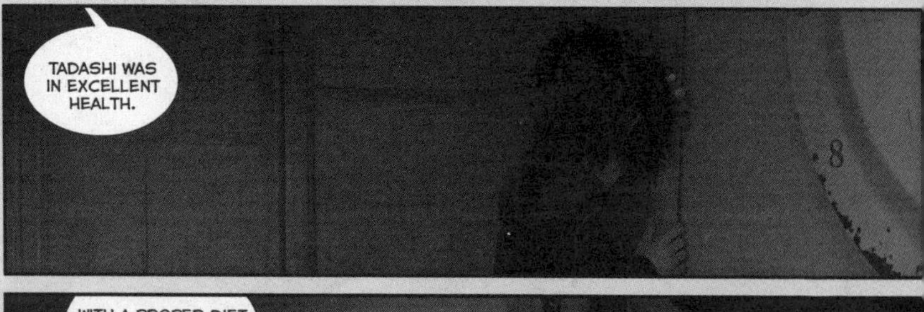
TADASHI WAS IN EXCELLENT HEALTH.

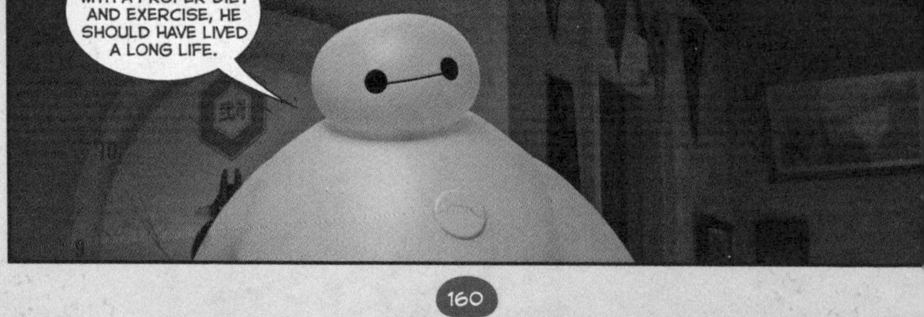
WITH A PROPER DIET AND EXERCISE, HE SHOULD HAVE LIVED A LONG LIFE.

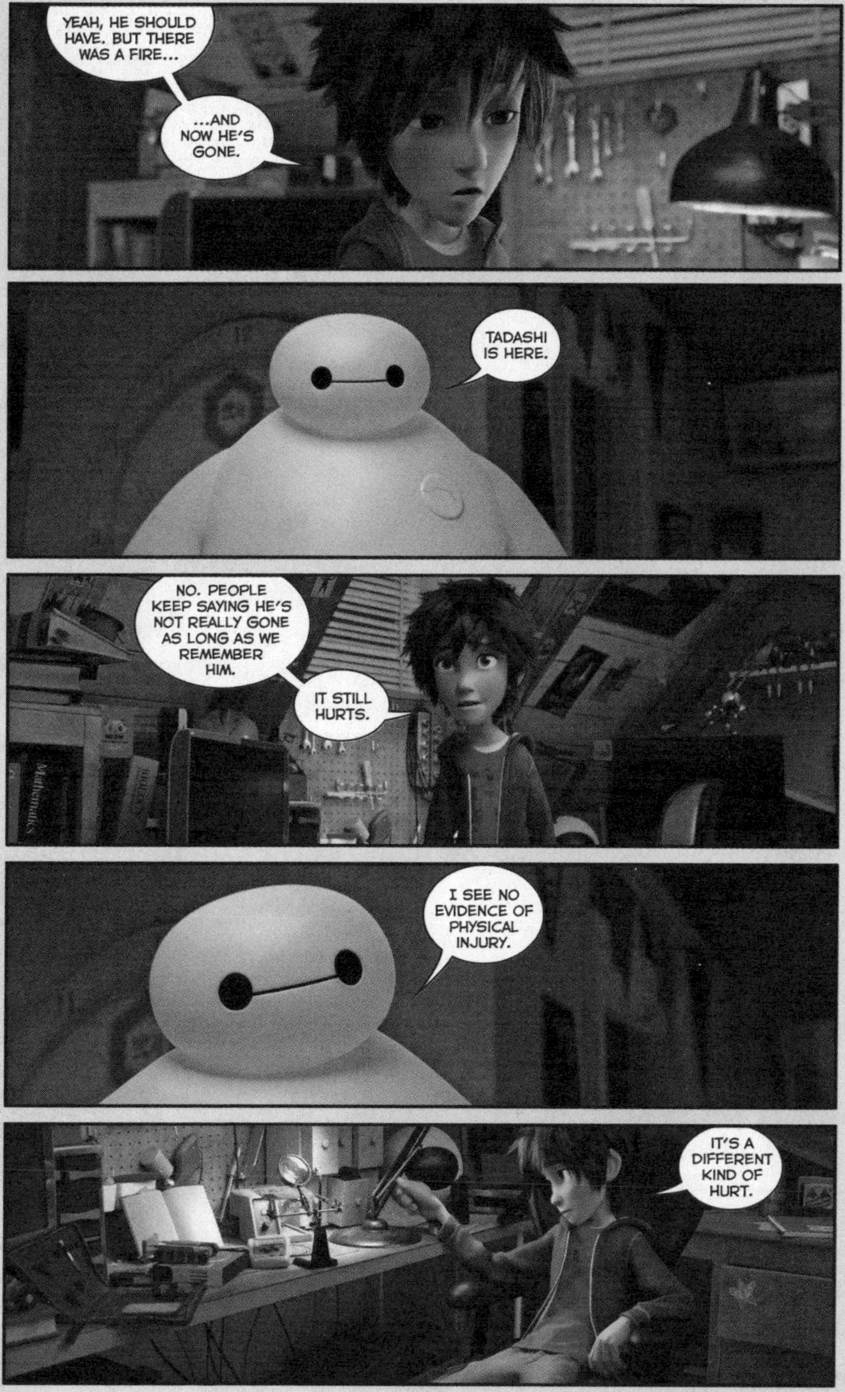
YEAH, HE SHOULD HAVE. BUT THERE WAS A FIRE...
...AND NOW HE'S GONE.
TADASHI IS HERE.
NO. PEOPLE KEEP SAYING HE'S NOT REALLY GONE AS LONG AS WE REMEMBER HIM.
IT STILL HURTS.
I SEE NO EVIDENCE OF PHYSICAL INJURY.
IT'S A DIFFERENT KIND OF HURT.

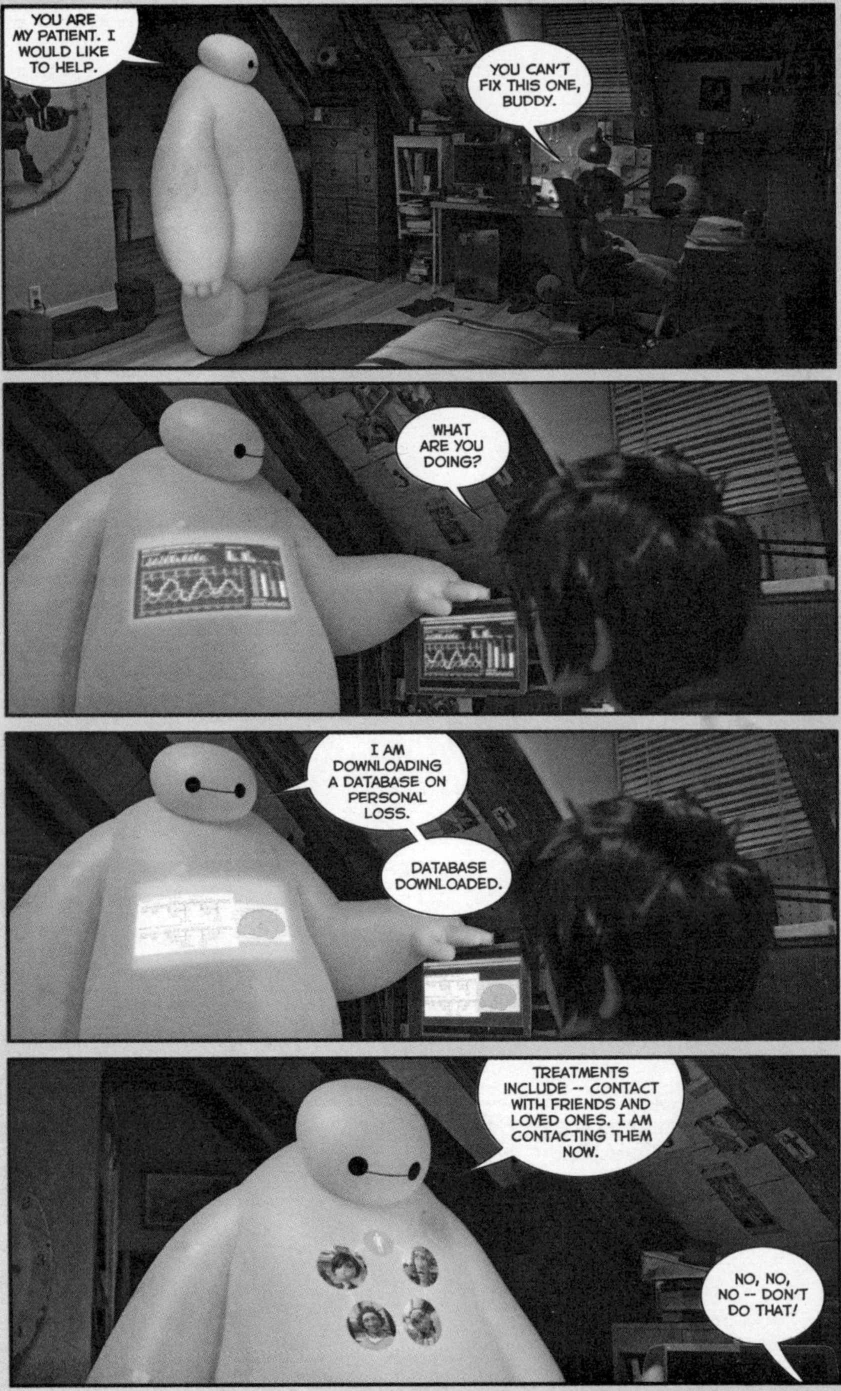
YOU ARE MY PATIENT. I WOULD LIKE TO HELP.
YOU CAN'T FIX THIS ONE, BUDDY.
WHAT ARE YOU DOING?
I AM DOWNLOADING A DATABASE ON PERSONAL LOSS.
DATABASE DOWNLOADED.
TREATMENTS INCLUDE -- CONTACT WITH FRIENDS AND LOVED ONES. I AM CONTACTING THEM NOW.
NO, NO, NO -- DON'T DO THAT!

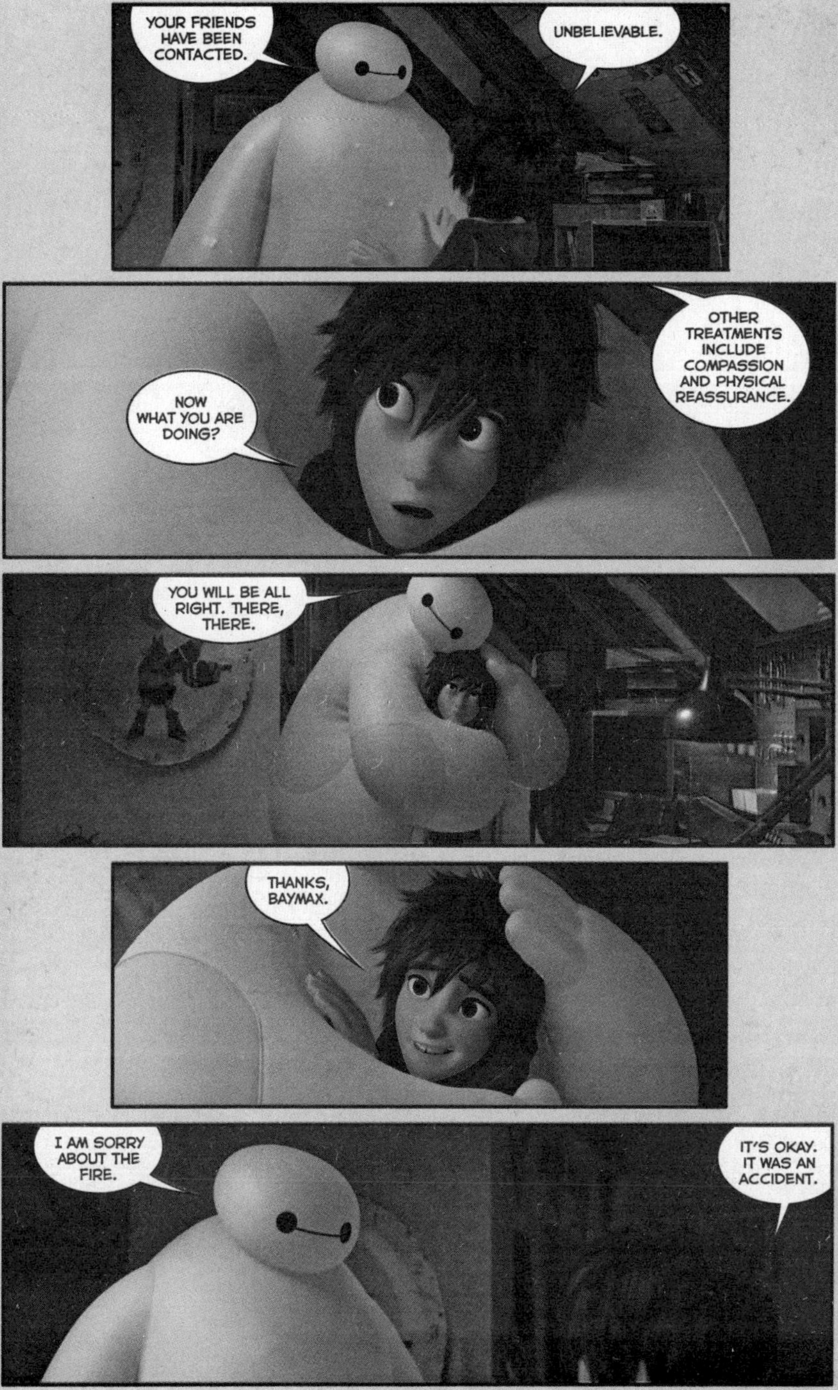
YOUR FRIENDS HAVE BEEN CONTACTED.
UNBELIEVABLE.
NOW WHAT YOU ARE DOING?
OTHER TREATMENTS INCLUDE COMPASSION AND PHYSICAL REASSURANCE.
YOU WILL BE ALL RIGHT. THERE, THERE.
THANKS, BAYMAX.
I AM SORRY ABOUT THE FIRE.
IT'S OKAY. IT WAS AN ACCIDENT.

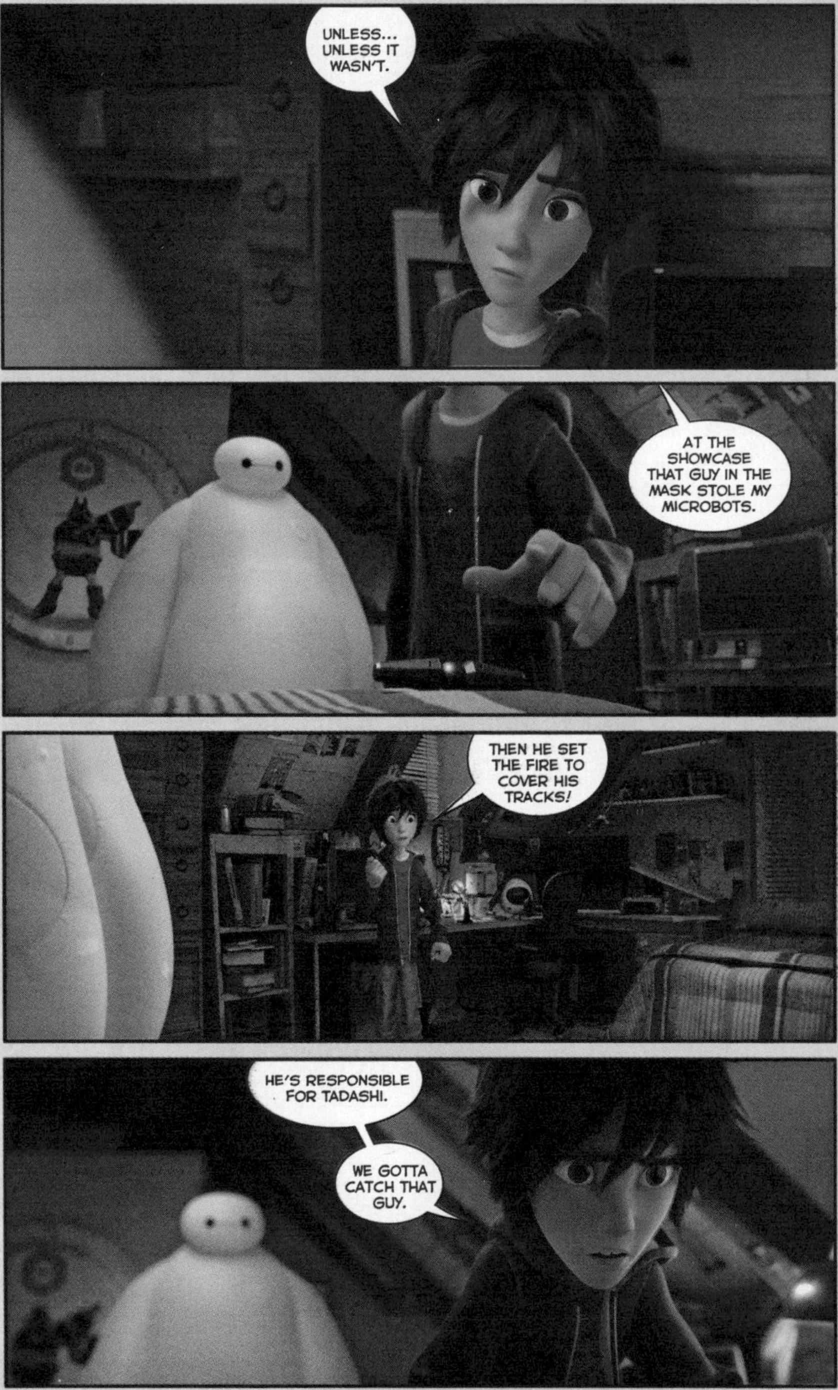
UNLESS... UNLESS IT WASN'T.
AT THE SHOWCASE THAT GUY IN THE MASK STOLE MY MICROBOTS.
THEN HE SET THE FIRE TO COVER HIS TRACKS!
HE'S RESPONSIBLE FOR TADASHI.
WE GOTTA CATCH THAT GUY.

DOWNSTAIRS IN THE GARAGE...

IF WE'RE GONNA CATCH THAT GUY, YOU'RE GONNA NEED SOME UPGRADES.

WILL APPREHENDING THE MAN IN THE MASK IMPROVE YOUR EMOTIONAL STATE?

ABSOLUTELY.

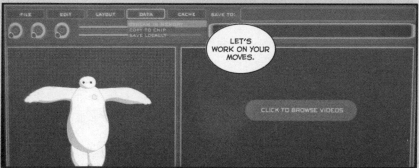

FILE   EDIT   LAYOUT   DATA   CACHE   SAVE TO:

STREAM IN BROWSER
COPY TO CHIP
SAVE LOCALLY

LET'S WORK ON YOUR MOVES.

CLICK TO BROWSE VIDEOS

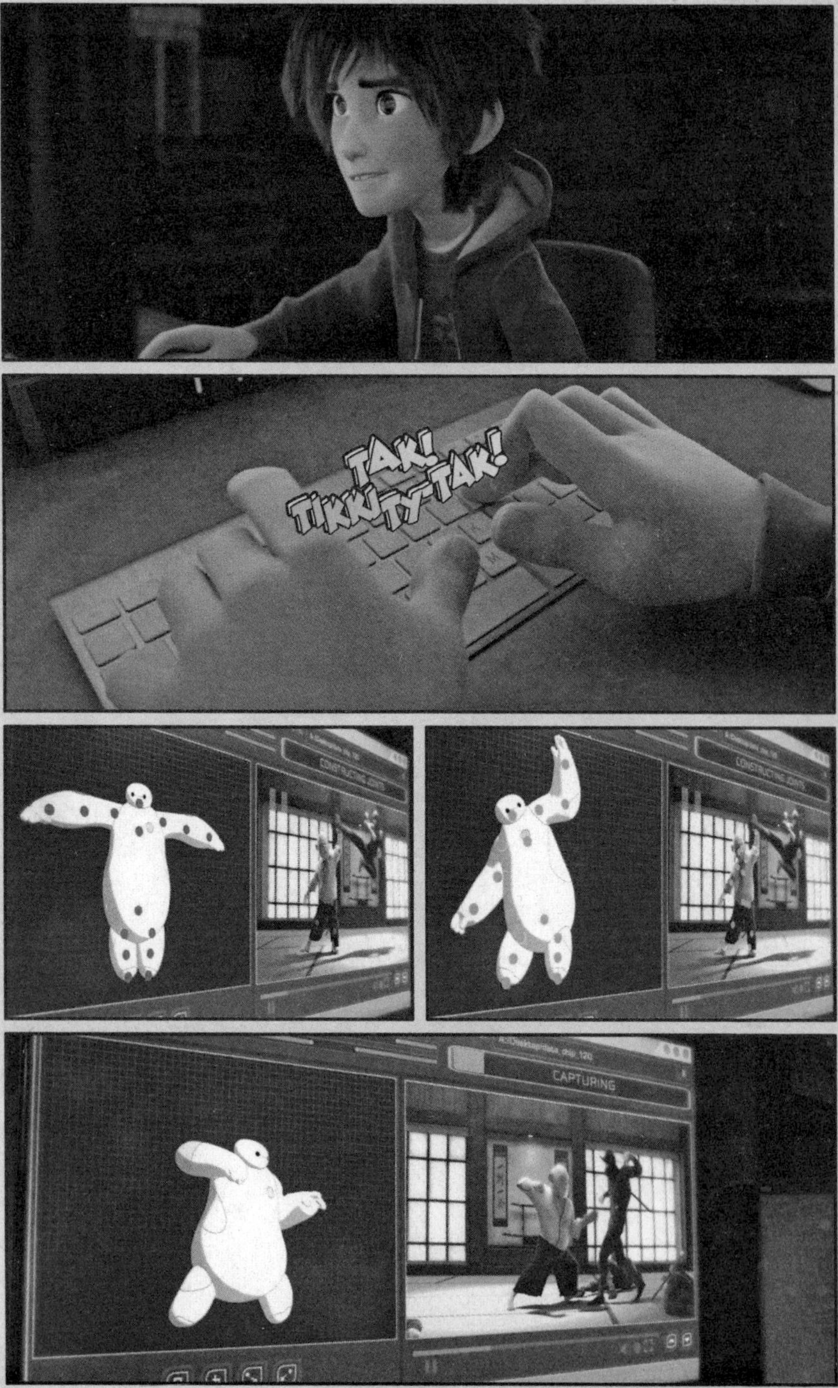
TAK!
TIKKITY-TAK!
CONSTRUCTING JOINTS
CONSTRUCTING JOINTS
CAPTURING

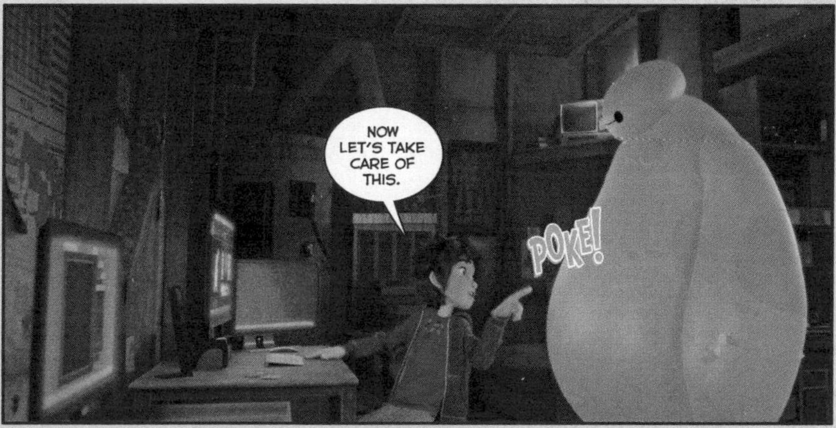
NOW LET'S TAKE CARE OF THIS.
POKE!

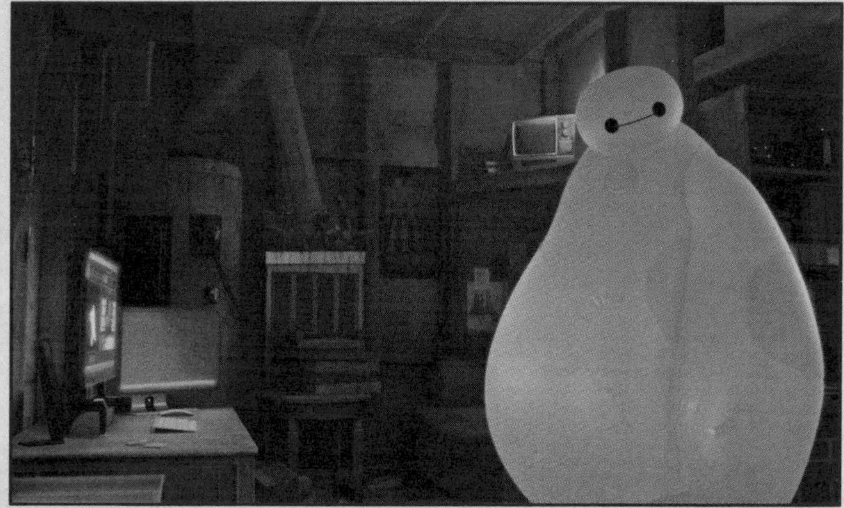

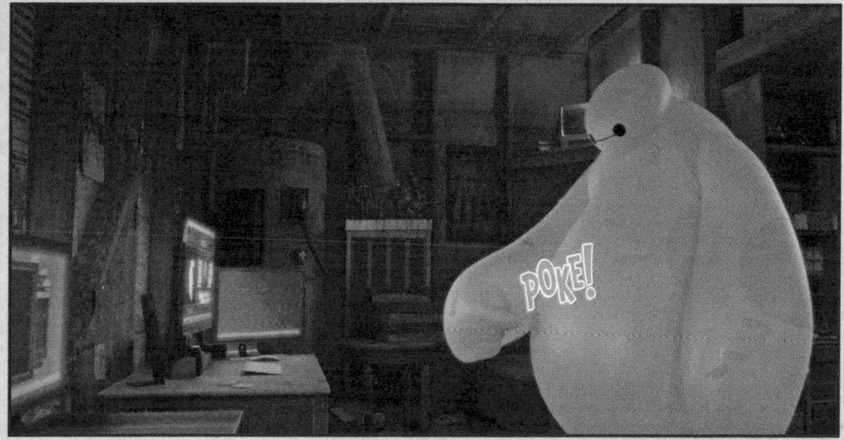
POKE!

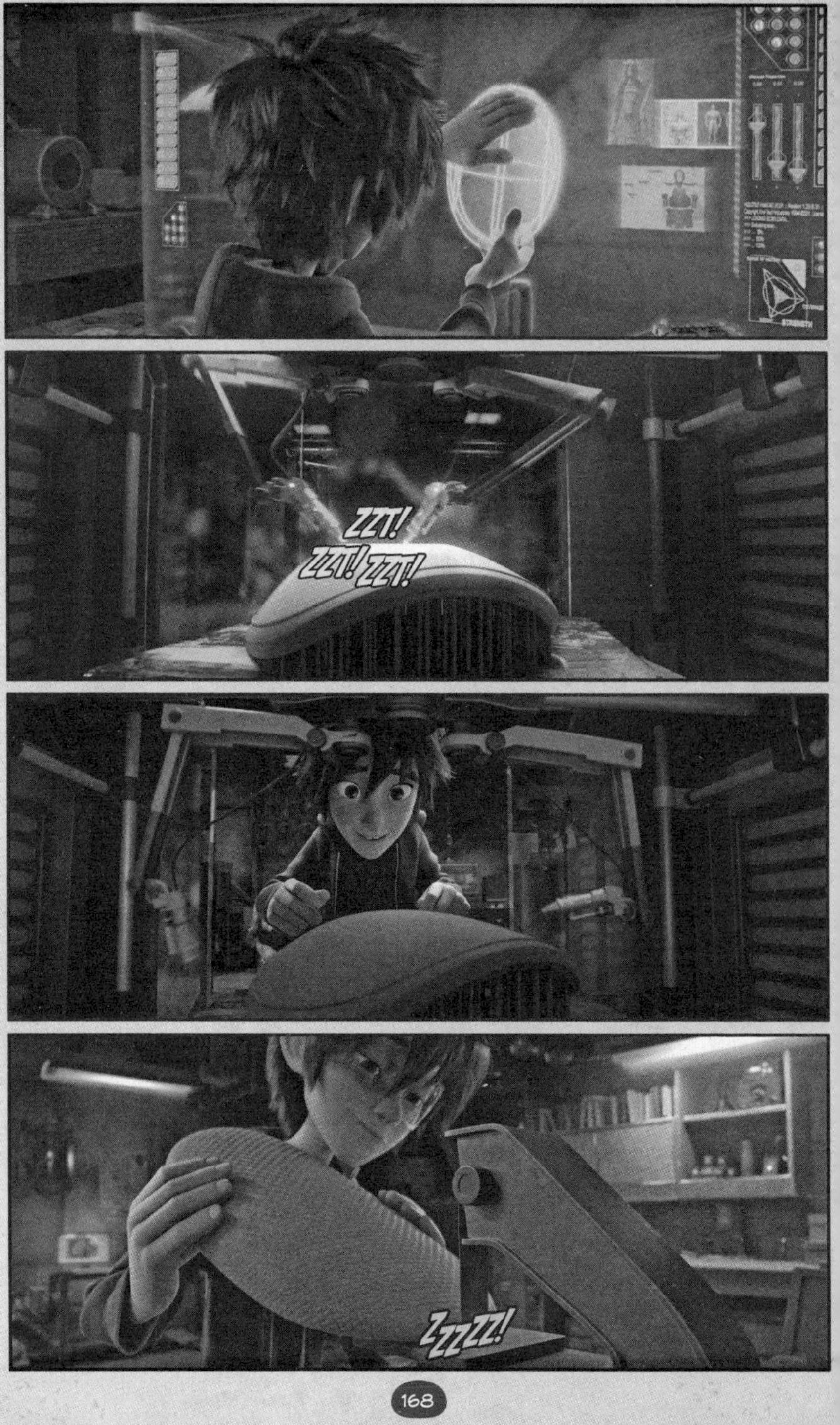
ZZT!
ZZT! ZZT!
ZZZZZ!

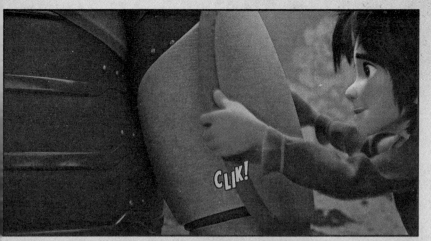

CLIK!

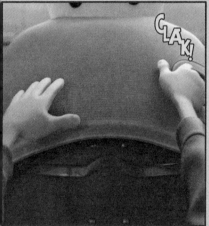

CLAK!

CLOK!

THERE...

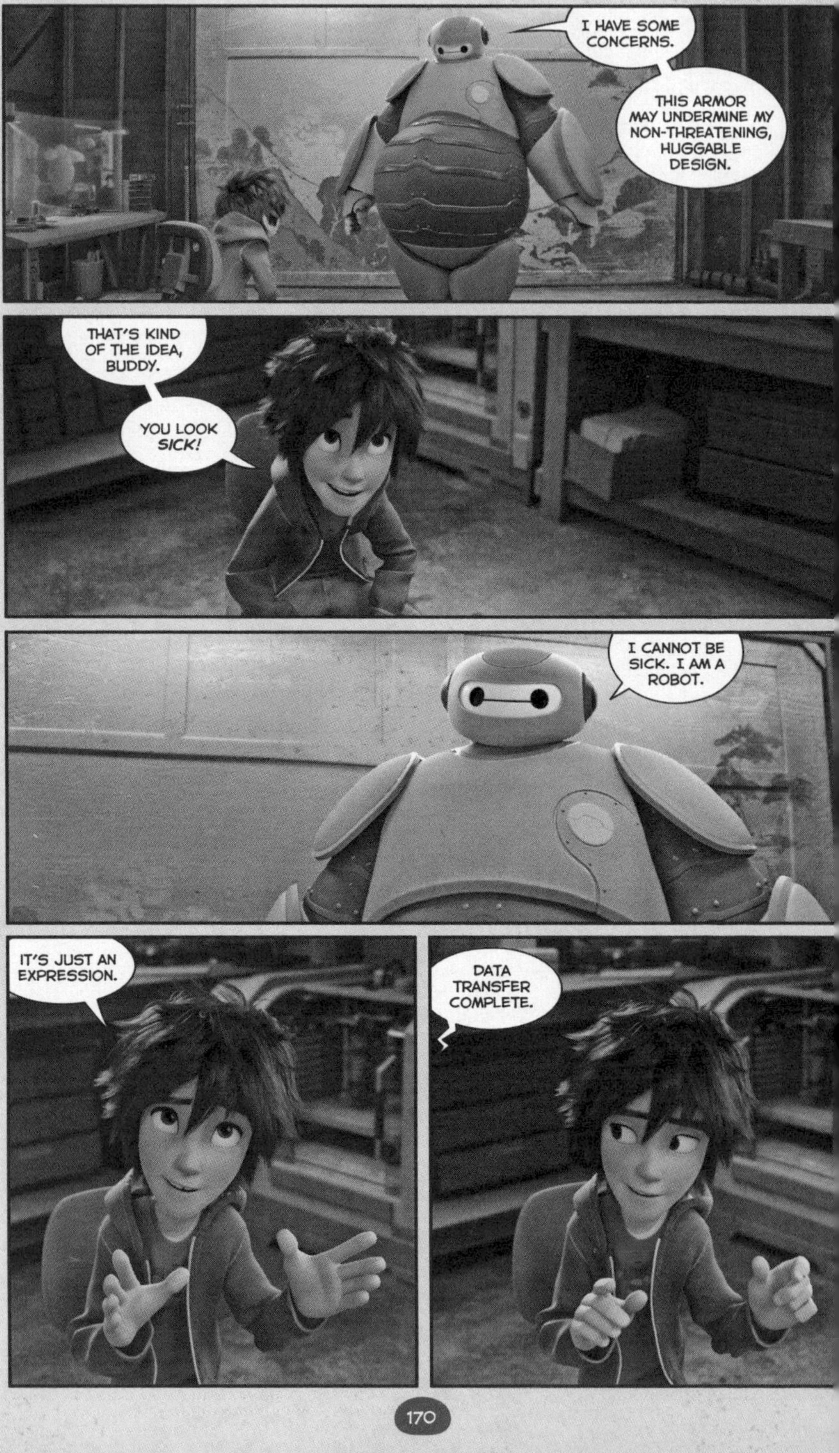
I HAVE SOME CONCERNS.
THIS ARMOR MAY UNDERMINE MY NON-THREATENING, HUGGABLE DESIGN.
THAT'S KIND OF THE IDEA, BUDDY.
YOU LOOK *SICK*!
I CANNOT BE SICK. I AM A ROBOT.
IT'S JUST AN EXPRESSION.
DATA TRANSFER COMPLETE.

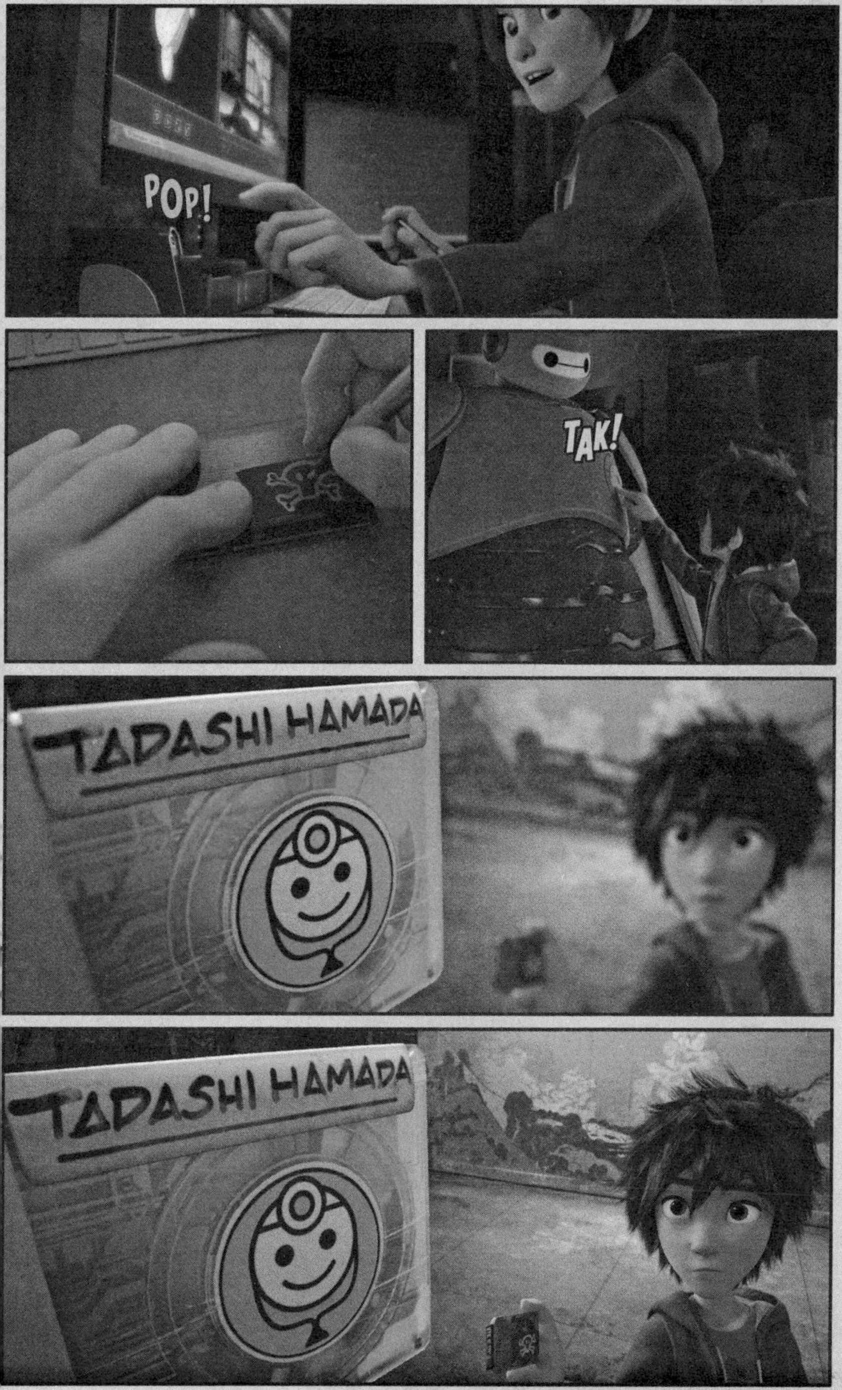
POP!
TAK!
TADASHI HAMADA
TADASHI HAMADA

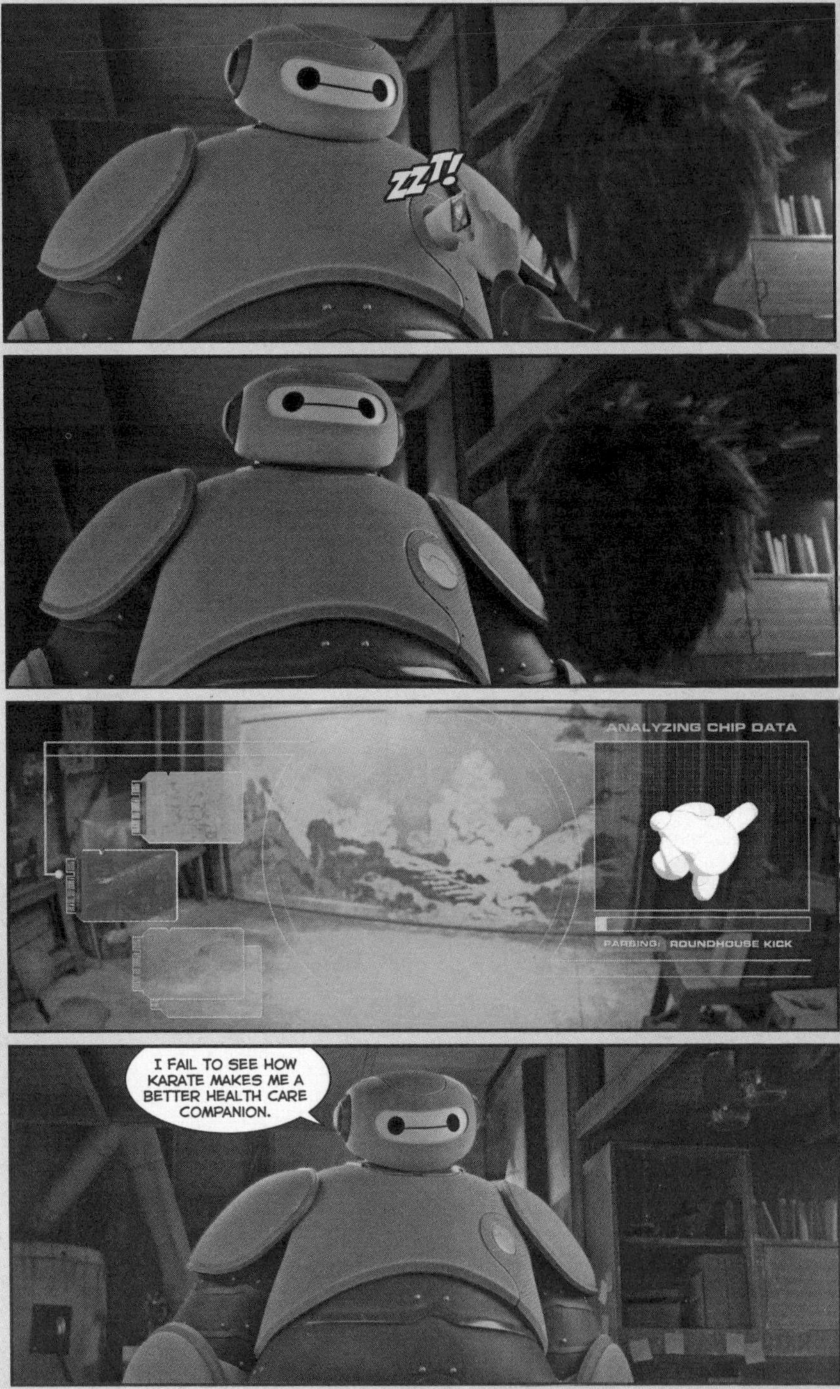
ZZT!
ANALYZING CHIP DATA
PARSING: ROUNDHOUSE KICK
I FAIL TO SEE HOW KARATE MAKES ME A BETTER HEALTH CARE COMPANION.

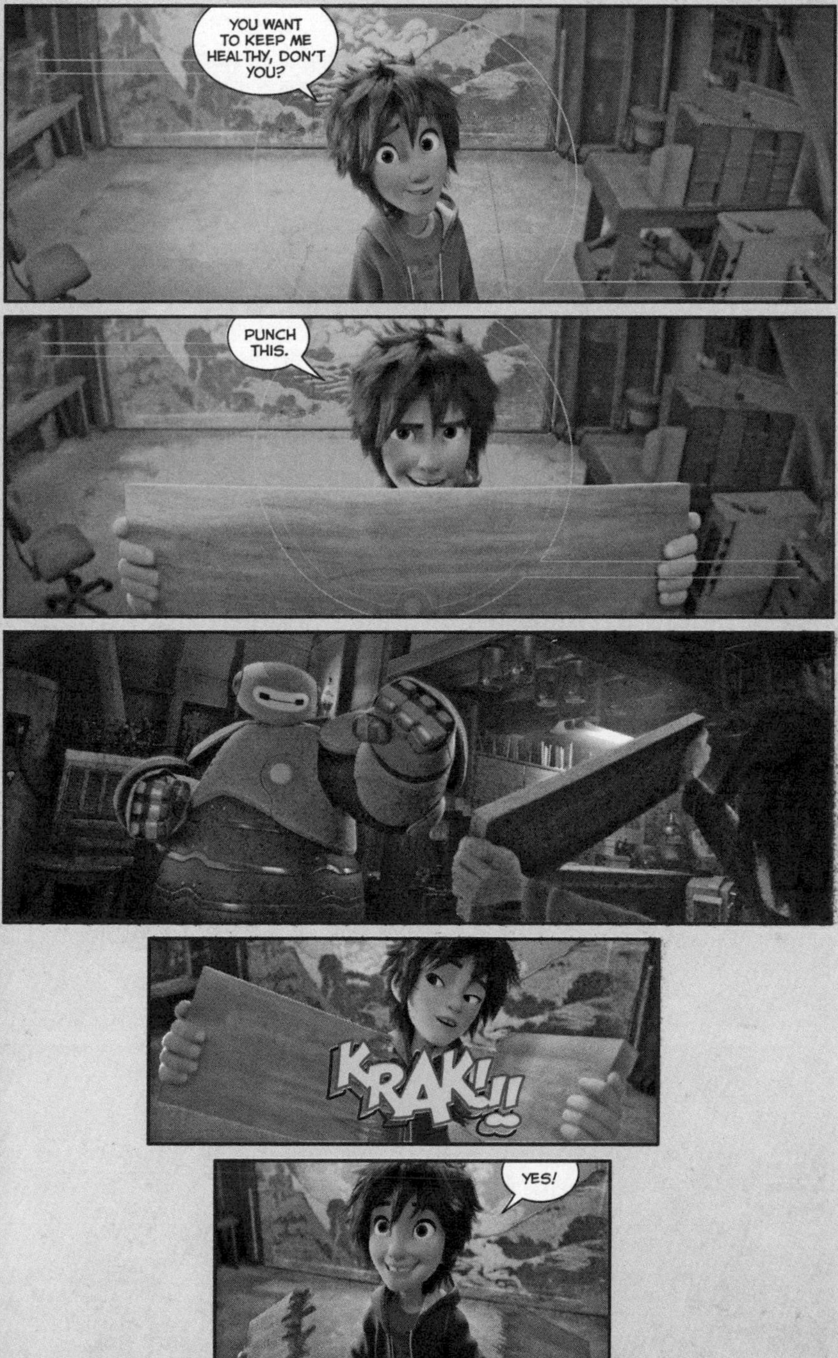
YOU WANT TO KEEP ME HEALTHY, DON'T YOU?
PUNCH THIS.
KRAK!!
YES!

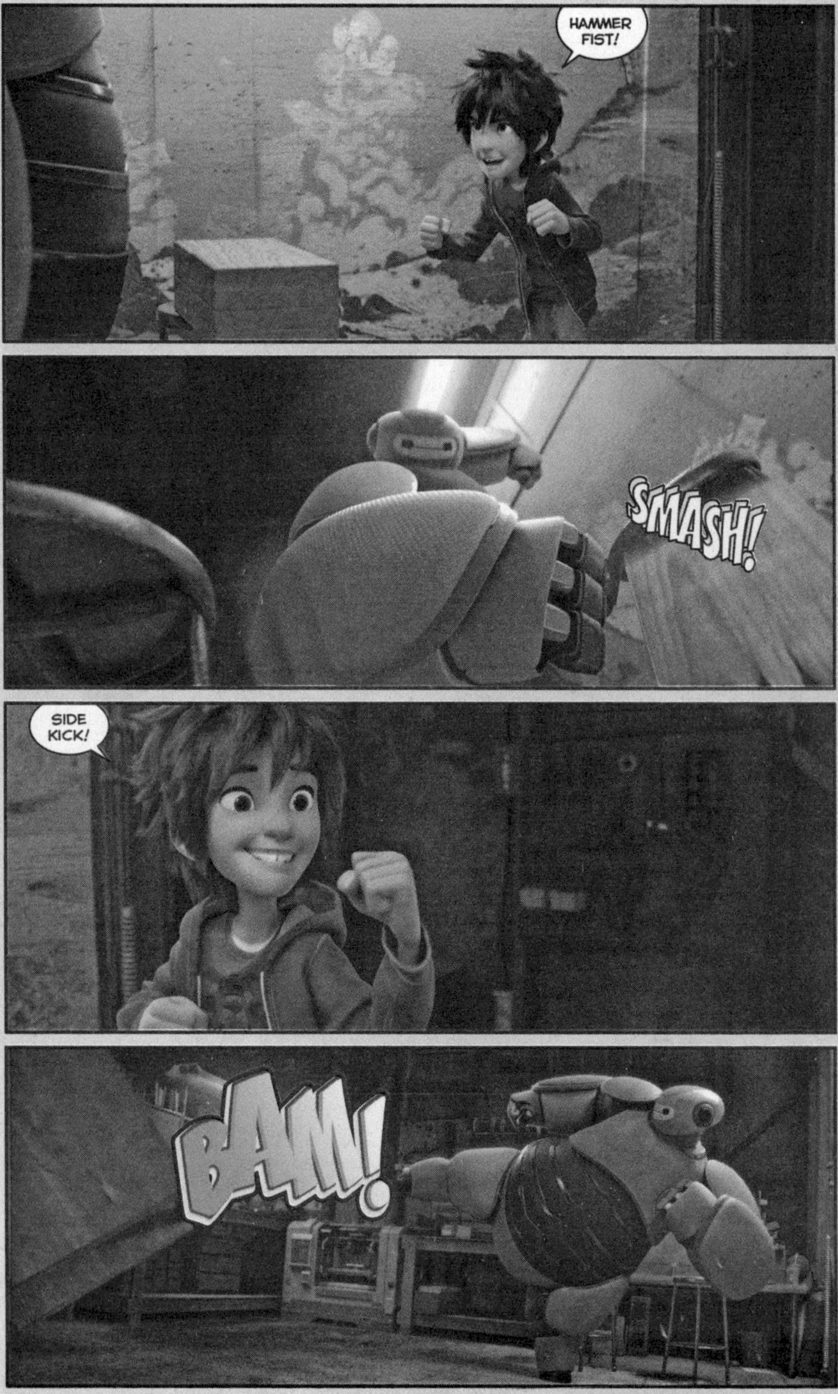
HAMMER FIST!
SMASH!
SIDE KICK!
BAM!

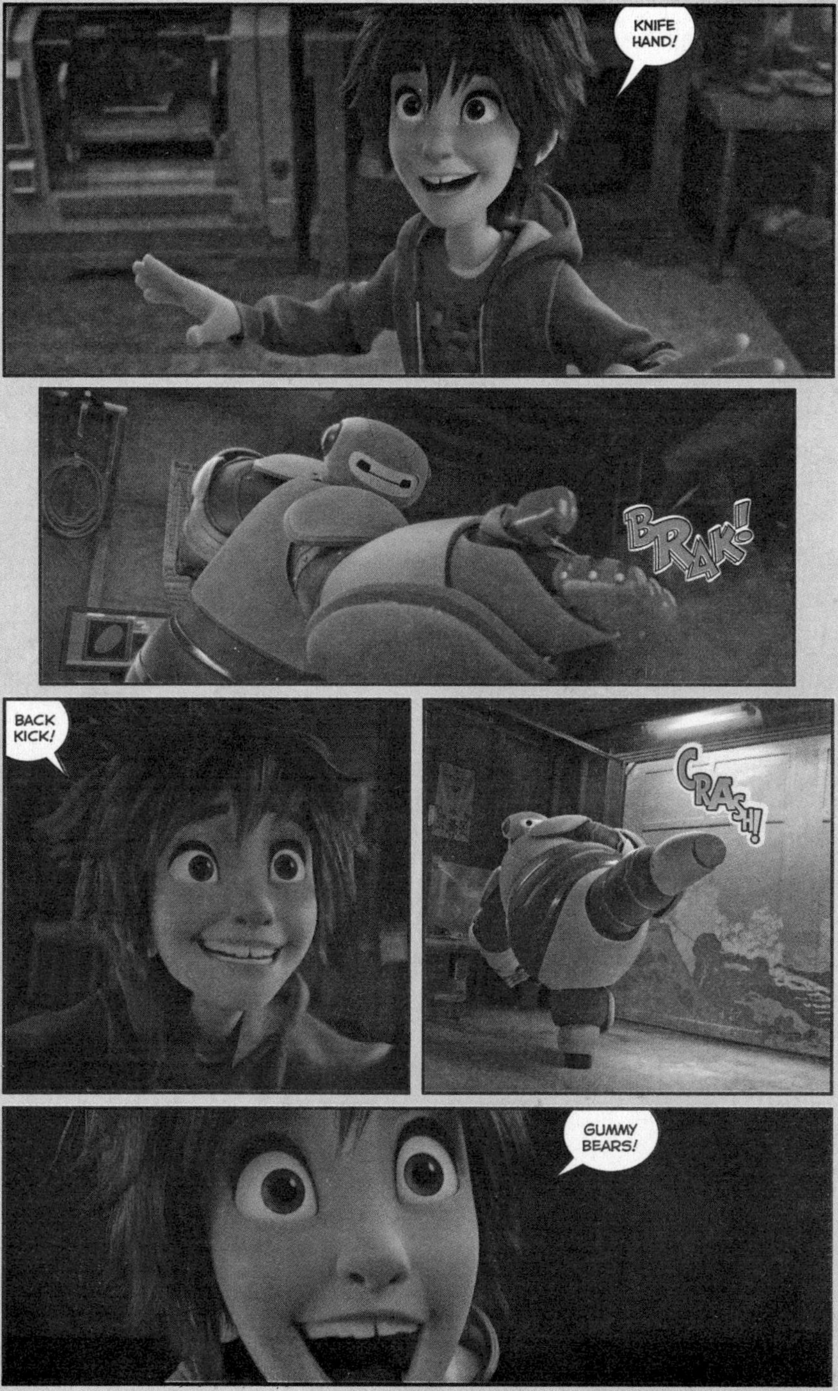
KNIFE HAND!
BRAK!
BACK KICK!
CRASH!
GUMMY BEARS!

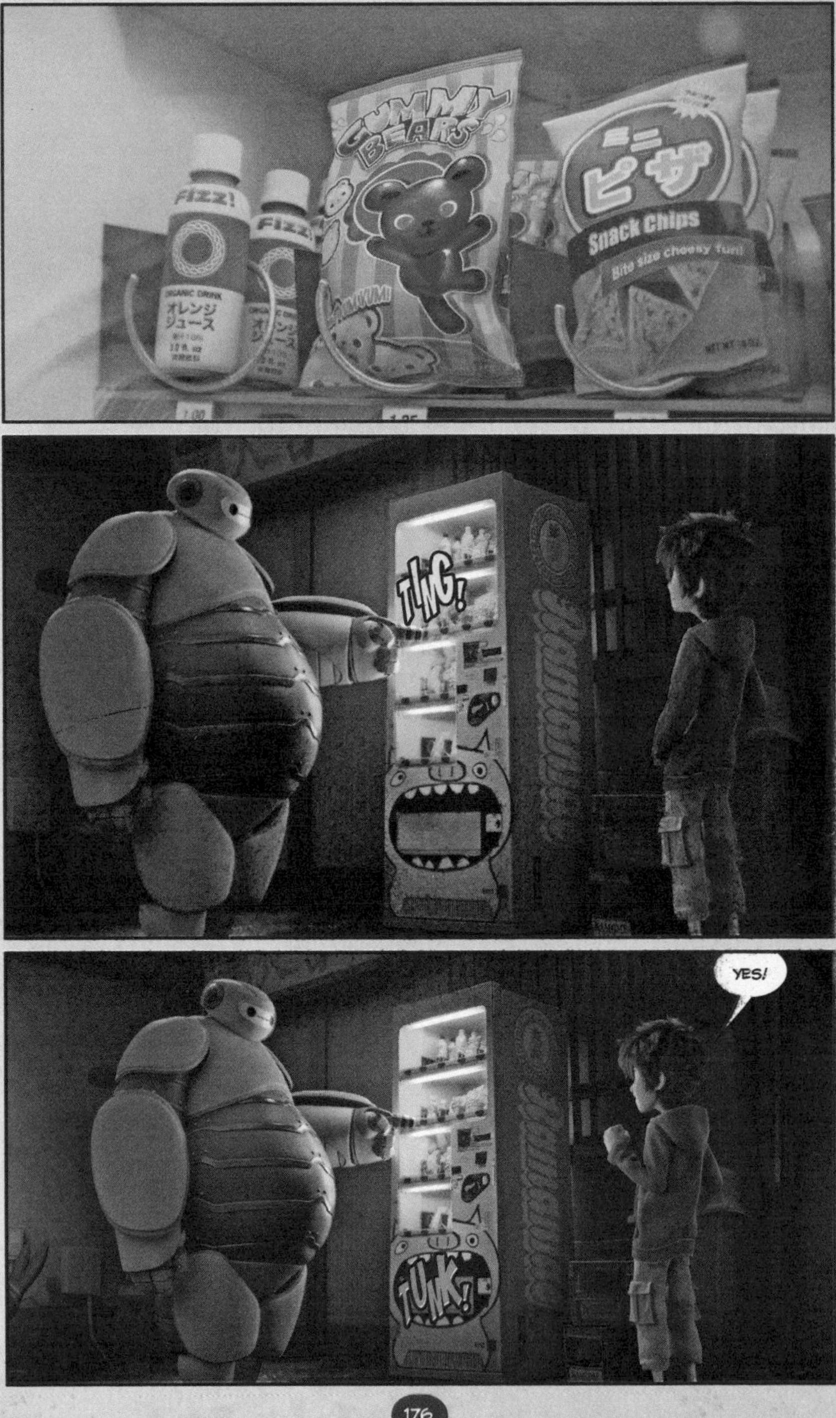
FIZZ!
ORGANIC DRINK
オレンジ
ジュース
GUMMY BEARS
ミニ
ピザ
Snack Chips
Bite size cheesy fun!
TING!
YES!
TUNK!

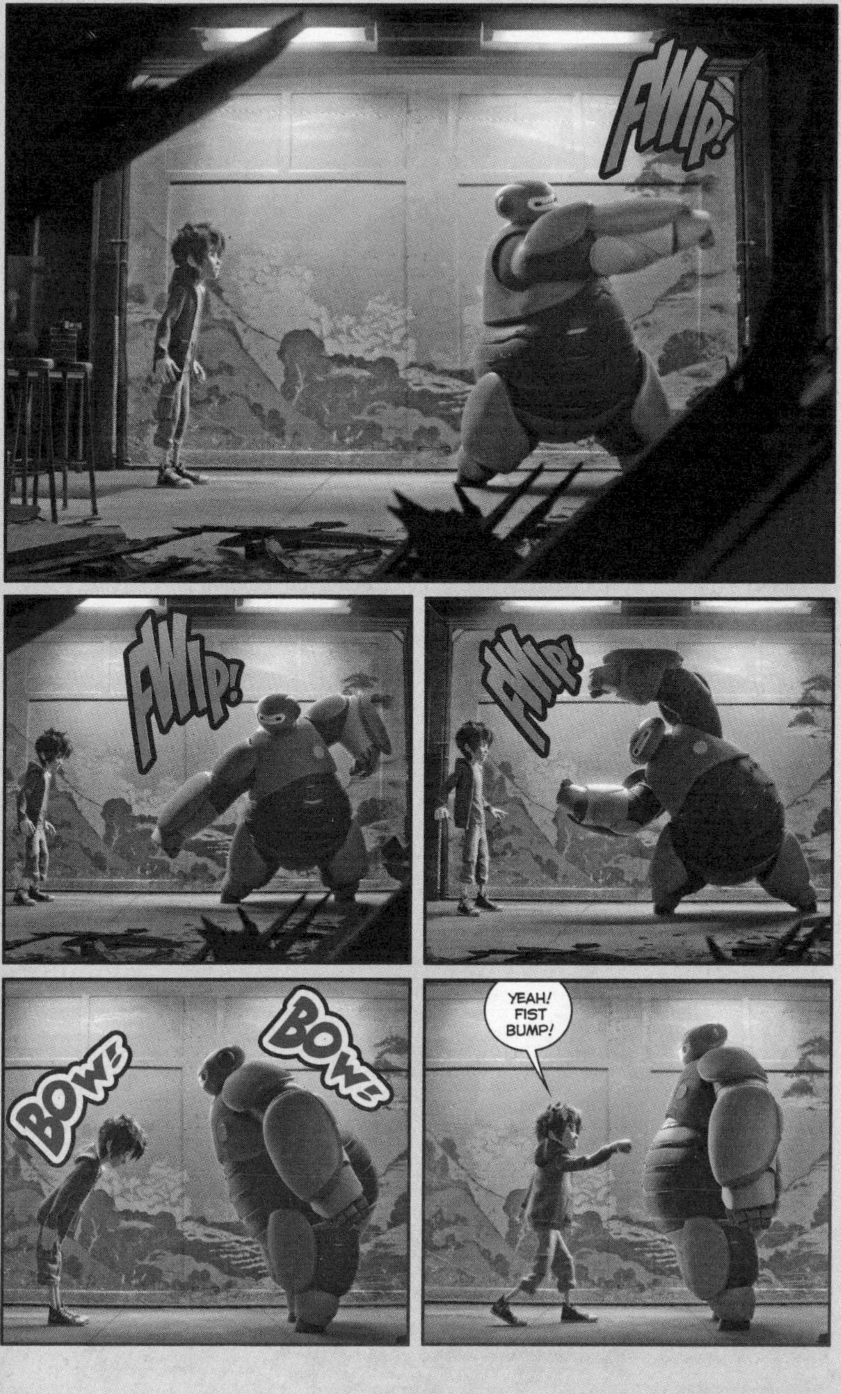
FWIP!
FWIP!
FWIP!
BOW!
BOW!
YEAH! FIST BUMP!

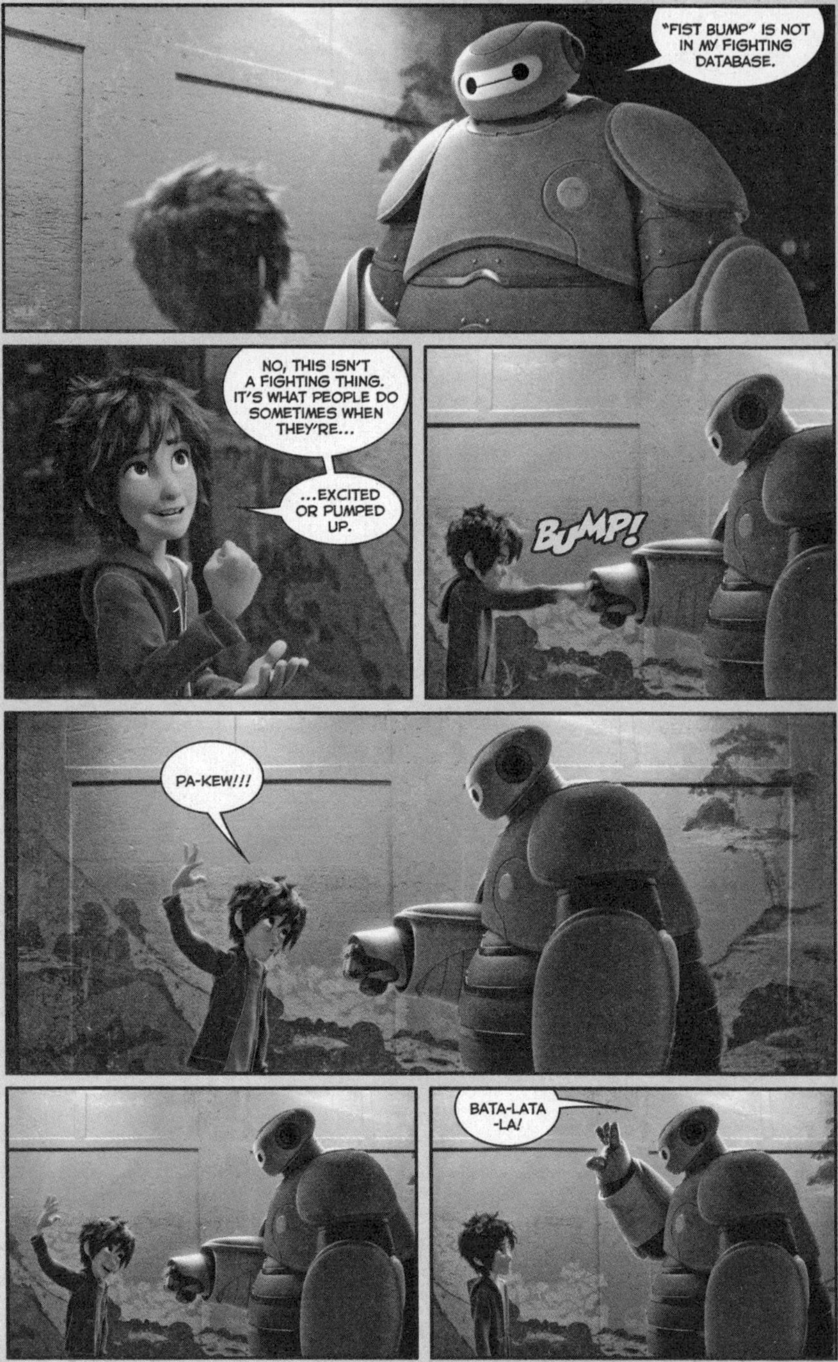

"FIST BUMP" IS NOT IN MY FIGHTING DATABASE.
NO, THIS ISN'T A FIGHTING THING. IT'S WHAT PEOPLE DO SOMETIMES WHEN THEY'RE...
...EXCITED OR PUMPED UP.
BUMP!
PA-KEW!!!
BATA-LATA -LA!

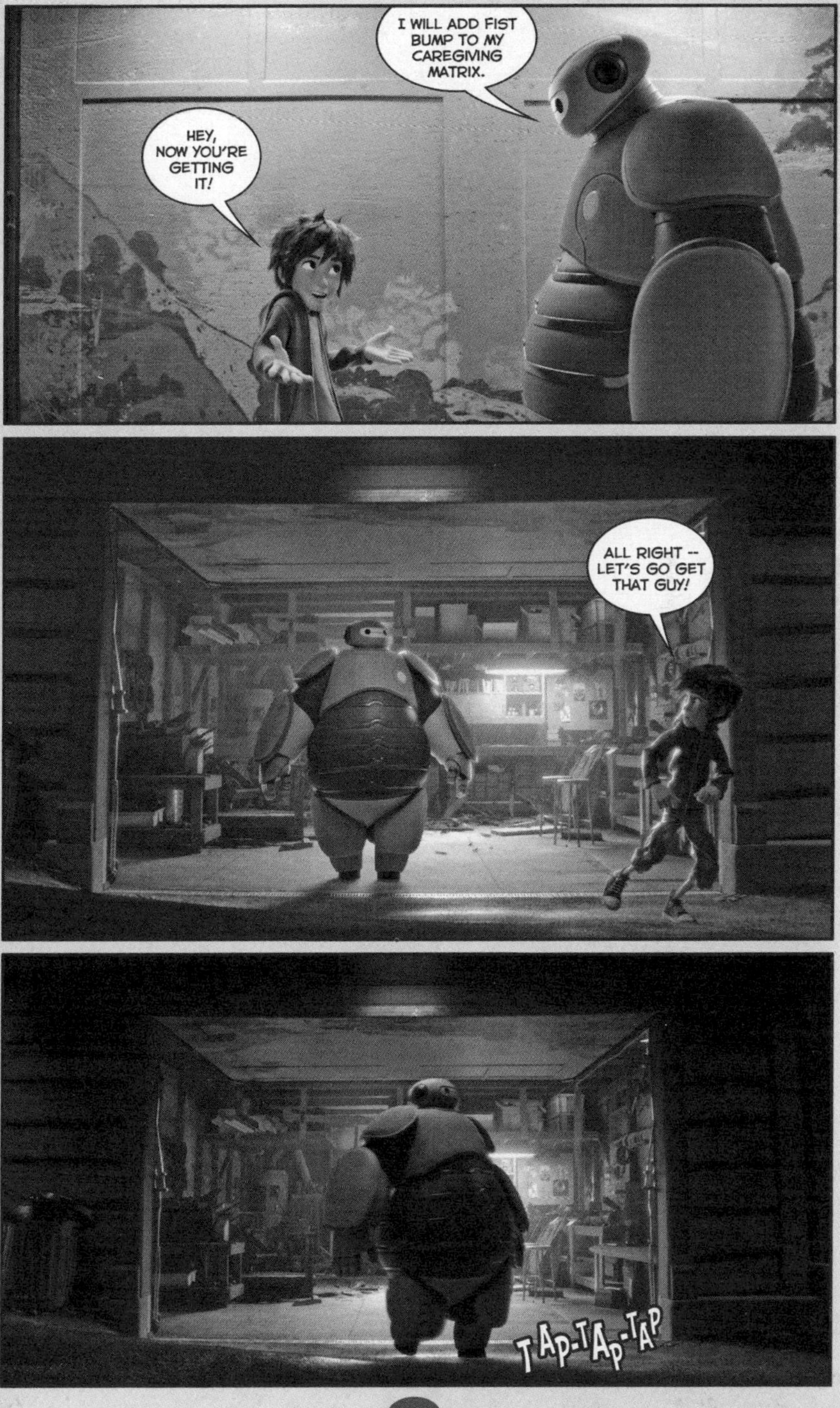
HEY, NOW YOU'RE GETTING IT!
I WILL ADD FIST BUMP TO MY CAREGIVING MATRIX.
ALL RIGHT -- LET'S GO GET THAT GUY!
TAP-TAP-TAP

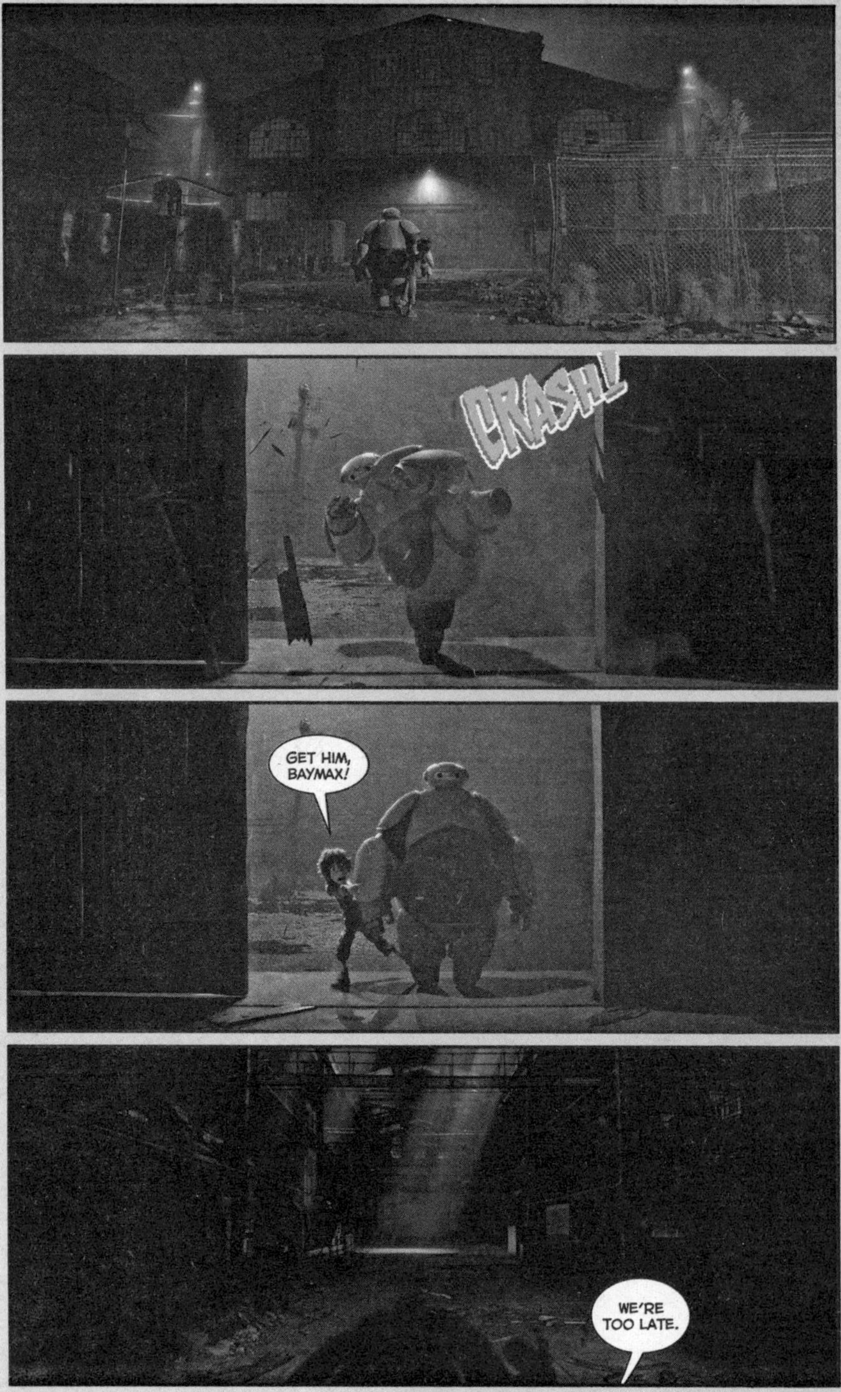
CRASH!
GET HIM, BAYMAX!
WE'RE TOO LATE.

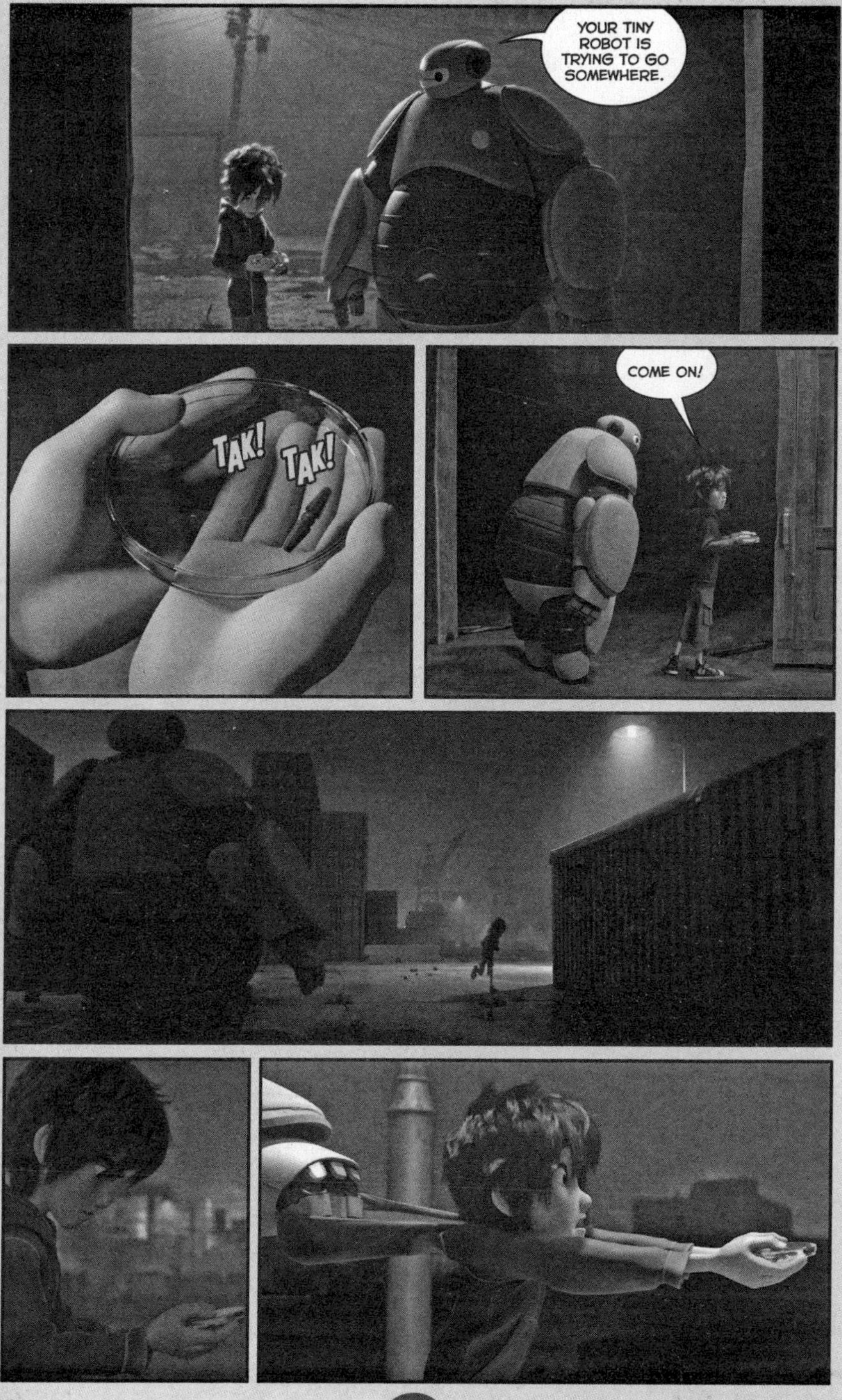
YOUR TINY ROBOT IS TRYING TO GO SOMEWHERE.
TAK!
TAK!
COME ON!

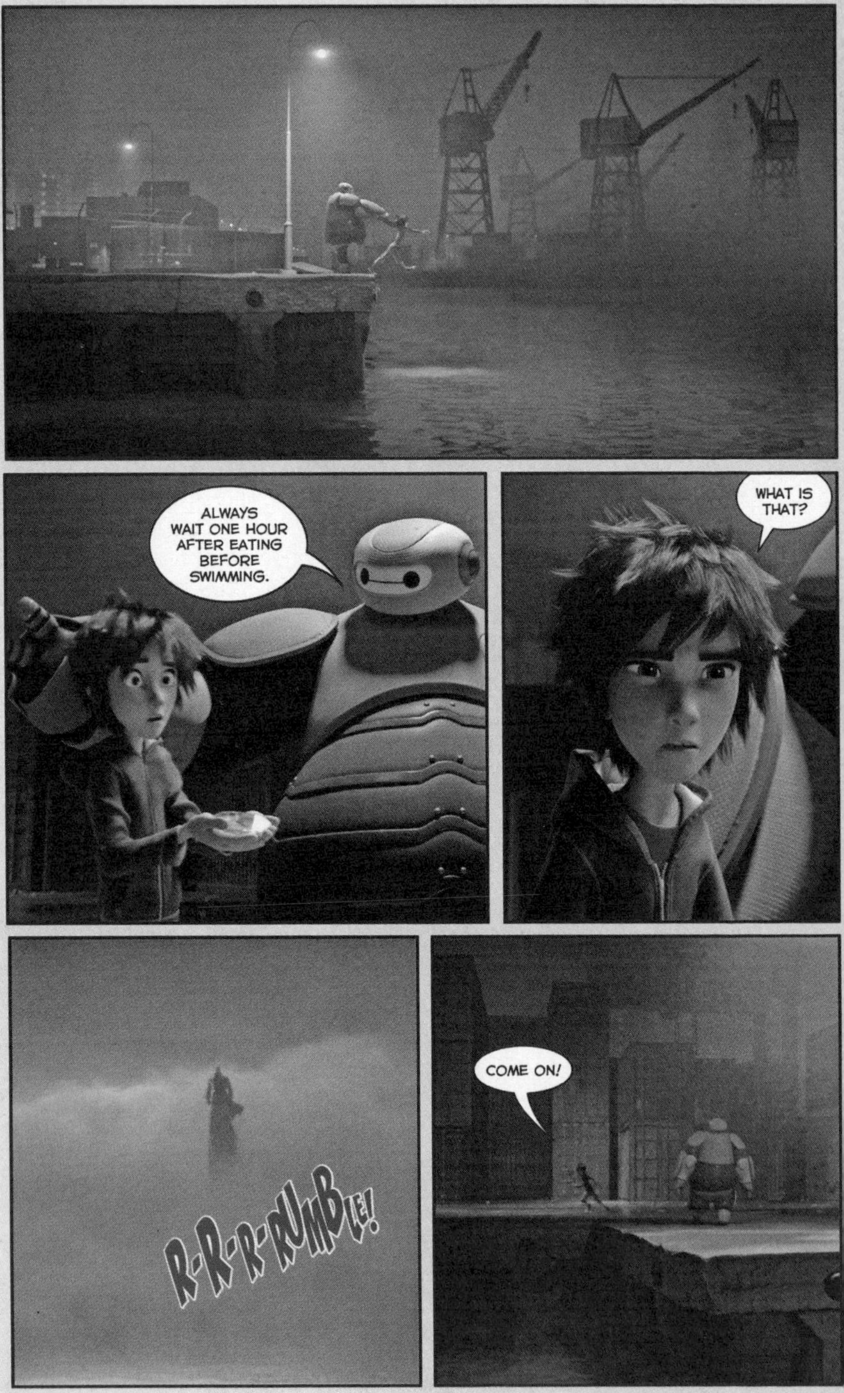
ALWAYS WAIT ONE HOUR AFTER EATING BEFORE SWIMMING.
WHAT IS THAT?
R-R-R-RUMBLE!
COME ON!

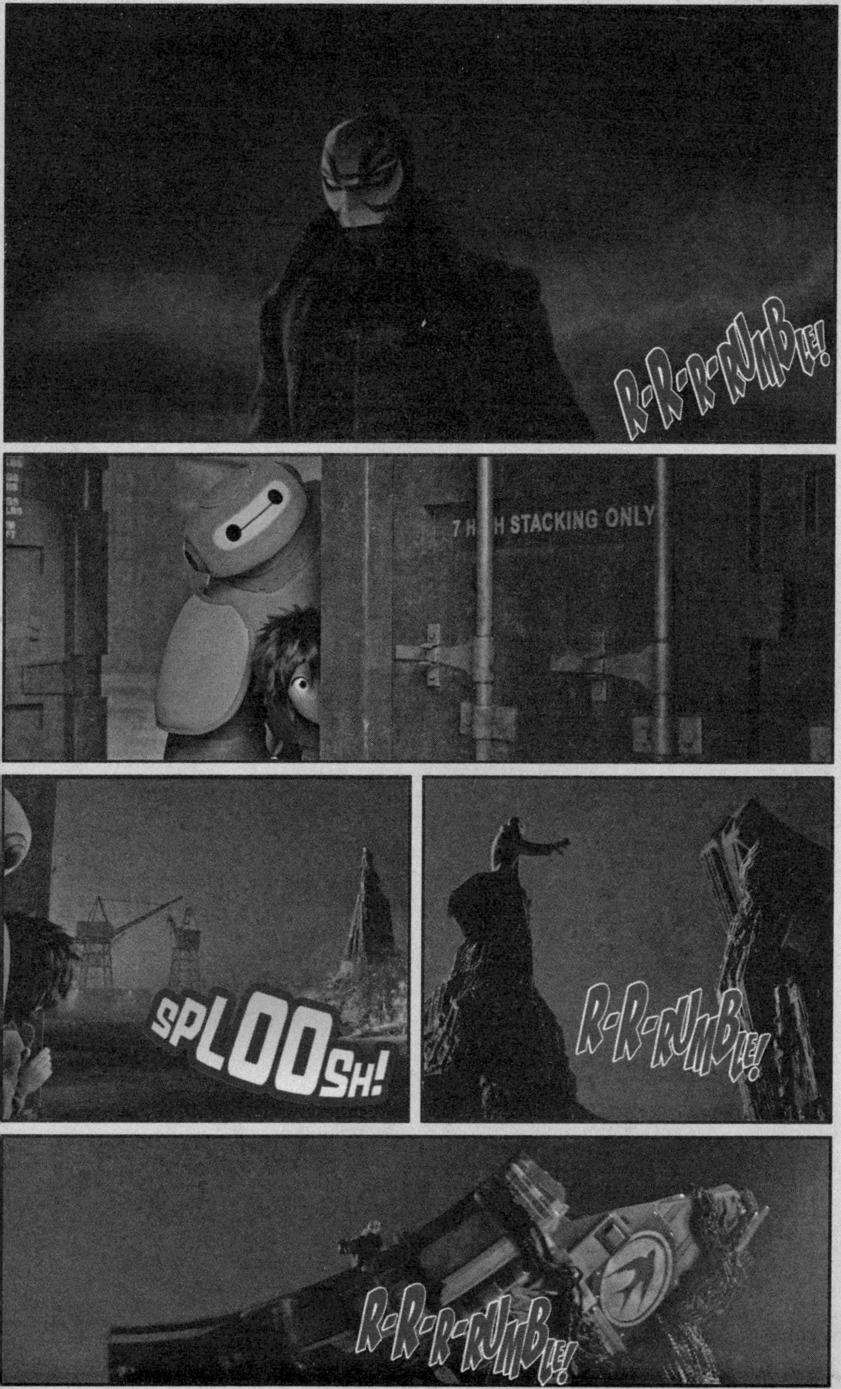
R-R-R-RUMBLE!
7 H H STACKING ONLY
SPLOOSH!
R-R-RUMBLE!
R-R-R-RUMBLE!

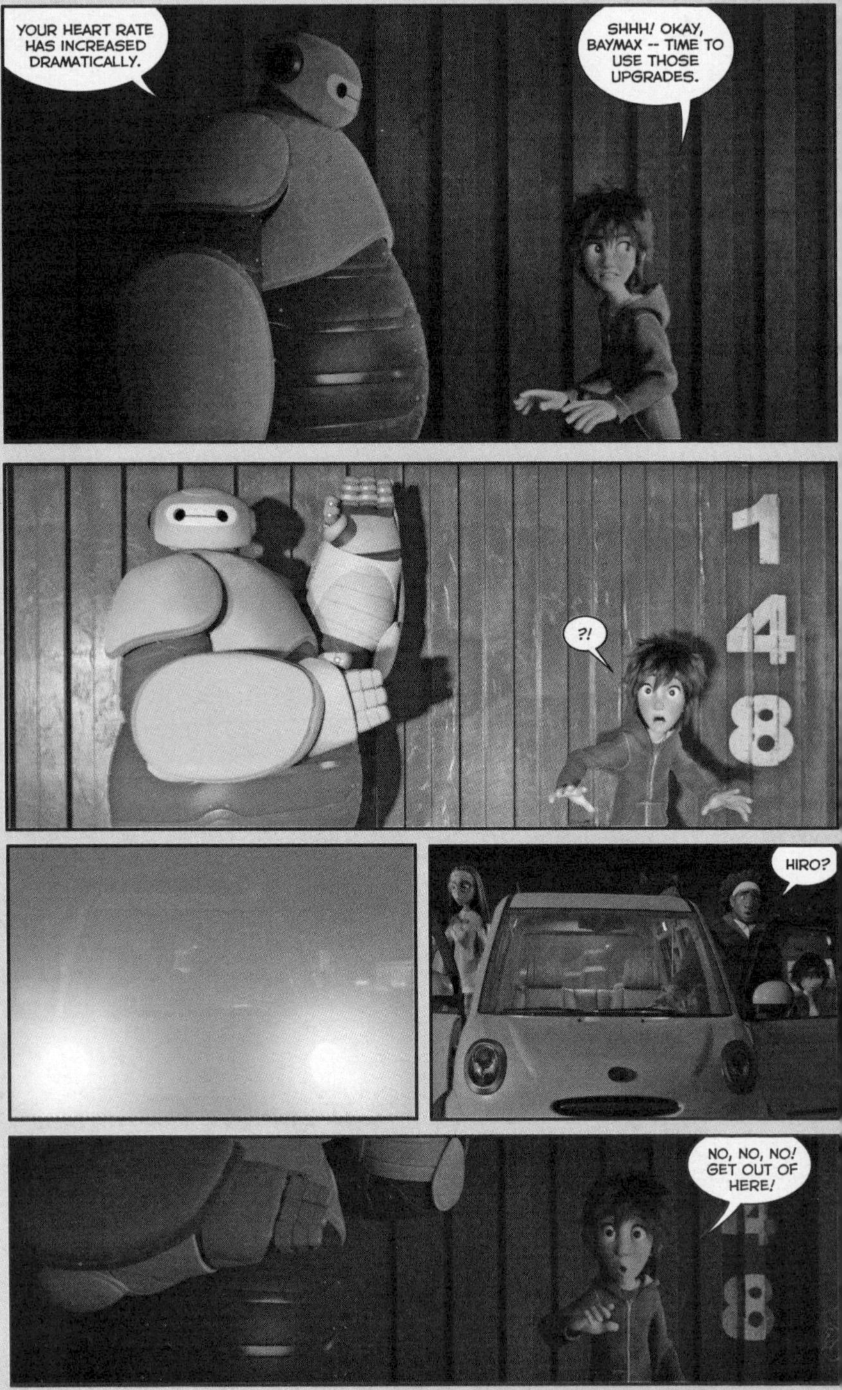
YOUR HEART RATE HAS INCREASED DRAMATICALLY.
SHHH! OKAY, BAYMAX -- TIME TO USE THOSE UPGRADES.
1 4 8
?!
HIRO?
NO, NO, NO! GET OUT OF HERE!

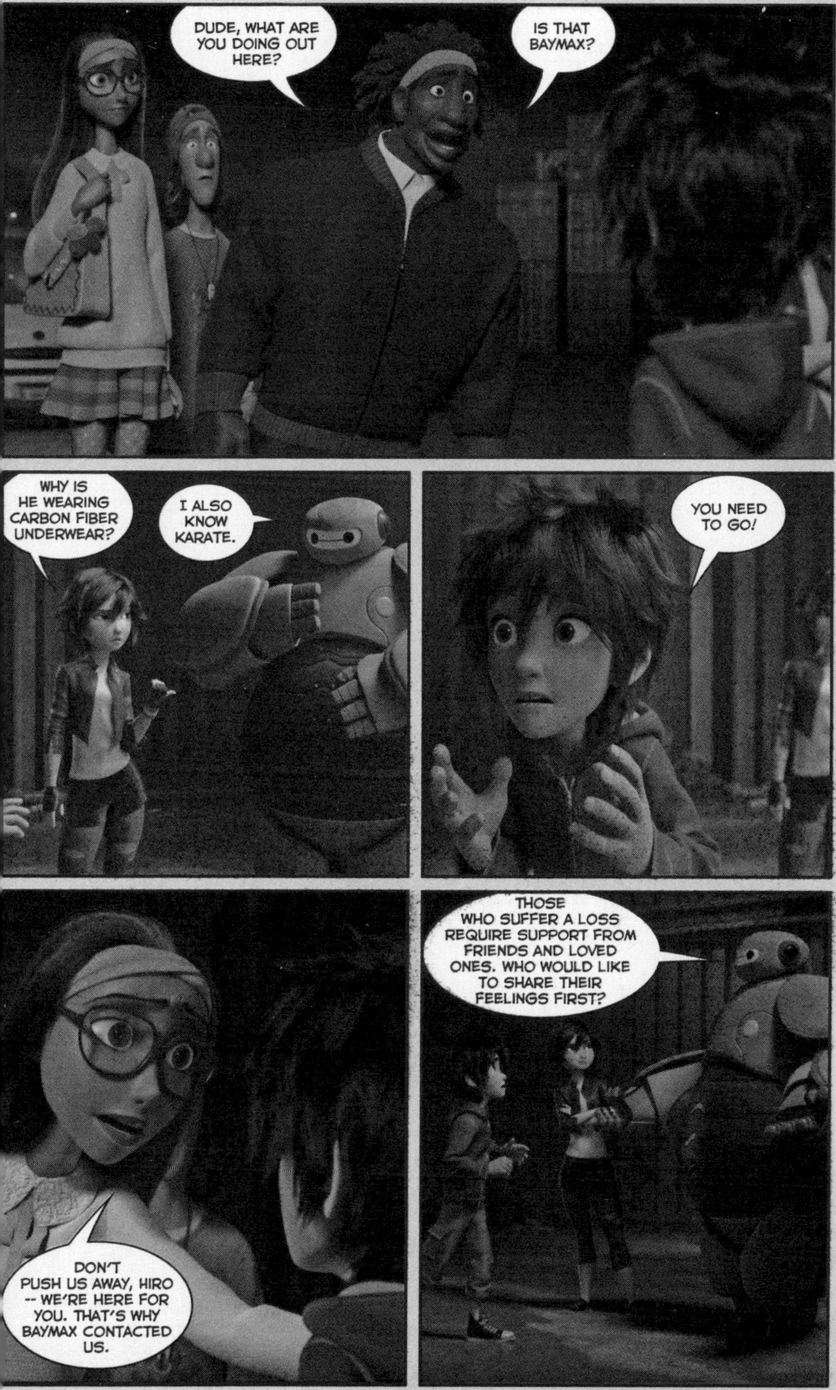
DUDE, WHAT ARE YOU DOING OUT HERE?
IS THAT BAYMAX?
WHY IS HE WEARING CARBON FIBER UNDERWEAR?
I ALSO KNOW KARATE.
YOU NEED TO GO!
DON'T PUSH US AWAY, HIRO -- WE'RE HERE FOR YOU. THAT'S WHY BAYMAX CONTACTED US.
THOSE WHO SUFFER A LOSS REQUIRE SUPPORT FROM FRIENDS AND LOVED ONES. WHO WOULD LIKE TO SHARE THEIR FEELINGS FIRST?

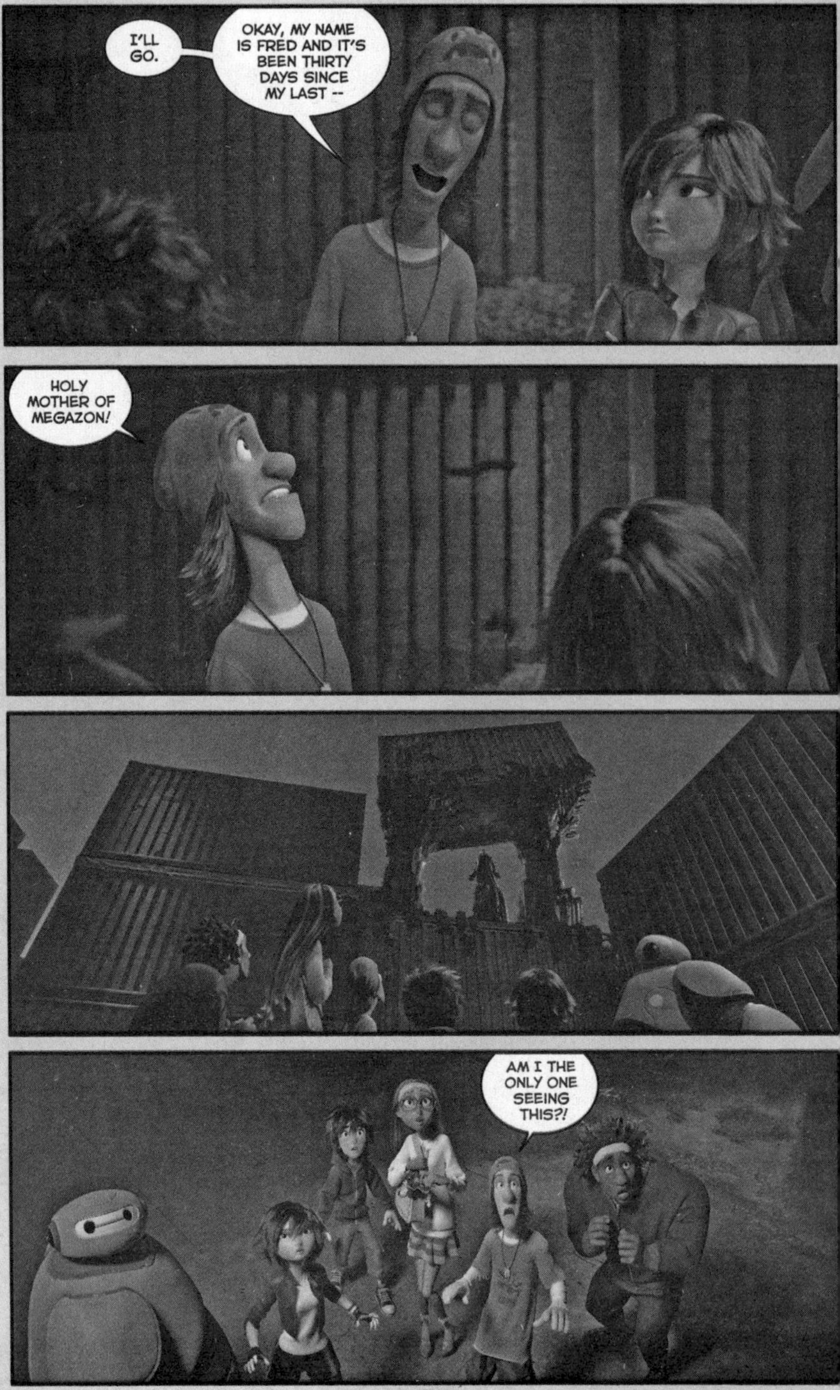
I'LL GO.
OKAY, MY NAME IS FRED AND IT'S BEEN THIRTY DAYS SINCE MY LAST --
HOLY MOTHER OF MEGAZON!
AM I THE ONLY ONE SEEING THIS?!

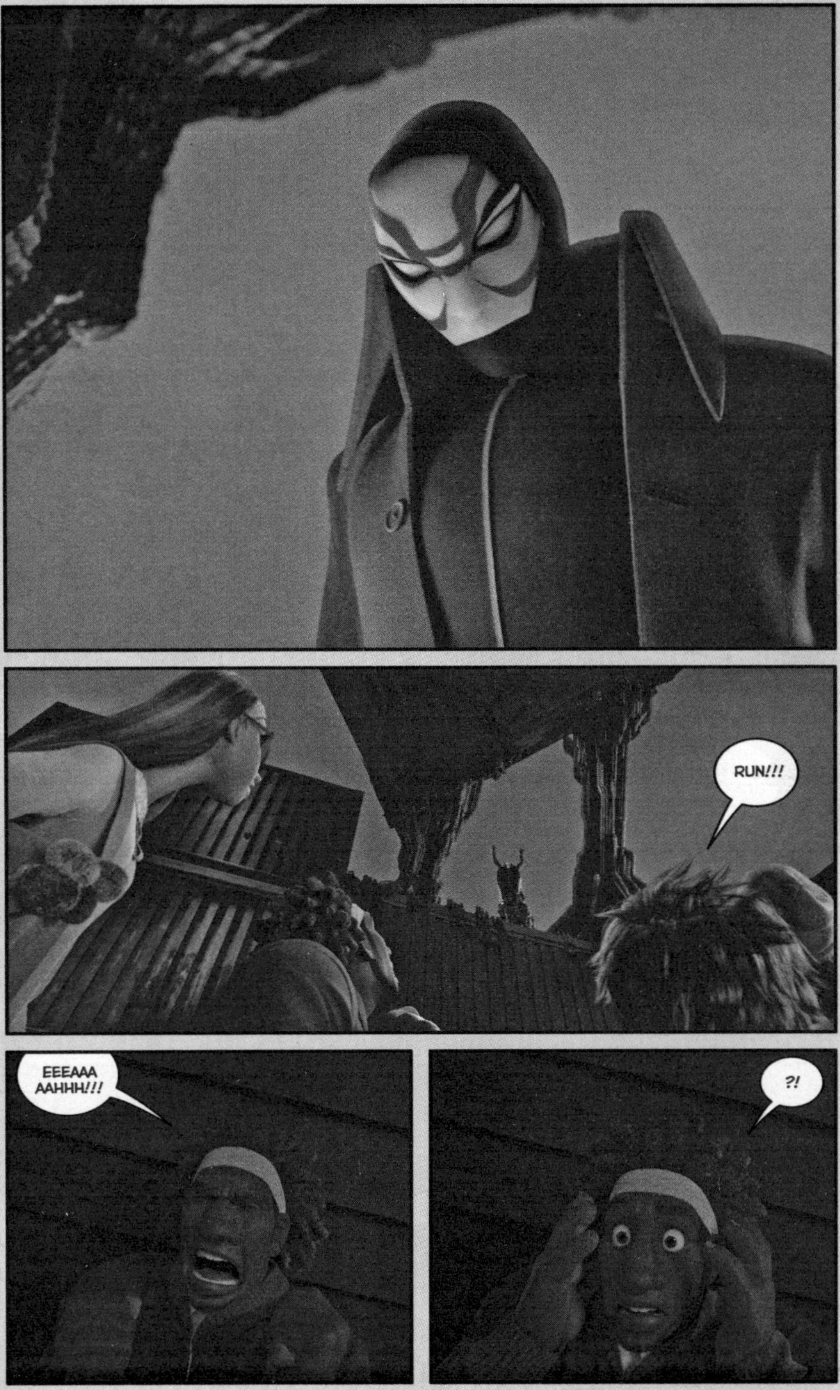
RUN!!!
EEEAAA
AAHHH!!!
?!

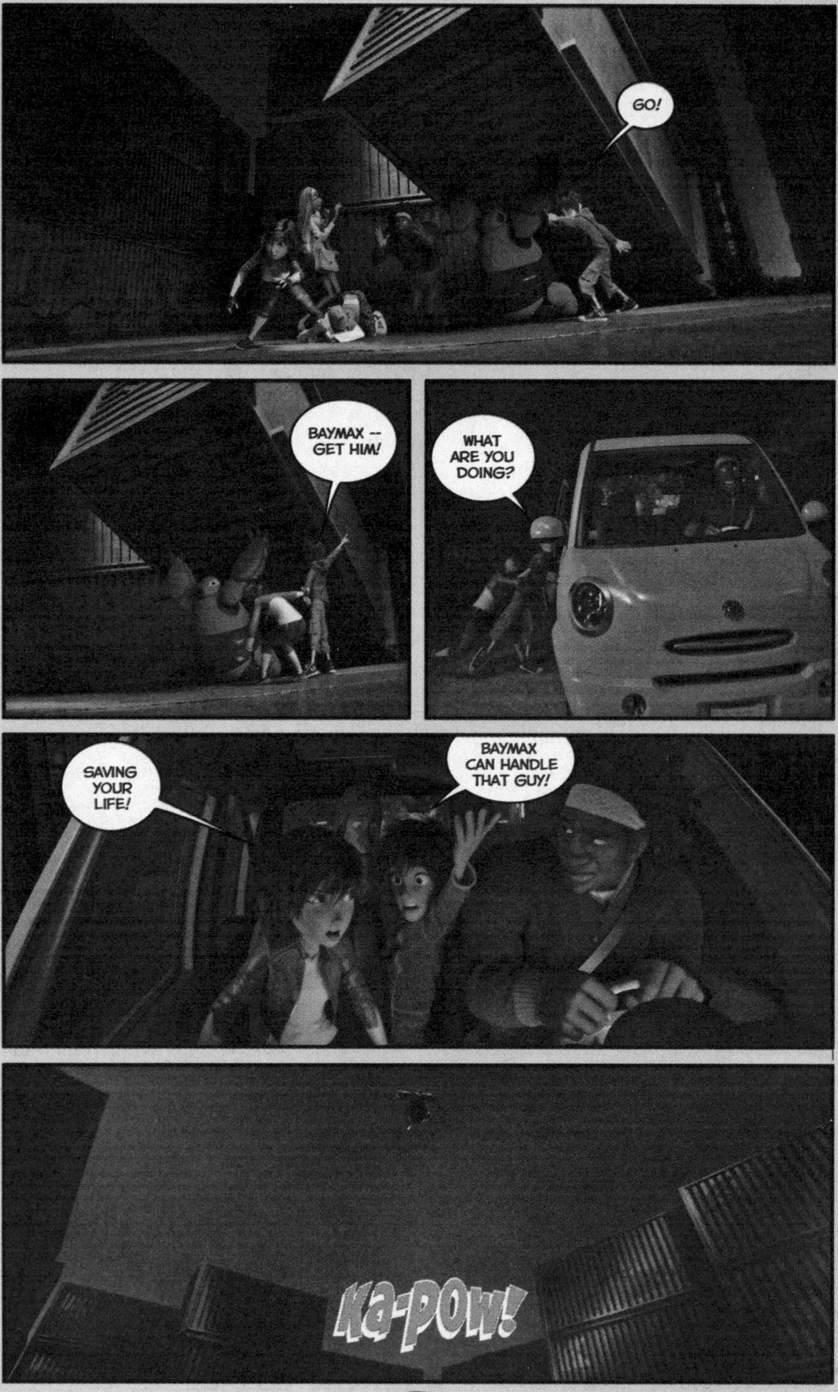
GO!
BAYMAX -- GET HIM!
WHAT ARE YOU DOING?
SAVING YOUR LIFE!
BAYMAX CAN HANDLE THAT GUY!
KA-POW!

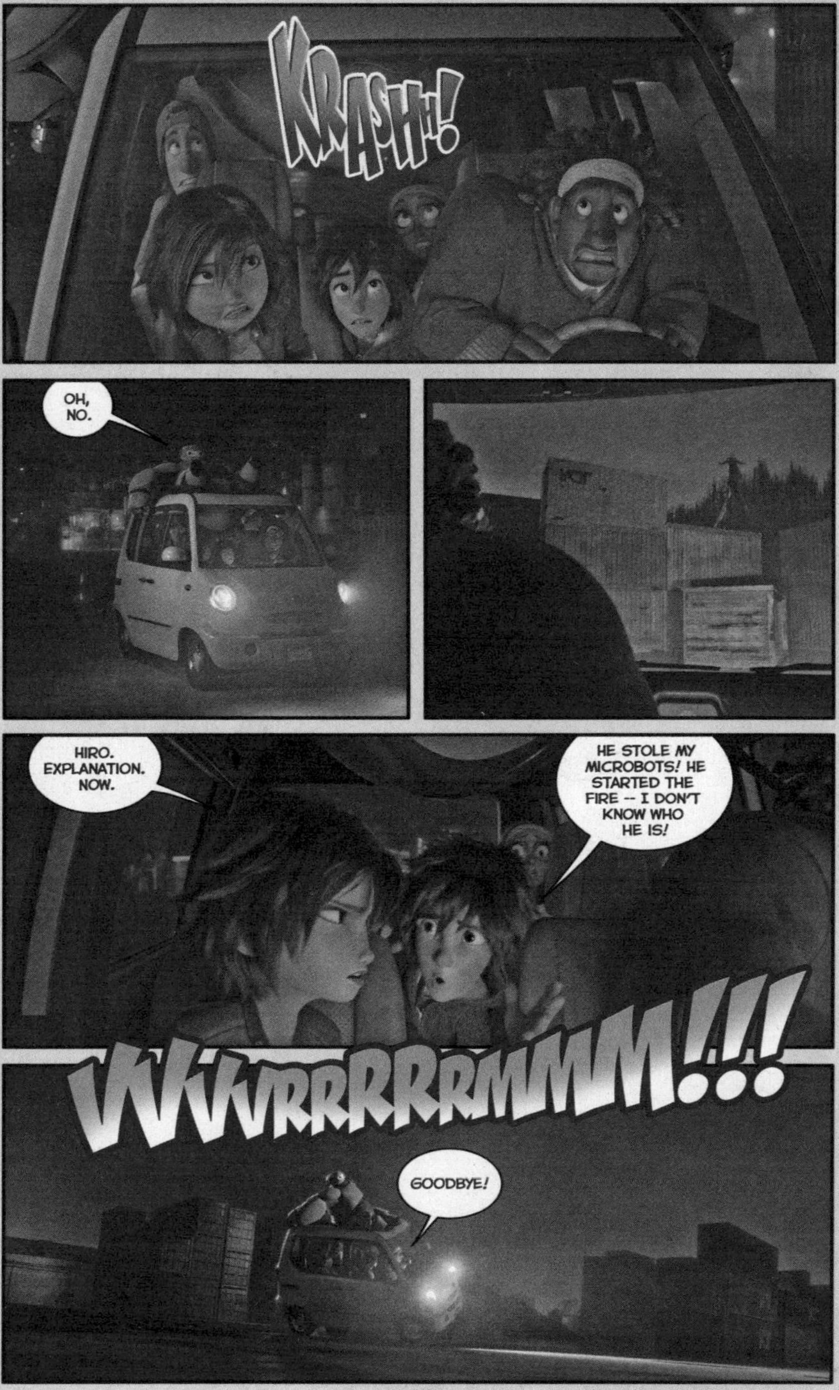

KRASHH!
OH, NO.
HIRO. EXPLANATION. NOW.
HE STOLE MY MICROBOTS! HE STARTED THE FIRE -- I DON'T KNOW WHO HE IS!
WVVRRRRRMMMM!!!
GOODBYE!

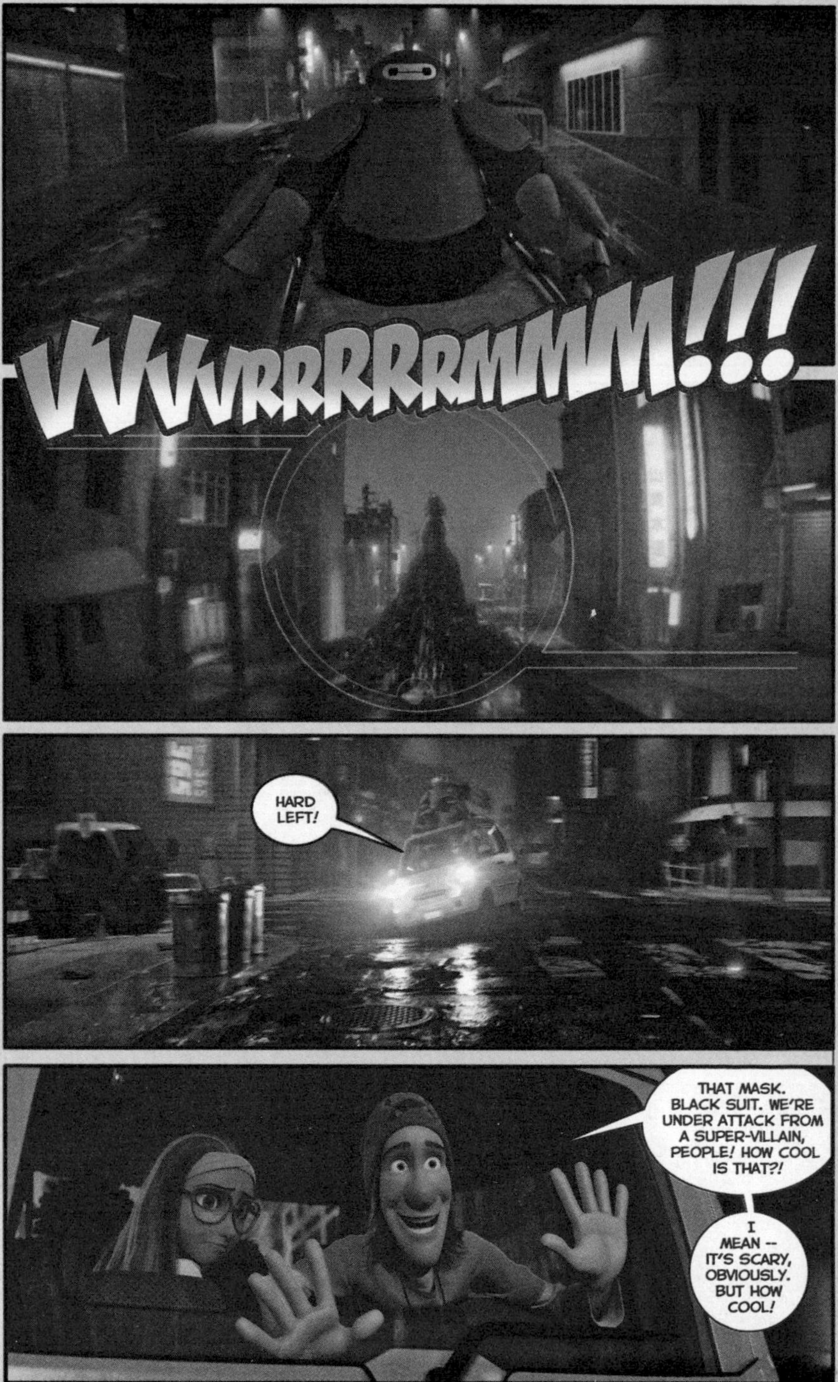
VVVVRRRRRRMMMM!!!
HARD LEFT!
THAT MASK. BLACK SUIT. WE'RE UNDER ATTACK FROM A SUPER-VILLAIN, PEOPLE! HOW COOL IS THAT?!
I MEAN -- IT'S SCARY, OBVIOUSLY. BUT HOW COOL!

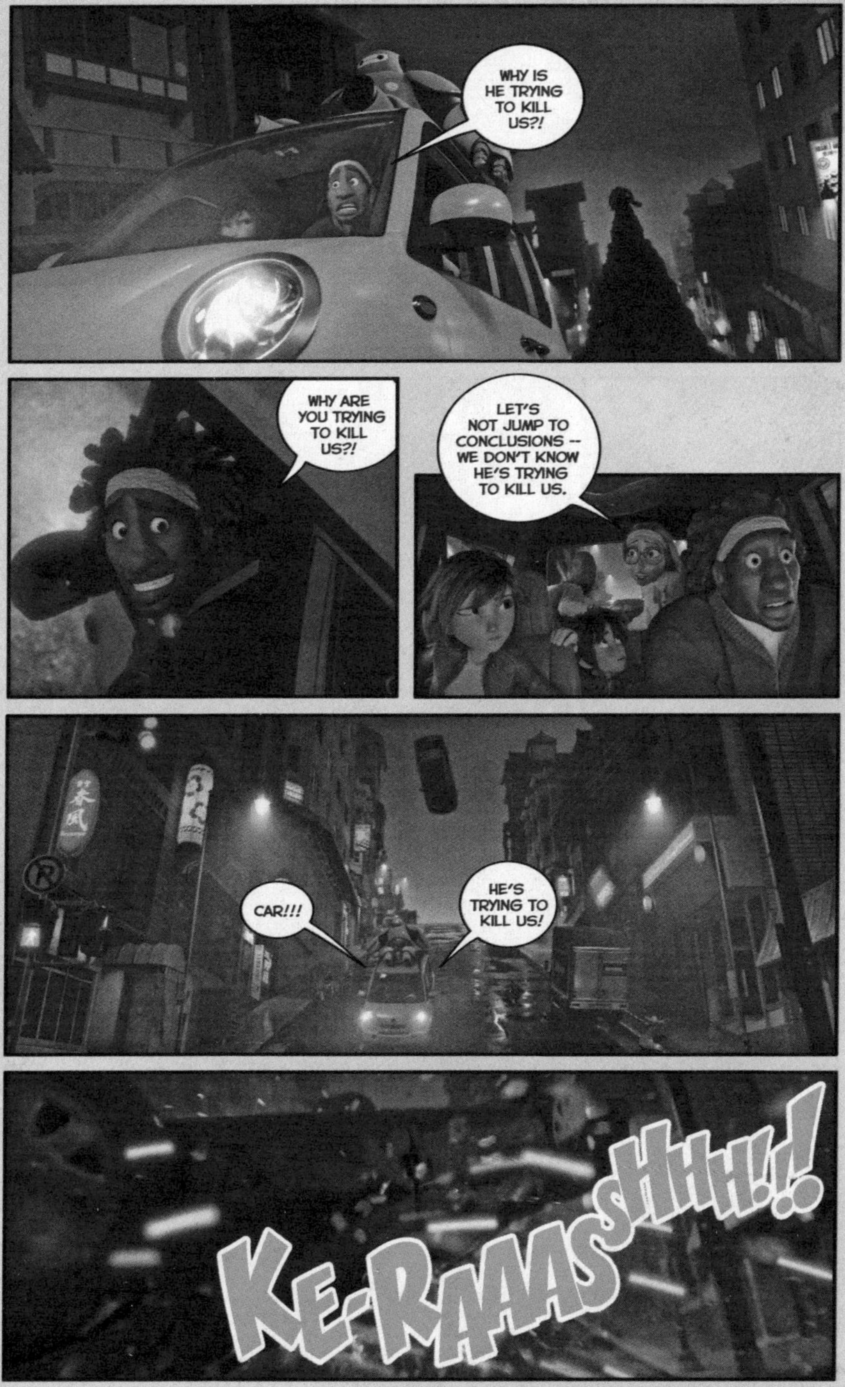
WHY IS HE TRYING TO KILL US?!
WHY ARE YOU TRYING TO KILL US?!
LET'S NOT JUMP TO CONCLUSIONS -- WE DON'T KNOW HE'S TRYING TO KILL US.
CAR!!!
HE'S TRYING TO KILL US!
KE-RAAASHHH!!!

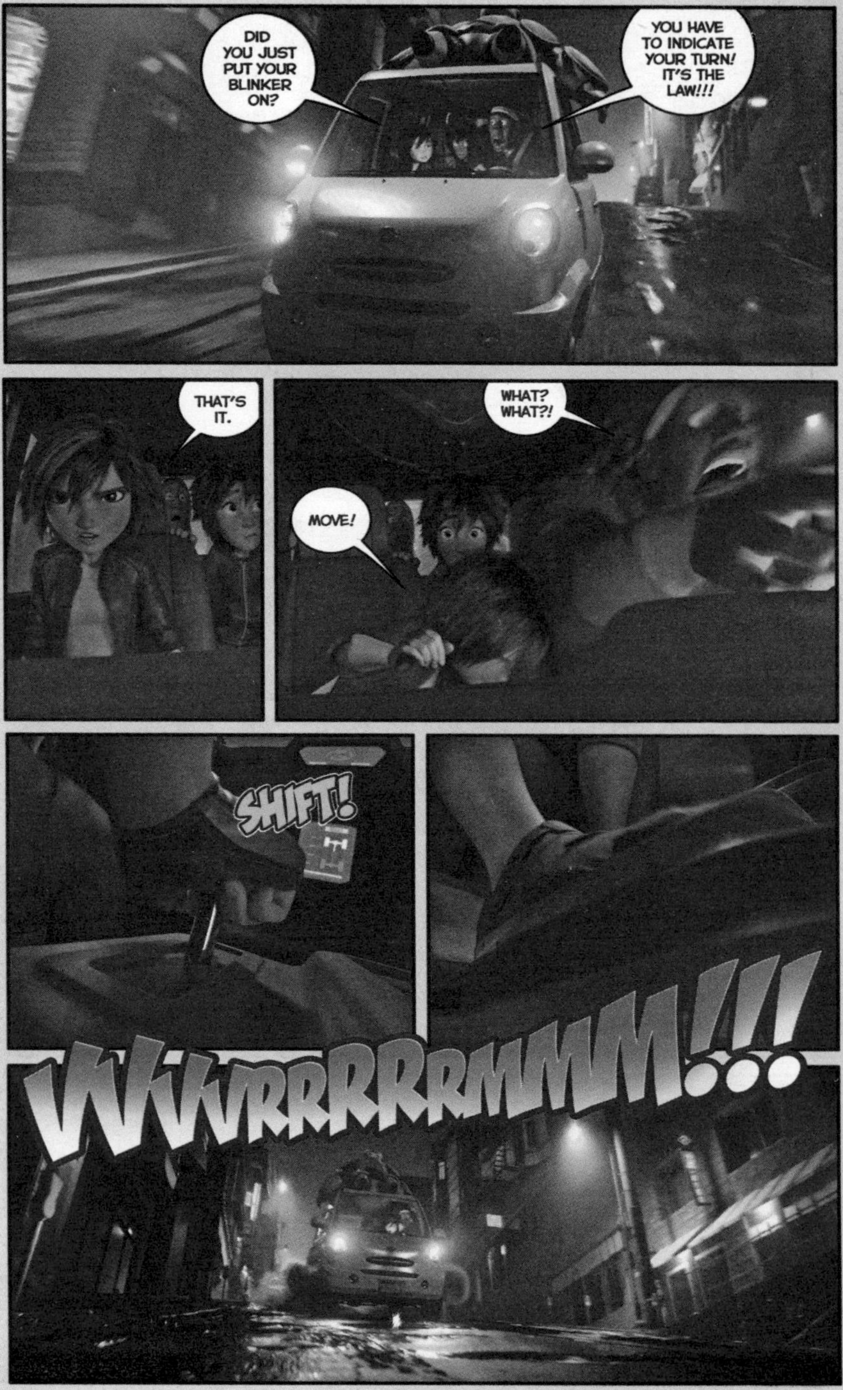
DID YOU JUST PUT YOUR BLINKER ON?
YOU HAVE TO INDICATE YOUR TURN! IT'S THE LAW!!!
THAT'S IT.
WHAT? WHAT?!
MOVE!
SHIFT!
WWWRRRRRMMMM!!!

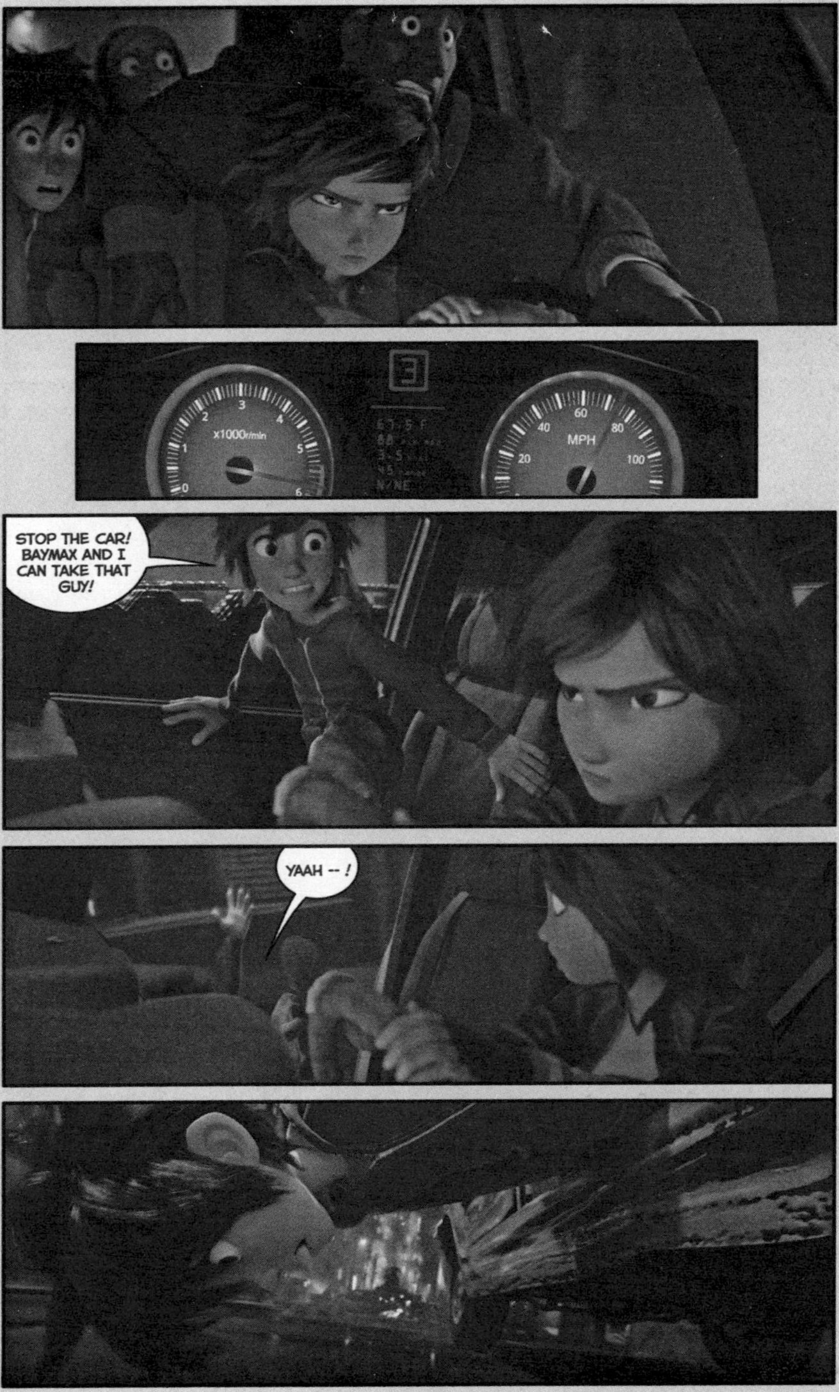

STOP THE CAR! BAYMAX AND I CAN TAKE THAT GUY!
YAAH -- !

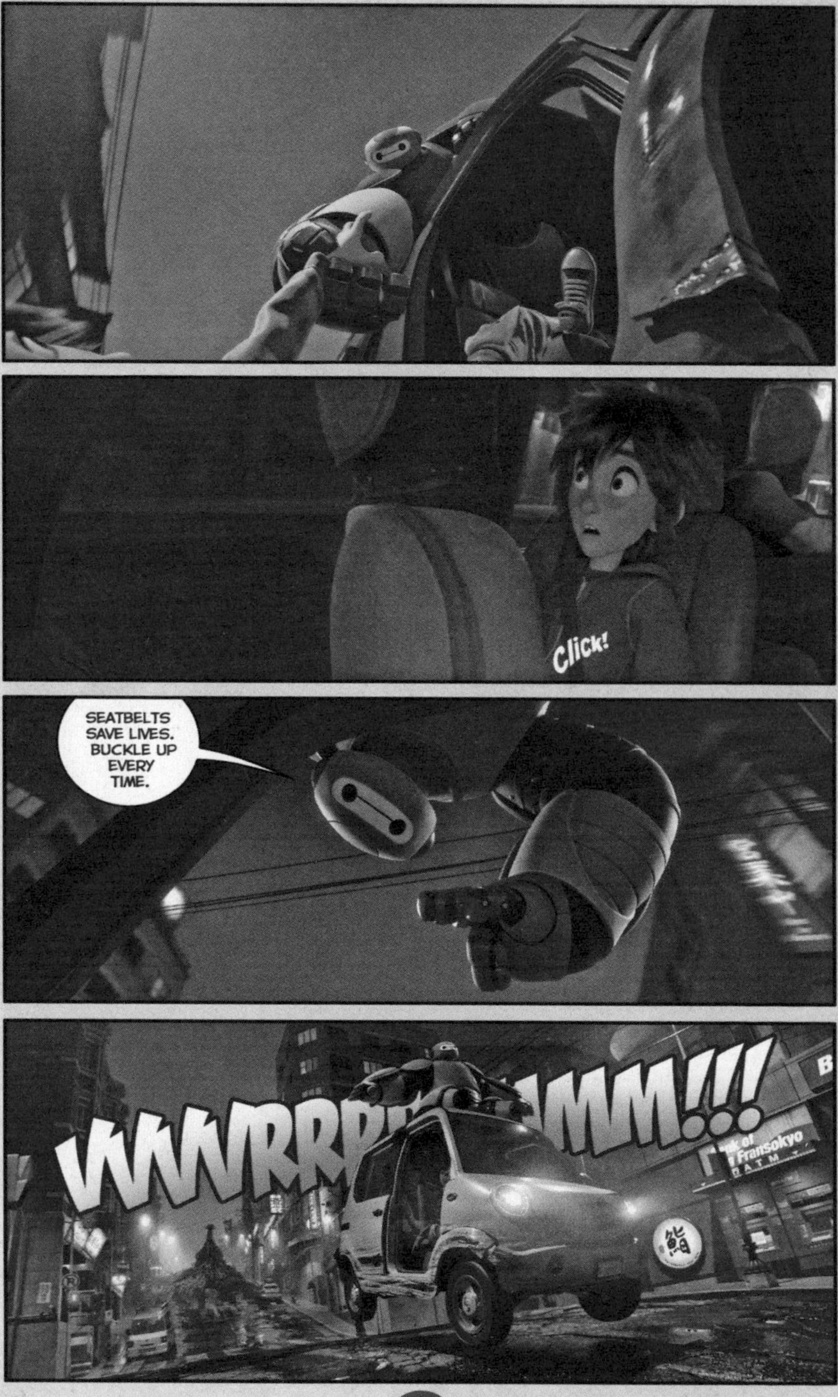
Click!
SEATBELTS SAVE LIVES. BUCKLE UP EVERY TIME.

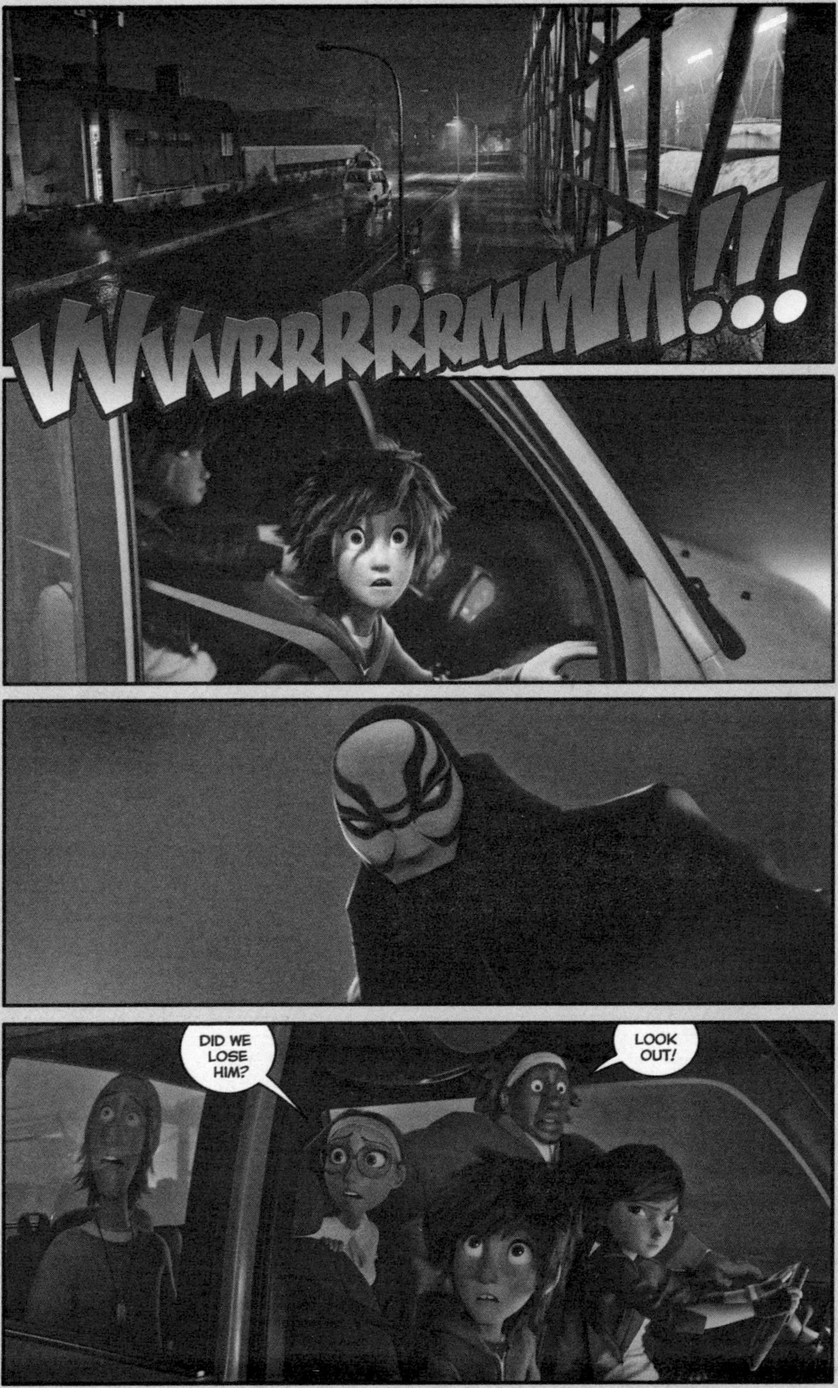
WWRRRRRMMMM!!!
DID WE LOSE HIM?
LOOK OUT!

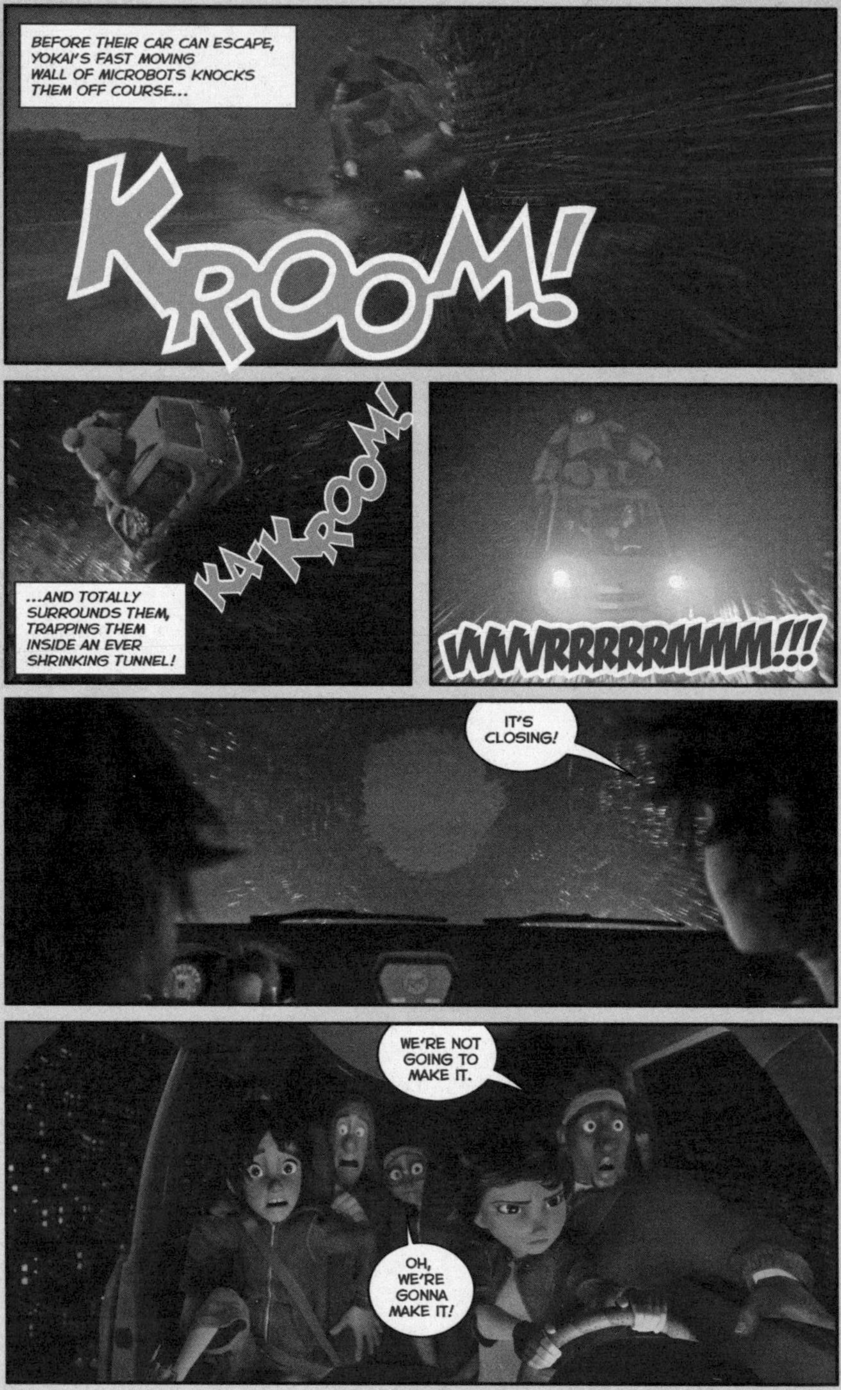
BEFORE THEIR CAR CAN ESCAPE, YOKAI'S FAST MOVING WALL OF MICROBOTS KNOCKS THEM OFF COURSE...
KROOM!
KA-KROOM!
...AND TOTALLY SURROUNDS THEM, TRAPPING THEM INSIDE AN EVER SHRINKING TUNNEL!
WWWRRRRRMMM!!!
IT'S CLOSING!
WE'RE NOT GOING TO MAKE IT.
OH, WE'RE GONNA MAKE IT!

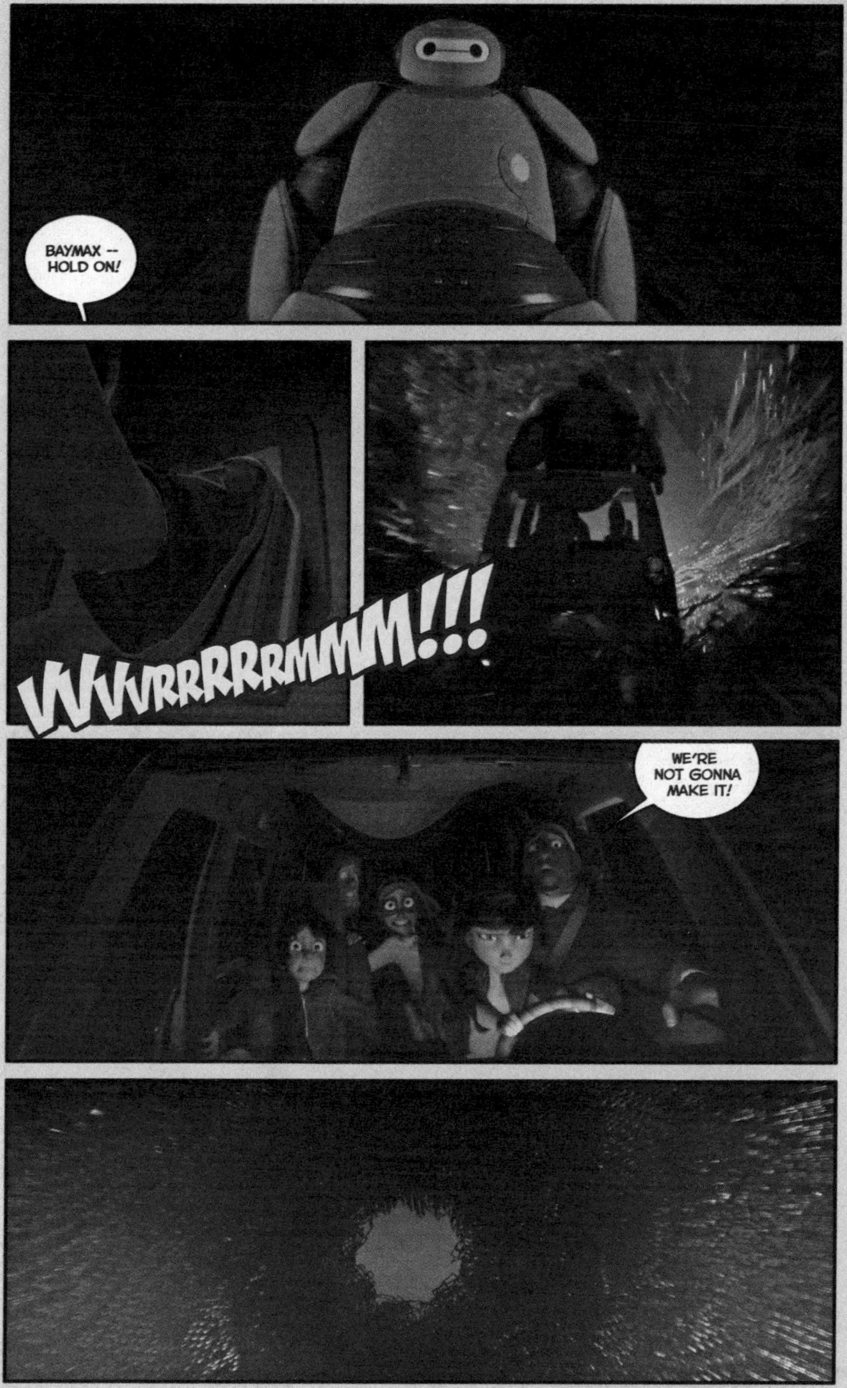
BAYMAX -- HOLD ON!
WVVRRRRRMMMM!!!
WE'RE NOT GONNA MAKE IT!

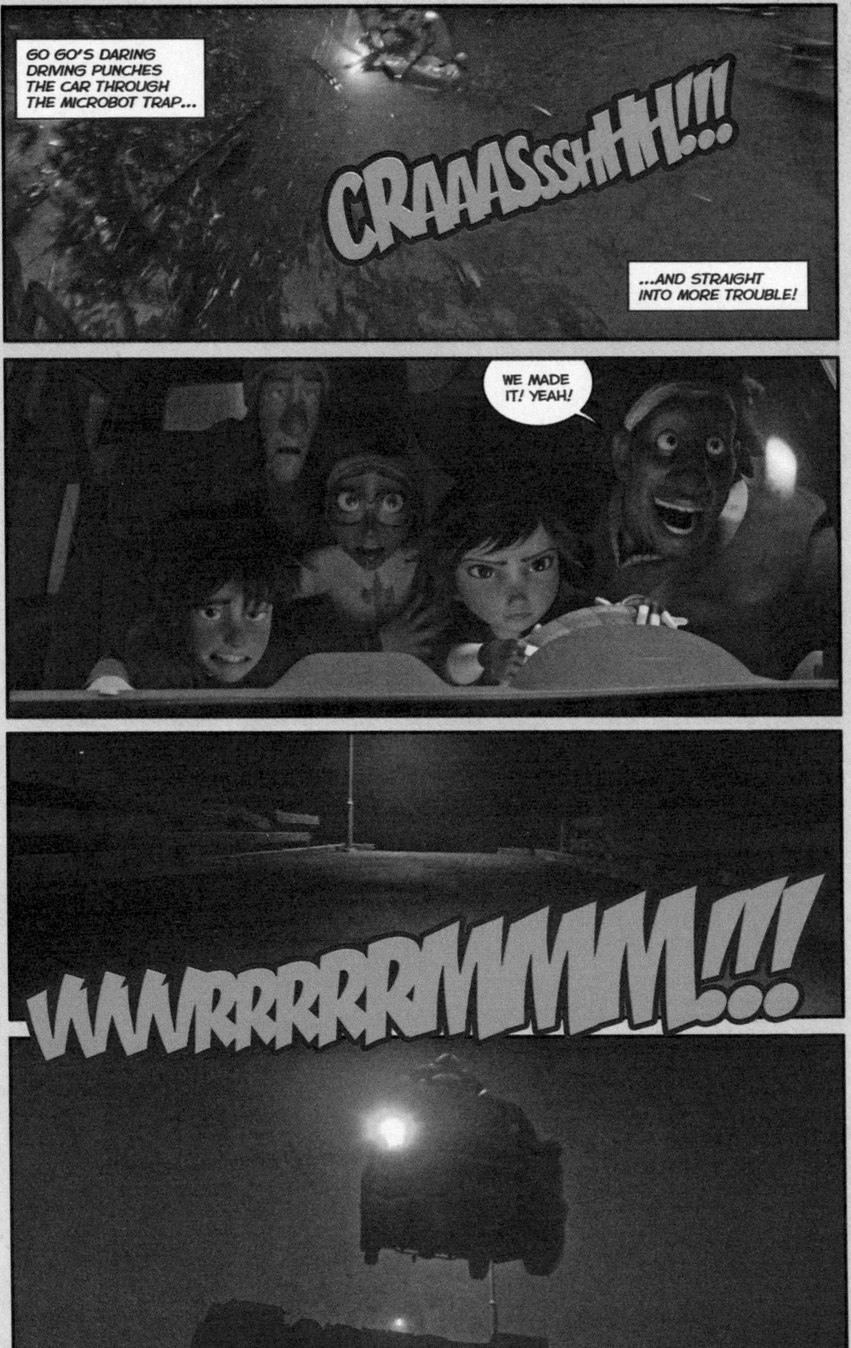
GO GO'S DARING DRIVING PUNCHES THE CAR THROUGH THE MICROBOT TRAP...
CRAAASSSHHH!!!
...AND STRAIGHT INTO MORE TROUBLE!
WE MADE IT! YEAH!
WWRRRRRMMMM!!!

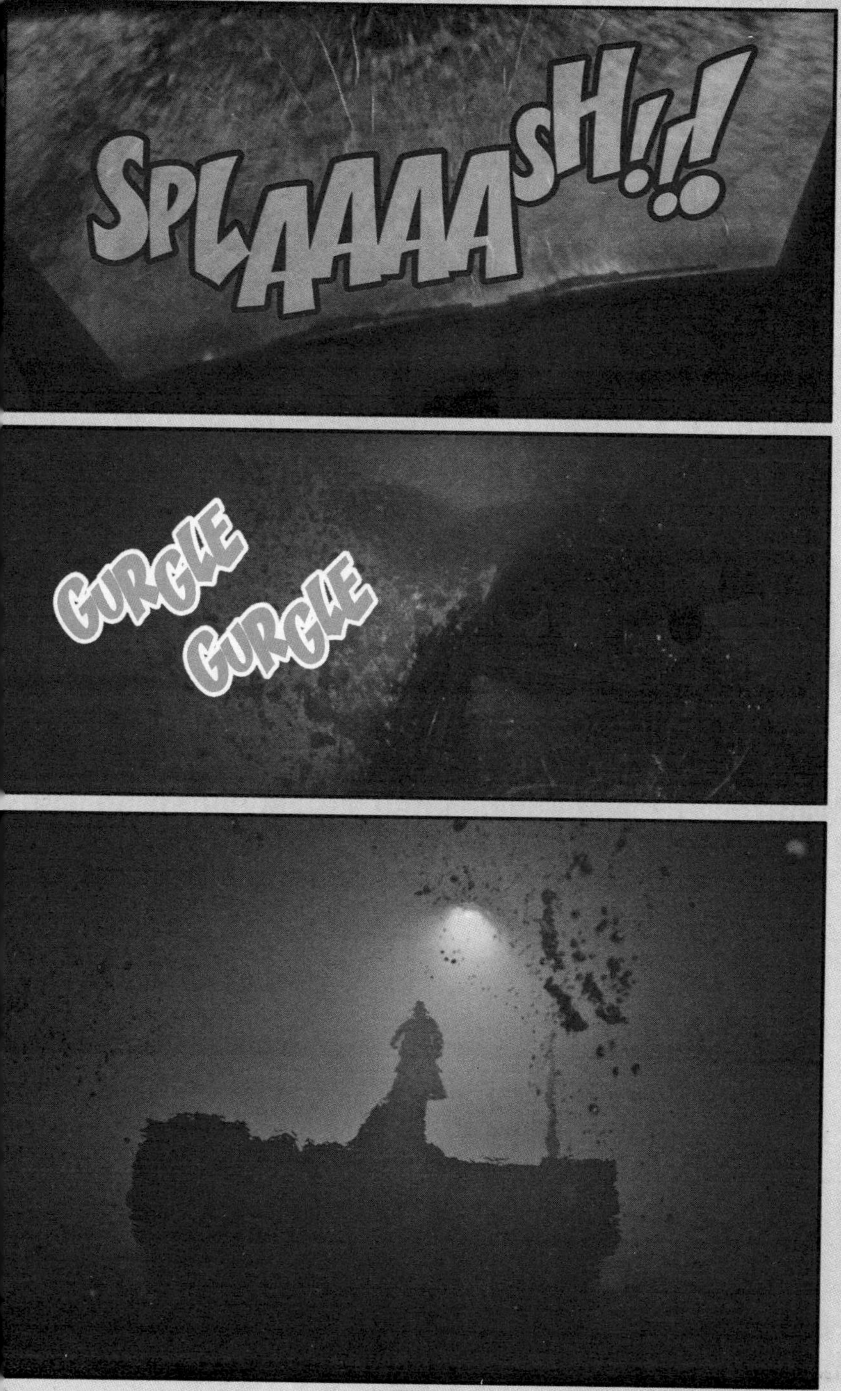
SPLAAAASH!!!
GURGLE
GURGLE

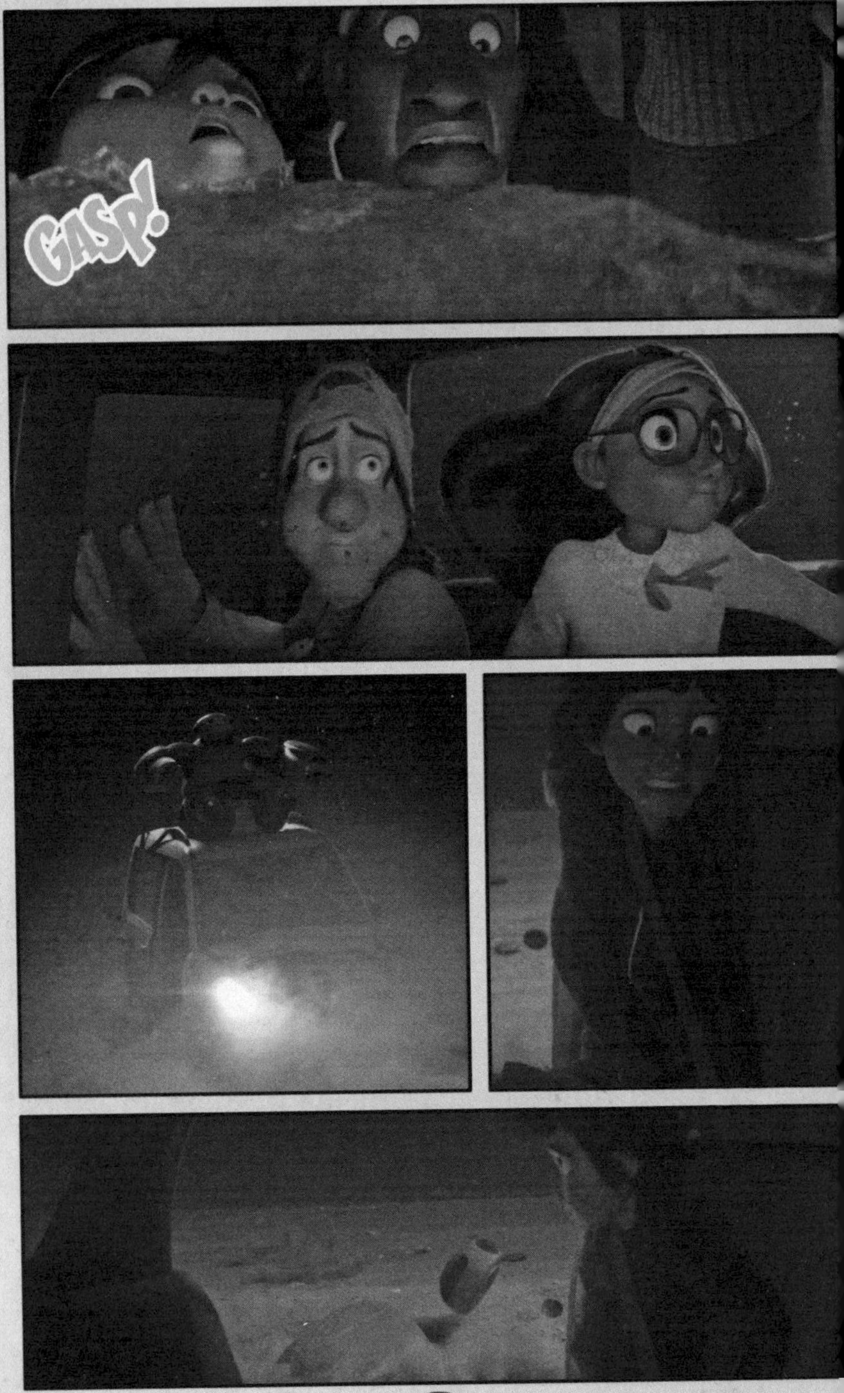
GASP!

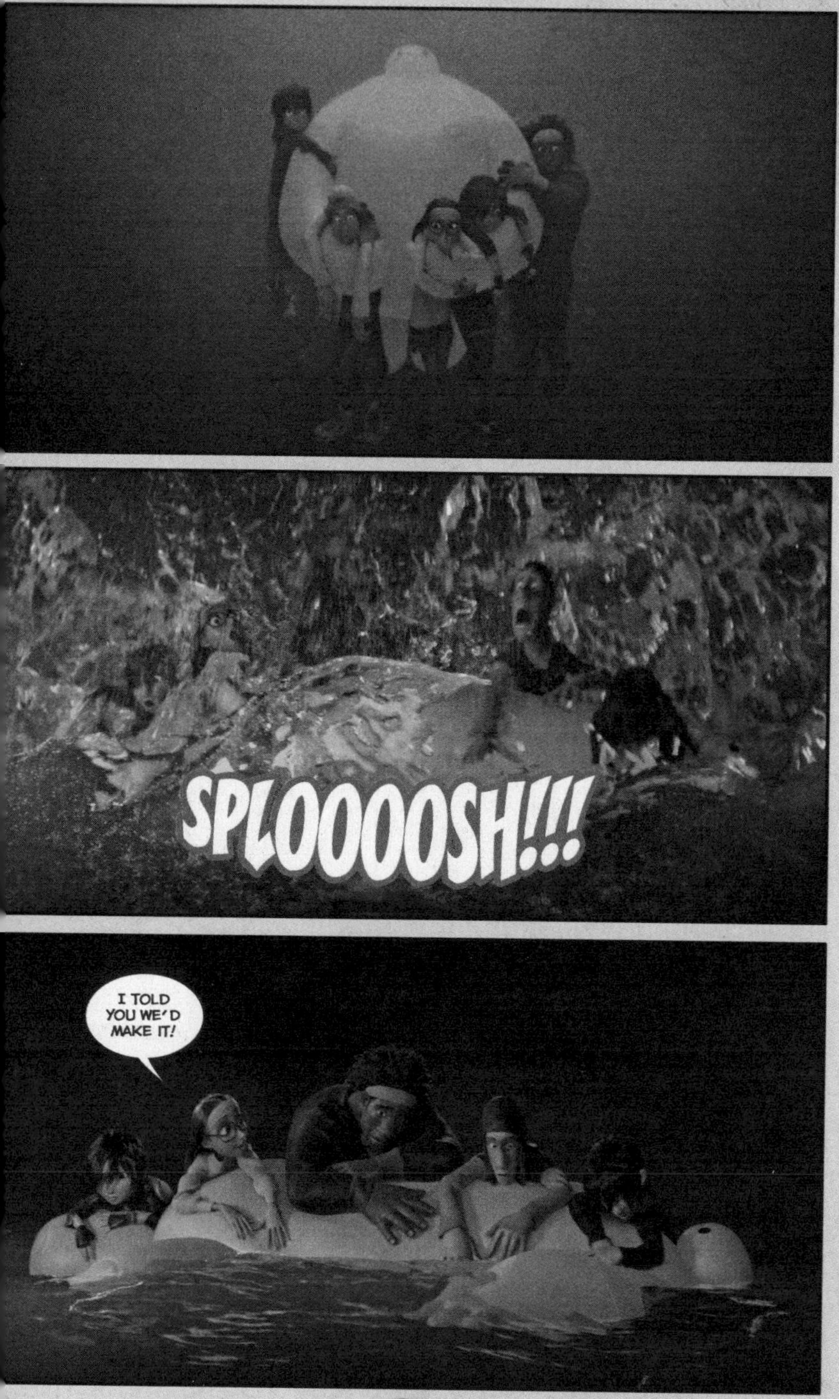
SPLOOOOSH!!!
I TOLD YOU WE'D MAKE IT!

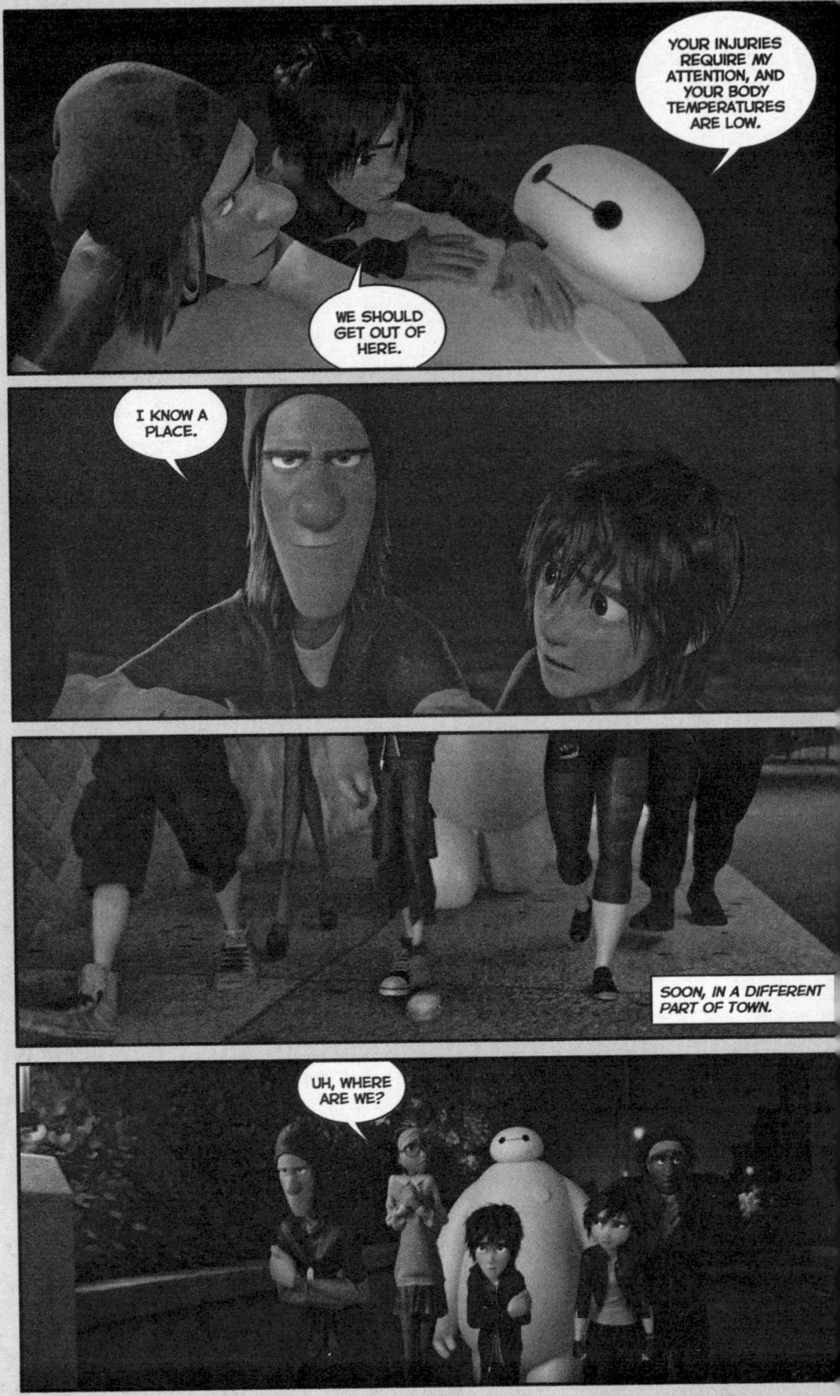
YOUR INJURIES REQUIRE MY ATTENTION, AND YOUR BODY TEMPERATURES ARE LOW.
WE SHOULD GET OUT OF HERE.
I KNOW A PLACE.
SOON, IN A DIFFERENT PART OF TOWN.
UH, WHERE ARE WE?

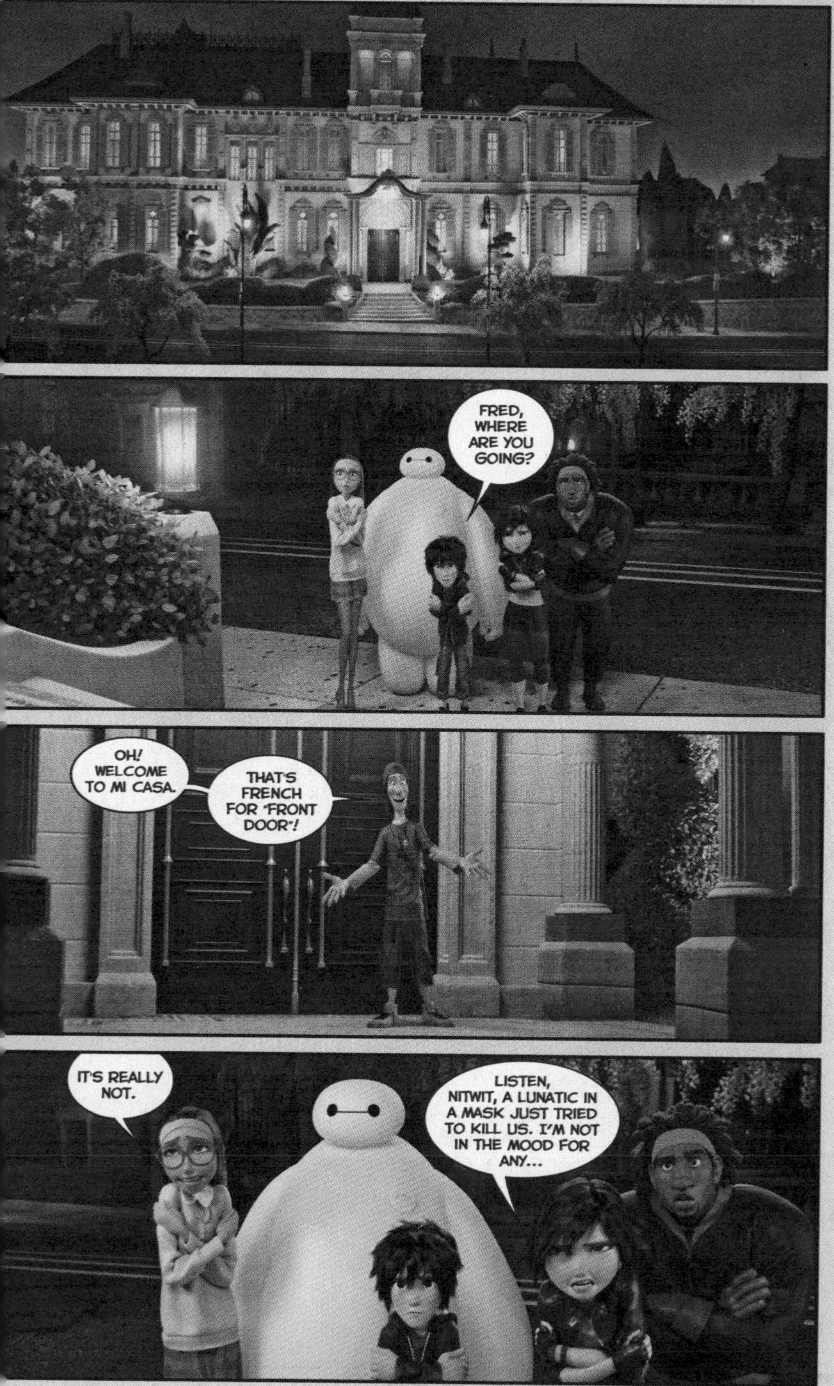
FRED, WHERE ARE YOU GOING?
OH! WELCOME TO MI CASA.
THAT'S FRENCH FOR "FRONT DOOR"!
IT'S REALLY NOT.
LISTEN, NITWIT, A LUNATIC IN A MASK JUST TRIED TO KILL US. I'M NOT IN THE MOOD FOR ANY...

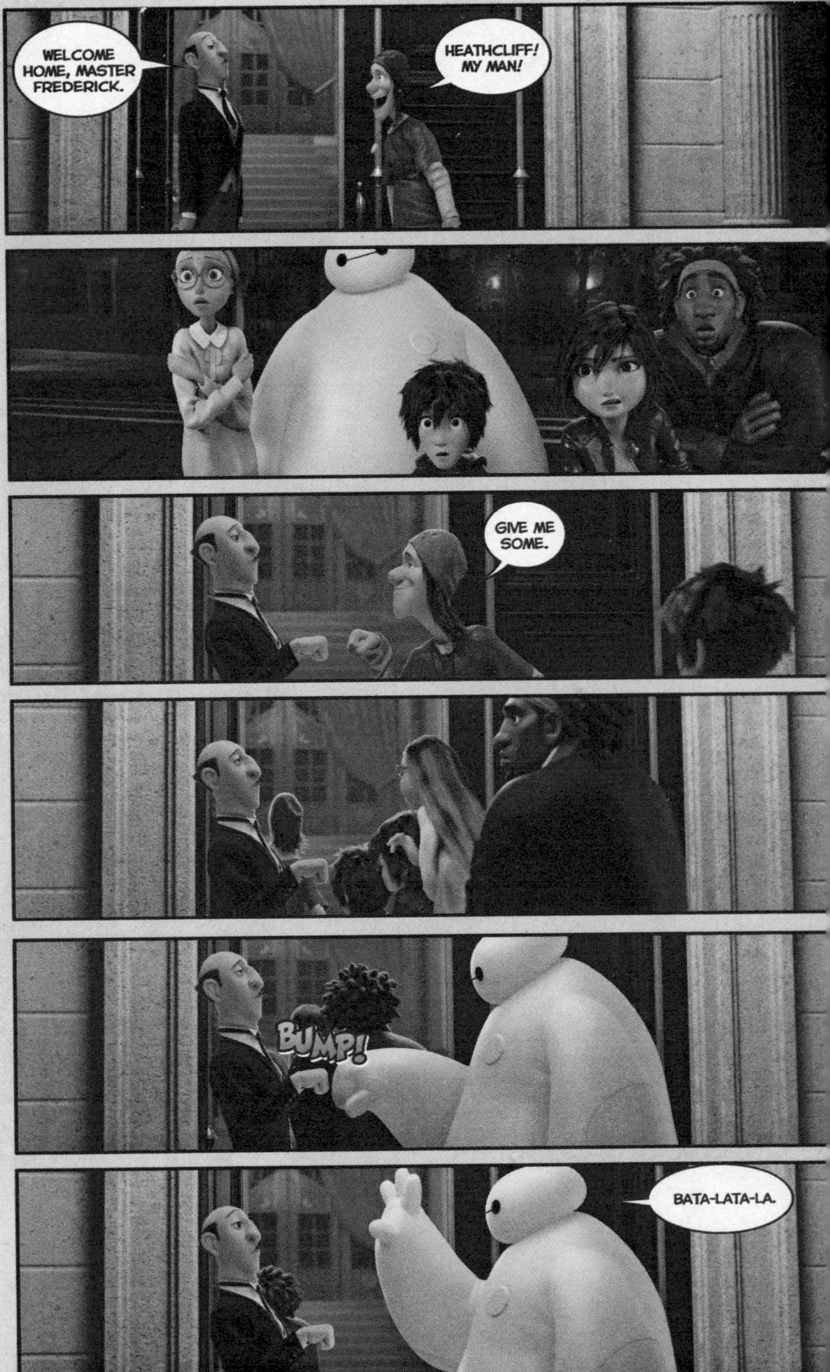
WELCOME HOME, MASTER FREDERICK.
HEATHCLIFF! MY MAN!
GIVE ME SOME.
BUMP!
BATA-LATA-LA.

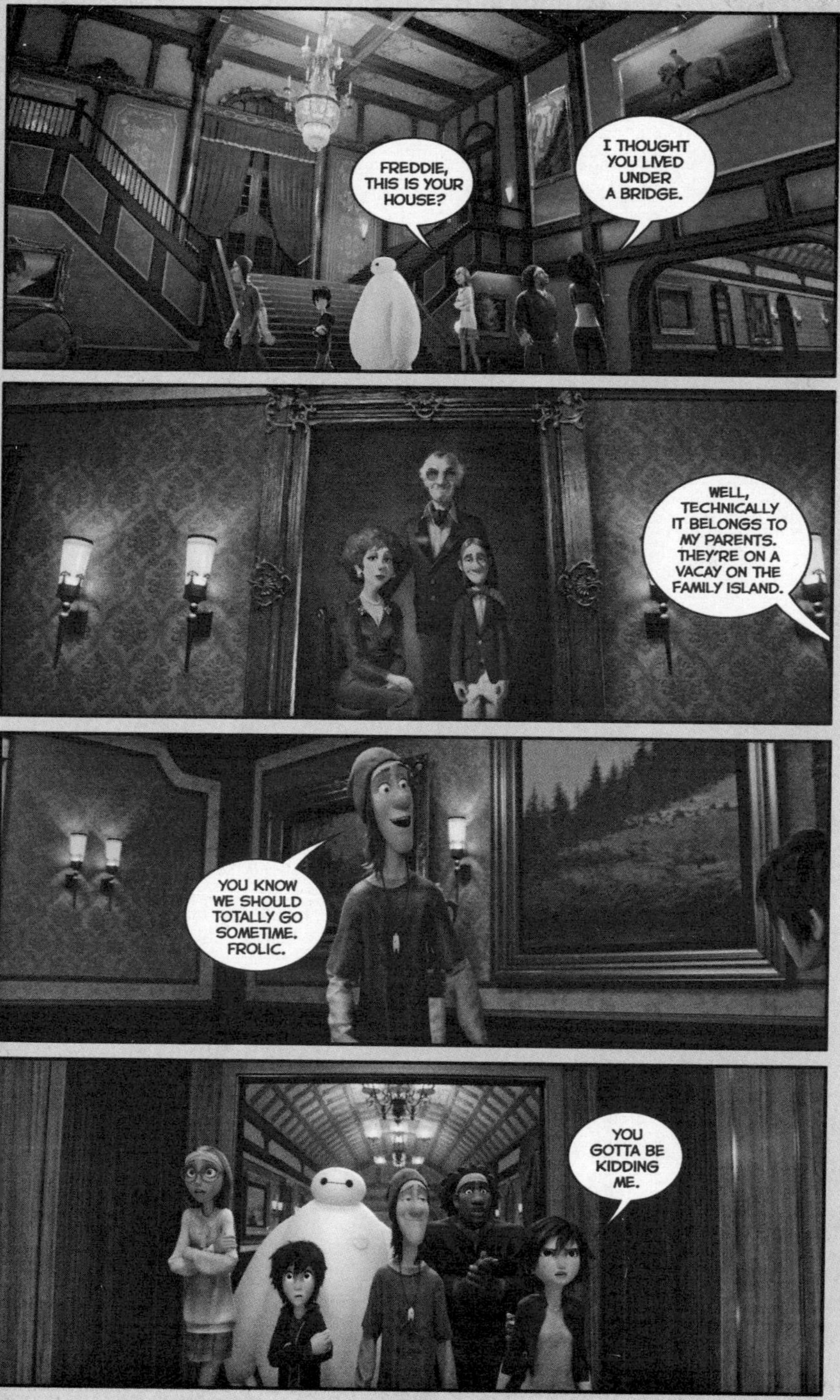
FREDDIE, THIS IS YOUR HOUSE?
I THOUGHT YOU LIVED UNDER A BRIDGE.
WELL, TECHNICALLY IT BELONGS TO MY PARENTS. THEY'RE ON A VACAY ON THE FAMILY ISLAND.
YOU KNOW WE SHOULD TOTALLY GO SOMETIME. FROLIC.
YOU GOTTA BE KIDDING ME.

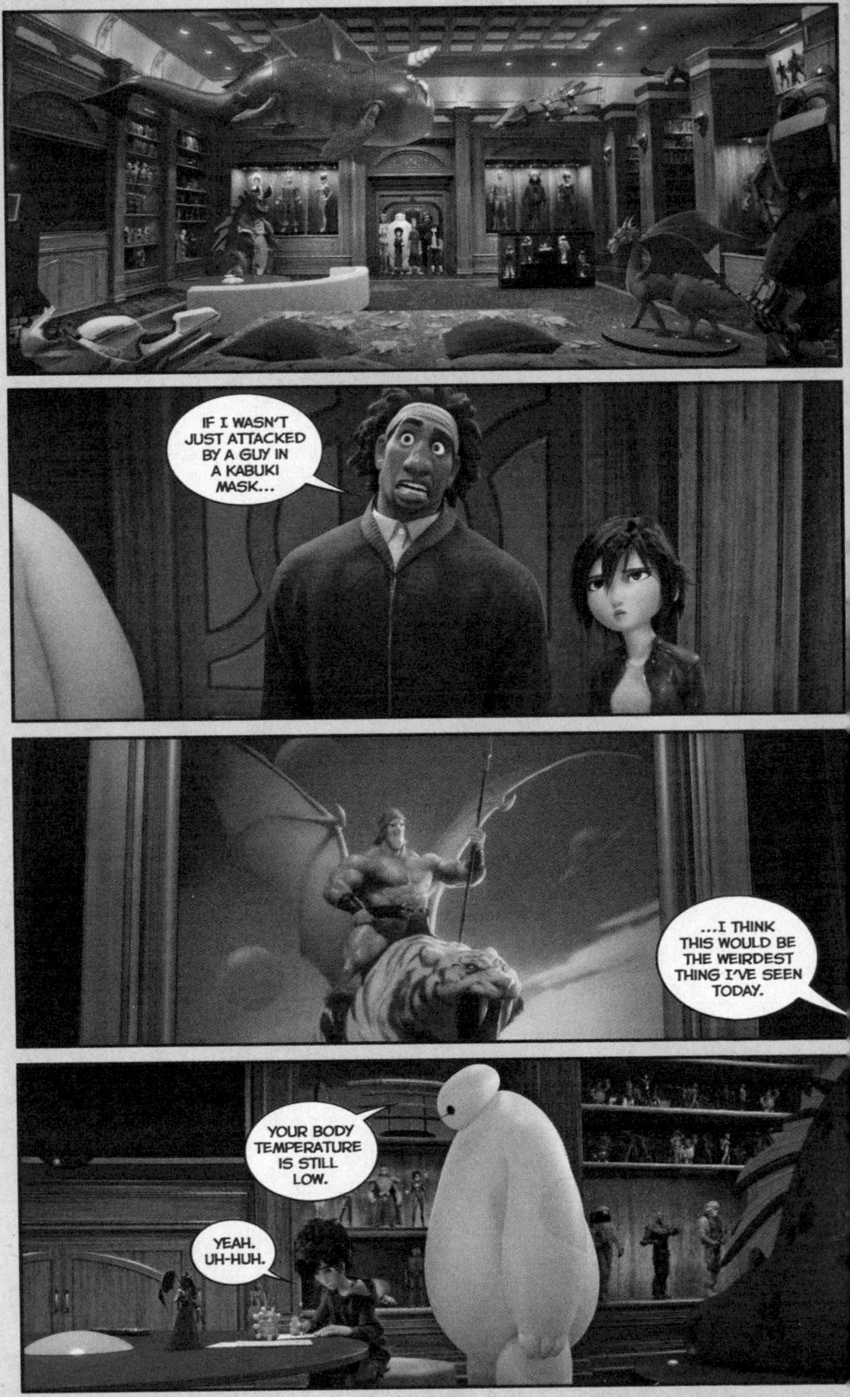
IF I WASN'T JUST ATTACKED BY A GUY IN A KABUKI MASK...
...I THINK THIS WOULD BE THE WEIRDEST THING I'VE SEEN TODAY.
YOUR BODY TEMPERATURE IS STILL LOW.
YEAH. UH-HUH.

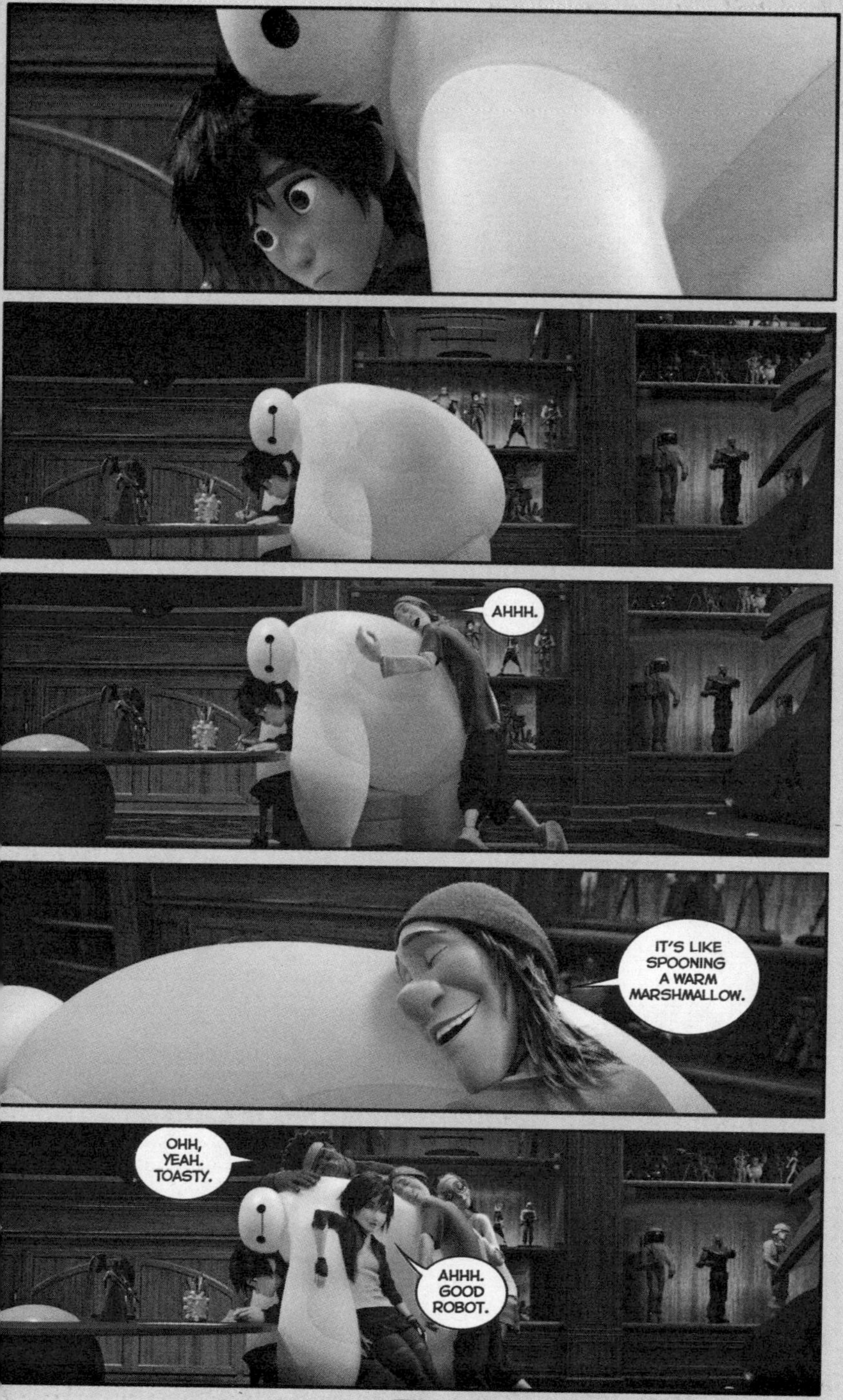
AHHH.
IT'S LIKE SPOONING A WARM MARSHMALLOW.
OHH, YEAH. TOASTY.
AHHH. GOOD ROBOT.

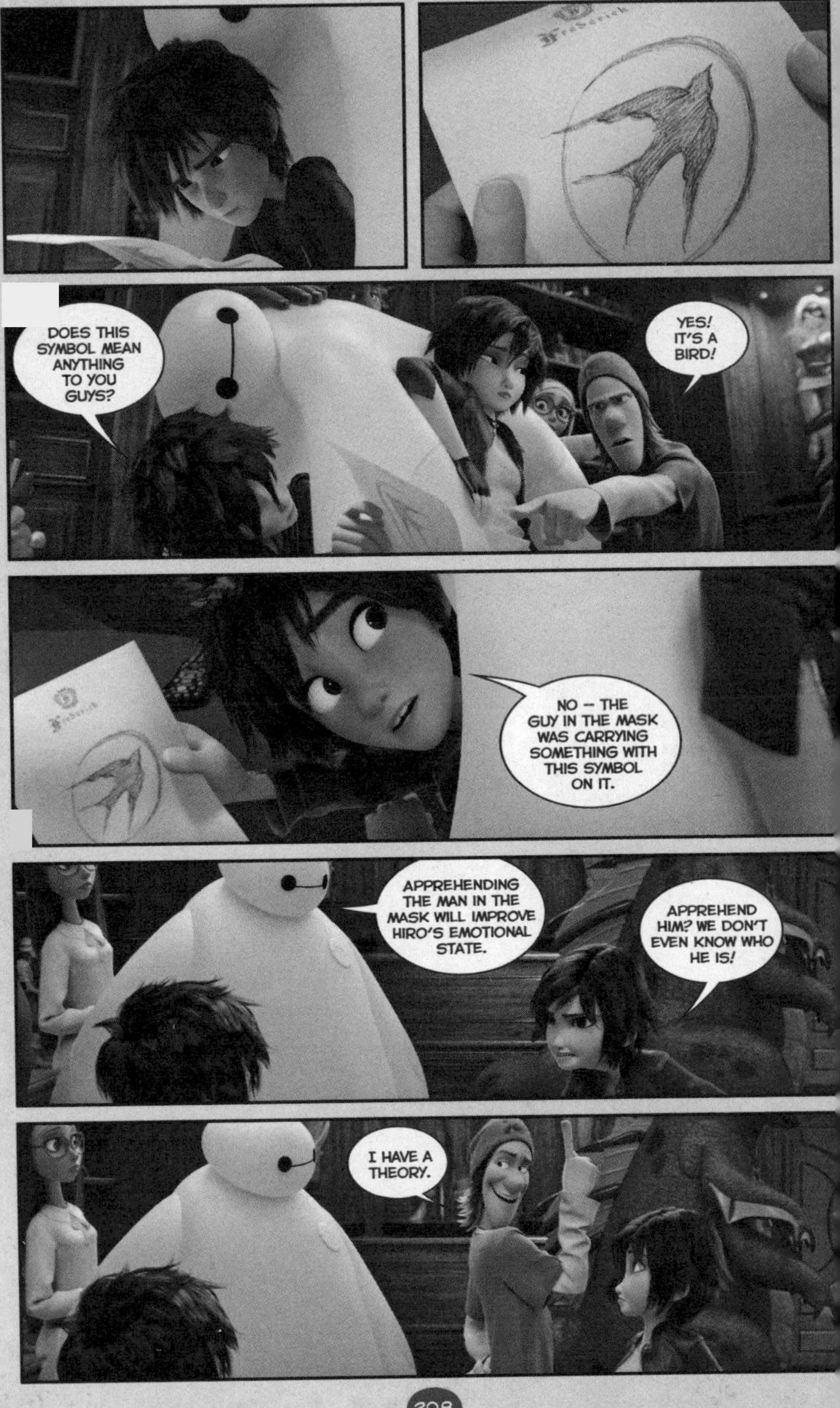
DOES THIS SYMBOL MEAN ANYTHING TO YOU GUYS?
YES! IT'S A BIRD!
NO -- THE GUY IN THE MASK WAS CARRYING SOMETHING WITH THIS SYMBOL ON IT.
APPREHENDING THE MAN IN THE MASK WILL IMPROVE HIRO'S EMOTIONAL STATE.
APPREHEND HIM? WE DON'T EVEN KNOW WHO HE IS!
I HAVE A THEORY.

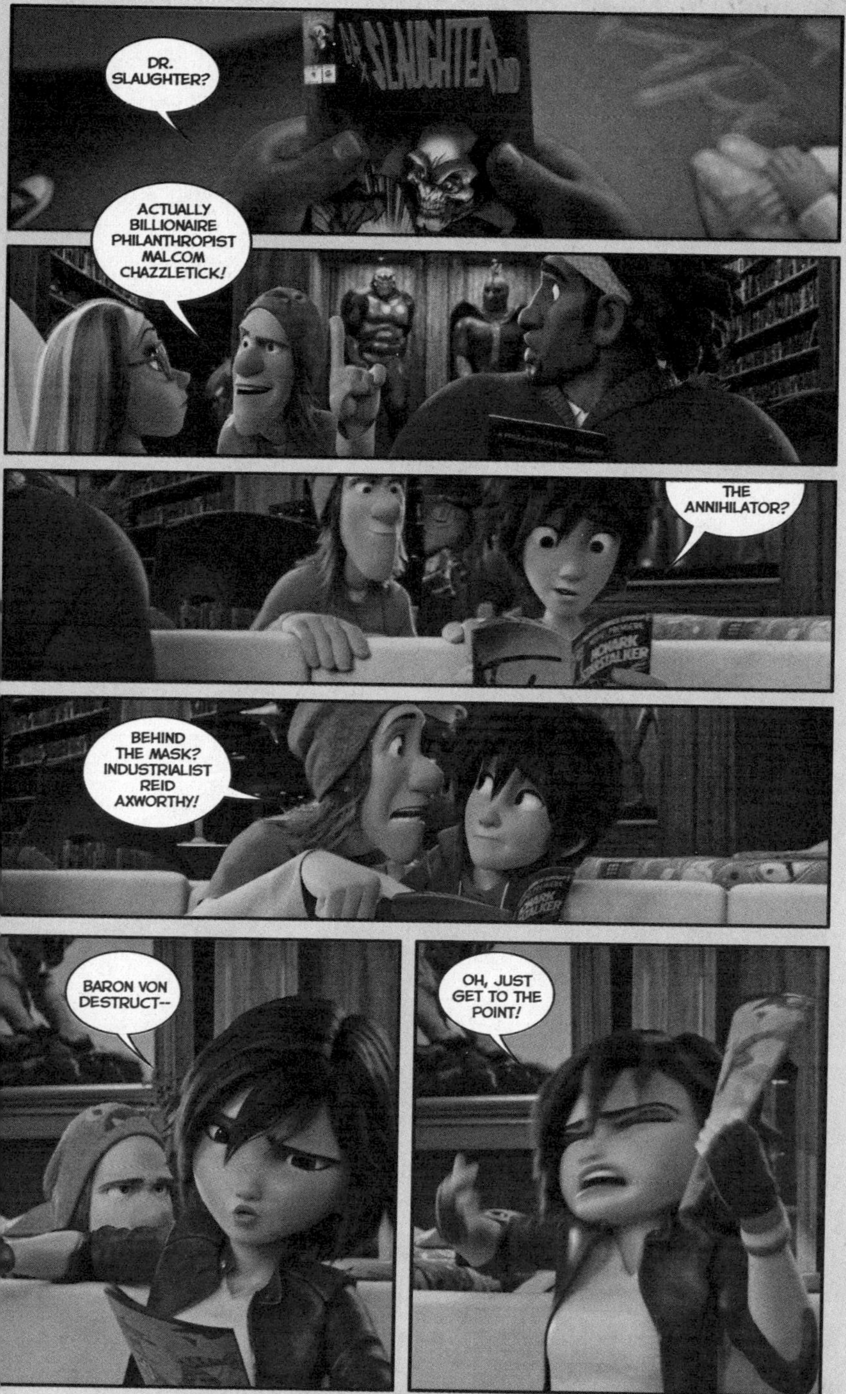
DR. SLAUGHTER?
ACTUALLY BILLIONAIRE PHILANTHROPIST MALCOM CHAZZLETICK!
THE ANNIHILATOR?
BEHIND THE MASK? INDUSTRIALIST REID AXWORTHY!
BARON VON DESTRUCT--
OH, JUST GET TO THE POINT!

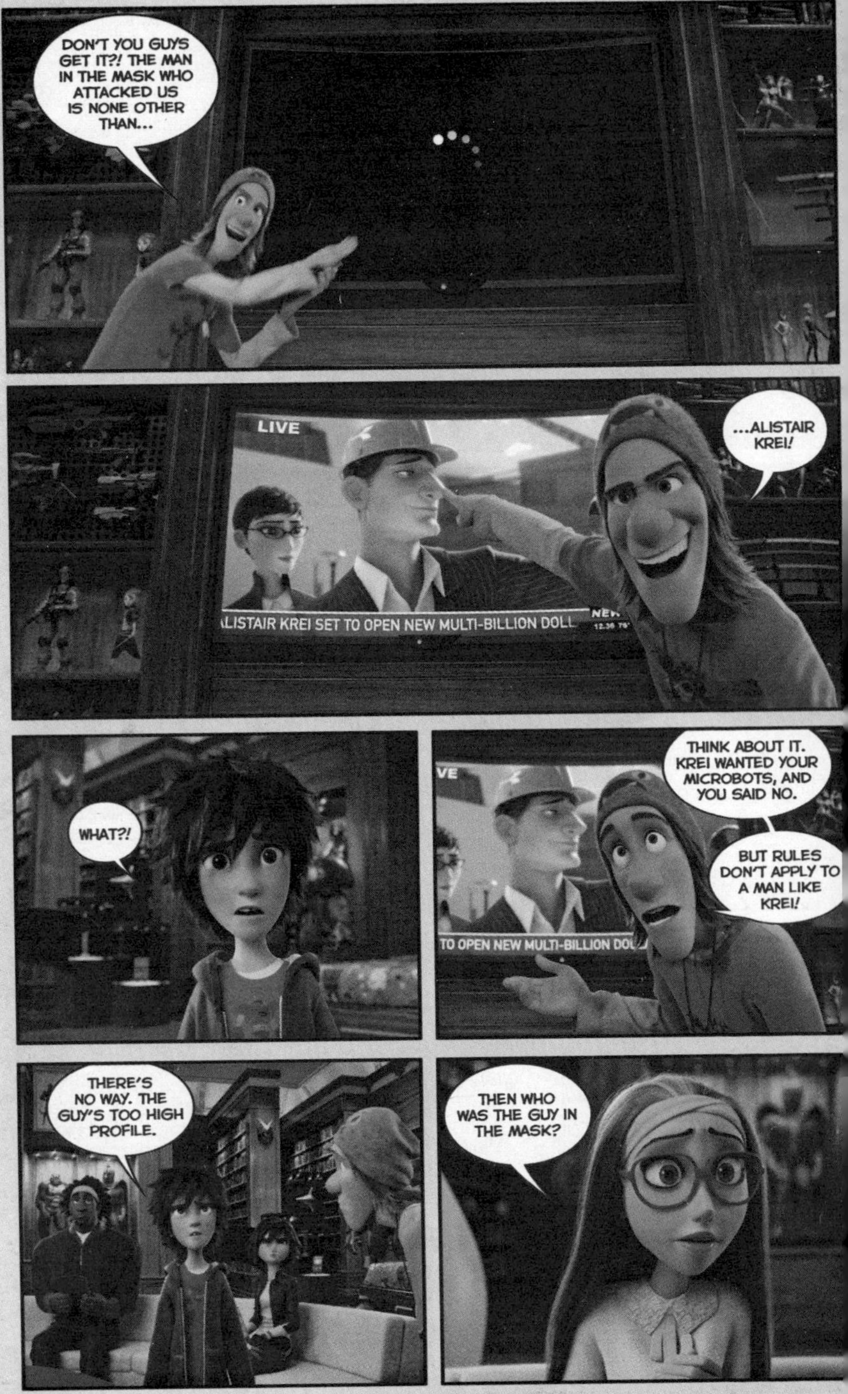
DON'T YOU GUYS GET IT?! THE MAN IN THE MASK WHO ATTACKED US IS NONE OTHER THAN...
LIVE
LISTAIR KREI SET TO OPEN NEW MULTI-BILLION DOLL
...ALISTAIR KREI!
WHAT?!
THINK ABOUT IT. KREI WANTED YOUR MICROBOTS, AND YOU SAID NO.
BUT RULES DON'T APPLY TO A MAN LIKE KREI!
TO OPEN NEW MULTI-BILLION DOL
THERE'S NO WAY. THE GUY'S TOO HIGH PROFILE.
THEN WHO WAS THE GUY IN THE MASK?

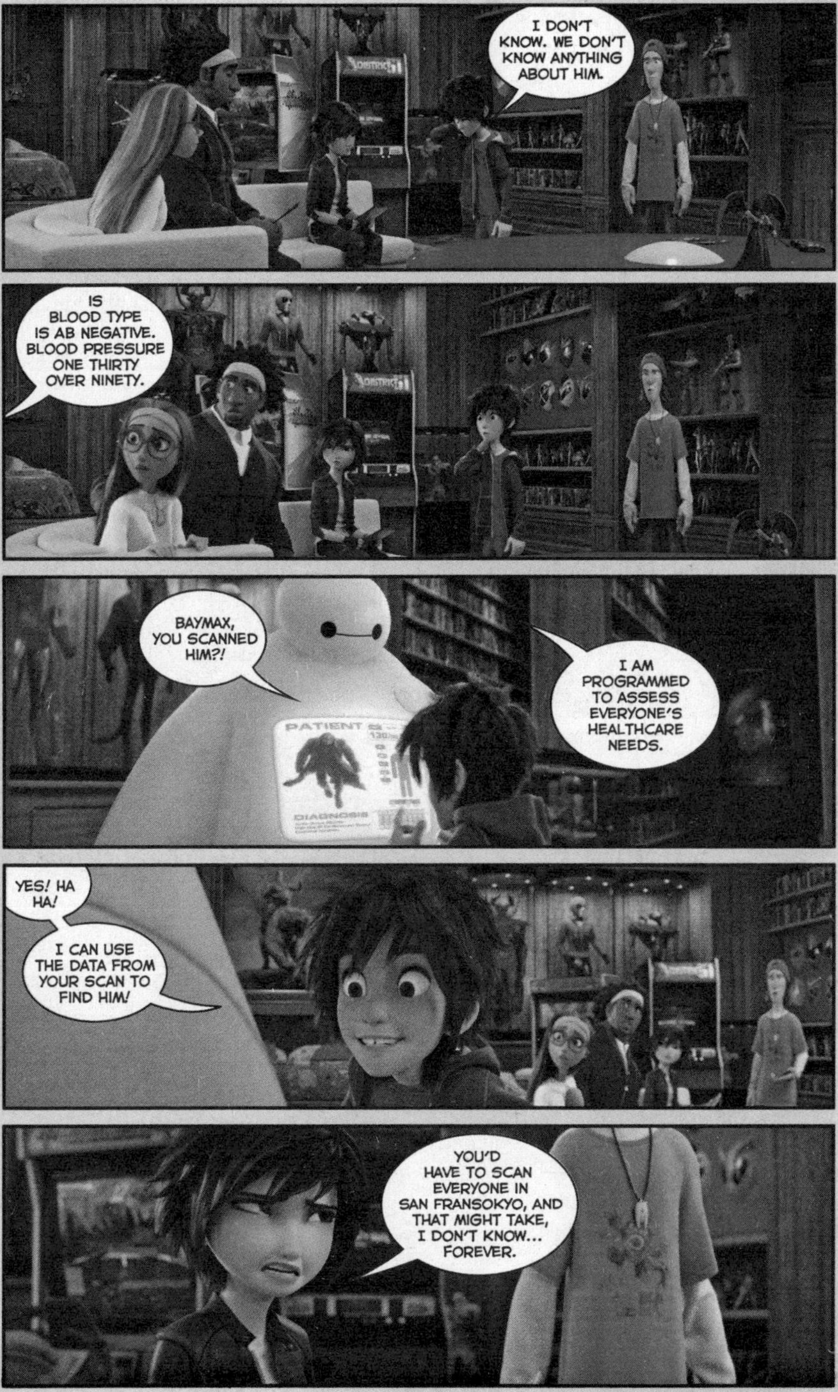

I DON'T KNOW. WE DON'T KNOW ANYTHING ABOUT HIM.
IS BLOOD TYPE IS AB NEGATIVE. BLOOD PRESSURE ONE THIRTY OVER NINETY.
BAYMAX, YOU SCANNED HIM?!
I AM PROGRAMMED TO ASSESS EVERYONE'S HEALTHCARE NEEDS.
PATIENT
DIAGNOSIS
YES! HA HA!
I CAN USE THE DATA FROM YOUR SCAN TO FIND HIM!
YOU'D HAVE TO SCAN EVERYONE IN SAN FRANSOKYO, AND THAT MIGHT TAKE, I DON'T KNOW... FOREVER.

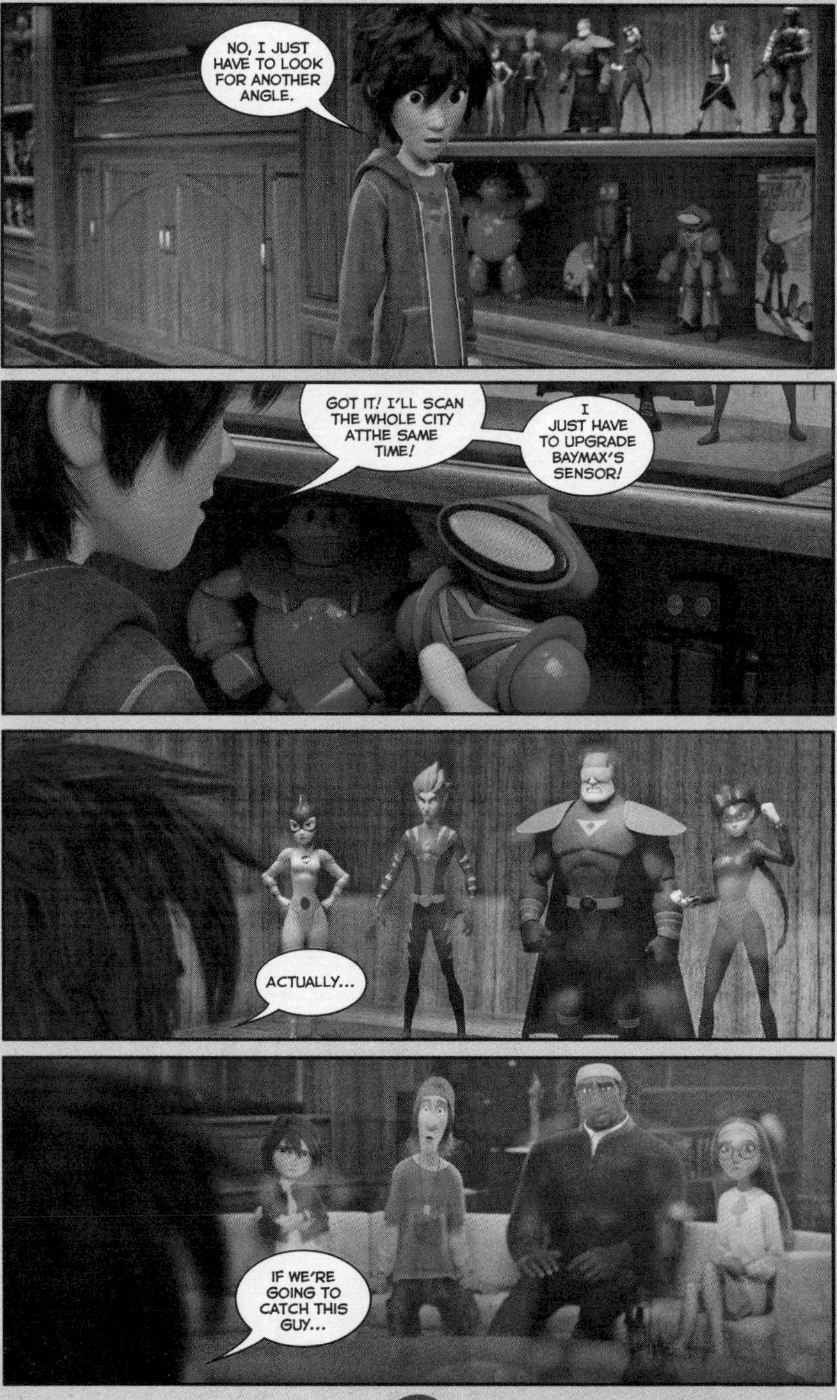
NO, I JUST HAVE TO LOOK FOR ANOTHER ANGLE.
GOT IT! I'LL SCAN THE WHOLE CITY ATTHE SAME TIME!
I JUST HAVE TO UPGRADE BAYMAX'S SENSOR!
ACTUALLY...
IF WE'RE GOING TO CATCH THIS GUY...

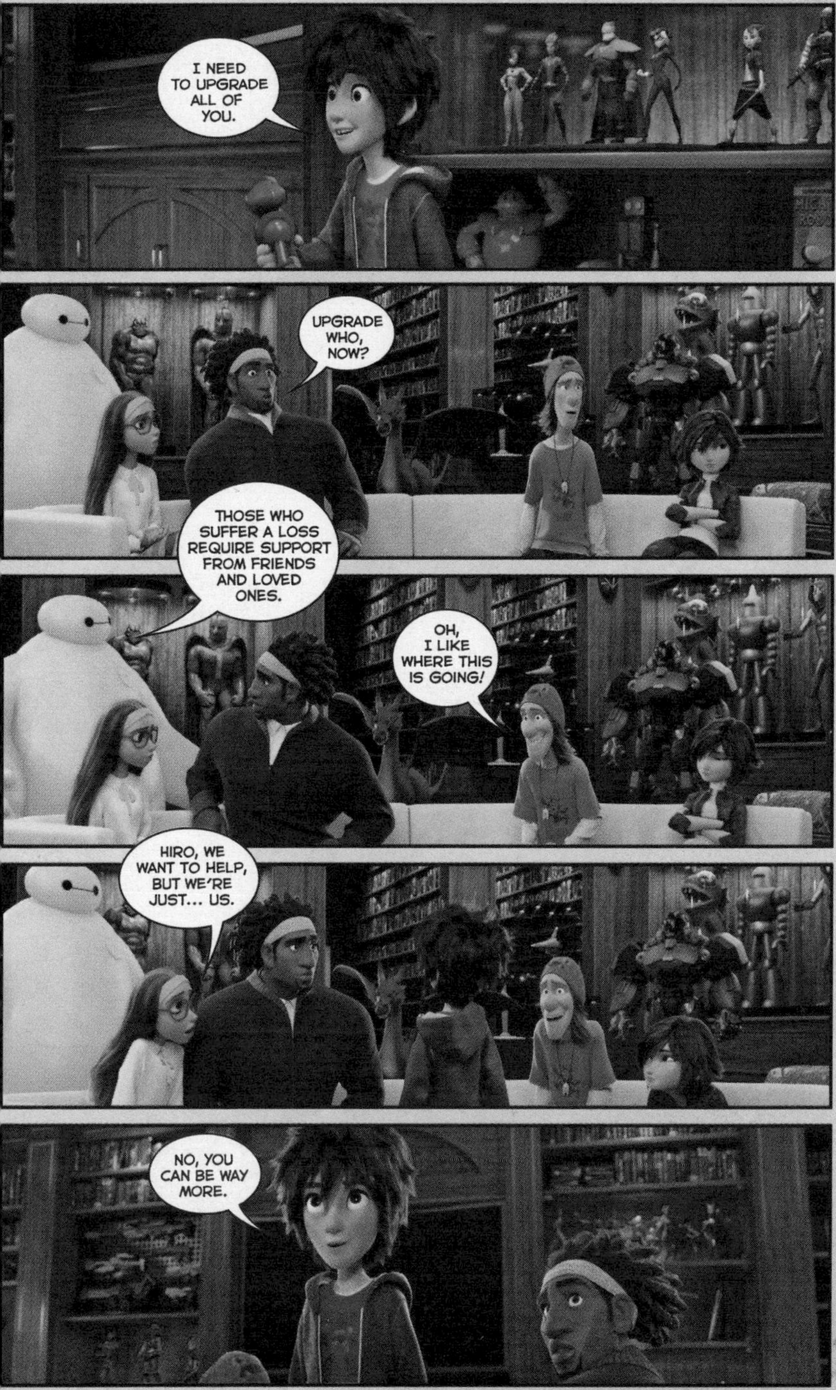
I NEED TO UPGRADE ALL OF YOU.
UPGRADE WHO, NOW?
THOSE WHO SUFFER A LOSS REQUIRE SUPPORT FROM FRIENDS AND LOVED ONES.
OH, I LIKE WHERE THIS IS GOING!
HIRO, WE WANT TO HELP, BUT WE'RE JUST... US.
NO, YOU CAN BE WAY MORE.

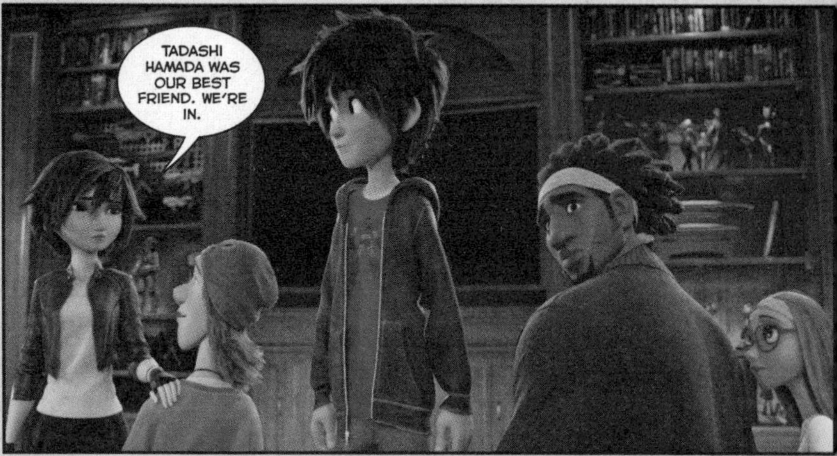
TADASHI HAMADA WAS OUR BEST FRIEND. WE'RE IN.

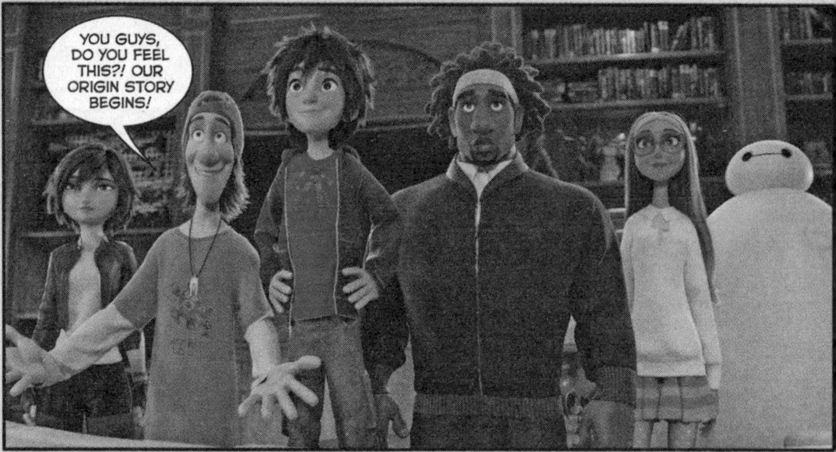
YOU GUYS, DO YOU FEEL THIS?! OUR ORIGIN STORY BEGINS!

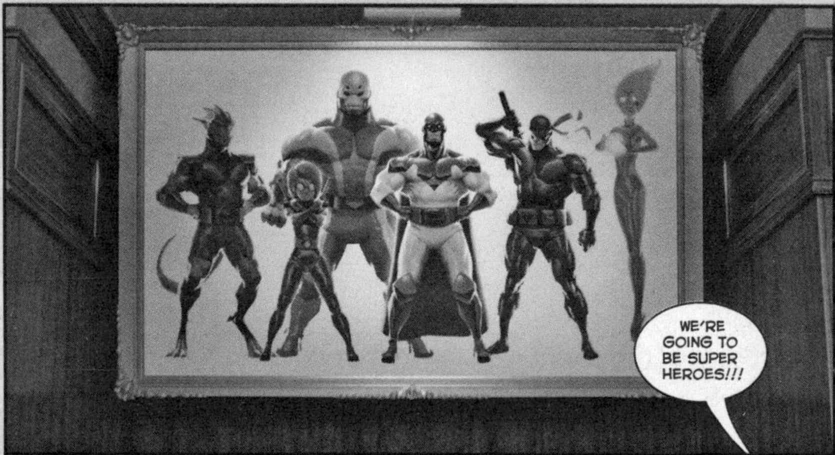
WE'RE GOING TO BE SUPER HEROES!!!

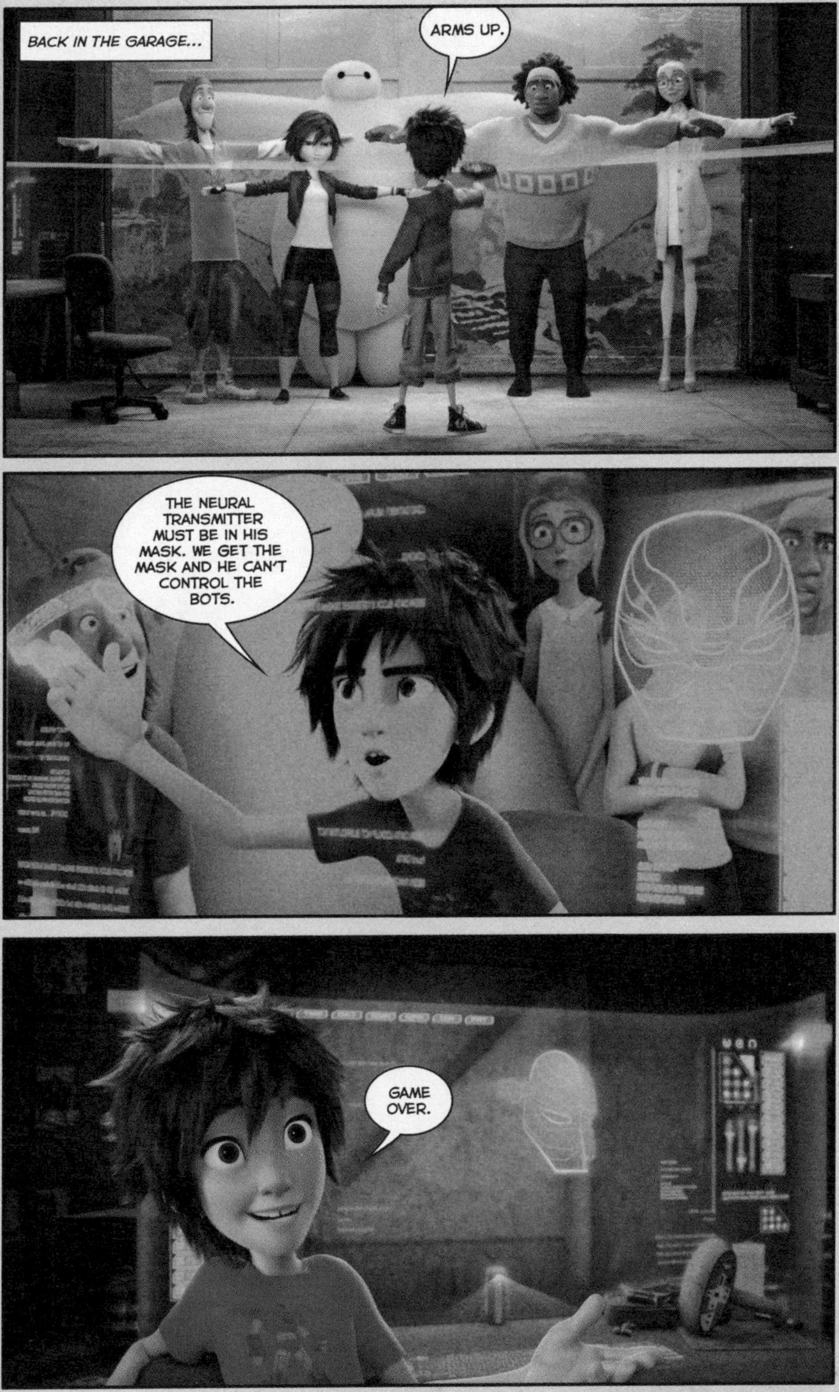
BACK IN THE GARAGE...
ARMS UP.
THE NEURAL TRANSMITTER MUST BE IN HIS MASK. WE GET THE MASK AND HE CAN'T CONTROL THE BOTS.
GAME OVER.

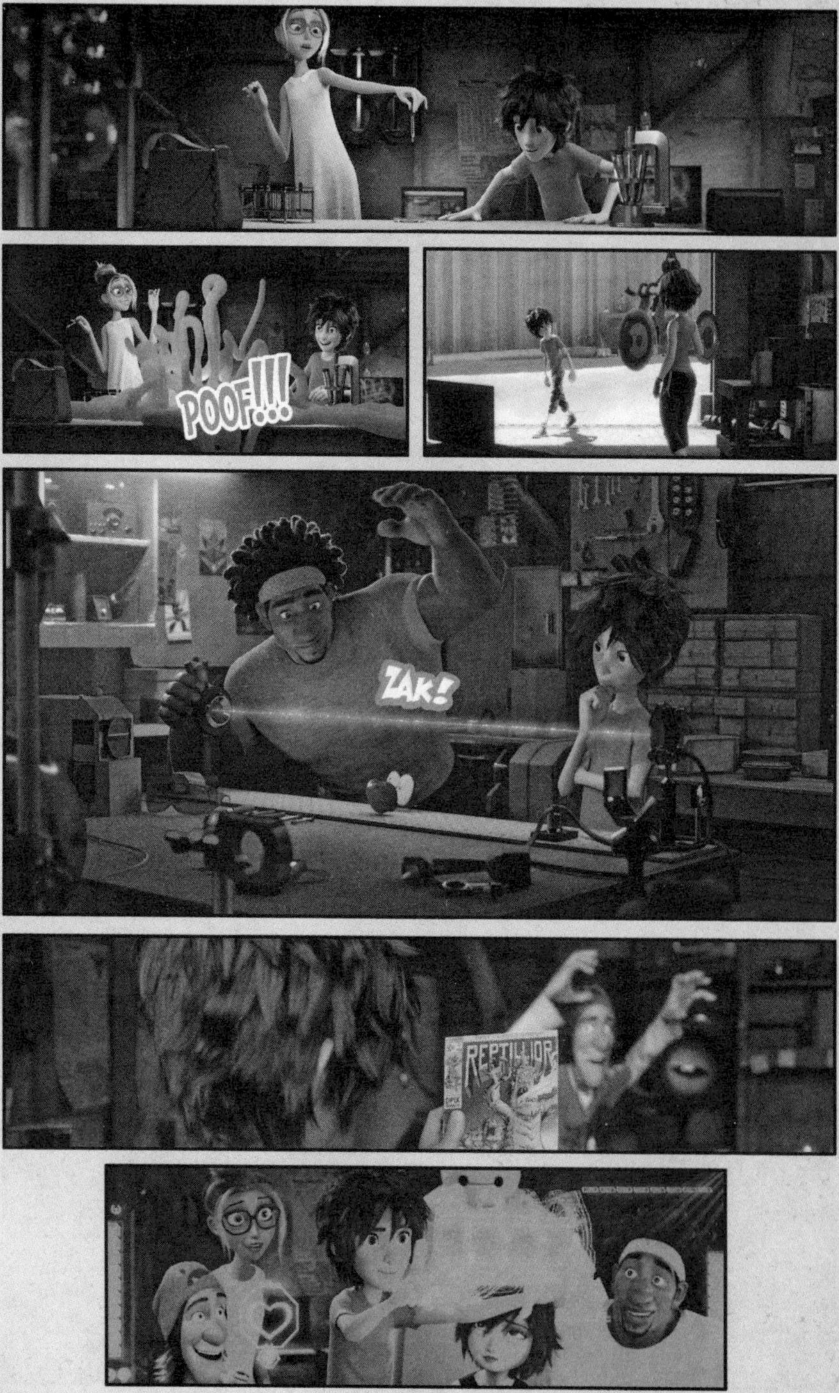
POOF!!!
ZAK!
REPTILLIOR

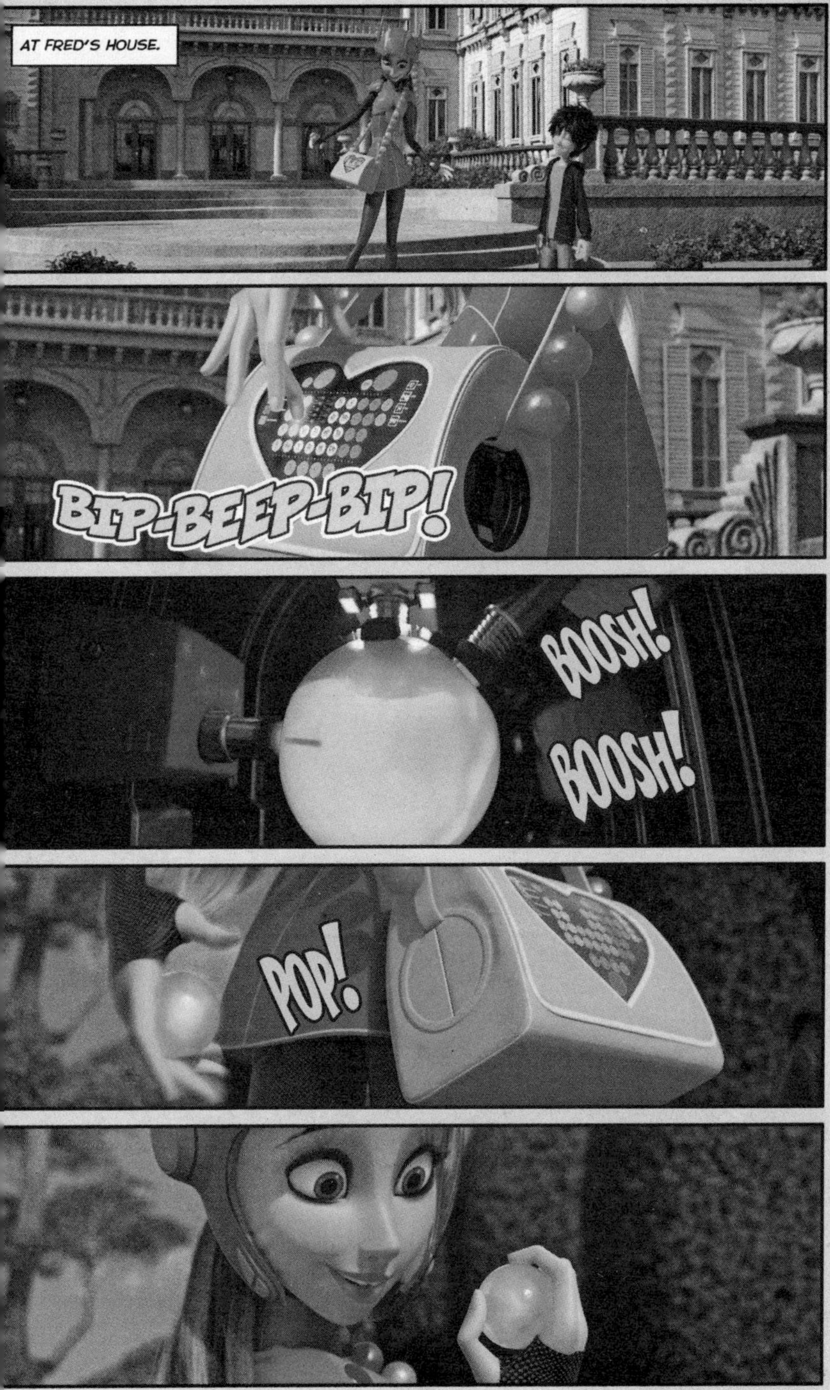

AT FRED'S HOUSE.
BIP-BEEP-BIP!
BOOSH!
BOOSH!
POP!

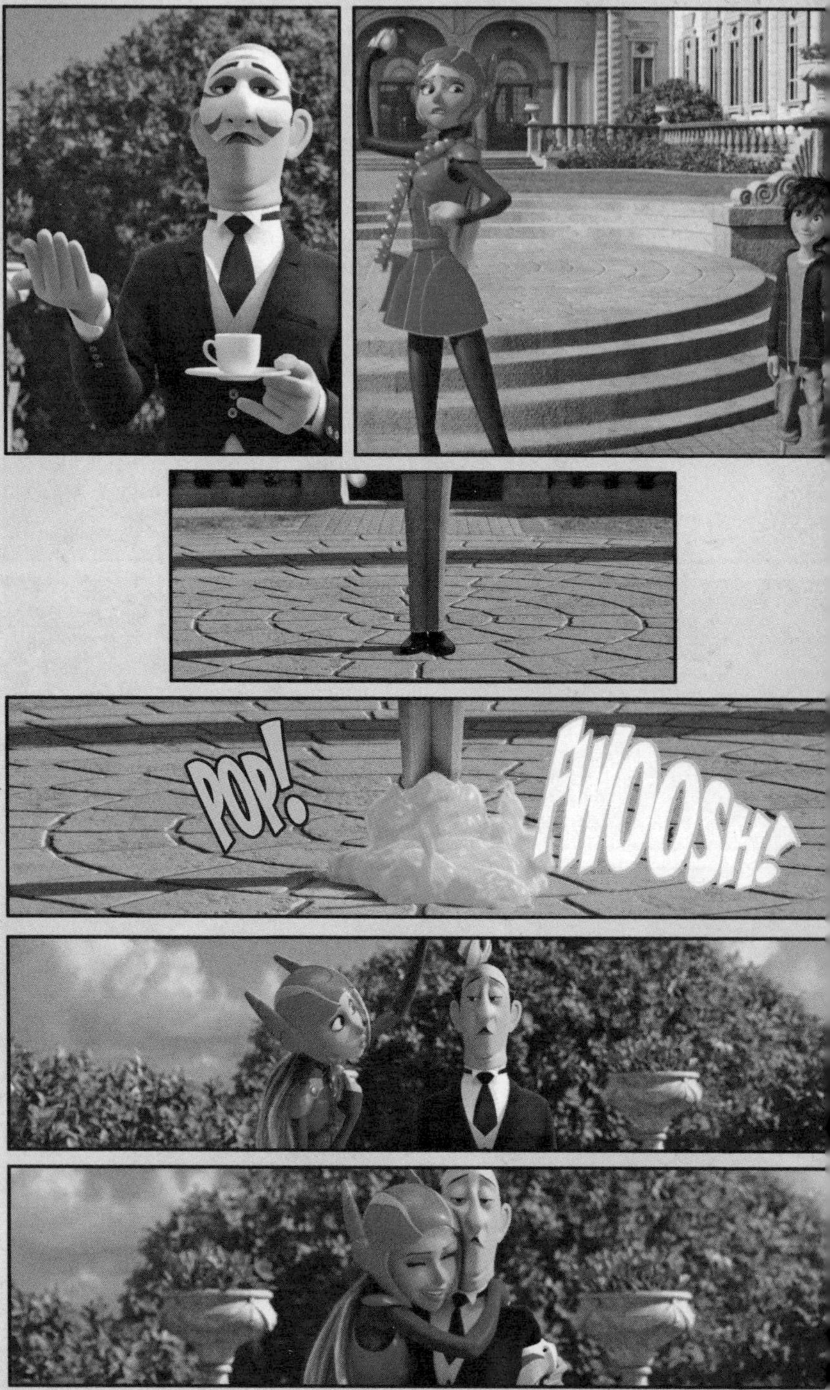
POP!
FWOOSH!

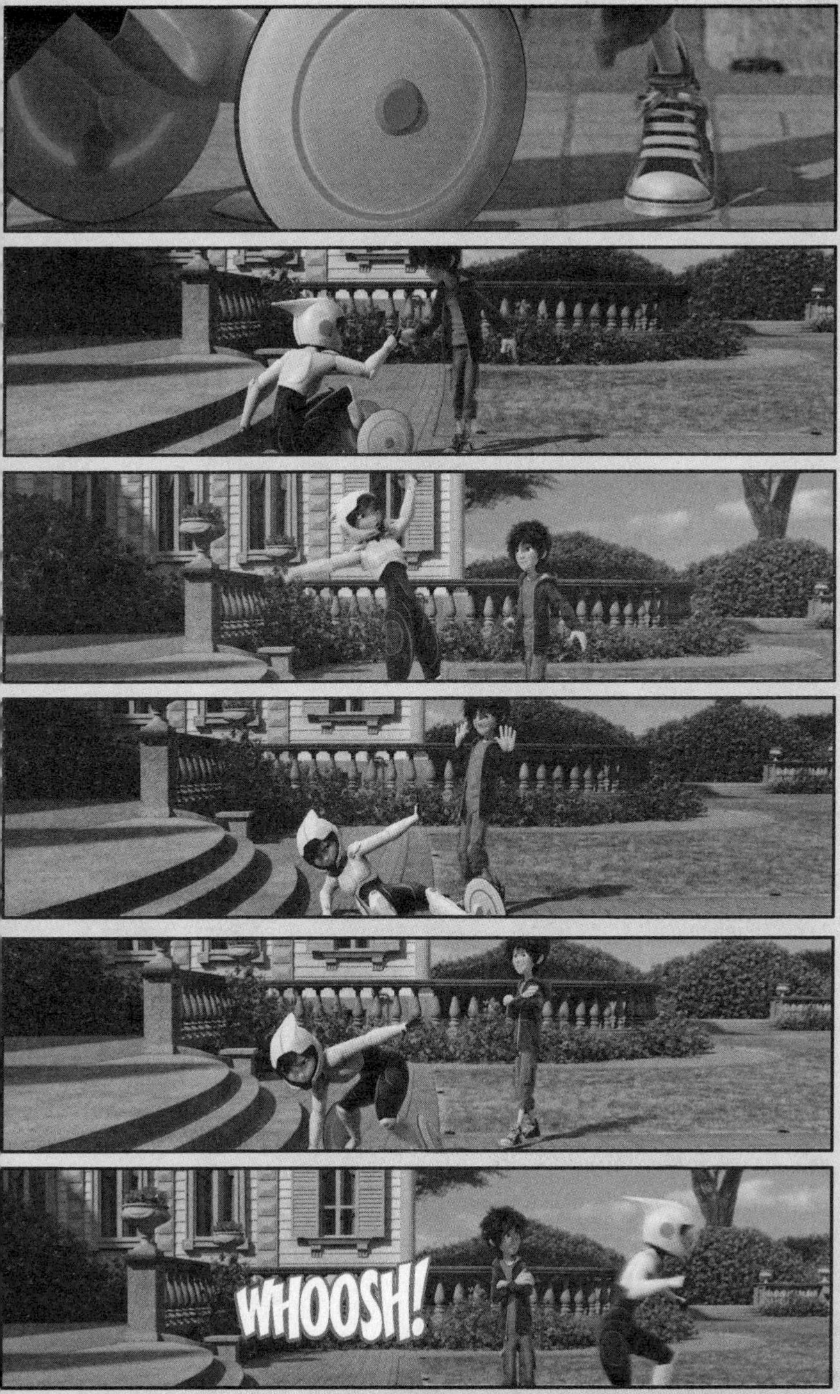
WHOOSH!

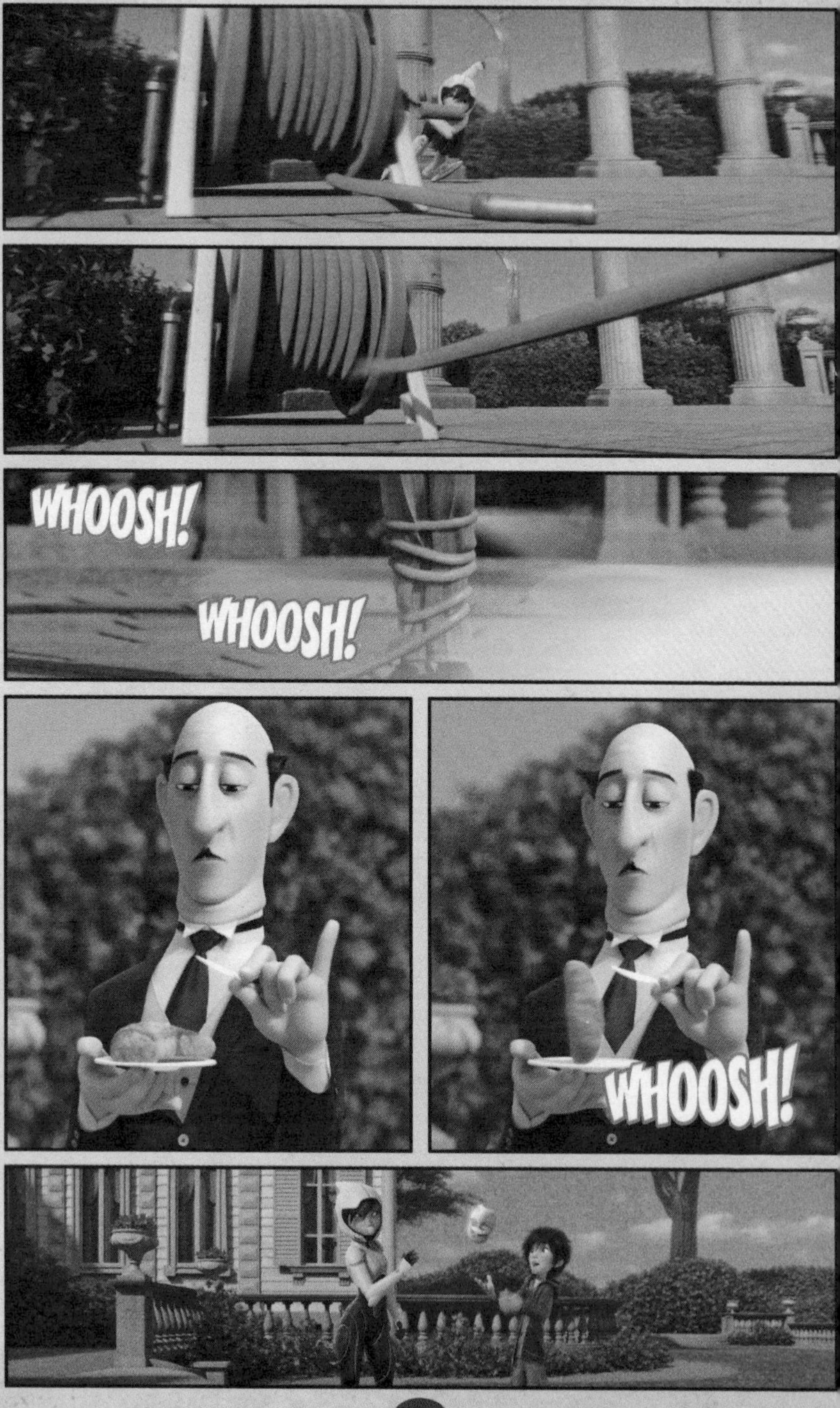
WHOOSH!
WHOOSH!
WHOOSH!

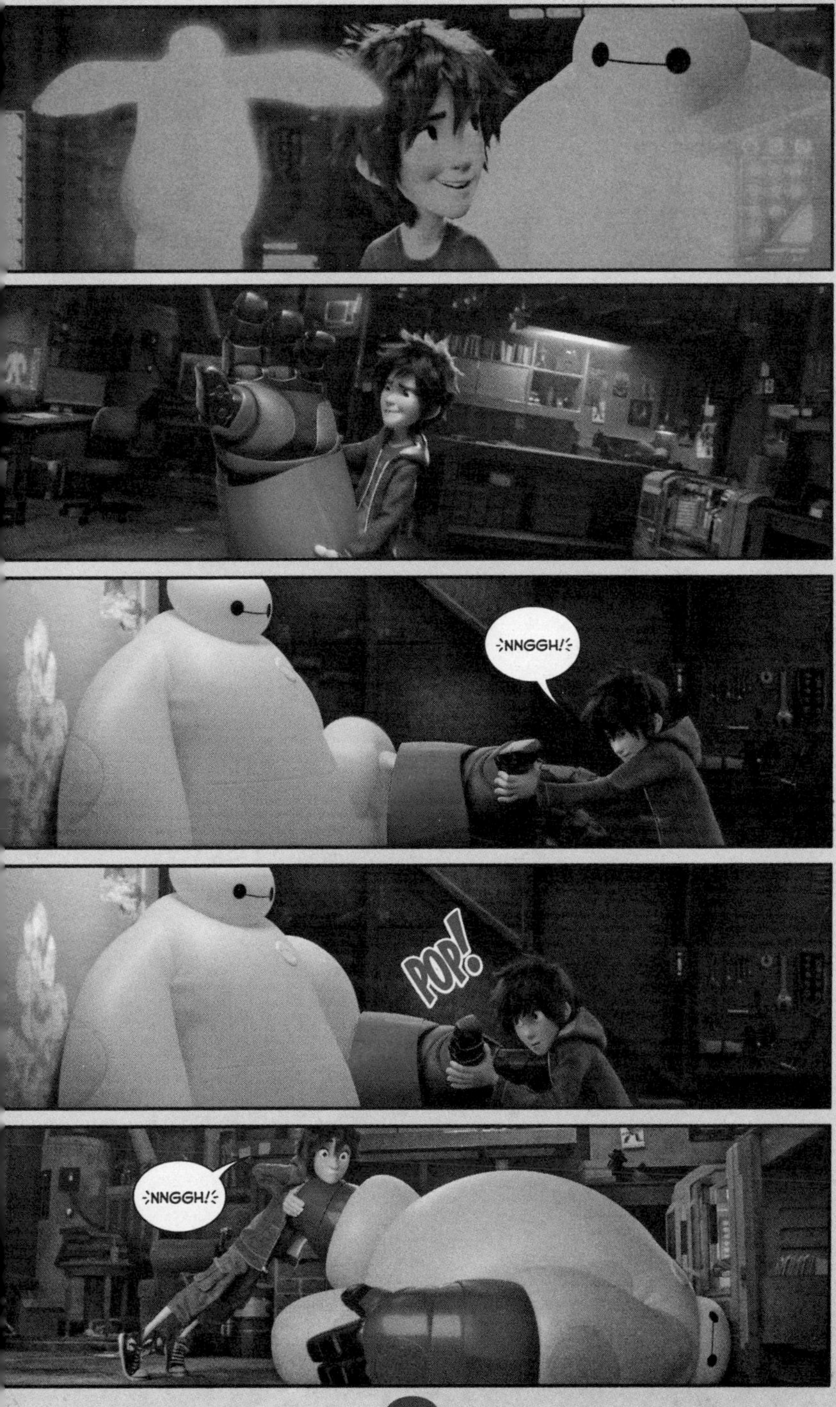
NNGGH!
POP!
NNGGH!

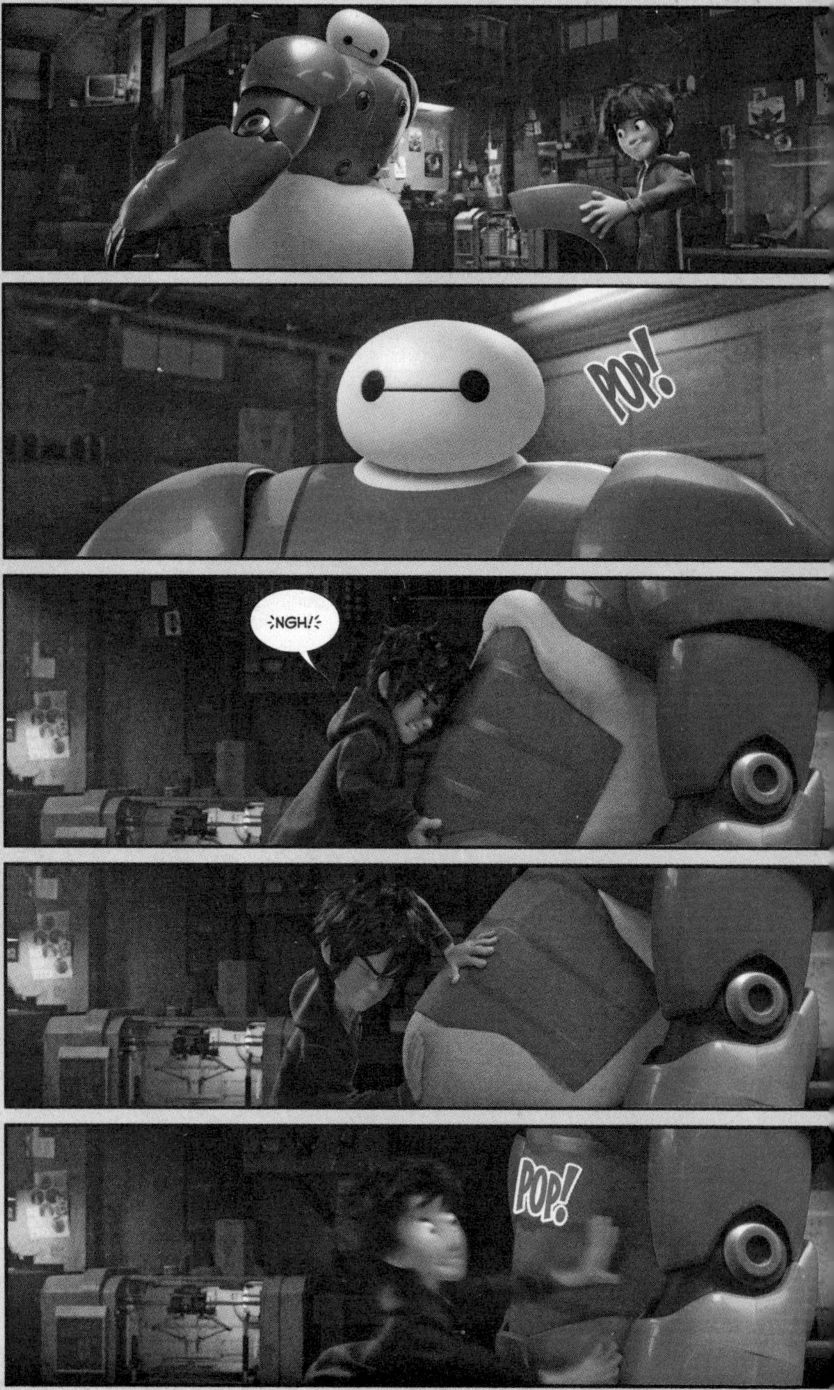
POP!
NGH!
POP!

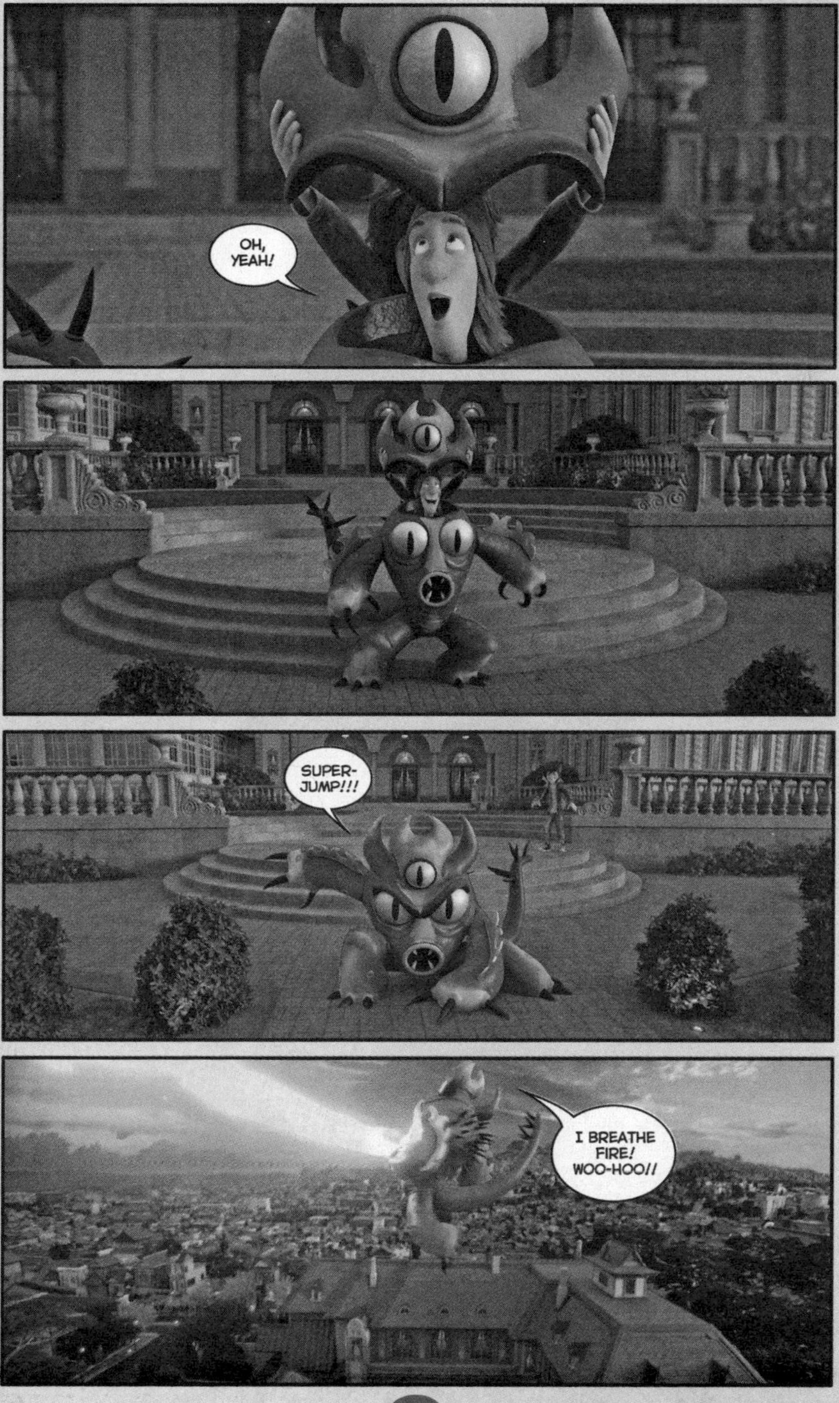
OH, YEAH!
SUPER-JUMP!!!
I BREATHE FIRE! WOO-HOO!!

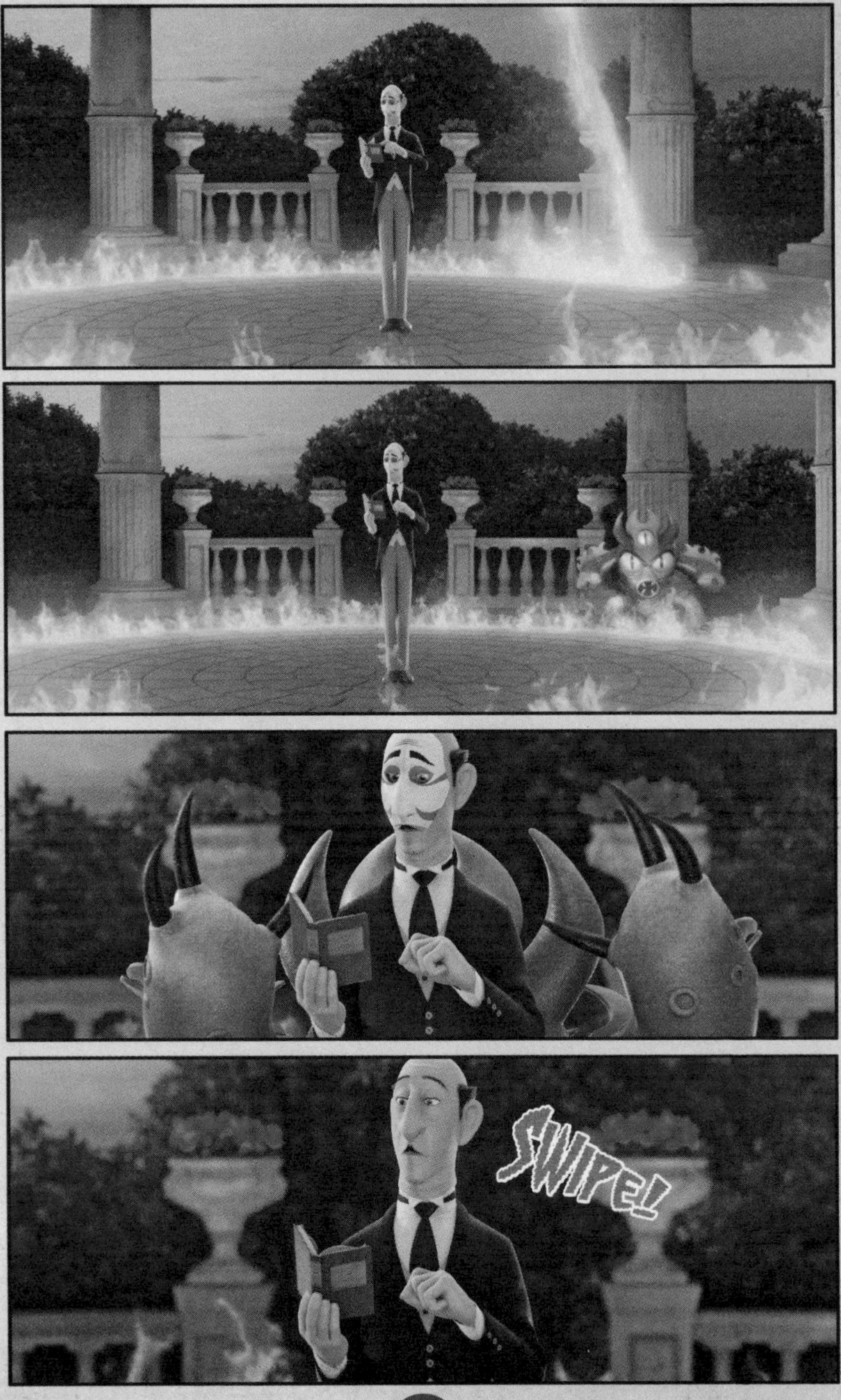
SWIPE!

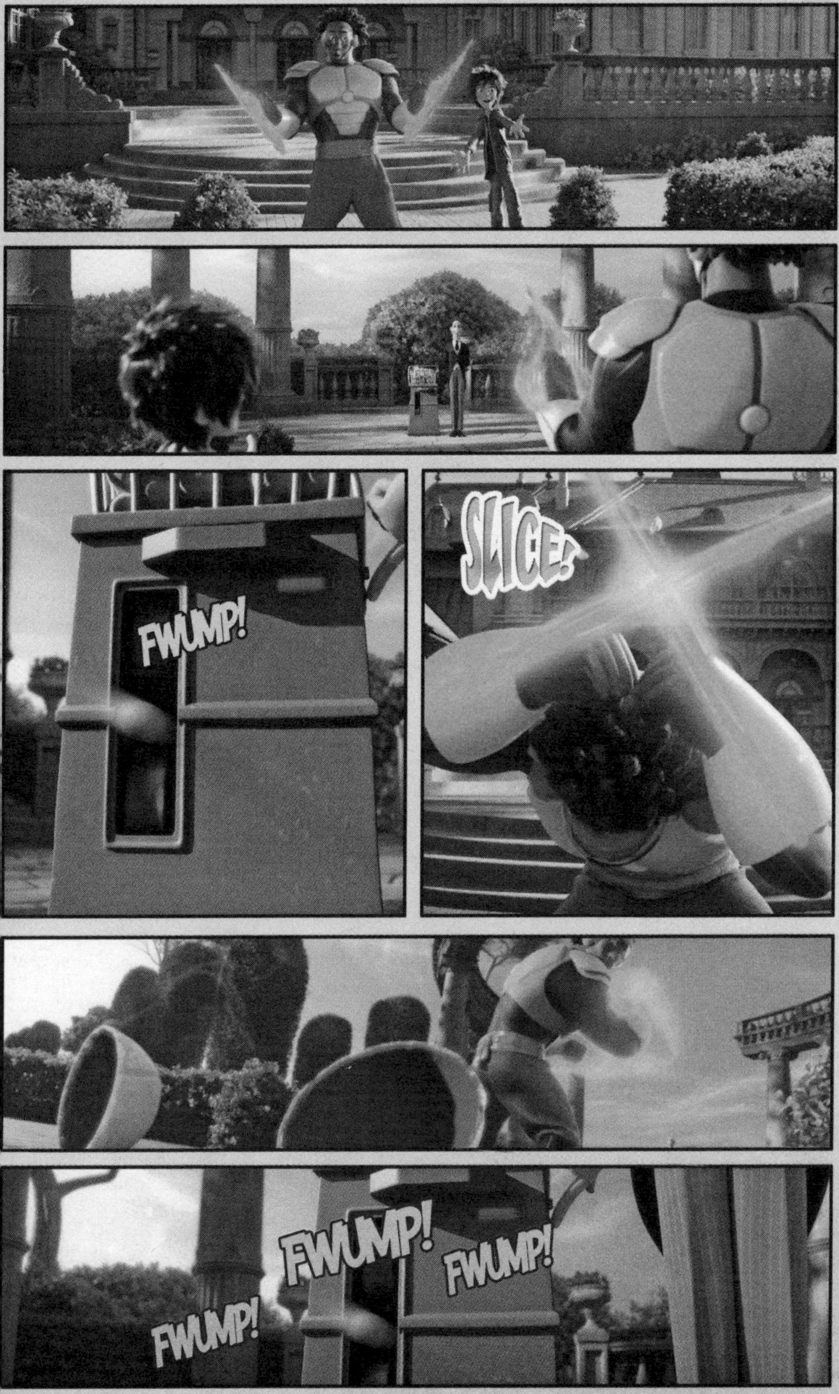
FWUMP!
SLICE!
FWUMP!
FWUMP!
FWUMP!

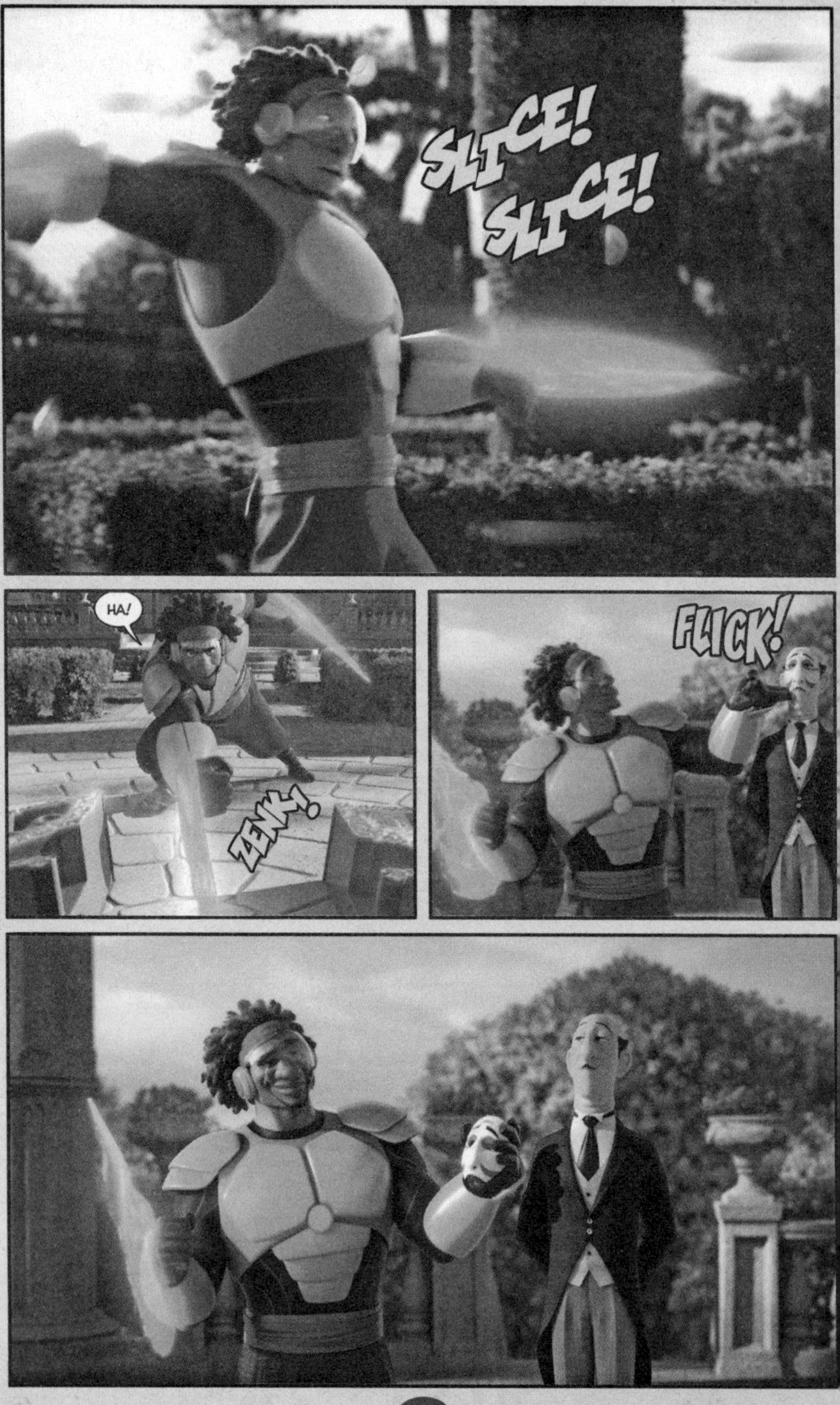
SLICE!
SLICE!
HA!
ZENK!
FLICK!

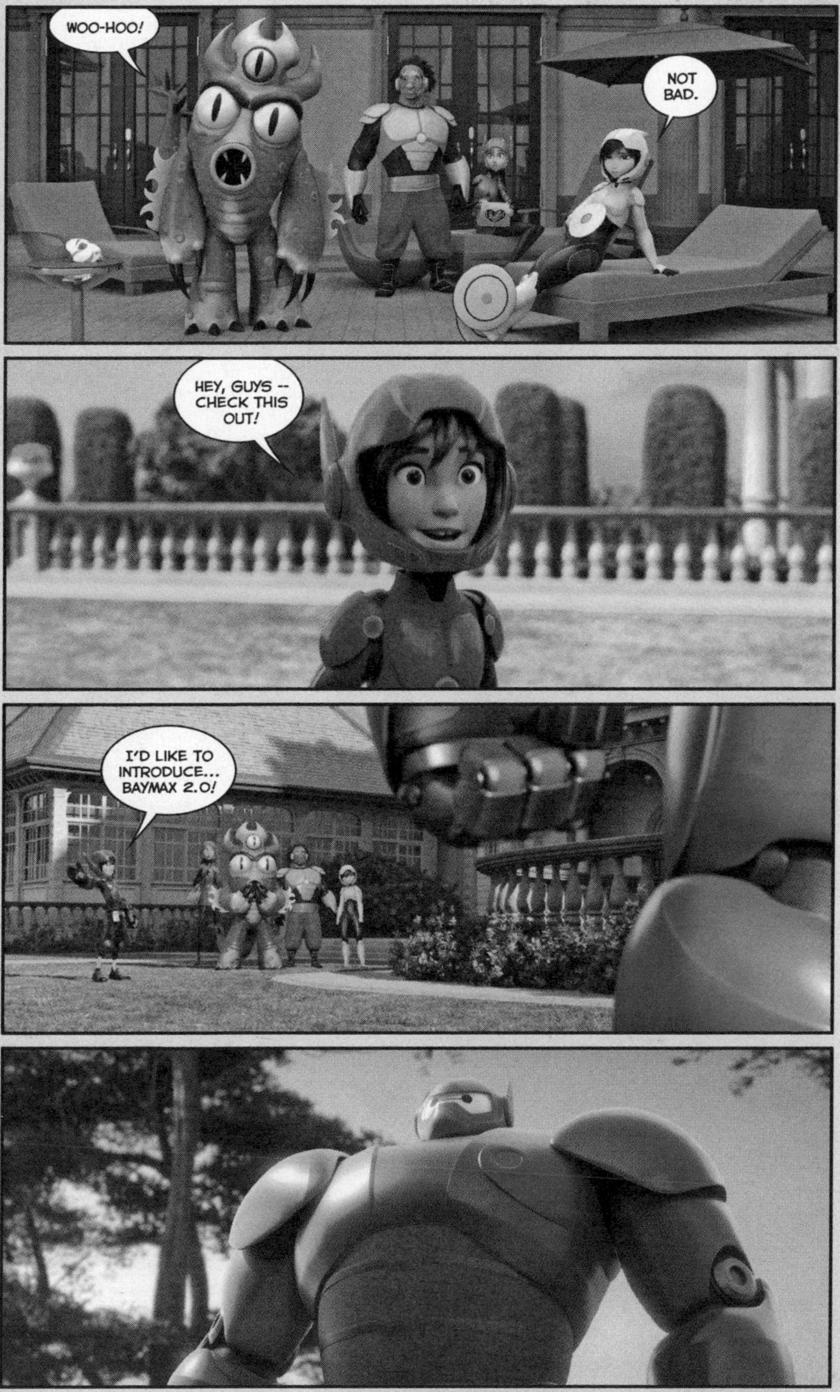
WOO-HOO!
NOT BAD.
HEY, GUYS -- CHECK THIS OUT!
I'D LIKE TO INTRODUCE... BAYMAX 2.0!

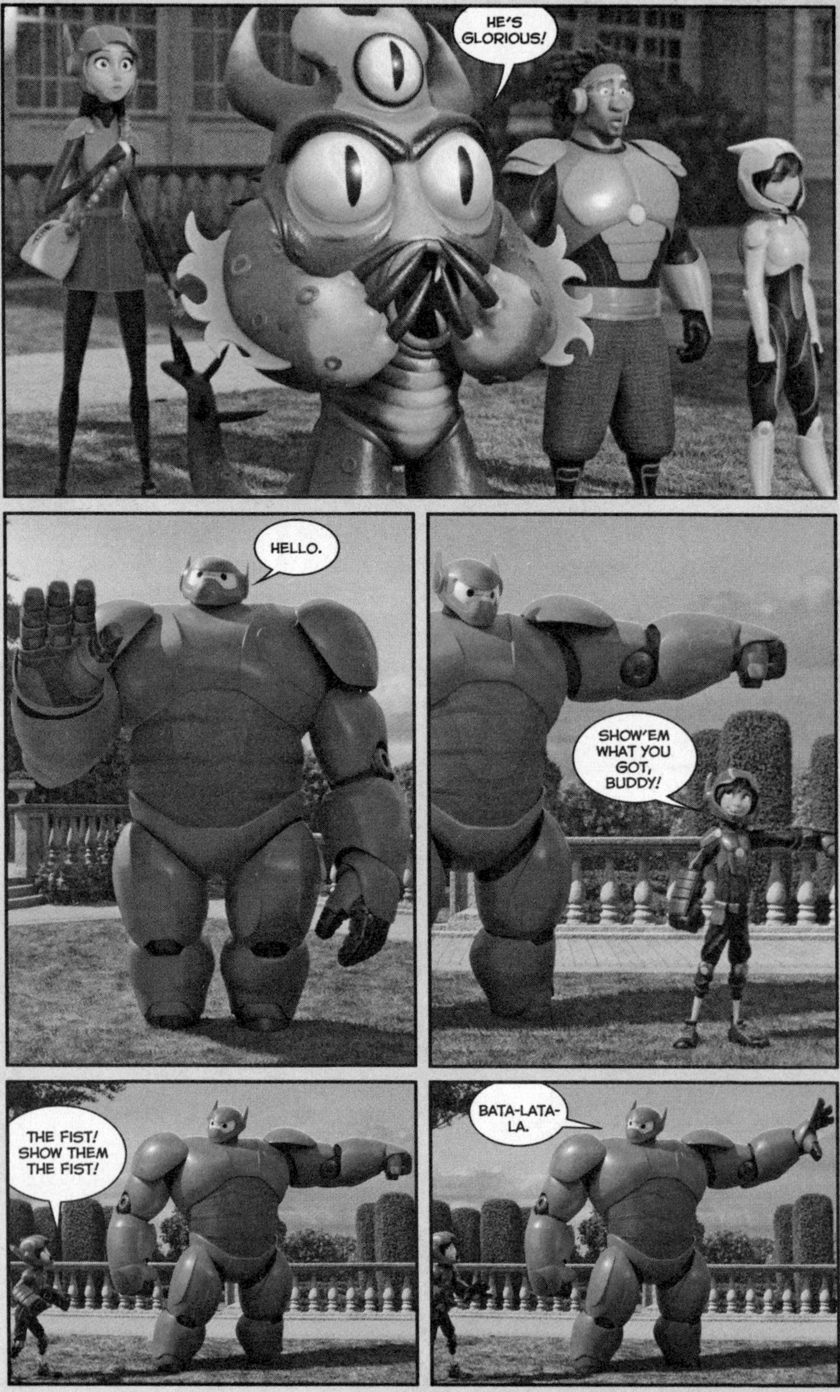
HE'S GLORIOUS!
HELLO.
SHOW'EM WHAT YOU GOT, BUDDY!
THE FIST! SHOW THEM THE FIST!
BATA-LATA-LA.

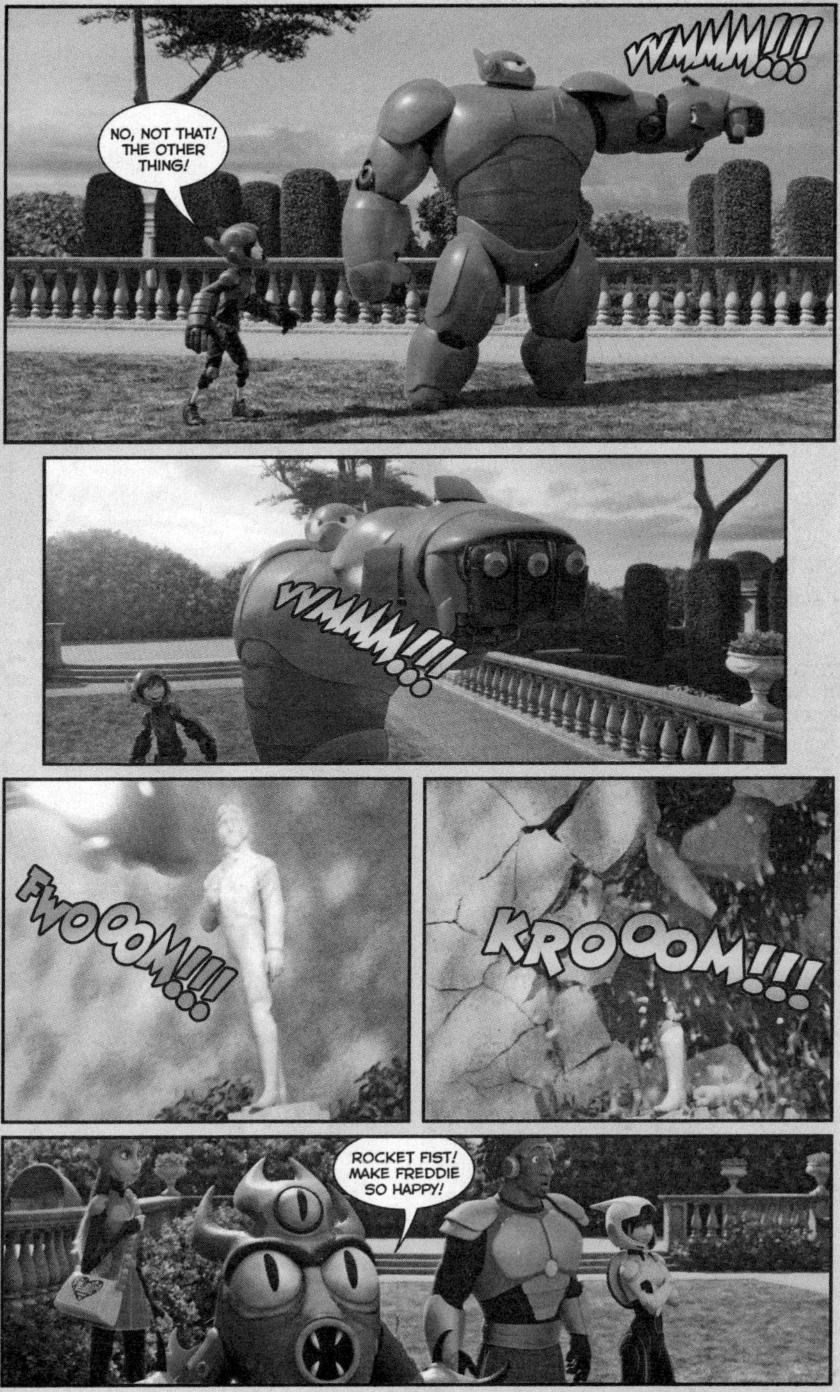

VVMMM!!!
NO, NOT THAT! THE OTHER THING!
VVMMM!!!
FWOOOM!!!
KROOOM!!!
ROCKET FIST! MAKE FREDDIE SO HAPPY!

THAT'S JUST ONE OF HIS NEW UPGRADES!

TUNK!

BAYMAX -- WINGS!

FLICK!

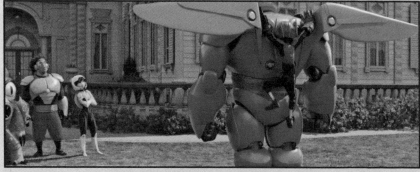

TAK!

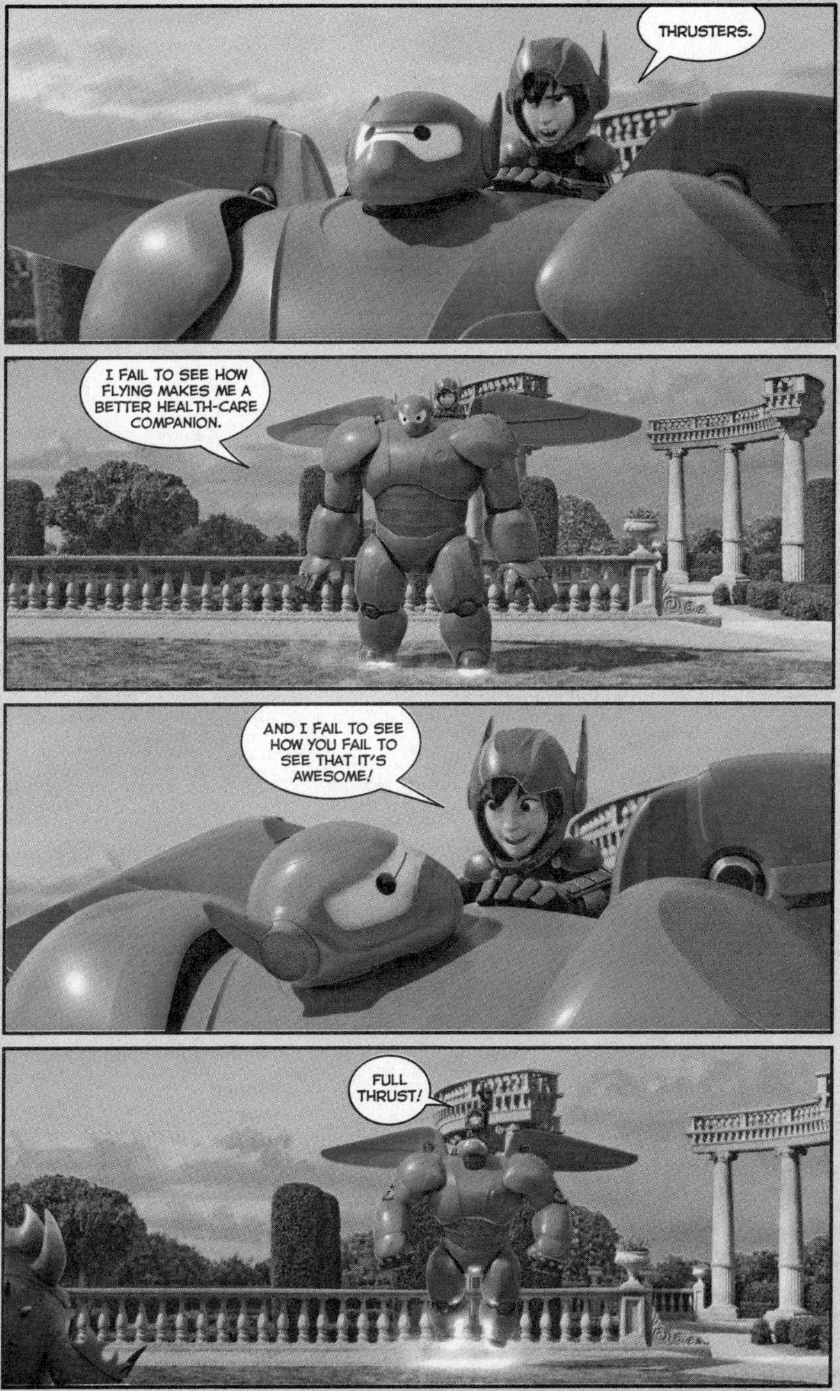
THRUSTERS.
I FAIL TO SEE HOW FLYING MAKES ME A BETTER HEALTH-CARE COMPANION.
AND I FAIL TO SEE HOW YOU FAIL TO SEE THAT IT'S AWESOME!
FULL THRUST!

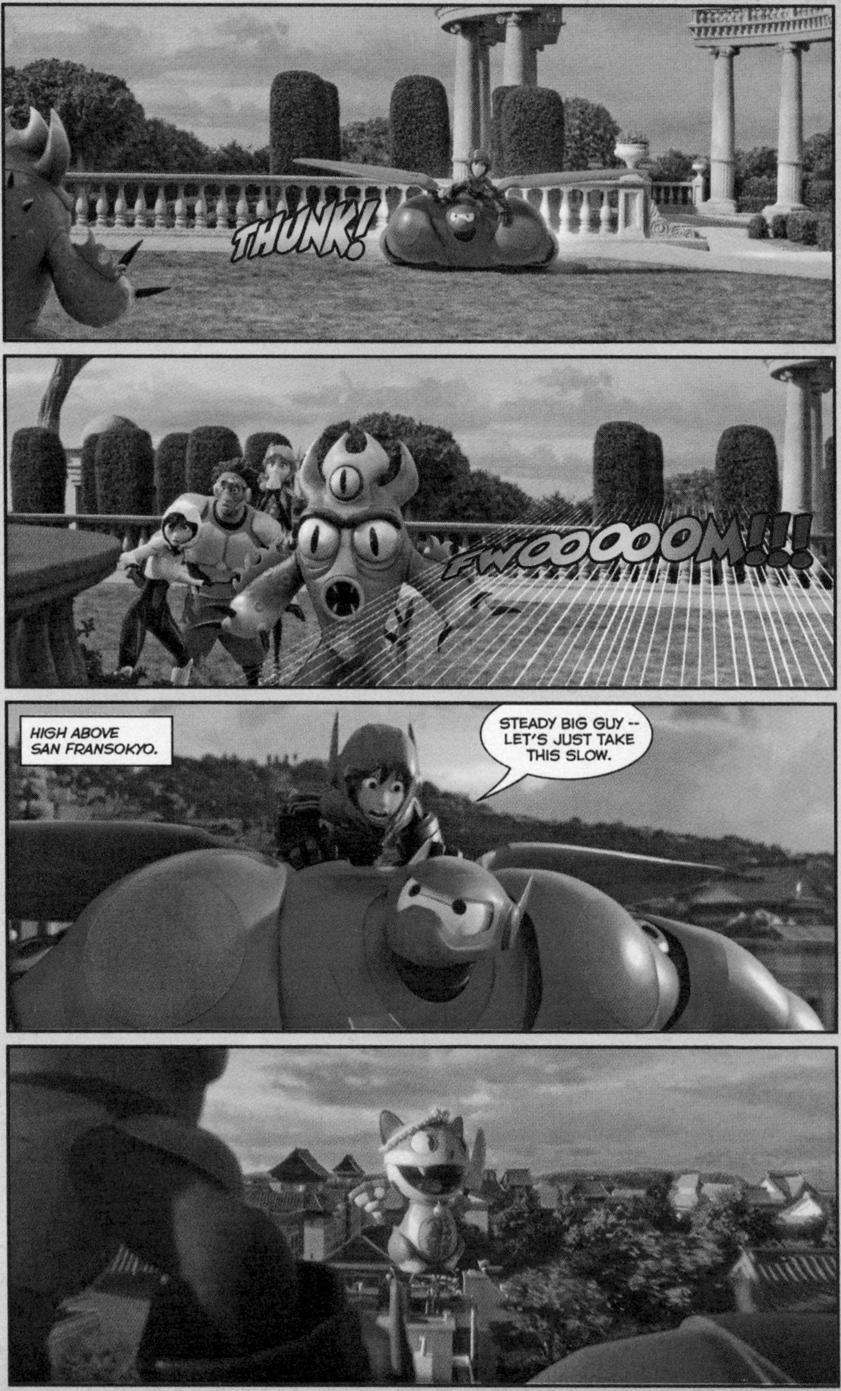
THUNK!
FWOOOOOOM!!!
HIGH ABOVE SAN FRANSOKYO.
STEADY BIG GUY -- LET'S JUST TAKE THIS SLOW.

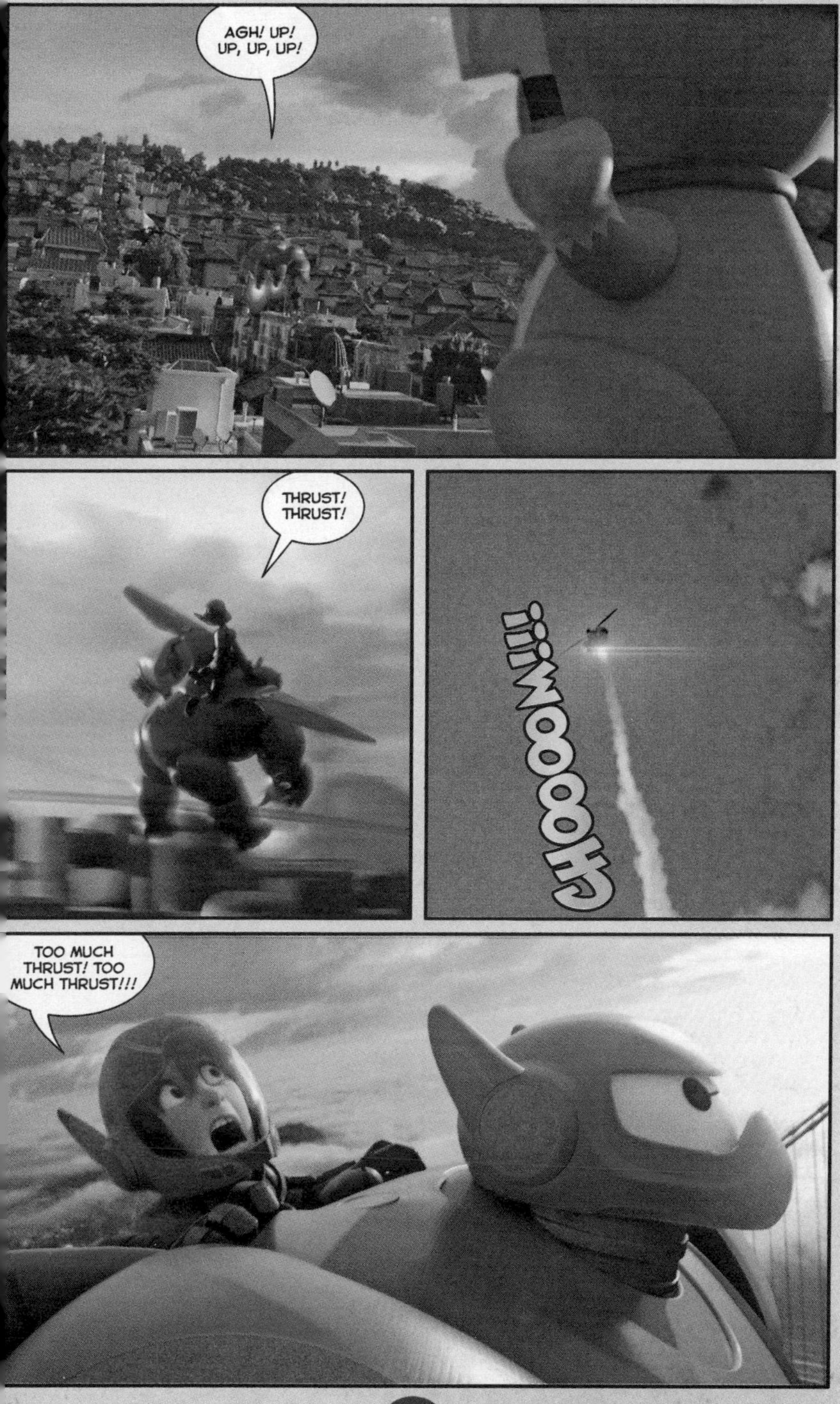
AGH! UP! UP, UP, UP!
THRUST! THRUST!
CHOOOOOM!!!
TOO MUCH THRUST! TOO MUCH THRUST!!!

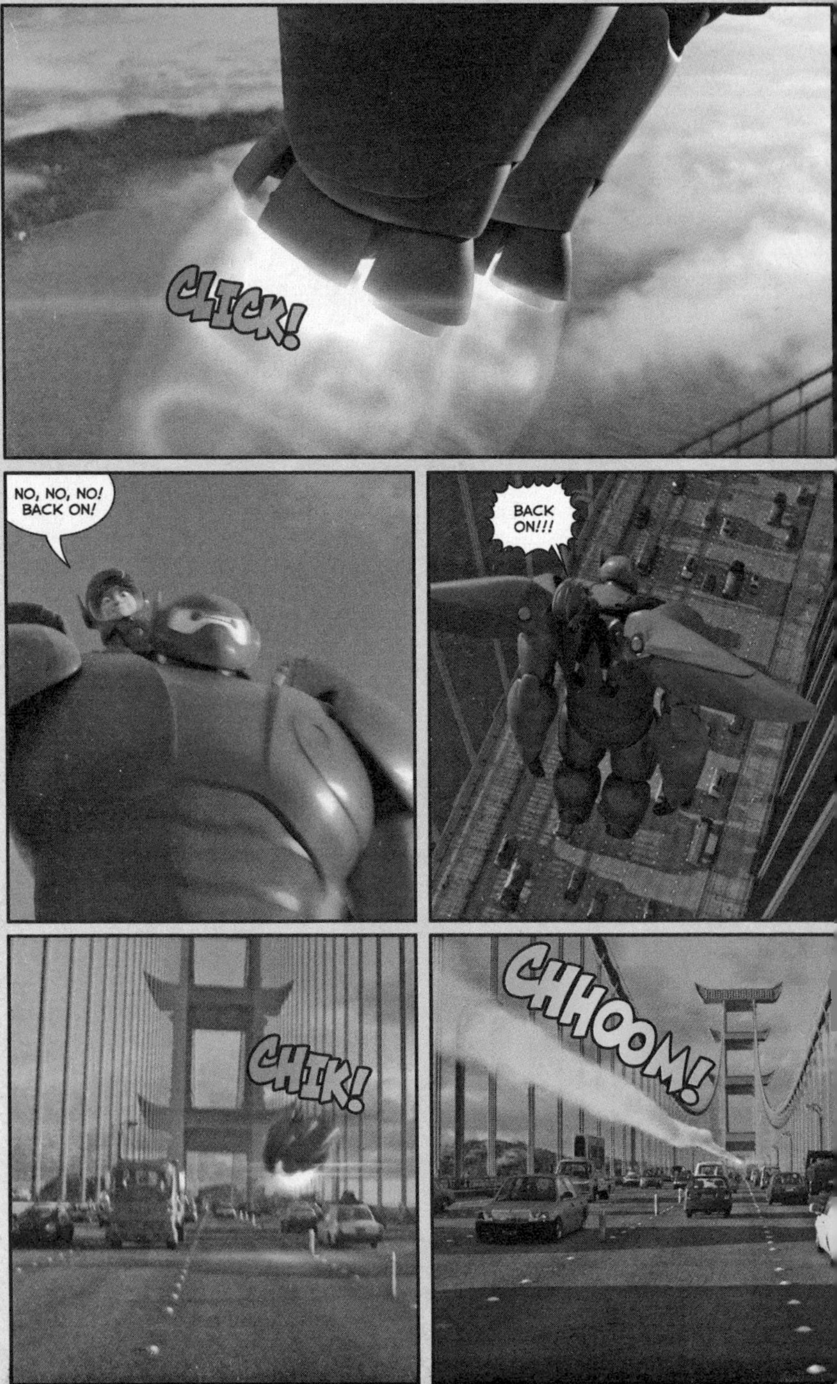
CLICK!
NO, NO, NO!
BACK ON!
BACK
ON!!!
CHIK!
CHHOOM!

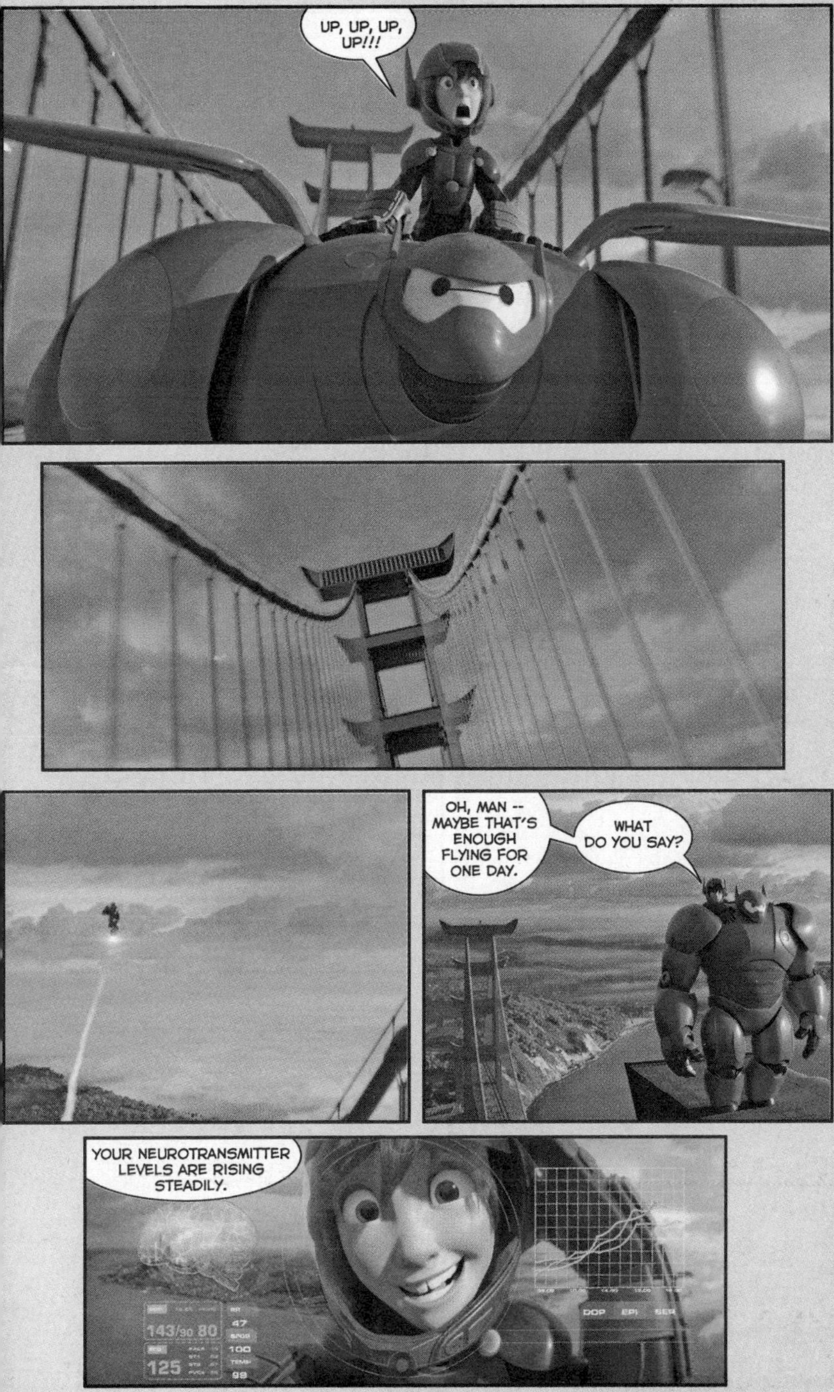
UP, UP, UP, UP!!!
OH, MAN -- MAYBE THAT'S ENOUGH FLYING FOR ONE DAY.
WHAT DO YOU SAY?
YOUR NEUROTRANSMITTER LEVELS ARE RISING STEADILY.
143/90 80
125
47
100
99
DOP
EPI
SER

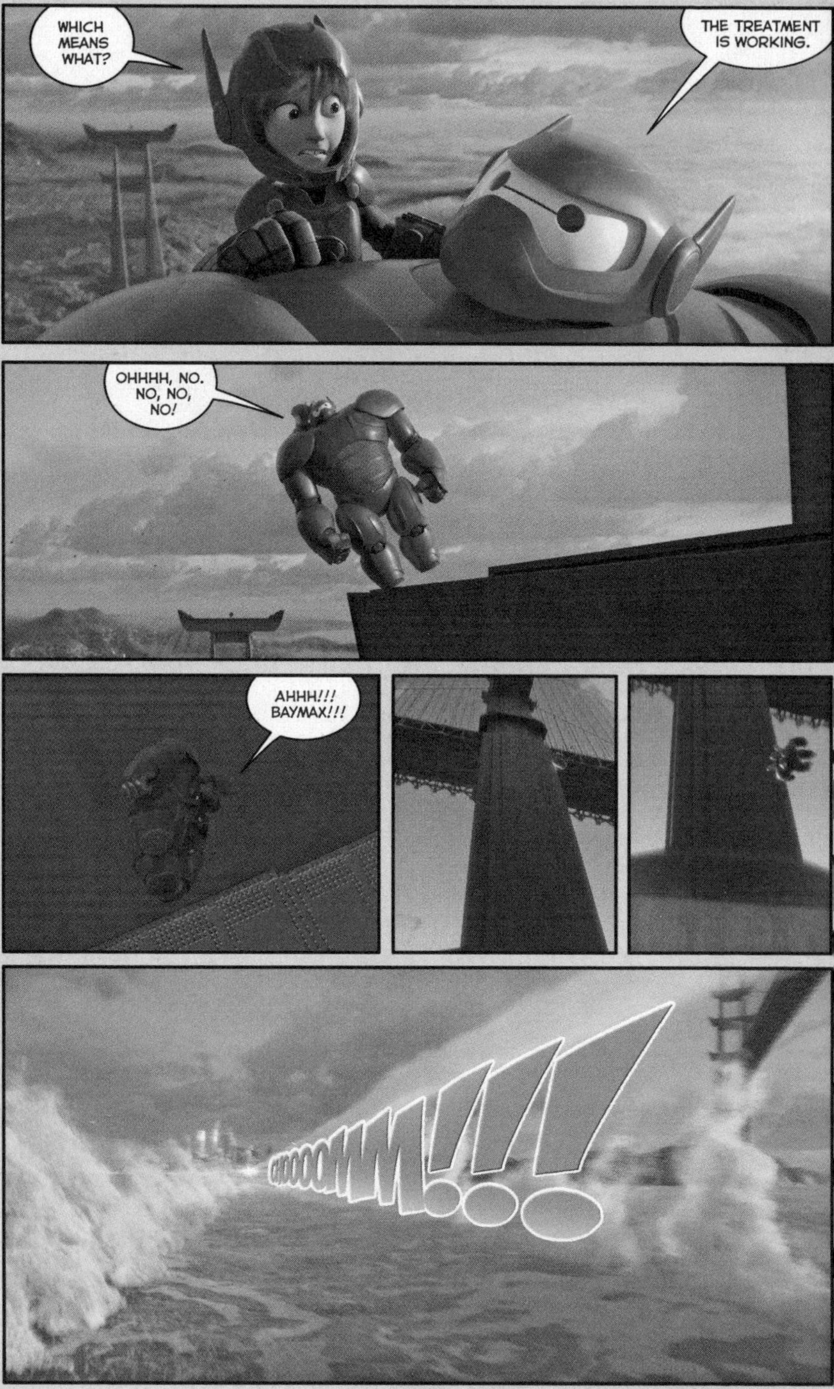
WHICH MEANS WHAT?
THE TREATMENT IS WORKING.
OHHHH, NO. NO, NO, NO!
AHHH!!! BAYMAX!!!

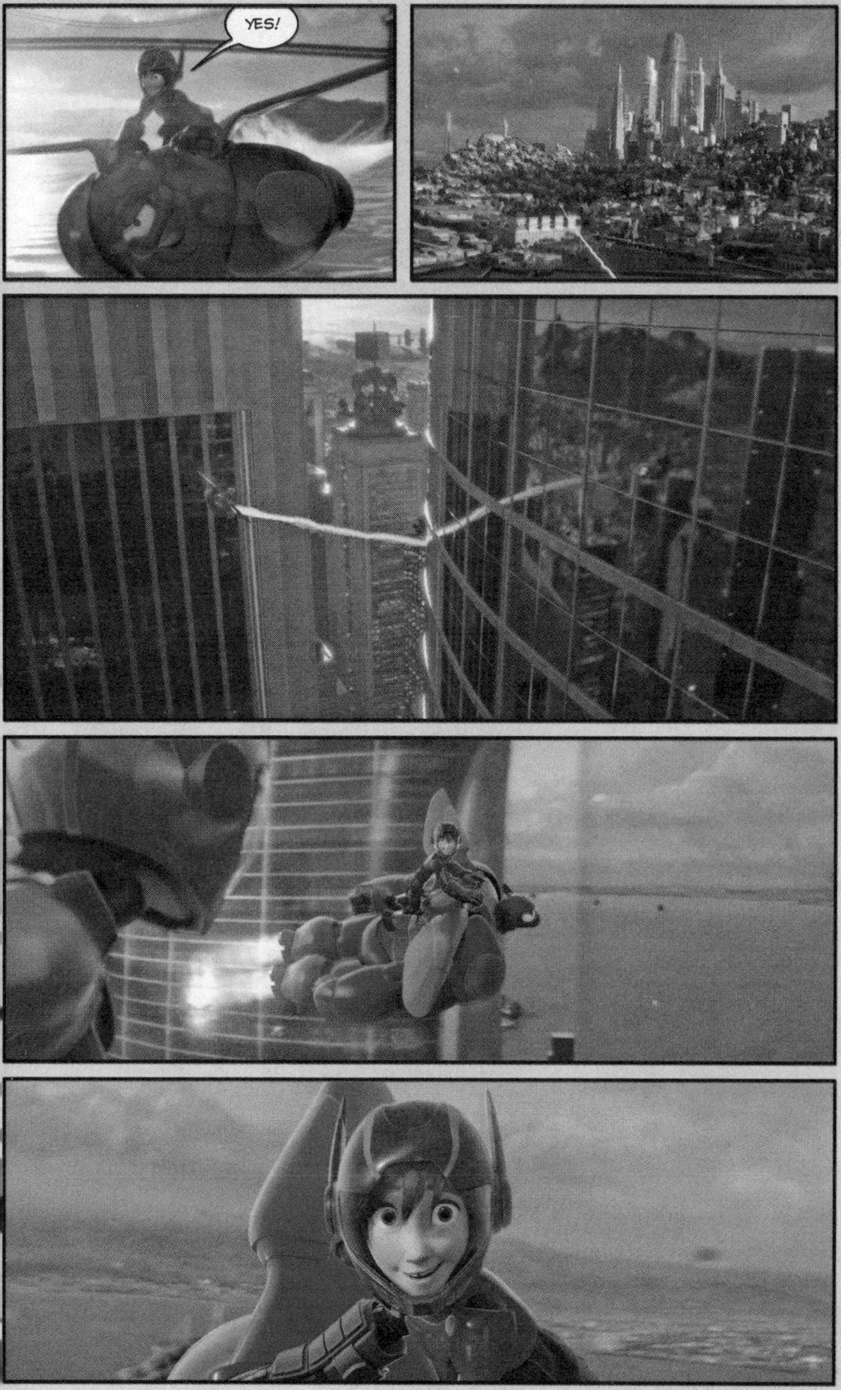
YES!

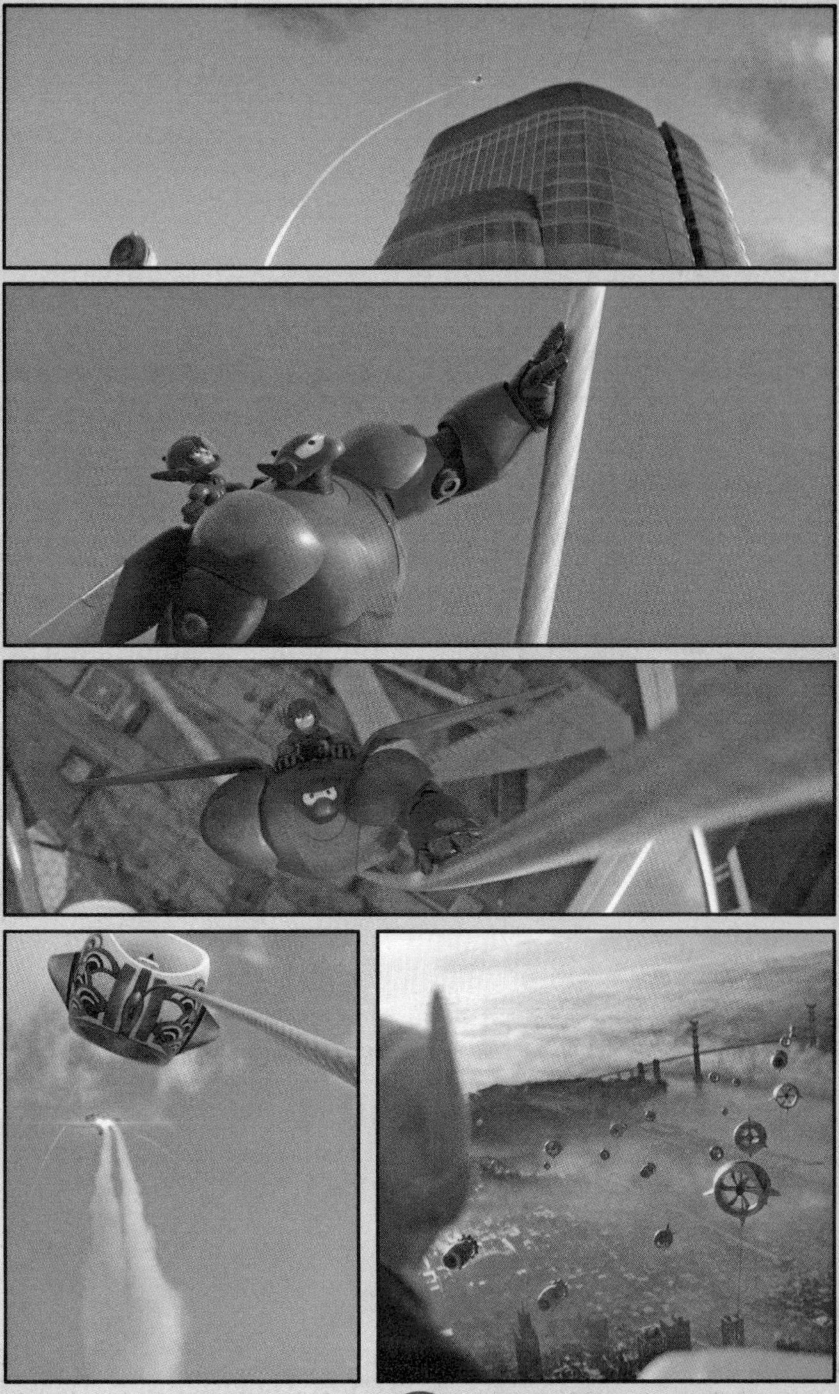

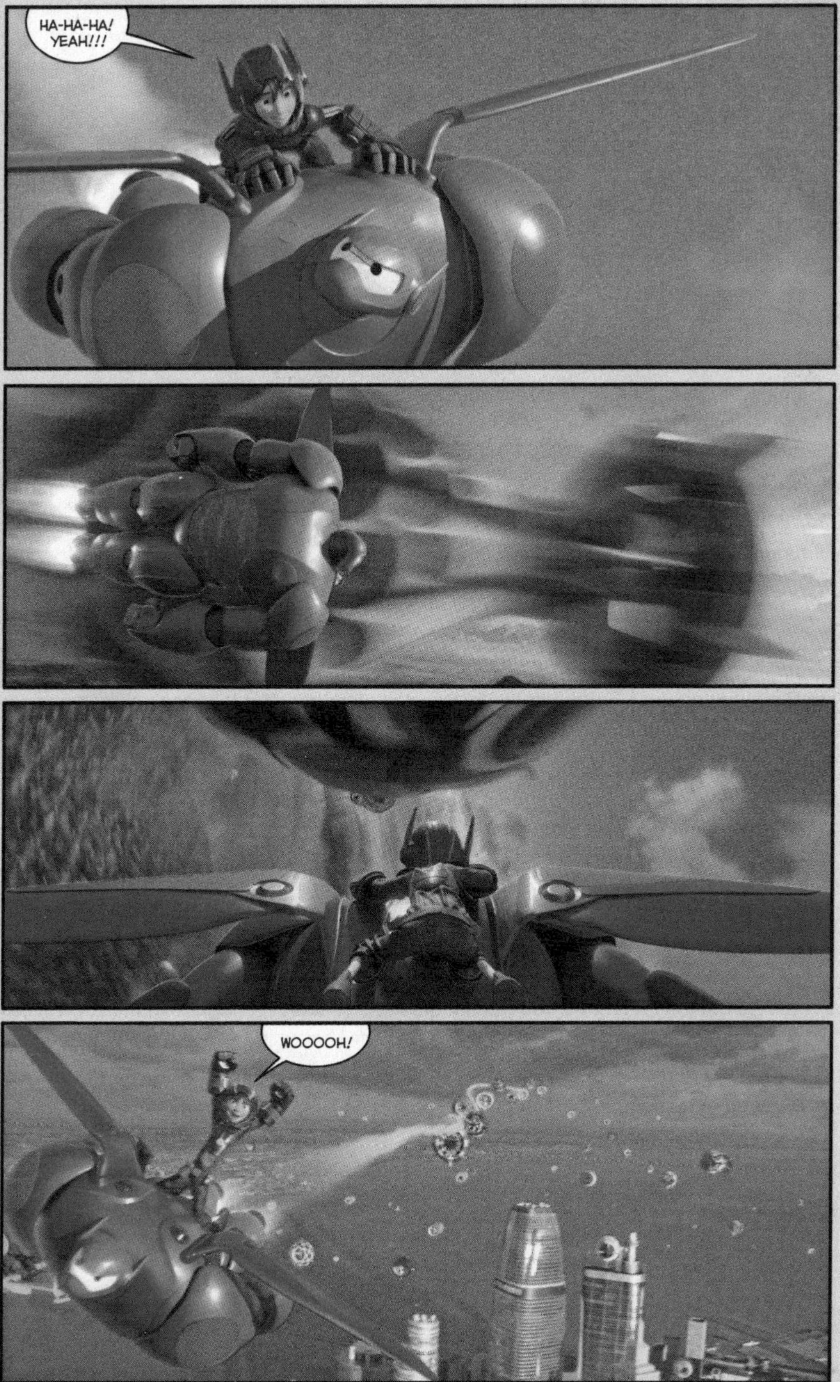
HA-HA-HA! YEAH!!!
WOOOOH!

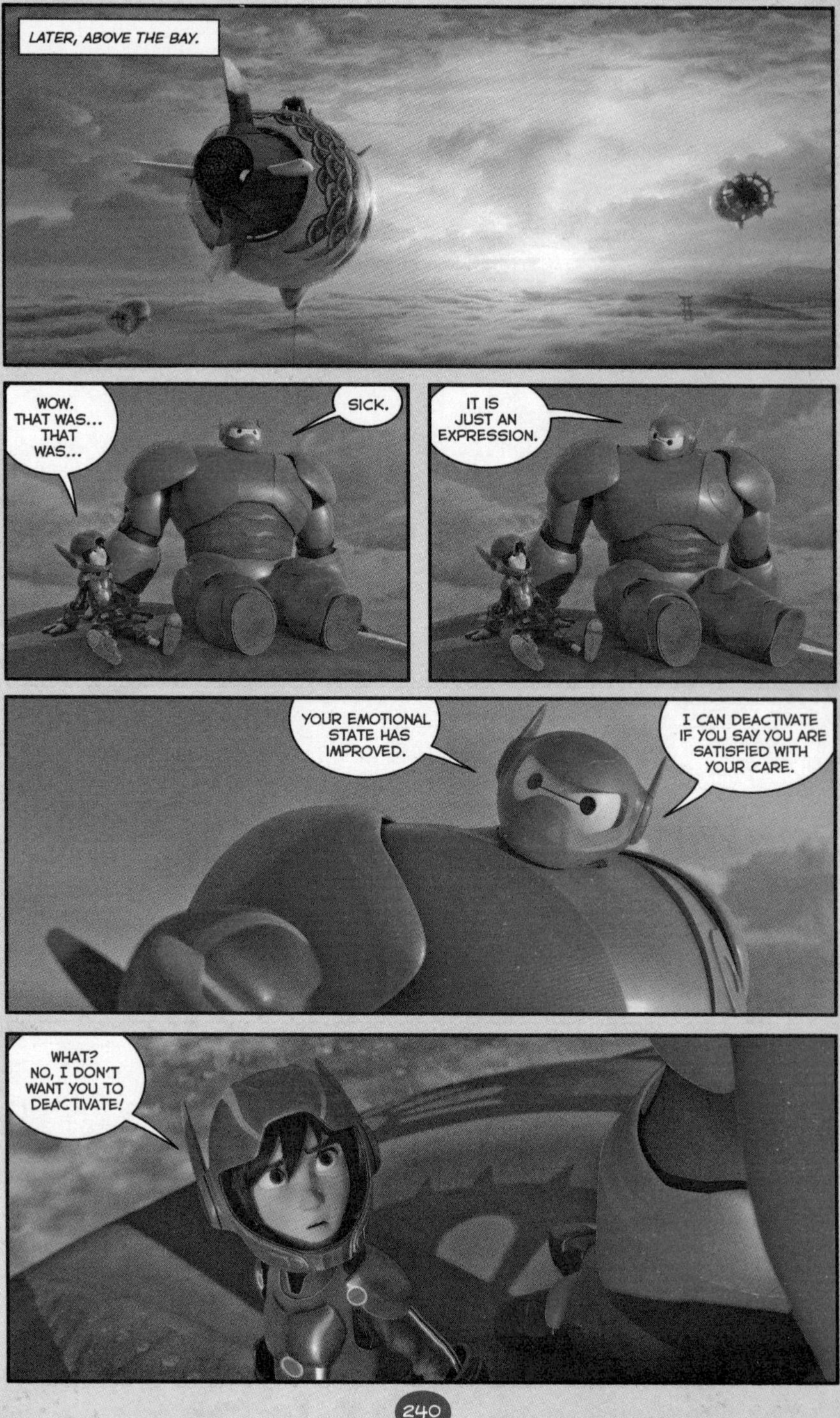
LATER, ABOVE THE BAY.
WOW. THAT WAS... THAT WAS...
SICK.
IT IS JUST AN EXPRESSION.
YOUR EMOTIONAL STATE HAS IMPROVED.
I CAN DEACTIVATE IF YOU SAY YOU ARE SATISFIED WITH YOUR CARE.
WHAT? NO, I DON'T WANT YOU TO DEACTIVATE!

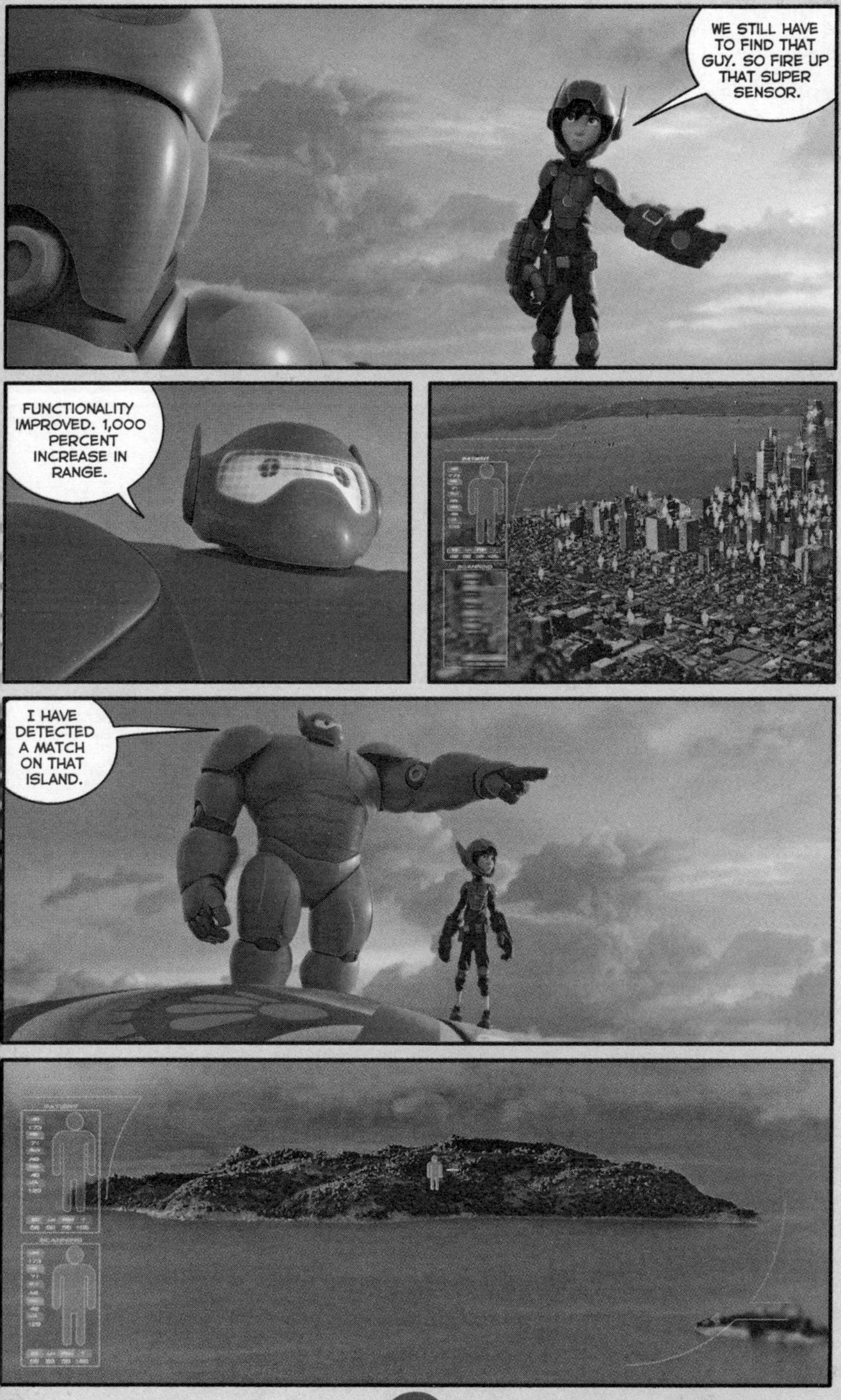
WE STILL HAVE TO FIND THAT GUY. SO FIRE UP THAT SUPER SENSOR.
FUNCTIONALITY IMPROVED. 1,000 PERCENT INCREASE IN RANGE.
I HAVE DETECTED A MATCH ON THAT ISLAND.

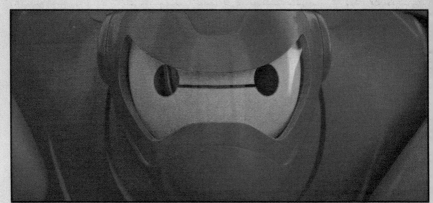

KILLER VIEW.

YEAH, IF I WASN'T TERRIFIED OF HEIGHTS, I'D PROBABLY LOVE THIS!

BUT I'M TERRIFIED OF HEIGHTS, SO I DON'T LOVE THIS!

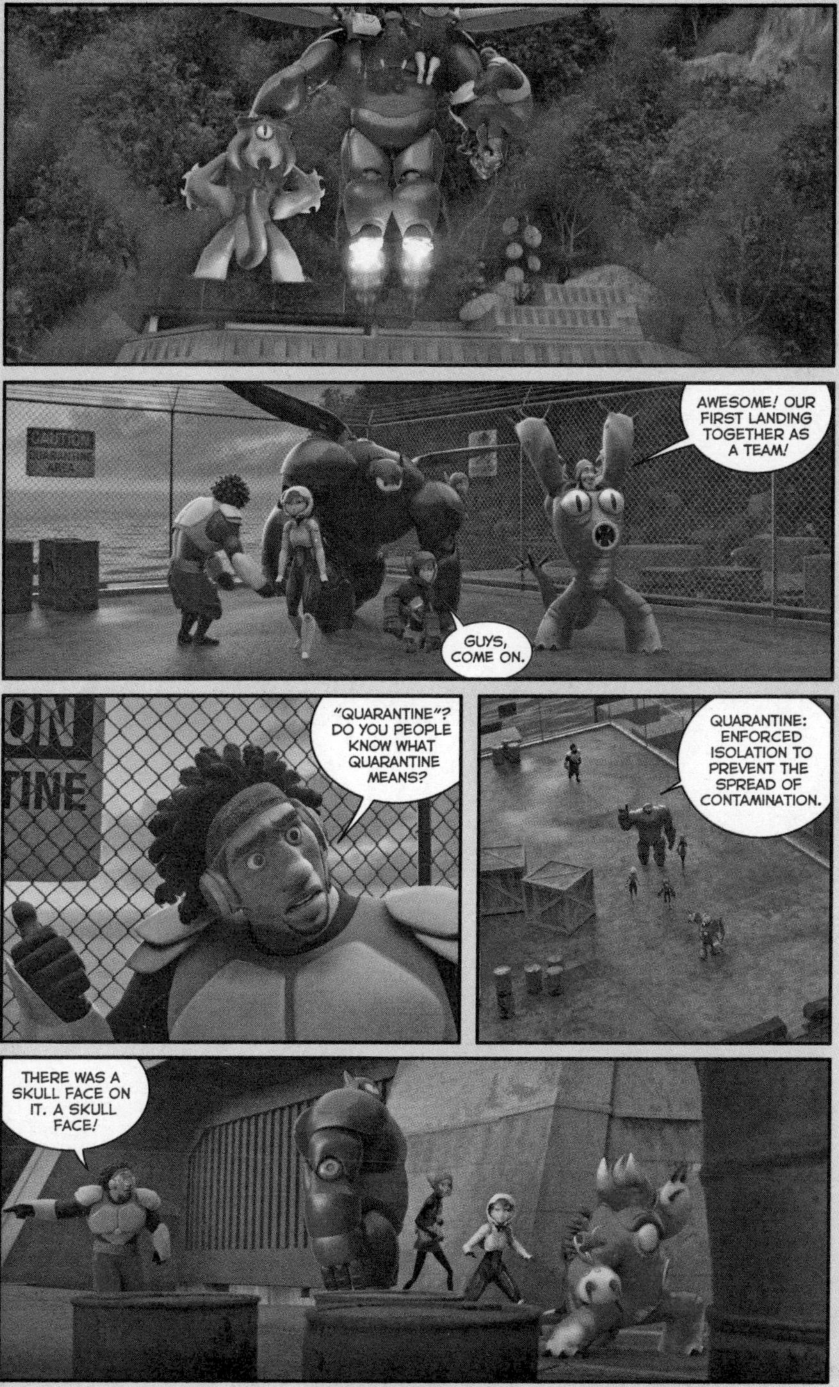
CAUTION
QUARANTINE AREA
AWESOME! OUR FIRST LANDING TOGETHER AS A TEAM!
GUYS, COME ON.
"QUARANTINE"? DO YOU PEOPLE KNOW WHAT QUARANTINE MEANS?
QUARANTINE: ENFORCED ISOLATION TO PREVENT THE SPREAD OF CONTAMINATION.
THERE WAS A SKULL FACE ON IT. A SKULL FACE!

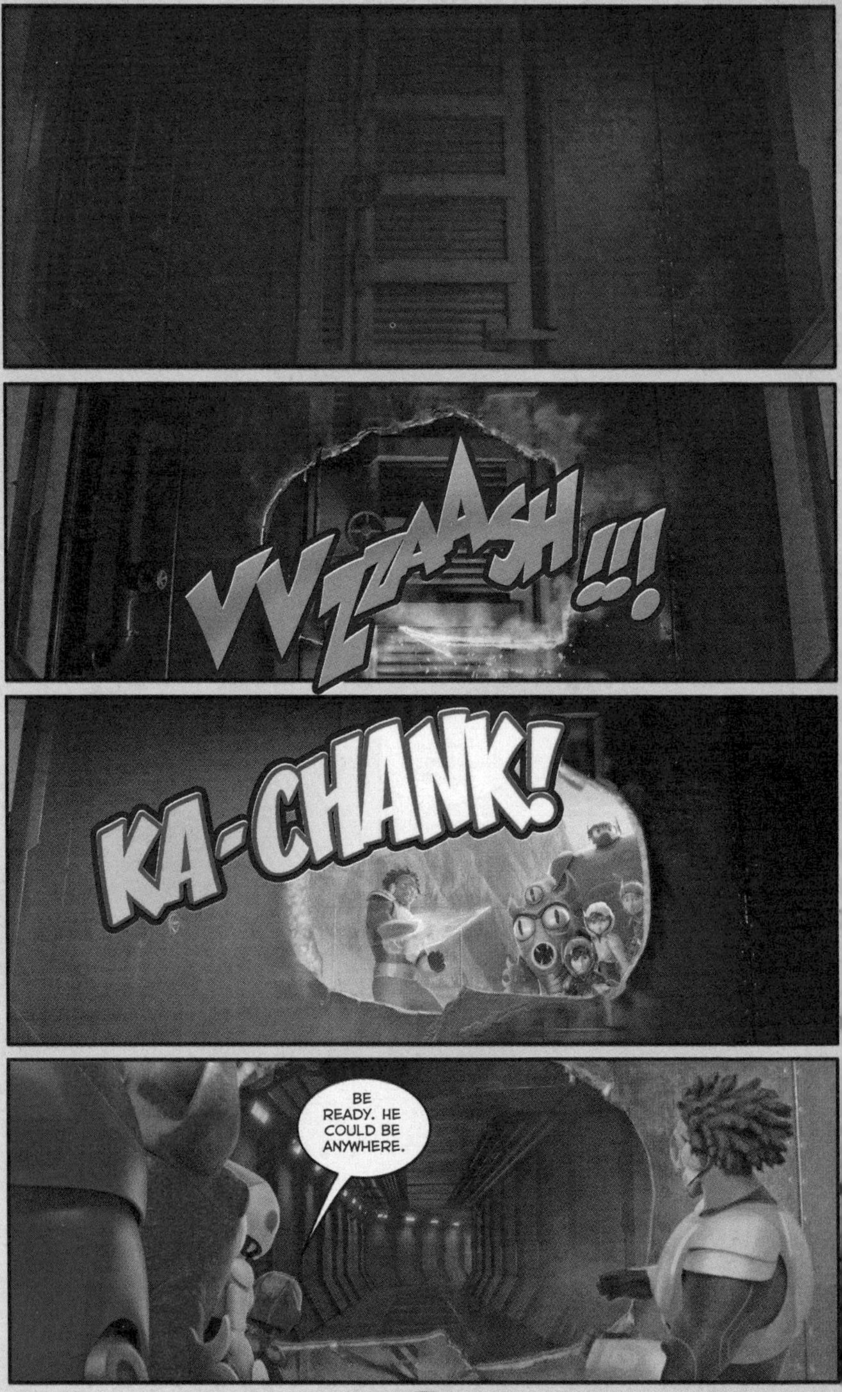
VVZZAASH!!!
KA-CHANK!
BE READY. HE COULD BE ANYWHERE.

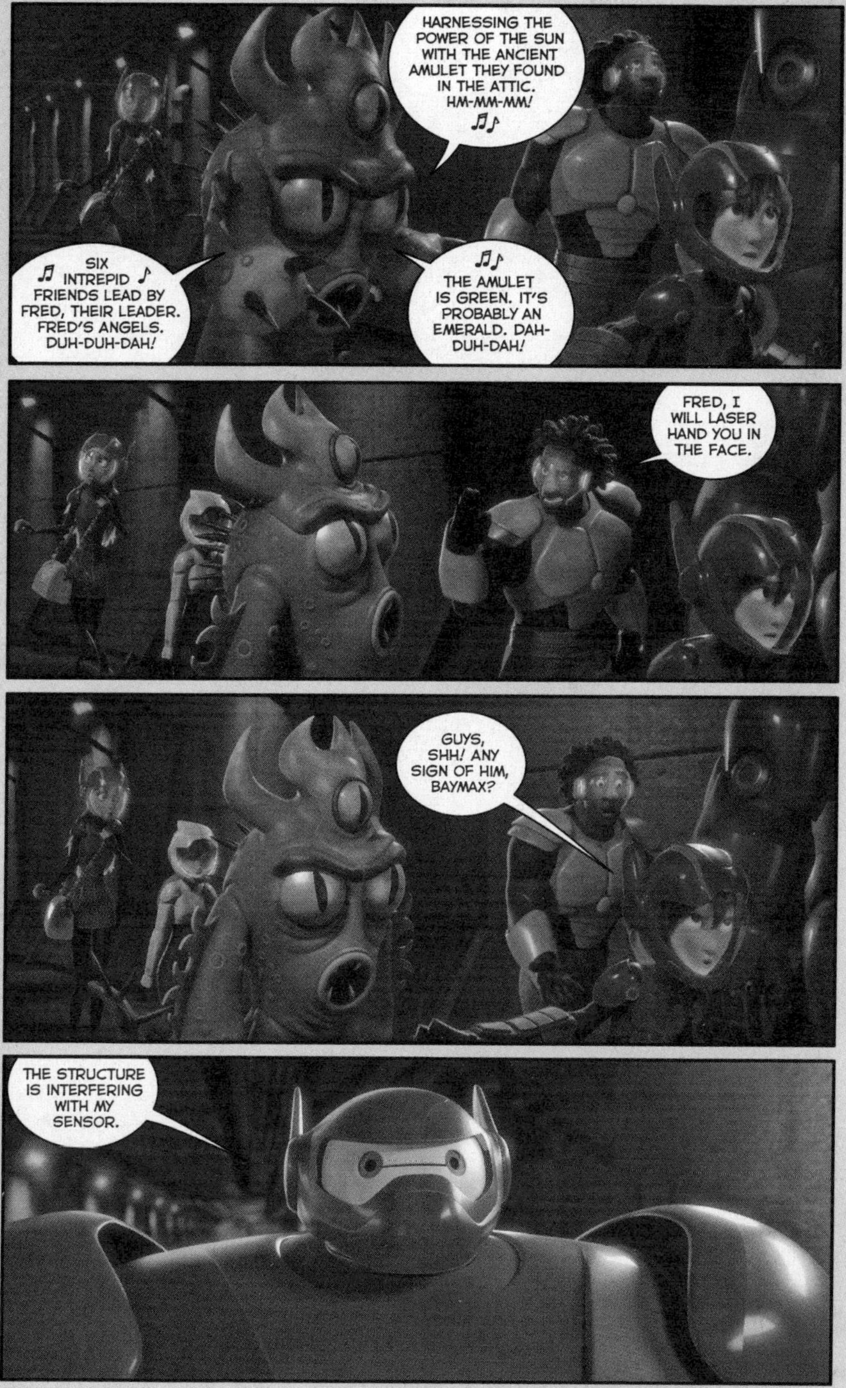
HARNESSING THE POWER OF THE SUN WITH THE ANCIENT AMULET THEY FOUND IN THE ATTIC. HM-MM-MM! ♫♪
♫ SIX INTREPID ♪ FRIENDS LEAD BY FRED, THEIR LEADER. FRED'S ANGELS. DUH-DUH-DAH!
♫♪ THE AMULET IS GREEN. IT'S PROBABLY AN EMERALD. DAH-DUH-DAH!
FRED, I WILL LASER HAND YOU IN THE FACE.
GUYS, SHH! ANY SIGN OF HIM, BAYMAX?
THE STRUCTURE IS INTERFERING WITH MY SENSOR.

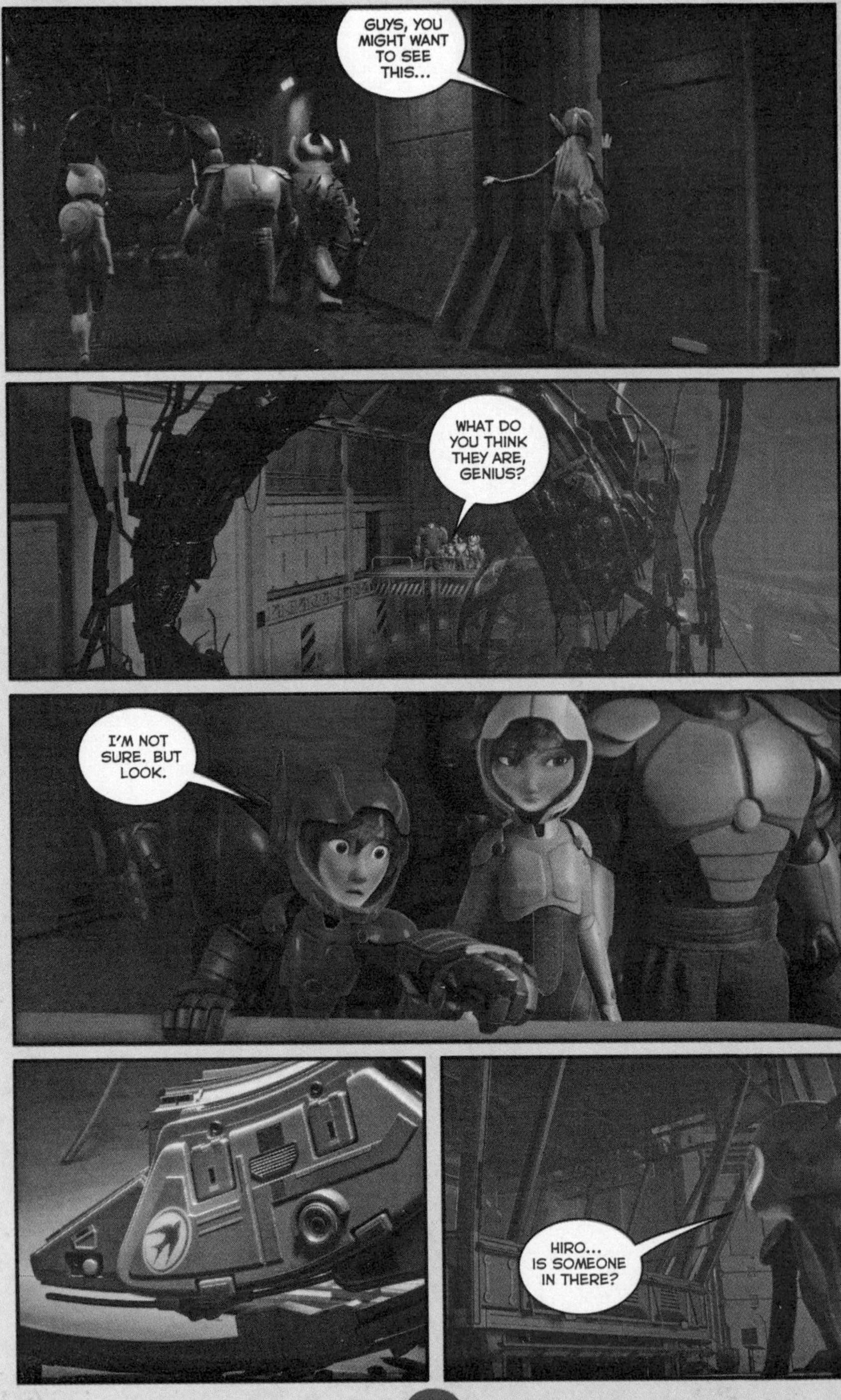
GUYS, YOU MIGHT WANT TO SEE THIS...
WHAT DO YOU THINK THEY ARE, GENIUS?
I'M NOT SURE. BUT LOOK.
HIRO... IS SOMEONE IN THERE?

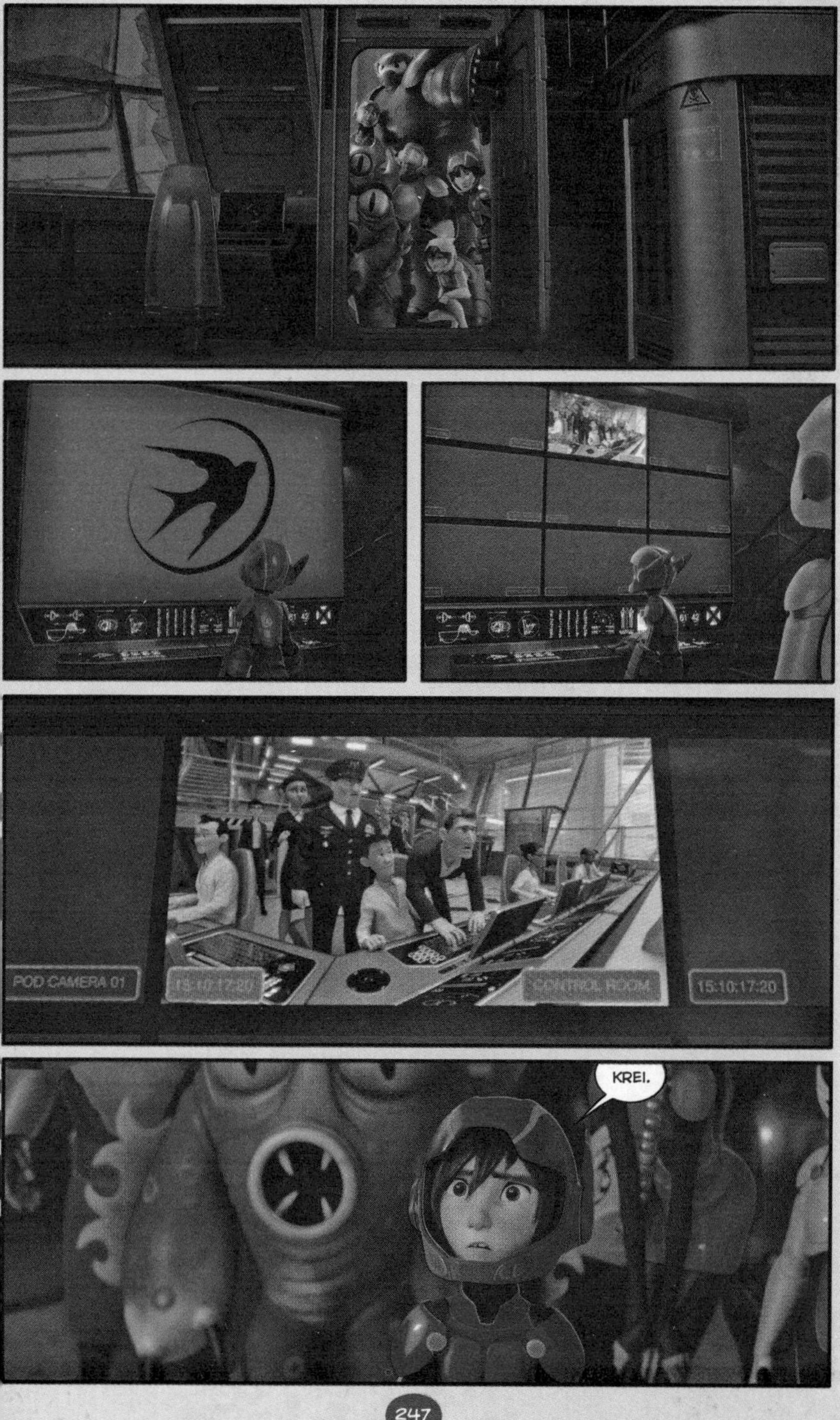
POD CAMERA 01
15:10:17:20
CONTROL ROOM
15:10:17:20
KREI.

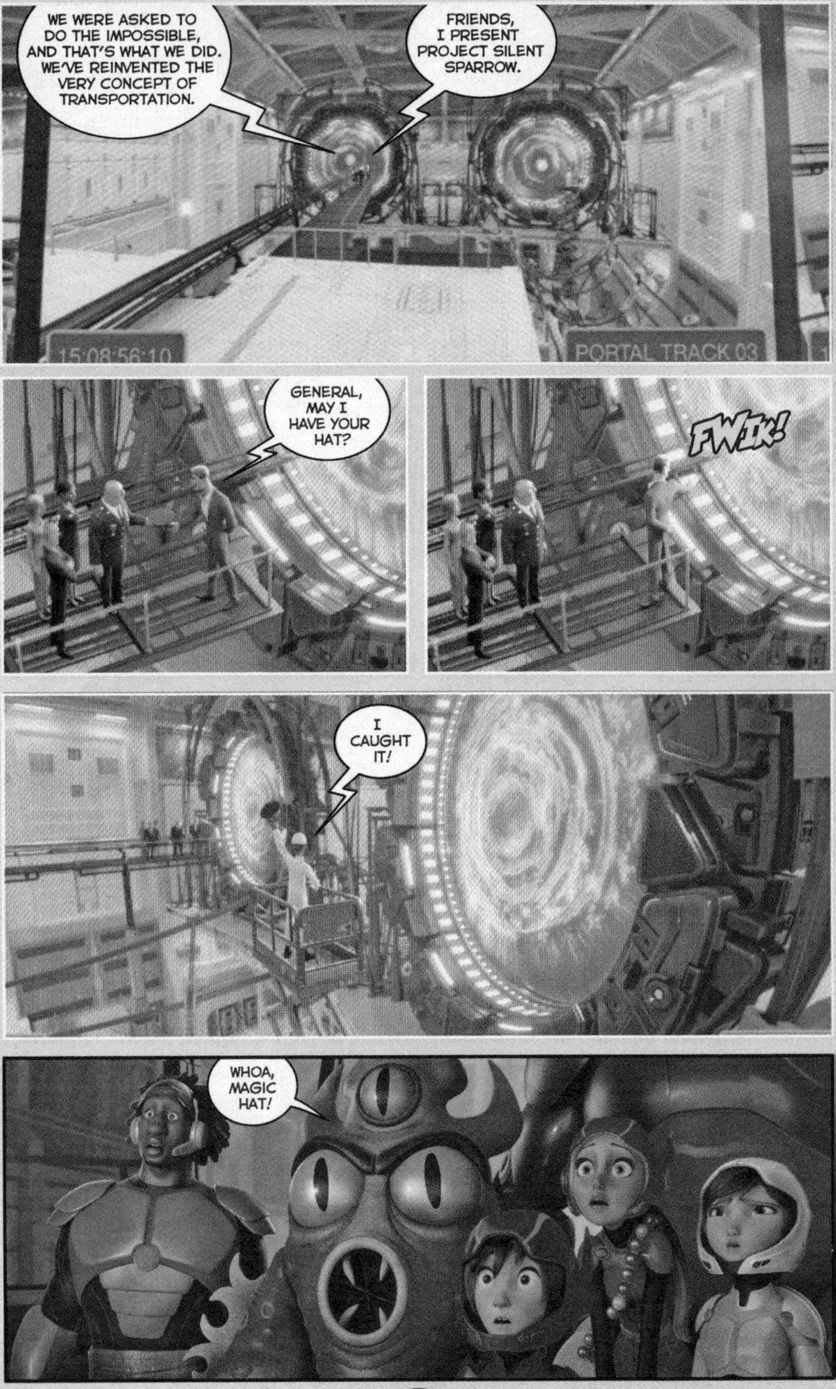
WE WERE ASKED TO DO THE IMPOSSIBLE, AND THAT'S WHAT WE DID. WE'VE REINVENTED THE VERY CONCEPT OF TRANSPORTATION.
FRIENDS, I PRESENT PROJECT SILENT SPARROW.
15:08:56:10
PORTAL TRACK 03
GENERAL, MAY I HAVE YOUR HAT?
FWIK!
I CAUGHT IT!
WHOA, MAGIC HAT!

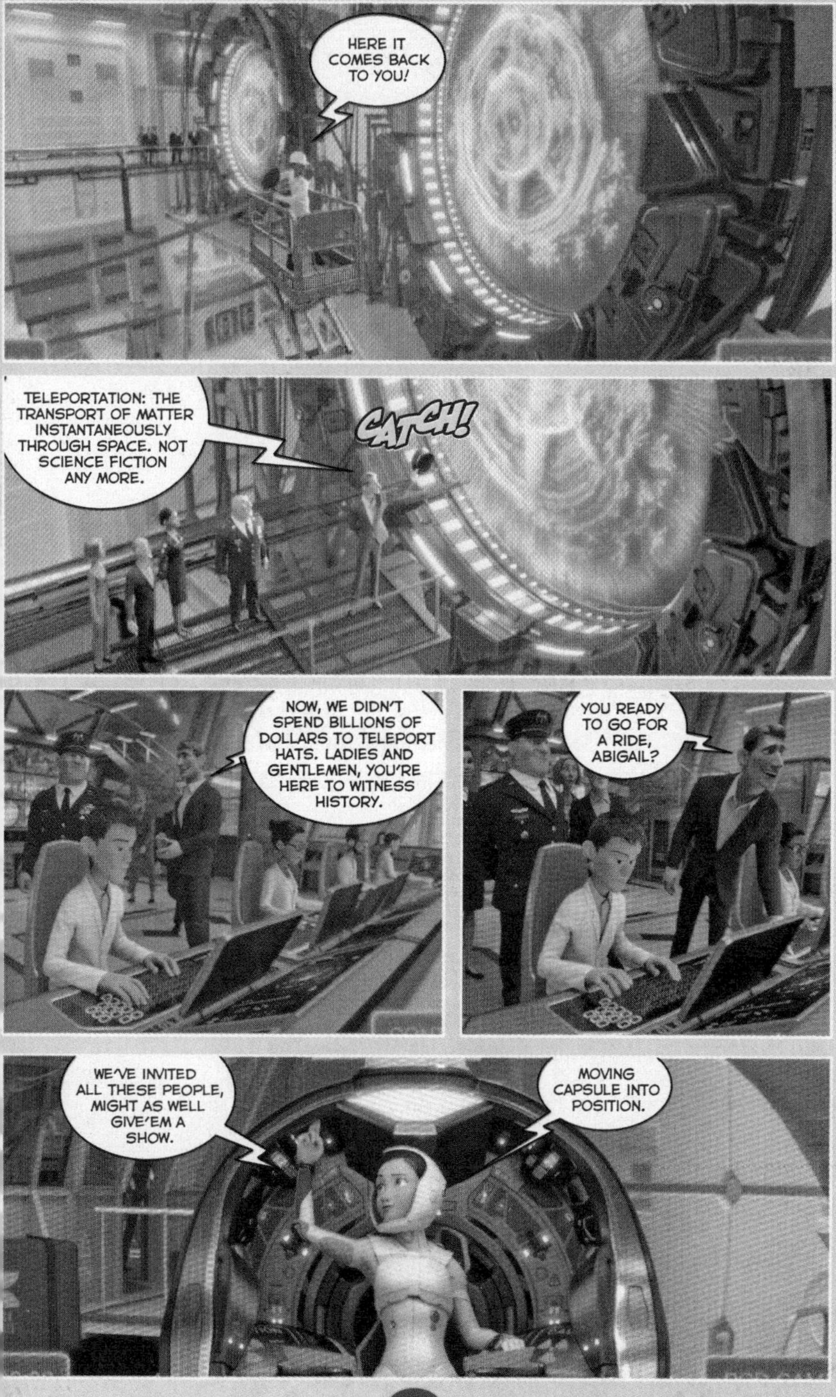
HERE IT COMES BACK TO YOU!
TELEPORTATION: THE TRANSPORT OF MATTER INSTANTANEOUSLY THROUGH SPACE. NOT SCIENCE FICTION ANY MORE.
CATCH!
NOW, WE DIDN'T SPEND BILLIONS OF DOLLARS TO TELEPORT HATS. LADIES AND GENTLEMEN, YOU'RE HERE TO WITNESS HISTORY.
YOU READY TO GO FOR A RIDE, ABIGAIL?
WE'VE INVITED ALL THESE PEOPLE, MIGHT AS WELL GIVE'EM A SHOW.
MOVING CAPSULE INTO POSITION.

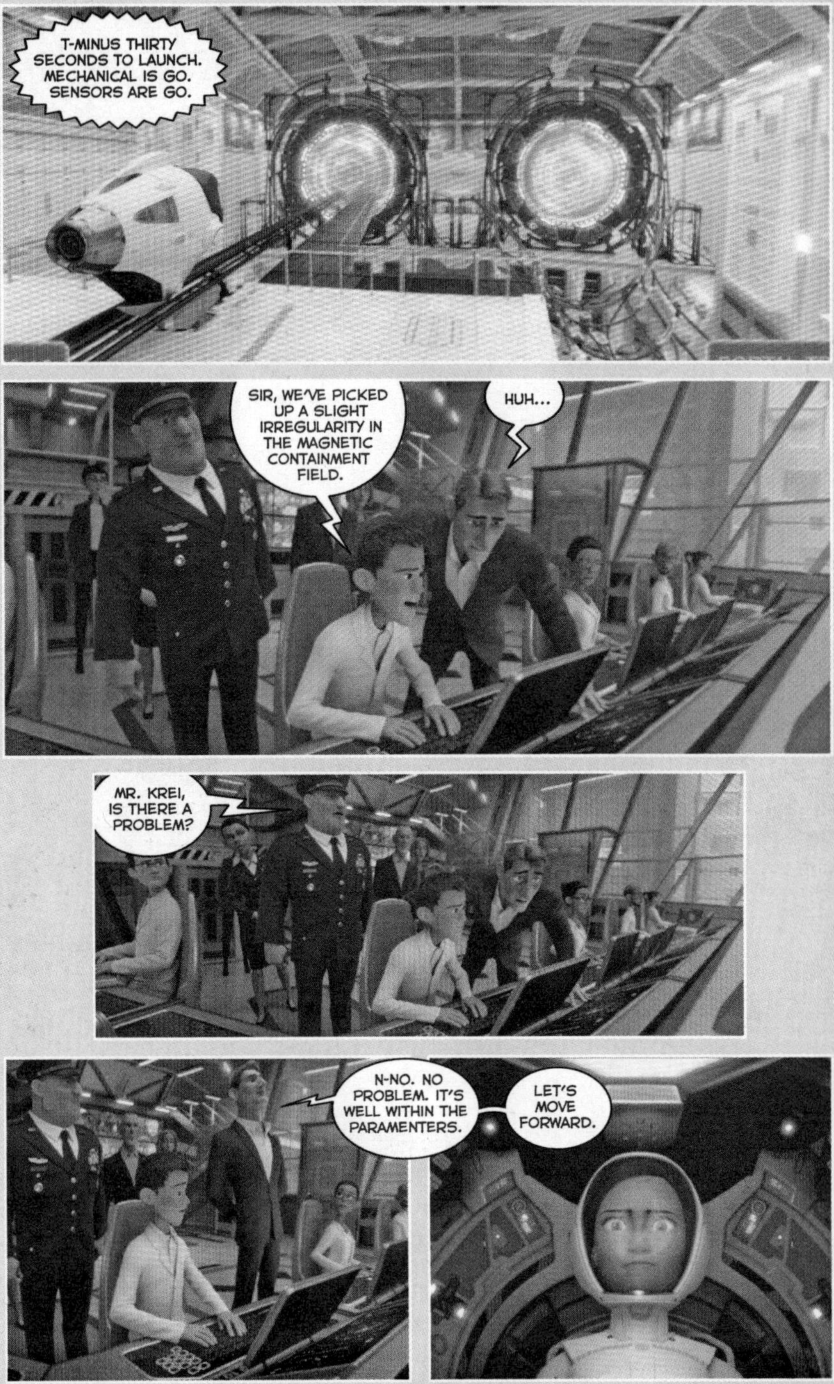
T-MINUS THIRTY SECONDS TO LAUNCH. MECHANICAL IS GO. SENSORS ARE GO.
SIR, WE'VE PICKED UP A SLIGHT IRREGULARITY IN THE MAGNETIC CONTAINMENT FIELD.
HUH...
MR. KREI, IS THERE A PROBLEM?
N-NO. NO PROBLEM. IT'S WELL WITHIN THE PARAMENTERS.
LET'S MOVE FORWARD.

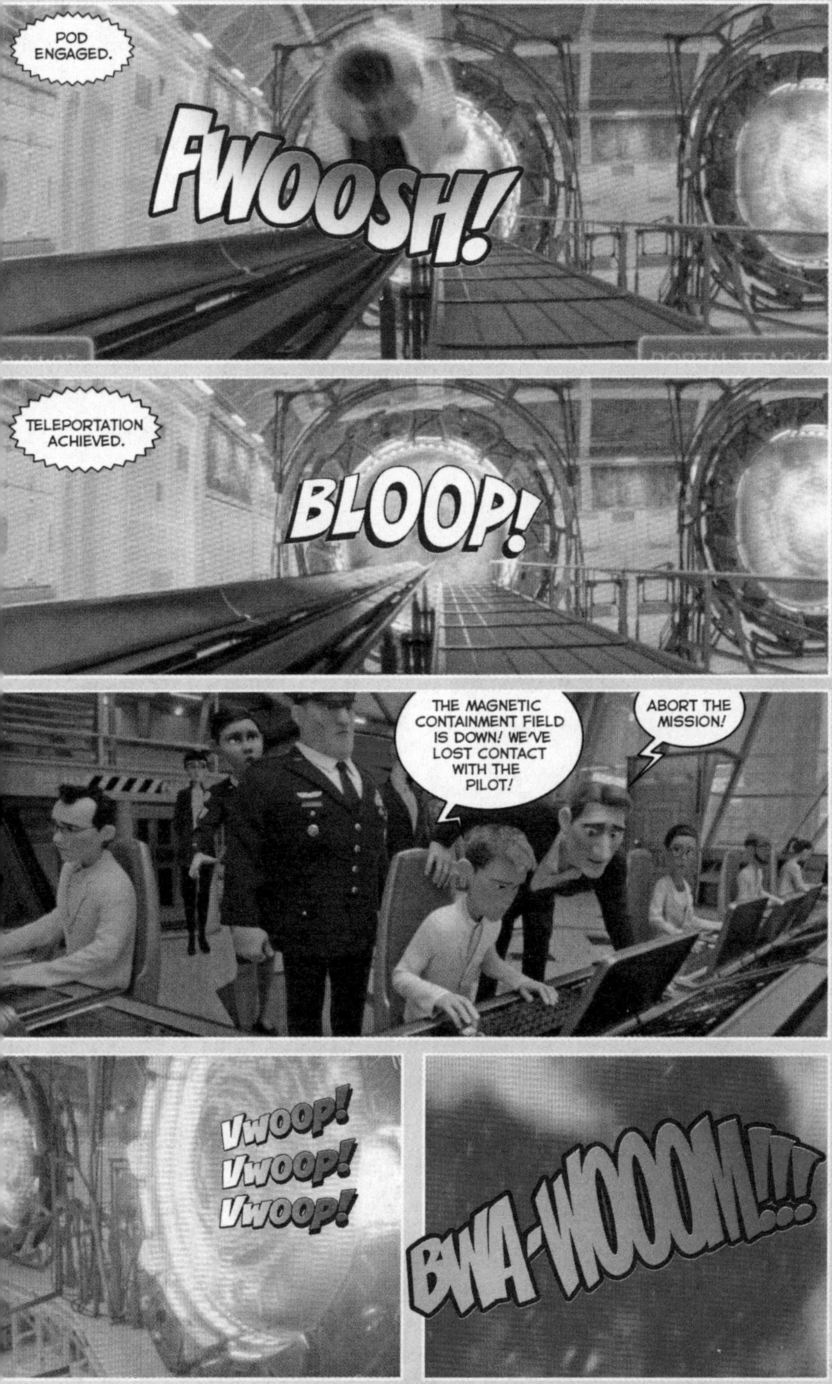
POD ENGAGED.
FWOOSH!
TELEPORTATION ACHIEVED.
BLOOP!
THE MAGNETIC CONTAINMENT FIELD IS DOWN! WE'VE LOST CONTACT WITH THE PILOT!
ABORT THE MISSION!
VWOOP! VWOOP! VWOOP!
BWA-WOOOM!!!

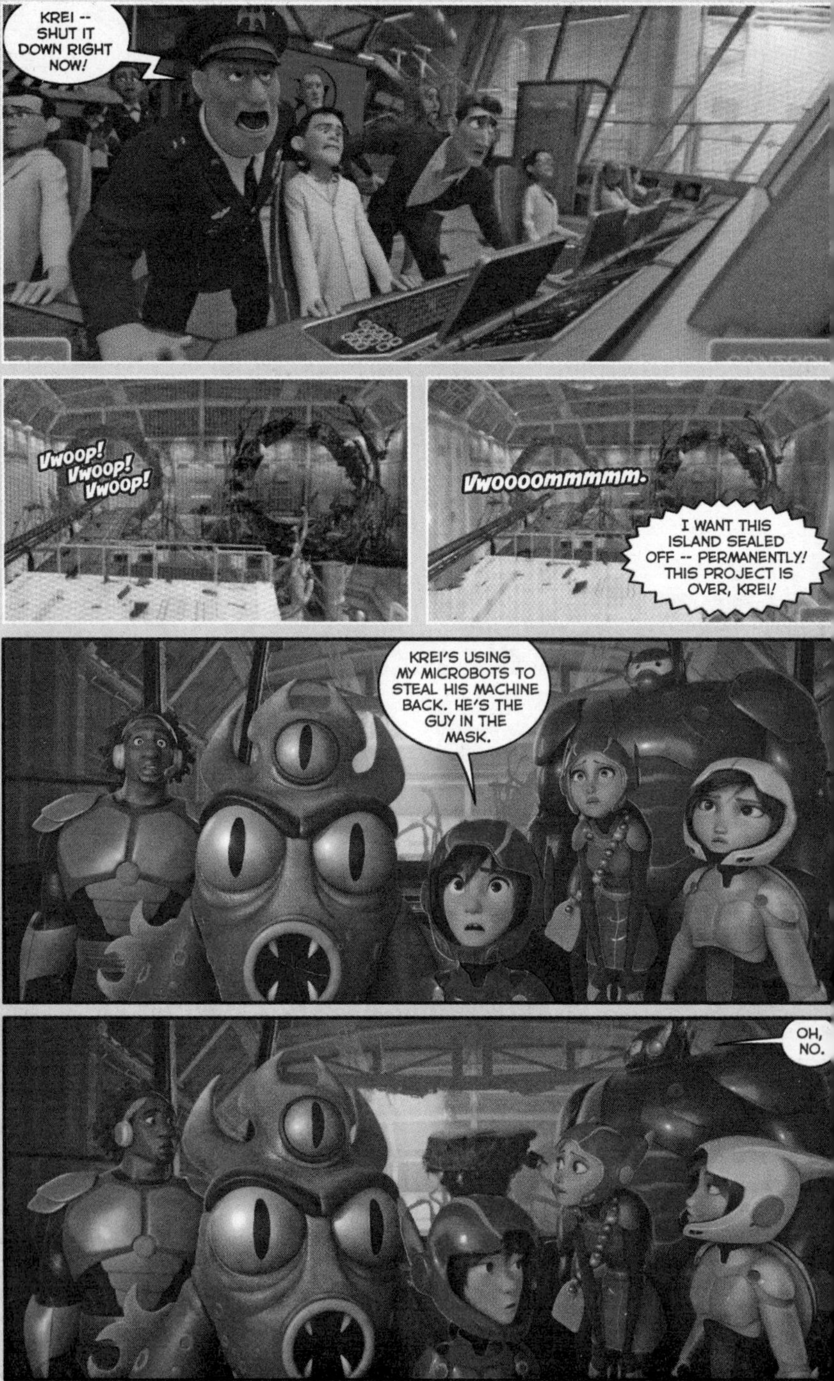
KREI -- SHUT IT DOWN RIGHT NOW!
VWOOP! VWOOP! VWOOP!
VWOOOOMMMMMM.
I WANT THIS ISLAND SEALED OFF -- PERMANENTLY! THIS PROJECT IS OVER, KREI!
KREI'S USING MY MICROBOTS TO STEAL HIS MACHINE BACK. HE'S THE GUY IN THE MASK.
OH, NO.

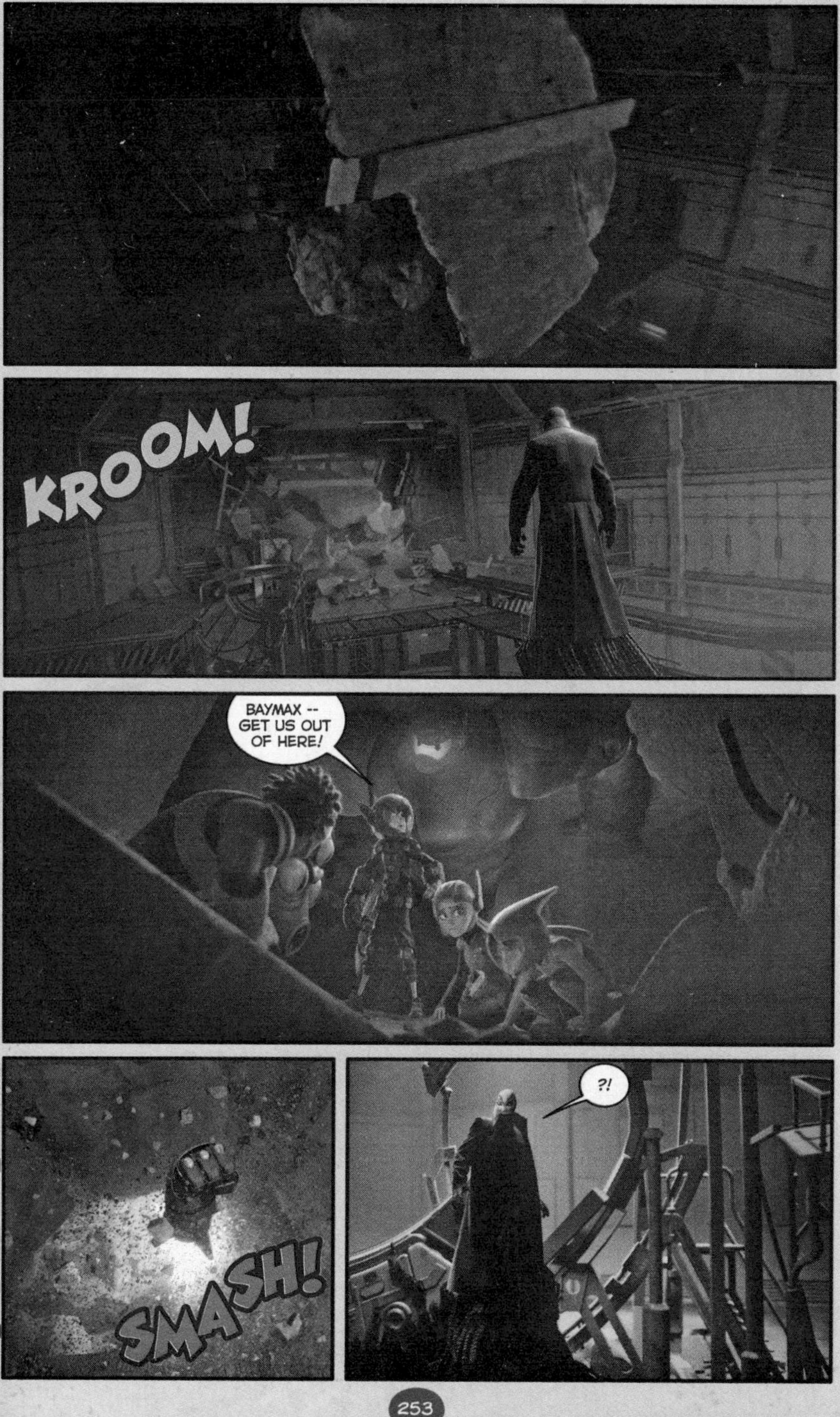
KROOM!
BAYMAX -- GET US OUT OF HERE!
SMASH!
?!

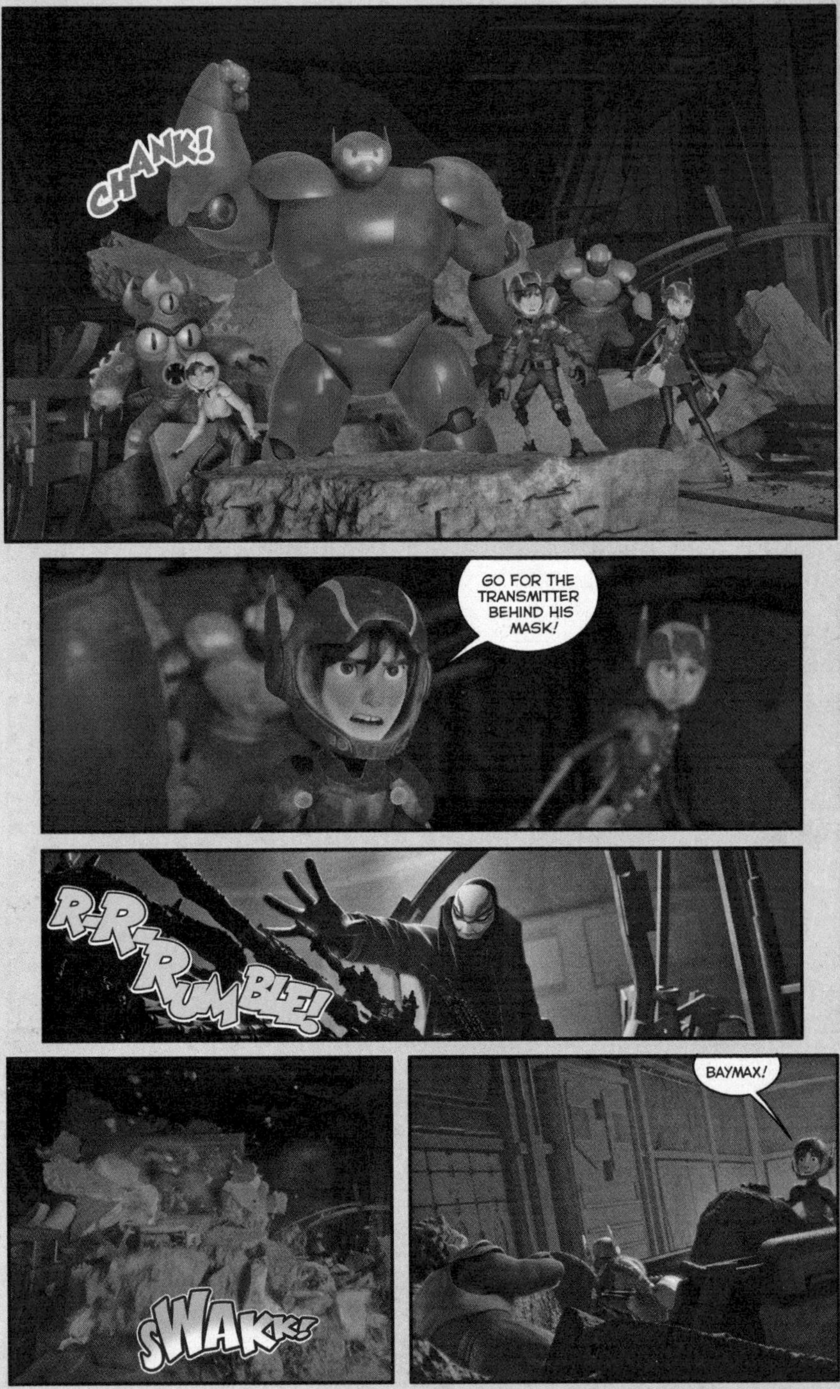
CHANK!
GO FOR THE TRANSMITTER BEHIND HIS MASK!
R-R-R-RUMBLE!
SWAKK!
BAYMAX!

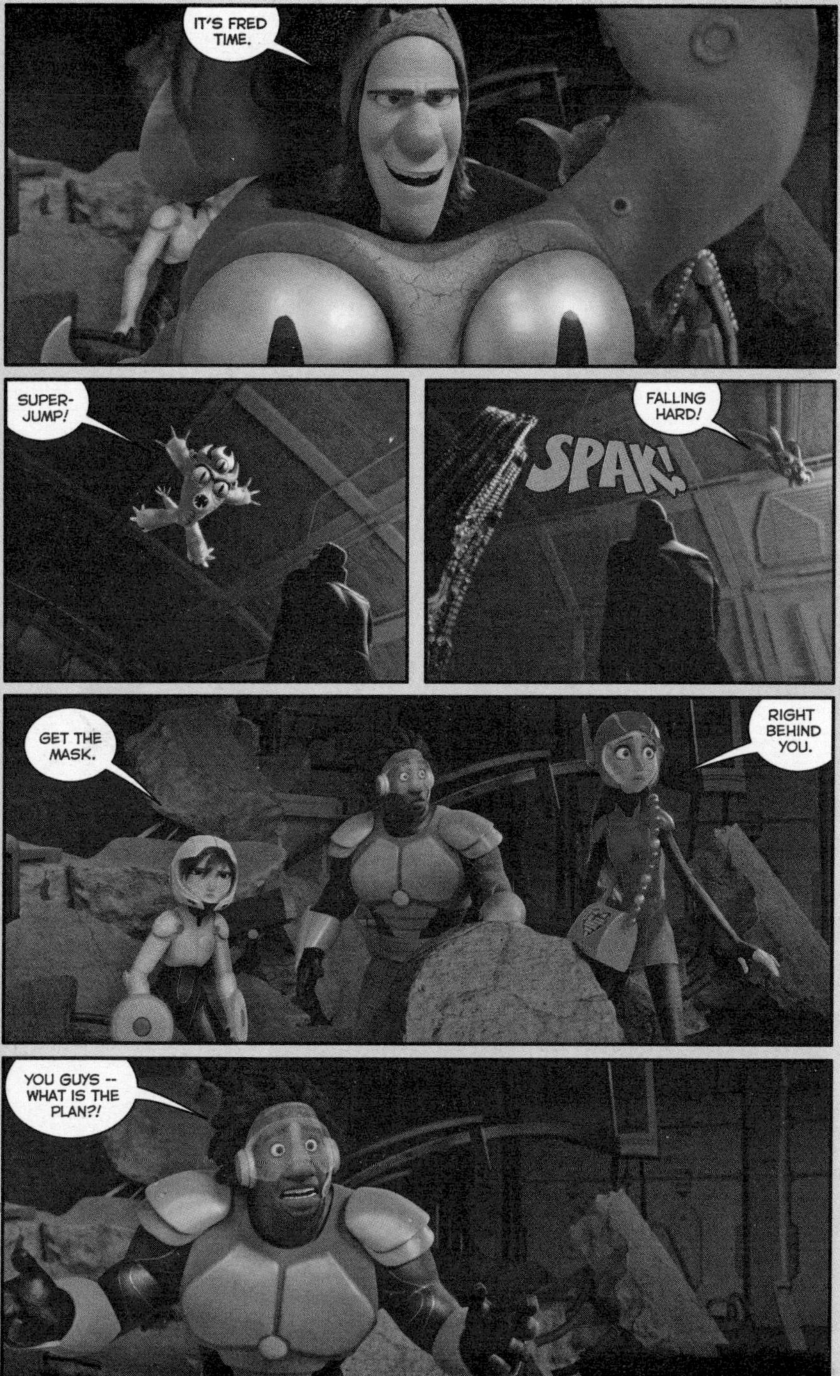
IT'S FRED TIME.
SUPER-JUMP!
SPAK!
FALLING HARD!
GET THE MASK.
RIGHT BEHIND YOU.
YOU GUYS -- WHAT IS THE PLAN?!

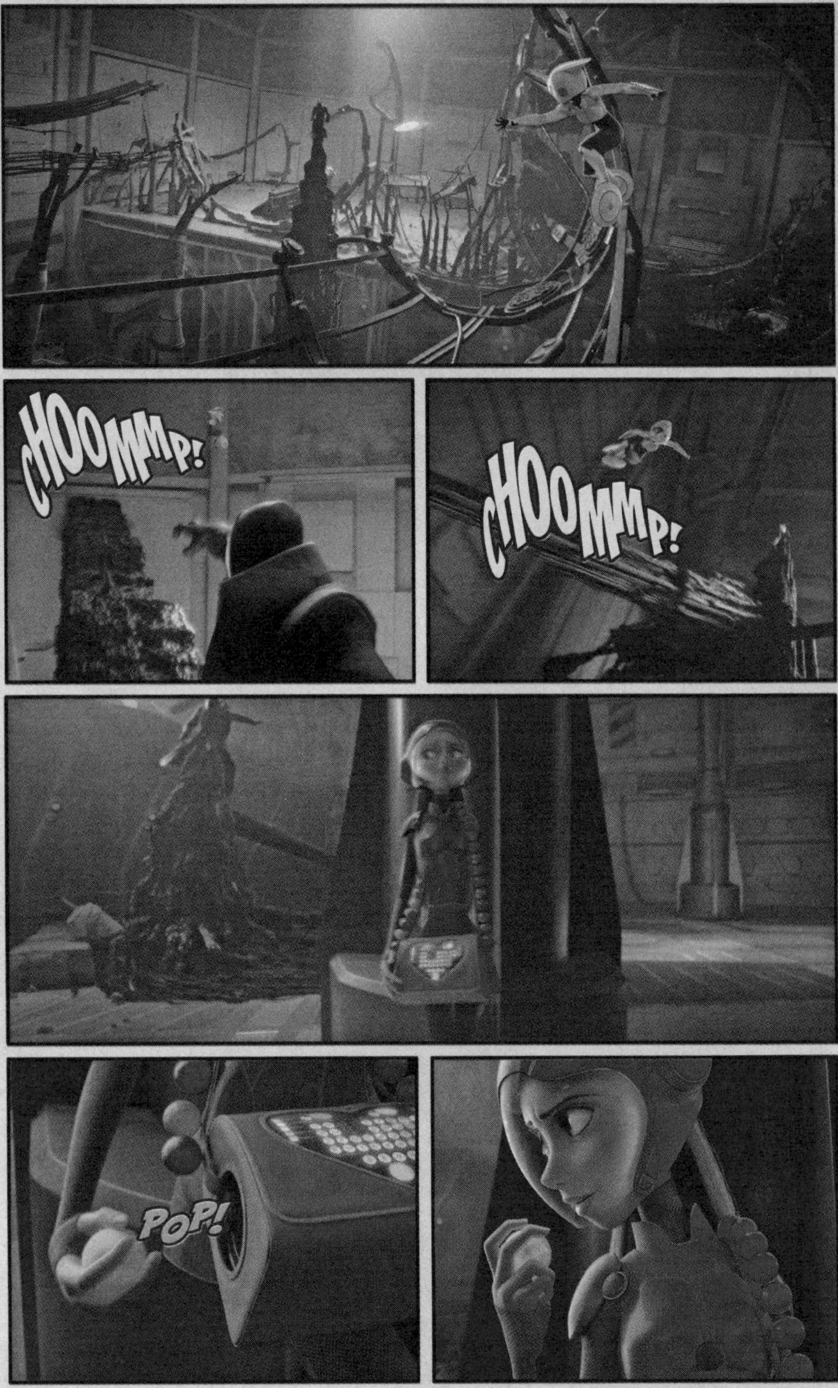
CHOOMMP!
CHOOMMMP!
POP!

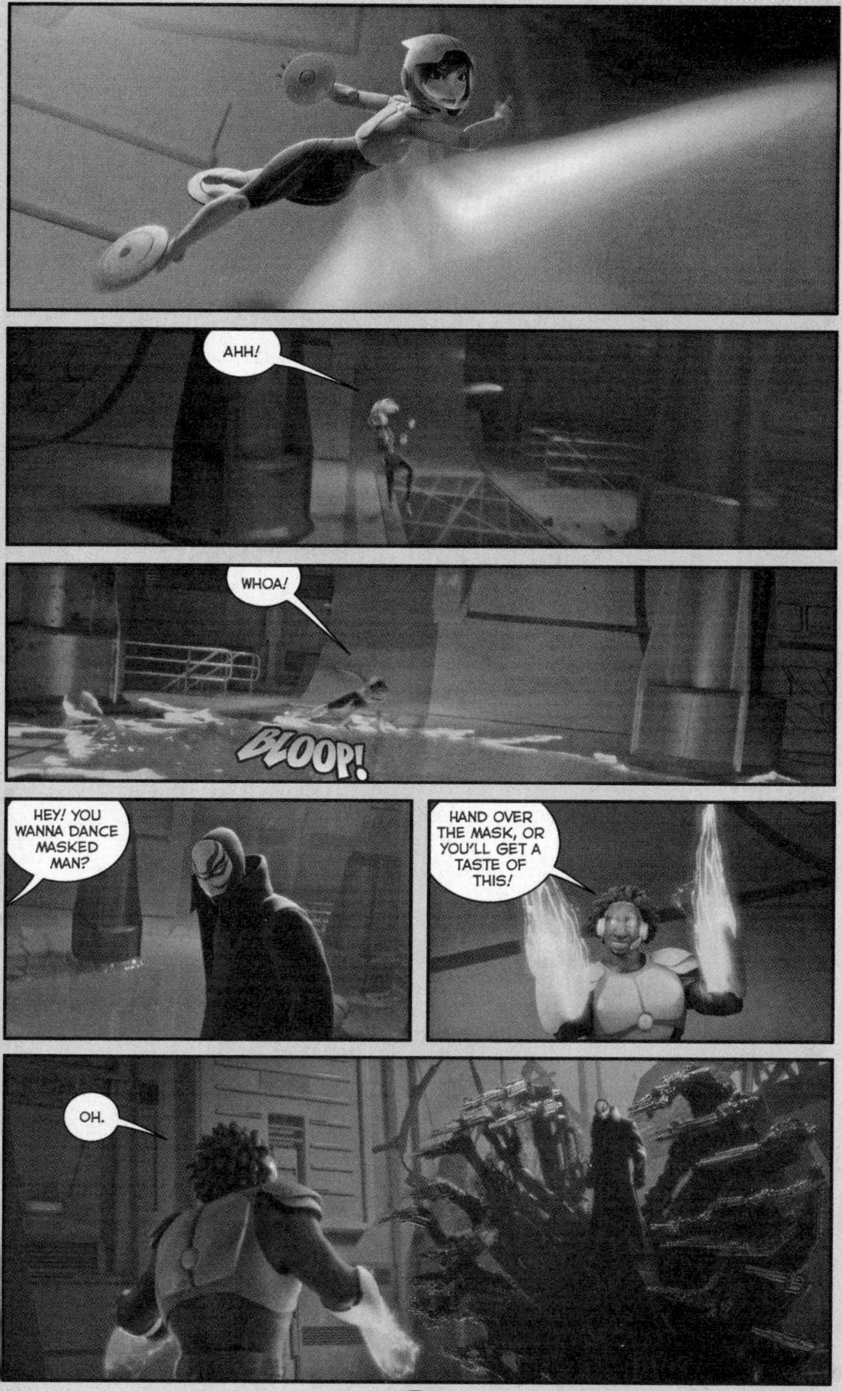
AHH!
WHOA!
BLOOP!
HEY! YOU WANNA DANCE MASKED MAN?
HAND OVER THE MASK, OR YOU'LL GET A TASTE OF THIS!
OH.

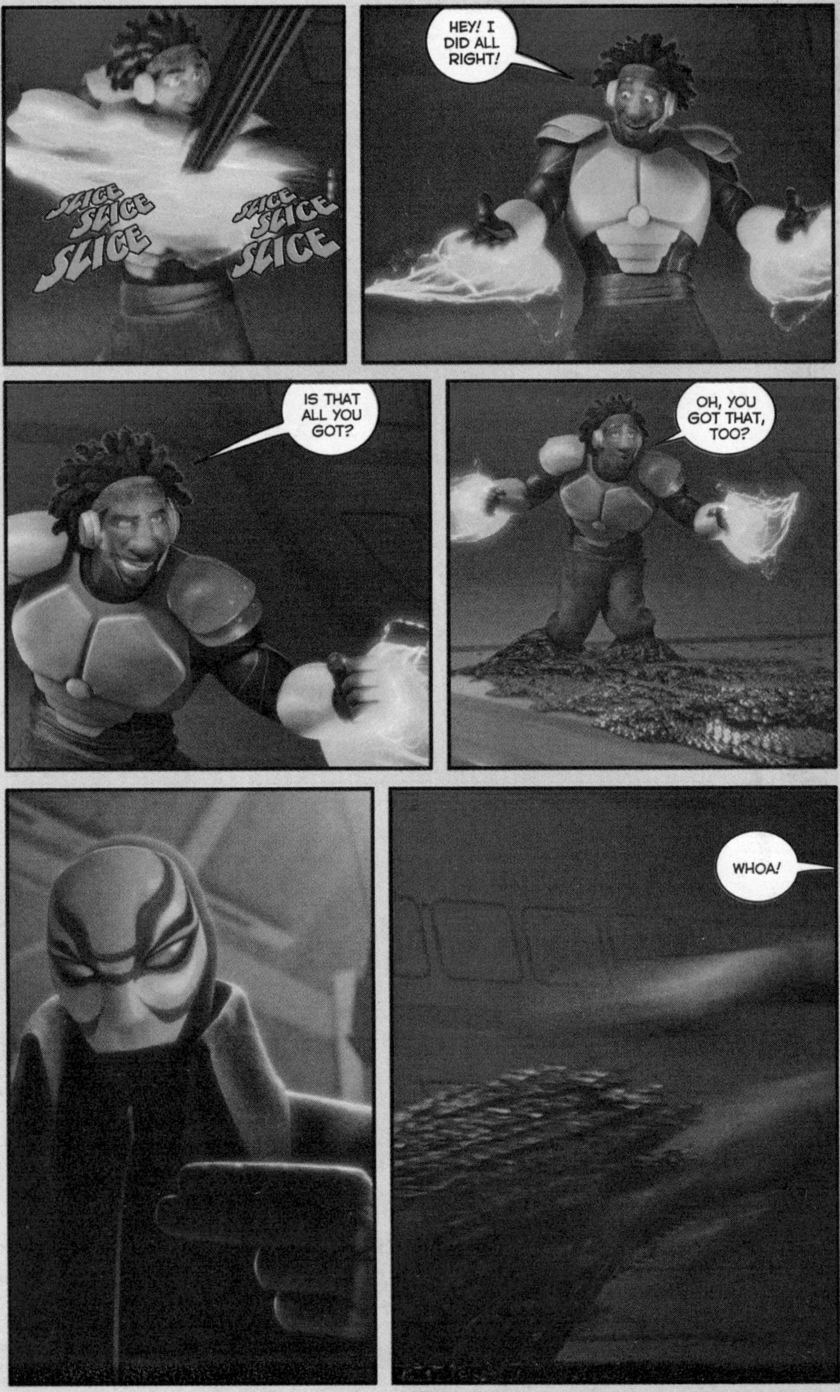
SLICE SLICE SLICE
SLICE SLICE SLICE
HEY! I DID ALL RIGHT!
IS THAT ALL YOU GOT?
OH, YOU GOT THAT, TOO?
WHOA!

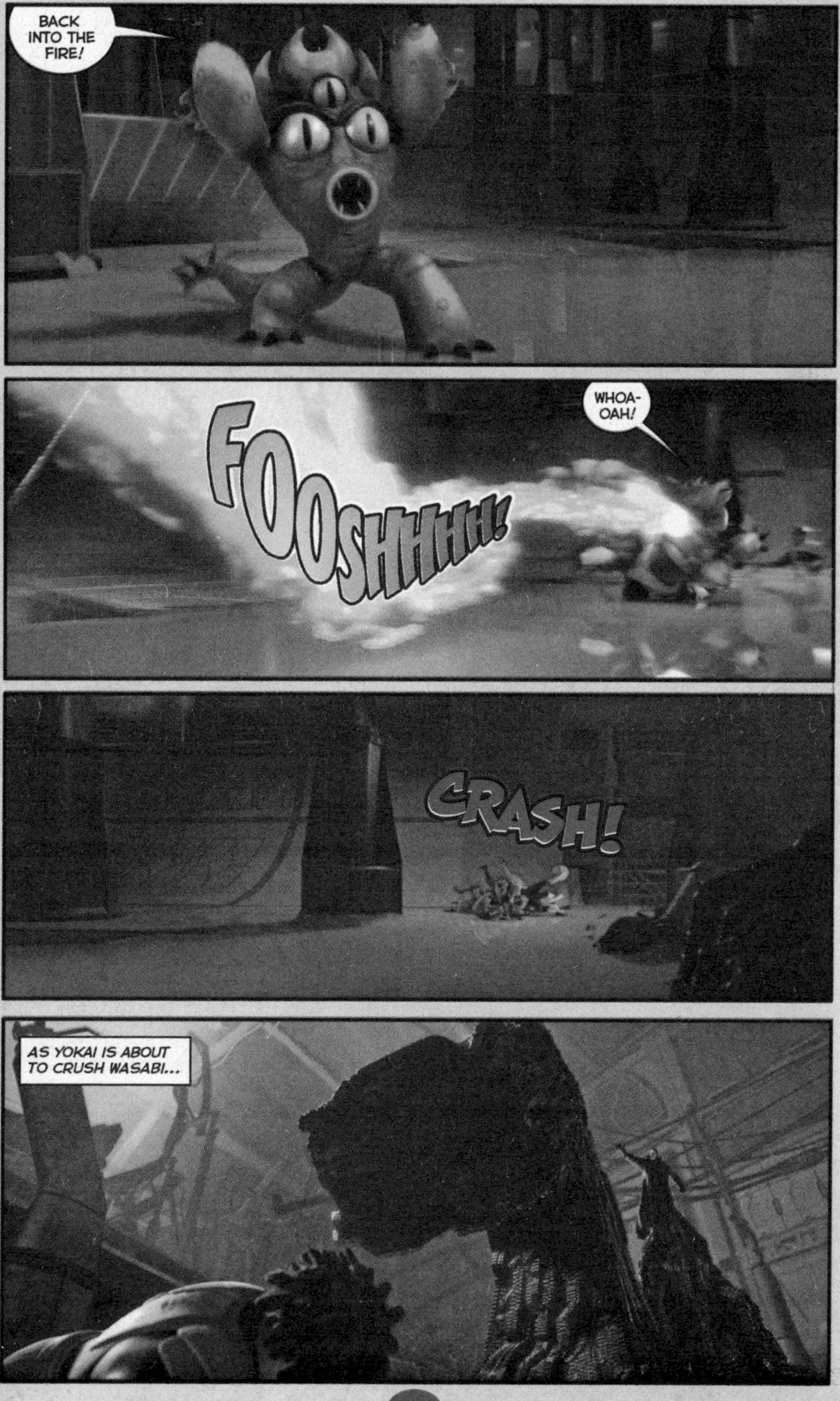
BACK INTO THE FIRE!
FOOSHHHH!
WHOA-OAH!
CRASH!
AS YOKAI IS ABOUT TO CRUSH WASABI...

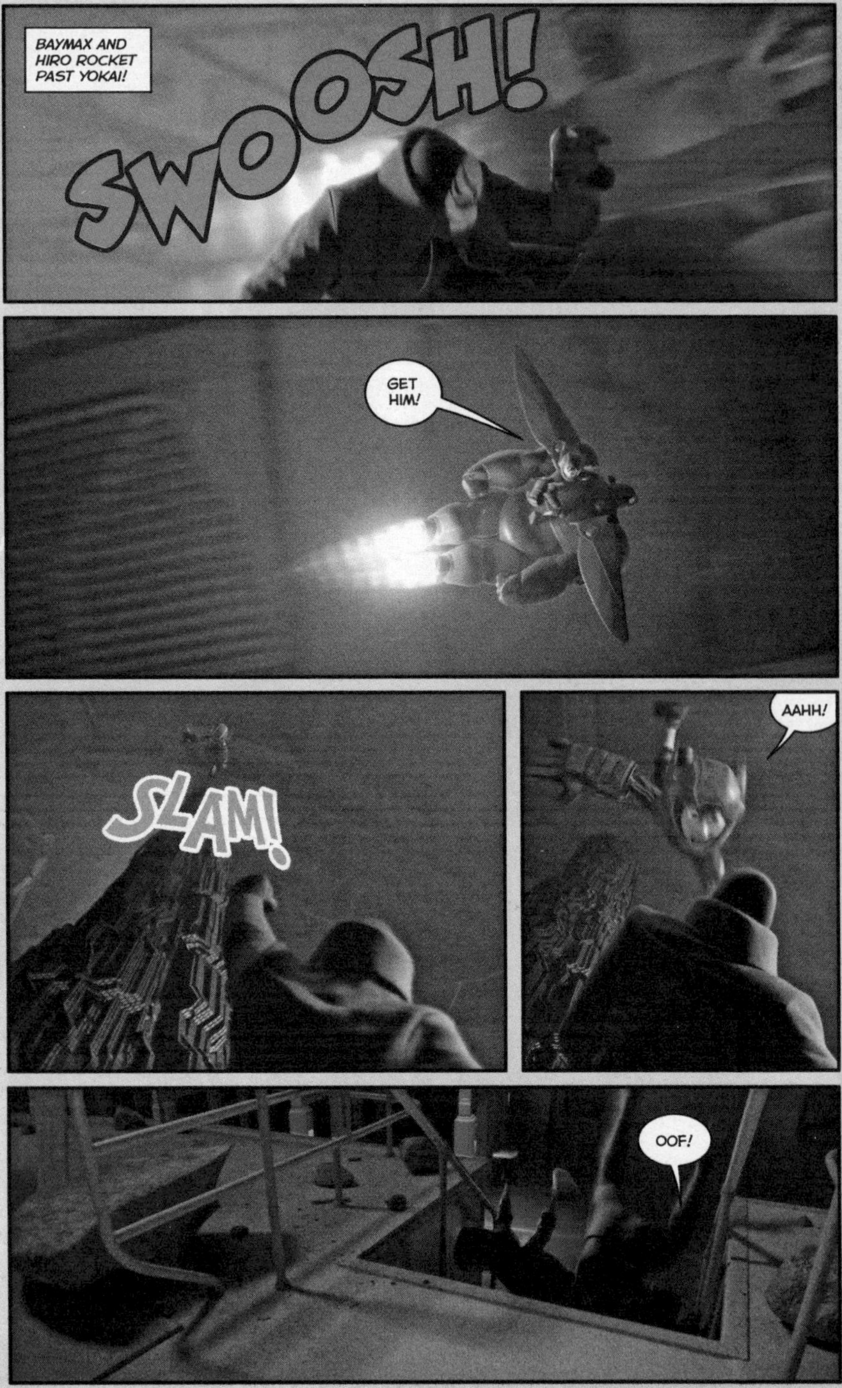
BAYMAX AND HIRO ROCKET PAST YOKAI!
SWOOSH!
GET HIM!
SLAM!
AAHH!
OOF!

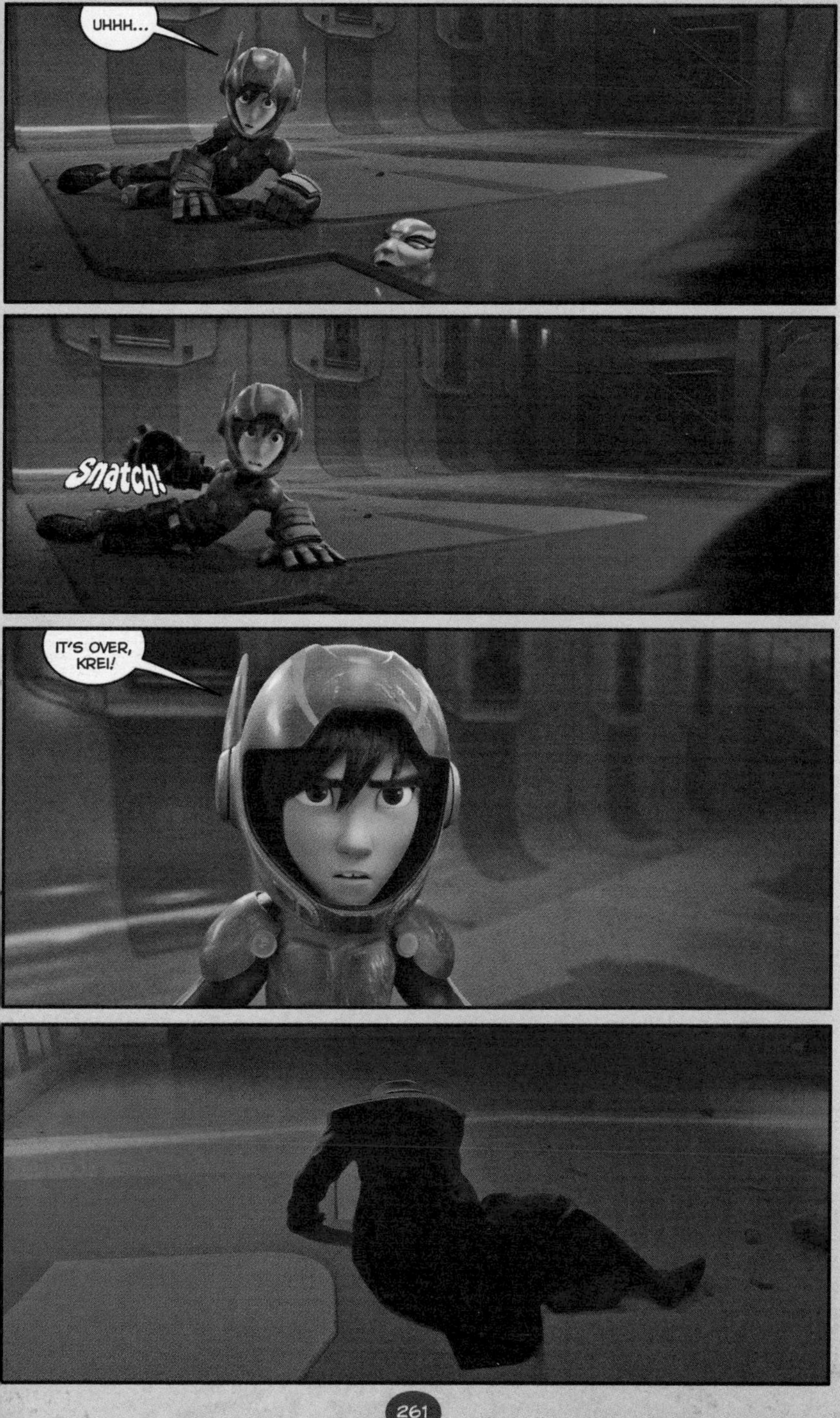
UHHH...
Snatch!
IT'S OVER, KREI!

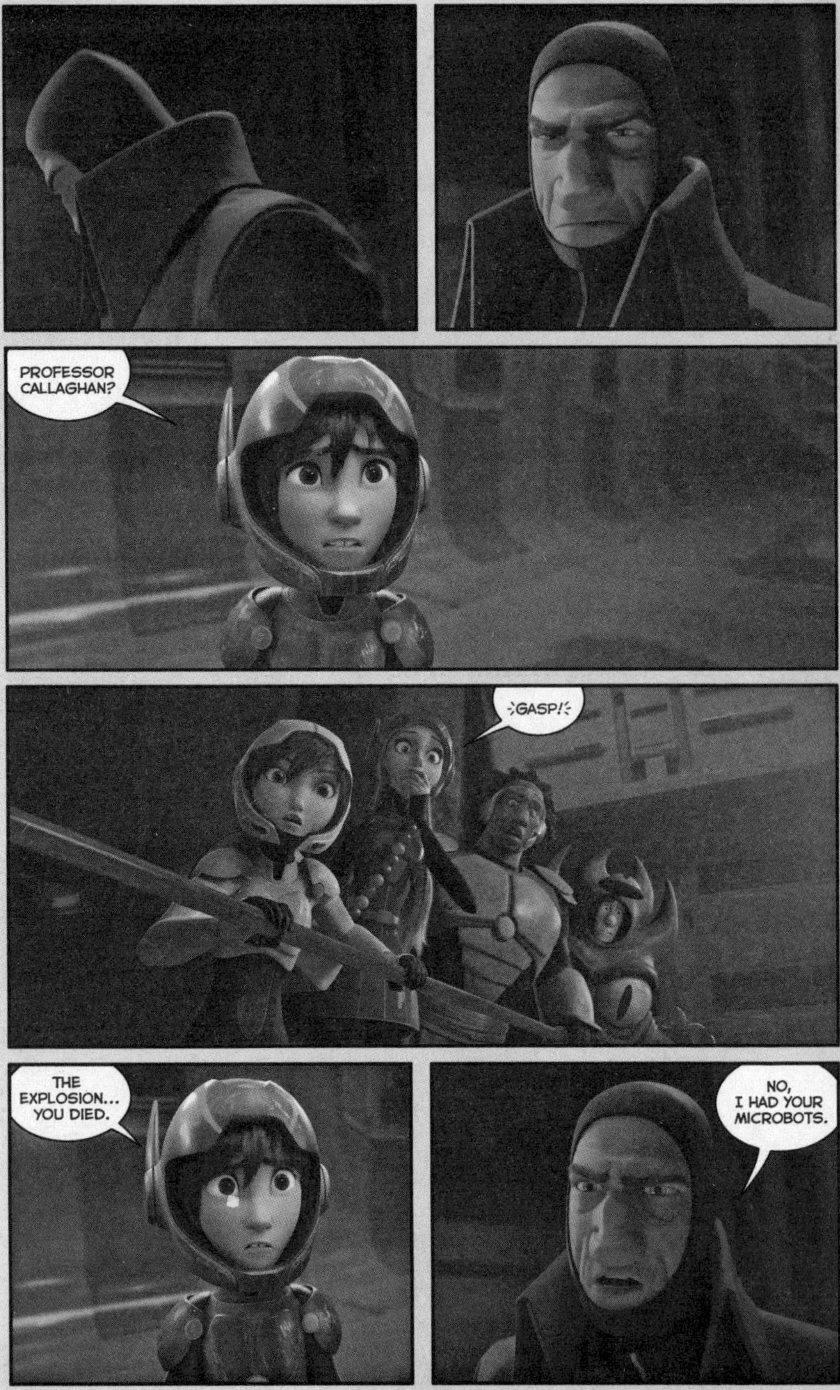
PROFESSOR CALLAGHAN?
GASP!
THE EXPLOSION... YOU DIED.
NO, I HAD YOUR MICROBOTS.

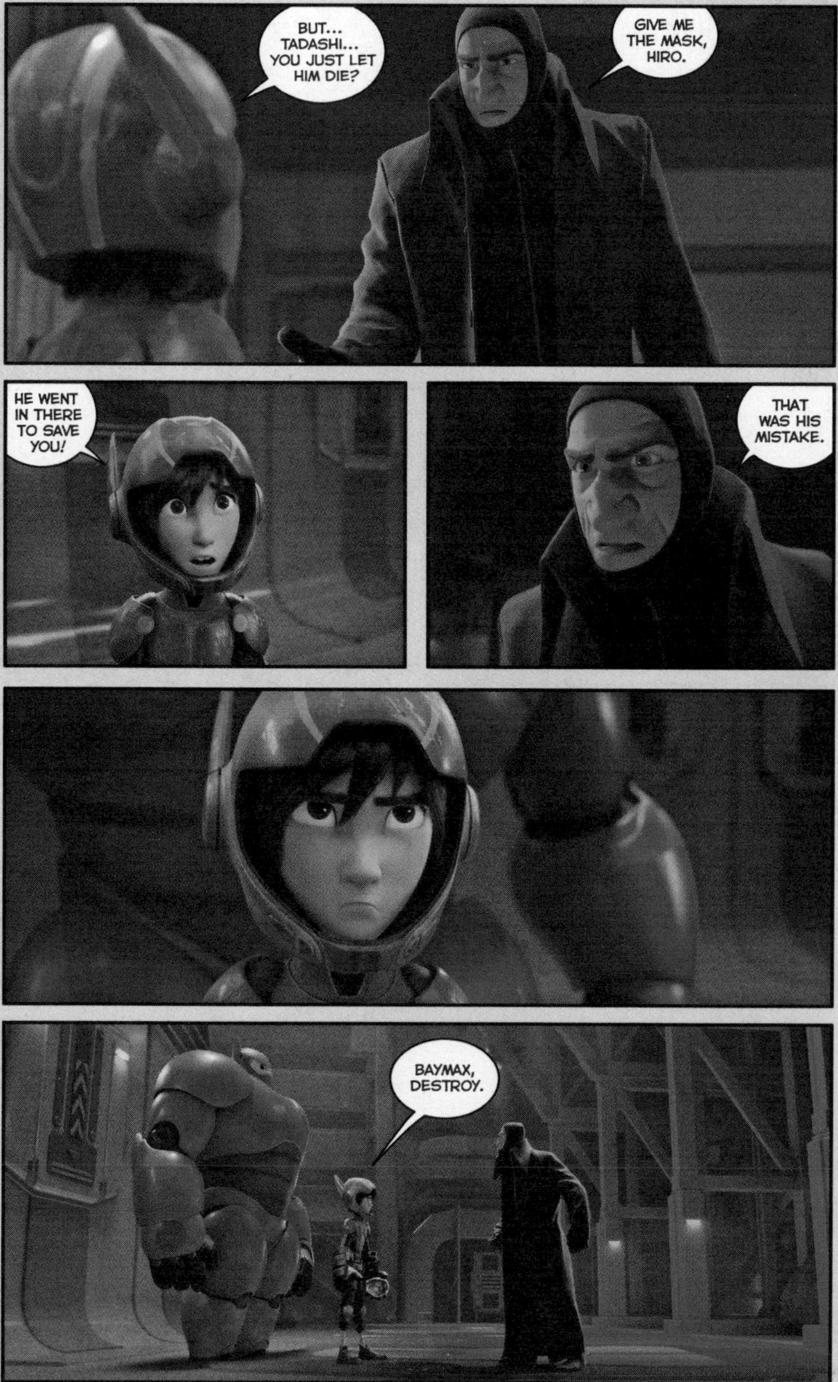
BUT... TADASHI... YOU JUST LET HIM DIE?
GIVE ME THE MASK, HIRO.
HE WENT IN THERE TO SAVE YOU!
THAT WAS HIS MISTAKE.
BAYMAX, DESTROY.

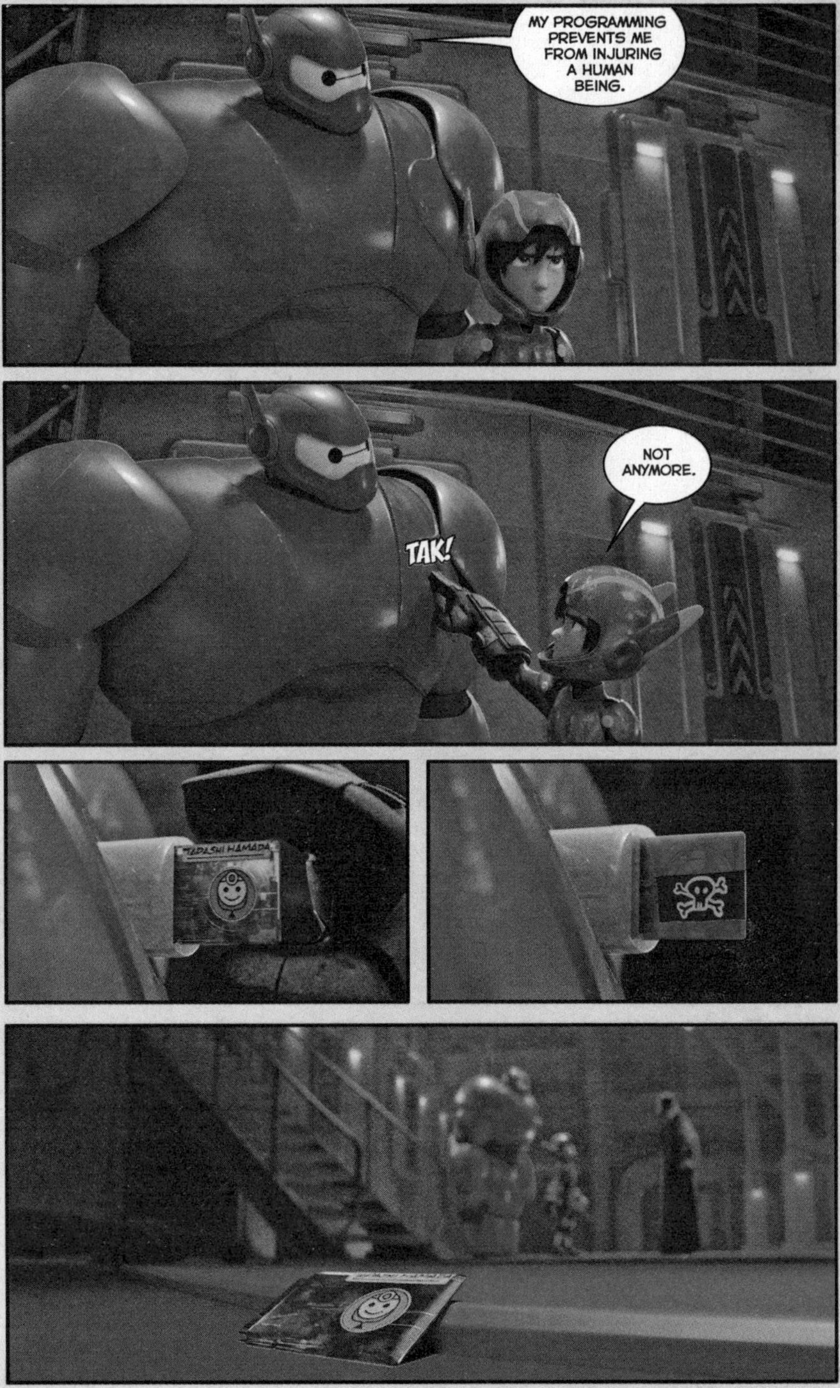
MY PROGRAMMING PREVENTS ME FROM INJURING A HUMAN BEING.
NOT ANYMORE.
TAK!
TADASHI HAMADA

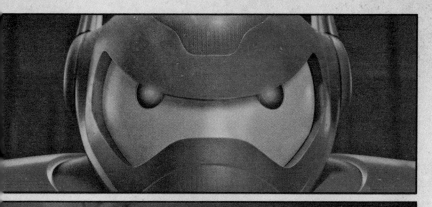

DO IT, BAYMAX. DESTROY HIM!

BOOM!

KROOM!

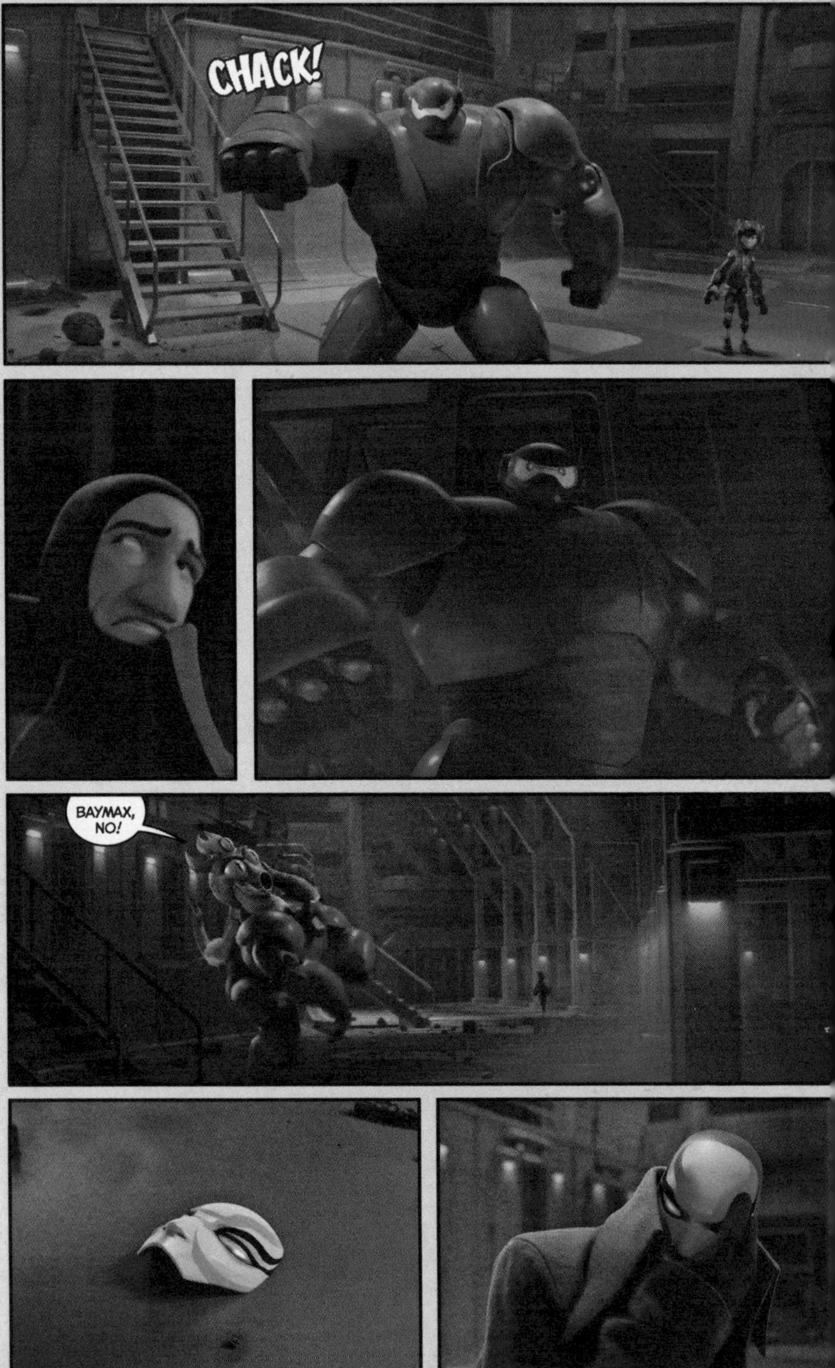
CHACK!
BAYMAX, NO!

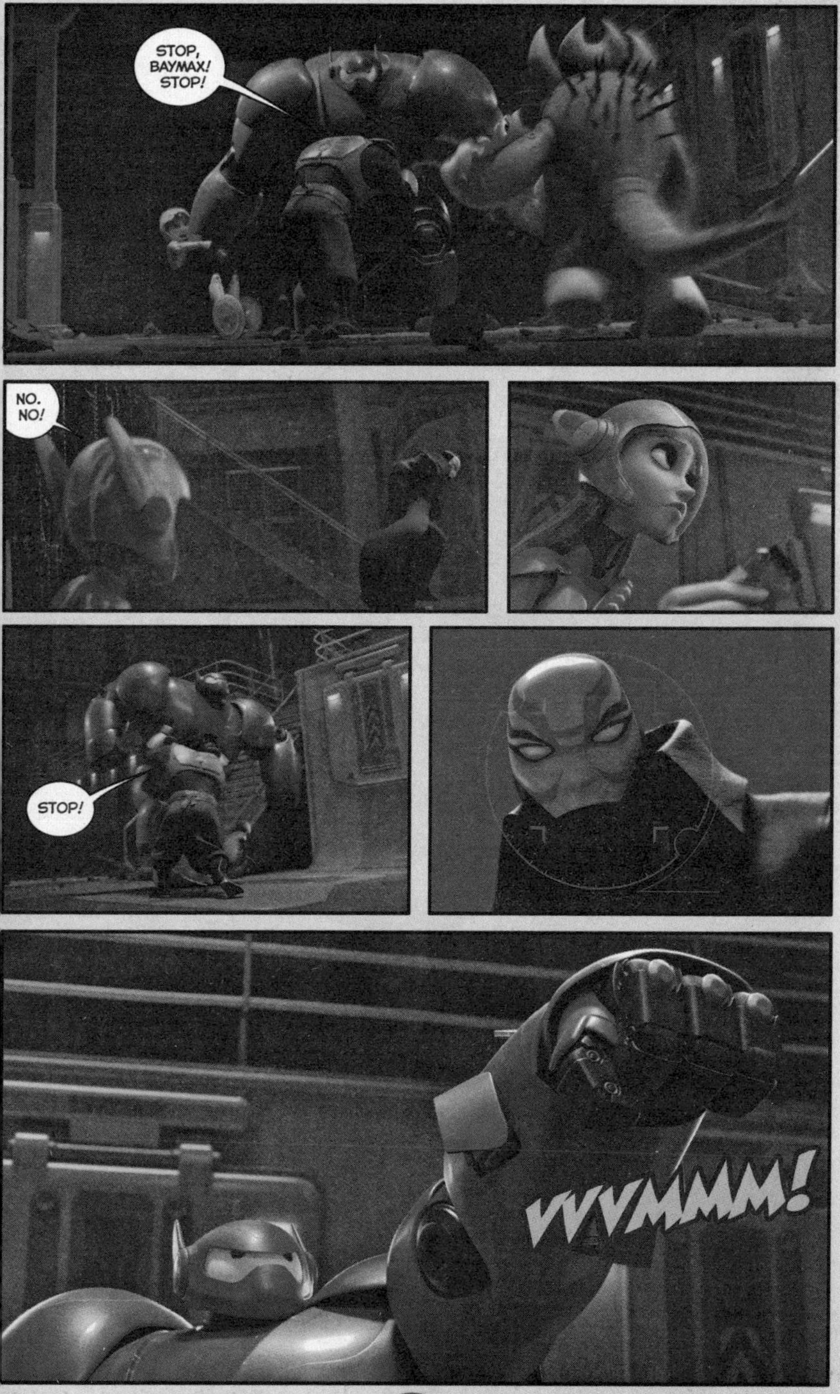
STOP, BAYMAX! STOP!
NO. NO!
STOP!
VVVMMM!

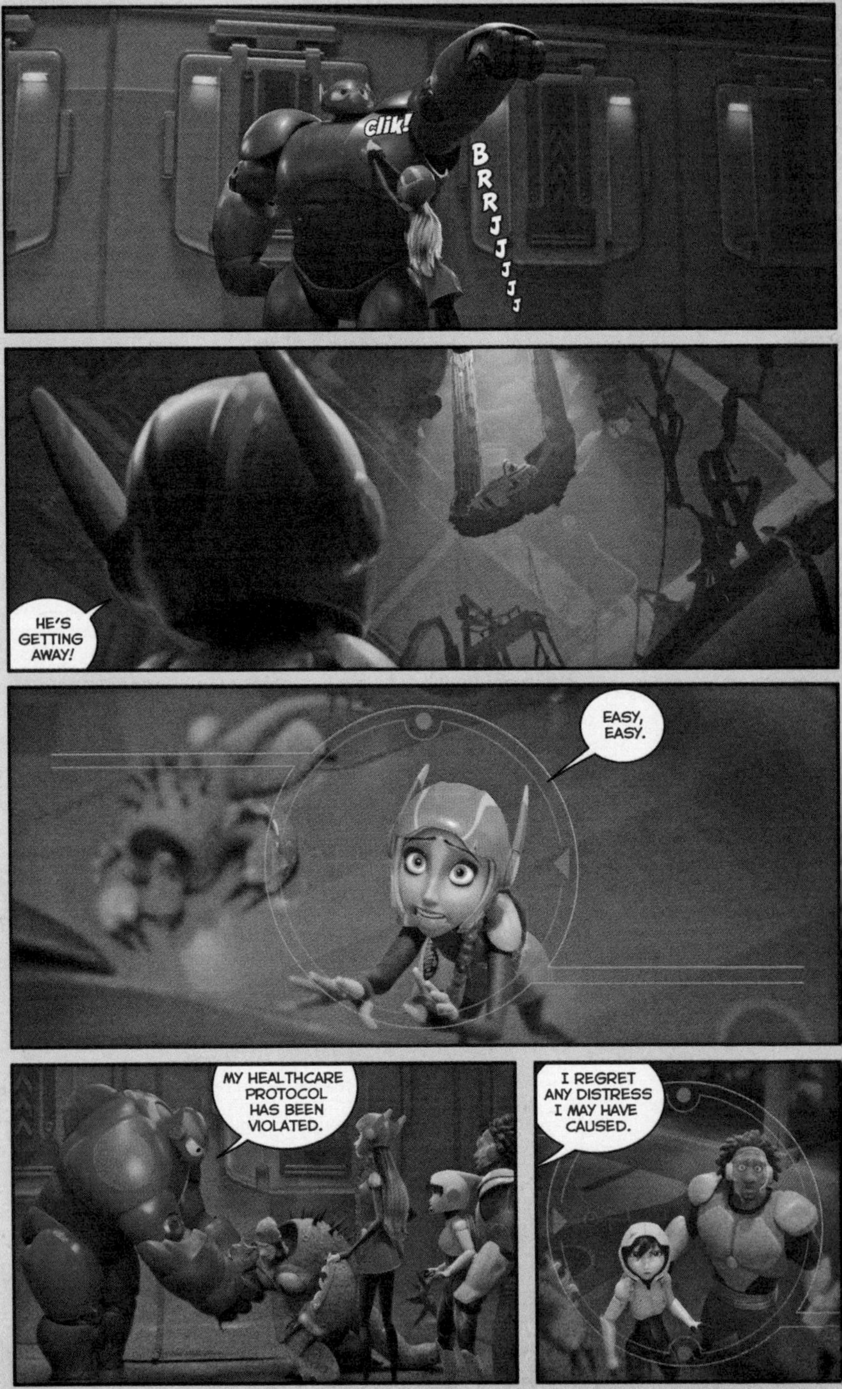
clik!
BRRJJJJJ
HE'S GETTING AWAY!
EASY, EASY.
MY HEALTHCARE PROTOCOL HAS BEEN VIOLATED.
I REGRET ANY DISTRESS I MAY HAVE CAUSED.

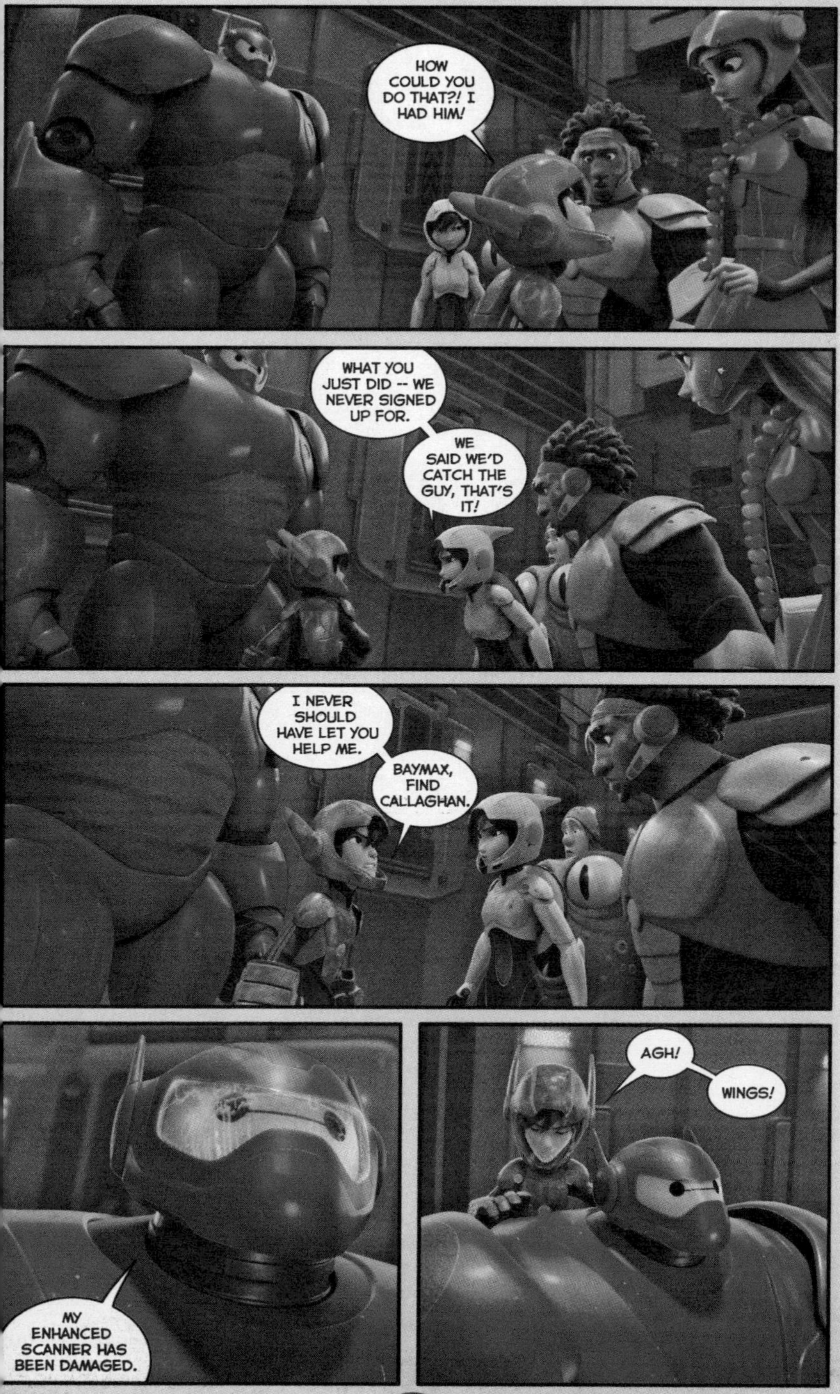
HOW COULD YOU DO THAT?! I HAD HIM!
WHAT YOU JUST DID -- WE NEVER SIGNED UP FOR.
WE SAID WE'D CATCH THE GUY, THAT'S IT!
I NEVER SHOULD HAVE LET YOU HELP ME.
BAYMAX, FIND CALLAGHAN.
MY ENHANCED SCANNER HAS BEEN DAMAGED.
AGH!
WINGS!

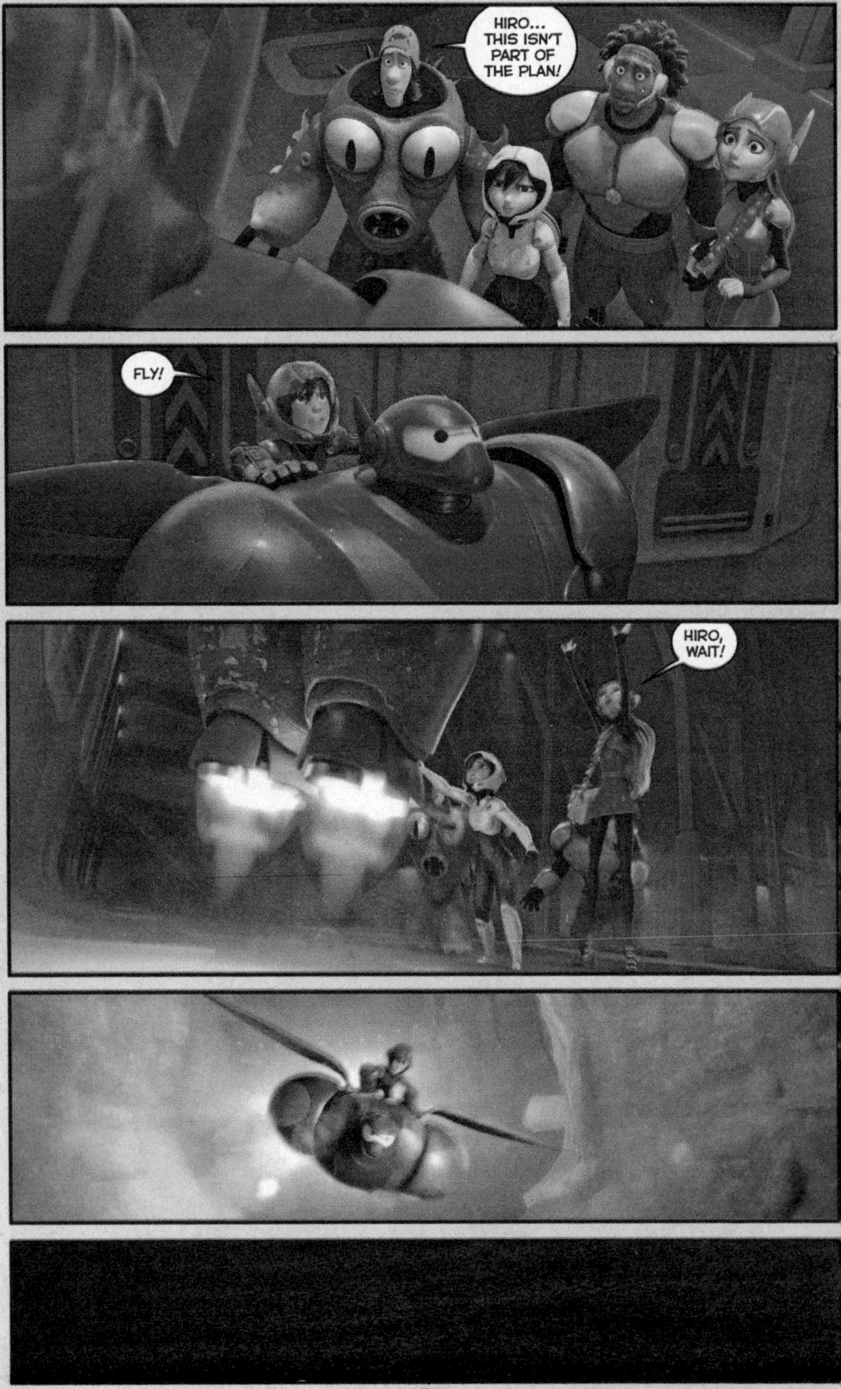
HIRO... THIS ISN'T PART OF THE PLAN!
FLY!
HIRO, WAIT!

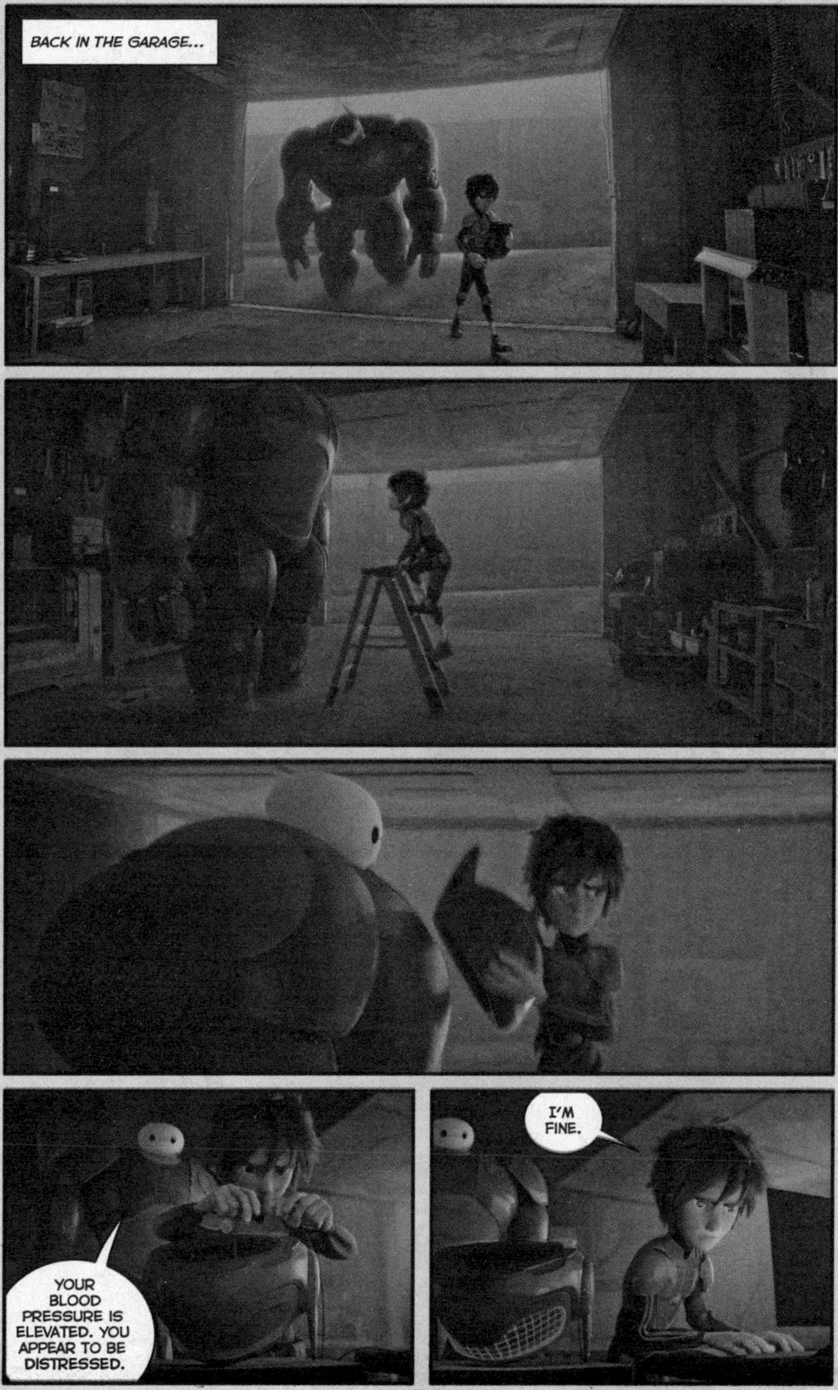
BACK IN THE GARAGE...
YOUR BLOOD PRESSURE IS ELEVATED. YOU APPEAR TO BE DISTRESSED.
I'M FINE.

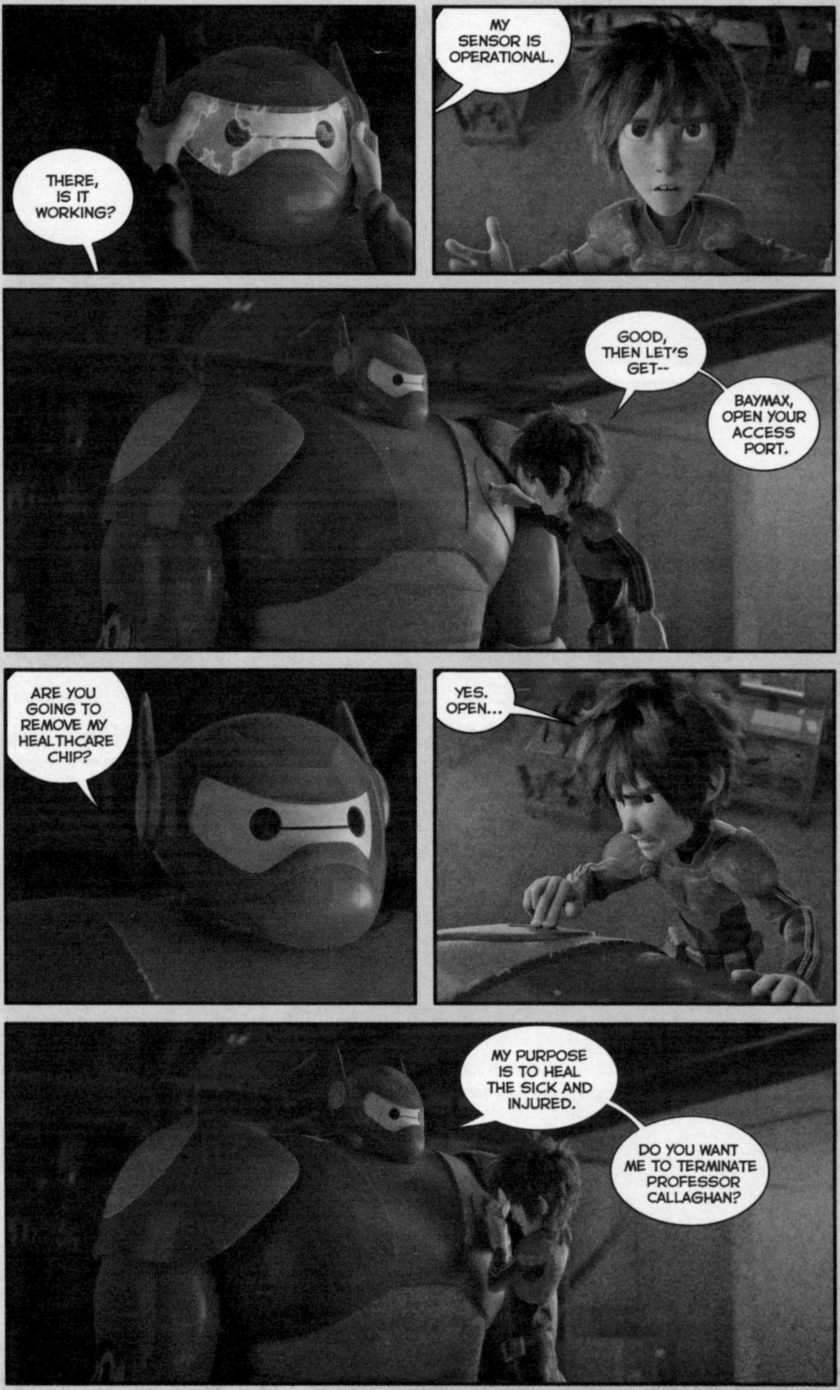
THERE, IS IT WORKING?
MY SENSOR IS OPERATIONAL.
GOOD, THEN LET'S GET--
BAYMAX, OPEN YOUR ACCESS PORT.
ARE YOU GOING TO REMOVE MY HEALTHCARE CHIP?
YES. OPEN...
MY PURPOSE IS TO HEAL THE SICK AND INJURED.
DO YOU WANT ME TO TERMINATE PROFESSOR CALLAGHAN?

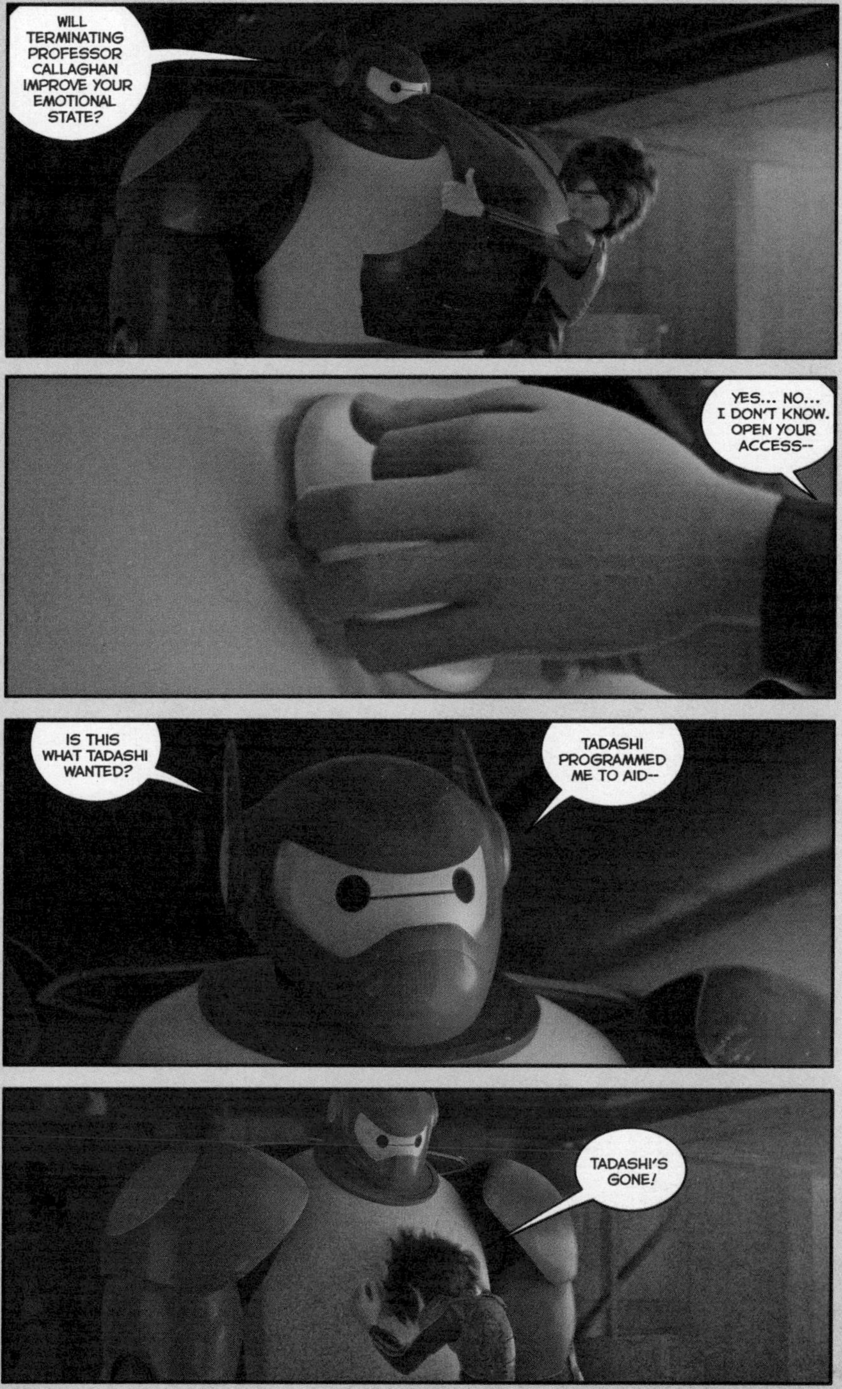
WILL TERMINATING PROFESSOR CALLAGHAN IMPROVE YOUR EMOTIONAL STATE?
YES... NO... I DON'T KNOW. OPEN YOUR ACCESS--
IS THIS WHAT TADASHI WANTED?
TADASHI PROGRAMMED ME TO AID--
TADASHI'S GONE!

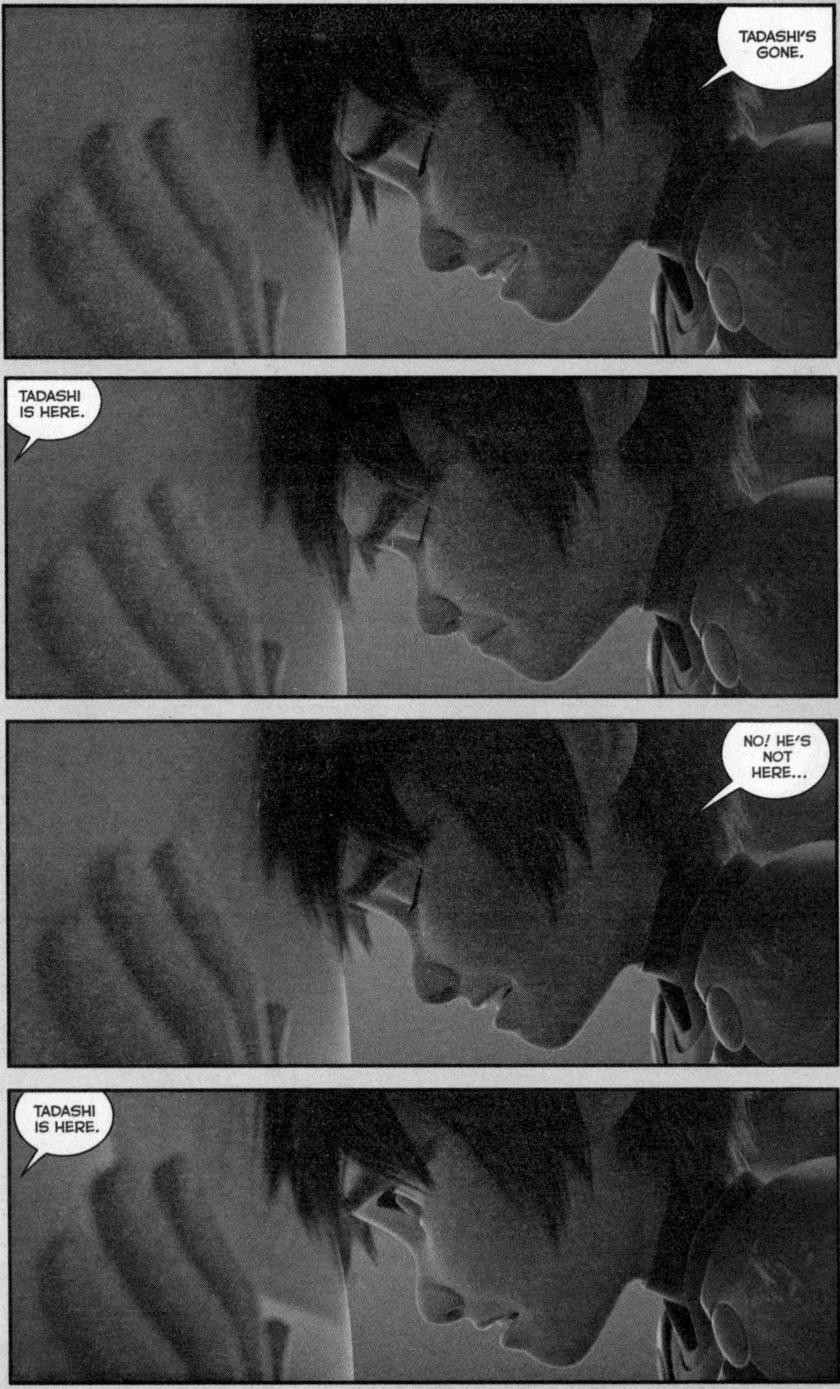
TADASHI'S GONE.
TADASHI IS HERE.
NO! HE'S NOT HERE...
TADASHI IS HERE.

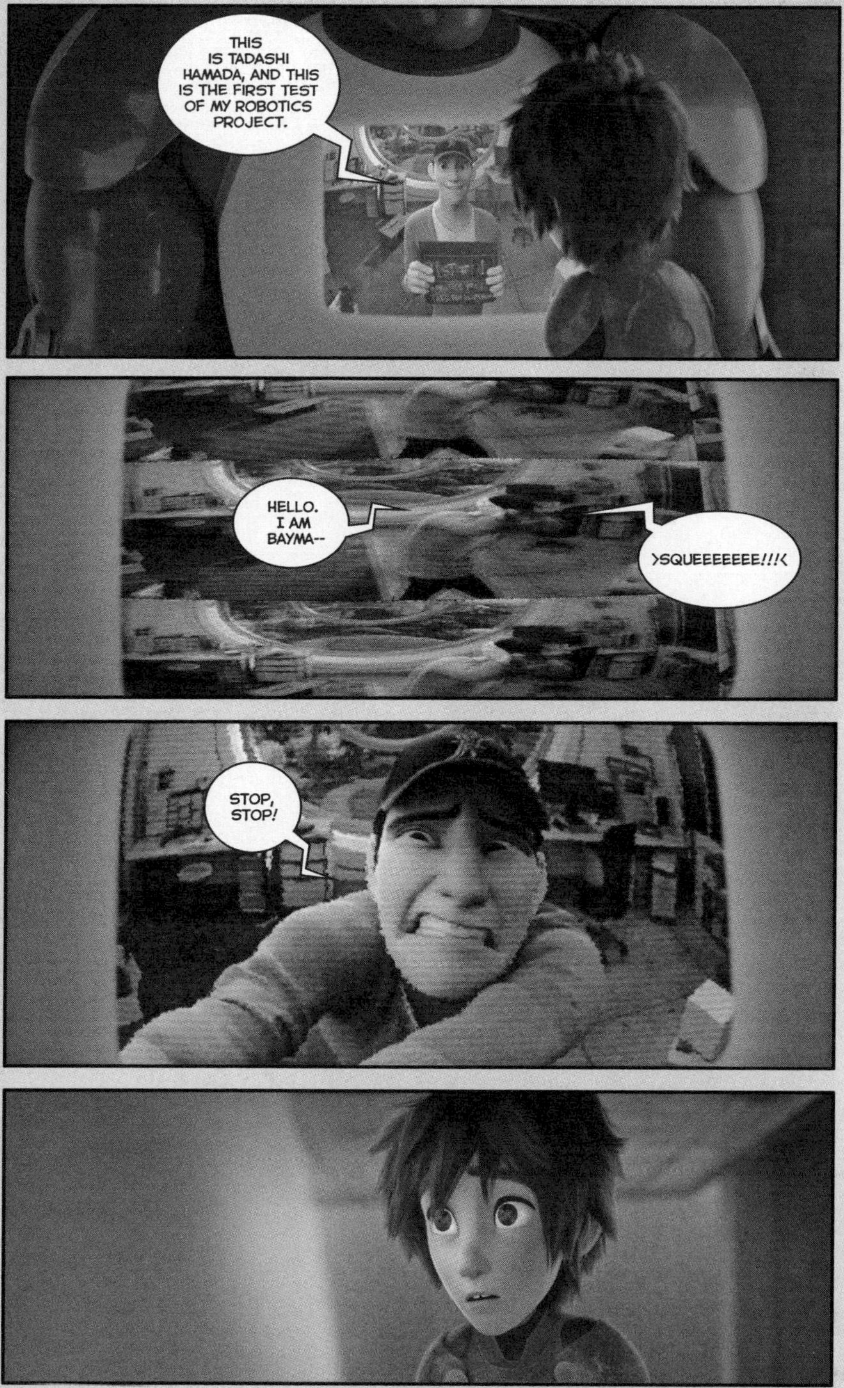
THIS IS TADASHI HAMADA, AND THIS IS THE FIRST TEST OF MY ROBOTICS PROJECT.
HELLO. I AM BAYMA--
>SQUEEEEEEEE!!!<
STOP, STOP!

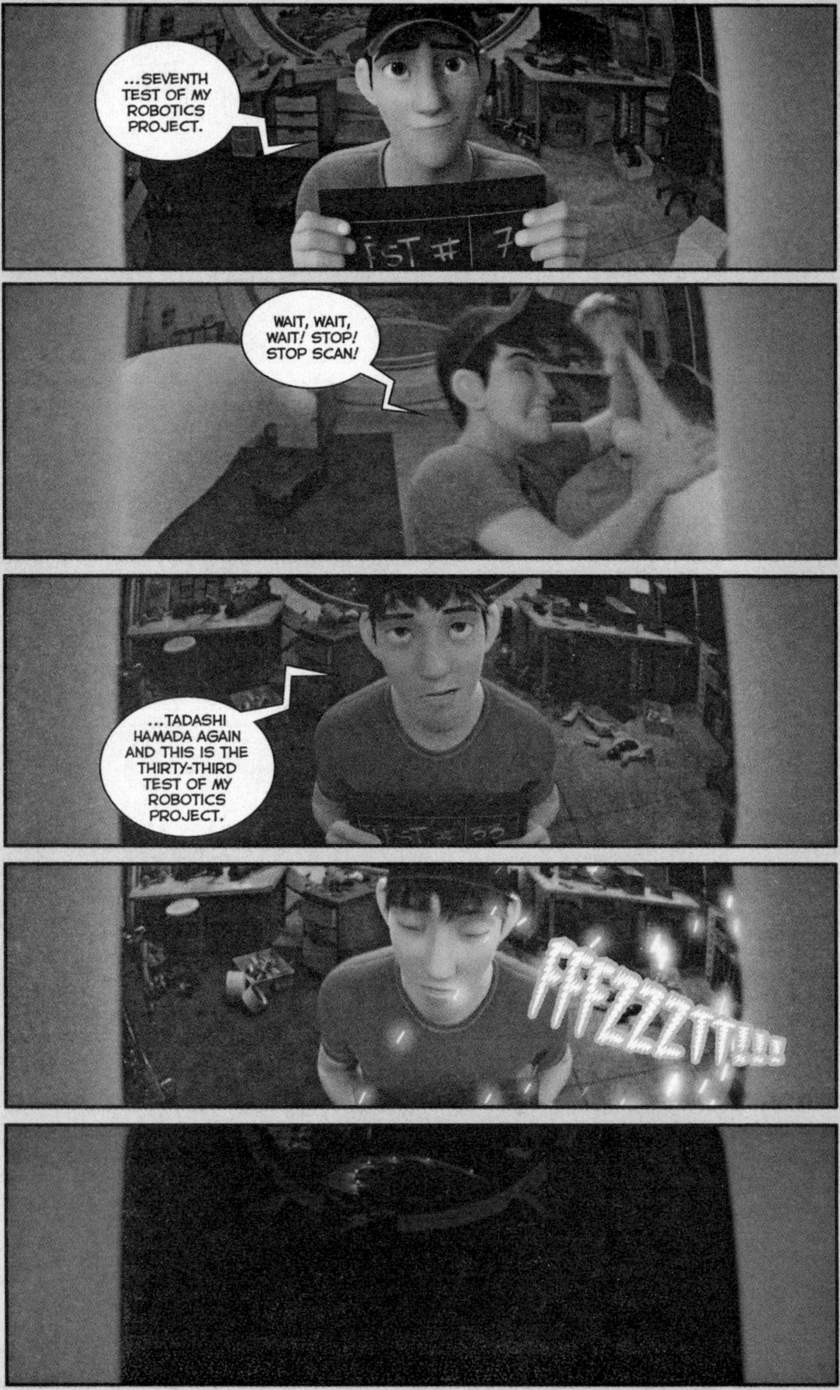
...SEVENTH TEST OF MY ROBOTICS PROJECT.
WAIT, WAIT, WAIT! STOP! STOP SCAN!
...TADASHI HAMADA AGAIN AND THIS IS THE THIRTY-THIRD TEST OF MY ROBOTICS PROJECT.
FFFZZZTT!!!

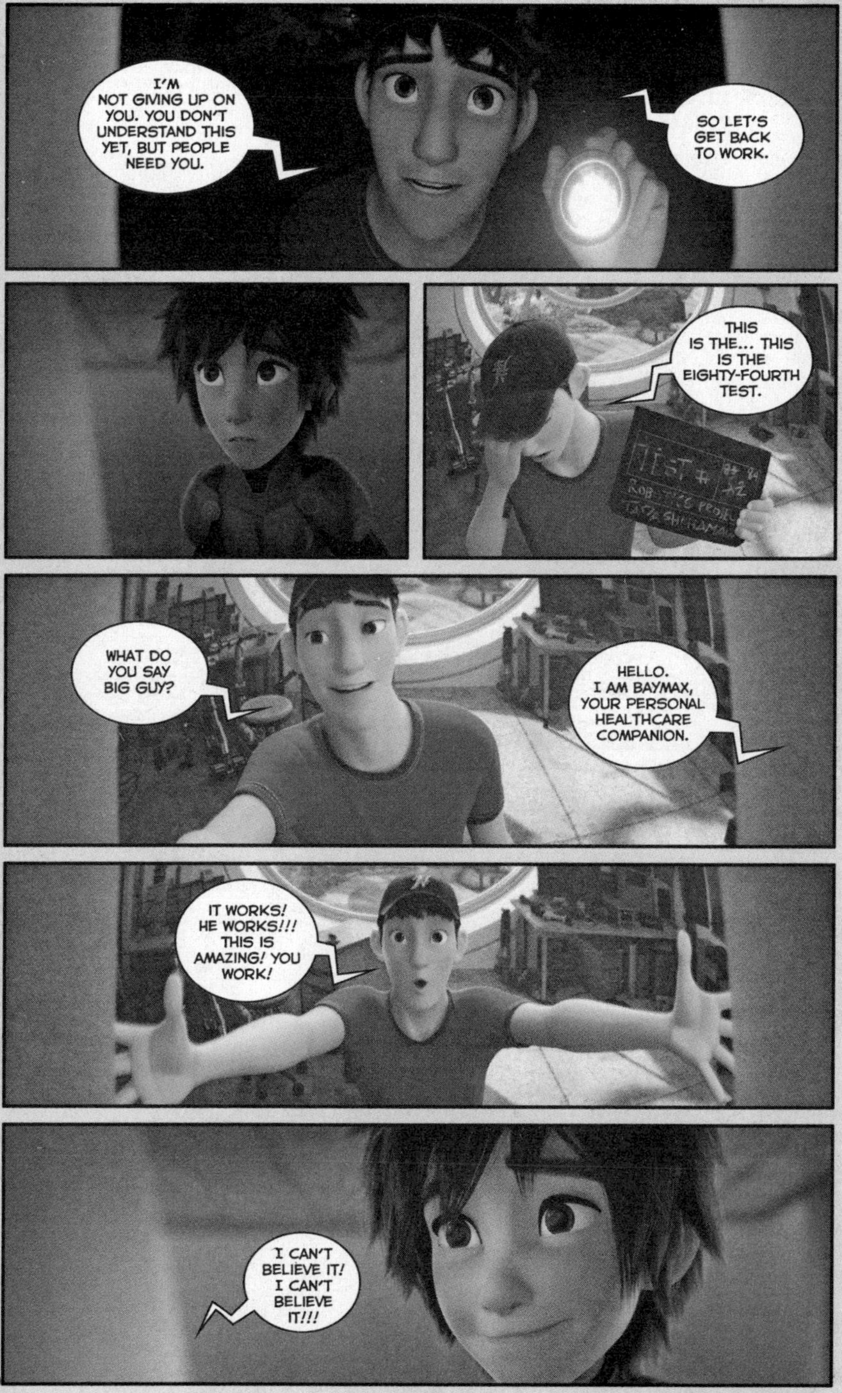
I'M NOT GIVING UP ON YOU. YOU DON'T UNDERSTAND THIS YET, BUT PEOPLE NEED YOU.
SO LET'S GET BACK TO WORK.
THIS IS THE... THIS IS THE EIGHTY-FOURTH TEST.
WHAT DO YOU SAY BIG GUY?
HELLO. I AM BAYMAX, YOUR PERSONAL HEALTHCARE COMPANION.
IT WORKS! HE WORKS!!! THIS IS AMAZING! YOU WORK!
I CAN'T BELIEVE IT! I CAN'T BELIEVE IT!!!

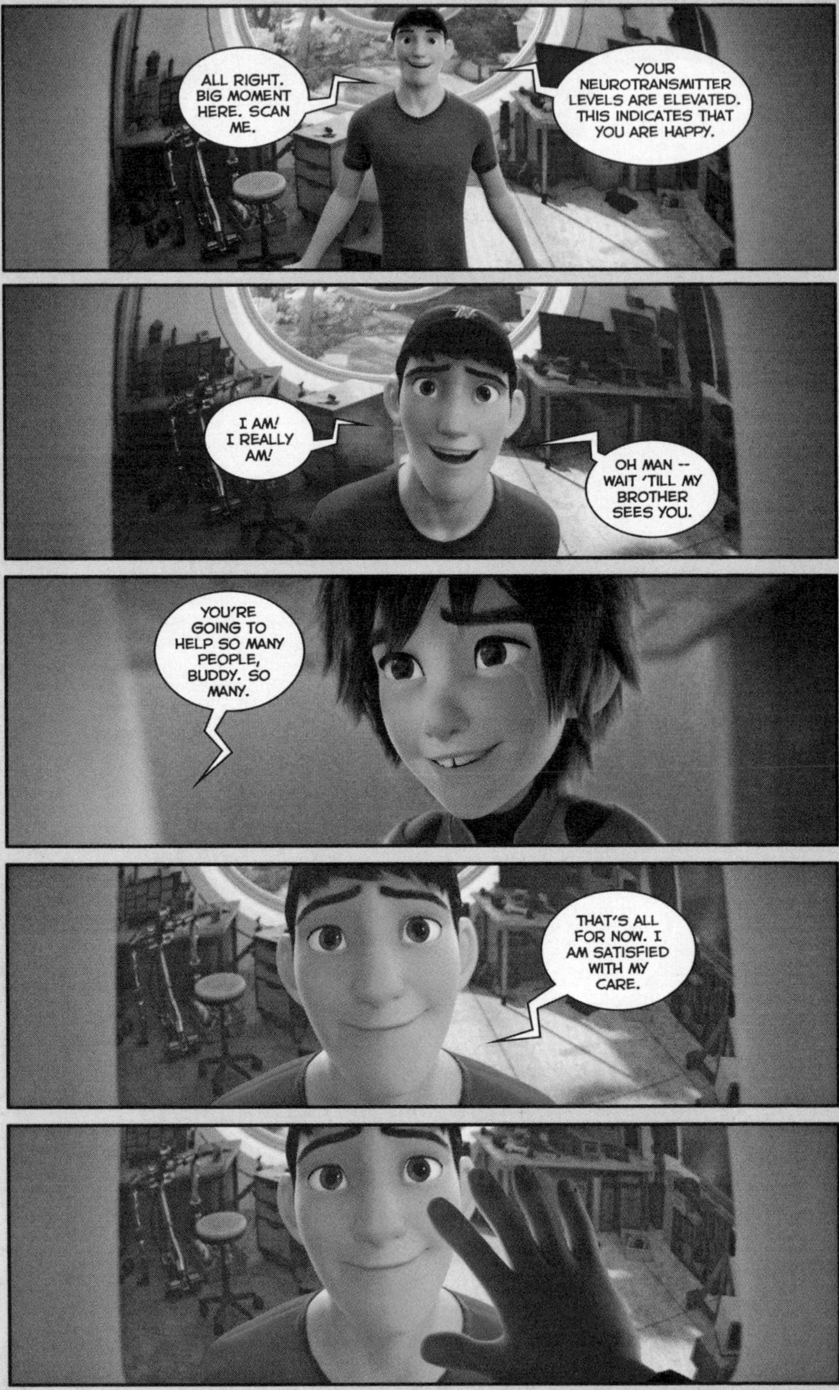
ALL RIGHT. BIG MOMENT HERE. SCAN ME.
YOUR NEUROTRANSMITTER LEVELS ARE ELEVATED. THIS INDICATES THAT YOU ARE HAPPY.
I AM! I REALLY AM!
OH MAN -- WAIT 'TILL MY BROTHER SEES YOU.
YOU'RE GOING TO HELP SO MANY PEOPLE, BUDDY. SO MANY.
THAT'S ALL FOR NOW. I AM SATISFIED WITH MY CARE.

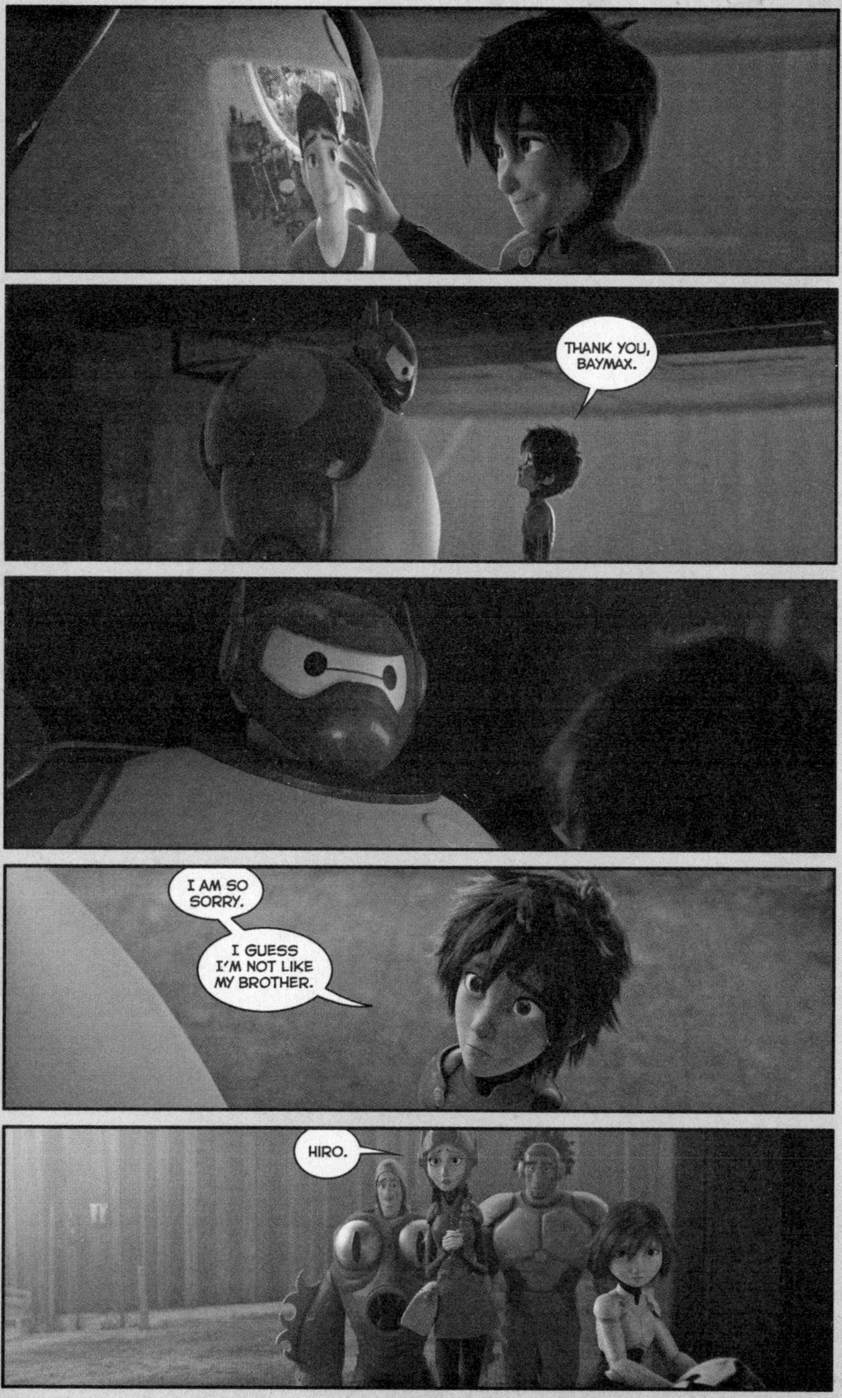
THANK YOU, BAYMAX.
I AM SO SORRY.
I GUESS I'M NOT LIKE MY BROTHER.
HIRO.

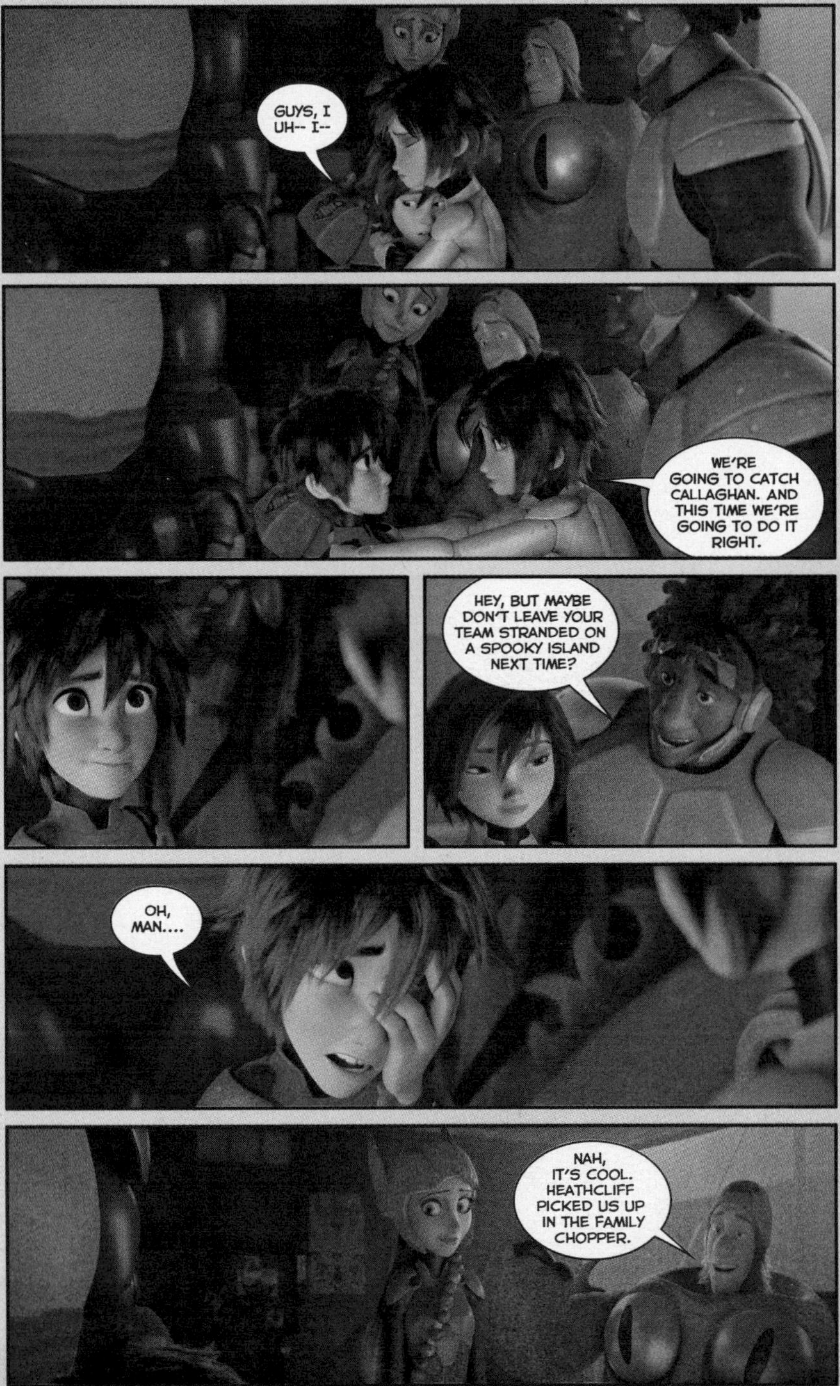
GUYS, I UH-- I--
WE'RE GOING TO CATCH CALLAGHAN. AND THIS TIME WE'RE GOING TO DO IT RIGHT.
HEY, BUT MAYBE DON'T LEAVE YOUR TEAM STRANDED ON A SPOOKY ISLAND NEXT TIME?
OH, MAN....
NAH, IT'S COOL. HEATHCLIFF PICKED US UP IN THE FAMILY CHOPPER.

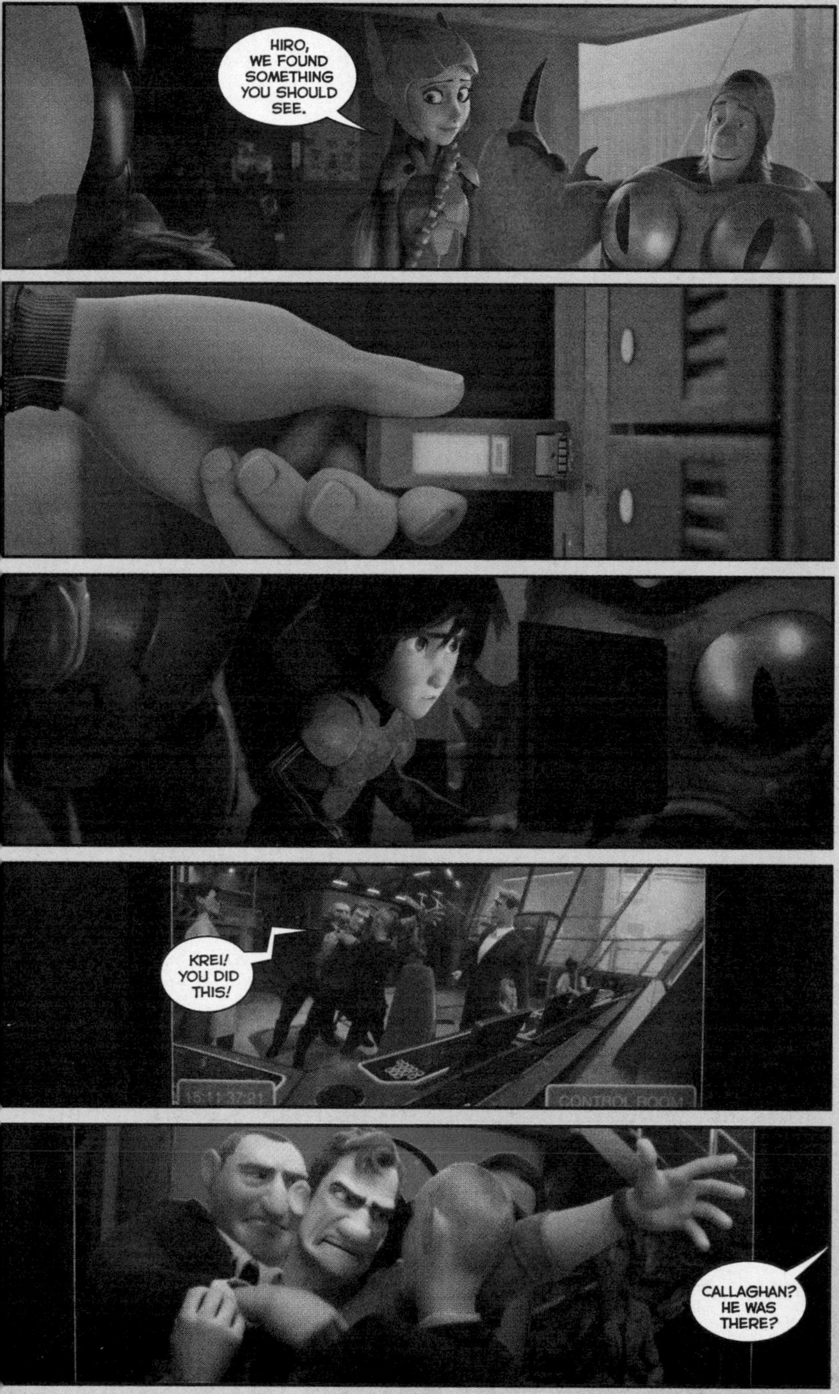
HIRO, WE FOUND SOMETHING YOU SHOULD SEE.
KREI! YOU DID THIS!
CONTROL ROOM
CALLAGHAN? HE WAS THERE?

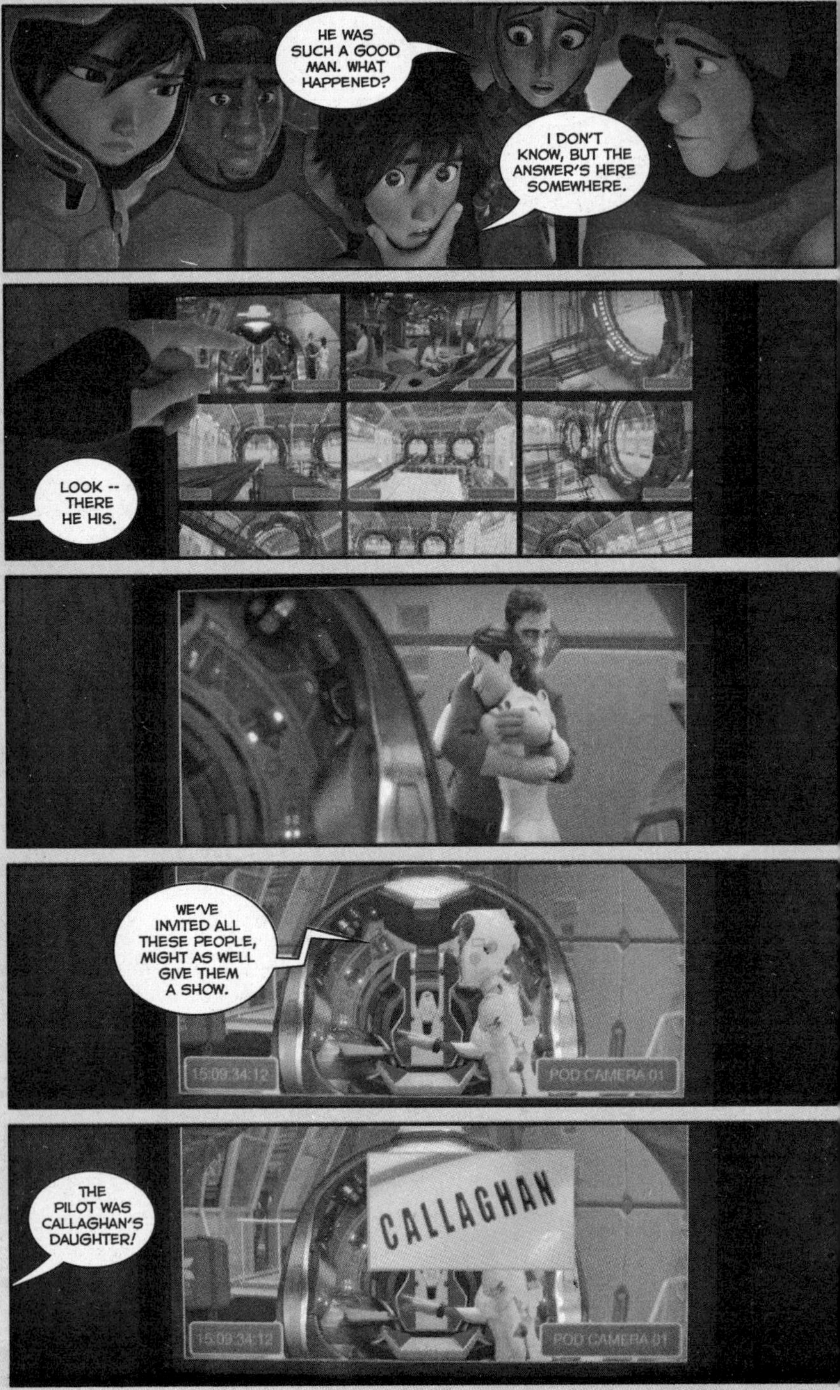
HE WAS SUCH A GOOD MAN. WHAT HAPPENED?
I DON'T KNOW, BUT THE ANSWER'S HERE SOMEWHERE.
LOOK -- THERE HE HIS.
WE'VE INVITED ALL THESE PEOPLE, MIGHT AS WELL GIVE THEM A SHOW.
15:09:34:12
POD CAMERA 01
THE PILOT WAS CALLAGHAN'S DAUGHTER!
CALLAGHAN
15:09:34:12
POD CAMERA 01

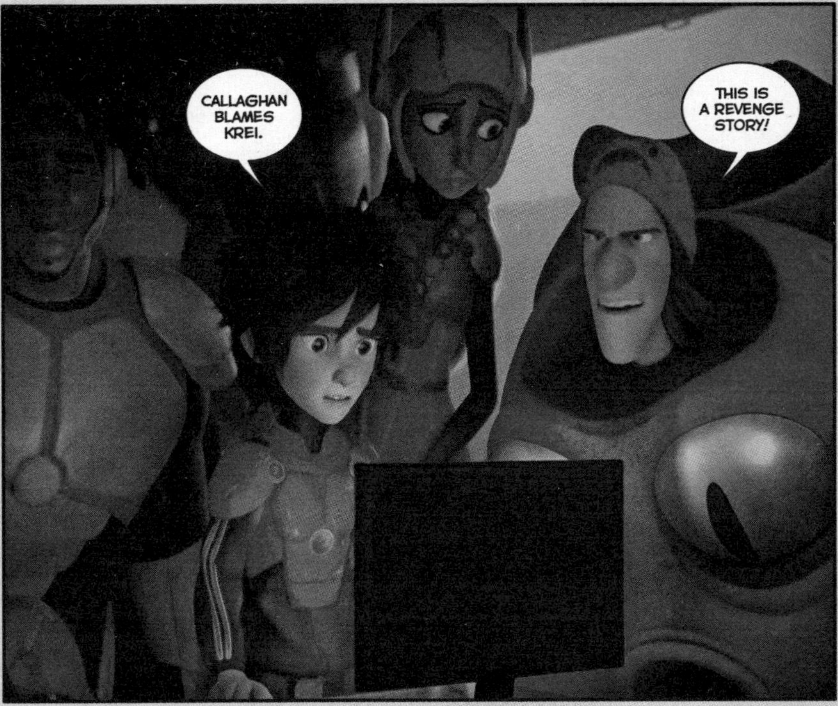
CALLAGHAN BLAMES KREI.
THIS IS A REVENGE STORY!

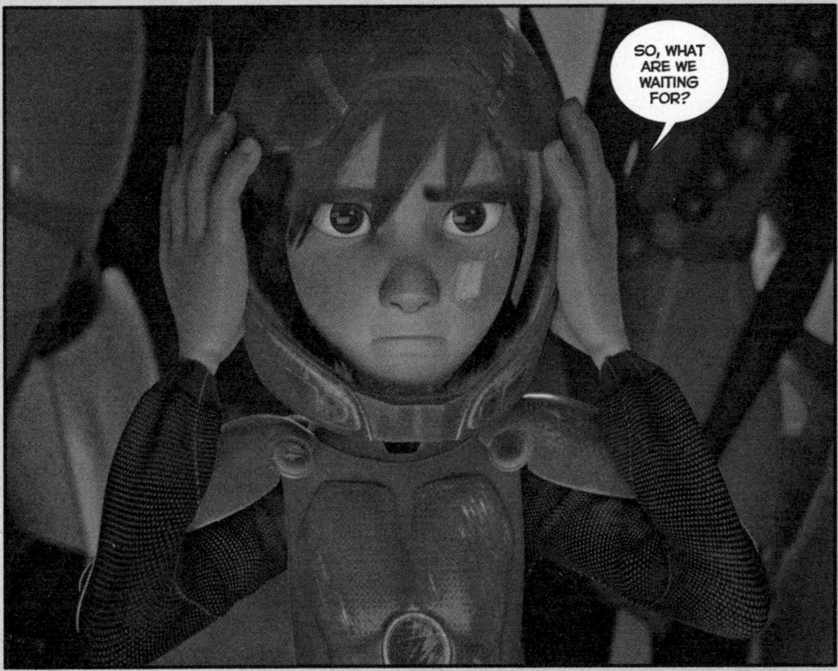
SO, WHAT ARE WE WAITING FOR?

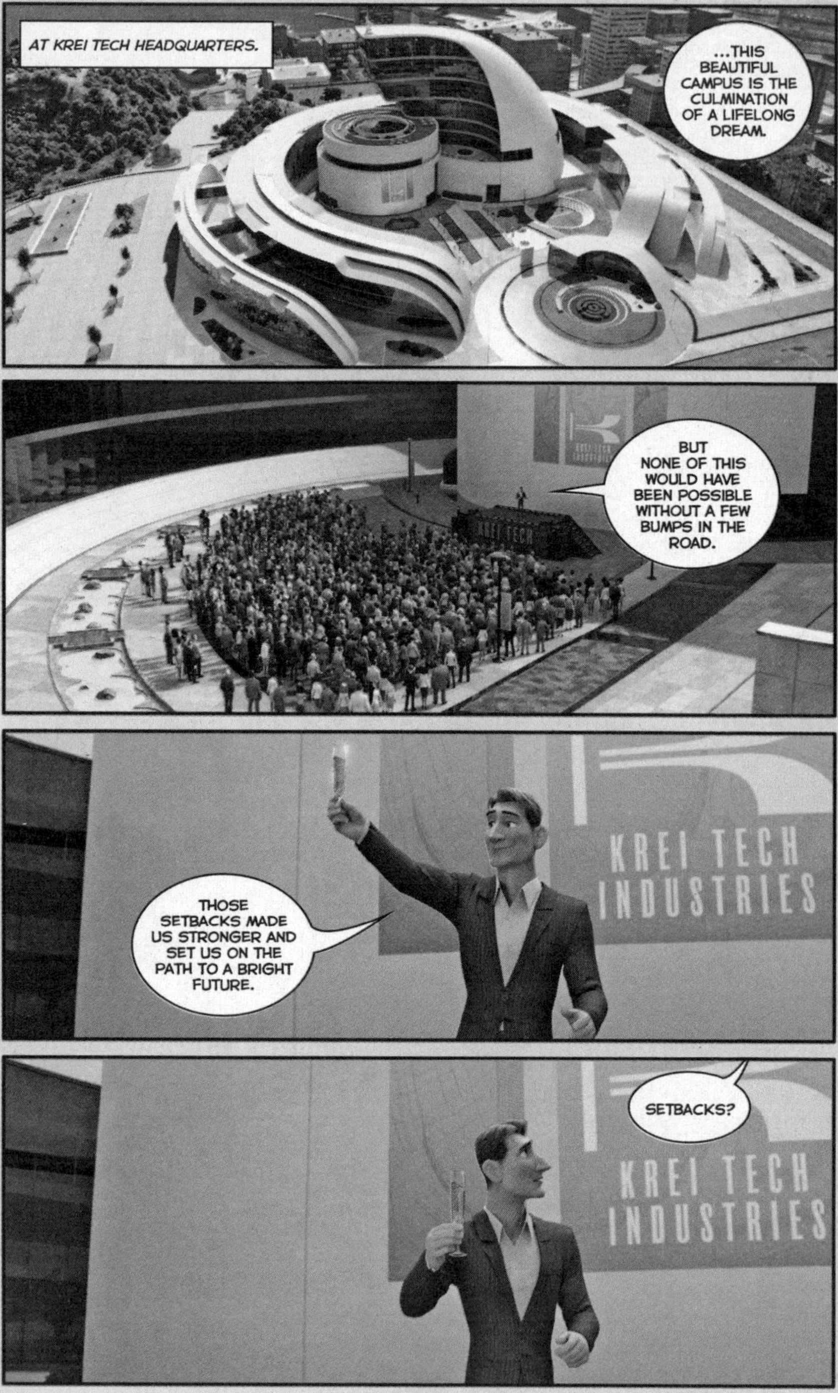
AT KREI TECH HEADQUARTERS.
...THIS BEAUTIFUL CAMPUS IS THE CULMINATION OF A LIFELONG DREAM.
BUT NONE OF THIS WOULD HAVE BEEN POSSIBLE WITHOUT A FEW BUMPS IN THE ROAD.
KREI TECH INDUSTRIES
THOSE SETBACKS MADE US STRONGER AND SET US ON THE PATH TO A BRIGHT FUTURE.
SETBACKS?
KREI TECH INDUSTRIES

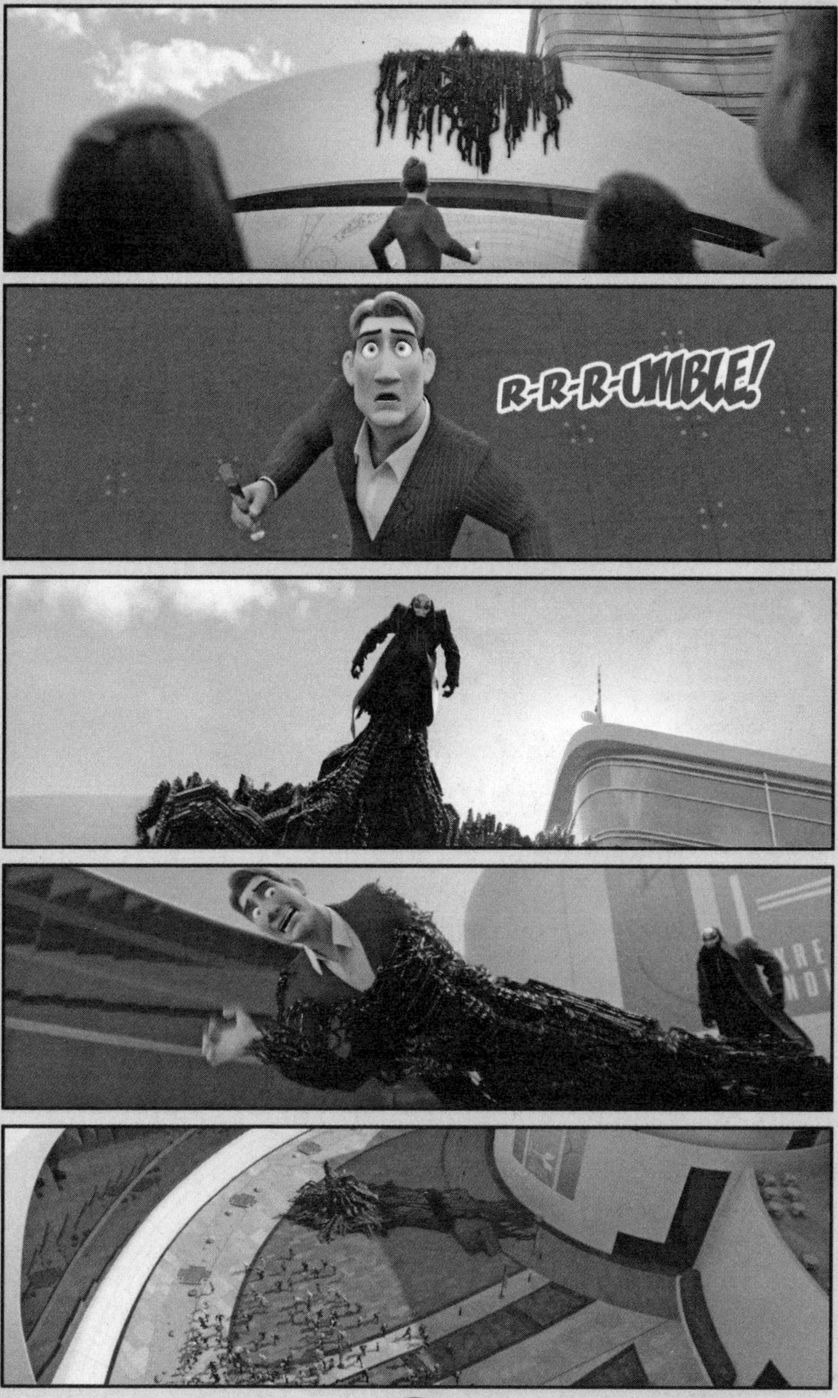
R-R-R-UMBLE!

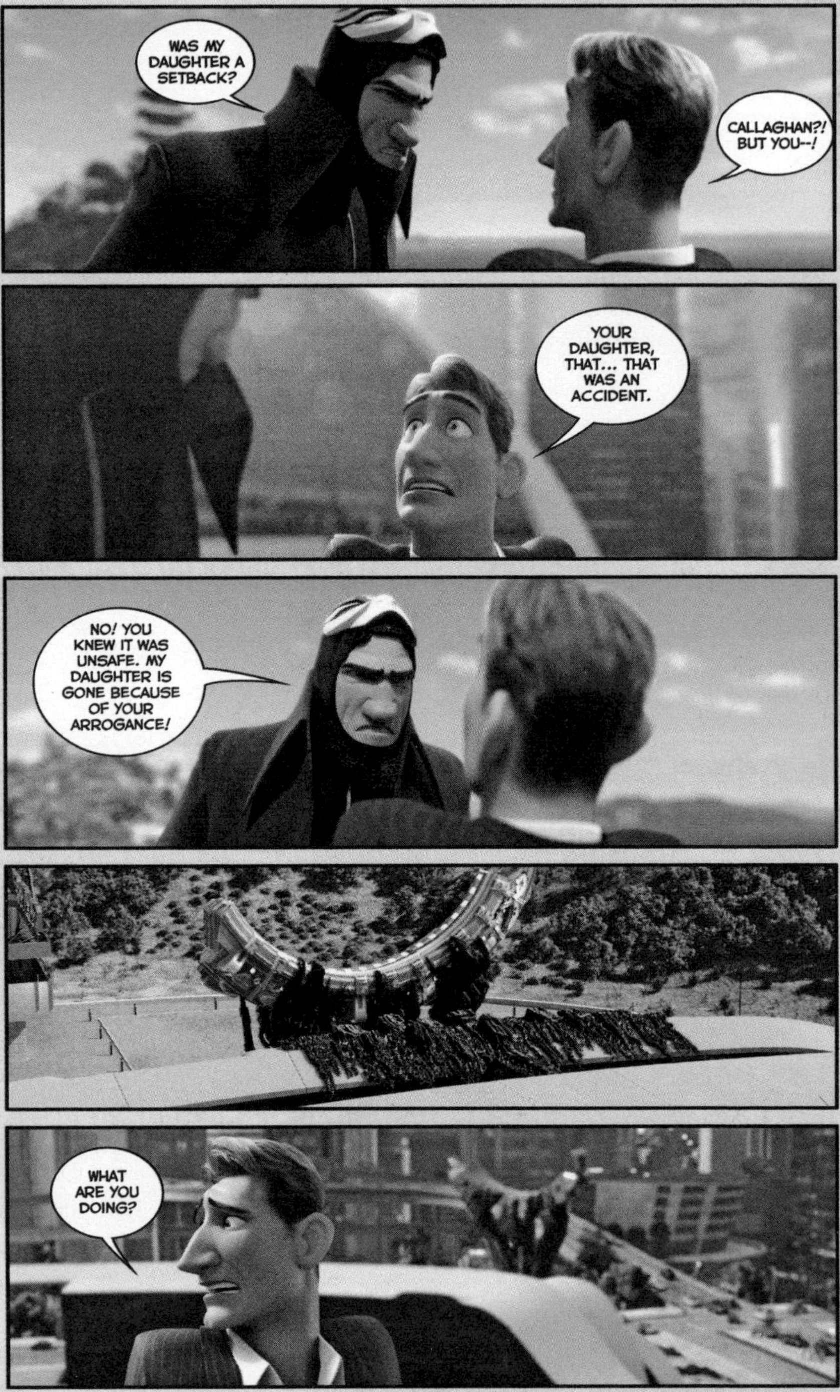
WAS MY DAUGHTER A SETBACK?
CALLAGHAN?! BUT YOU--!
YOUR DAUGHTER, THAT... THAT WAS AN ACCIDENT.
NO! YOU KNEW IT WAS UNSAFE. MY DAUGHTER IS GONE BECAUSE OF YOUR ARROGANCE!
WHAT ARE YOU DOING?

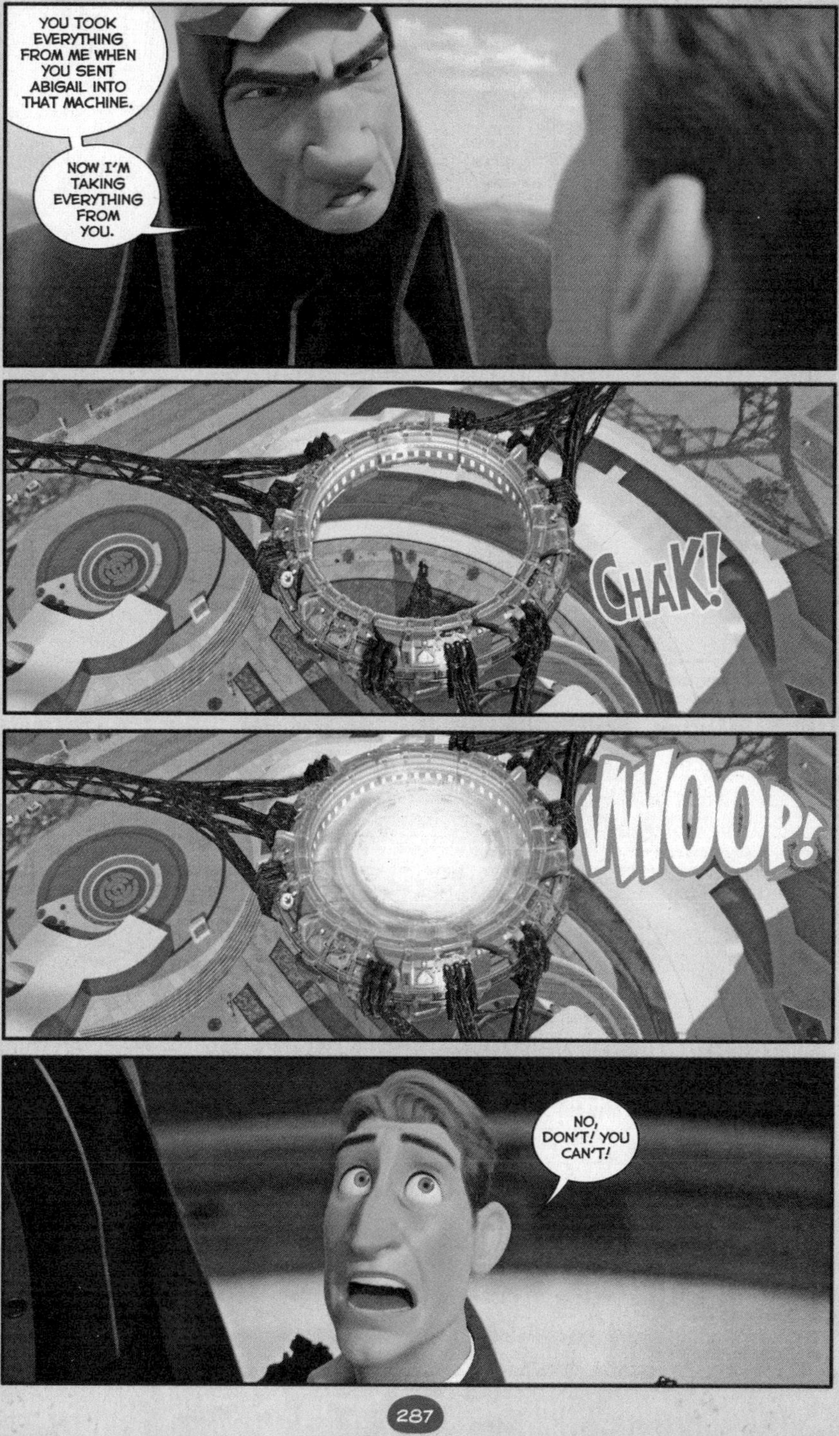
YOU TOOK EVERYTHING FROM ME WHEN YOU SENT ABIGAIL INTO THAT MACHINE.
NOW I'M TAKING EVERYTHING FROM YOU.
CHAK!
VWOOP!
NO, DON'T! YOU CAN'T!

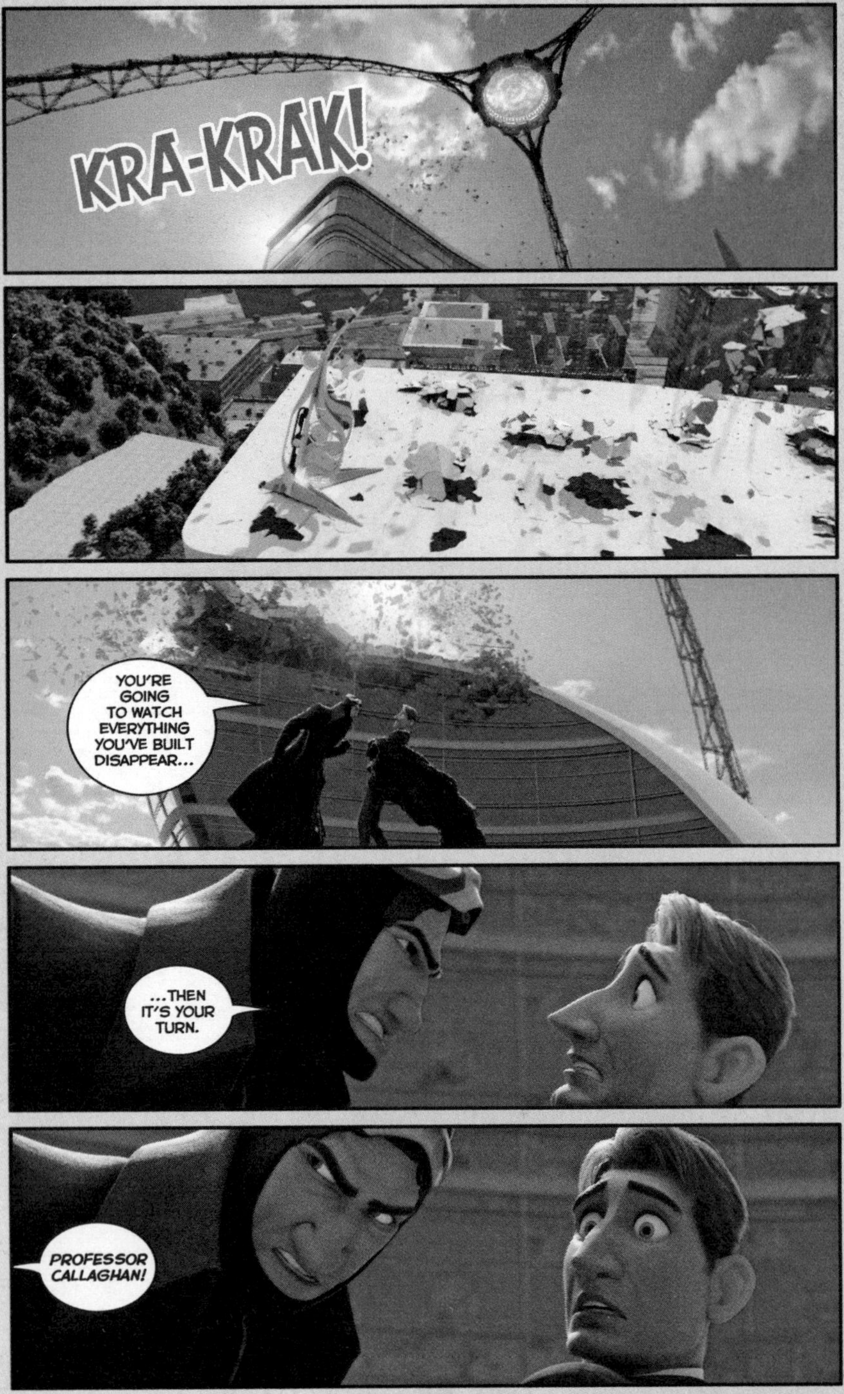
KRA-KRAK!
YOU'RE GOING TO WATCH EVERYTHING YOU'VE BUILT DISAPPEAR...
...THEN IT'S YOUR TURN.
PROFESSOR CALLAGHAN!

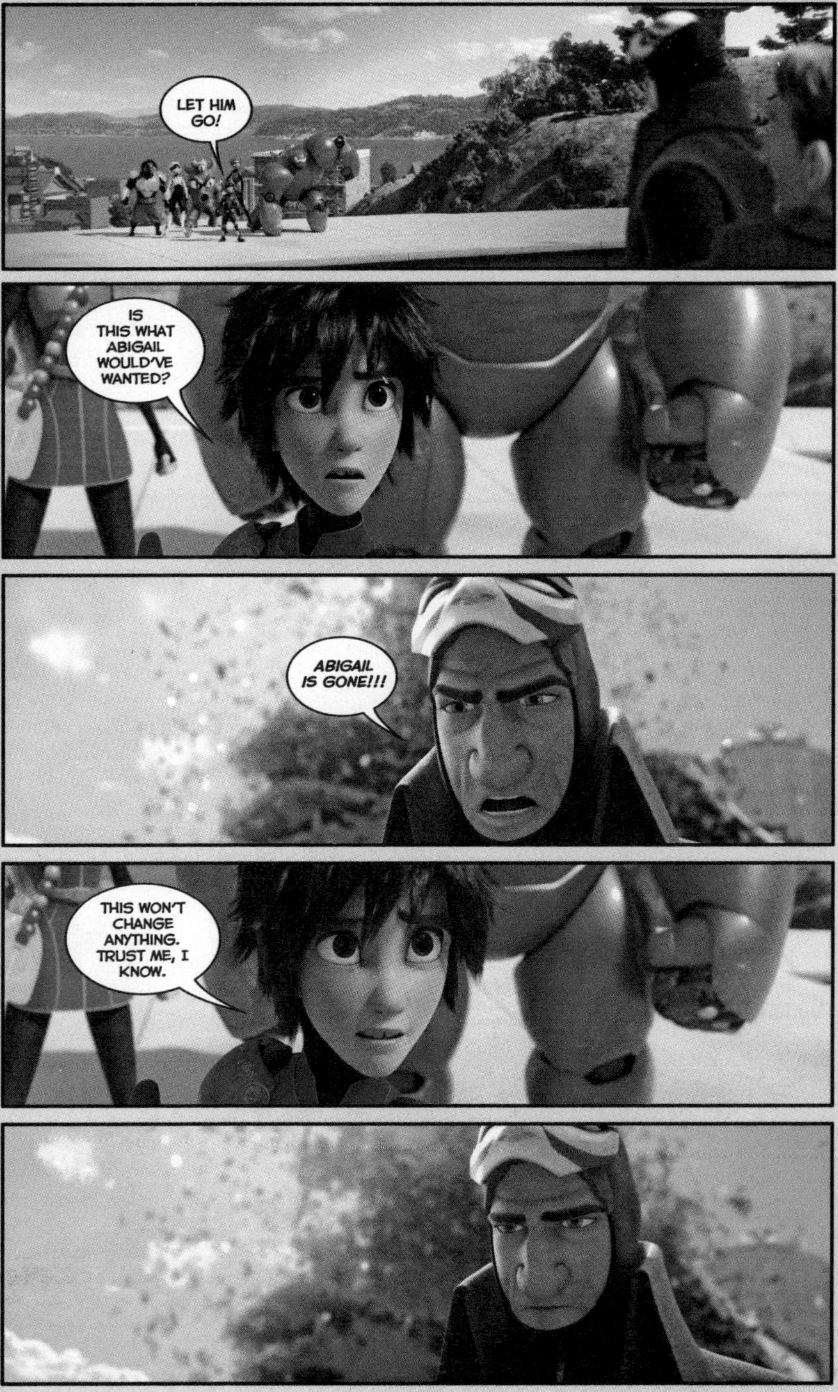
LET HIM GO!
IS THIS WHAT ABIGAIL WOULD'VE WANTED?
ABIGAIL IS GONE!!!
THIS WON'T CHANGE ANYTHING. TRUST ME, I KNOW.

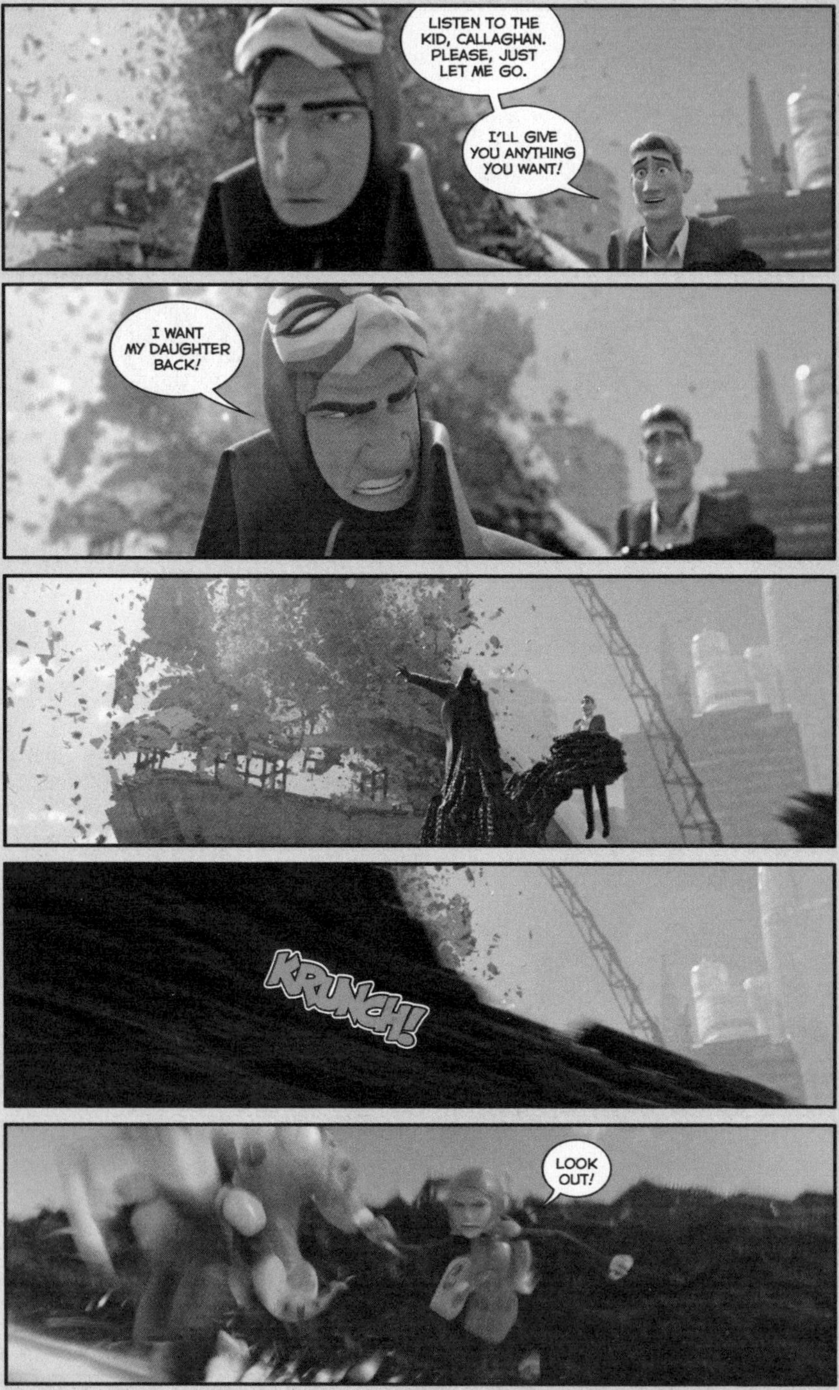
LISTEN TO THE KID, CALLAGHAN. PLEASE, JUST LET ME GO.
I'LL GIVE YOU ANYTHING YOU WANT!
I WANT MY DAUGHTER BACK!
KRUNCH!
LOOK OUT!

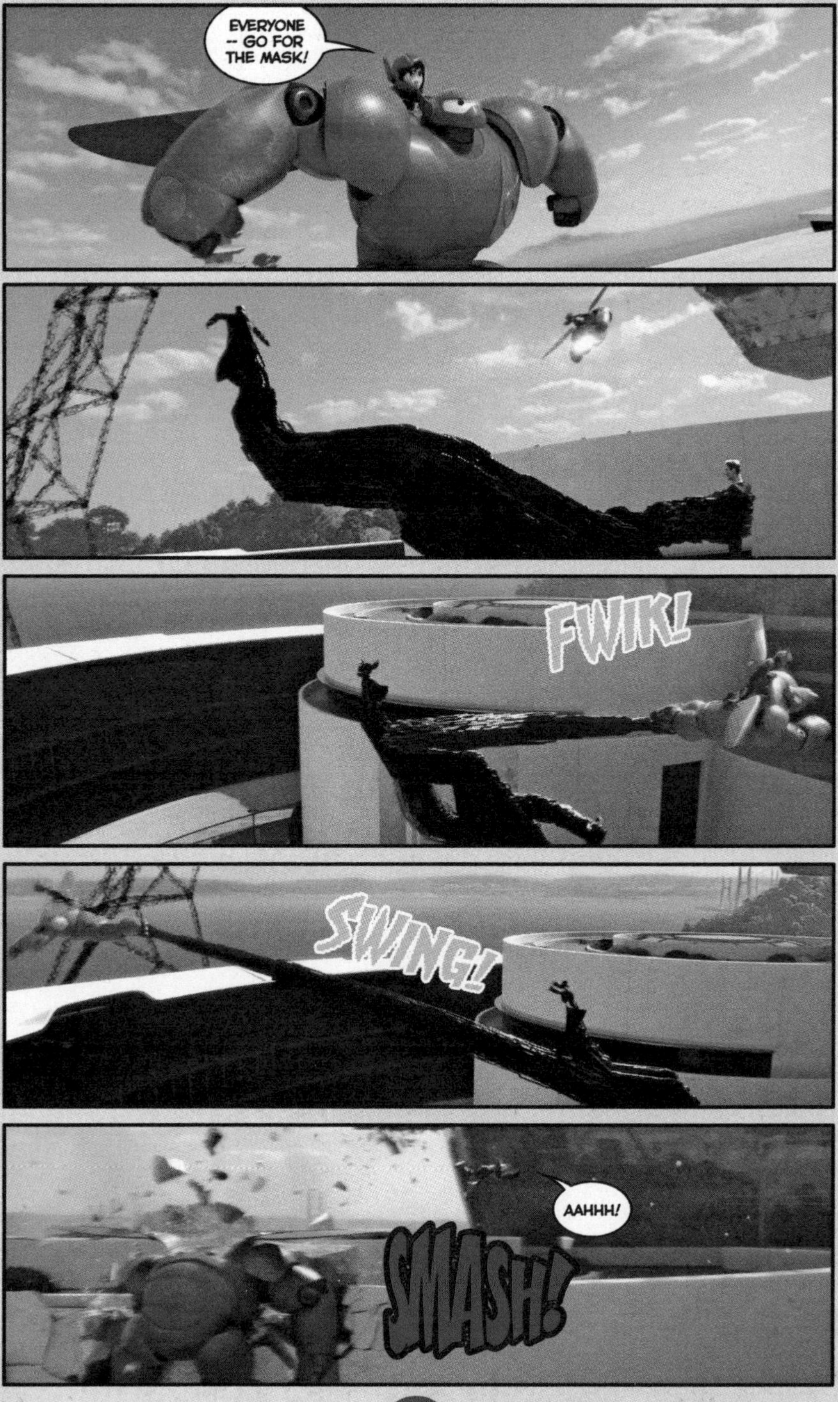
EVERYONE -- GO FOR THE MASK!
FWIK!
SWING!
AAHHH!
SMASH!

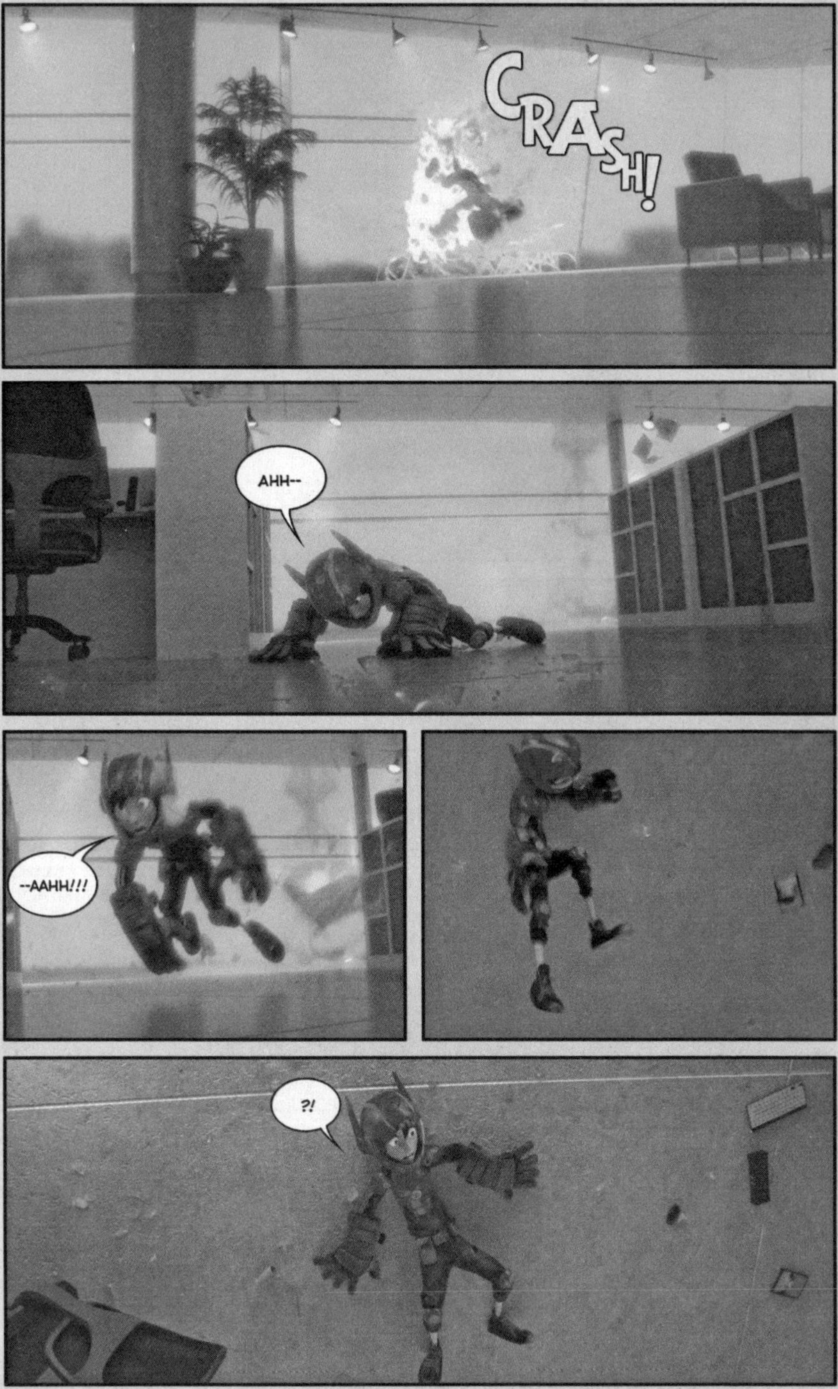
CRASH!
AHH--
--AAHH!!!
?!

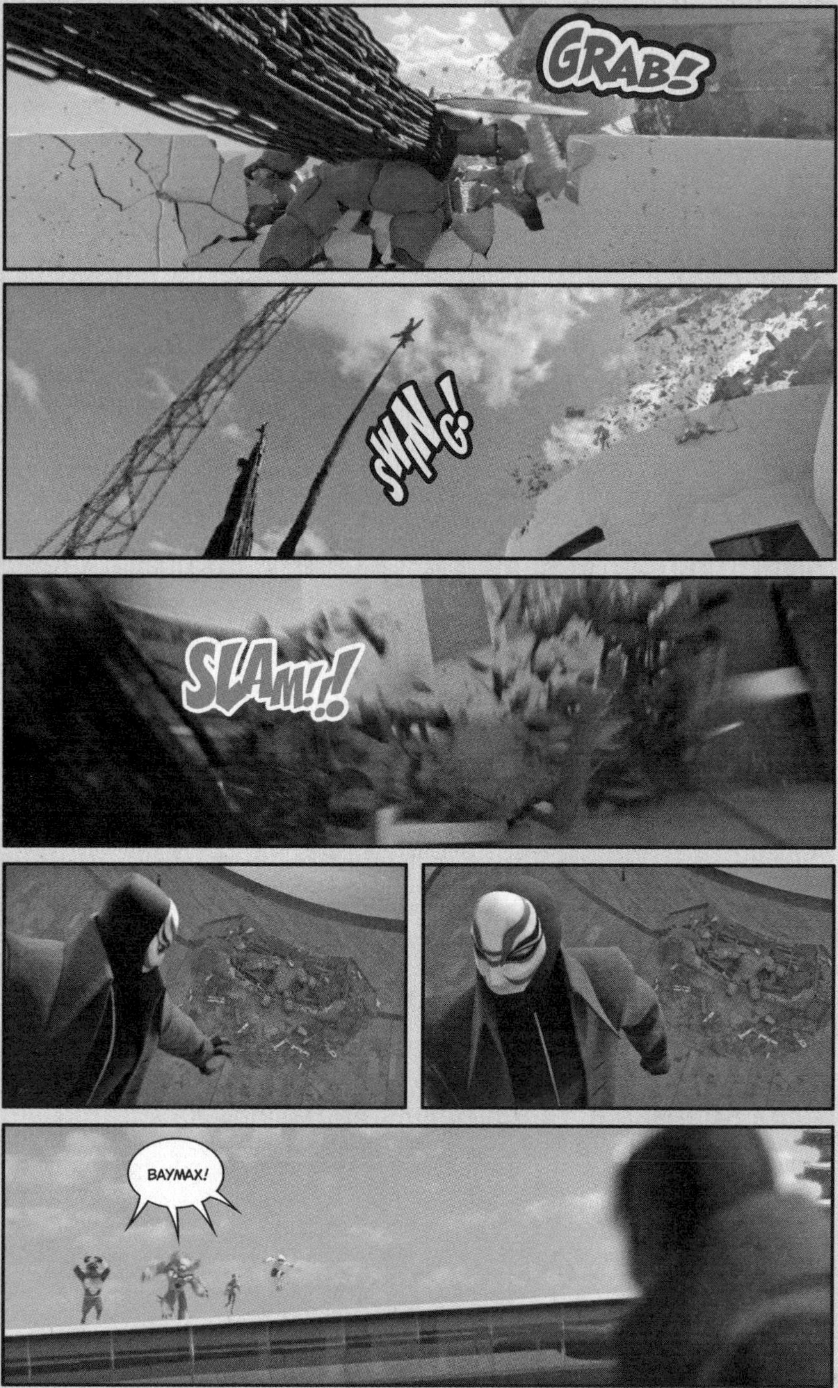
GRAB!
SWING!
SLAM!!!
BAYMAX!

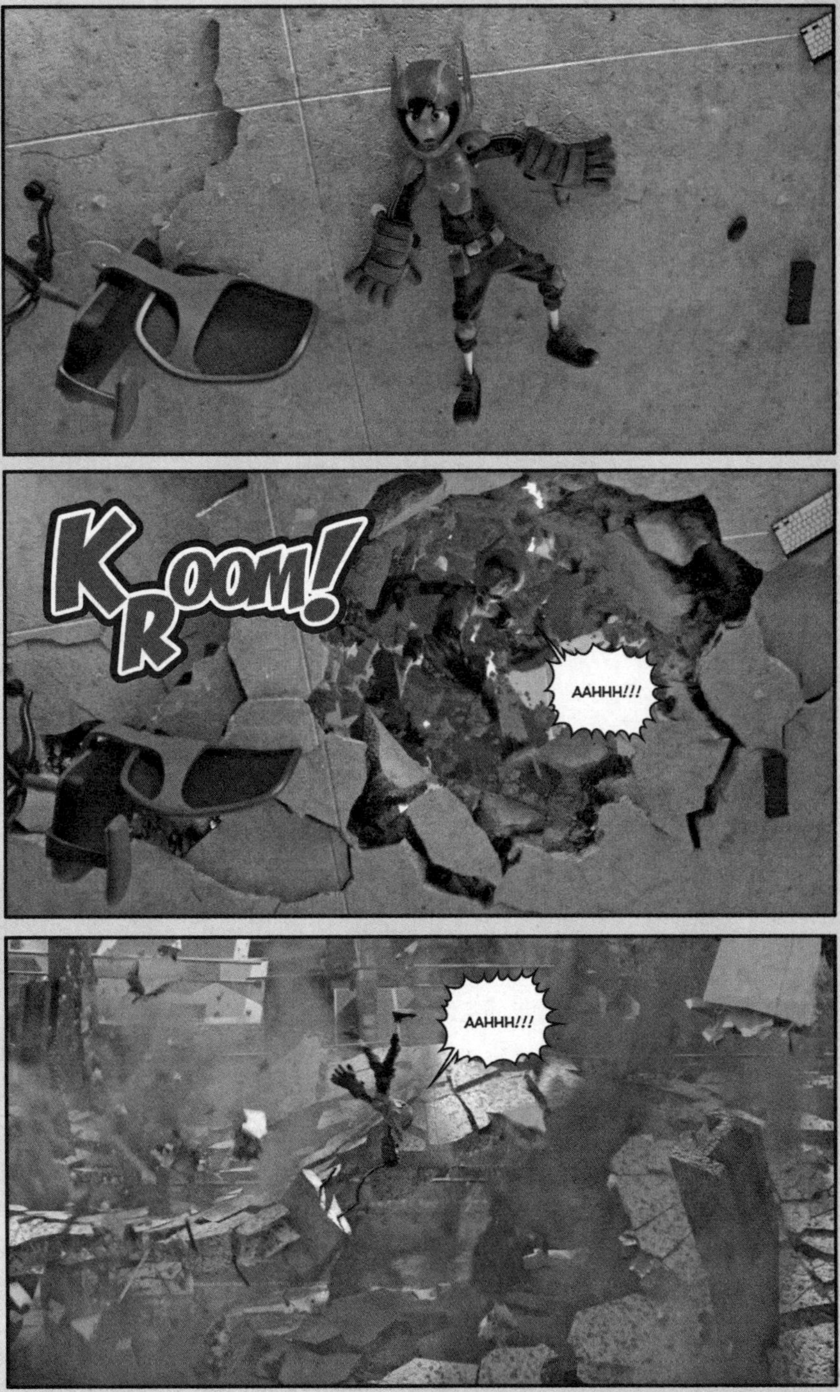

KROOM!
AAHHH!!!
AAHHH!!!

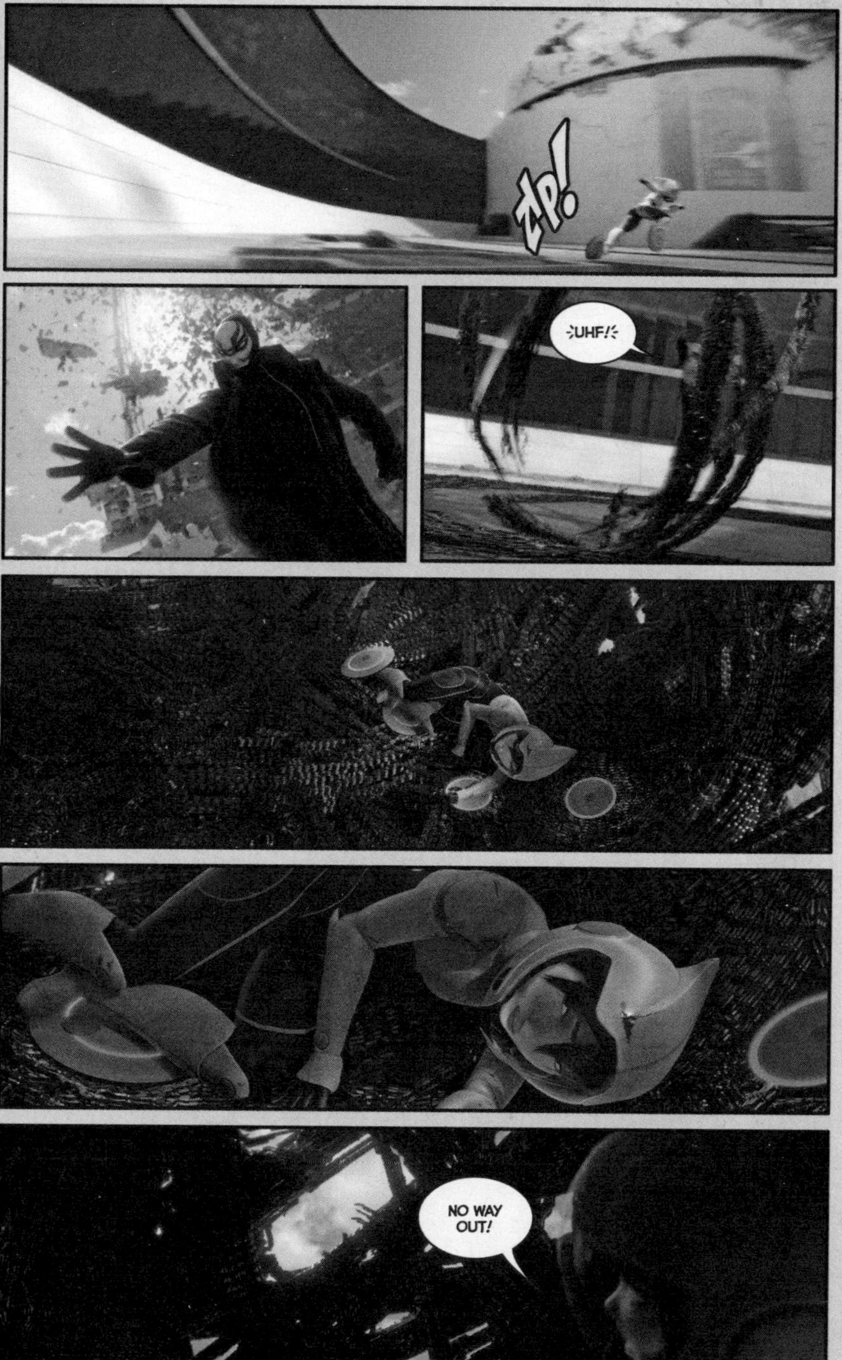
ZIP!
UHF!
NO WAY OUT!

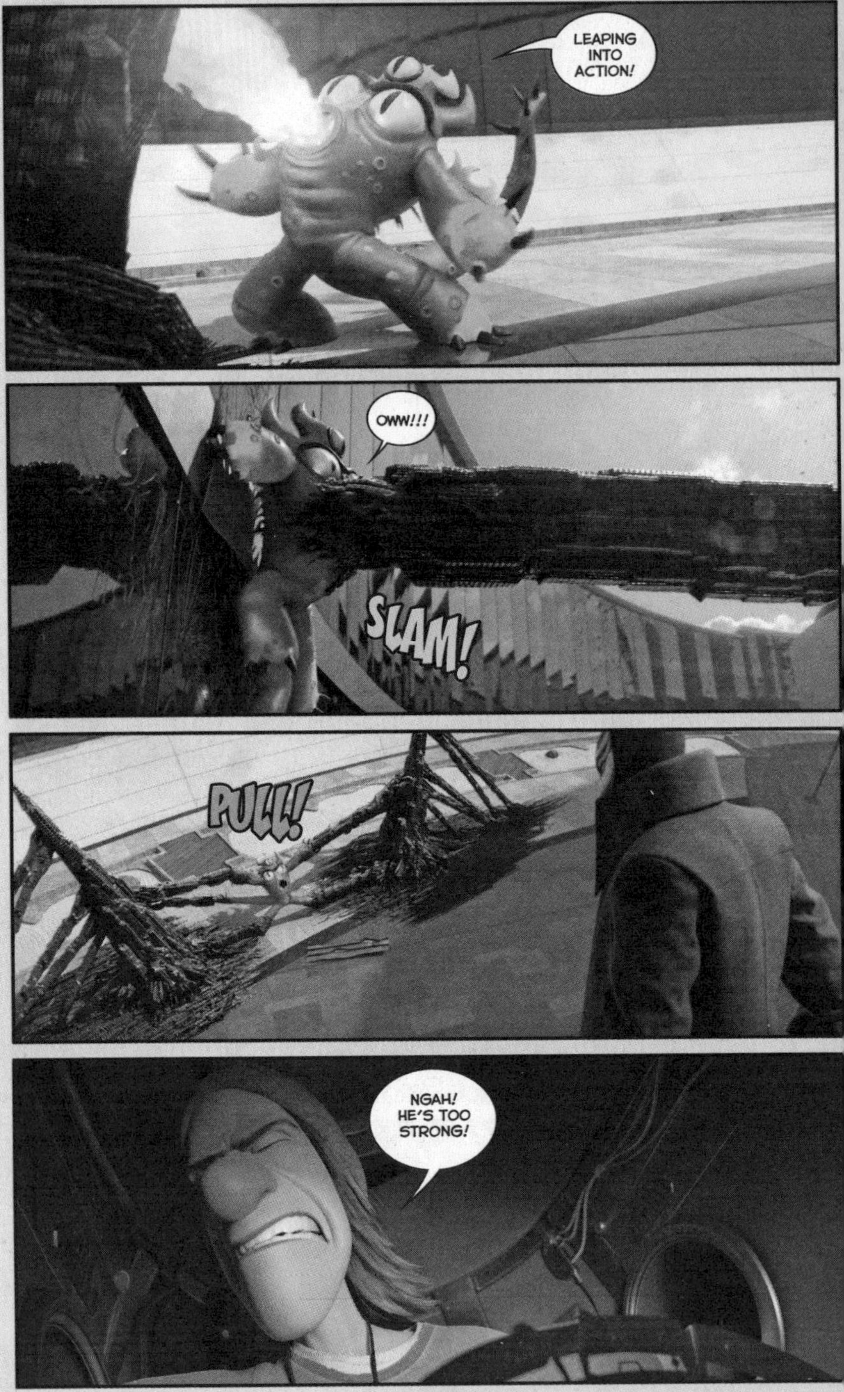
LEAPING INTO ACTION!
OWW!!!
SLAM!
PULL!
NGAH! HE'S TOO STRONG!

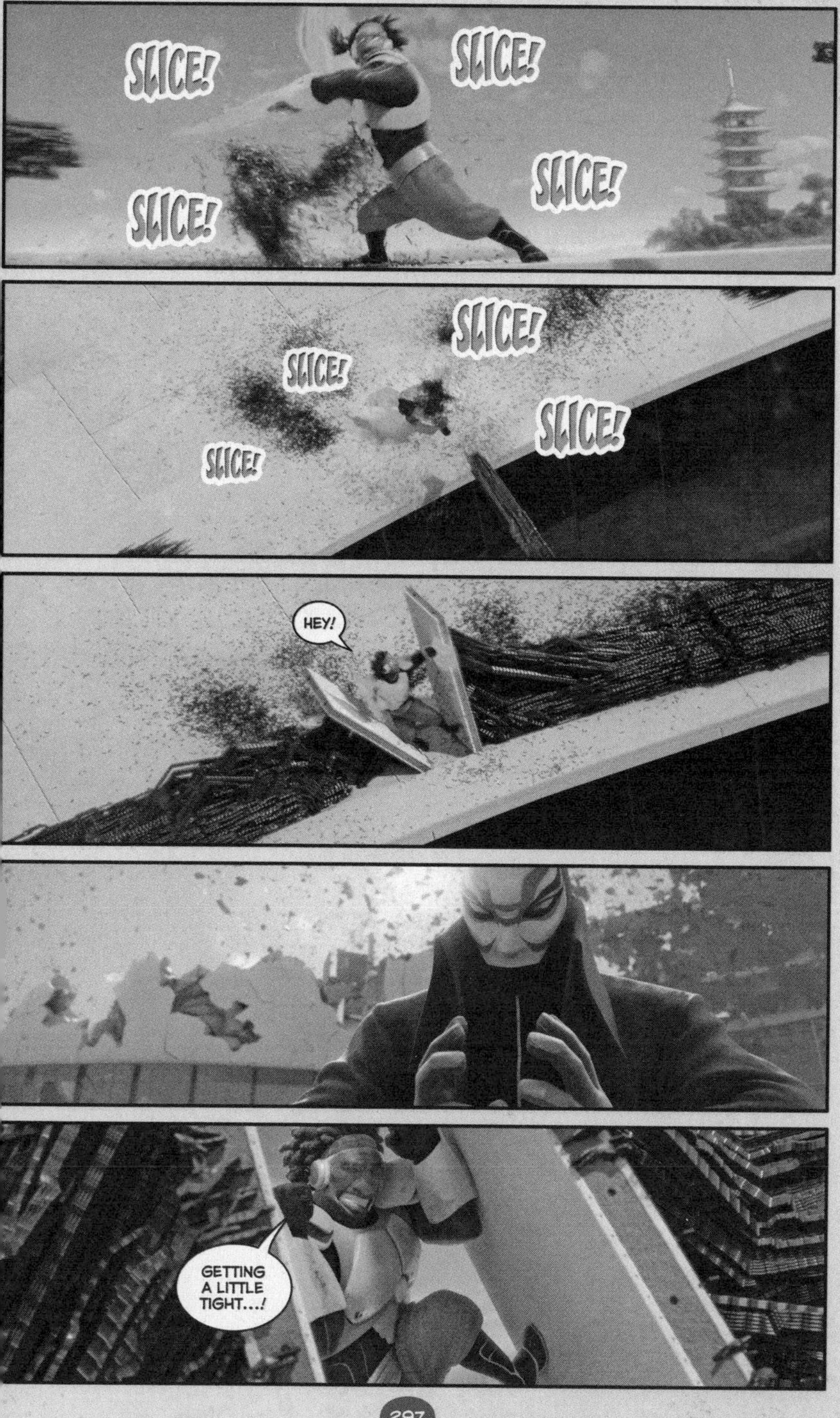
SLICE!
SLICE!
SLICE!
SLICE!
SLICE!
SLICE!
SLICE!
SLICE!
HEY!
GETTING A LITTLE TIGHT...!

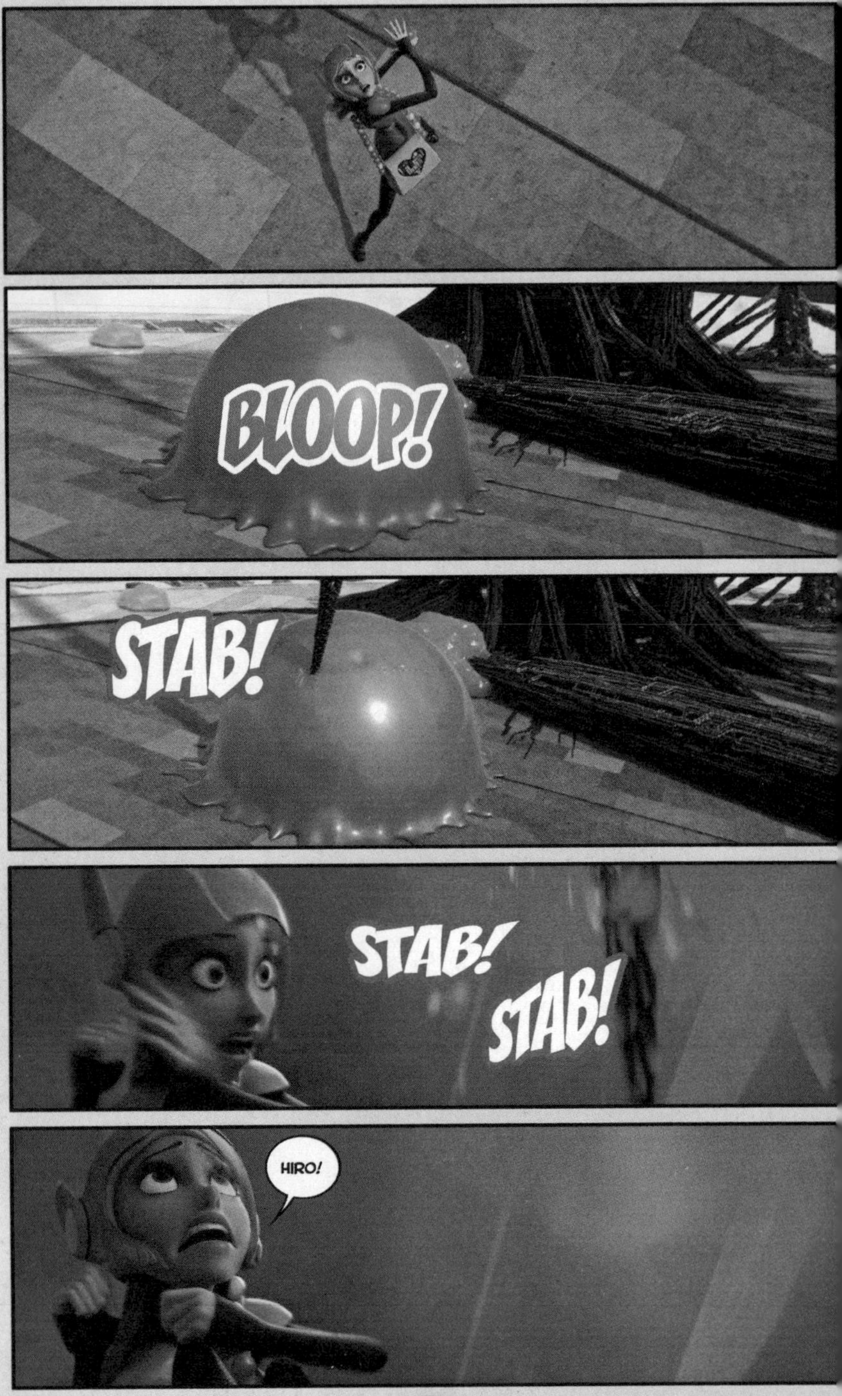
BLOOP!
STAB!
STAB!
STAB!
HIRO!

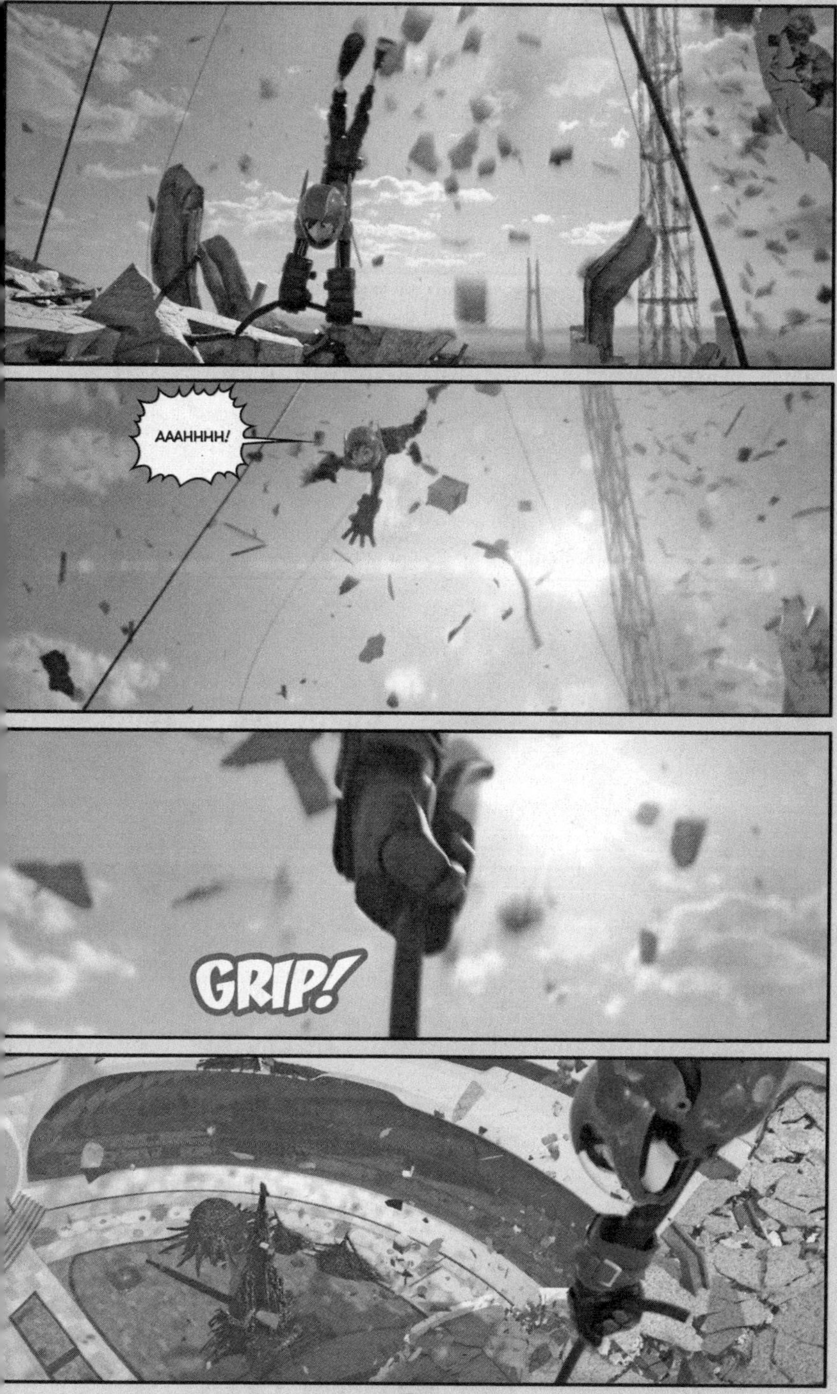
AAAHHHH!
GRIP!

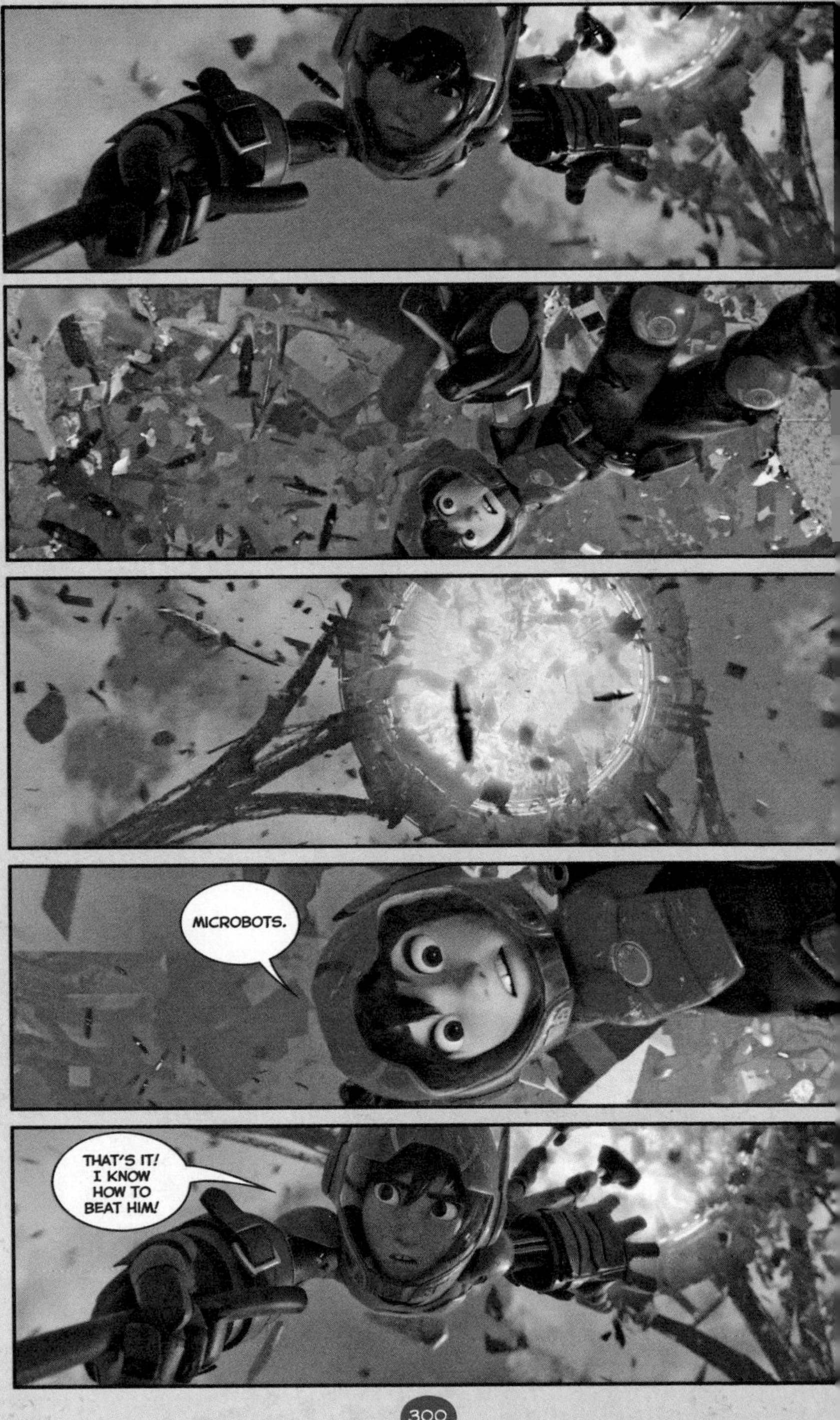
MICROBOTS.
THAT'S IT! I KNOW HOW TO BEAT HIM!

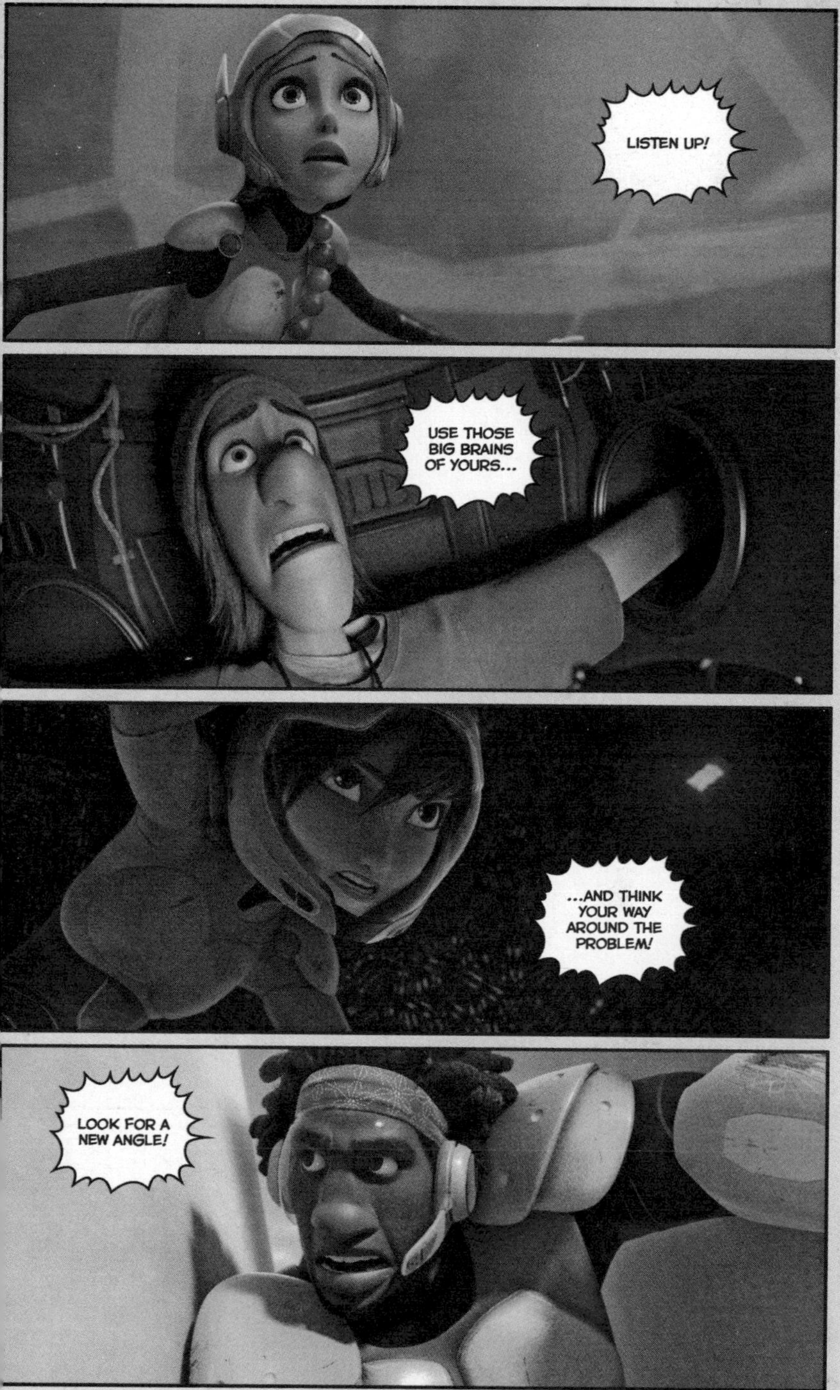
LISTEN UP!
USE THOSE BIG BRAINS OF YOURS...
...AND THINK YOUR WAY AROUND THE PROBLEM!
LOOK FOR A NEW ANGLE!

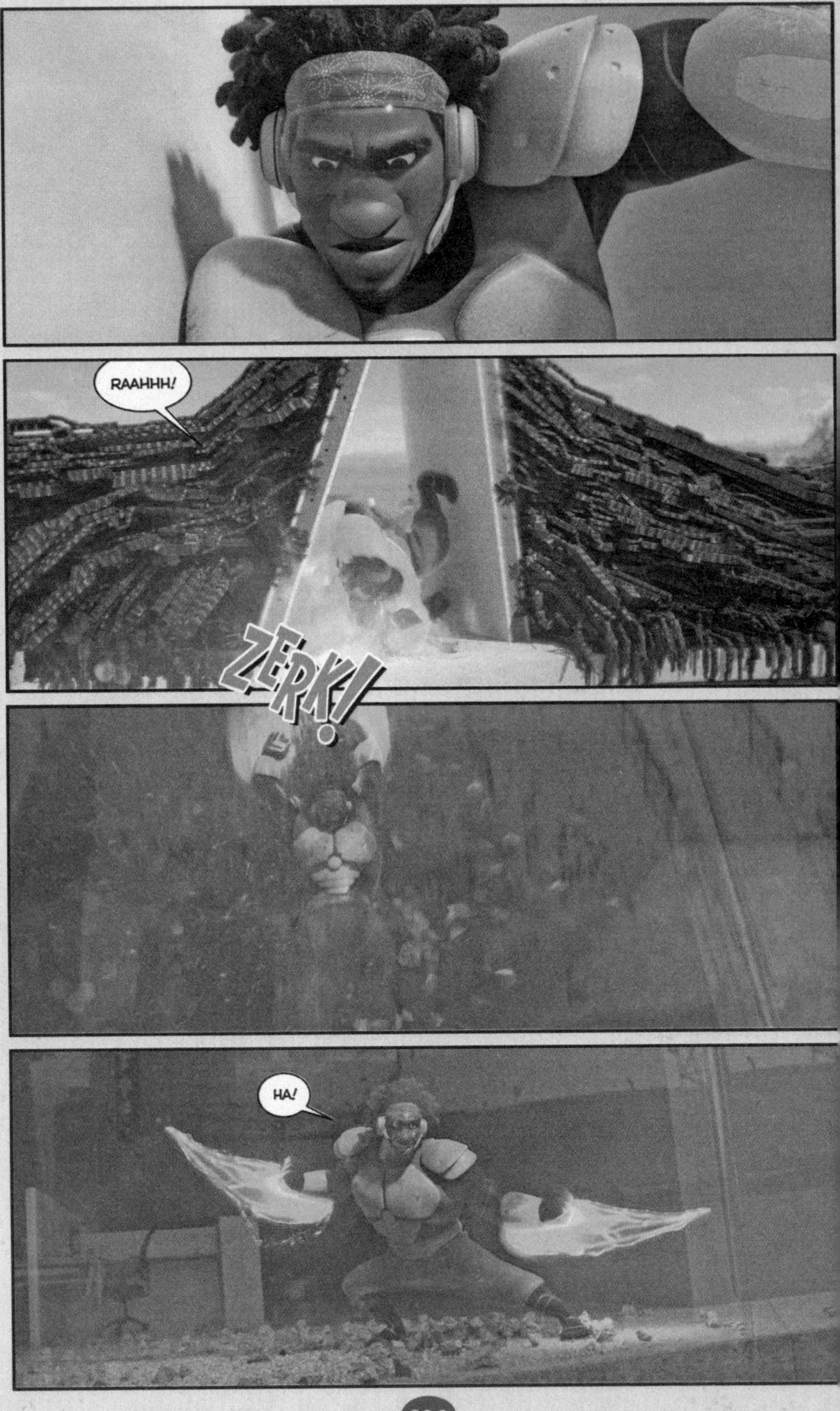
RAAHHH!
ZERK!
HA!

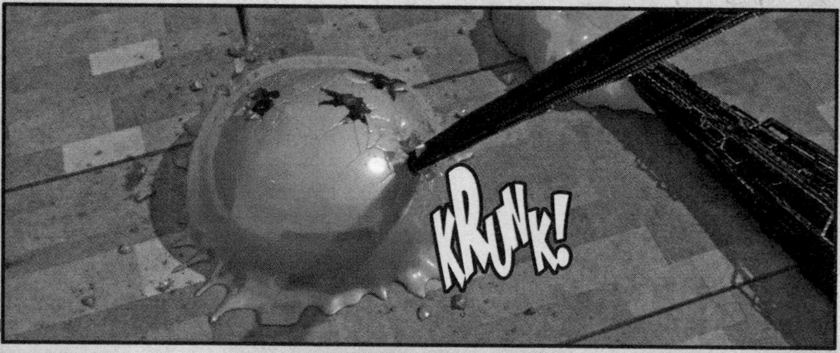
KRUNK!

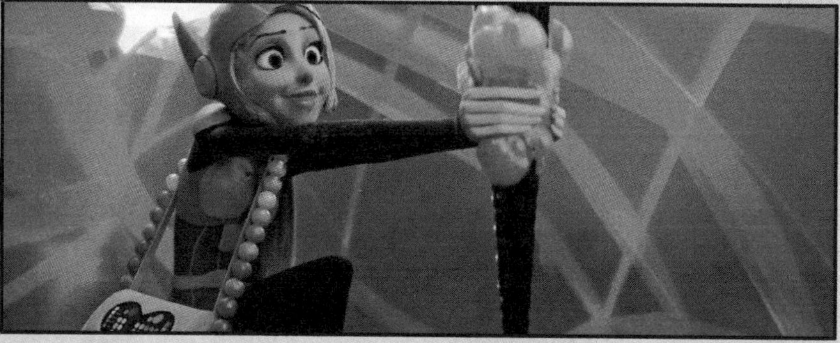

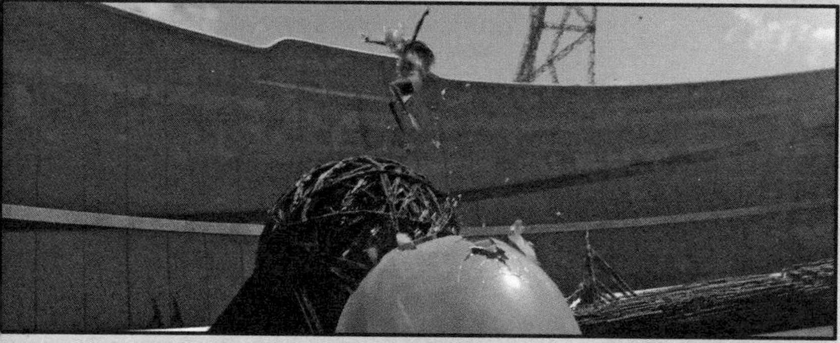

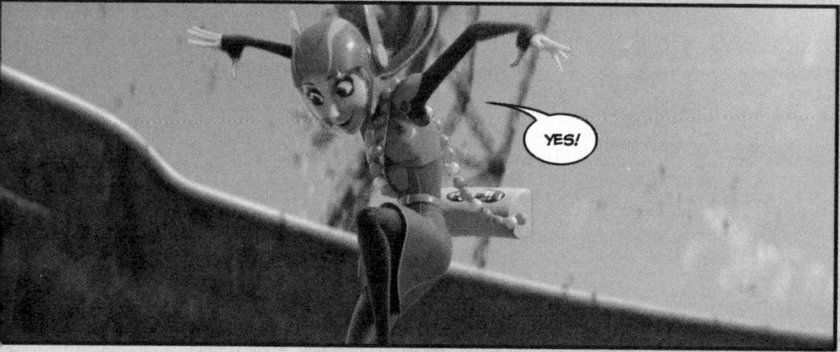
YES!

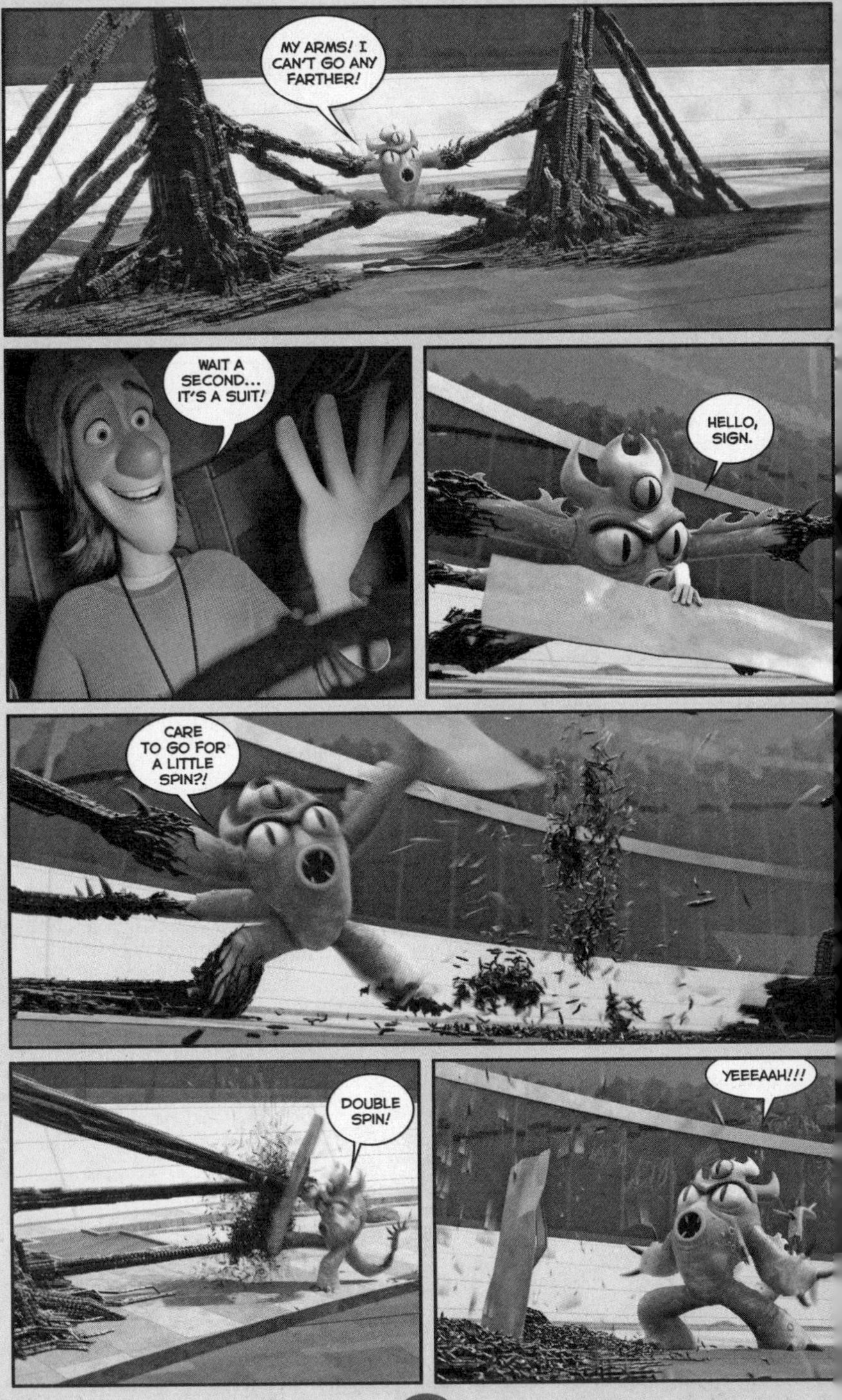
MY ARMS! I CAN'T GO ANY FARTHER!
WAIT A SECOND... IT'S A SUIT!
HELLO, SIGN.
CARE TO GO FOR A LITTLE SPIN?!
DOUBLE SPIN!
YEEEAAH!!!

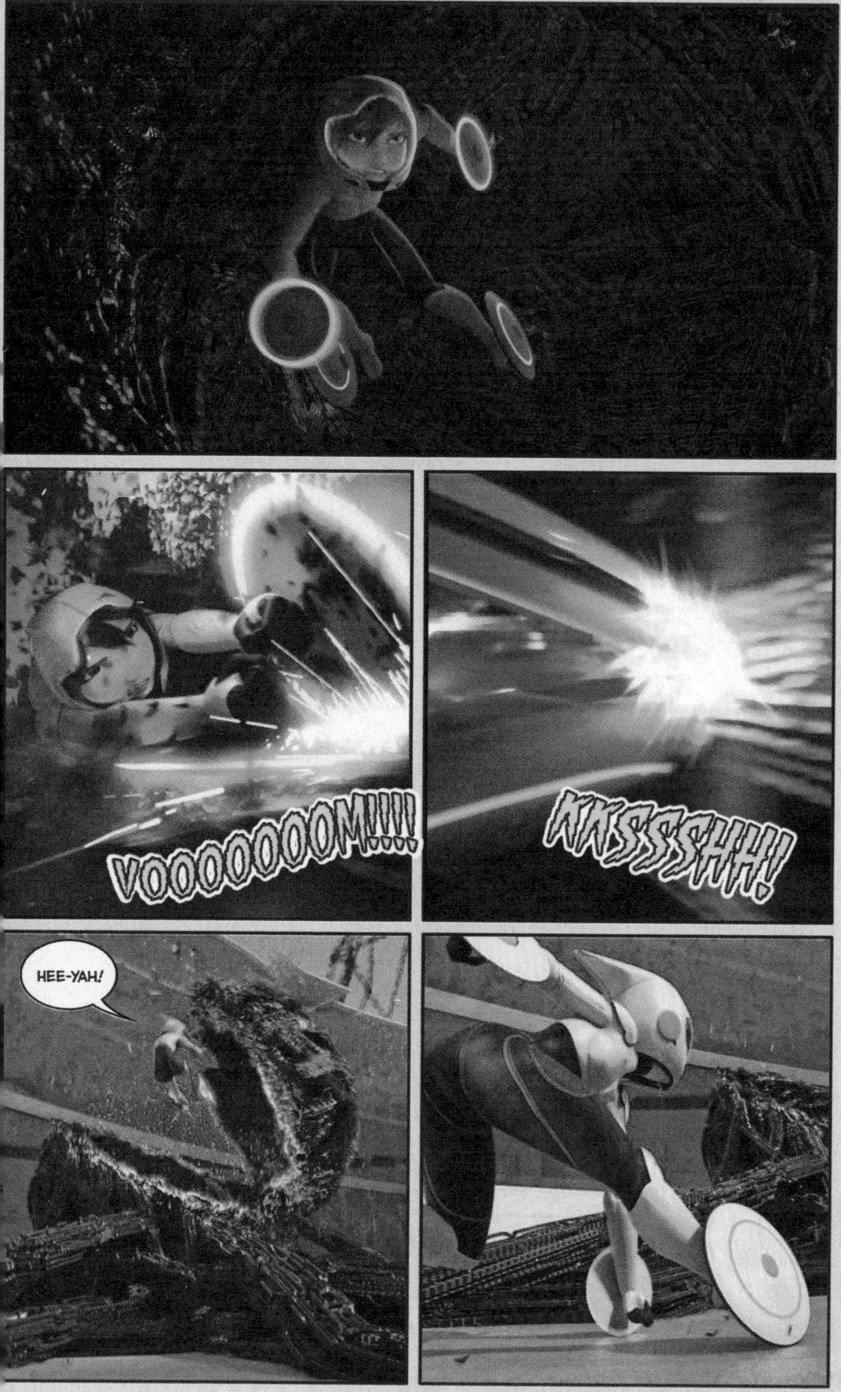
VOOOOOOOM!!!!
KKSSSSHH!
HEE-YAH!

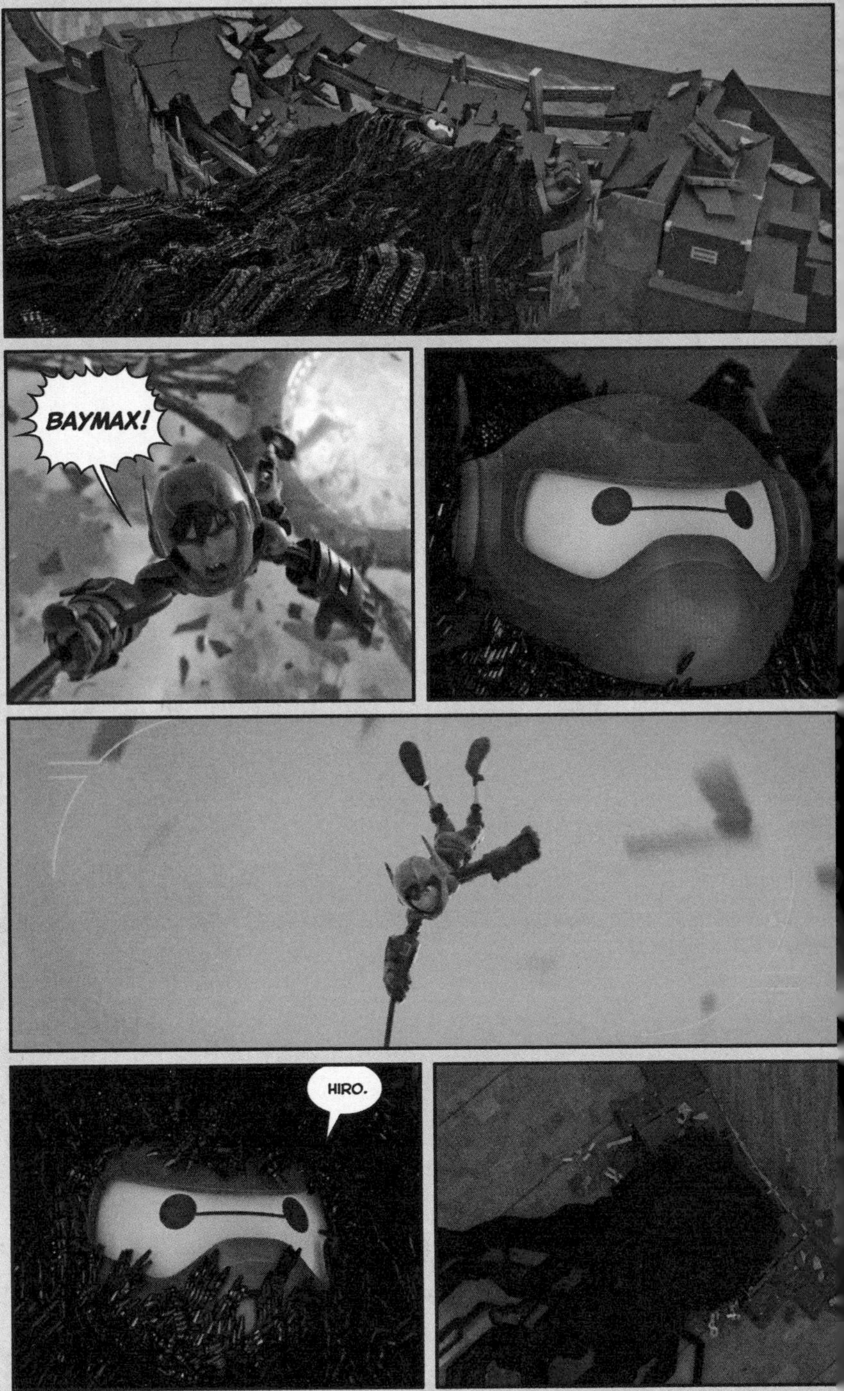
BAYMAX!
HIRO.

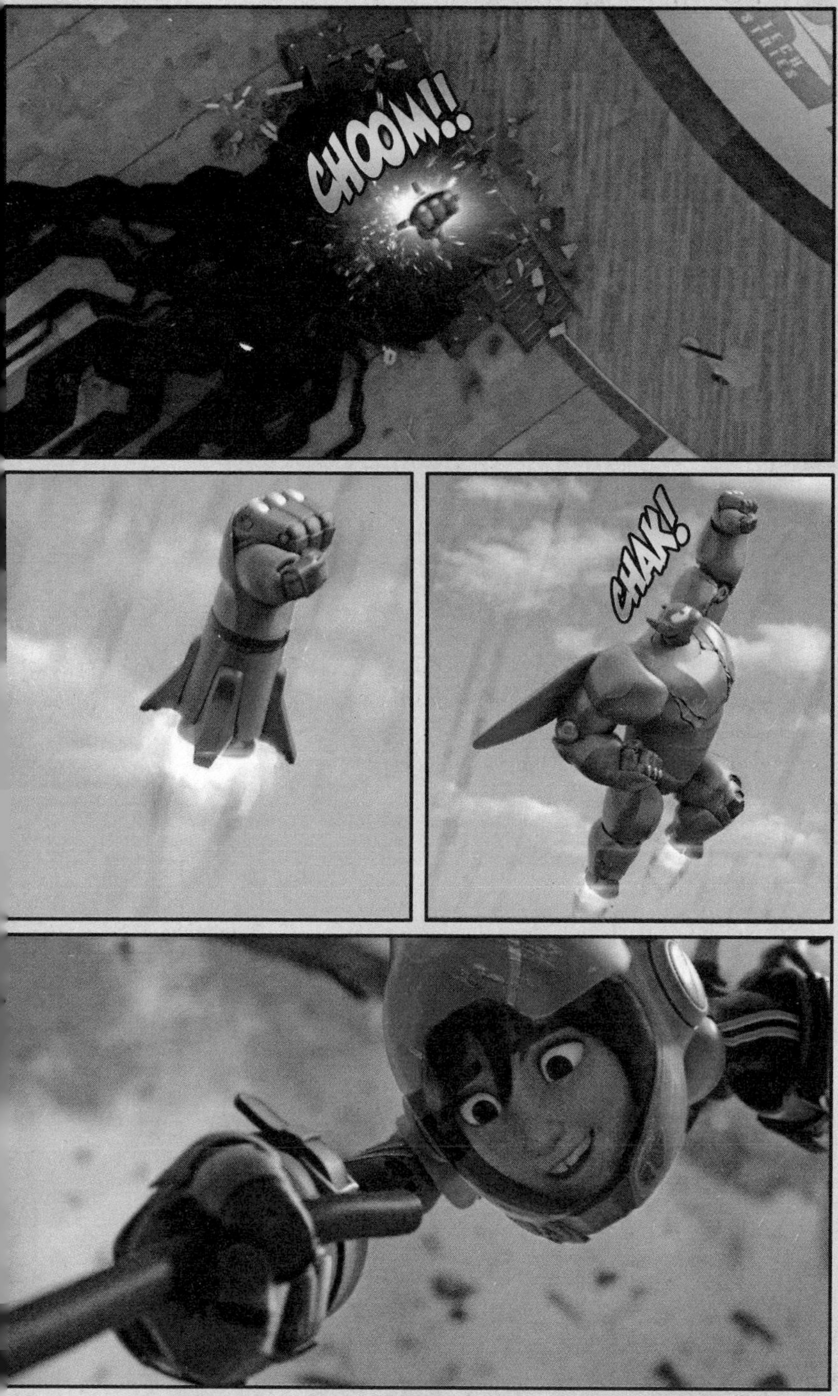
CHOOM!!
CHAK!

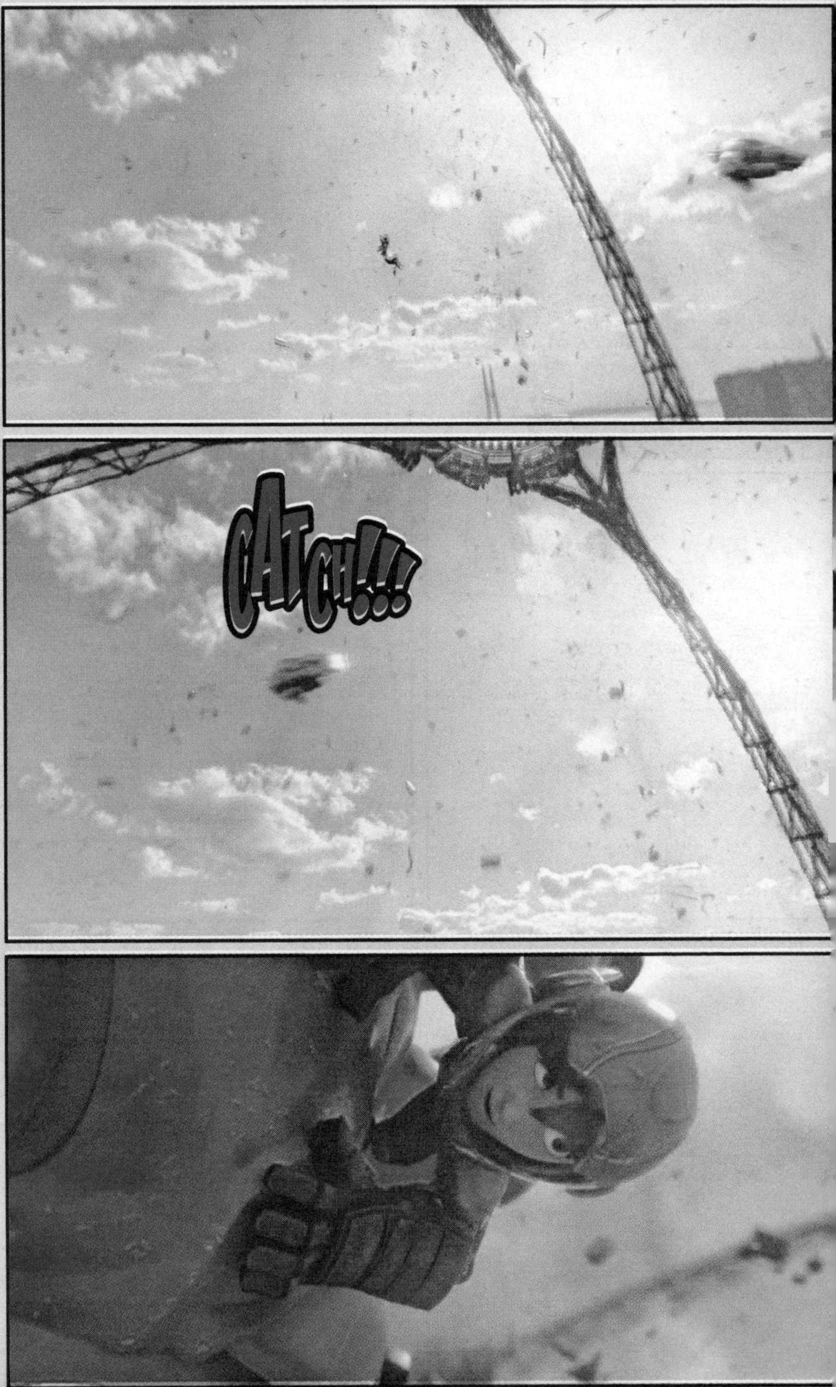
CATCH!!!

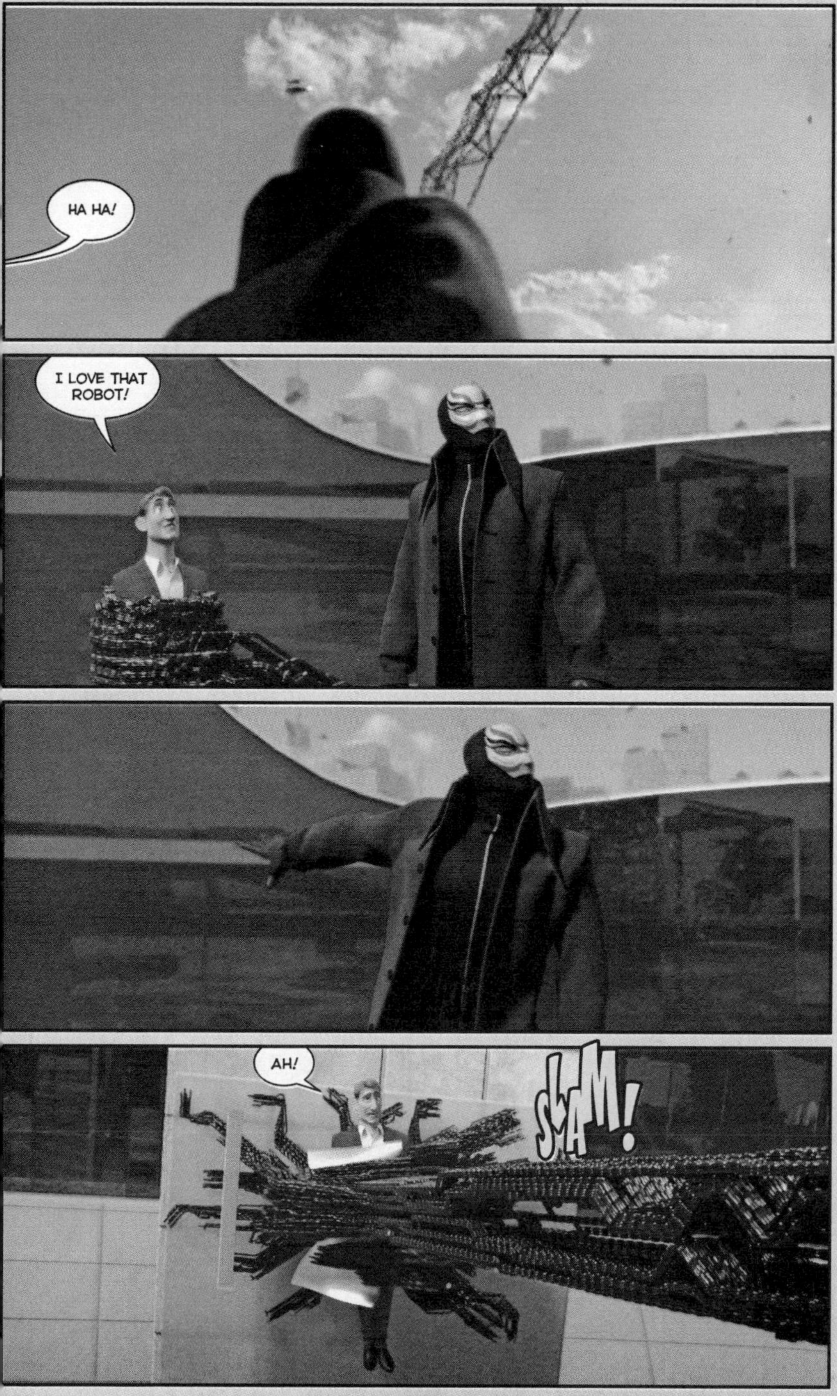
HA HA!
I LOVE THAT ROBOT!
AH!
SLAM!

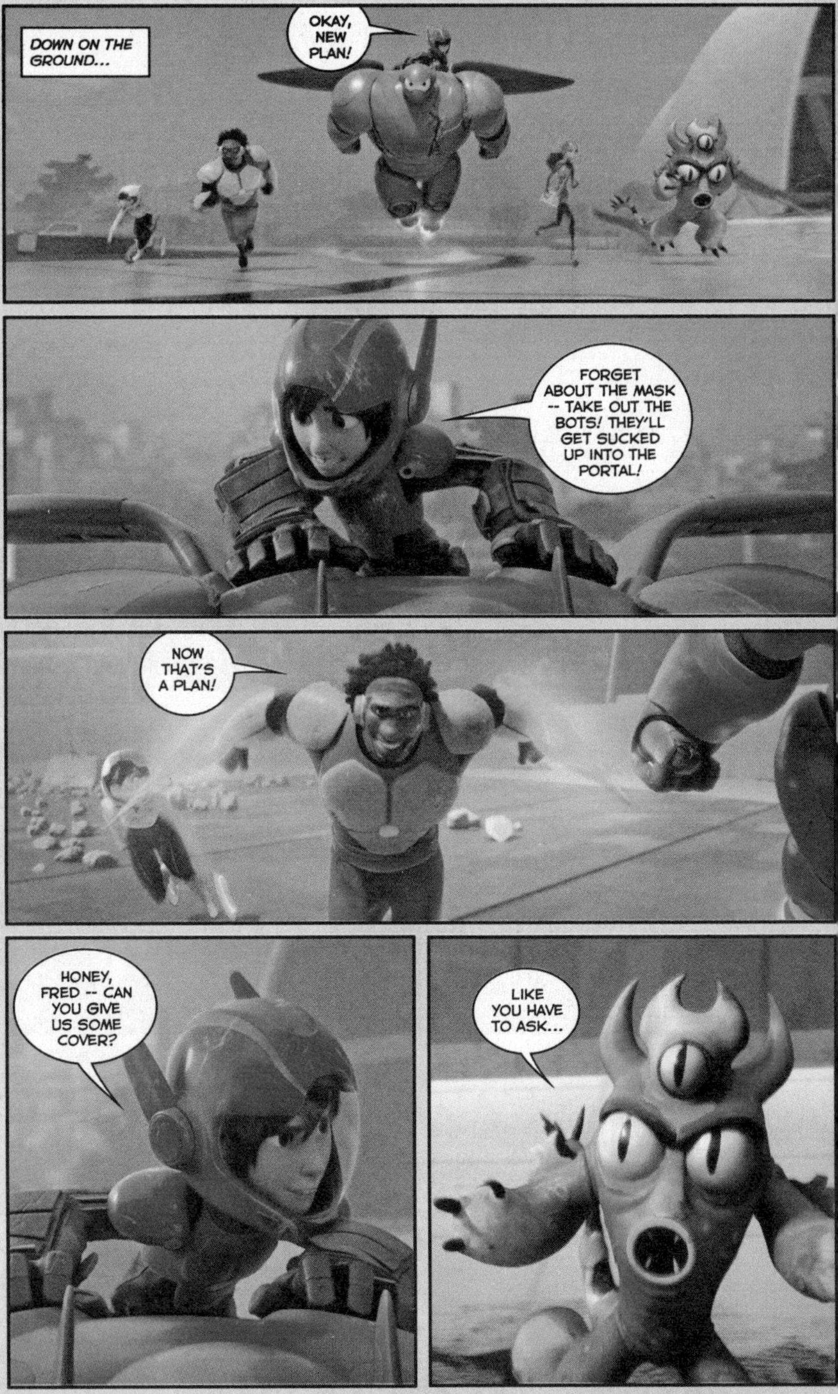
DOWN ON THE GROUND...
OKAY, NEW PLAN!
FORGET ABOUT THE MASK -- TAKE OUT THE BOTS! THEY'LL GET SUCKED UP INTO THE PORTAL!
NOW THAT'S A PLAN!
HONEY, FRED -- CAN YOU GIVE US SOME COVER?
LIKE YOU HAVE TO ASK...

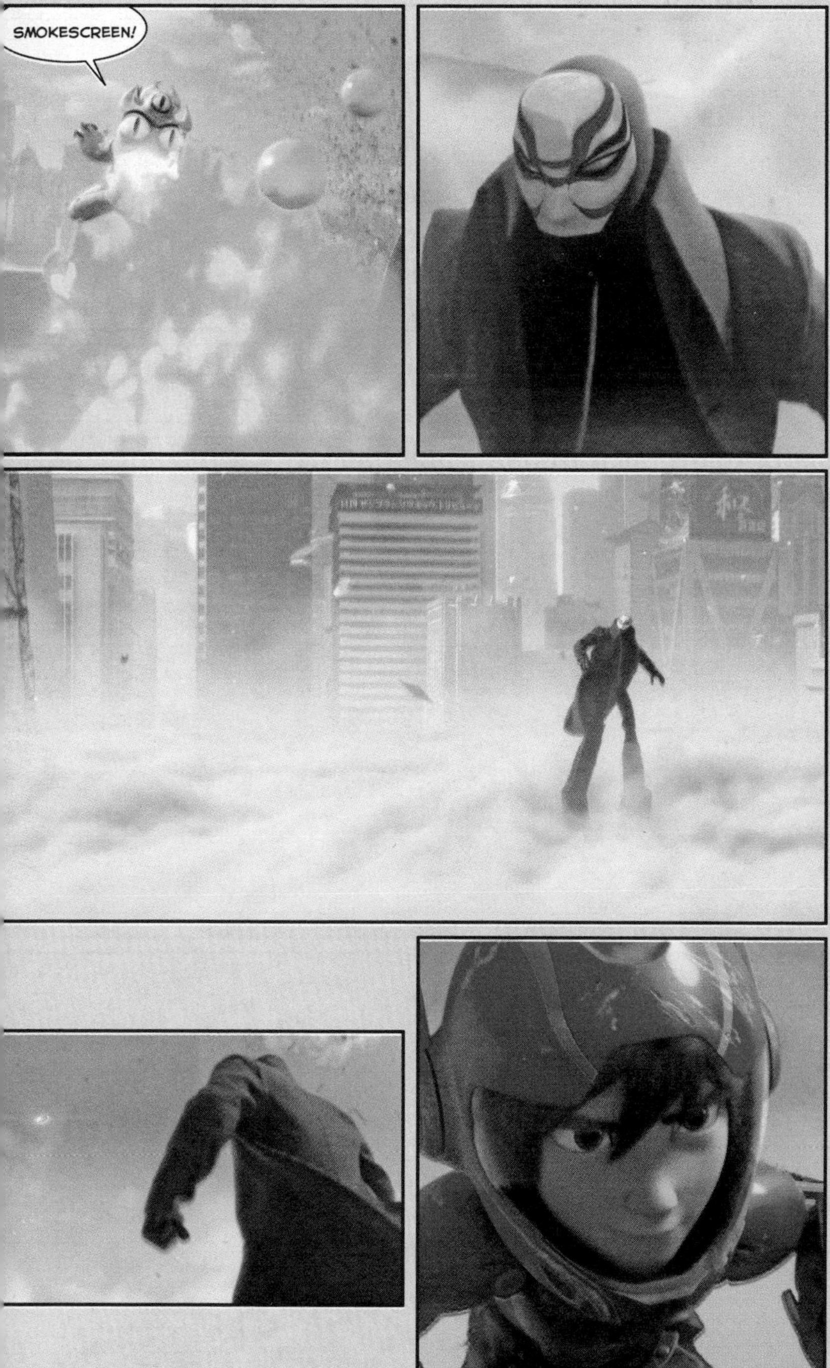
SMOKESCREEN!

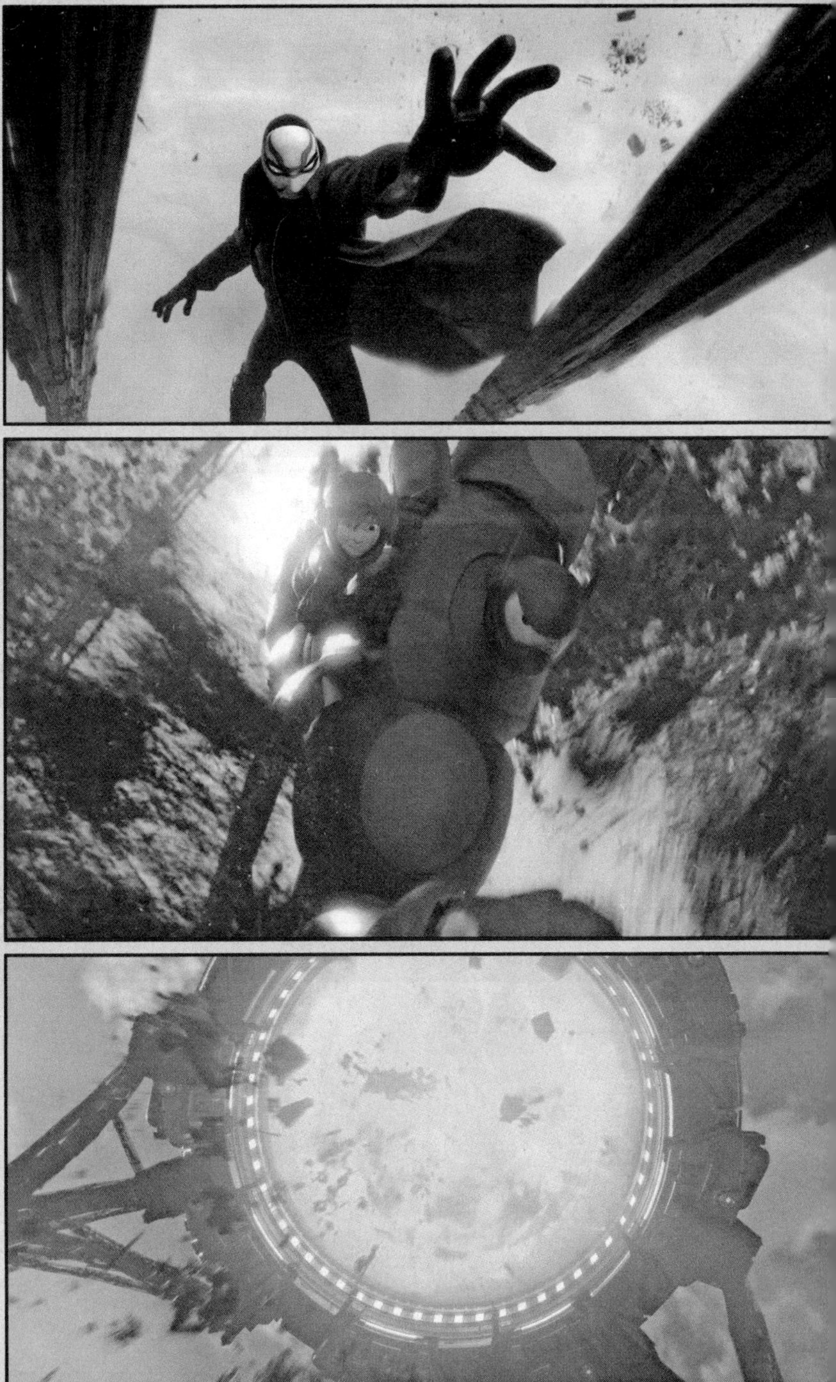

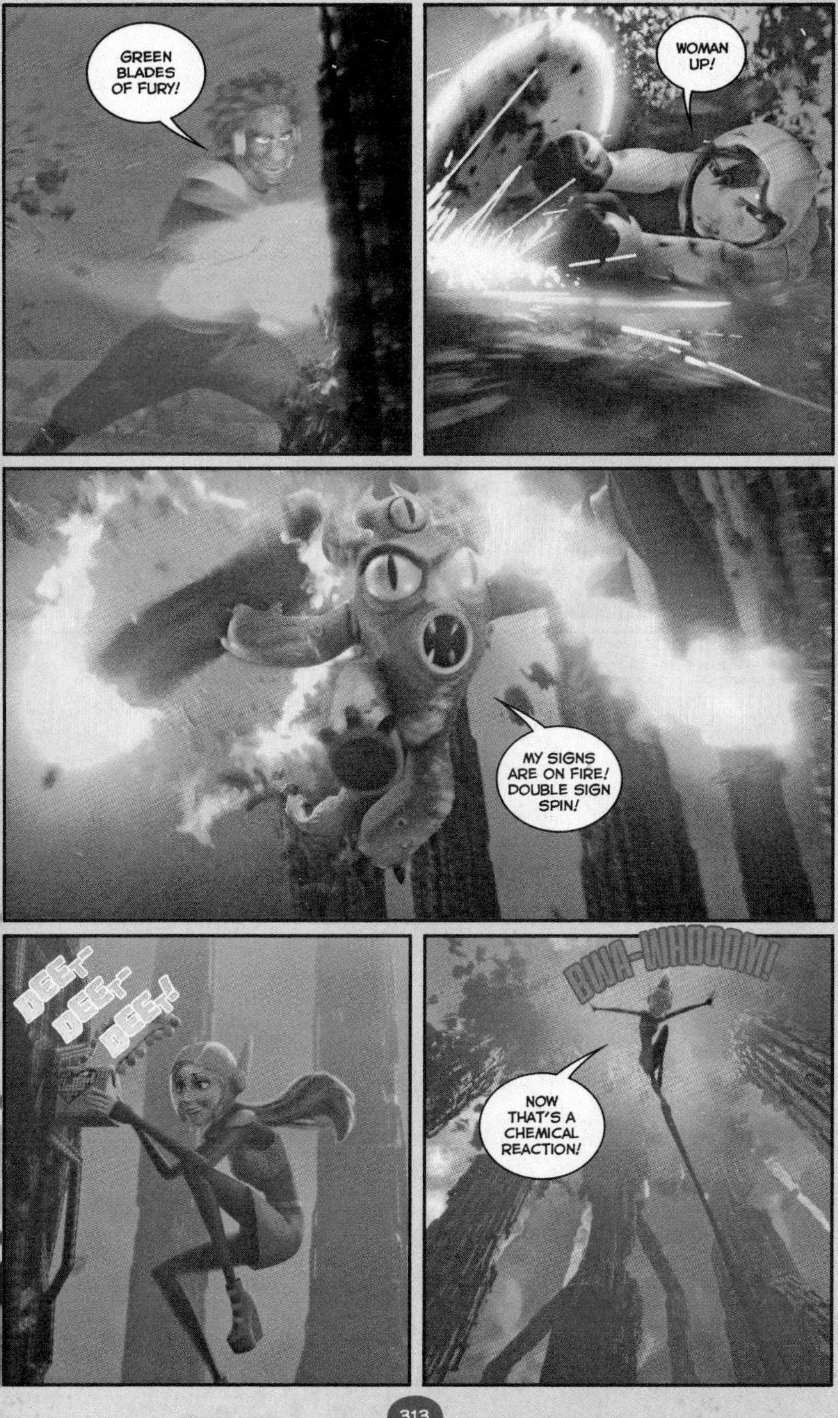
GREEN BLADES OF FURY!
WOMAN UP!
MY SIGNS ARE ON FIRE! DOUBLE SIGN SPIN!
DEET-DEET-DEET!
BWA-WHOOOM!
NOW THAT'S A CHEMICAL REACTION!

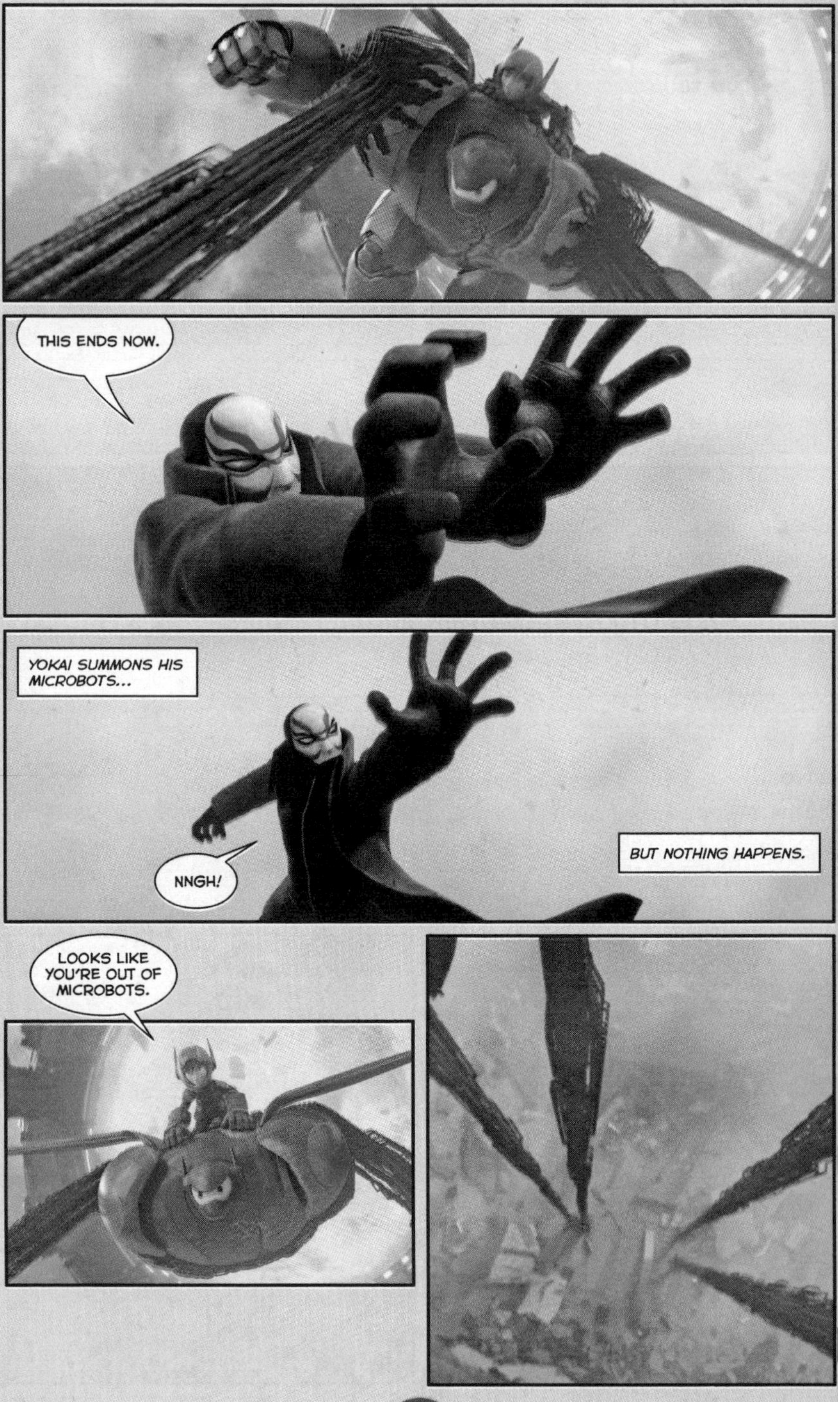
THIS ENDS NOW.
YOKAI SUMMONS HIS MICROBOTS...
NNGH!
BUT NOTHING HAPPENS.
LOOKS LIKE YOU'RE OUT OF MICROBOTS.

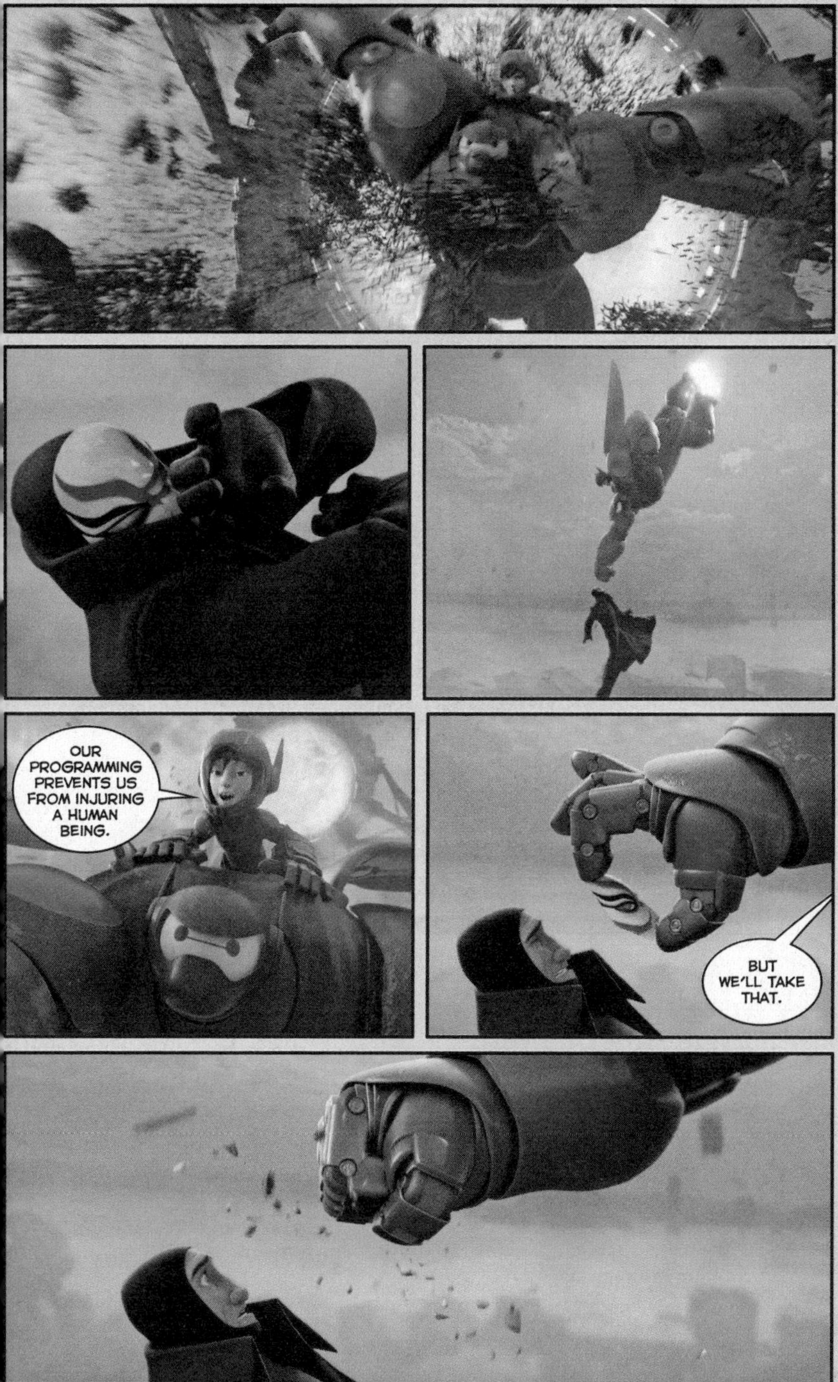
OUR PROGRAMMING PREVENTS US FROM INJURING A HUMAN BEING.
BUT WE'LL TAKE THAT.

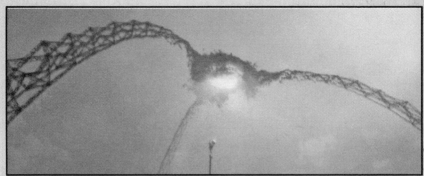

WHA-WHOA!

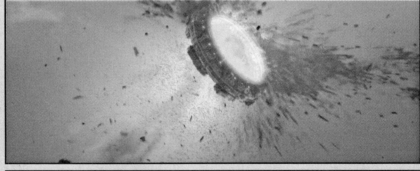

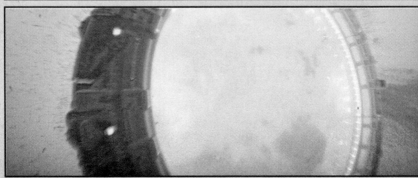

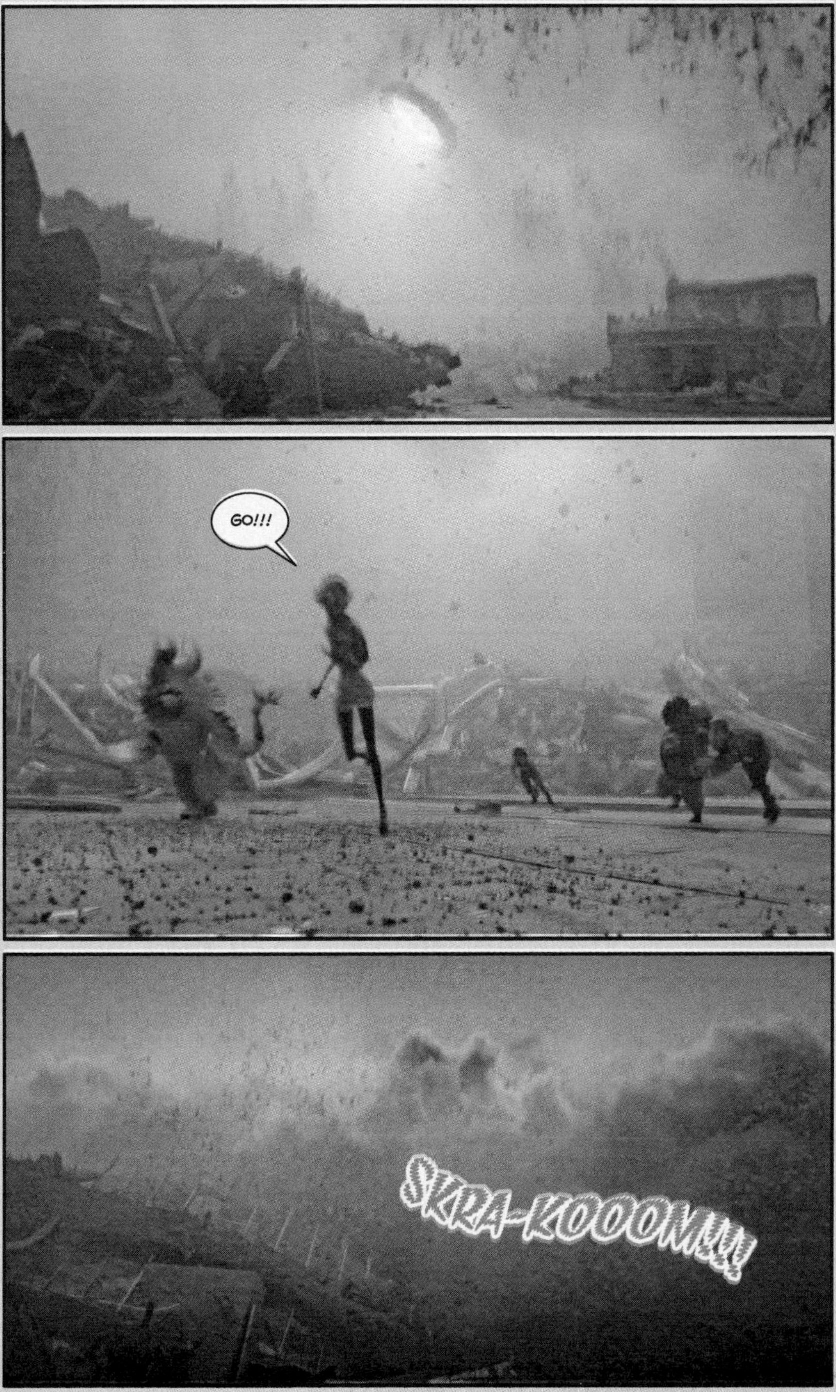
GO!!!
SKRA-KOOOM!!!

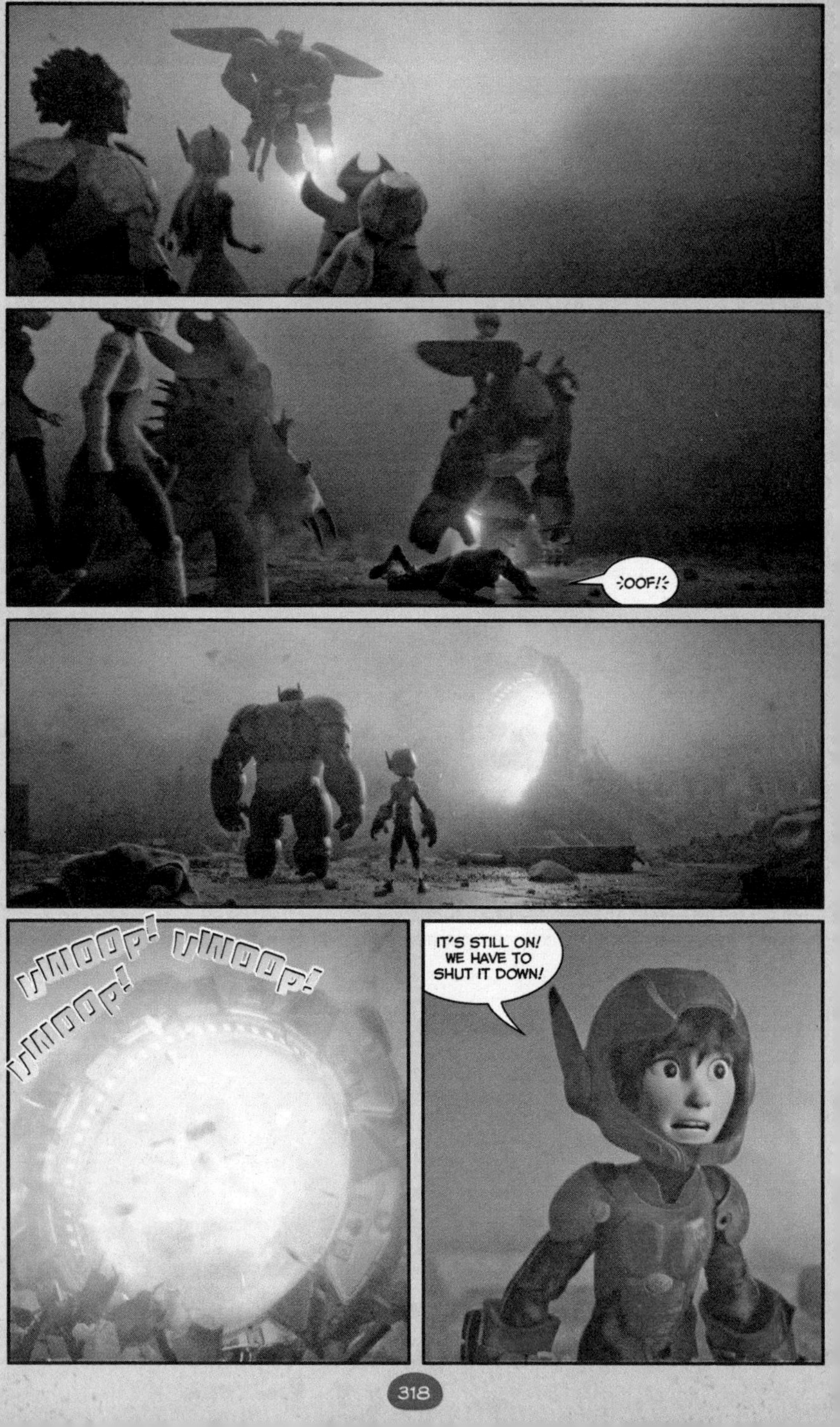
OOF!
VWOOP!
VWOOP!
VWOOP!
IT'S STILL ON! WE HAVE TO SHUT IT DOWN!

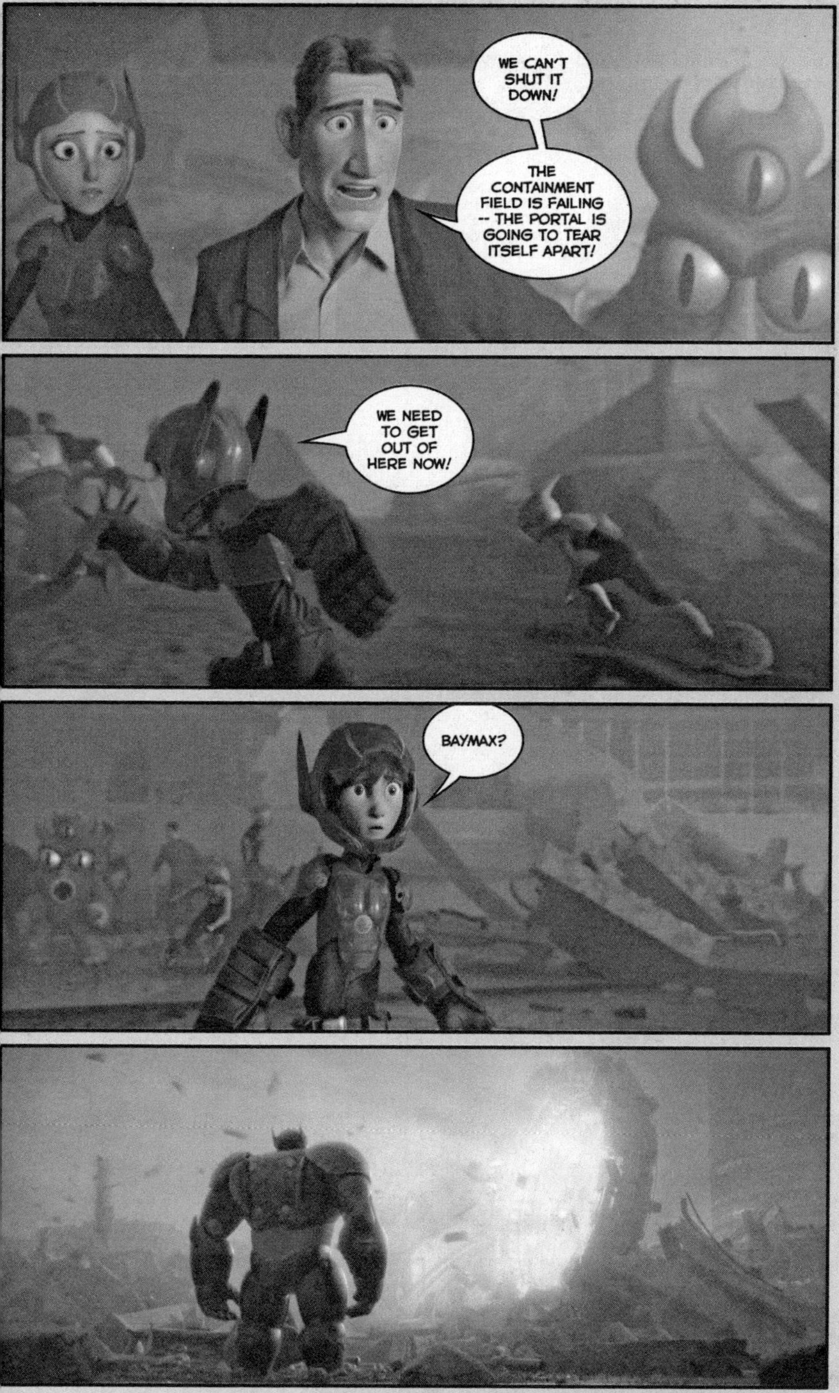
WE CAN'T SHUT IT DOWN!
THE CONTAINMENT FIELD IS FAILING -- THE PORTAL IS GOING TO TEAR ITSELF APART!
WE NEED TO GET OUT OF HERE NOW!
BAYMAX?

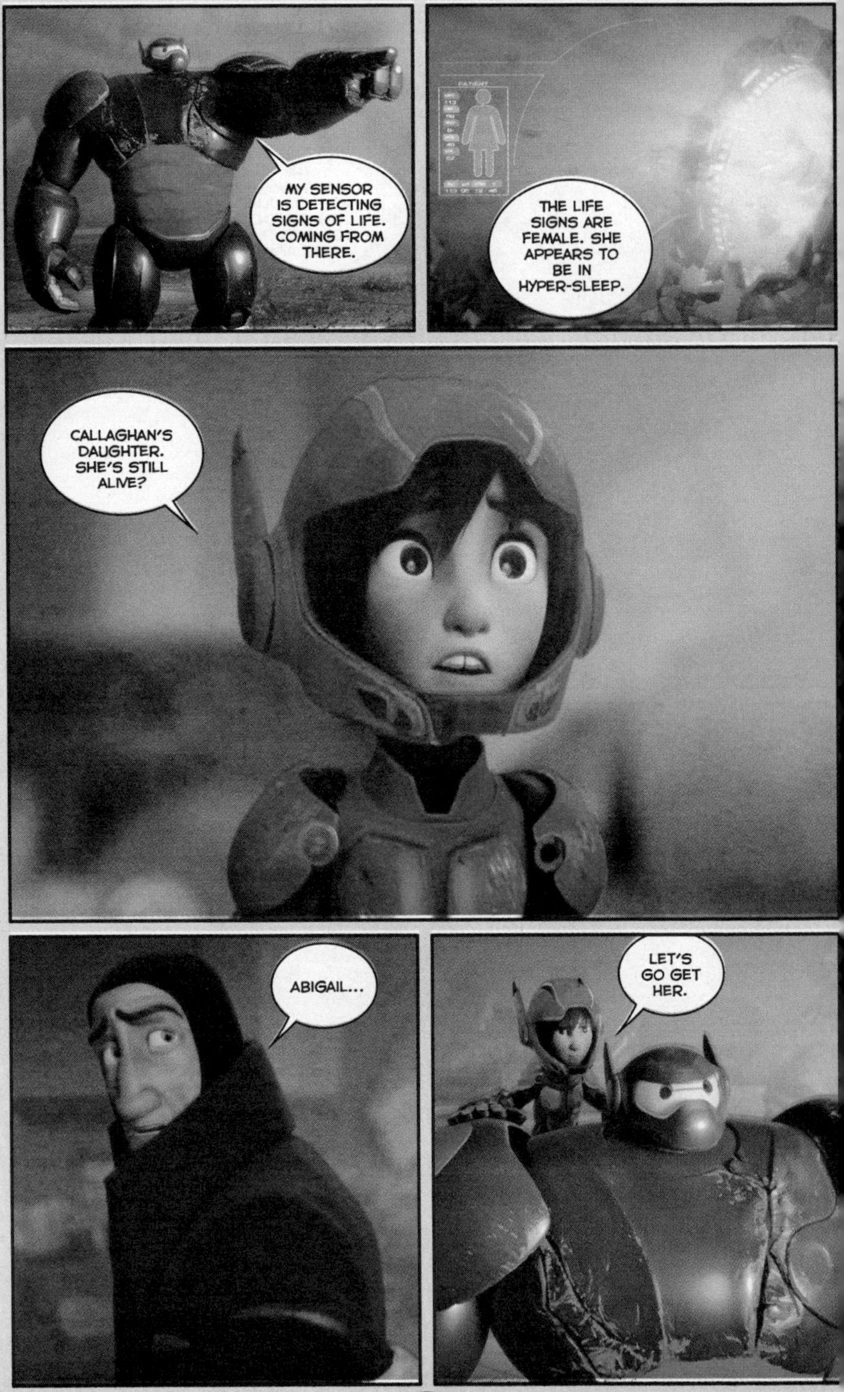
MY SENSOR IS DETECTING SIGNS OF LIFE. COMING FROM THERE.
THE LIFE SIGNS ARE FEMALE. SHE APPEARS TO BE IN HYPER-SLEEP.
CALLAGHAN'S DAUGHTER. SHE'S STILL ALIVE?
ABIGAIL...
LET'S GO GET HER.

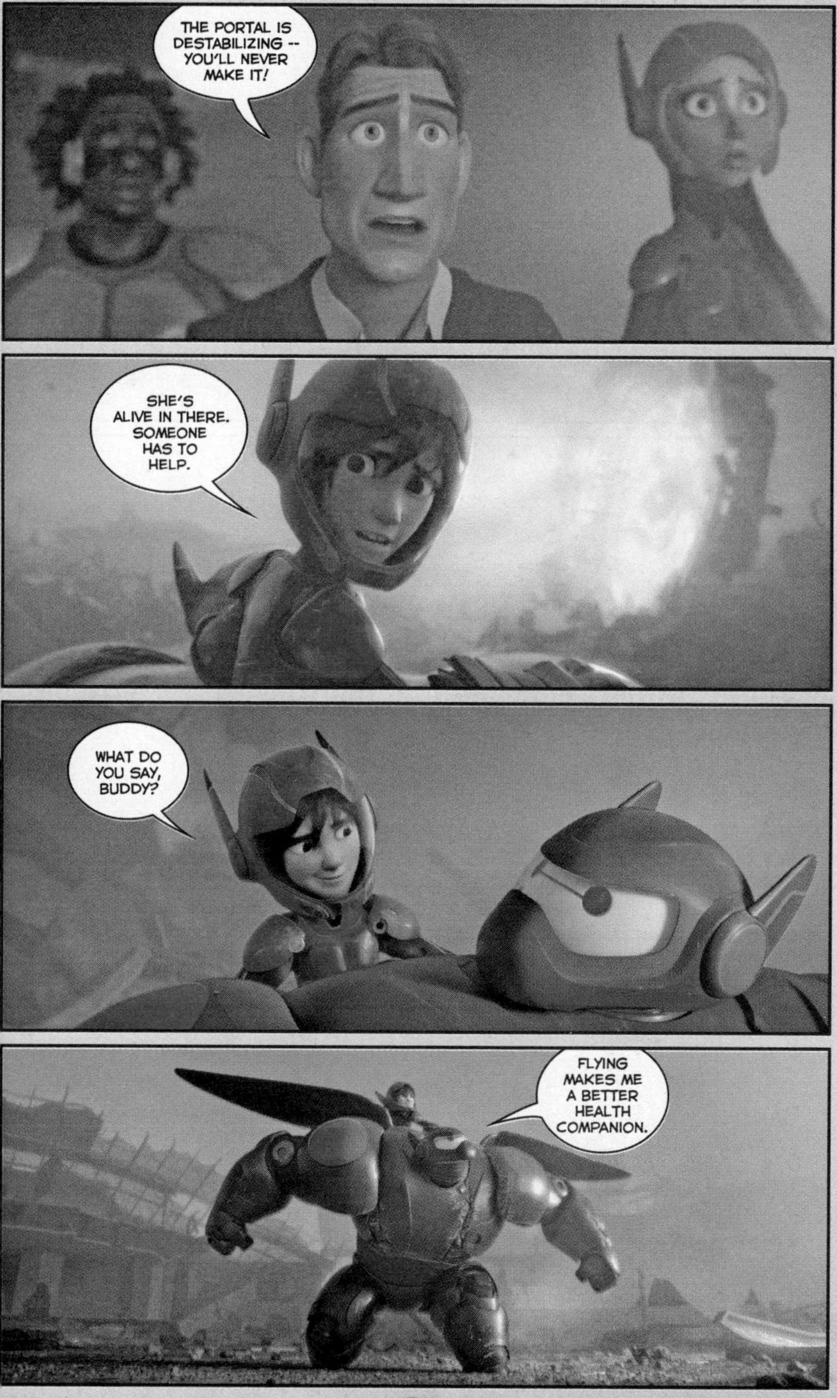
THE PORTAL IS DESTABILIZING -- YOU'LL NEVER MAKE IT!
SHE'S ALIVE IN THERE. SOMEONE HAS TO HELP.
WHAT DO YOU SAY, BUDDY?
FLYING MAKES ME A BETTER HEALTH COMPANION.

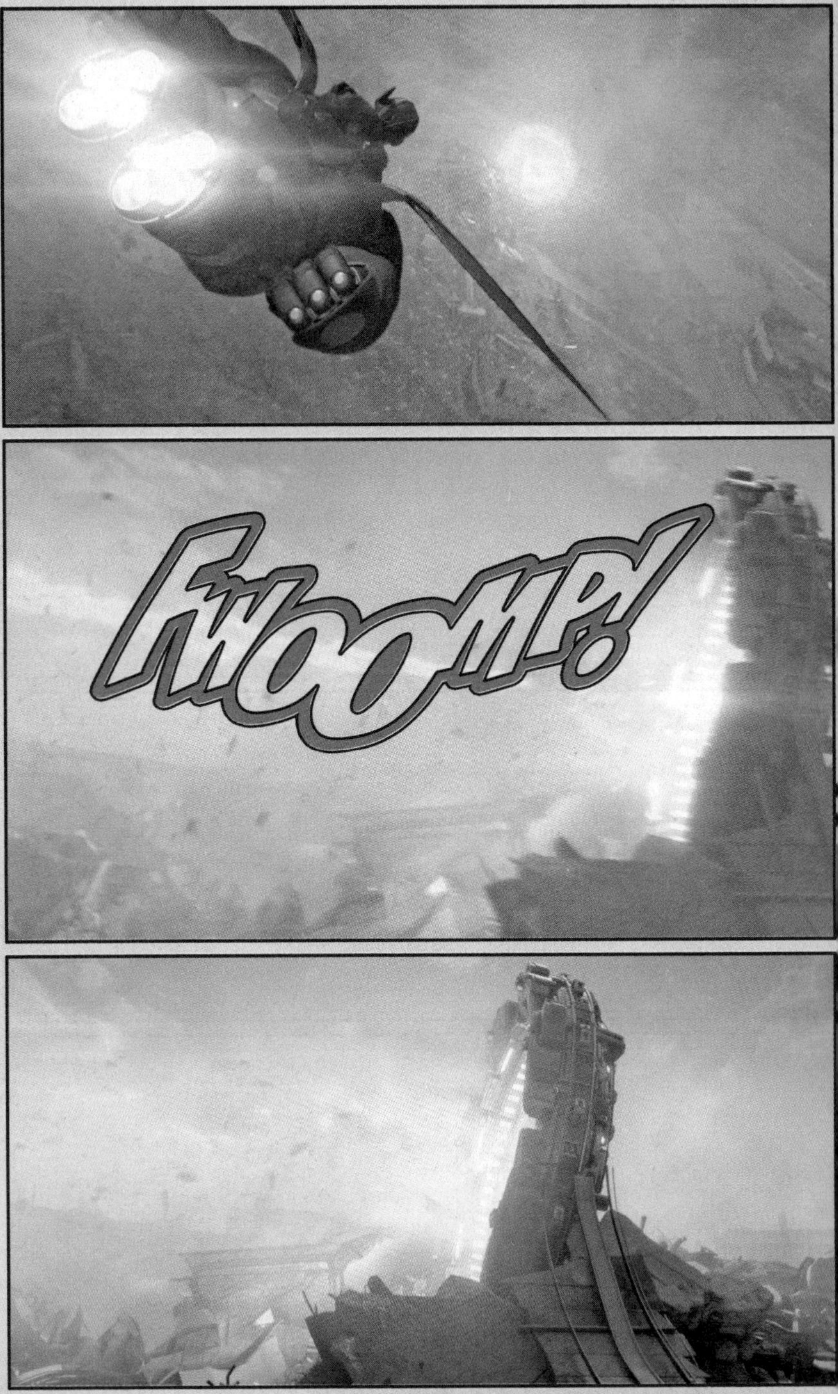
FWOOMP!

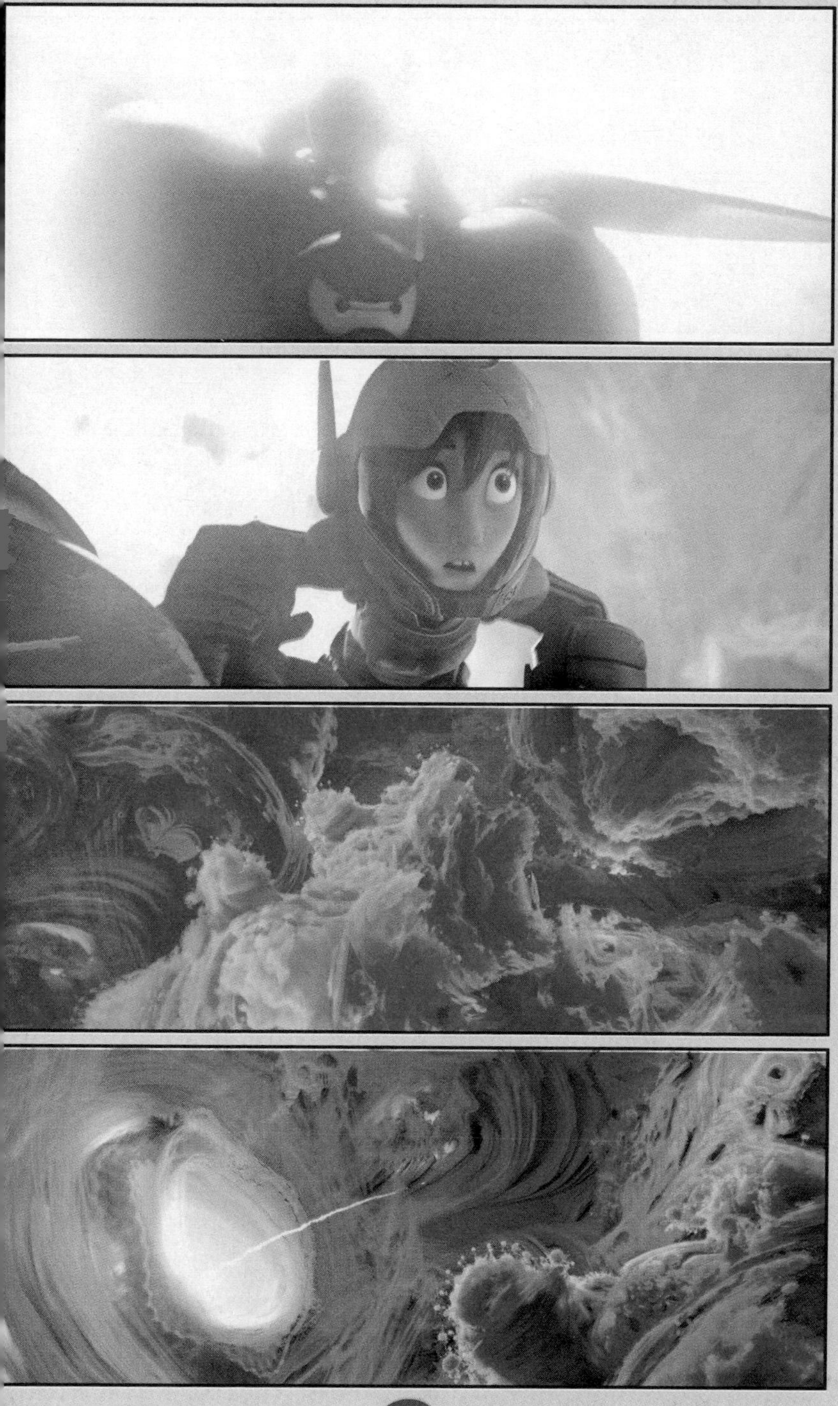

BE CAREFUL -- THERE'S KREI TECH DEBRIS EVERYWHERE.

I HAVE LOCATED THE PATIENT.

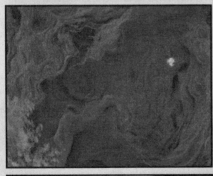

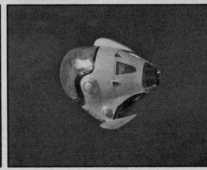

HURRY!

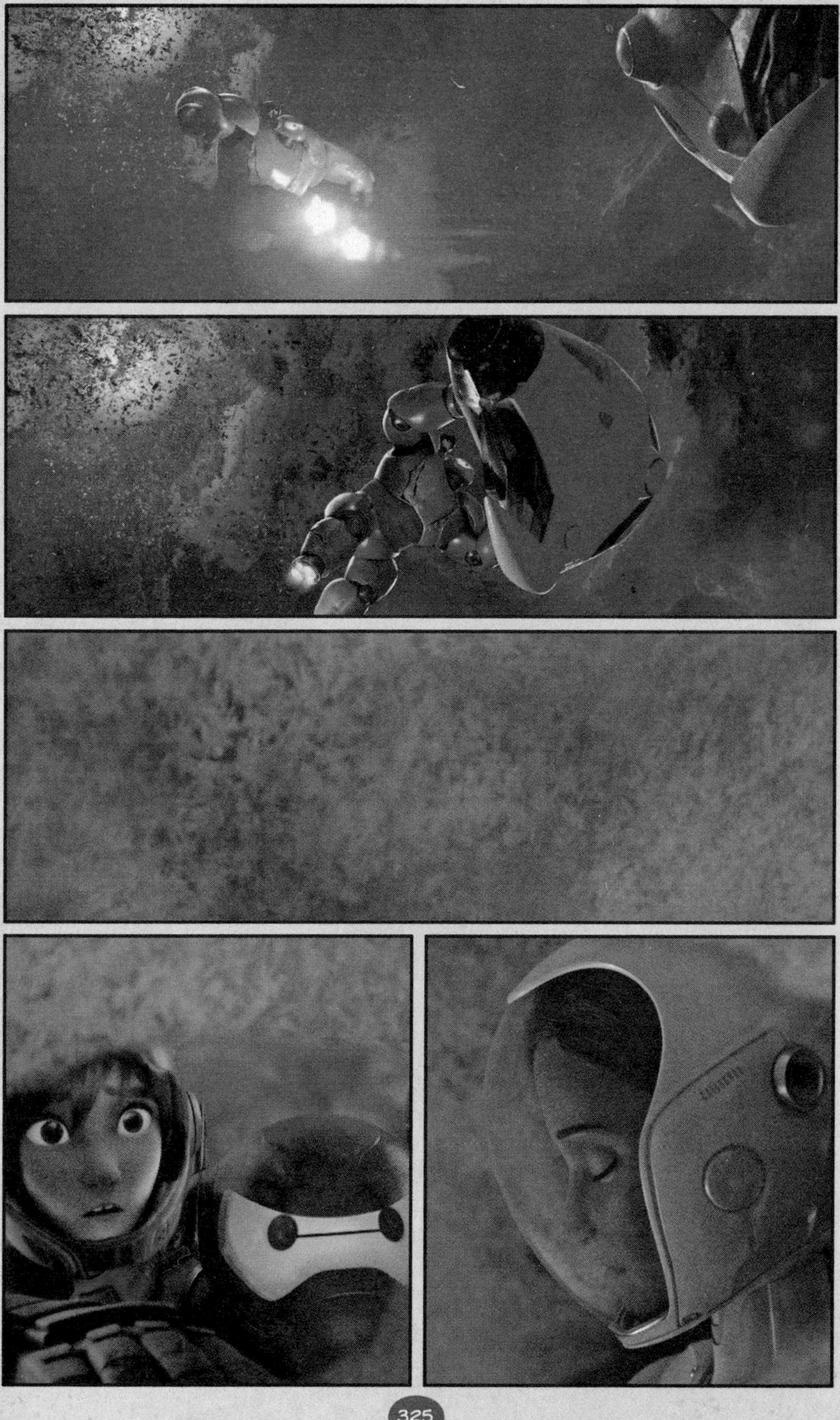

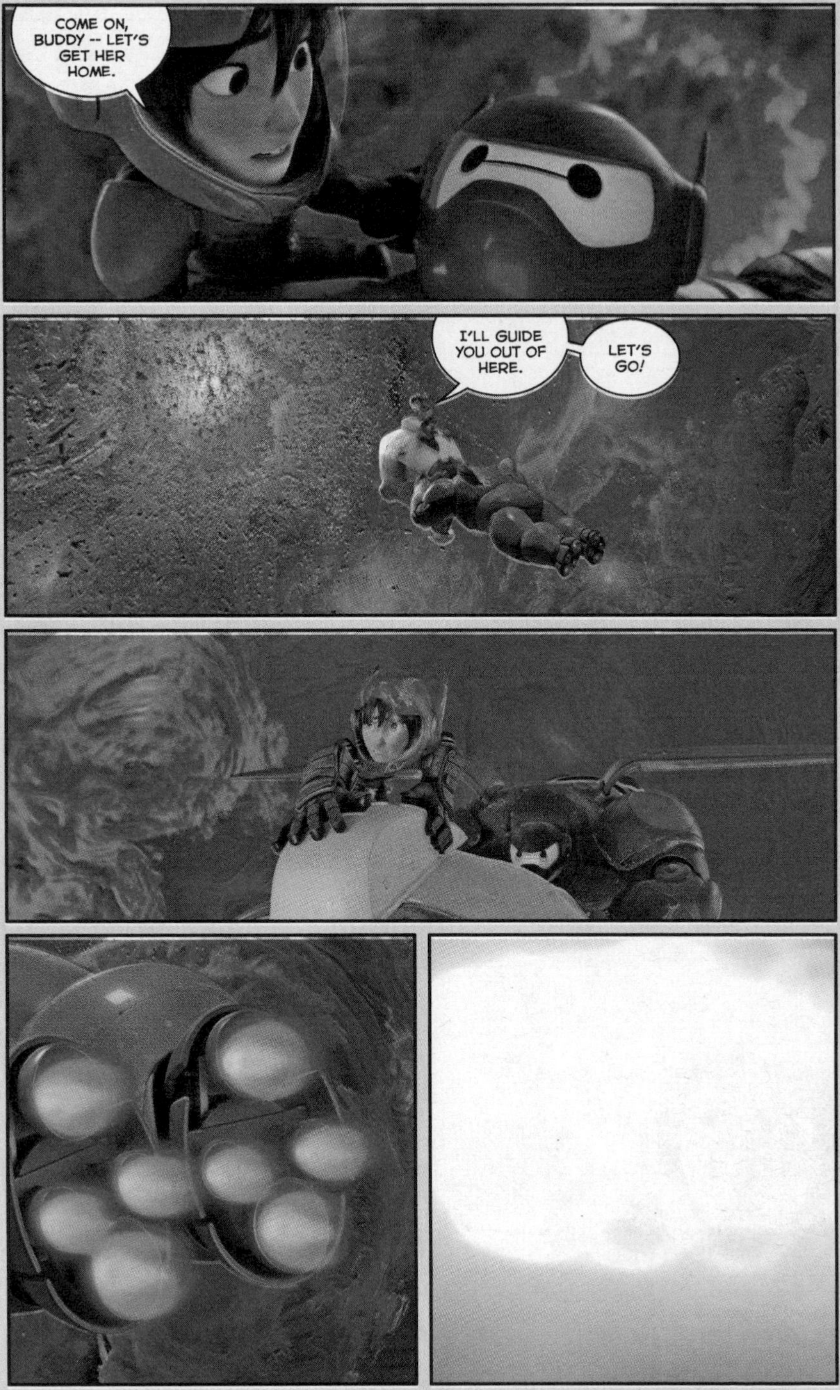
COME ON, BUDDY -- LET'S GET HER HOME.
I'LL GUIDE YOU OUT OF HERE.
LET'S GO!

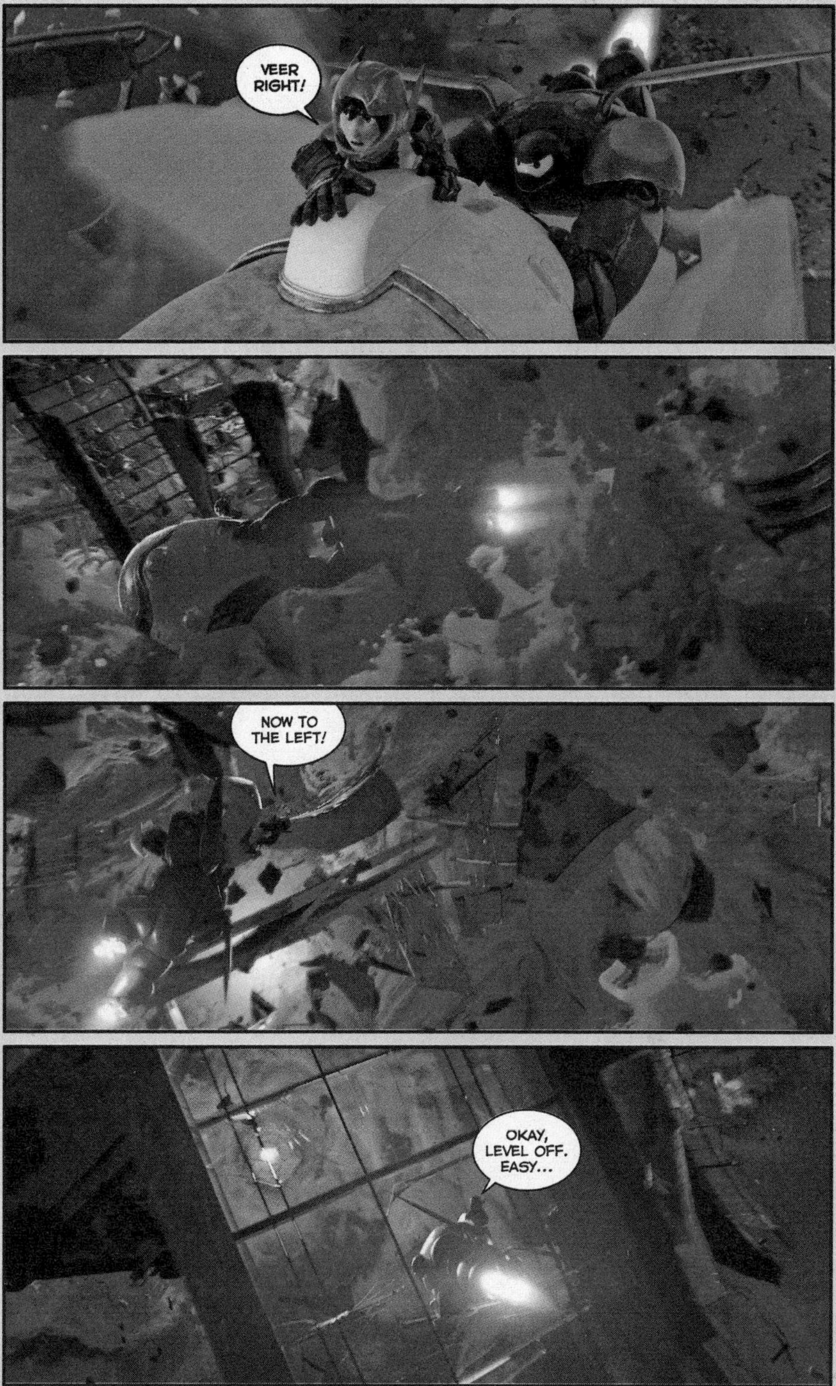
VEER RIGHT!
NOW TO THE LEFT!
OKAY, LEVEL OFF. EASY...

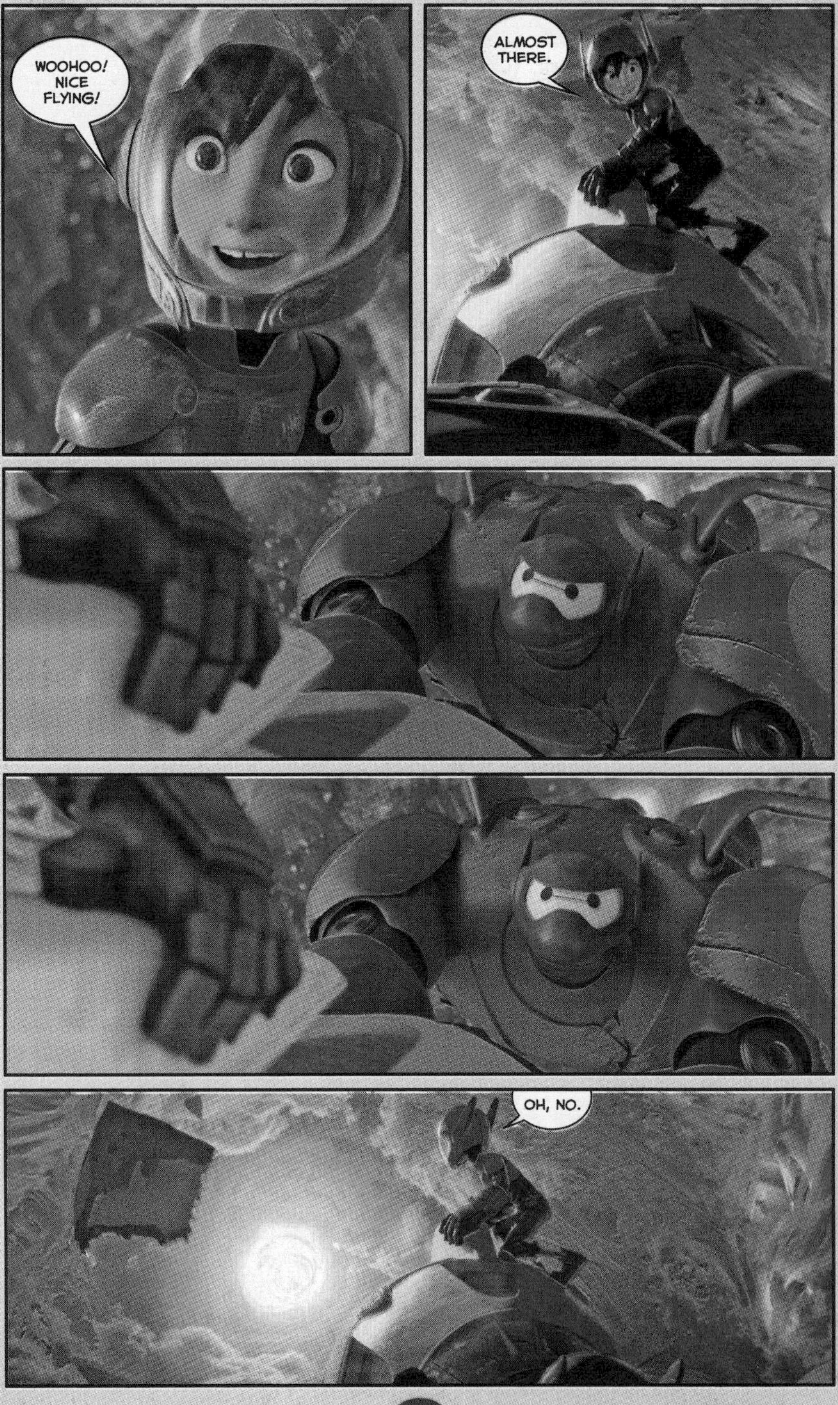
WOOHOO! NICE FLYING!
ALMOST THERE.
OH, NO.

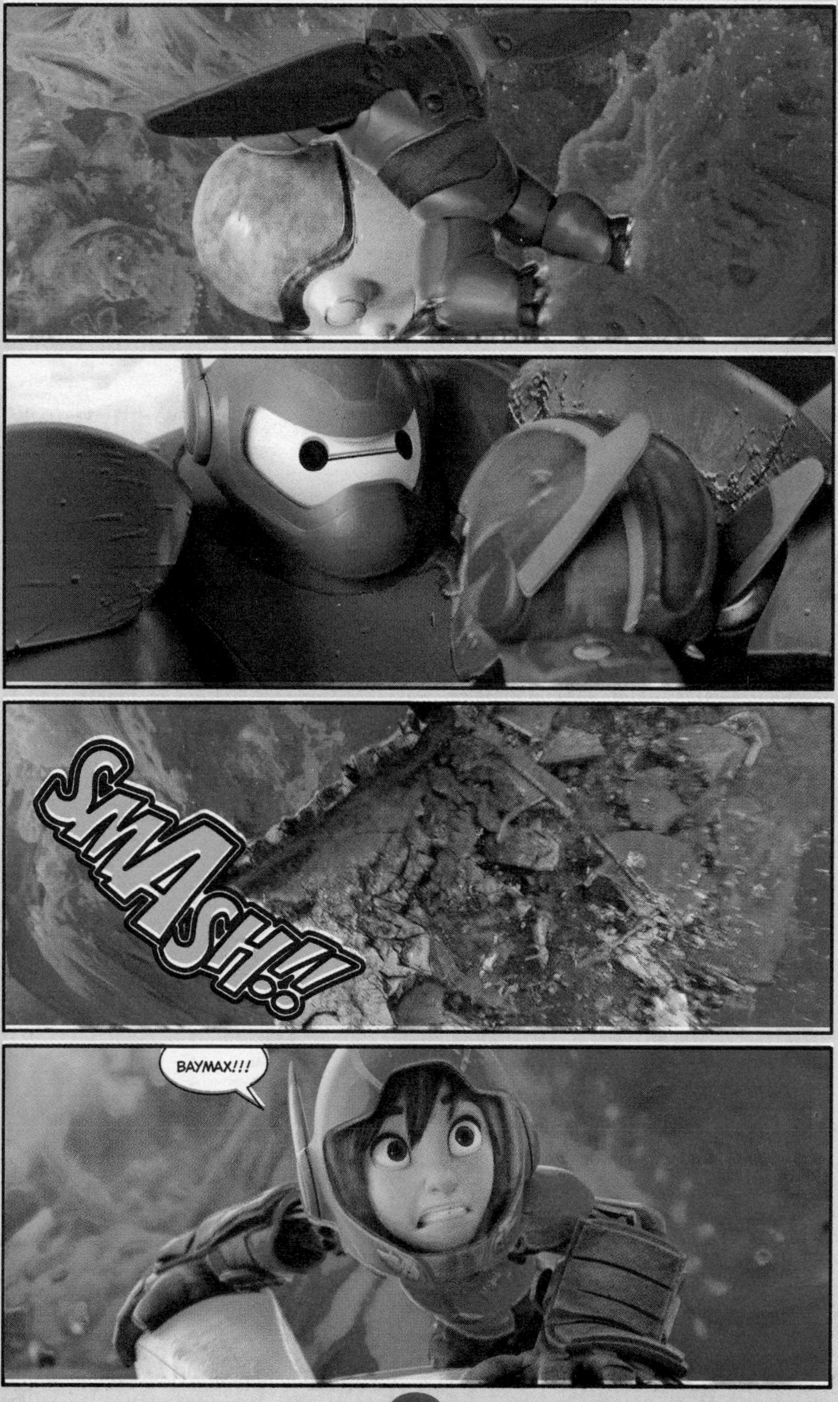
SMASH!!
BAYMAX!!!

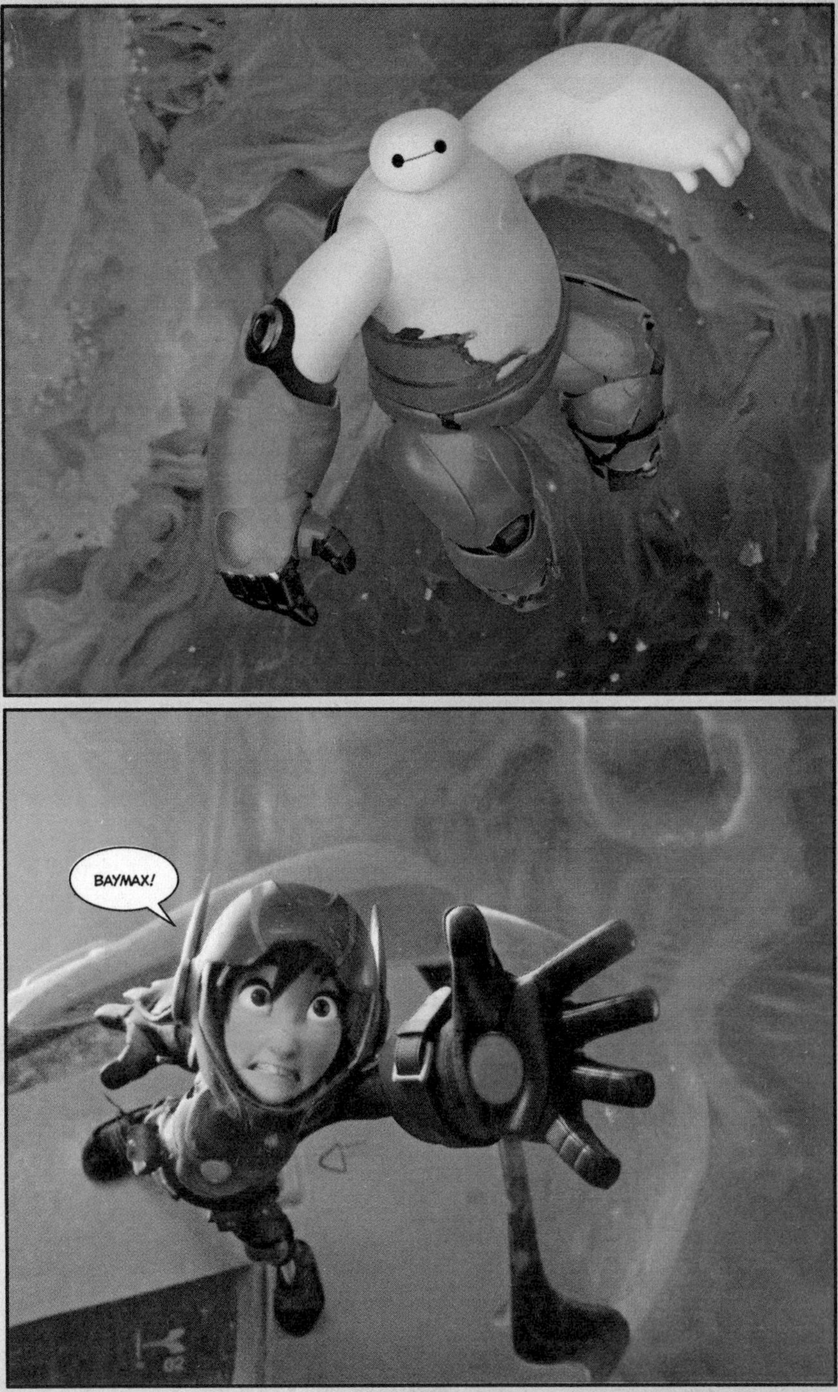
BAYMAX!

VZZT! VZZT!

MY THRUSTERS ARE INOPERABLE.

JUST GRAB HOLD!

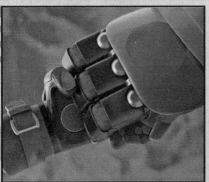

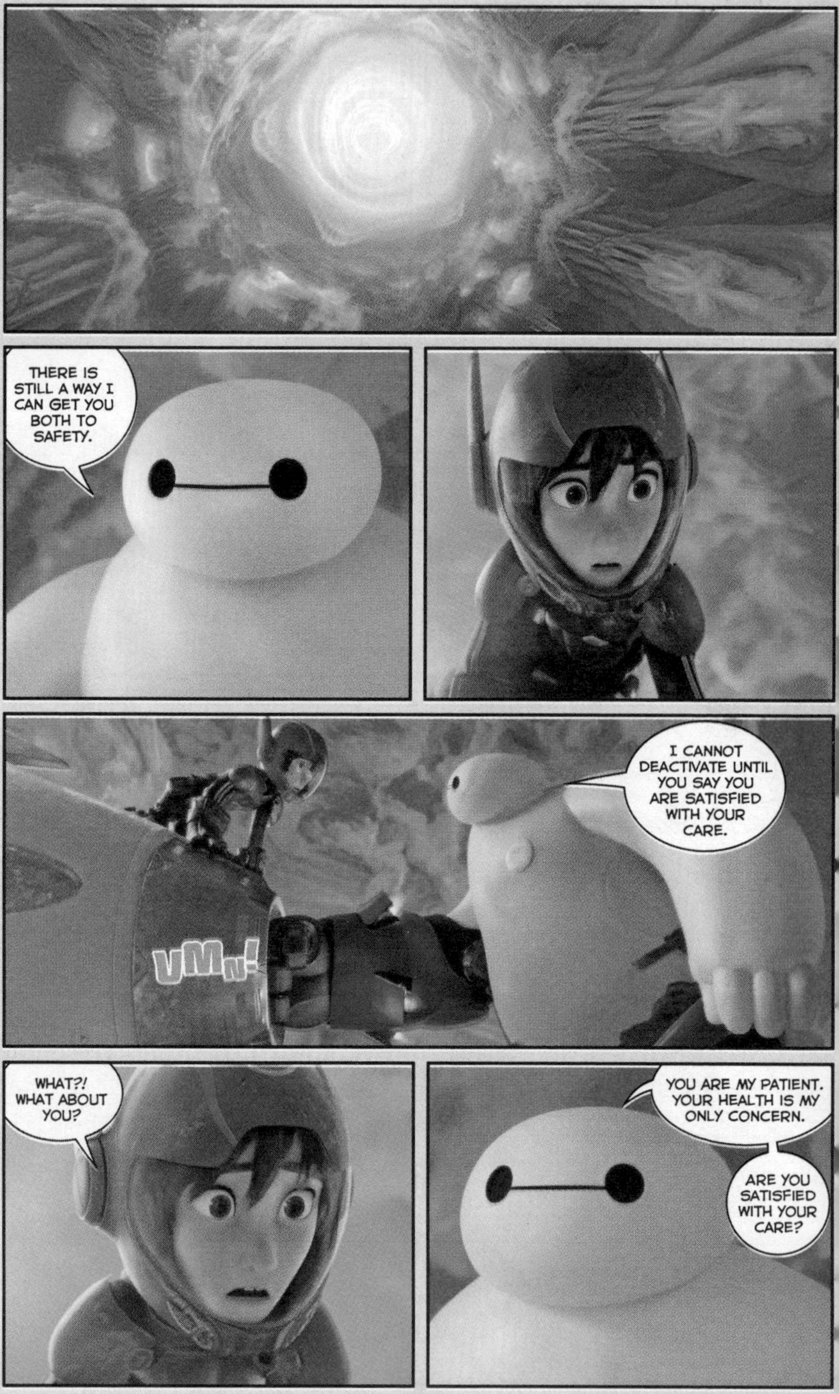
THERE IS STILL A WAY I CAN GET YOU BOTH TO SAFETY.
I CANNOT DEACTIVATE UNTIL YOU SAY YOU ARE SATISFIED WITH YOUR CARE.
UMN!
WHAT?! WHAT ABOUT YOU?
YOU ARE MY PATIENT. YOUR HEALTH IS MY ONLY CONCERN.
ARE YOU SATISFIED WITH YOUR CARE?

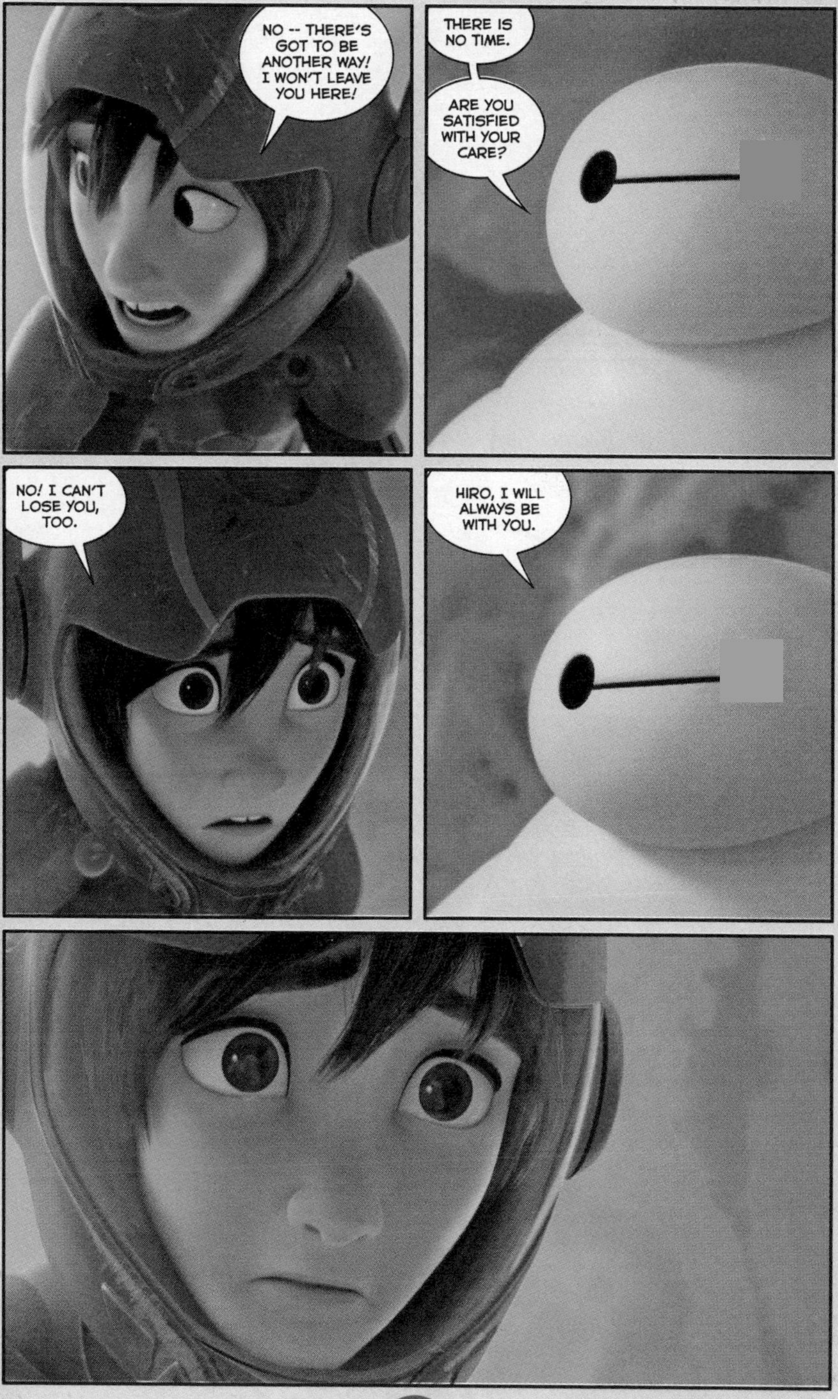
NO -- THERE'S GOT TO BE ANOTHER WAY! I WON'T LEAVE YOU HERE!
THERE IS NO TIME.
ARE YOU SATISFIED WITH YOUR CARE?
NO! I CAN'T LOSE YOU, TOO.
HIRO, I WILL ALWAYS BE WITH YOU.

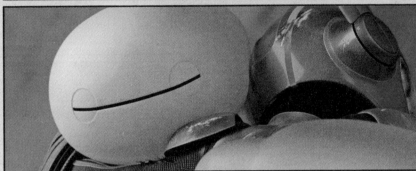

I AM SATISFIED WITH MY CARE.

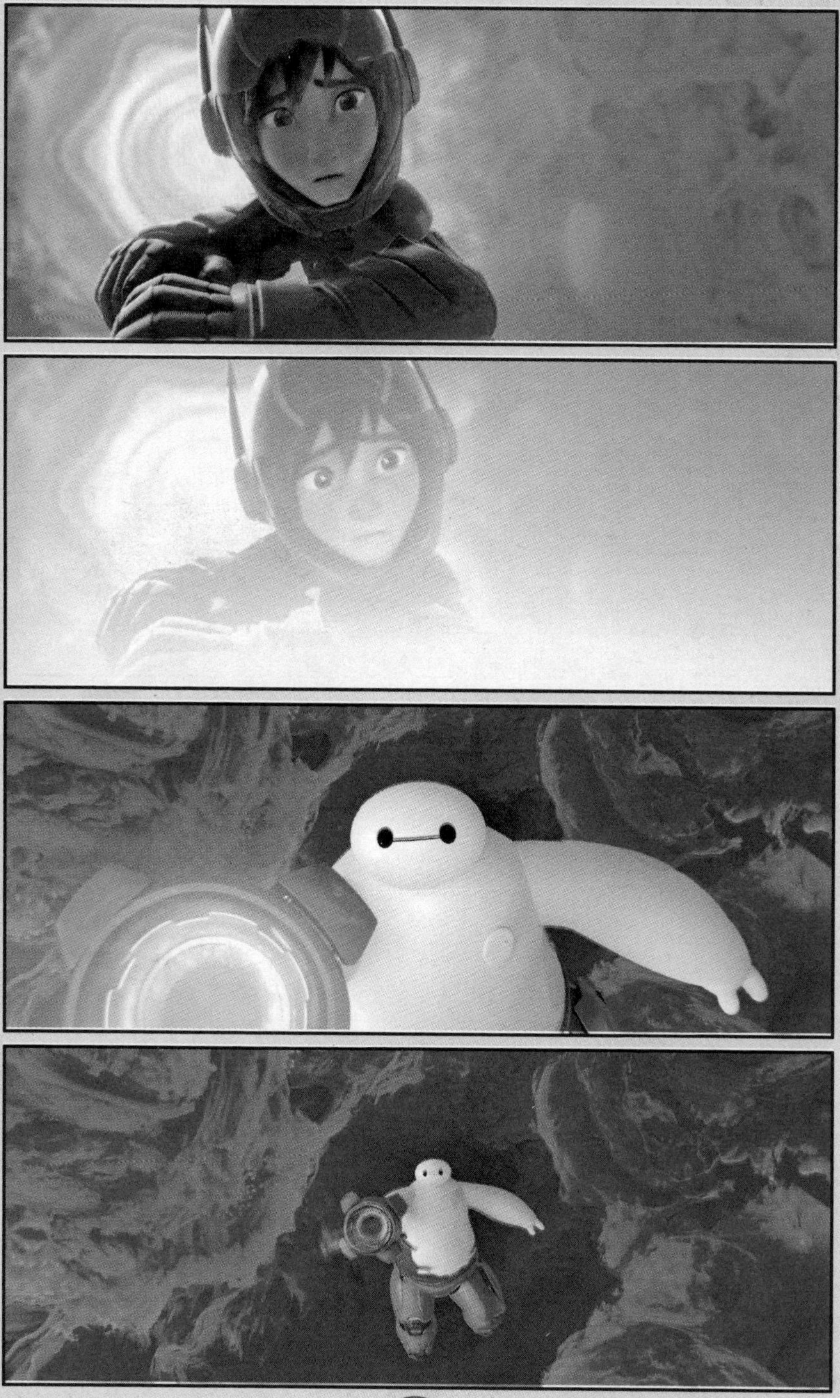

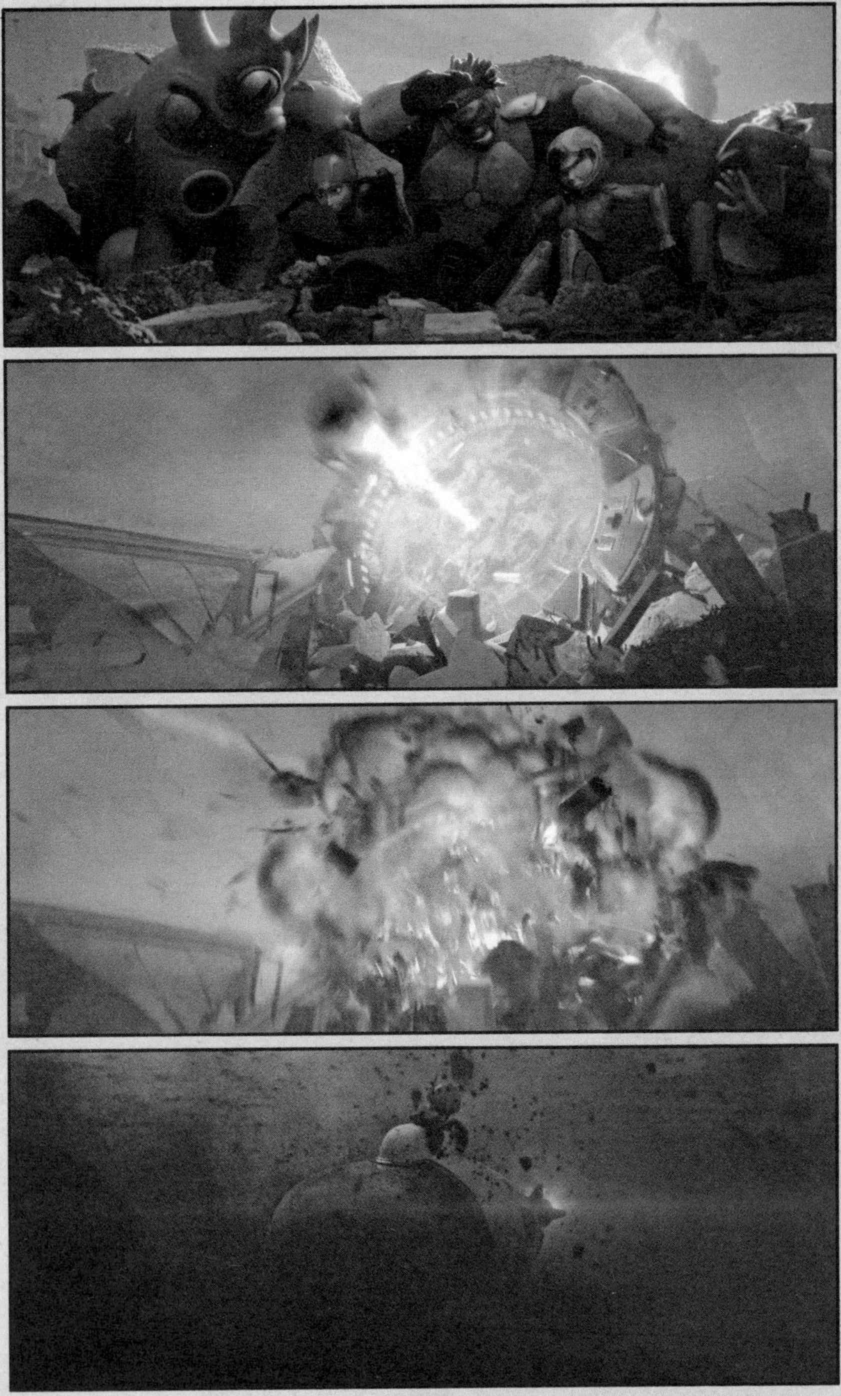

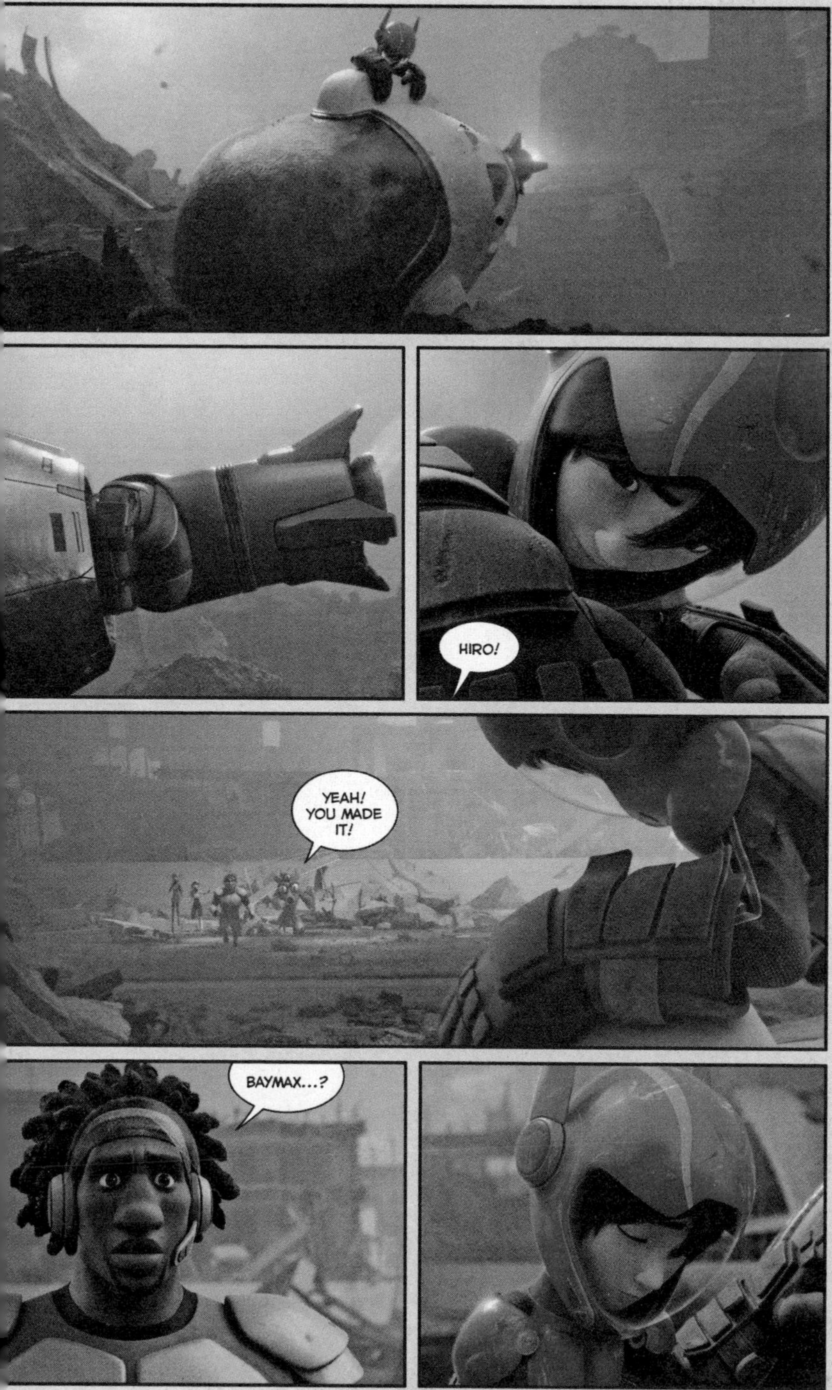
HIRO!
YEAH! YOU MADE IT!
BAYMAX...?

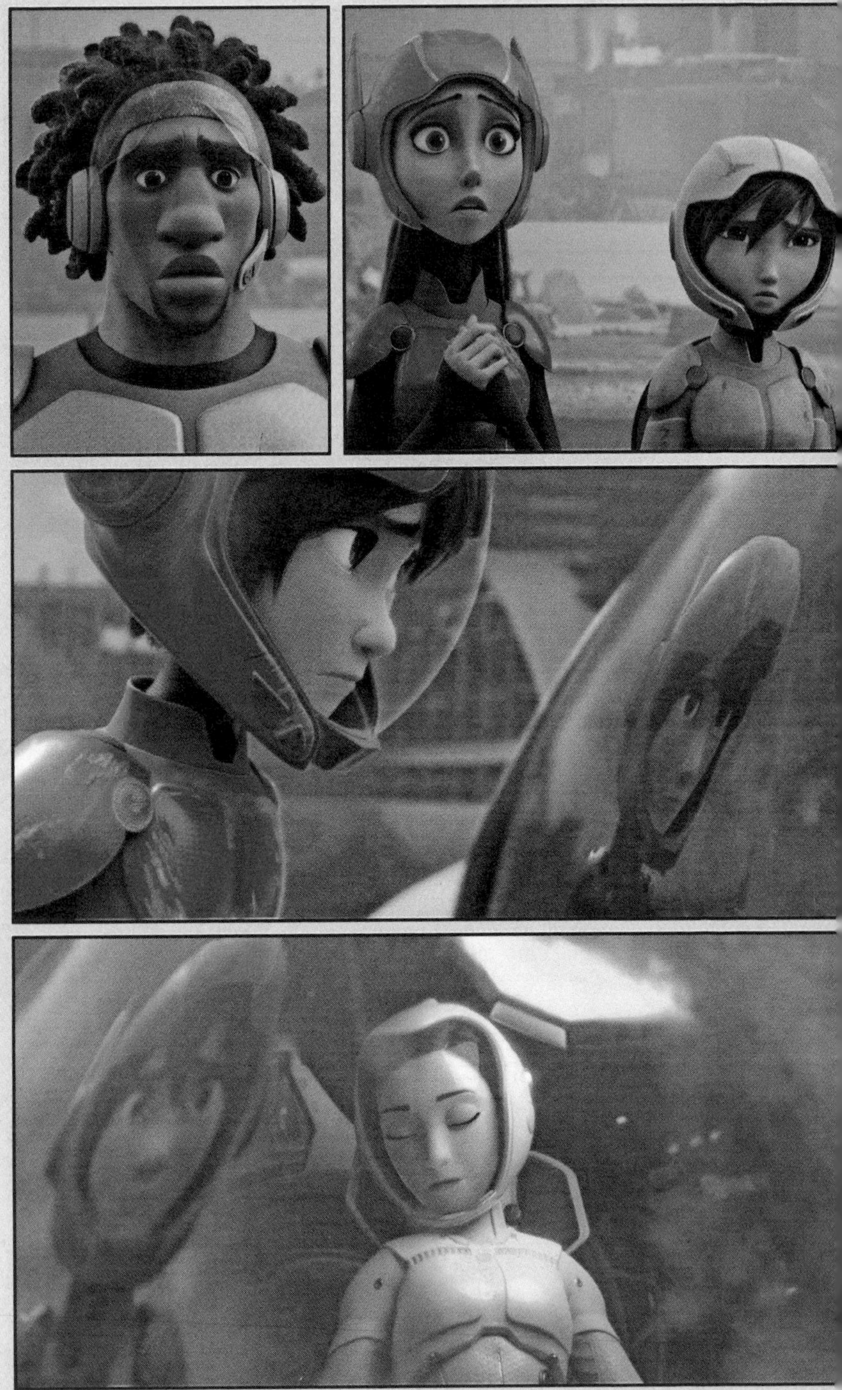

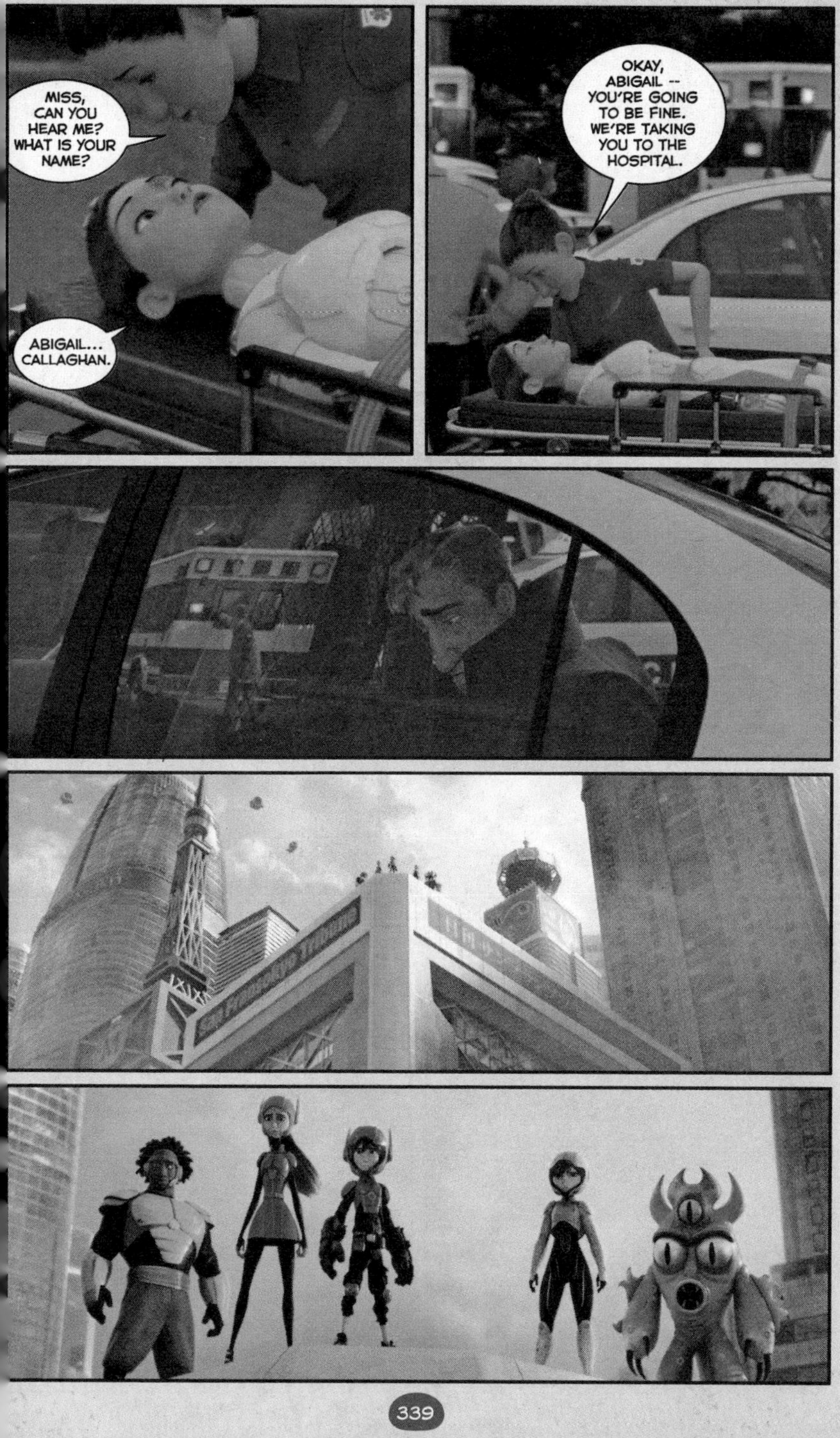
MISS, CAN YOU HEAR ME? WHAT IS YOUR NAME?
ABIGAIL... CALLAGHAN.
OKAY, ABIGAIL -- YOU'RE GOING TO BE FINE. WE'RE TAKING YOU TO THE HOSPITAL.

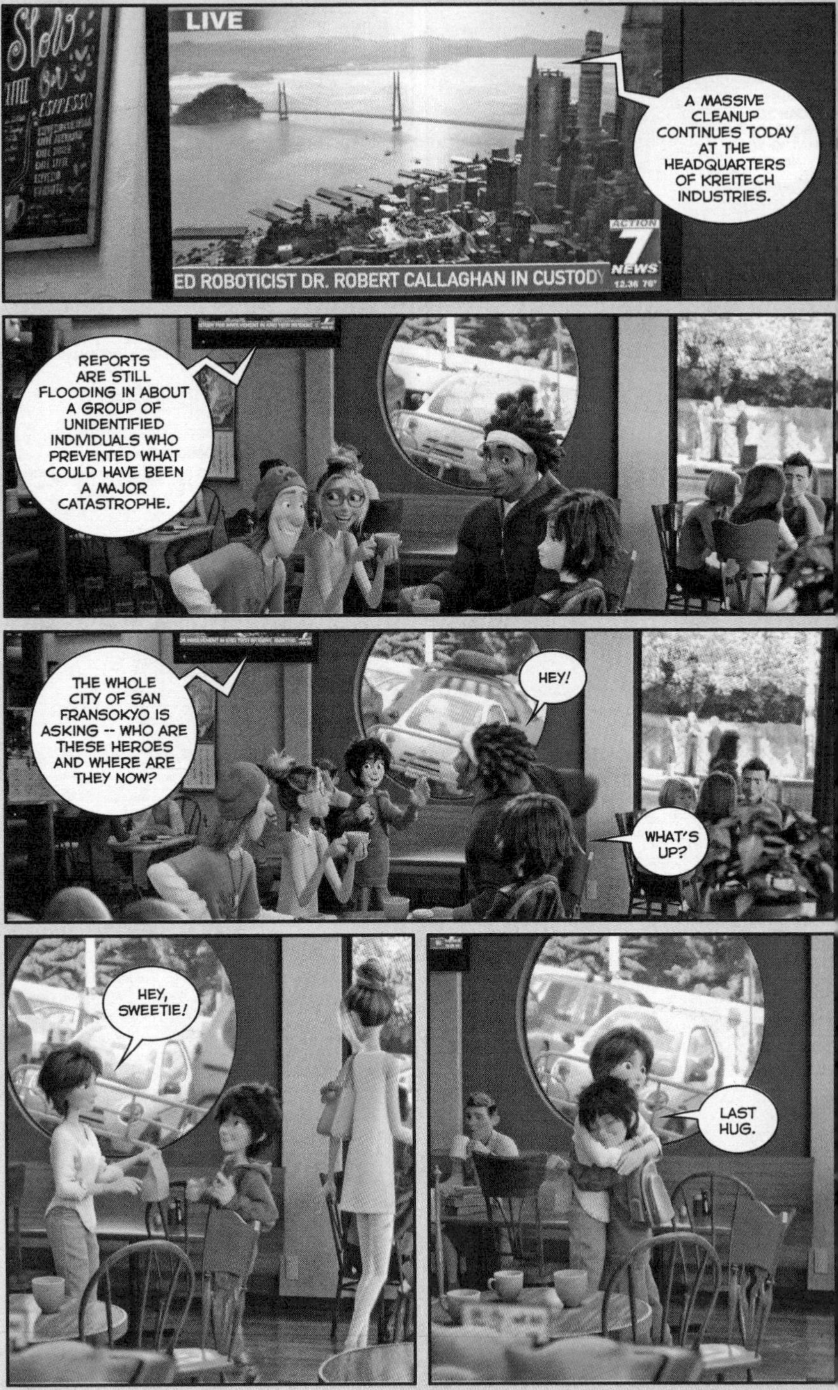
LIVE
A MASSIVE CLEANUP CONTINUES TODAY AT THE HEADQUARTERS OF KREITECH INDUSTRIES.
ACTION 7 NEWS
ED ROBOTICIST DR. ROBERT CALLAGHAN IN CUSTODY
REPORTS ARE STILL FLOODING IN ABOUT A GROUP OF UNIDENTIFIED INDIVIDUALS WHO PREVENTED WHAT COULD HAVE BEEN A MAJOR CATASTROPHE.
THE WHOLE CITY OF SAN FRANSOKYO IS ASKING -- WHO ARE THESE HEROES AND WHERE ARE THEY NOW?
HEY!
WHAT'S UP?
HEY, SWEETIE!
LAST HUG.

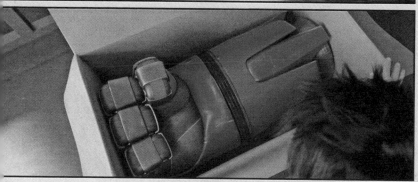

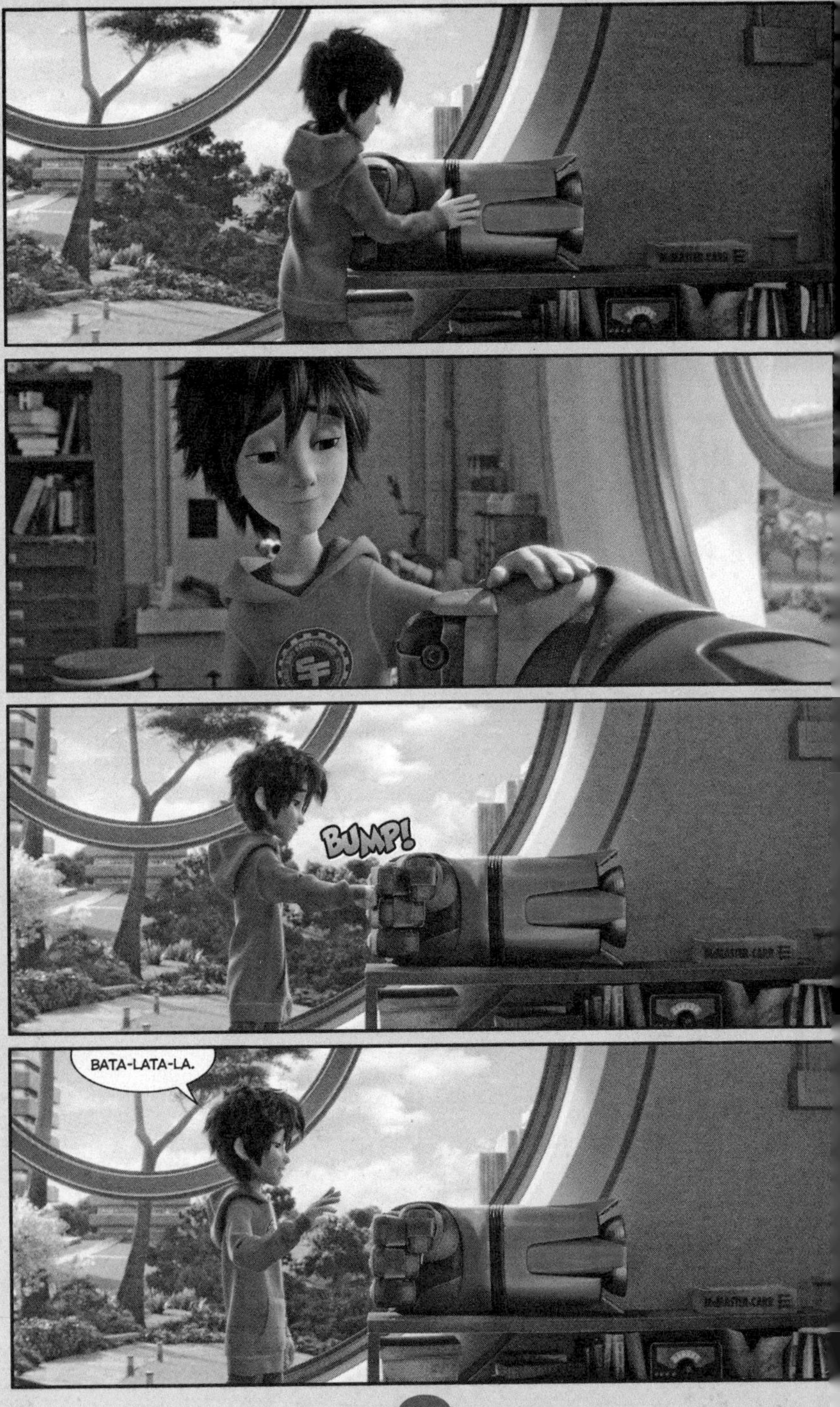
BUMP!
BATA-LATA-LA.

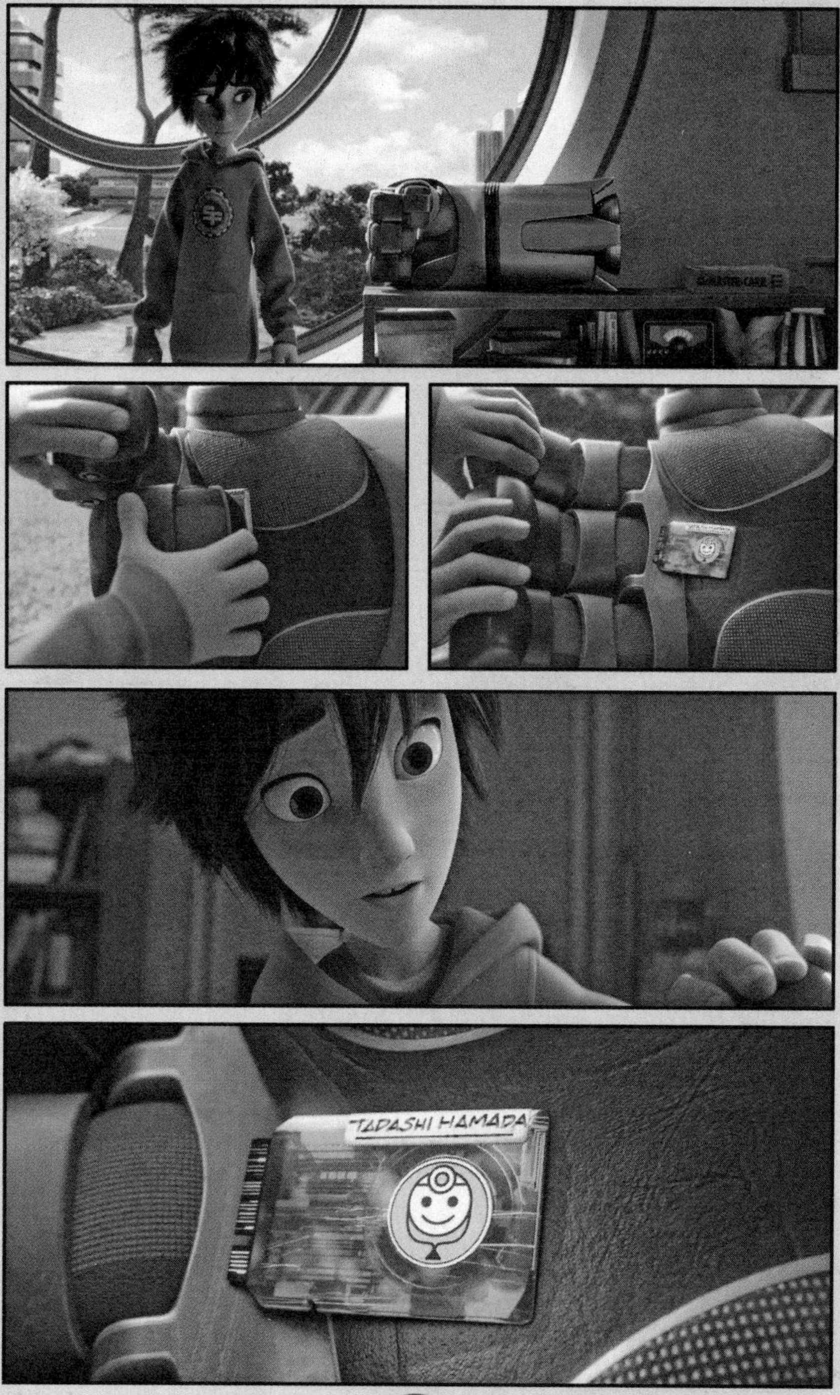
TADASHI HAMADA

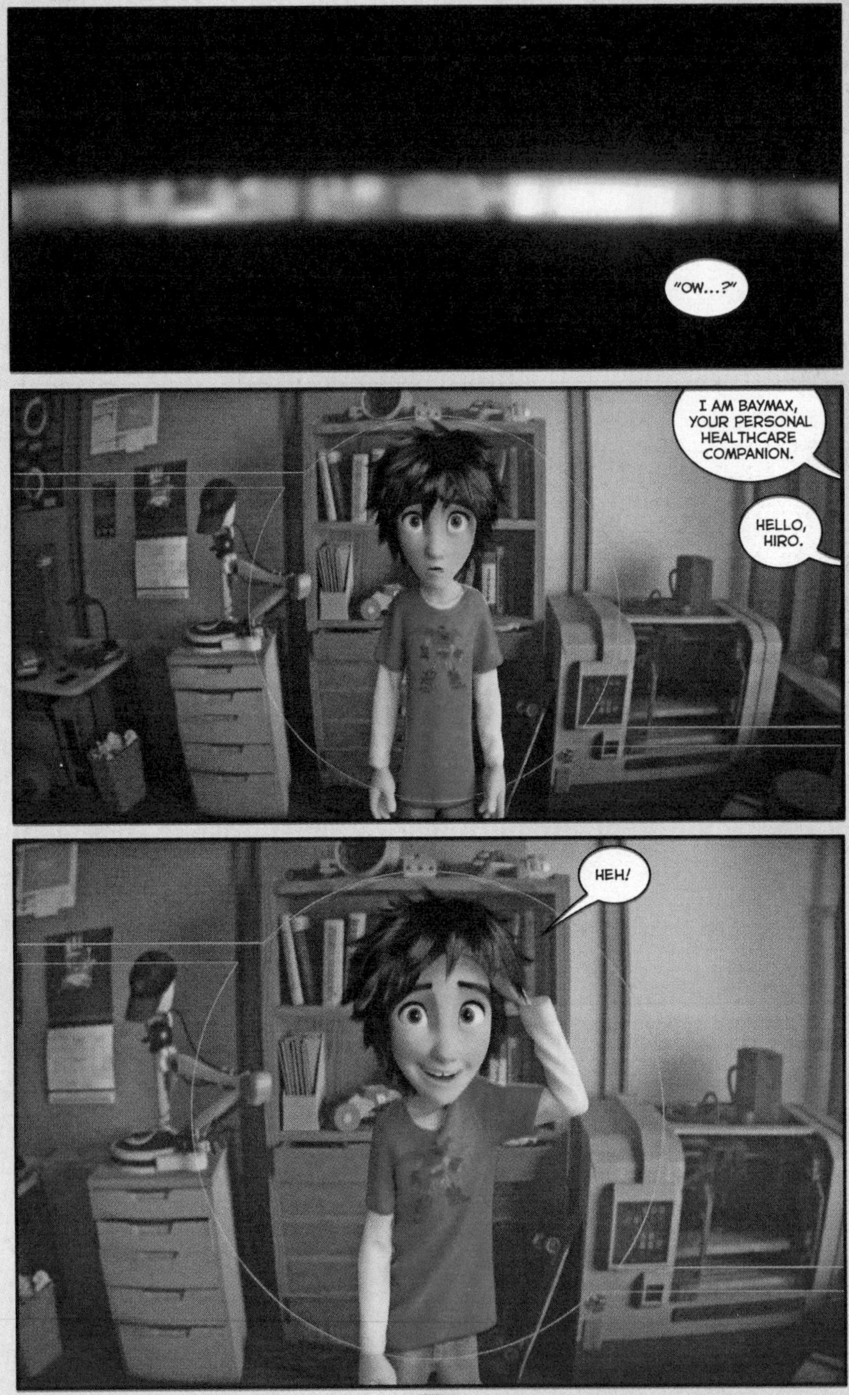
"OW...?"
I AM BAYMAX, YOUR PERSONAL HEALTHCARE COMPANION.
HELLO, HIRO.
HEH!

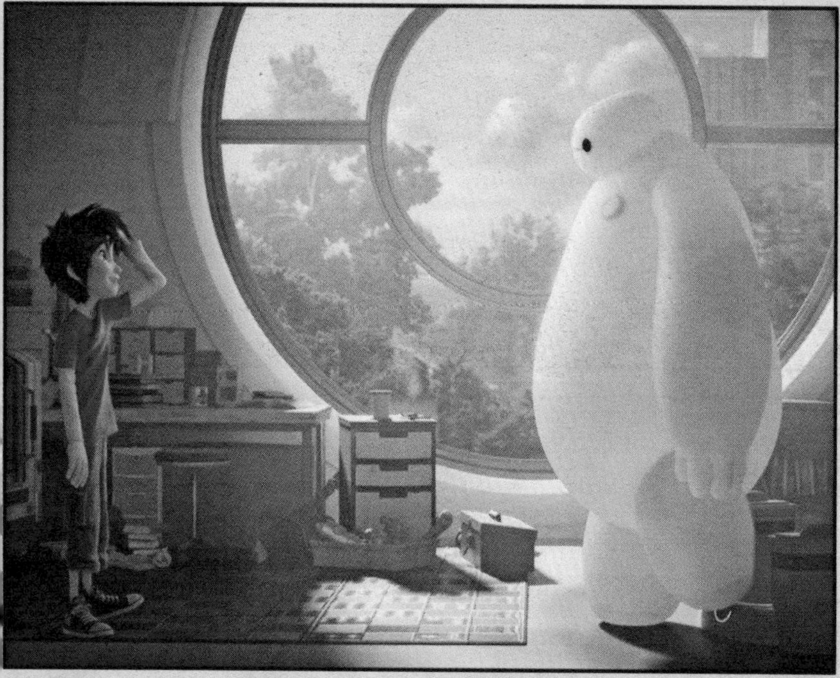

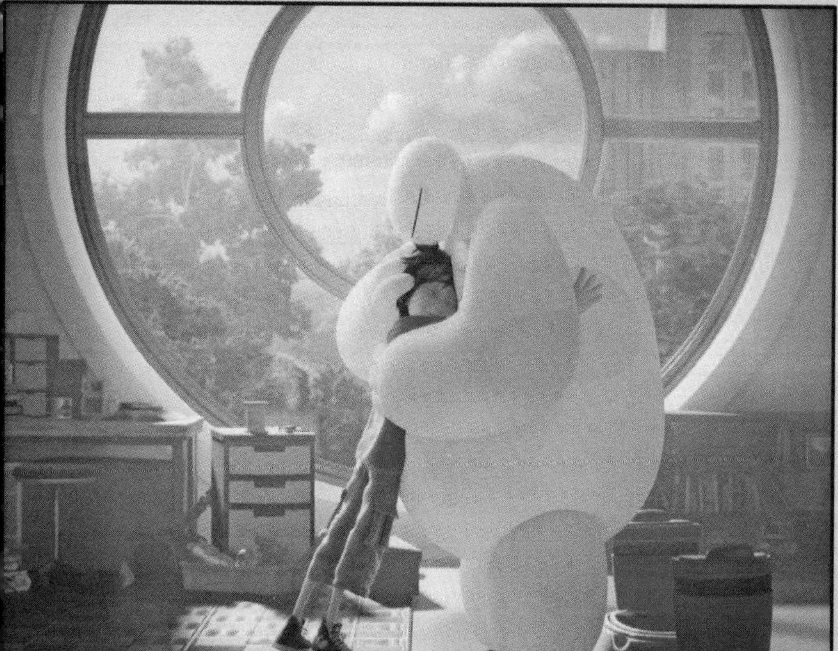

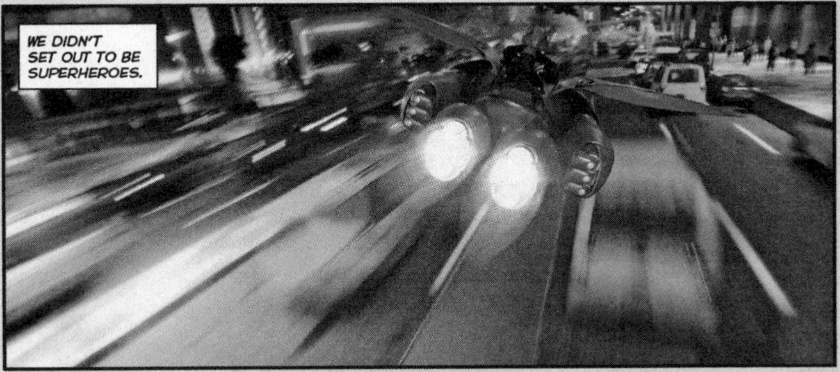
WE DIDN'T SET OUT TO BE SUPERHEROES.

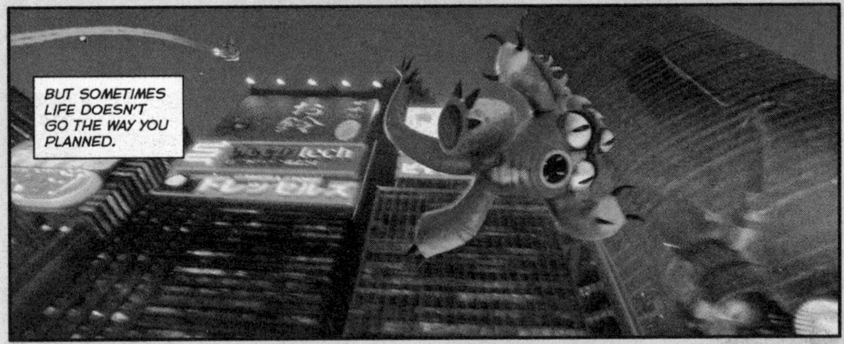
BUT SOMETIMES LIFE DOESN'T GO THE WAY YOU PLANNED.

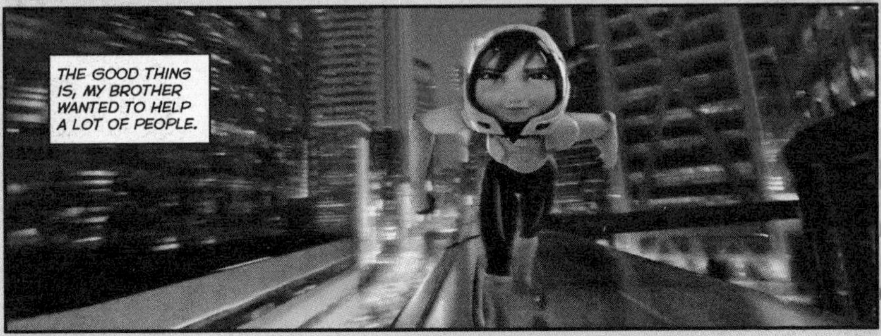
THE GOOD THING IS, MY BROTHER WANTED TO HELP A LOT OF PEOPLE.

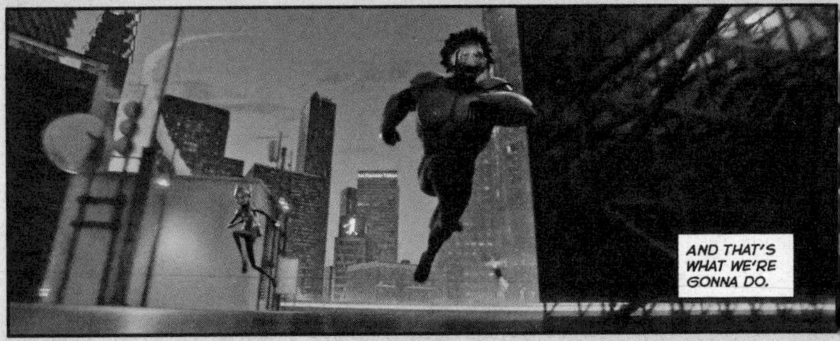
AND THAT'S WHAT WE'RE GONNA DO.

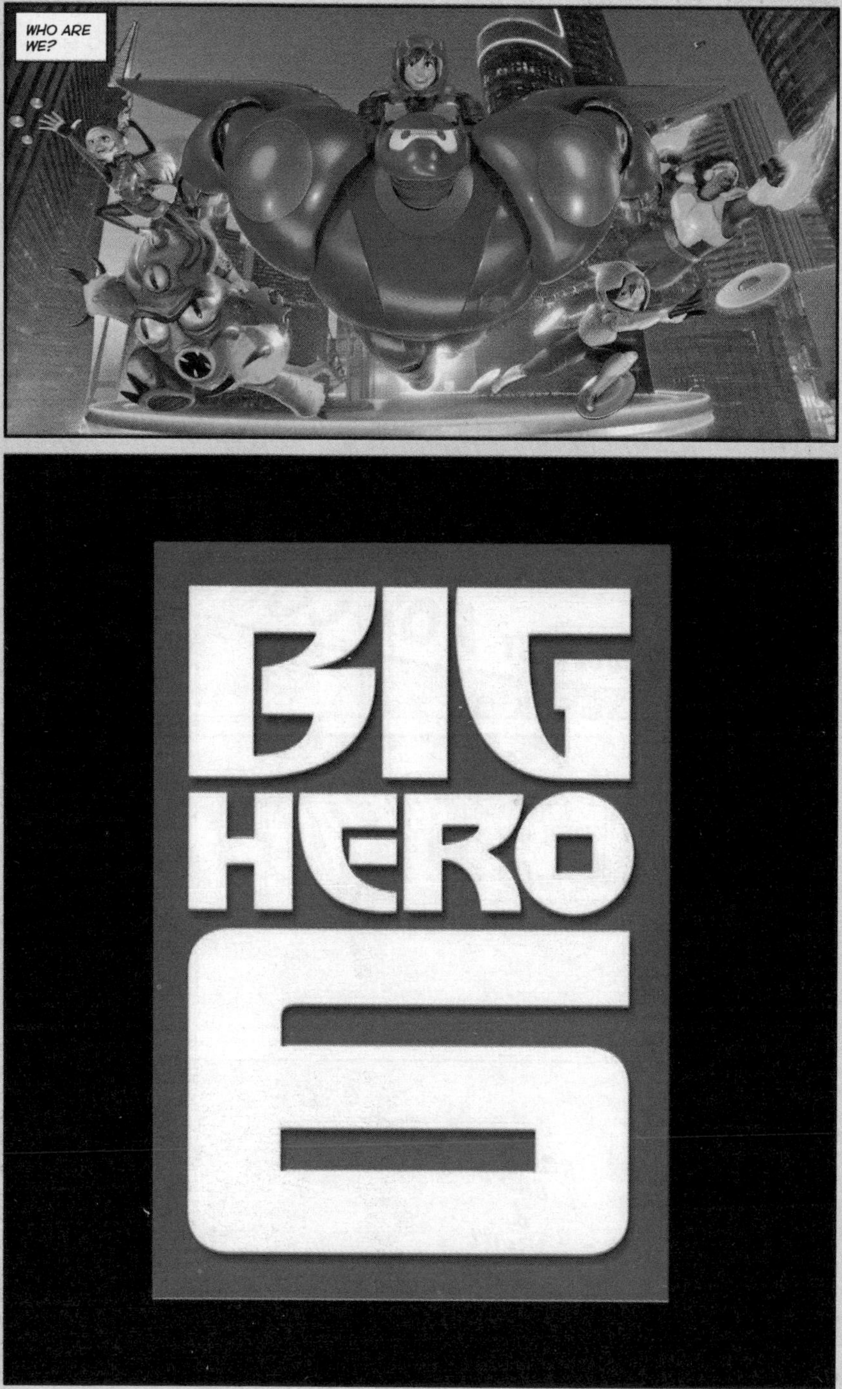
WHO ARE WE?
BIG HERO 6

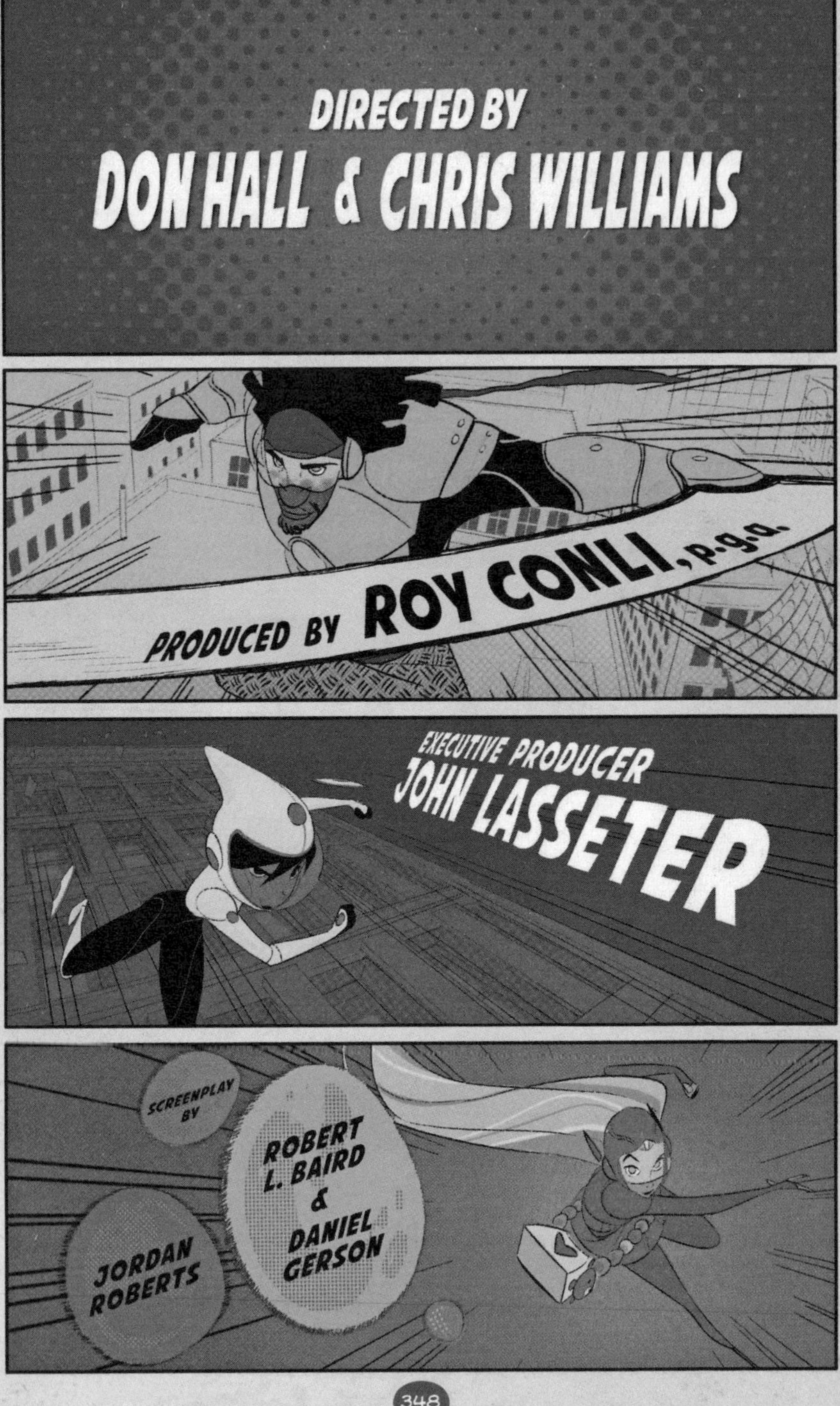
DIRECTED BY
DON HALL & CHRIS WILLIAMS
PRODUCED BY ROY CONLI, p.g.a.
EXECUTIVE PRODUCER
JOHN LASSETER
SCREENPLAY BY
ROBERT L. BAIRD & DANIEL GERSON
JORDAN ROBERTS

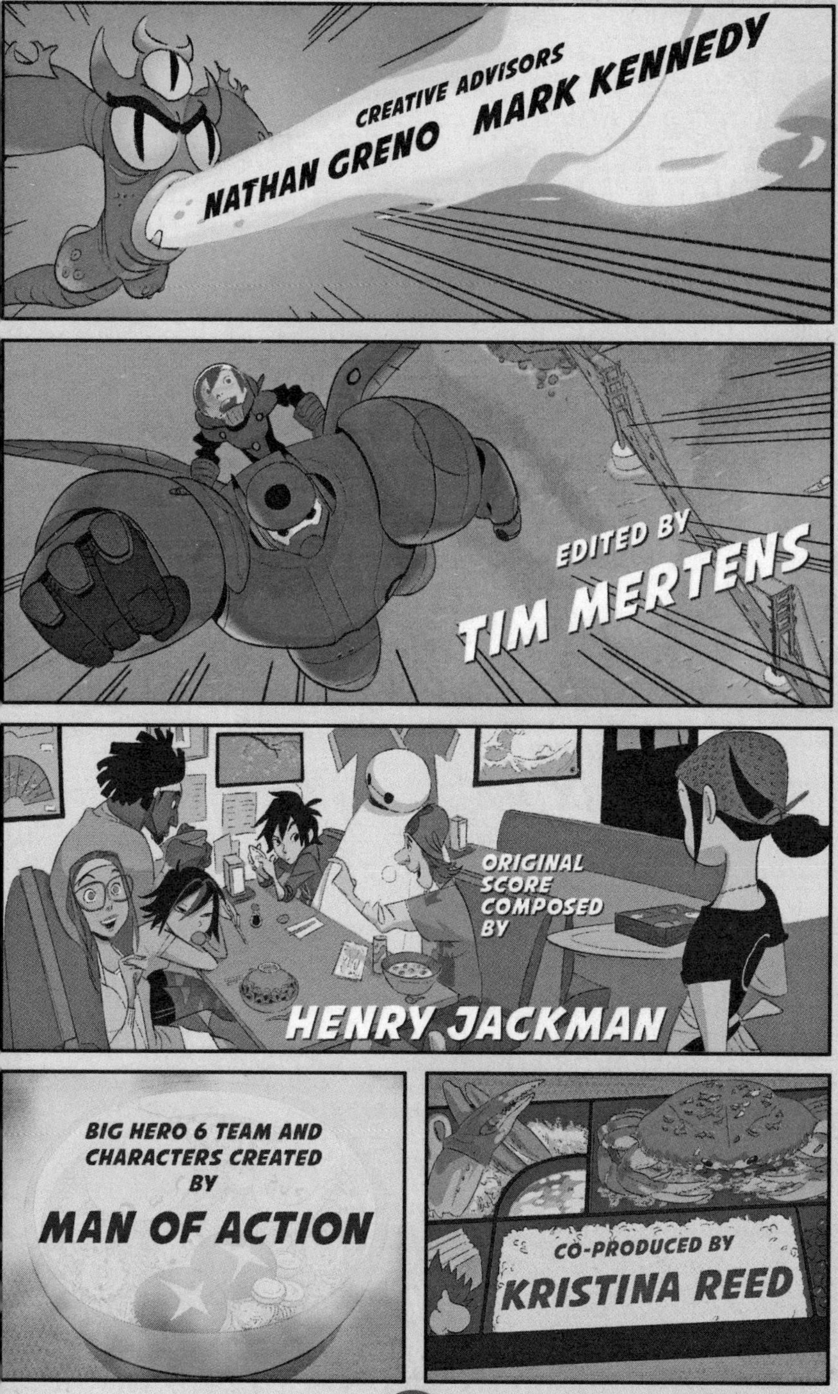
CREATIVE ADVISORS
NATHAN GRENO MARK KENNEDY
EDITED BY
TIM MERTENS
ORIGINAL SCORE COMPOSED BY
HENRY JACKMAN
BIG HERO 6 TEAM AND CHARACTERS CREATED BY
MAN OF ACTION
CO-PRODUCED BY
KRISTINA REED

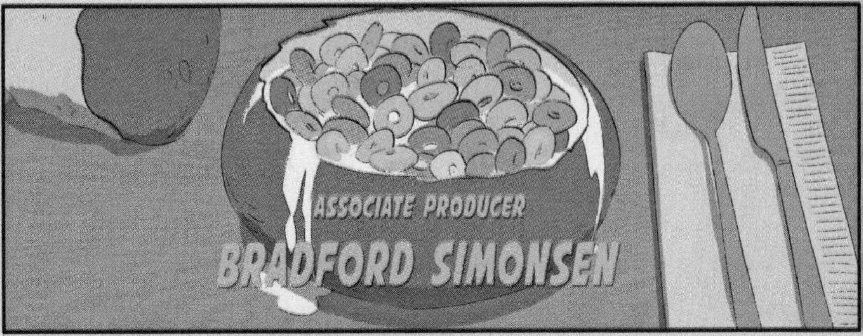
ASSOCIATE PRODUCER
BRADFORD SIMONSEN

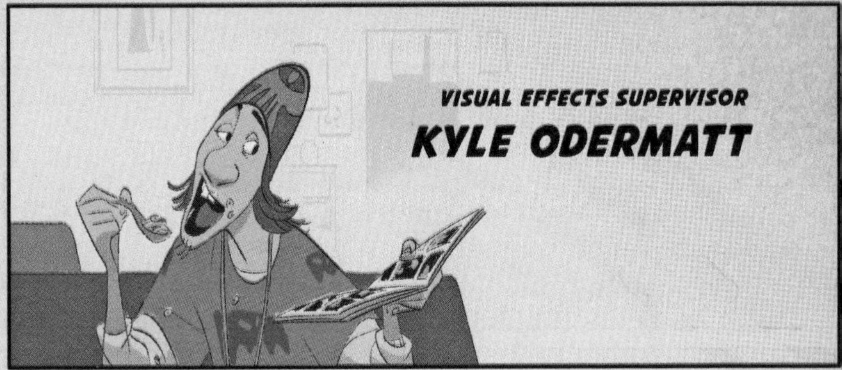
VISUAL EFFECTS SUPERVISOR
KYLE ODERMATT

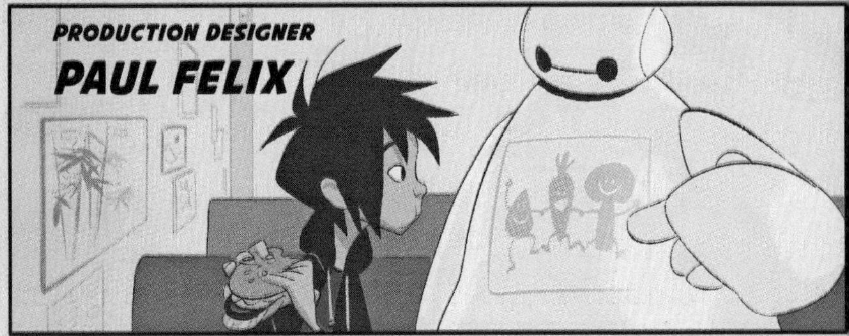
PRODUCTION DESIGNER
PAUL FELIX

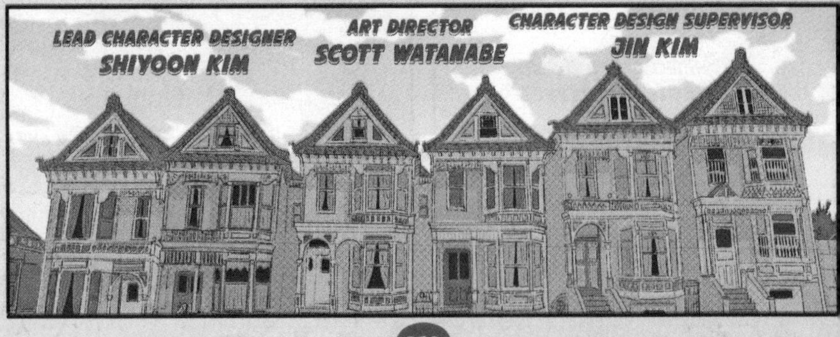
LEAD CHARACTER DESIGNER
SHIYOON KIM
ART DIRECTOR
SCOTT WATANABE
CHARACTER DESIGN SUPERVISOR
JIN KIM

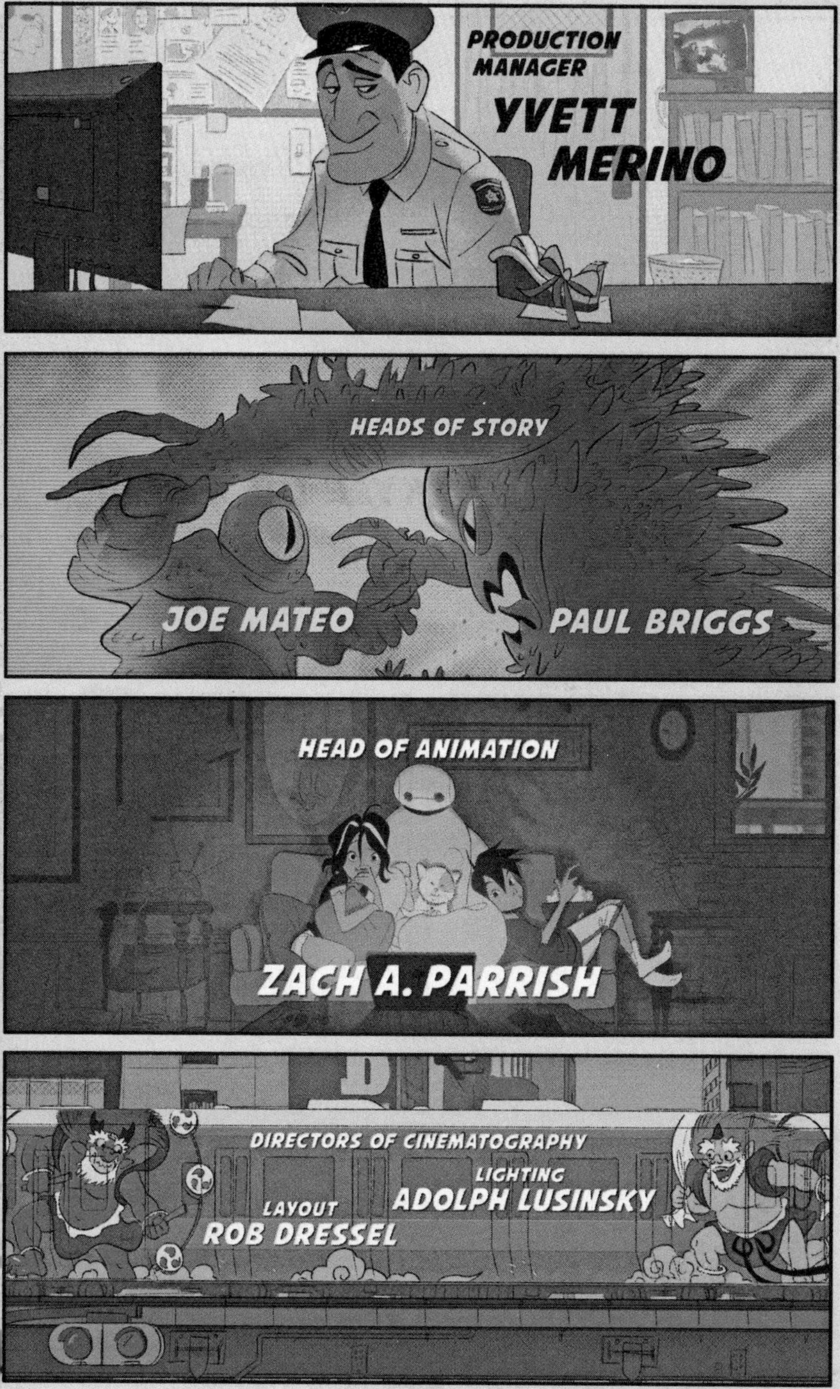
PRODUCTION MANAGER
YVETT MERINO
HEADS OF STORY
JOE MATEO
PAUL BRIGGS
HEAD OF ANIMATION
ZACH A. PARRISH
DIRECTORS OF CINEMATOGRAPHY
LIGHTING
ADOLPH LUSINSKY
LAYOUT
ROB DRESSEL

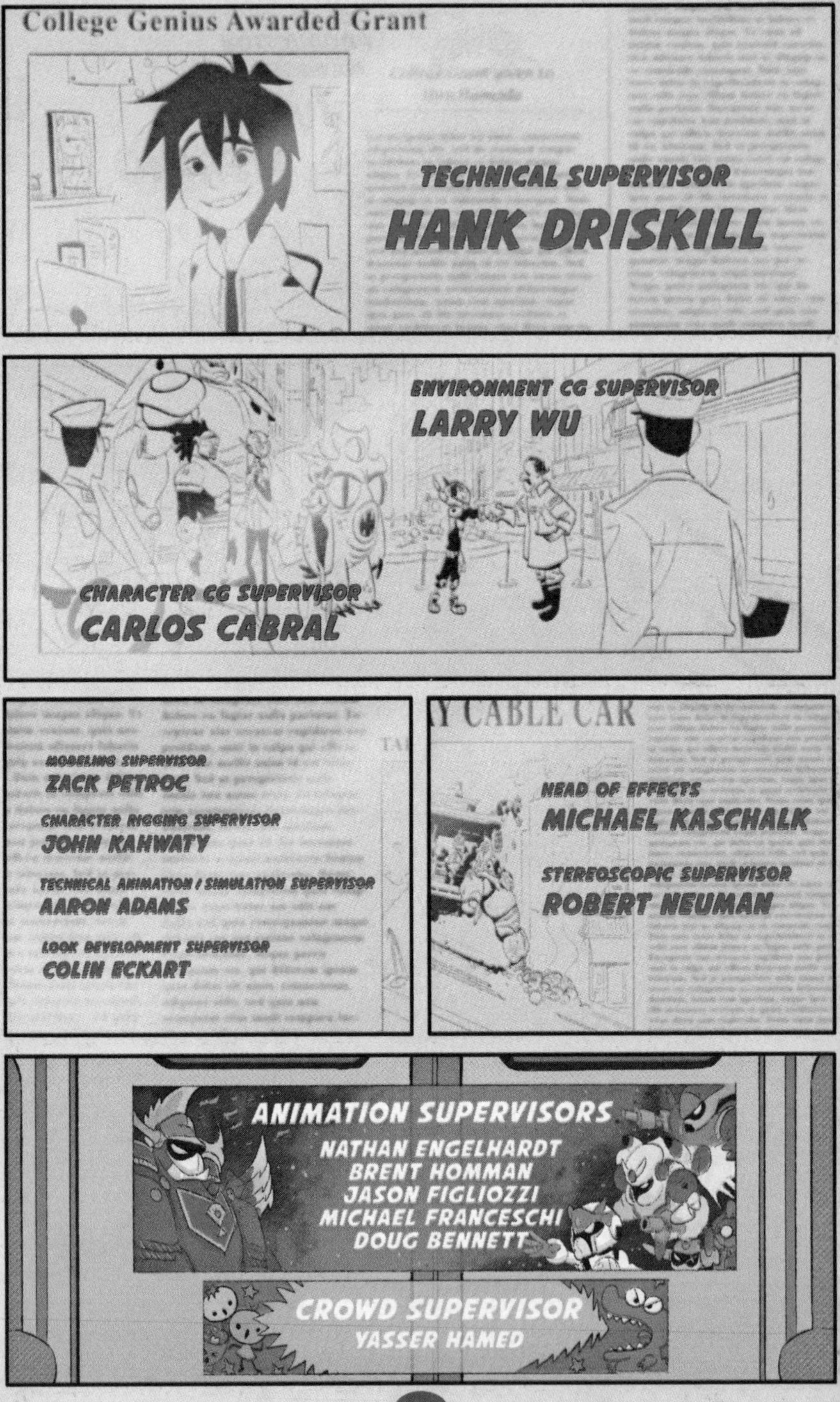
College Genius Awarded Grant
TECHNICAL SUPERVISOR
HANK DRISKILL
ENVIRONMENT CG SUPERVISOR
LARRY WU
CHARACTER CG SUPERVISOR
CARLOS CABRAL
MODELING SUPERVISOR
ZACK PETROC
CHARACTER RIGGING SUPERVISOR
JOHN KAHWATY
TECHNICAL ANIMATION / SIMULATION SUPERVISOR
AARON ADAMS
LOOK DEVELOPMENT SUPERVISOR
COLIN ECKART
Y CABLE CAR
HEAD OF EFFECTS
MICHAEL KASCHALK
STEREOSCOPIC SUPERVISOR
ROBERT NEUMAN
ANIMATION SUPERVISORS
NATHAN ENGELHARDT
BRENT HOMMAN
JASON FIGLIOZZI
MICHAEL FRANCESCHI
DOUG BENNETT
CROWD SUPERVISOR
YASSER HAMED

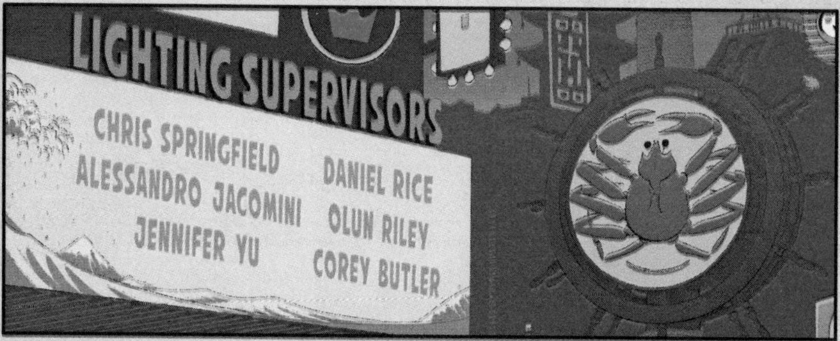
LIGHTING SUPERVISORS
CHRIS SPRINGFIELD
ALESSANDRO JACOMINI
JENNIFER YU
DANIEL RICE
OLUN RILEY
COREY BUTLER

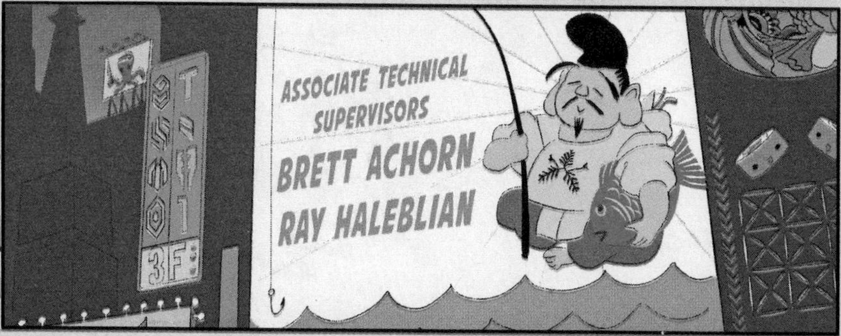
ASSOCIATE TECHNICAL SUPERVISORS
BRETT ACHORN
RAY HALEBLIAN

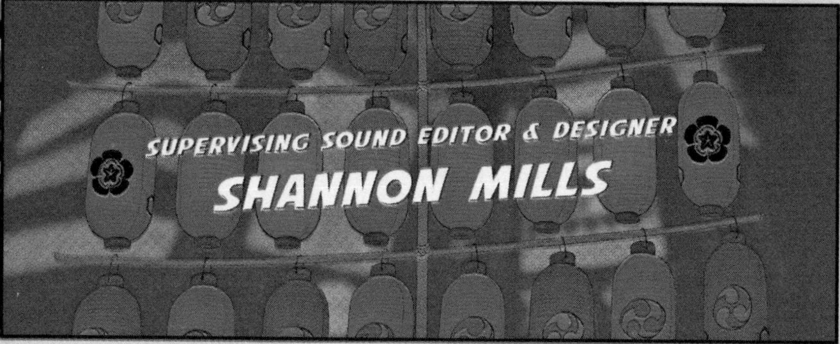
SUPERVISING SOUND EDITOR & DESIGNER
SHANNON MILLS

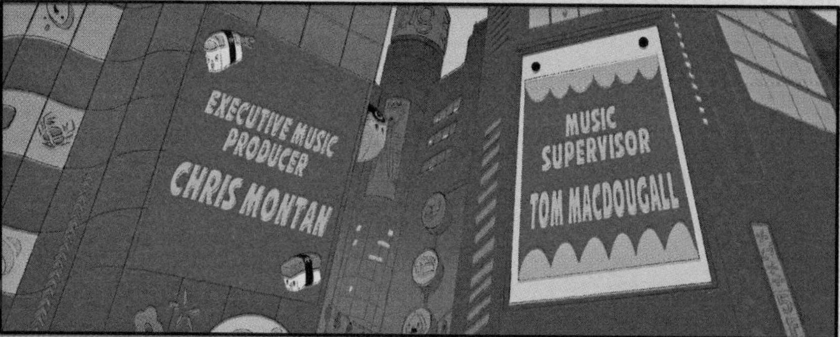
EXECUTIVE MUSIC PRODUCER
CHRIS MONTAN
MUSIC SUPERVISOR
TOM MACDOUGALL

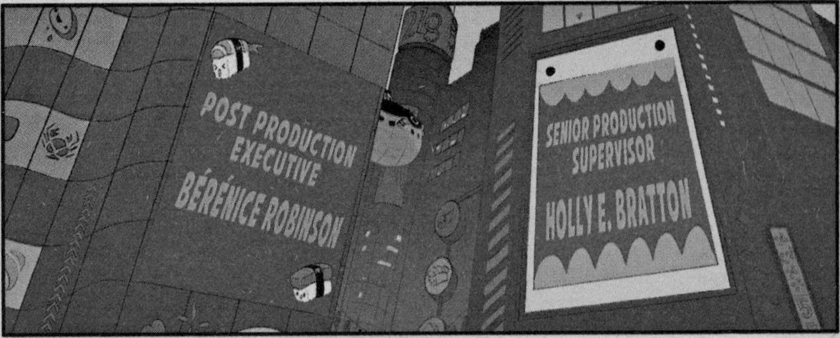
POST PRODUCTION EXECUTIVE
BÉRÉNICE ROBINSON
SENIOR PRODUCTION SUPERVISOR
HOLLY E. BRATTON

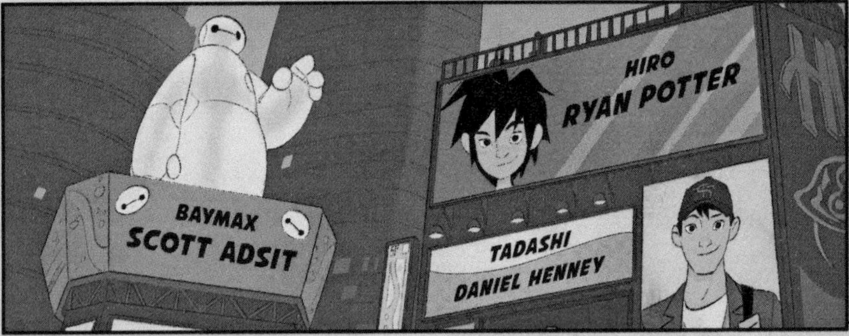
HIRO
RYAN POTTER
BAYMAX
SCOTT ADSIT
TADASHI
DANIEL HENNEY

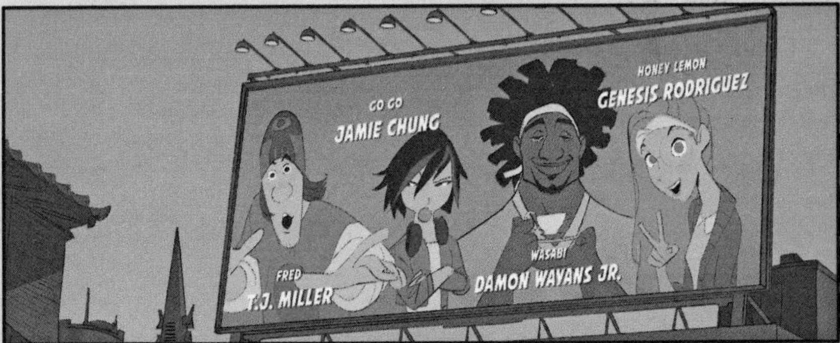
GO GO
JAMIE CHUNG
HONEY LEMON
GENESIS RODRIGUEZ
FRED
T.J. MILLER
WASABI
DAMON WAYANS JR.

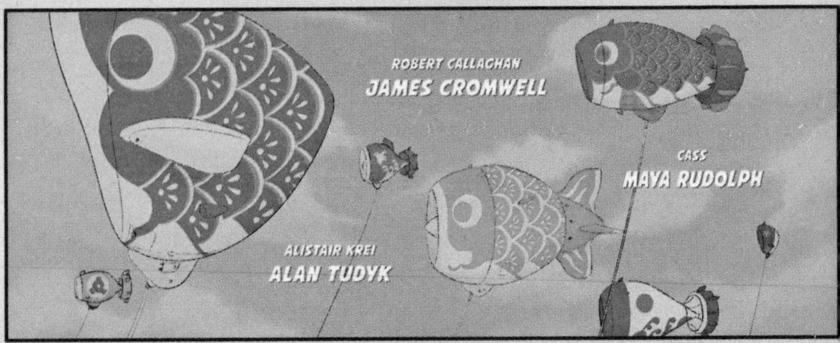
ROBERT CALLAGHAN
JAMES CROMWELL
CASS
MAYA RUDOLPH
ALISTAIR KREI
ALAN TUDYK

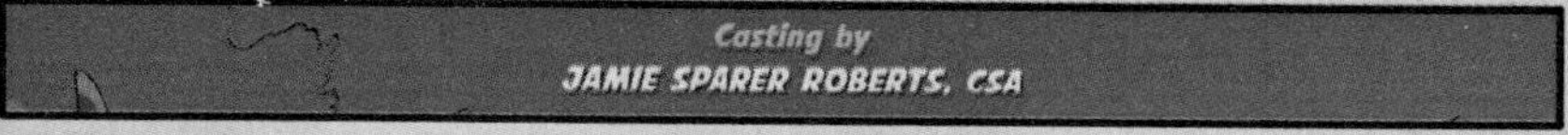
Casting by
JAMIE SPARER ROBERTS, CSA

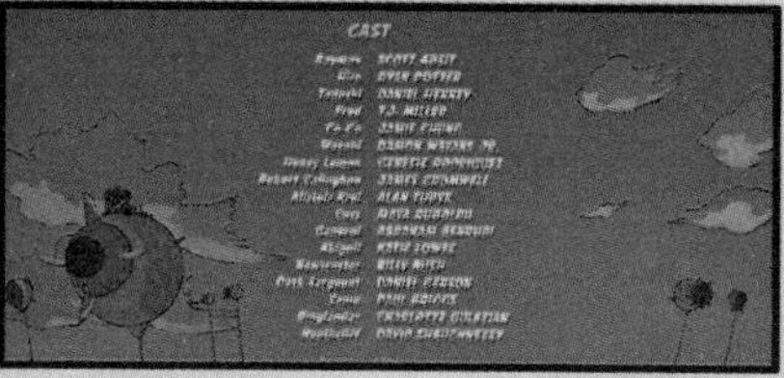
CAST

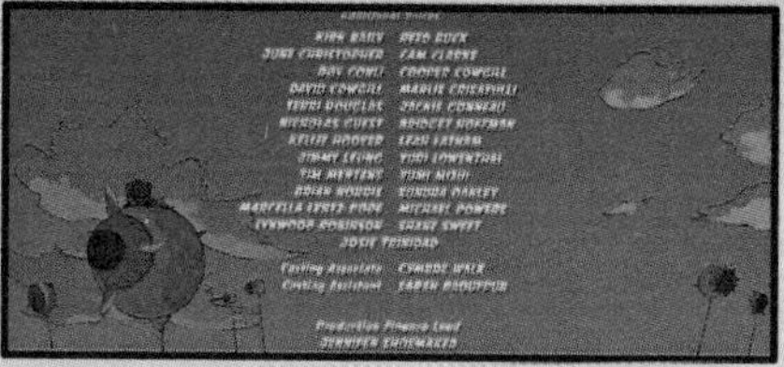
KIRK BAILY REED BUCK
JUNE CHRISTOPHER CAM CLARKE
ROY CONLI COOPER COWGILL
DAVID COWGILL MARLIE CRISAFULLI
TERRI DOUGLAS
NICHOLAS GUEST BRIDGET HOFFMAN
KELLY HOOVER LEAH LATHAM
JIMMY LEUNG YURI LOWENTHAL
TIM MERTENS YUMI MIZUI
MARCELLA LENTZ-POPE MICHAEL POWERS
LYNWOOD ROBINSON SHANE SWEET
JOSIE TRINIDAD

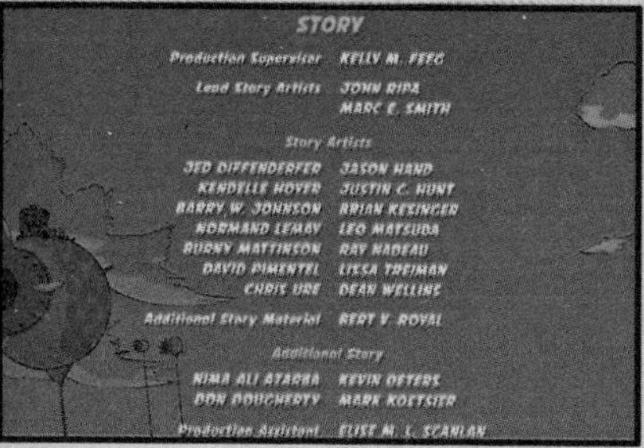
STORY
Production Supervisor KELLY M. FEEG
Lead Story Artists JOHN RIPA
MARC E. SMITH
Story Artists
JED DIFFENDERFER JASON HAND
KENDELLE HOYER JUSTIN C. HUNT
BARRY W. JOHNSON BRIAN KESINGER
NORMAND LEMAY LEO MATSUDA
BURNY MATTINSON RAY NADEAU
DAVID PIMENTEL LISSA TREIMAN
CHRIS URE DEAN WELLINS
Additional Story Material BERT V. ROYAL
Additional Story
NIMA ALI ATARBA KEVIN DETERS
DON DOUGHERTY MARK KOETSIER
Production Assistant ELISE M. L. SCANLAN

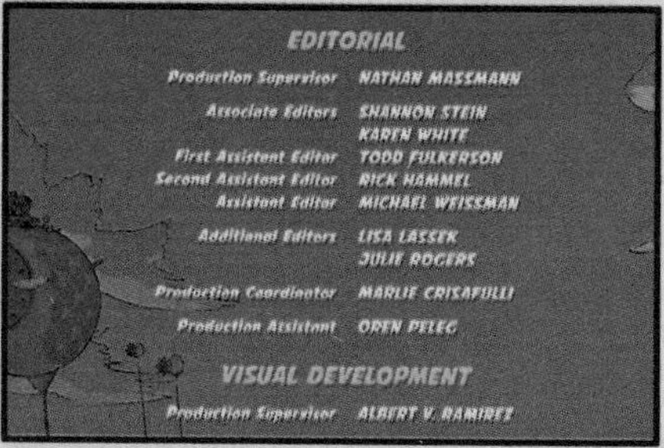
EDITORIAL
Production Supervisor NATHAN MASSMANN
Associate Editors SHANNON STEIN
KAREN WHITE
First Assistant Editor TODD FULKERSON
Second Assistant Editor RICK HAMMEL
Assistant Editor MICHAEL WEISSMAN
Additional Editors LISA LASSEK
JULIE ROGERS
Production Coordinator MARLIE CRISAFULLI
Production Assistant OREN PELEG
VISUAL DEVELOPMENT
Production Supervisor ALBERT V. RAMIREZ

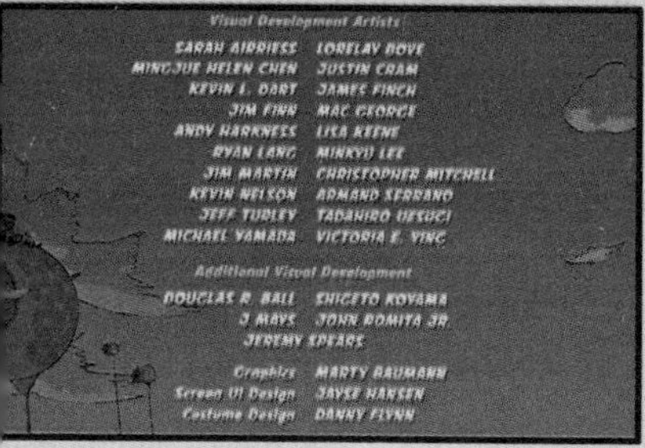
Visual Development Artists
SARAH AIRRIESS LORELAY BOVE
MINGJUE HELEN CHEN JUSTIN CRAM
KEVIN L. DART JAMES FINCH
JIM FINN MAC GEORGE
ANDY HARKNESS LISA KEENE
RYAN LANG MINKYU LEE
JIM MARTIN CHRISTOPHER MITCHELL
KEVIN NELSON ARMAND SERRANO
JEFF TURLEY TADAHIRO UESUGI
MICHAEL YAMADA VICTORIA E. YING
Additional Visual Development
DOUGLAS R. BALL SHIGETO KOYAMA
J MAYS JOHN ROMITA JR.
JEREMY SPEARS
Graphics MARTY BAUMANN
Screen UI Design JAYSE HANSEN
Costume Design DANNY FLYNN

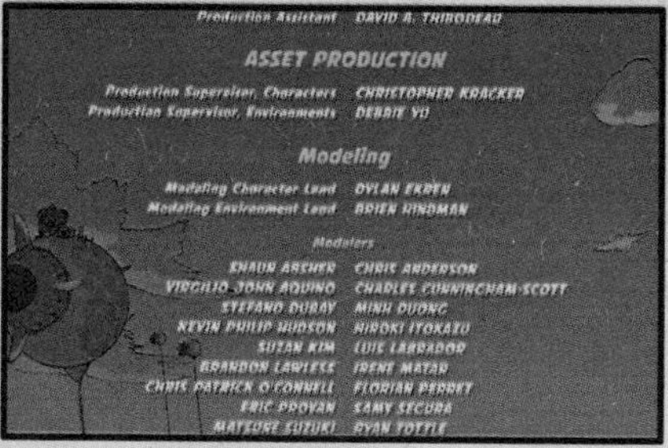
Production Assistant DAVID A. THIBODEAU
ASSET PRODUCTION
Production Supervisor, Characters CHRISTOPHER KRACKER
Production Supervisor, Environments DEBBIE YU
Modeling
Modeling Character Lead DYLAN EKREN
Modeling Environment Lead BRIEN HINDMAN
Modelers
SHAUN ABSHER CHRIS ANDERSON
VIRGILIO JOHN AQUINO CHARLES CUNNINGHAM-SCOTT
STEFANO DUBAY MINH DUONG
KEVIN PHILIP HUDSON HIROKI ITOKAZU
SUZAN KIM LUIS LABRADOR
BRANDON LAWLESS IRENE MATAR
CHRIS PATRICK O'CONNELL FLORIAN PERRET
ERIC PROVAN SAMY SEGURA
MATSUNE SUZUKI RYAN TOTTLE

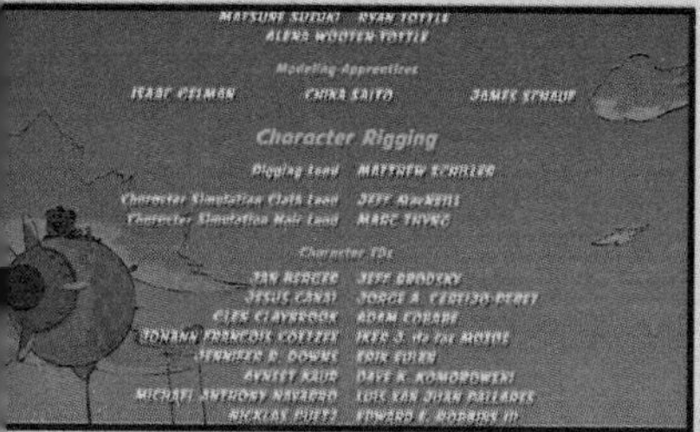
MATSUNE SUZUKI RYAN TOTTLE
ALENA WOOTEN-TOTTLE
Modeling Apprentices
ISAAC CELMAN CHIKA SAITO JAMES STRAUF
Character Rigging
Rigging Lead MATTHEW SCHILLER
Character Simulation Cloth Lead JEFF ALACNEILL
Character Simulation Hair Lead MARC THYNG
Character TDs
JAN BERGER JEFF BRODSKY
JESUS CANAL JORGE A. CEREIJO-PEREZ
GLEN CLAYBROOK ADAM CORABE
JOHANN FRANCOIS COETZEE IKER J. DE LOS MOZOS
JENNIFER R. DOWNS ERIK EULEN
AVNEET KAUR DAVE K. KOMOROWSKI
MICHAEL ANTHONY NAVARRO LUIS SAN JUAN PALLARES
NICKLAS PUETZ EDWARD E. ROBBINS III

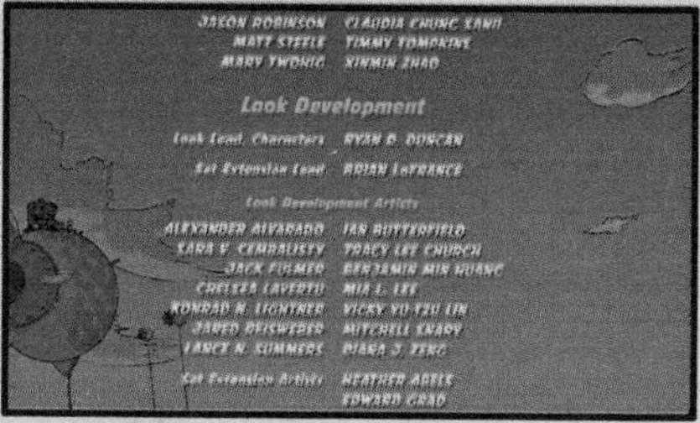
JASON ROBINSON CLAUDIA CHUNG SANII
MATT STEELE TIMMY TOMPKINS
MARY TWOHIG XINMIN ZHAO
Look Development
Look Lead, Characters RYAN D. DUNCAN
Set Extension Lead BRIAN LeFRANCE
Look Development Artists
ALEXANDER ALVARADO IAN BUTTERFIELD
SARA V. CEMBALISTY TRACY LEE CHURCH
JACK FULMER BENJAMIN MIN HUANG
CHELSEA LAVERTU MIA L. LEE
KONRAD R. LIGHTNER VICKY YU-TZU LIN
JARED REISWEBER MITCHELL SNARY
LANCE N. SUMMERS DIANA J. ZENG
Set Extension Artists HEATHER ABELS
EDWARD GRAD

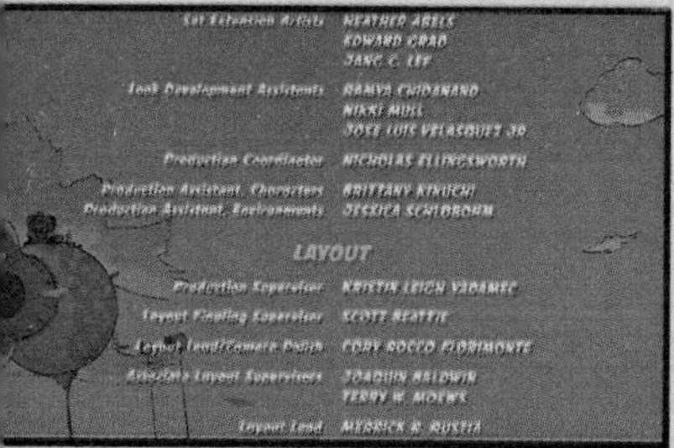
Set Extension Artists HEATHER ABELS
EDWARD GRAD
JANG C. LEE
Look Development Assistants RAMYA CHIDANAND
NIKKI MULL
JOSE LUIS VELASQUEZ JR.
Production Coordinator NICHOLAS ELLINGSWORTH
Production Assistant, Characters BRITTANY KIKUCHI
Production Assistant, Environments JESSICA SCHLOBOHM
LAYOUT
Production Supervisor KRISTIN LEIGH YADAMEC
Layout Finaling Supervisor SCOTT BEATTIE
Layout Lead/Camera Polish CORY ROCCO FLORIMONTE
Associate Layout Supervisors JOAQUIN BALDWIN
TERRY W. MOEWS
Layout Lead MERRICK R. RUSTIA

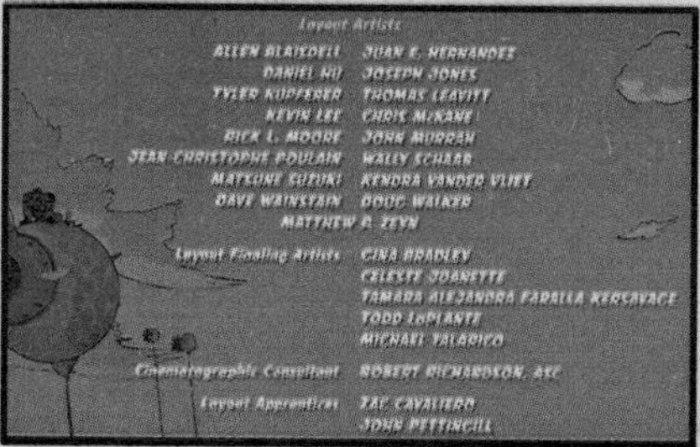
Layout Artists
ALLEN BLAISDELL JUAN E. HERNANDEZ
DANIEL HU JOSEPH JONES
TYLER KUPFERER THOMAS LEAVITT
KEVIN LEE CHRIS McKANE
RICK L. MOORE JOHN MURRAH
JEAN-CHRISTOPHE POULAIN WALLY SCHAAB
MATSUNE SUZUKI KENDRA VANDER VLIET
DAVE WAINSTAIN DOUG WALKER
MATTHEW R. ZEYN
Layout Finaling Artists GINA BRADLEY
CELESTE JOANETTE
TAMARA ALEJANDRA FARALLA KERSAVAGE
TODD LaPLANTE
MICHAEL TALARICO
Cinematographic Consultant ROBERT RICHARDSON, ASC
Layout Apprentices ZAC CAVALIERO
JOHN PETTINGILL

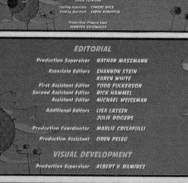

Layout Apprentices ZAC CAVALIERO
JOHN PETTINGILL
LINDSEY ST. PIERRE

Layout TDs MIKE HARRIS
JEFF SADLER
SHWETA VISWANATHAN

Production Coordinator ALLISON OSBORNE

Production Assistants DANIELLE BEVERSON
JAMES ROMO

ANIMATION

Lead Production Supervisor KAREN RYAN

Production Supervisor TUCKER GILMORE

Lead 2D Animator MARK HENN

Animators

ALBERTO ABRIL   ABRAHAM AGUILAR   DAN BARKER
GUILLAUME BELANGER   TONY BONILLA   REBECCA WILSON BRESSE

DARRIN BUTTERS   ANDREW CHESWORTH   YOUNGJAE CHOI
SHAWN CLARK   CHRISTOPHER CORDINGLEY   RAHUL DABHOLKAR
PATRICK DANAHER   MARAT DAVLETSHIN   RIANNON DELANOV
VALENTIN AMADOR DIAZ   DANIEL EDWARDS   JEFFREY ENGEL
ANDREW FELICIANO   CHADD FERRON   MARIO FURMANCZYK
MINOR JOSE GAYTAN   DANIEL GONZALES III   EMILIE COULET
ADAM GREEN   RYAN HOBBIERBURKEN   DARRELL JOHNSON
MACK KABLAN   BERT KLEIN   MICHAEL KLIM
DANIEL JAMES KLUG   CALLUM LaPRAIRIE   ANDREW LAWSON
HYUN-MIN LEE   DAVID LISRE   KEVIN MacLEAN
KELLY McCLANAHAN   BRIAN F. MENZ   MATTHEW MEYER
MARK MITCHELL   KYLE MOHR   MARLON HOWE
PATRICK OSBORNE   RYAN PAGE   DANIEL MARTIN PEIXE
MALCOM B. PIERCE III   BOBBY PONTILLAS   NICOLAS PROTHAIS
MITJA BARAD   SVETLA RADIVOEVA   JOEL REID
GREGORY RIZZI   RURKE ROANE   JASON RYAN
FRANK SACCO   BRIAN SCOTT   BENSON SHUM
JUSTIN SKLAR   JOSHUA SLICE   AMY LAWSON SMEED
ALEXANDER SNOW   CHRISTIAN EO   RASTKO STEFANOVIĆ
WAYNE UNTEN   JOHN VASSALLO   LESLIE WATTERS

GEOFFREY WHEELER   MARK WILLIAMS   JEFF WILLIAMS
JOHN WONG   MICHAEL WOODSIDE   NARA YOUN
                       SHAOFU ZHANG

Animating Assistants

FRANK E. ABNEY III   JORGE E. RUIZ CANO
TONY CHAU   TRENT CORREY
JORGE GARCIA   AMANDA WAGNER
                      JUSTIN WEBER

Animation Apprentices

KITTY LAI CHING FUNG   ALA'A ABU HANISH
KIM HAZEL   YUNG H. PHAM
                      JOON SHIK SONG

Animation TDs

FABRICE CEUGNIET   SUMIT DAS
CHRISTOPHER OTTO GALLAGHER   NATT MINTRASAK
          REBECCA VALLERA-THOMPSON

Production Coordinators BRANDON HOLMES
MONICA FOROUZESH
SAMMY PERLMUTTER

Production Assistants MADISON BOEHME
JOE ORLANDO

TECHNICAL ANIMATION

Production Supervisor DAVE KOHUT

Associate Technical Animation Supervisors HUBERT LEO
CHRISTOPHER EVART

Technical Animation Artists

ARTURO AGUILAR   KATHLEEN M. BAILEY   COREY BOLWYN
AARON CAMPBELL   GLEN CLAYBROOK   JOHANN FRANCOIS COETZEE
MITCHELL COUNSELL   IKER J. de los MOZOS   MARK EMPEY
GARRETT C. EVES   JAY CAMBELL   FRANK HANNED
ROSE IBANHA   ANDREW JENNINGS   WILLIAM D. KASTAK
KI-NYUNG KIM   KATE KIRBY-O'CONNELL   IAN KREBS-SMITH
ADAM REED LEVY   PETE MEGOW   MICHAEL ANTHONY NAVARRO

MAIA NEUBIG   SCOTT PETERS   NAVIN MARTIN PINTO
GARRETT RAINE   JASON ROBINSON   ANDY ROMINE
JOSH SOBEL   JASON STELLWAG   MICHAEL W. STIEBER
JOHN TRUONG   MARY TWOHIG   RICHARD M. VAN CLEAVE
                     WALTER YODER

Production Assistants

JORDAN BEDER   DEREK MANZELLA

Crowd Animation

Crowd Artists ERIN J. ELLIOTT
TUAN NGUYEN
ALBERTO LUCEÑO ROS
MARK THIELEN

Production Coordinator STEPH GODTZ

EFFECTS

Production Supervisor NATHAN CURTIS

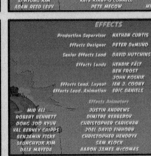

EFFECTS

Production Supervisor NATHAN CURTIS

Effects Designer PETER DeMUND

Senior Effects Lead DAVID HUTCHINS

Effects Leads HENDRIK PÄLT
BEN FROST
JOHN KOSNIK

Effects Lead, Layout IAN J. COONY

Effects Lead, Animation ERIC DANIELS

Effects Animators

MID ALI   JUSTIN ANDREWS   ERIC W. ARAUJO
ROBERT BENNETT   DIMITRE BERBEROV   BRETT BOGGS
DONG JOO RYUN   CHRISTOPHER CARIGNAN   PAUL CARMAN
VAL BERNEY CRIPPS   JOEL DAVID FINHORN   JESSE ERICKSON
BENJAMIN FISKE   CHRISTOPHER HENDRYX   JOHN HUGHES
SEUNGCHUK KIM   SAM KLOCK   JAMES DeV. MANSFIELD
DALE MAVEDA   AARON JAMES McCOMAS   TIM MOLINDER

HIROAKI NARITA   MIKE NAVARRO   HENDRIK PANZ
BLAIR PIERPONT   DAVE RAND   RATTANIN SIRINARUEMARN
KEE NAM SUONG   LE JOYCE TONG   SCOTT TOWNSEND
CESAR VELAZQUEZ   ZUBIN WADIA   JIN WATANABE
THOMAS WICKES   BRUCE WRIGHT   JAE HYUN YOO
                      XIAO ZHANG

Effects TDs

TONY CHAI   JONATHAN F. GARCIA   NEELIMA KARANAM

Additional Effects LUCA PATARACCHIA

Production Coordinator BLAIR BRADLEY

Production Assistant CHRISTIANA MARIE CUNANAN

LIGHTING

Production Supervisor MIKE HUANG

Lighting Character Lead AMY PFAFFINGER

Lighting Artists

BRIAN ADAMS   BUS BRUTSCHE   ONNY CARR
JEFF CHUNG   MATTHEW CLUBB   GREGORY CULP
CHERYL DAVIE   RYAN DeYOUNG   JUSTIN DOBIES
KAORI DOI   SHANT ERGENIAN   PATRICK FINLEY
JOSHUA FRY   ALEX GARCIA   LOGAN GLOOR
PAULA GOLDSTEIN   DYLAN GOTTLING   RICHARD HOGGE
HARRY CUNDGREEN   THOMAS HOLLIER   BENJAMIN MIN HOANG
ADRIAN IEO   KATHERINE IRZYK   IVA ITCHEVERA-BRAIN
ARTHUR JEPPE   JONGO   KURT KAMINSKI
BLAINE KENNISON   HOLLY KIM-ANGEL   ASURA TONDA KINNEY
MACDUFF KNOX   KEVIN KONEVAL   YOGESH LAKHANI
ROGER LEE   RICHARD Z. LENHAGN   BENJAMIN FRANKLIN LICURA
JASON MARTINO   VINH KAO MAHONEY   ROBERT E. MILES
JONATHAN FLETCHER MOORE   CRISTIAN C. MORAS   EDDIE MARHOLT
DEREK NELSON   JAMES NEWLAND   STEPHEN NOEL
JORGE OBREGÓN   EILEEN O'NEILL   WINSTON QUITASOL
KATIE DEINMAN   FRANK "CHERMAN" ENRIA JR. HYEKYUNG SHIN
ROBERT SHOWALTER   MARK SIEGEL   SARAH M. SWEENEY
KA VON TAR   FATEMA TARTI   EMILY TSE

ELIZABETH WILLY   NASHEET ZAMAN

Marketing Visual Effects Supervisor JOSH STAUB

Lighting Assistants

JEFF GIBSON   MOHAMMED HASSAN
KYLE HUMPHREY   RYAN CHRISTOPHER LANG
          ANGELA McBRIDE

Lighting Apprentices

ALEXANDRE CAZALS   CHRISTOPHER KENT ERICKSON
NATALIE GREENHILL   LUKE YONGMIN LEE
MATT SULLIVAN   MIGUEL LLERAS VILLAVECES
          YETI KUE

Lighting TDs

DEXTER CHENG   KAY CLOUD
MARC COOPER   ALLEN M. CORCORDAN
ANDREW B. GARTNER   KELSEY HURLEY
KIMBERLY W. KEECH   VAL L. LANCASTER
THADDEUS P. MILLER   LAUDALEA OTIS
          LEWIS N. SIEGEL

LEWIS N. SIEGEL

Assistant TDs

GABRIELA HERNANDEZ   BRANDON LEE JARRATT
NORMAN MOSES JOSEPH JUSTIN KEON
KAILEEN KRAKMER   CARI REICHE
          ABRAHAM FRANKLIN TSENG

Production Coordinators

CAITLIN PEAK COONE   LAURA M. MEREDITH
AUSTIN M. SALMI   KIT TURLEY

Production Assistants

SARAH KAMBARA   ALEXANDRA "LEXY" POSTON
          KARA RAMOS

STEREO

Production Supervisor MARISA K. CASTRO

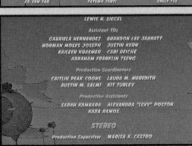

Stereo Artists

MICHAEL R.W. ANDERSON THOMAS BAKER
VANESSA SALAS CASTILLO ANITA NAUFAL EDWARDS
ROB ENGLE KATIE A. FICO
HEIDI FRIESE ALYSSA BRULE GORENCE
TROY GRIFFIN ELISSA CORDERO HANSEN
MARK HENLEY DARREN SIMPSON

PRODUCTION

Production Supervisor, Sweatbox CHARLYN GO-GIAMPA

Production Supervisor, Publicity ANDY SINUR
Production Assistant, Publicity LAUREN NICOLE BROWN

Assistant to Producer LINDSAY HENRY
Assistant to Directors HALIMA HUDSON

Production Tracking Specialist PAUL FIEBIGER
Production Finance Analyst CHRISTINA W. CHEN

ADDITIONAL PRODUCTION SUPPORT

JEFF CHASIN JOHN A. DANKO, III
STEPHANIE HACHEM KEIKO OKISADA
ERNEST J. PETTI JENNIFER CHRISTINE VERA

MUSIC

Original Score Produced by HENRY JACKMAN
Score Recorded and Mixed by ALAN MEYERSON
Score Conducted by NICK GLENNIE-SMITH
Score Orchestrations by STEPHEN COLEMAN
Music Editor, Production EARL GHAFFARI
Music Editor, Score DANIEL PINDER
Music Production Director ANDREW PAGE
Music Business Affairs DONNA COLE-BRULÉ
Music Production Coordinator ASHLEY CHAFIN
Executive Music Assistant JILL HEFFLEY
Music Production Assistant JIMMY TSAI
Music Preparation by BOOKER WHITE-WALT DISNEY MUSIC
Score Contracted by PETER ROTTER

Score Choir Contracted and Conducted by JASPER RANDALL
Digital Score Recordist KEVIN GLOBERMAN
Additional Music DOMINIC LEWIS
PAUL MOUNSEY
Mix Assistant JOHN CHAPMAN
Score Technicians VICTOR CHAGA
VIVIAN AGUIAR-BUFF
Score Production Services TAMMY SAUNT
Score Coordinator MATTHEW K. JUSTMANN
Assistant Music Editor DANIEL WALDMAN
Additional Temp Music Editor DOMINICK CERTO

Score Choir

TAMARA BEVARD KAREN HOGLE BROWN
HAYDEN EBERHART CARRAH FLAHIVE
AMY FOGERSON HARRIET FRASER
AYANA HAVIV JENNIFER HAYDN-JONES
MICHELE HEMMINGS CALLISTA HOFFMAN
ELISSA JOHNSTON KASONDRA KAZANJIAN
LESLEY LEIGHTON SARAH LYNCH
ADRIANA MANFREDI CINDY MARTY

JESSICA ROTTER KAREN WHIPPLE SCHNURR
HOLLY SEDILLOS NIKE ST. CLAIR
NANCY SULAHIAN KIMBERLY SWITZER
KRISTEN TOEDTMAN SUZANNE WATERS
ELYSE WILLIS

"IMMORTALS"
Performed by Fall Out Boy
Written by Andy Hurley, Joe Trohman, Patrick Stump and Pete Wentz
Produced by Butch Walker
Engineered by Todd Stopera and Patrick Stump
Additional Production & Engineering and Mixed by Jake Sinclair
Fall Out Boy appears courtesy of Island Records, A Division of UMG Recordings, Inc.

"BOCA DULCE BOCA"
Written by F. Estefano Salgado, Flavio Enrique Santander
Performed by Jose Luis Rodriguez
Courtesy of Sony Music (US) Latin, LLC
By Arrangement with Sony Music Licensing

"EYE OF THE TIGER"
Written by James Michael Peterik, Frank Sullivan
Performed by Survivor
Courtesy of Volcano Entertainment III, LLC
By Arrangement with Sony Music Licensing

POST PRODUCTION

Post Production Supervisor DAVID OKEY

Post Production Coordinator BRYCE OLSON
Original Dialogue Mixers GABRIEL GUY, CAS
DOC KANE

Post Production Sound Services by SKYWALKER SOUND
A LUCASFILM LTD. COMPANY
MARIN COUNTY, CALIFORNIA

DISNEY DIGITAL STUDIO SERVICES

Re-Recording Mixers DAVID E. FLUHR, CAS

GABRIEL GUY, CAS
Re-Recording Mix Technician STEVE SCHATZ
Sound Effects Editors ADDISON TEAGUE
DAVID C. HUGHES
NIA HANSEN
JEREMY BOWKER
Supervising Dialogue Editor KIM FOSCATO
Supervising ADR Editor DANIEL LAURIE
Foley Editors ROBERT SHOUP
JIM LIKOWSKI
First Assistant Sound Editor JACOB RIEHLE
Foley Artists JOHN ROESCH
ALYSON DEE MOORE
Foley Mixer MARY JO LANG
Assistant Re-Recording Mixer BONNIE WILD
Client Services Coordinator EVA PORTER

Skywalker Sound Executive Staff
General Manager JOSH LOWDEN
Director of Engineering STEVE MORRIS

ADR Group Voice Casting TERRI DOUGLAS
THE LOOP TROOP
Digital Imaging Specialist ROBERT H. BAGLEY
Digital Colorist ELIOT MILBOURN
End Title Design SCARLET LETTERS
Film Color Timer DAN MUSCARELLA
Film Lab FOTOKEM
Transfer Room/Theater Operators LUTZNER RODRIGUEZ
GABRIEL STEWART

TECHNOLOGY

Technology Directors DAN CANDELA
JONATHAN E. GEIBEL

Sr. Research Scientist RASMUS TAMSTORF

Technology Coordinator DAWN HALLORAN

Sr. Graphic Designer JAMES LAVRAKAS

Animation Technology

Technology Manager EVAN GOLDBERG

Principal Software Engineer MARK A. McLAUGHLIN

JOSE LUIS GOMEZ DIAZ CATHERINE LAM
GENE S. LEE CHUNG-AN ANDY LIN
ANDY MILNE DMITRIY PINSKIY
JAY STEELE ALEXANDRE D. TORIJA-PARIS
JUSTIN WALKER BRIAN WHITED

Look/Effects/Dynamics

Technology Manager RAJESH SHARMA

DAVID AGUILAR LAWRENCE CHAI
KELLY WARD HAMMEL YING LIU
JOSEPH W. LONGSON ALEKA McADAMS
MARYANN SIMMONS ALEKEY DMITRIEVICH STOMAKHIN

Disney's Hyperion Renderer

Leadership

BRENT BURLEY SEAN D. JENKINS
CHUCK TAPPAN

Developers

DAVID M. ADLER MATT JEN-YUAN CHIANG
CHRISTIAN EISENACHER RALF HABEL
PETER KUTZ GREG NICHOLS
JAN NOVÁK ANDREW SELLE
BEN SPENCER DANIEL TEECE

Additional Development

BENEDIKT BITTERLI STELLA HSIN-HUEI CHENG
GABOR LIKTOR ULRICH V. MUELLER
OSIRIS PÉREZ MAGADALENA PRUS
SERGE SRETSCHINSKY

Software Infrastructure

Senior Technology Manager KEVIN GAMBREL

Business Integration Project Manager KRISTA HALEY

MARTY ALCHIN NEIL P. BARBER
DALE BECK JORDI CARRILLO BOSCH
MARK R. CARLSON KYLE D. HAYES
PAUL HILDEBRANDT JEAN HIMEBAUGH
HIDE A. HIRASE MICHAEL D. KLIEWER
STEFAN LUKA CHRISTOPHER D. MIHALY
C. KEVIN MORGAN JOHN ROBERT PERRY
WENDY M. TAM ROY TURNER
JOANNA ZETA

Systems

Technology Managers JAMES COLBY BETTE
RONALD L. JOHNSON
MATTHEW SCHNITTKER

Technology Assistant Manager DAVRA B. MELTZER

Database Engineering
STUART McDOUGAL   ZACHARY STOKES

Linux Engineering
JAY HILLIARD   DANNY JEWELL
STEVEN SEED

Mac Engineering
GREG NEAGLE

Media Engineering
JASON L. BERGMAN   JEFFREY R. CORNISH
GLENN DAKAKE   NORBERT FAERSTAIN
KAMALDEEP TUMKUR SRINATH   JAMES A. WARGOWSKI

Network Engineering
JAMES MacBURNEY

Production Engineering
KEVIN C. CONSTANTINE   ROSIE WACHA
GRAHAM B. WHITTED IV

Systems Mobile Development
DIANA STONE   TRUONG VO

Systems Operations
VINCENT D'AMORE   CARLOS "CHARLIE" ESTIANDAN
ERIC N. GARCIA   MATTHEW GOODMAN
ALAN A. PATEL

Technical Support
NATALIE ACOSTA   PETER LEE CHUN
MICHAEL DOBSON   MICHAEL M. FUKUMOTO
JOHN READICK   GRACE H. SHIRADO

Disney Research
MARKUS GROSS   JESSICA HODGINS
WOJCIECH JAROSZ   PETER KAUFMANN
JASON HINTZ LLOPIS   FABRICE ROUSSELLE
ALEXANDER SORKINE-HORNUNG   OLIVER WANG
HENNING ZIMMER

THE STAFF OF WALT DISNEY ANIMATION STUDIOS

Studio Leadership
JOHN LASSETER   ED CATMULL   ANDREW MILLSTEIN
GREG COLEMAN   ROY CONLI   PETER DEL VECHO
ANDY HENDRICKSON   ALAN KEITH   ANN LE CAM
SEAN LURIE   MAGGIE MALONE   JOHN I. McGUIRE
DOROTHY McKIM   KRISTINA REED   OSNAT SHURER
CLARK SPENCER

Creative Leadership

Creative Leadership
STEVE ANDERSON   CHRIS BUCK   JARED BUSH
RON CLEMENTS   KEVIN DETERS   NATHAN GRENO
DON HALL   BYRON HOWARD   JENNIFER LEE
RICH MOORE   JOHN MUSKER   DEAN WELLINS
STEVIE WERMERS-SKELTON   CHRIS WILLIAMS

Departmental Leadership
SCOTT BEATTIE   PAUL BRIGGS   CARLOS CABRAL
RENATO dos ANJOS   JEFF DRAHEIM   ROB DRESSEL
HANK DRISKILL   COLIN ECKART   PAUL FELIX
KATIE A. FICO   MIKE GABRIEL   DAVE GOETZ
STEVE GOLDBERG   MARK HAMMEL   FRANK HANNER
NICOLE P. HEARON   DARIN HOLLINGS   ALESSANDRO JACOMINI
SEAN JENKINS   MOHIT KALLIANPUR   MICHAEL KASCHALK
MARK KENNEDY   SCOTT KERSAVAGE   DAVE K. KOMOROWSKI
MONICA LAGO-KAYTIS   BRIAN LEACH   ADOLPH LUSINSKY
YVETT MERINO   TIM MERTENS   THADDEUS P. MILLER
TERRY W. MOEWS   JOHN MURRAH   ROBERT NEUMAN
KYLE ODERMATT   PATRICK OSBORNE   ZACK PETROC
ERNEST J. PETTI   BÉRÉNICE ROBINSON   AIMEE SCRIBNER

ERNEST J. PETTI   BÉRÉNICE ROBINSON   AIMEE SCRIBNER
BRADFORD SIMONSEN   AMY LAWSON SMEED   MARC E. SMITH
JOSH STAUB   CHADD STUBBLEFIELD   CHUCK TAPPAN
CESAR VELAZQUEZ   JENNIFER CHRISTINE VERA   MARLON WEST

Executive Administrative Support
PATTI CONKLIN   HEATHER FENG-YANU
MICHELLE MORETTA LIGHTNER   TANYA OSKANIAN
BONNIE POPP   TERRI SHEVY
WENDY DALE TANZILLO

Artist Management
MEI-MING CASINO
VICKI CASE   JEREMY COSTELLO   JACQUELYN COLOMB-PEREZ
KELLIE HOOVER   SHELLEY KATAYAMA   COLLIN LARKINS
MELISSA ROBERTS   LESLEY BENTIVEGNA   STEPHANIE MORSE

Development
KAREN TENKHOFF   KYLE GABRIEL   BRYAN DAVIDSON
JESSICA JULIUS   ELISE ALIBERTI   KELLY EISERT
SCOTT HUMMEL   BOO KURTZ-LOPEZ   LAUREN KAY LEFFINGWELL

NICHOLAS RUSSELL   SAM STRATTON   RUTH STROTHER
FELICITY TREVIÑO

Marketing & Publicity
AMY ASTLEY   MELANIE BEARD   DAVID BESS
GARTH BURKHARD   JOE DUNN   HOWARD GREEN
MIKE GORTZ   AMY KREUTZEN   SHANNON PETRANO
DAVID SAMETH   MICHAEL SIMMS   ELENA TIMMAN
KYLE ZABALA

Business & Legal Affairs
CHRISTINE CHRISMAN   DOUG BRUNSWICK
MONA SHOKRAI   GUS AVILA
JARVIS GEORGE   TIM GREER
JERI HOWARD

Finance
JULIANNE HALE   DIRAN BANDAZIAN   LAURIE L. AU
JENNIFER "JEJO" SLEEPER   LINDA MATSUOKA-NARMORE   TOM BODY
FRANK WILLIAM KNITTEL JR.   ANGELA M. SABETTA   MARCELA COUCH

Environment & Events
TANJA KNOBLICH   CARLOS AREVALO   REY CERVANTES JR.
DANIEL COSGROVE   BENITO DeFRANCO   GARY DENES
MELISSA COLE FANFASSIAN   KEN LEWIS   BRUCE PARKER
EDUARDO RUIZ   KEVIN WALDVOGEL-DeMONACO   COLLIN MAPP

Human Resources
LINDSAY NADLER   KIM COSTELLO
DENISE IRWIN STASTNY   HILDE VAN GOOL
GINGER WEI-HSIEN CHEN   KATHERINE QUINTERO

Artistic & Production Recruiting
CAMILLE EDEN   SCOTT CAMPBELL
ROBYN PALMER   CHRISTINE PRANIEWICZ
MATT ROBERTS   DOERI WELCH GREINER

Talent Development & Outreach
DAWN ERNSTER YAMAZI   NINA HARAGUCHI
ERIN ONG   KATIE REESE

Talent Development & Outreach
DAWN ERNSTER YAMAZI   NINA HARAGUCHI
ERIN ONG   KATIE REESE
ANNIE SEVAREID   KELSI WIGGINS TAGLANG
ZULEMA URIARTE

Training
TRACY BOVASSO CAMPBELL   ROSS BLOCHER
CHRIS CHAVEZ   NANCY EVANS

Digital Art Services
KENT GORDON

Caffeination
CARLOS BENAVIDES

Special Projects
DAVID A. BOSSERT   ASHLEIGH BATEMAN   BRANDON BLOCH
DAVID BLOCK   MINNIE CHEN   LIANE ABEL DIETZ
DARIN HOLLINGS   JAMES HULL   DEV KARNA

RICARDO NADU   CAMERON RAMSAY   ANDRE W. STUPPERT
LURELINE WEATHERLY   HAN YU

Animation Research Library
LELLA F. SMITH
MARY WALSH
JILL BREZNICAN   FOX F. CARNEY   TAMMY CROSSON
MARK M. DAWSON   DOUG ENGALLA   IDRIS ERBA
MAT FRETSCHEL   ANN W. HANSEN   LEON INGRAM
RICHARD N. KANNO   TAMARA N. KHALAF   TRACY ANN LEACH
MARISA LEONARDI   KRISTEN McCORMICK   HEATHER McLAUGHLIN
JAMIE PANETTA   TOM PNIEWSKI   MIKE PUCHER
JACKIE VASQUEZ   ELDA "TITA" VENEGAS   PATRICK WHITE

Ink & Paint
RIKKI CHOBANIAN   JIM LUSBY
ANTONIO PELAYO   SHERRI VANDOLI

Security
NORMAN GREEN   MICHELLE HOWARD
FORREST IWASZEWSKI   TERRY LA RAIA

Security
NORMAN GREEN   MICHELLE HOWARD
FORREST IWASZEWSKI   TERRY LA RAIA
ALAN MERCHANT   JERRY M. ROMERO
DARRYL VONTOURE   CHRIS A. VARNEY

THE FILMMAKERS WOULD LIKE TO THANK

Marvel Entertainment
JOE QUESADA   JEPH LOEB

Carnegie Mellon University
The Robotics Institute
CHRIS ATKESON, PROFESSOR OF ROBOTICS

Massachusetts Institute of Technology
NEIL GERSHENFELD, DIRECTOR, CENTER FOR BITS AND ATOMS

University of Tokyo
Dept. of Mechano-Informatics
YOSHIHIKO NAKAMURA, PROFESSOR

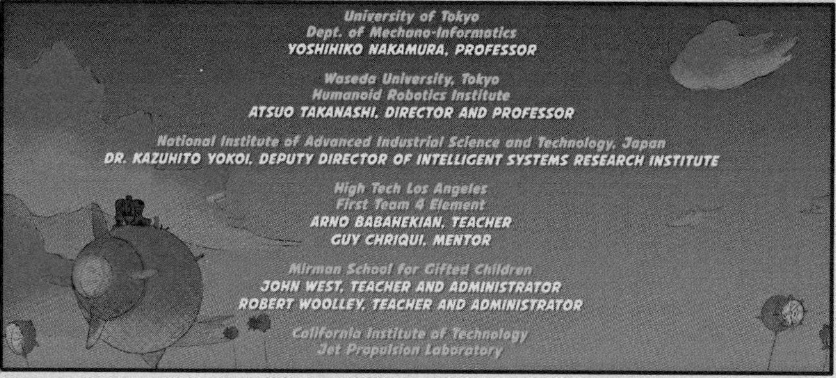
University of Tokyo
Dept. of Mechano-Informatics
YOSHIHIKO NAKAMURA, PROFESSOR
Waseda University, Tokyo
Humanoid Robotics Institute
ATSUO TAKANASHI, DIRECTOR AND PROFESSOR
National Institute of Advanced Industrial Science and Technology, Japan
DR. KAZUHITO YOKOI, DEPUTY DIRECTOR OF INTELLIGENT SYSTEMS RESEARCH INSTITUTE
High Tech Los Angeles
First Team 4 Element
ARNO BABAHEKIAN, TEACHER
GUY CHRIQUI, MENTOR
Mirman School for Gifted Children
JOHN WEST, TEACHER AND ADMINISTRATOR
ROBERT WOOLLEY, TEACHER AND ADMINISTRATOR
California Institute of Technology
Jet Propulsion Laboratory

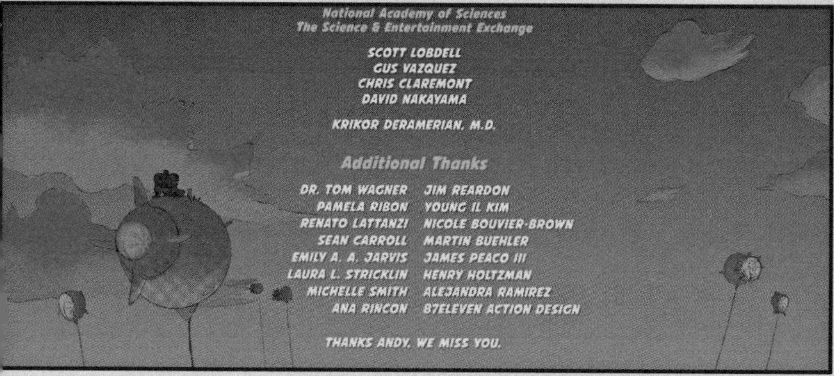
National Academy of Sciences
The Science & Entertainment Exchange
SCOTT LOBDELL
GUS VAZQUEZ
CHRIS CLAREMONT
DAVID NAKAYAMA
KRIKOR DERAMERIAN, M.D.
Additional Thanks
DR. TOM WAGNER
PAMELA RIBON
RENATO LATTANZI
SEAN CARROLL
EMILY A. A. JARVIS
LAURA L. STRICKLIN
MICHELLE SMITH
ANA RINCON
JIM REARDON
YOUNG IL KIM
NICOLE BOUVIER-BROWN
MARTIN BUEHLER
JAMES PEACO III
HENRY HOLTZMAN
ALEJANDRA RAMIREZ
87ELEVEN ACTION DESIGN
THANKS ANDY, WE MISS YOU.

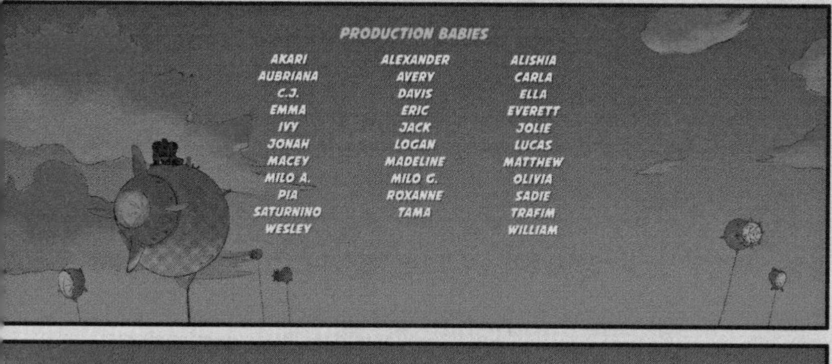
PRODUCTION BABIES
AKARI
AUBRIANA
C.J.
EMMA
IVY
JONAH
MACEY
MILO A.
PIA
SATURNINO
WESLEY
ALEXANDER
AVERY
DAVIS
ERIC
JACK
LOGAN
MADELINE
MILO G.
ROXANNE
TAMA
ALISHIA
CARLA
ELLA
EVERETT
JOLIE
LUCAS
MATTHEW
OLIVIA
SADIE
TRAFIM
WILLIAM

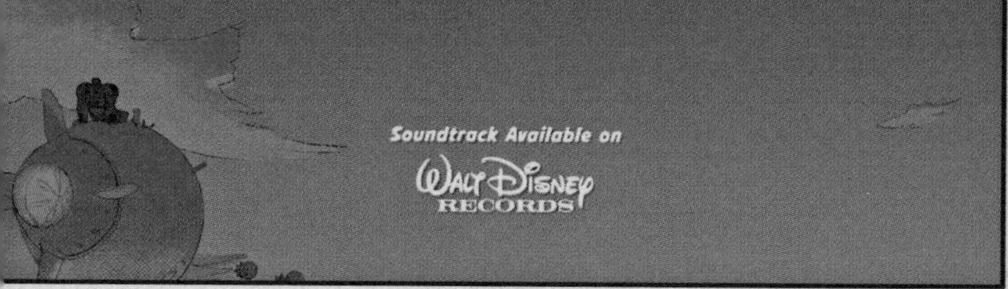
Soundtrack Available on
WALT DISNEY RECORDS

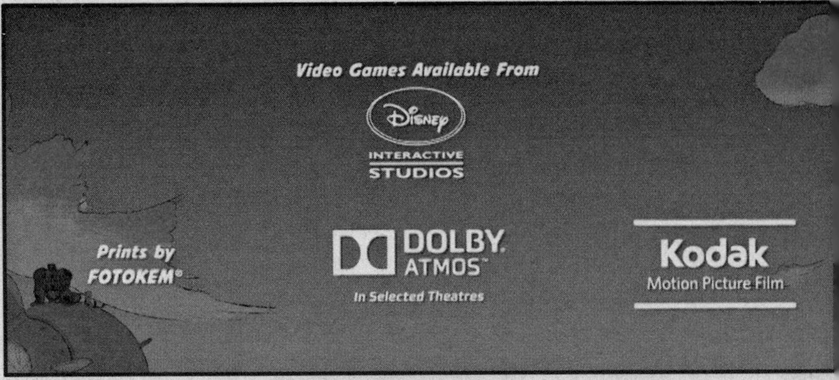
Video Games Available From
Disney
INTERACTIVE
STUDIOS
Prints by
FOTOKEM®
DOLBY
ATMOS™
In Selected Theatres
Kodak
Motion Picture Film

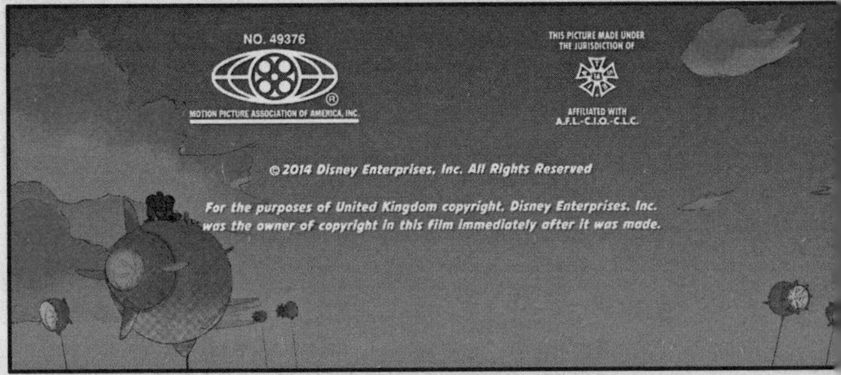
NO. 49376
MOTION PICTURE ASSOCIATION OF AMERICA, INC.
THIS PICTURE MADE UNDER
THE JURISDICTION OF
AFFILIATED WITH
A.F.L.-C.I.O.-C.L.C.
©2014 Disney Enterprises, Inc. All Rights Reserved
For the purposes of United Kingdom copyright, Disney Enterprises, Inc.
was the owner of copyright in this film immediately after it was made.

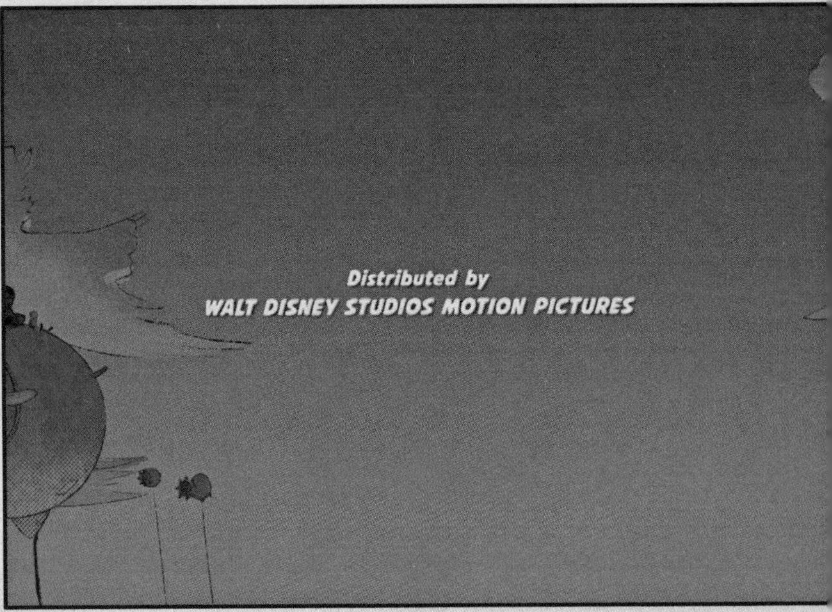
Distributed by
WALT DISNEY STUDIOS MOTION PICTURES

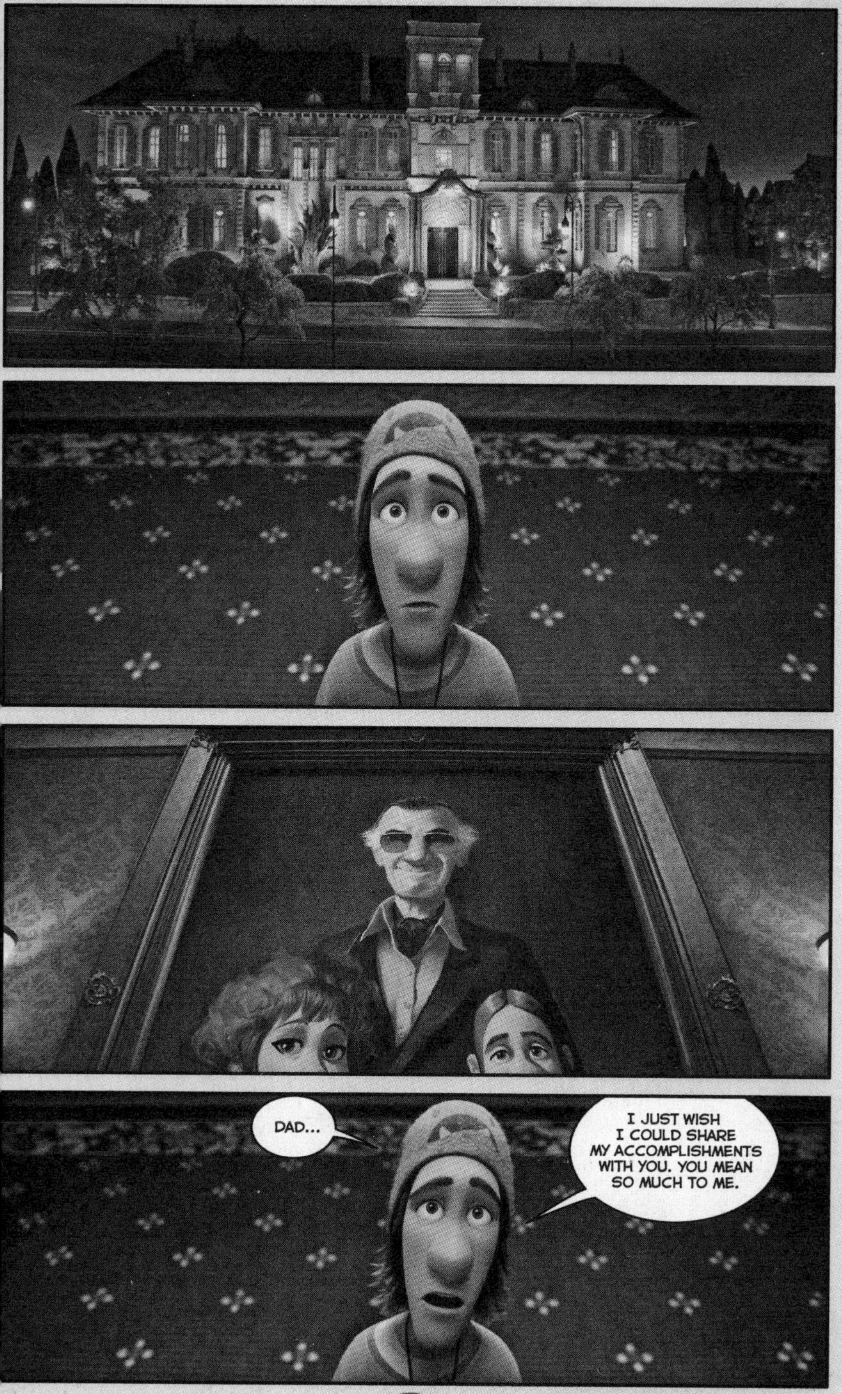
DAD...
I JUST WISH I COULD SHARE MY ACCOMPLISHMENTS WITH YOU. YOU MEAN SO MUCH TO ME.

AND HONESTLY, I'VE ALWAYS FELT A DISTANCE WHAT WITH YOU BEING ON THE FAMILY ISLAND ALL THE TIME.

I JUST WISH YOU COULD SEE--

CLICK!

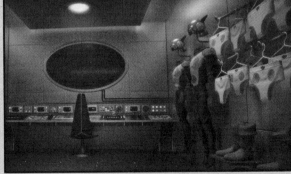

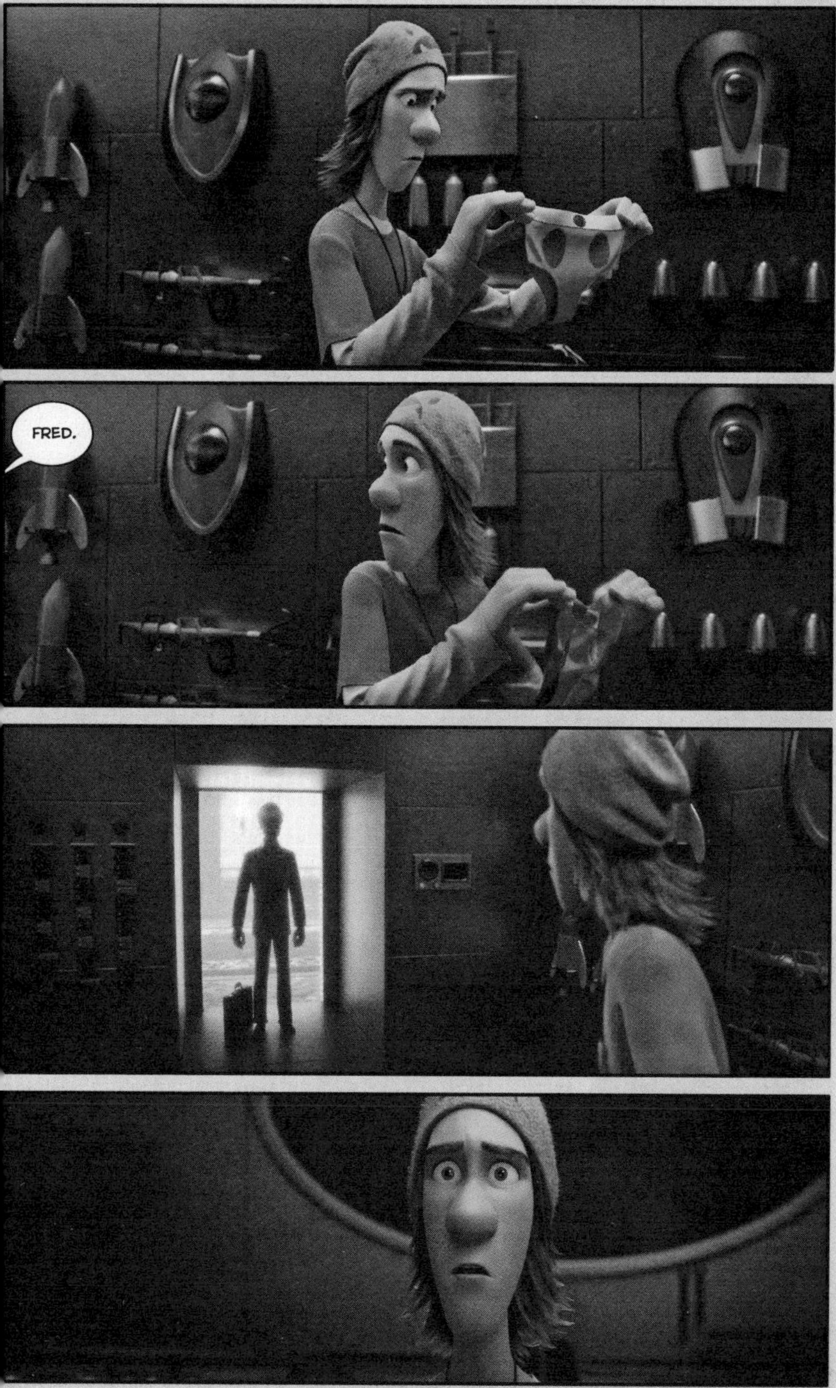
FRED.

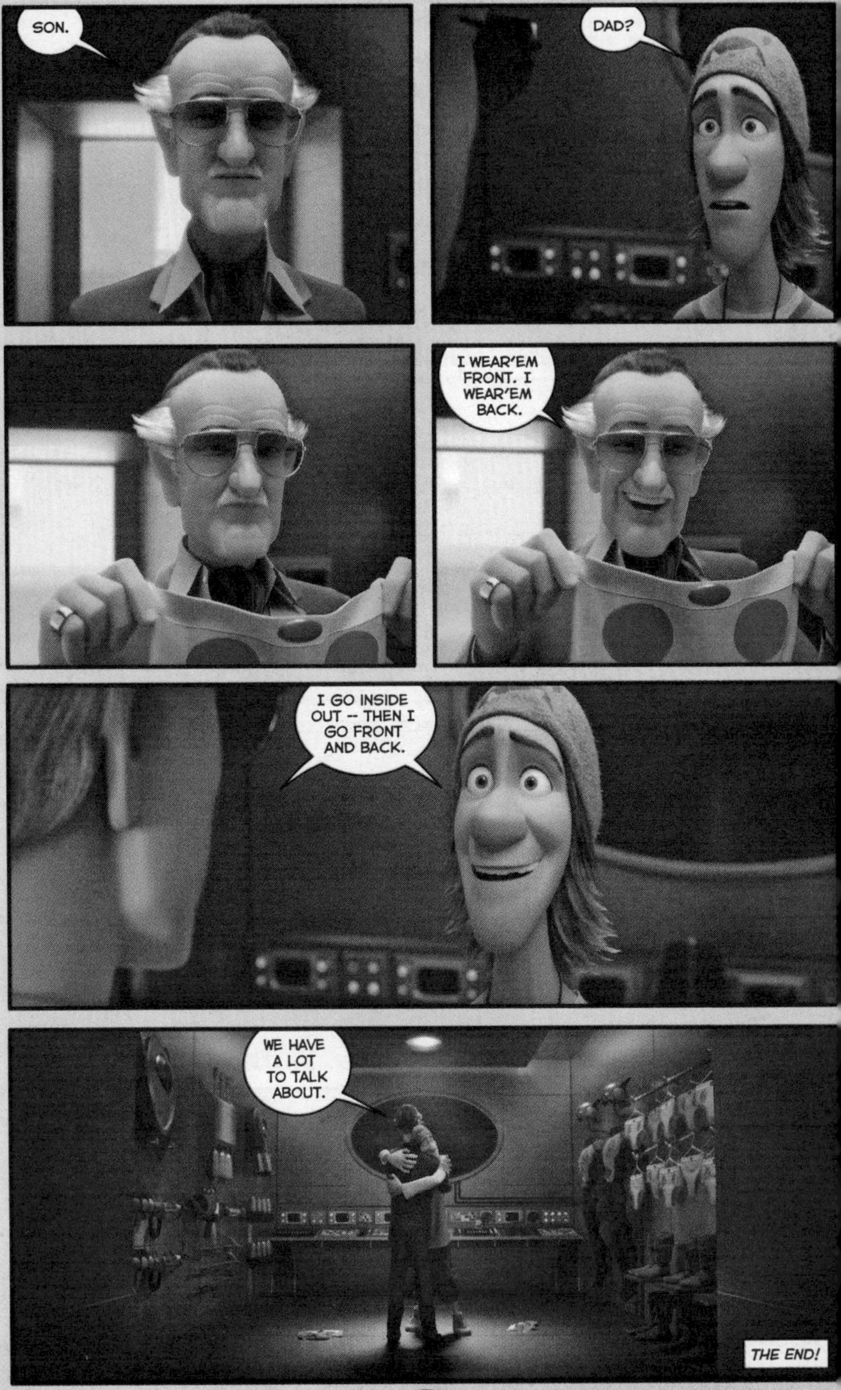
SON.
DAD?
I WEAR'EM FRONT. I WEAR'EM BACK.
I GO INSIDE OUT -- THEN I GO FRONT AND BACK.
WE HAVE A LOT TO TALK ABOUT.
THE END!

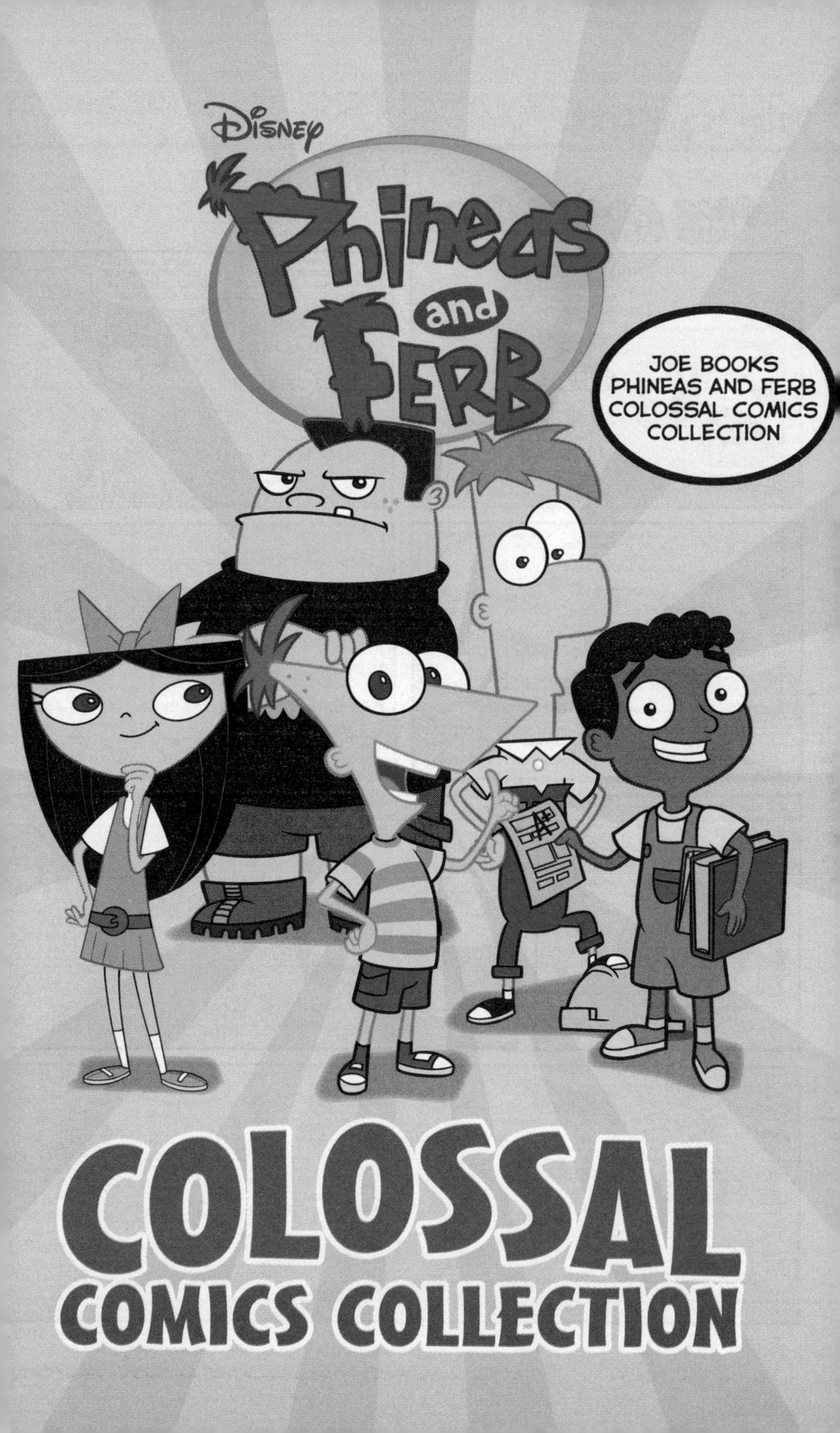
Disney
Phineas and Ferb
JOE BOOKS
PHINEAS AND FERB
COLOSSAL COMICS
COLLECTION
COLOSSAL
COMICS COLLECTION

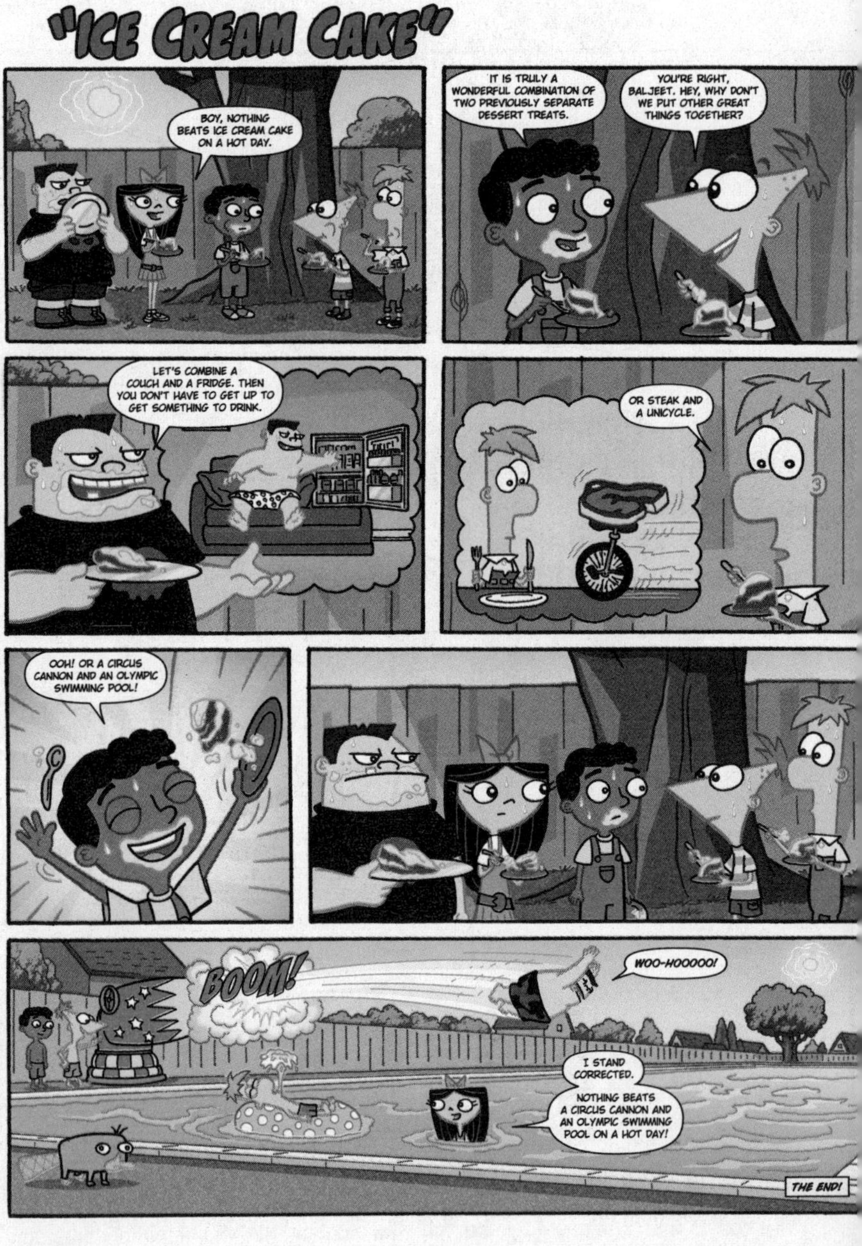
"ICE CREAM CAKE"
BOY, NOTHING BEATS ICE CREAM CAKE ON A HOT DAY.
IT IS TRULY A WONDERFUL COMBINATION OF TWO PREVIOUSLY SEPARATE DESSERT TREATS.
YOU'RE RIGHT, BALJEET. HEY, WHY DON'T WE PUT OTHER GREAT THINGS TOGETHER?
LET'S COMBINE A COUCH AND A FRIDGE. THEN YOU DON'T HAVE TO GET UP TO GET SOMETHING TO DRINK.
OR STEAK AND A UNICYCLE.
OOH! OR A CIRCUS CANNON AND AN OLYMPIC SWIMMING POOL!
BOOM!
WOO-HOOOOO!
I STAND CORRECTED.
NOTHING BEATS A CIRCUS CANNON AND AN OLYMPIC SWIMMING POOL ON A HOT DAY!
THE END!

"HEY, WHERE'S PERRY?"

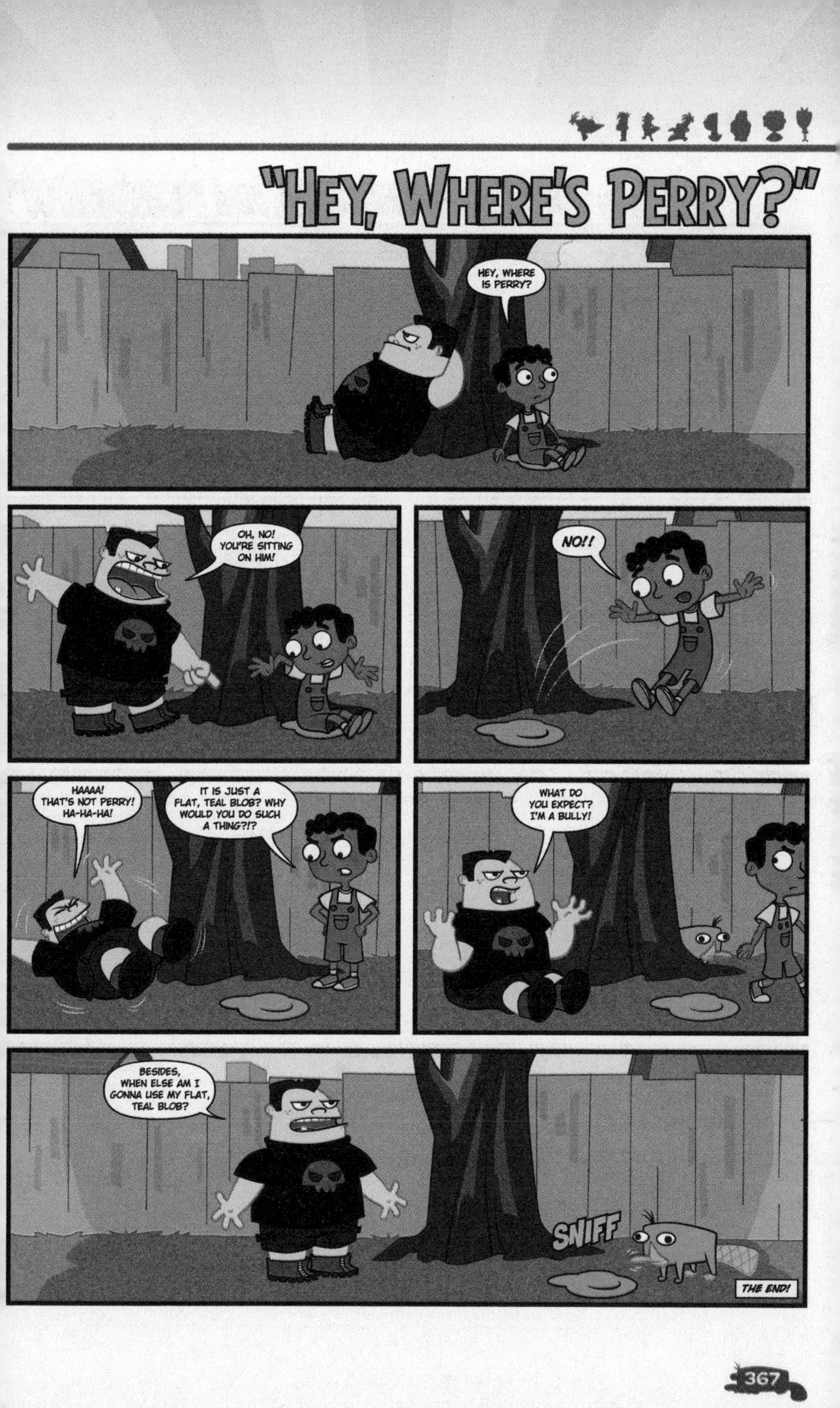
HEY, WHERE IS PERRY?
OH, NO! YOU'RE SITTING ON HIM!
NO!!
HAAAA! THAT'S NOT PERRY! HA-HA-HA!
IT IS JUST A FLAT, TEAL BLOB? WHY WOULD YOU DO SUCH A THING?!?
WHAT DO YOU EXPECT? I'M A BULLY!
BESIDES, WHEN ELSE AM I GONNA USE MY FLAT, TEAL BLOB?
SNIFF
THE END!

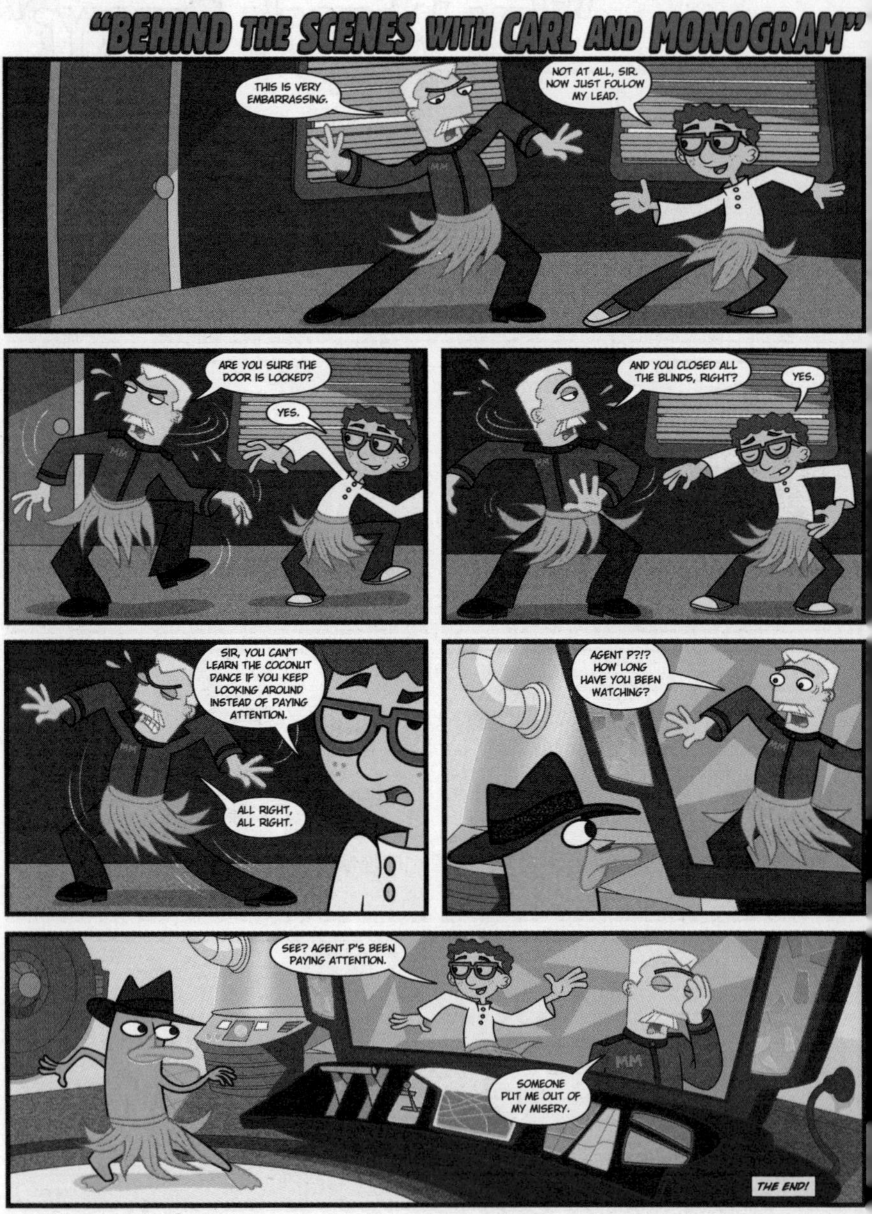
"BEHIND THE SCENES WITH CARL AND MONOGRAM"
THIS IS VERY EMBARRASSING.
NOT AT ALL, SIR. NOW JUST FOLLOW MY LEAD.
ARE YOU SURE THE DOOR IS LOCKED?
YES.
AND YOU CLOSED ALL THE BLINDS, RIGHT?
YES.
SIR, YOU CAN'T LEARN THE COCONUT DANCE IF YOU KEEP LOOKING AROUND INSTEAD OF PAYING ATTENTION.
ALL RIGHT, ALL RIGHT.
AGENT P?!? HOW LONG HAVE YOU BEEN WATCHING?
SEE? AGENT P'S BEEN PAYING ATTENTION.
SOMEONE PUT ME OUT OF MY MISERY.
THE END!

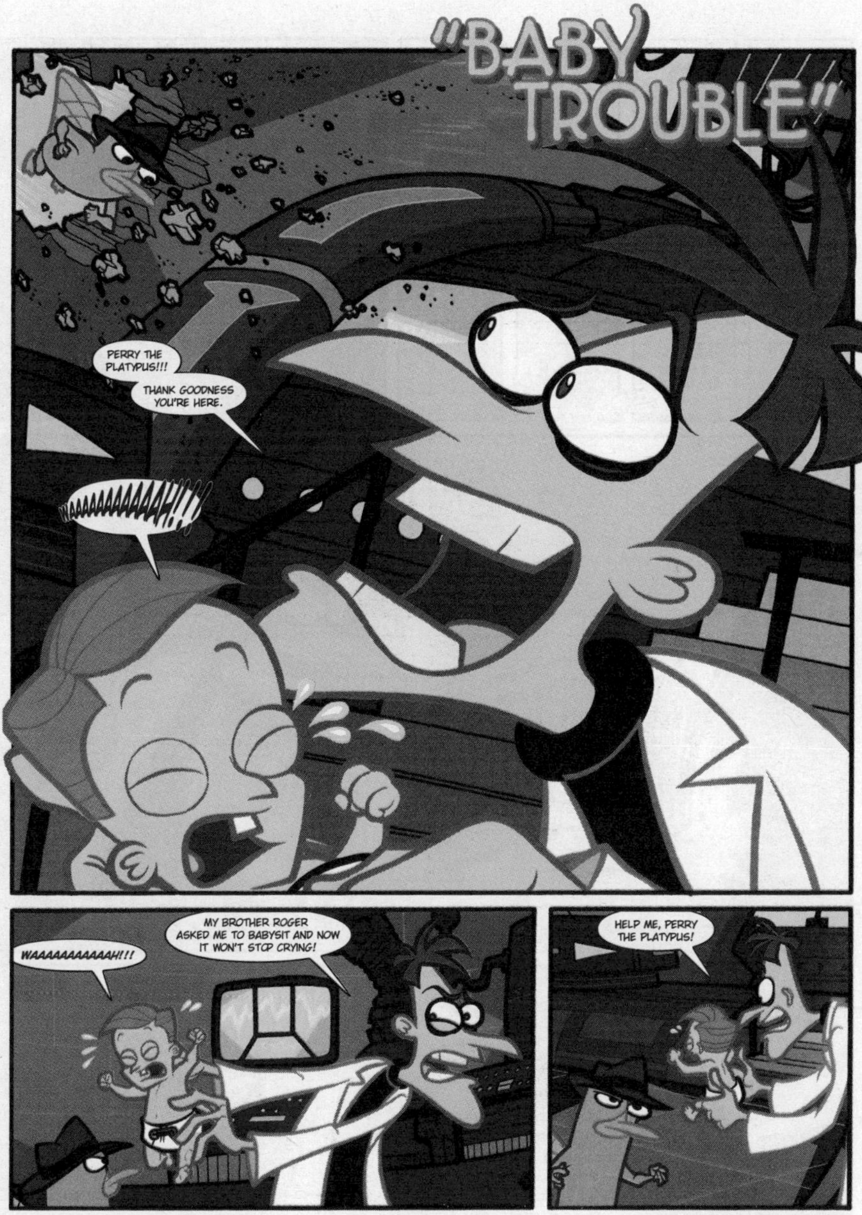
"BABY TROUBLE"
PERRY THE PLATYPUS!!!
THANK GOODNESS YOU'RE HERE.
WAAAAAAAAAAAH!!!
WAAAAAAAAAAAAH!!!
MY BROTHER ROGER ASKED ME TO BABYSIT AND NOW IT WON'T STOP CRYING!
HELP ME, PERRY THE PLATYPUS!

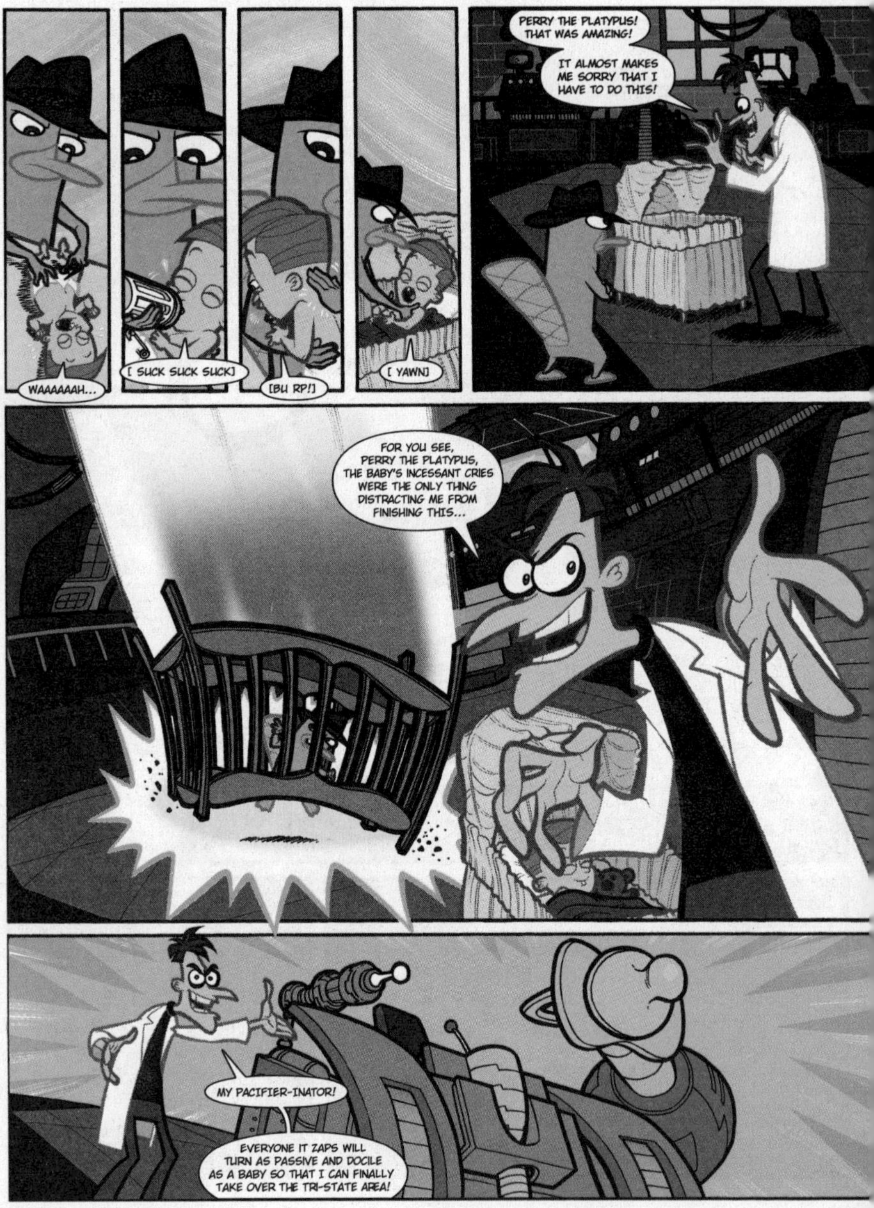
WAAAAAAH...
[SUCK SUCK SUCK]
[BU RP!]
[YAWN]
PERRY THE PLATYPUS! THAT WAS AMAZING!
IT ALMOST MAKES ME SORRY THAT I HAVE TO DO THIS!
FOR YOU SEE, PERRY THE PLATYPUS, THE BABY'S INCESSANT CRIES WERE THE ONLY THING DISTRACTING ME FROM FINISHING THIS...
MY PACIFIER-INATOR!
EVERYONE IT ZAPS WILL TURN AS PASSIVE AND DOCILE AS A BABY SO THAT I CAN FINALLY TAKE OVER THE TRI-STATE AREA!

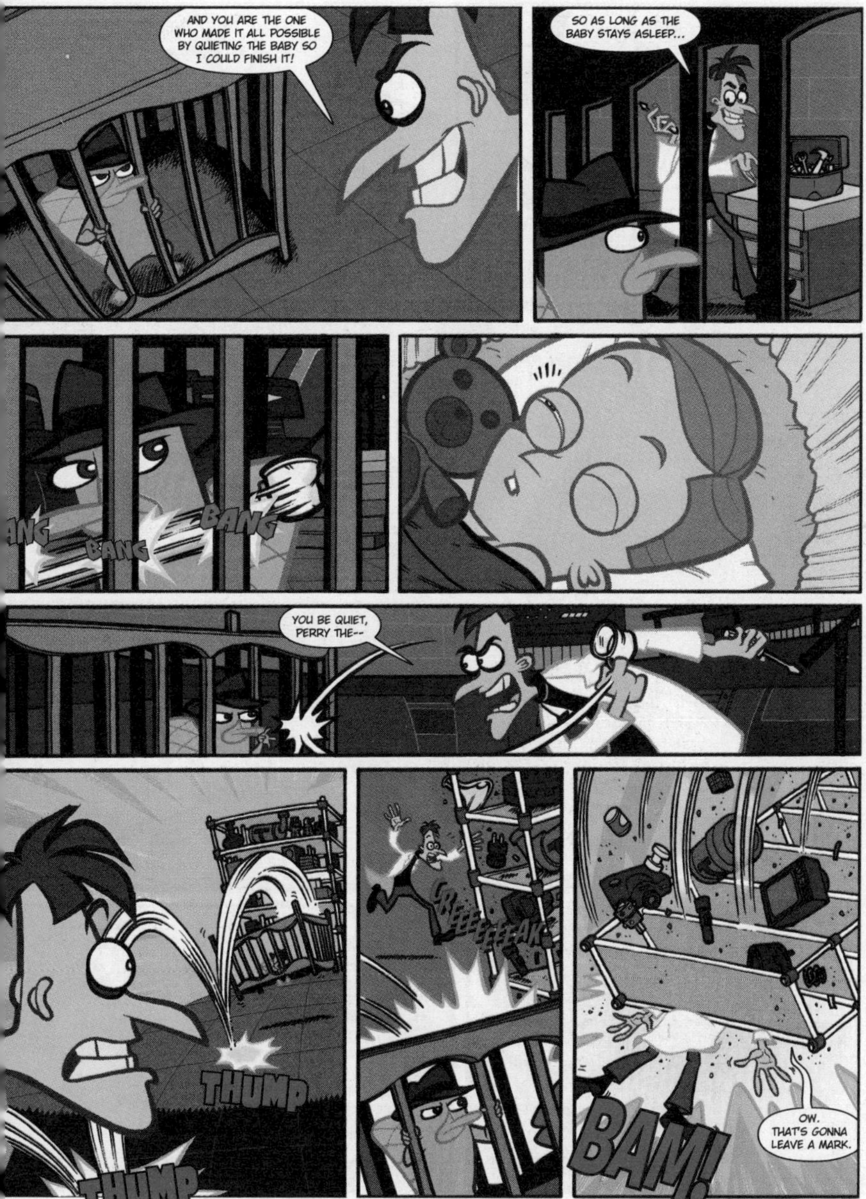
AND YOU ARE THE ONE WHO MADE IT ALL POSSIBLE BY QUIETING THE BABY SO I COULD FINISH IT!
SO AS LONG AS THE BABY STAYS ASLEEP...
BANG
BANG
BANG
YOU BE QUIET, PERRY THE--
THUMP
THUMP
CREEEEEEEAK
BAM!
OW. THAT'S GONNA LEAVE A MARK.

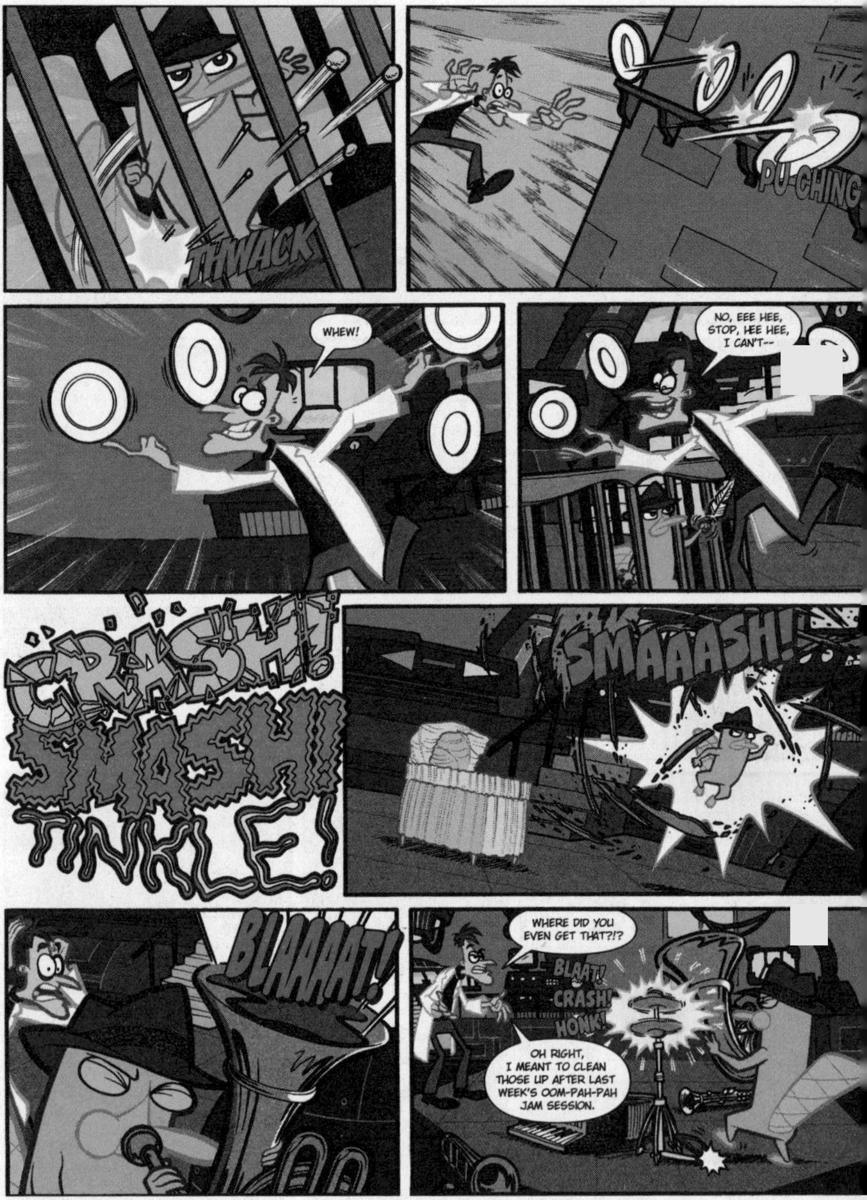
THWACK
PU-CHING
WHEW!
NO, EEE HEE, STOP, HEE HEE, I CAN'T--
CRASH! SMASH! TINKLE!
SMAAASH!
BLAAAAT!
WHERE DID YOU EVEN GET THAT?!?
BLAAT! CRASH! HONK!
OH RIGHT, I MEANT TO CLEAN THOSE UP AFTER LAST WEEK'S OOM-PAH-PAH JAM SESSION.

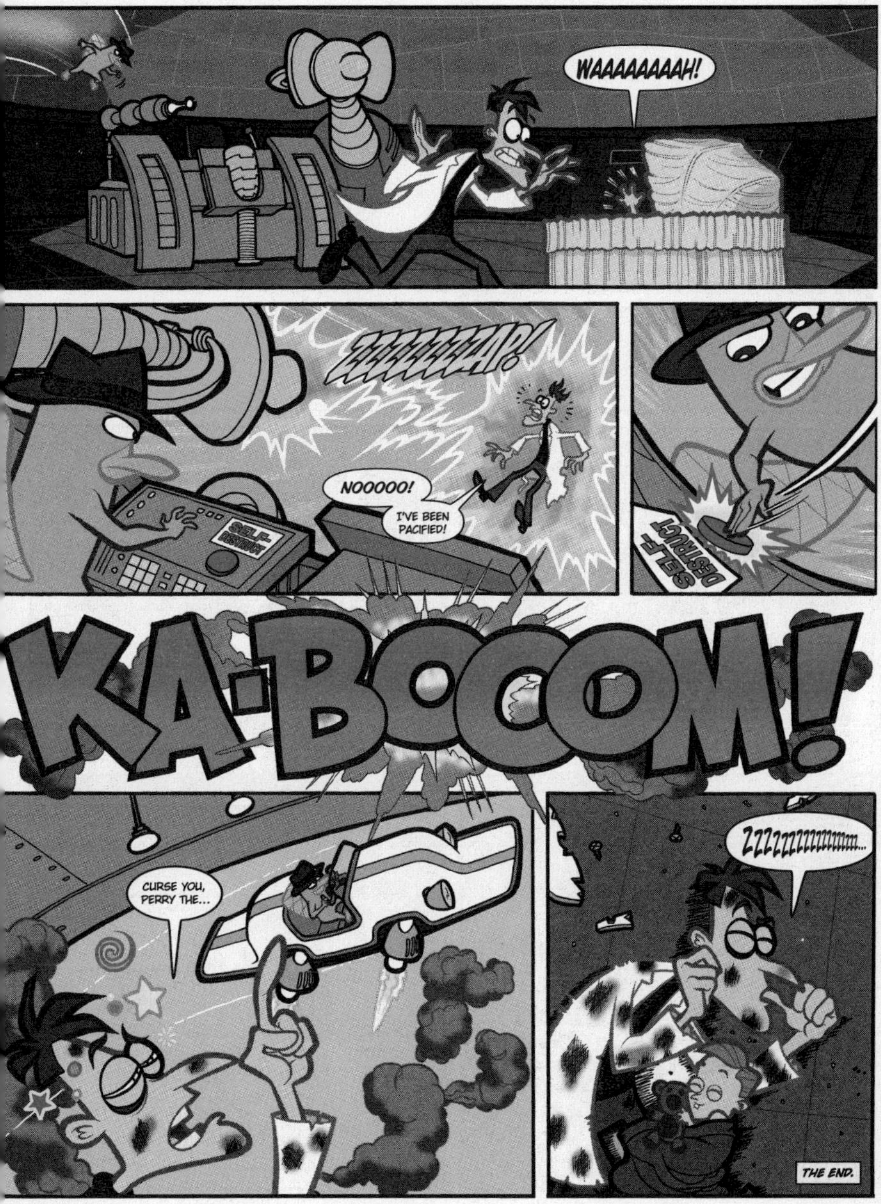
WAAAAAAAAH!
ZZZZZZZZAP!
NOOOOO!
I'VE BEEN PACIFIED!
SELF-DESTRUCT
SELF DESTRUCT
KA-BOOOM!
CURSE YOU, PERRY THE...
ZZZZzzzzzzzzzzmmm...
THE END.

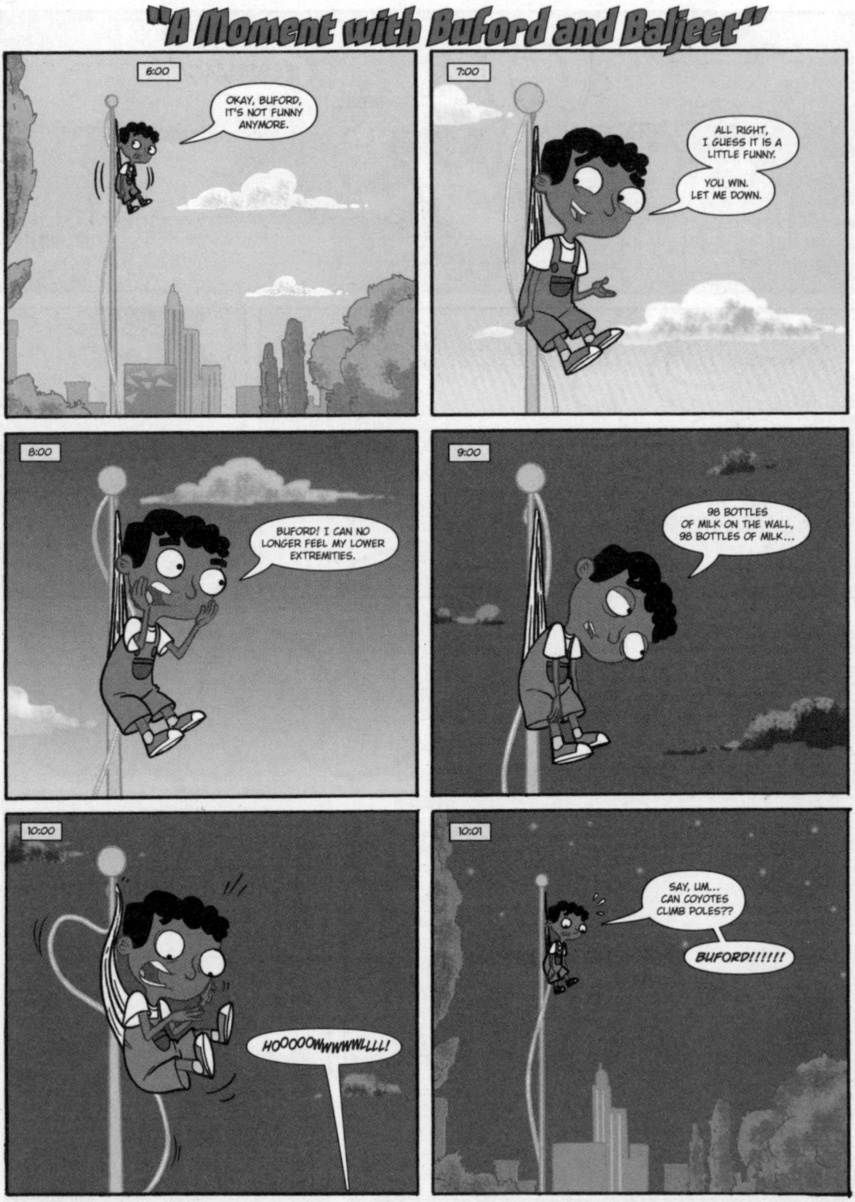
"A Moment with Buford and Baljeet"
6:00
OKAY, BUFORD, IT'S NOT FUNNY ANYMORE.
7:00
ALL RIGHT, I GUESS IT IS A LITTLE FUNNY.
YOU WIN. LET ME DOWN.
8:00
BUFORD! I CAN NO LONGER FEEL MY LOWER EXTREMITIES.
9:00
98 BOTTLES OF MILK ON THE WALL, 98 BOTTLES OF MILK...
10:00
HOOOOOWWWWLLLL!
10:01
SAY, UM... CAN COYOTES CLIMB POLES??
BUFORD!!!!!!

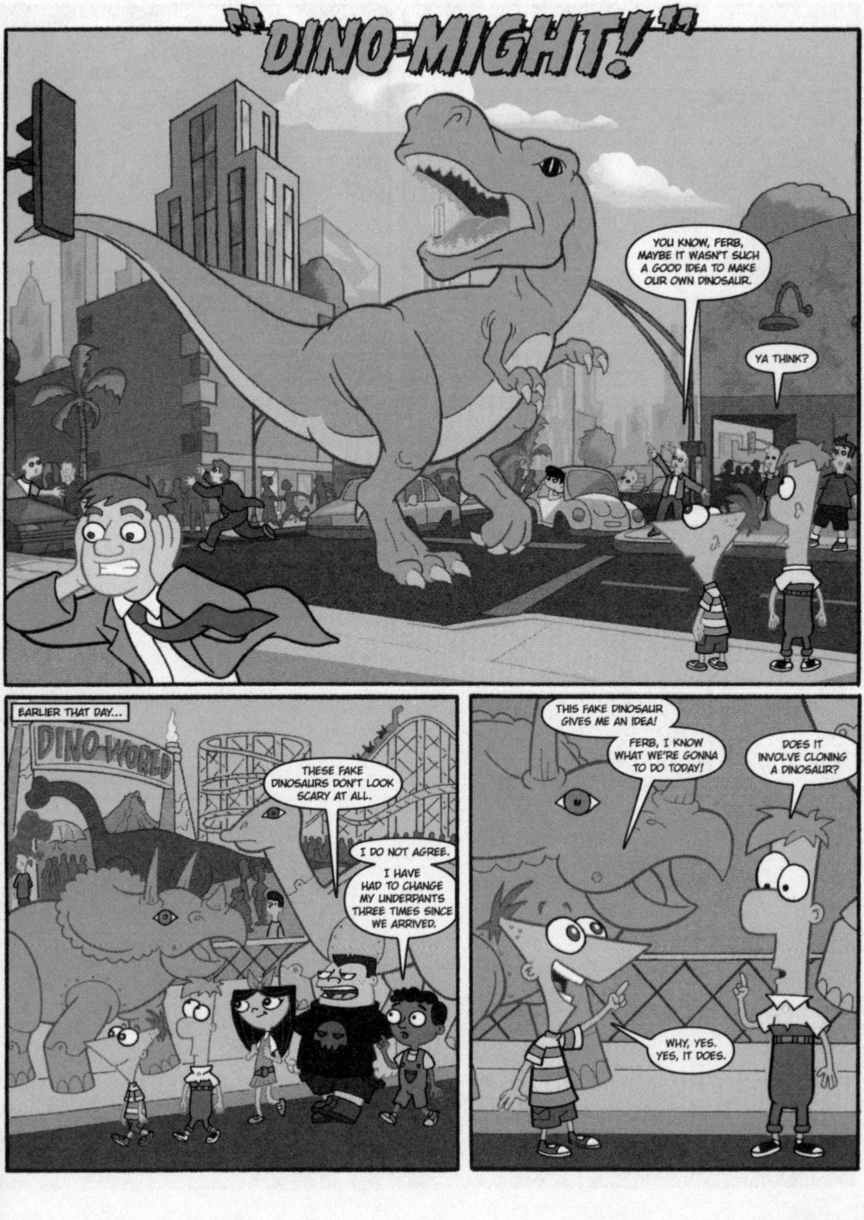
"DINO-MIGHT!"
YOU KNOW, FERB, MAYBE IT WASN'T SUCH A GOOD IDEA TO MAKE OUR OWN DINOSAUR.
YA THINK?
EARLIER THAT DAY...
DINO-WORLD
THESE FAKE DINOSAURS DON'T LOOK SCARY AT ALL.
I DO NOT AGREE.
I HAVE HAD TO CHANGE MY UNDERPANTS THREE TIMES SINCE WE ARRIVED.
THIS FAKE DINOSAUR GIVES ME AN IDEA!
FERB, I KNOW WHAT WE'RE GONNA TO DO TODAY!
DOES IT INVOLVE CLONING A DINOSAUR?
WHY, YES. YES, IT DOES.

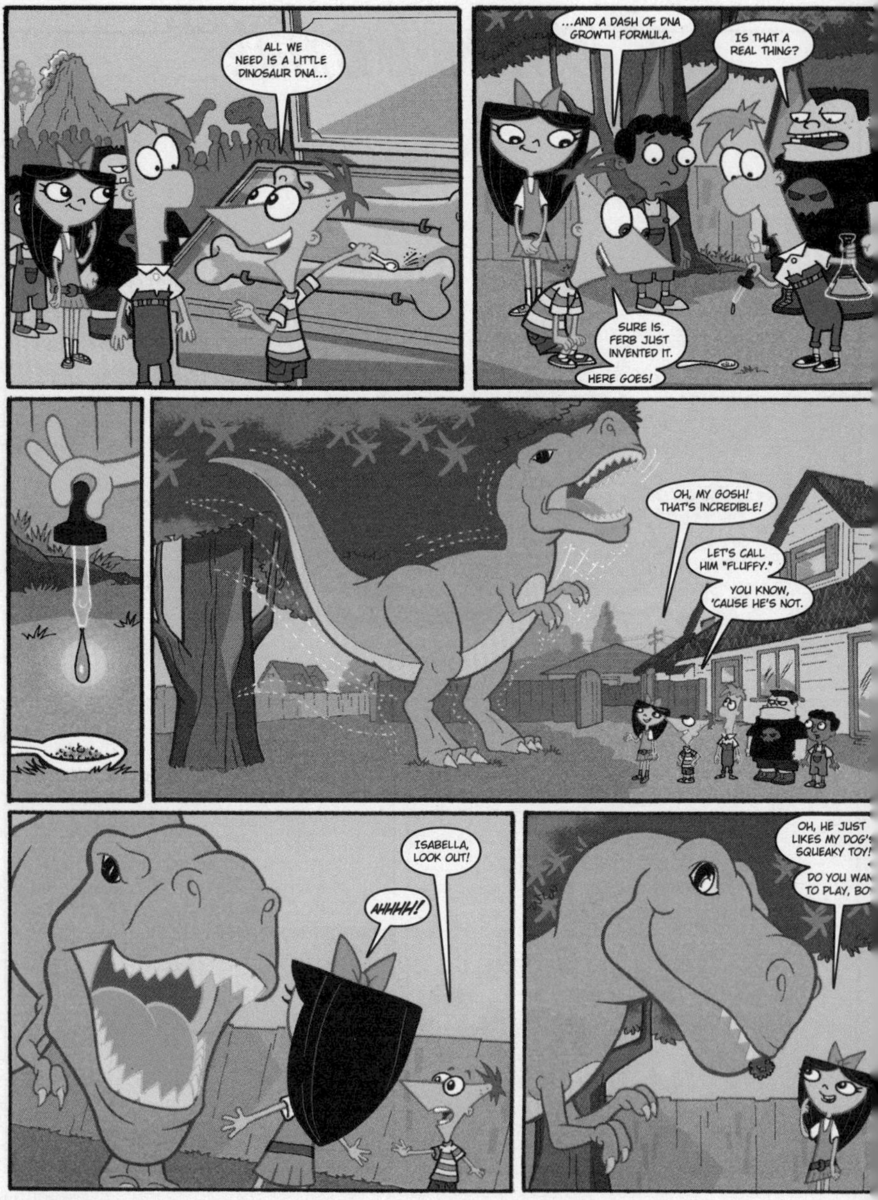
ALL WE NEED IS A LITTLE DINOSAUR DNA...
...AND A DASH OF DNA GROWTH FORMULA.
IS THAT A REAL THING?
SURE IS. FERB JUST INVENTED IT.
HERE GOES!
OH, MY GOSH! THAT'S INCREDIBLE!
LET'S CALL HIM "FLUFFY."
YOU KNOW, 'CAUSE HE'S NOT.
ISABELLA, LOOK OUT!
AHHHH!
OH, HE JUST LIKES MY DOG'S SQUEAKY TOY!
DO YOU WAN TO PLAY, BO

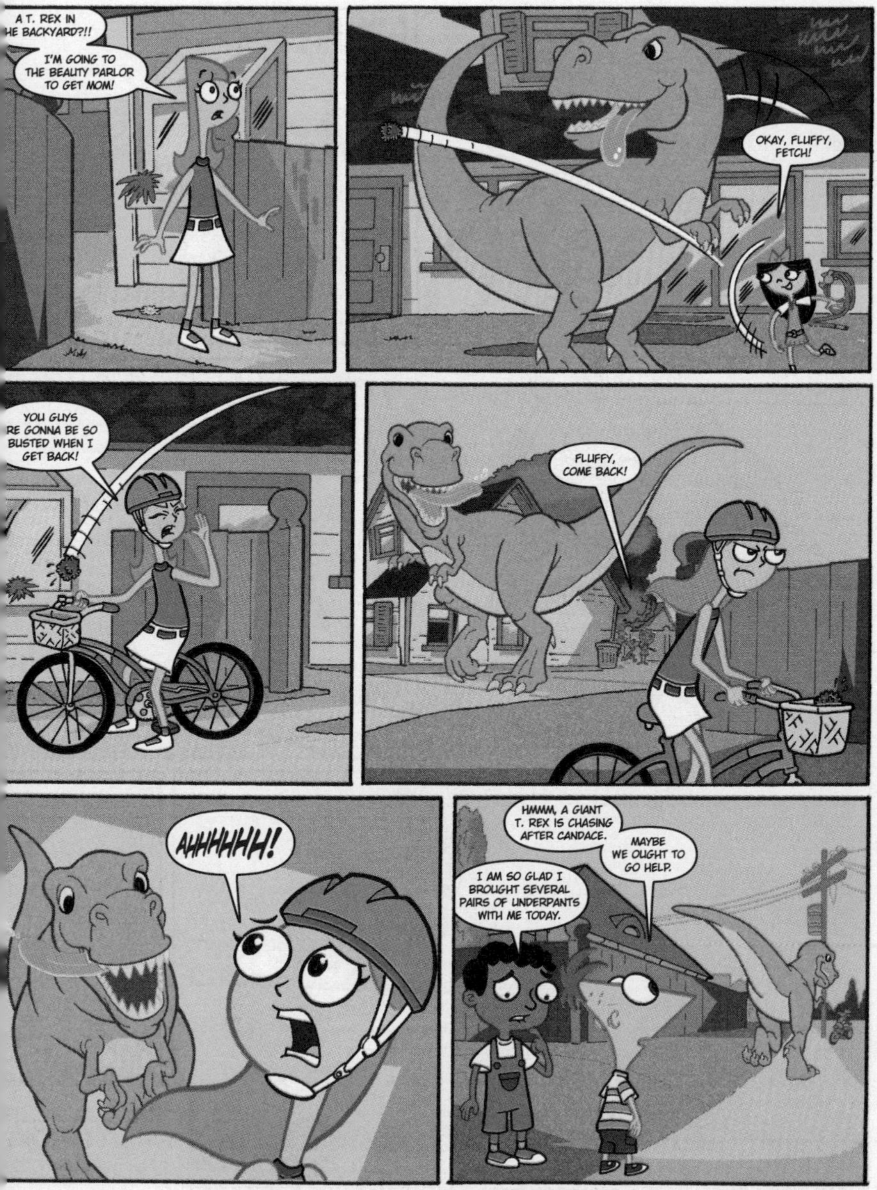
A T. REX IN
HE BACKYARD?!!
I'M GOING TO THE BEAUTY PARLOR TO GET MOM!
OKAY, FLUFFY, FETCH!
YOU GUYS
RE GONNA BE SO BUSTED WHEN I GET BACK!
FLUFFY, COME BACK!
AHHHHHH!
HMMM, A GIANT T. REX IS CHASING AFTER CANDACE.
MAYBE WE OUGHT TO GO HELP.
I AM SO GLAD I BROUGHT SEVERAL PAIRS OF UNDERPANTS WITH ME TODAY.

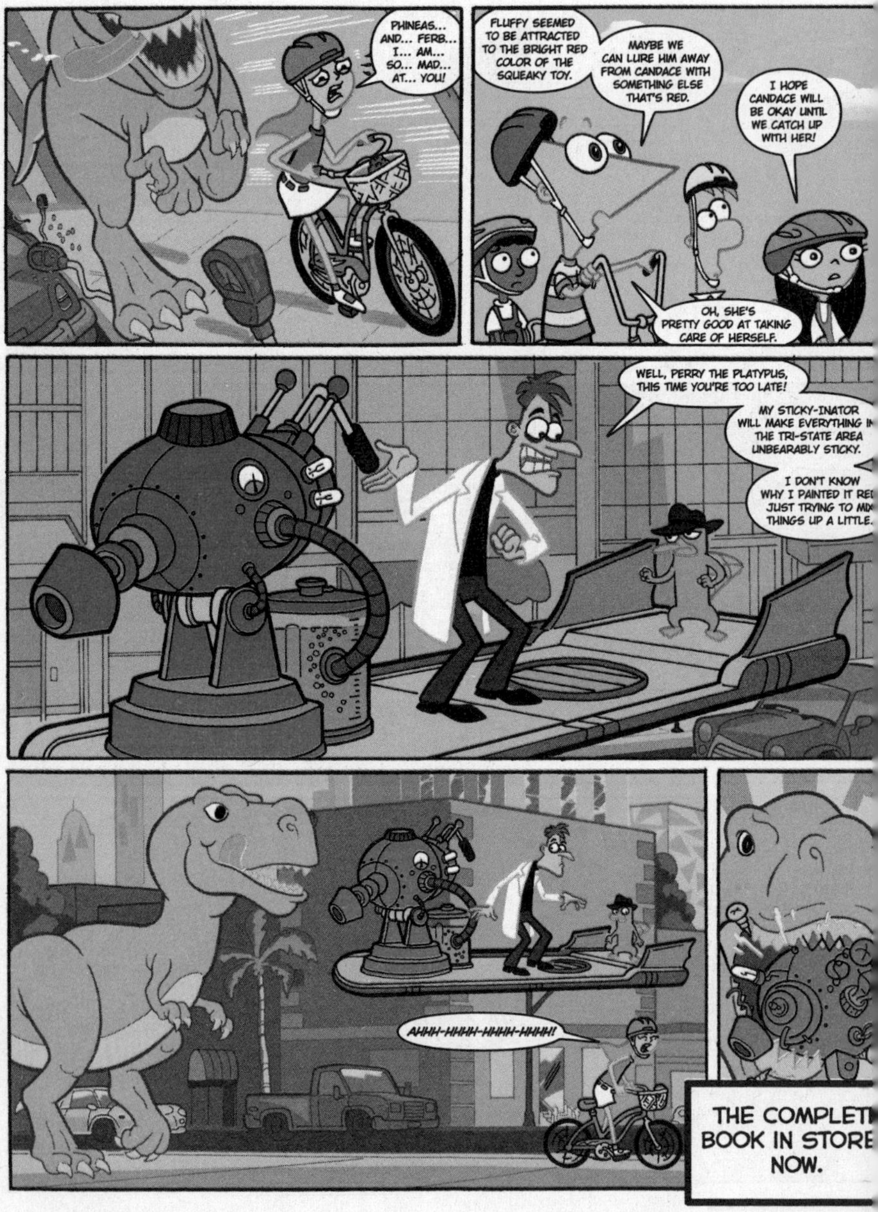
PHINEAS... AND... FERB... I... AM... SO... MAD... AT... YOU!
FLUFFY SEEMED TO BE ATTRACTED TO THE BRIGHT RED COLOR OF THE SQUEAKY TOY.
MAYBE WE CAN LURE HIM AWAY FROM CANDACE WITH SOMETHING ELSE THAT'S RED.
I HOPE CANDACE WILL BE OKAY UNTIL WE CATCH UP WITH HER!
OH, SHE'S PRETTY GOOD AT TAKING CARE OF HERSELF.
WELL, PERRY THE PLATYPUS, THIS TIME YOU'RE TOO LATE!
MY STICKY-INATOR WILL MAKE EVERYTHING I
THE TRI-STATE AREA UNBEARABLY STICKY.
I DON'T KNOW WHY I PAINTED IT RE
JUST TRYING TO MI
THINGS UP A LITTLE.
AHHH-HHHH-HHHH-HHHH!
THE COMPLET
BOOK IN STORE
NOW.